Newport Community Learning & Libraries
Cymuned ddysgu a Llyfrgelloedd Casnewydd

Newport
CITY COUNCIL
CYNGOR DINAS
Casnewydd

THIS ITEM SHOULD BE RETURNED OR
RENEWED BY THE LAST DATE
STAMPED BELOW.

To renew telephone: 656656 or 656657 (minicom)
or www.newport.gov.uk/libraries

Also by Catherine King

Without a Mother's Love

A Mother's Sacrifice

CATHERINE KING OMNIBUS

Silk and Steel

Women of Iron

sphere

SPHERE

This omnibus edition first published in Great Britain in 2010 by Sphere

Copyright © Catherine King 2010

Previously published separately:
Women of Iron first published in Great Britain in 2006 by Sphere
Paperback edition published in 2007 by Sphere
Reprinted 2007 (twice), 2008
Copyright © Catherine King 2006
Silk and Steel first published in Great Britain in 2007 by Sphere
Paperback edition published in 2008 by Sphere
Reprinted 2008
Copyright © Catherine King 2007

The moral right of the author has been asserted.

A CIP catalogue record for this book
is available from the British Library.

ISBN 978-0-7515-4441-1

Printed and bound in Great Britain by
Clays Ltd, St Ives plc

Sphere
An imprint of
Little, Brown Book Group
100 Victoria Embankment
London EC4Y 0DY

An Hachette UK Company
www.hachette.co.uk

www.littlebrown.co.uk

SILK AND STEEL

To the memory of Edmund Humphrey King

I should like to thank the staff and volunteers of Rotherham Archives, and the local history section of Rotherham Library, for enabling me to research the background to this book. Thanks, also, to my agent Judith Murdoch and editor Louise Davies for their sound advice in its development and writing. The inspiration for the story is my great-grandmother, who came from a family of tailors in Stokesley, North Yorkshire.

Chapter 1

1840

The vicar read quietly from his prayer book, his soft hand gently touching the chalk-white skin of the woman's forehead. He traced the shape of a cross and those slight movements signalled the end of life for Amelia Bowes.

Tears ran down the cheeks of her daughter Mariah as she grieved silently for her loss. While they had each other, their hardships in this house had been bearable, but how would she survive without her mother? How could she continue to live here without the only person in the world who loved her?

She could not call this house a home. A home was where she would have been welcome. But her father had regarded them both as his servants, and treated them no better than he did his labourers at the ironworks. England may have a woman on the throne, but men continued to do the ruling.

Mariah inhaled with a shudder as she tried to repress her sobs. During her mother's long and painful illness, she had not thought beyond caring for her. They had not been separated in all her nineteen years and she could not imagine a life without her.

She heard the front door slam and her body went rigid. She knew who it was because she had sent the stable lad to the works for him. Her father's heavy boots thumped on the stairs making the treads creak and groan. The door to the bedchamber flew open and banged against the wall.

'She's gone then.'

Ezekiel Bowes stood in the middle of the sparsely furnished chamber in his working clothes. His face was streaked and sweaty and his once white neckerchief hung, stained and greasy, around his damp, dusty neck.

'It took her long enough,' he added.

His ruddy face, hot from the furnace, showed no emotion, but then it would not unless he was angry. Mariah and her mother always knew when Ezekiel had been crossed, but never when he was pleased. Happiness was not part of his life. Or theirs. Amelia's life had been an austere one as the wife of Ezekiel Bowes.

Mariah sat quietly by the bed and thought that her mother looked peaceful now – more so than she had for many years. The vicar drew a white sheet over the still, serene face and murmured words of condolence to Ezekiel. Mariah saw the discomfort in her father's face. Ezekiel Bowes was not a church-going man and this new vicar was taking more of an interest in him than the old one had.

She had sent for him against her father's wishes because it was what her mother had wanted. Ezekiel was angry to see him in his house, but Mariah guessed he would let it pass for the sake of appearances. Appearances mattered to Ezekiel, but only to the world outside this house.

2

'Aye, well. You can leave now, Vicar,' he replied, with a surly nod.

The vicar added a few kind words to Mariah and hurried away. Mariah understood his haste.

'I suppose you sent for him?'

'Mother wanted him here at the end. You cannot begrudge her that, surely?'

Ezekiel turned on Mariah. He was a dark, swarthy man, toughened by years of manual labour. His hair was beginning to turn grey but he was still thick set and strong, for he still worked at the furnace with his men.

'I don't begrudge her anything now,' he said. 'Just get her out of here and clean up this chamber. I want everything of hers gone from this house. Do you hear me?'

'Yes, Father.'

'Get on with it, then!'

Mariah got to her feet and began to collect up the small comforts of nursing that had helped her mother through her last painful weeks. She knelt on the floor and piled the empty apothecary's bottles and soiled linen on a square of old calico and tied it into a bundle. She felt her father's domineering presence in the room and when she looked at him he was sneering at her mother's shroud.

Mariah's grief and anger rose against him. 'She was a good wife to you,' she cried.

'What would you know about it?'

'I know she was loyal to you, and you – you look as though you . . . hated her,' she replied quietly.

'Hated her? I married her, didn't I? Aye, I did that. And with you growing in her belly.'

Mariah had not known this and was surprised but not shocked. Many a bride was wed with her first child already on

3

the way. Indeed, any future husband would be pleased to know his betrothed was not barren. In a way, this knowledge cheered her and she remarked, 'You must have loved her once, then?'

He began to laugh, a low growling chuckle rumbled in his throat, but his brown eyes were hard. 'Is that what she told you?'

'Well, no. She did not talk of her – her early life.'

Ezekiel shook his head as though he had lost patience with her. 'Nigh on twenty years and she never told you.'

'It isn't a crime to be with child at the altar! Not if you loved each other—'

He let out a guffaw. 'And I thought you two were close! Well, I'll be damned! She never said!'

'We *were* close,' Mariah protested. 'Especially as I grew older and—' She choked on a sob. 'When she became ill, she needed me.'

Ezekiel's eyes glittered at her angrily. 'She needed *me*.' He spat out the words and his large frame towered over Mariah as she knelt by the bed.

'But you shunned her! You – you turned her away from your bedchamber, from your life, and treated her like a servant! What kind of marriage was that?'

'*Enough!*' Ezekiel shouted, closing in on her. 'You don't know what you're talking about! Don't you ever say things like that again! Do you hear me?'

Mariah's hazel eyes widened. He was standing right next to her and she could smell hot coal and metal on his leather boots and breeches. Anger radiated from him like the heat from his furnace.

'Stop this hatred of her, Father! Stop it! She's dead now.'

This seemed to calm him. But for how long? Mariah wondered.

4

'What did she tell you?' Ezekiel asked.

'Not much. Only that you always took care of her and that whatever you did to us, to remember that underneath it all you kept your promise.' Mariah gathered up her bundle and rose. 'As I said, you must have cared for her once. And she did try to be a good wife to you.'

'What else did she say?' he demanded.

'About what?' Mariah was a full-grown woman now and not frightened of him as she had been as a little girl. If her father had something to say to her, it was best out in the open.

'About you!' he barked. 'Look at you. Carrot hair, white skin and freckles. Not dark like the rest of us.'

What was he getting at? Her brother Henry was like his father with brown hair and eyes. Her mother's hair had had a coppery hue when she had been younger and a skin like her own that freckled in the summer sun and reddened if she did not keep it covered. 'I have my mother's hazel eyes,' she muttered.

He leaned forward and his eyes looked directly into hers. 'Oh aye, you're *her* lass all right. Same stubborn way with you. But you're not *mine*!'

Mariah's jaw dropped, her eyes rounded and she swayed. 'Y-you mean you are not my father?' She did not believe it! Her mother had lain with another man and carried his child. 'Did you know this when you married her?' she whispered.

'Of course I knew!'

'She never told me,' Mariah murmured. 'Not about this. Who is he, then? If you are not my father, who is my real father?'

Ezekiel sneered at her again. 'Don't go getting any fancy ideas. Your precious mother disgraced herself and her family with some coal miner who got killed in a pit fall. And there

5

was pretty little Amelia, left with no one to wed and a scandal on the way.'

'You knew about this and you married her?' Mariah thought it had been uncharacteristically generous on her father's part. There must have been some kindness in him all those years ago, although she had never seen much evidence of it in her lifetime. 'Then I was right, you must have loved her once.'

He did not answer but Mariah noticed his head shaking very slightly. Perhaps he had acted hastily and had regretted it ever since? Perhaps this was why he had spent most of his time at his ironworks, preferring to join his men for the heavy labouring in the yard?

'I never loved her,' he sneered. 'Not *her*.'

Mariah blinked as his face contorted to a sadness she had not seen before. 'Then why . . . why *did* you marry her?' she asked.

He appeared to recover quickly. There was no grief after all; no sense of loss for her mother. He raised his voice, filling the stuffy bedchamber with his venom. 'Do you think I did it for nowt!'

Mariah tensed again. Her father was using the language of his earlier, younger years, language he usually kept for his men at the works. This was a warning sign that he was really angry, frustrated with his furnace or his suppliers, or simply with himself. She thought he was not a man at ease with himself and the successful ironmaster he had become.

'They paid me ter marry 'er! So long as I took 'er away and never went back to 'em for owt else!' he yelled. 'Paid me well, an' all. They were tailors, you know. Her family were all tailors in the North Riding. Doing all right for theirsenns, and her ma 'ad an uncle who was building cottages for a mine owner. How do yer think I got set up here wi' me own furnace, when I were on'y a labourer in a quarry and a forge?'

Mariah felt herself go cold all over. 'You married her for money?' she whispered. 'They paid you to take her – and me – away?'

'Aye. That's what folk with means do with their wayward daughters.'

Mariah found it hard to imagine her mother as wayward. She had been a warm and loving parent to her, and had more than made up for her father's coldness towards them both. She must have been in love with Mariah's real father. Perhaps they were planning to marry when he was killed?

'Mother never spoke of her own folk. She told me she had no kin.'

'Aye, she would say that. They wanted nowt more to do with her, so she turned her back on them an' all. It suited me too.'

'But surely they will wish to know of her passing?'

'Why? As far as they are concerned, she is already dead. They were glad to see the back of her, let me tell you.' Ezekiel grimaced at the body of his late wife. 'And so am I.'

Mariah held her head in her hands. She knew her father could be unkind but to be this cruel to her mother's memory was too much for her to bear.

She cried out in anguish. 'She was your *wife*!'

'She was a whore with a bastard!' he retaliated. 'But she got me a share in the ironworks. That was the deal.'

'How can you be so disrespectful to the mother of your own child!'

'Aye. She bore me a son, all right. I'll give her that. He is all that matters to me.'

Mariah stood rigidly in front of him at the foot of the bed that cradled her mother's dead body. 'You *never* cared anything for her, did you? Never!'

7

'No.'

'Or me!'

'Even less for you! Some pit worker's bastard! I don't want you in my house reminding me of that!'

'What do you mean?'

'It's clear enough, i'n't it? Now your mother's gone, there's no need for you to stay here.'

'But you cannot turn me out! I have nowhere to go!'

'You look all right, don't you? That carrot hair is not to everybody's taste, but you haven't got boss eyes or black teeth. Or a limp. And if you're like yer ma you'll fall for a babby straight off to keep you out of mischief.'

Mariah was horrified. 'What on earth are you suggesting?'

'I am not suggesting, I am telling you. And if you value your mother's reputation you will do as you are told.'

'What do you mean?'

'I mean that if you do not obey me, I'll disown you for the bastard you are!'

'B-but people would think my mother was . . .'

'A whore? Aye, they would. So you'll do as I say and get yourself wed. And look sharp about it.'

'Be reasonable. I do not have a suitor.'

'I can find you one, don't you fret. A widower will do. One who won't be needing no dowry to have a bit o' young flesh in his bed of a night.'

'You cannot do that to me!'

His reply was slow and deliberate. 'I am your father, and until you are twenty-one I can do what I like with you and don't you forget it. Aye, I can find you a husband easy enough. And you'll marry him, by God. Before midsummer, or you'll be out on the streets selling yoursenn like your mother did afore you.'

8

'That is not true! How can you be so cruel? My mother would never have done such a thing.'

'How do you know she didn't? How do I know she wasn't at it here? She was never wanting for a new gown. Neither were you and I never paid for 'em. Where did they come from, I wonder?'

'What do you think she did all day while you were at work? Why do you think she kept the morning room for herself? You were never interested in anything she did!'

'Why should I want to know what women do with their time?'

'Why indeed,' Mariah responded wearily. 'All you are concerned about is your precious furnace.'

'You listen 'ere to me, Mariah Bowes, and listen well to what I'm saying, because I mean it. I gave you my name, didn't I? You should be grateful for that alone. But while you carry that name, you make sure everyone in this town knows what a good husband I was to yer ma, and what a proper father I am to you. Did I send you out to service as soon as you were old enough? No. The both o' you had a roof over your head and food on the table.'

'We were your *servants*!'

It was then he hit her. He raised his right arm and brought the back of his hand hard across her face, sending her reeling. She grasped the iron bedstead to stop herself falling and stumbled over the silent, cooling body of her darling mother. It was then she realised the full extent of Ezekiel Bowes' hatred for his wife and herself.

'I was a good husband and father and don't you forget it!' he retaliated loudly. 'As far as this town knows, we were – are – a decent family! If ever I hear any different from you – or from anybody in the Riding – I'll tell them what a whore your mother was and expose you for the bastard you are!'

His dark eyes were angry and his hands were clenched into fists as he continued to shout. 'And if your husband turns you out because o' that, it'll be your own doing. You'll be on the streets then, because I'll not have you back here. D'yer hear me? Never. Things are going to be different around here with yer ma and you out o' the road.'

Chapter 2

Ezekiel watched the coffin as it was lowered into the ground. It's over at last, he thought, and soon the daughter will be gone too, away from my house and that part of my life will be dead and buried for ever. He was a widower now, respectable, with a profitable business and an educated son to be proud of.

He had friends at the Freemason's lodge and they had turned out for him today, in their best black and polished boots. He was glad of that. The church service had been an ordeal for him but he felt stronger with his friends around him. Their wives and daughters were waiting for them in their own homes, the best place for womenfolk at times like these. None of them knew of his early life, and now his wife had gone and the bastard was on her way too, he could erase all those memories from his mind, push them away for ever deep down into the dark recesses of his past.

'Ashes to ashes, dust to dust . . .' the vicar droned on.

He was anxious for it to be finished. Churchmen made him uncomfortable, and this one, this new vicar, more so than most. He had never known the old vicar very well and he did not want to know this one either. In Ezekiel's book, God was unforgiving. God had made him a sinner and God had made him suffer. For the rest of his life he would suffer.

His face contorted with the hurt of remembering as he stood by the graveside. He saw the vicar looking at him. What did he know? he demanded silently. What did he know of growing up at the beck and call of his betters? Uneasily, he wondered where this new vicar came from and hoped it was not the North Riding.

'Father?'

A hand took his arm. It was Henry. My, what a fine gentleman he had become, dressed in a new black coat and tall hat. His heart swelled with pride when he looked at him. Henry was his salvation. A fine boy, his son from his own seed, schooled and confident, moving among the straggle of mourners, taking charge.

There was sherry wine and shortened biscuits laid out in the dining room at home. Ezekiel was cheered by the thought of going back to his works as soon as this was over. He knew who he was when he was there. He was the gaffer and the men deferred to him. He could have taken greater advantage of them but he did not. He was no longer the troublemaker of his younger years, he was a changed man. A family man. Respectable. He would wear his black armband for the required length of time. Henry would advise him.

Ezekiel managed a weak smile for the vicar before moving away, thankful this necessary show was over. There was old man Smith from the ironmongers in town. A widower like himself. Well, no, not quite like himself. He had a big family of growing lads and lasses. But they were a handful for him and it was rumoured he was looking for a wife. His shop was prospering and he had a bob or two from rents as well, so he'd make any lass a good husband.

'Mr Smith,' he called. 'Mr Smith, a word with you, if you please, sir.'

'Do you know about Father's plans, Henry?'

'Of course I do, Mariah. I am his son and heir. Father and I corresponded regularly when I was at school. The ironworks and this house are my future.' Henry sighed. 'It is a pity the house is so close to the works, for it is well proportioned and ideal for receiving callers.'

'It was very convenient for Father in the early days. I remember when Mother used to cook dinner for his labourers and feed them all in the kitchen. I helped her with the washing-up and cleaning.'

'I did not know we used to have *labourers* in our kitchen.'

'No. You were away at school for most of the time.'

Mariah had served her father and brother their breakfast in the dining room. When Ezekiel left for the works, instead of returning to the kitchen, she drew out a chair opposite Henry and sat down.

'Tell me about Father's plans, Henry.'

Henry had come home from school for his mother's funeral. At eighteen, he had worn new black clothes for the occasion but now he displayed only a black armband on his finely tailored coat. It was a fashionable maroon colour, made of good Yorkshire wool, Mariah noticed, and he wore pomade on his dark hair.

He sighed again. 'Mariah, I have already said that you do not need to concern yourself with these matters.' He frowned

13

and pursed his lips. 'And do remove your apron if you wish to join me at the table.'

Mariah ignored his request and watched him dispassionately as he picked an invisible speck of dust from his sleeve. He had grown into a handsome young man, with the dark hair and eyes of his father but without his swarthiness. Henry had inherited the smooth-textured skin of their mother. A feature he shared with her, except he had more warmth in his skin colouring and, of course, no freckles.

She felt plain and dowdy beside him. She had no money of her own and had sewn her mourning dress herself, from some black stuff already in her mother's workroom. She covered it with a large white pinafore most of the time as the cloth had been cheap and already showed signs of wear.

'But Father's plans do concern me, Henry,' she persisted, 'this is my home.'

'Not for much longer, I hear.' He measured out a small smile. 'Father has told me you will marry soon and become part of another family. That will be convenient for all of us. I know you are not a Bowes, and I no longer think of you as a sister.'

This was a shock for Mariah. Henry had grown apart from her in his years away at school and she no longer recognised him as her little brother.

'But I am your sister, Henry!' she protested. 'Your mother was my mother, too!'

'She was not a Bowes and never a part of Father's affairs.' He shrugged. 'She had no real claim to our family name. As Father's wife she was given it as a privilege.'

'Family name? What family name? Father was an ordinary labourer before he came to the South Riding.'

'If you take my advice, you will not let him hear you say that. He means to be a well-respected ironmaster in this town.'

14

Mariah thought he probably already was. As a young man he had invested his wife's generous dowry in a rundown furnace, repaired the crumbling brickwork and taken on men to labour alongside him. To give her father his due he had worked hard, but he could have done none of it without marrying Amelia.

She said firmly, 'It was my mother's money that bought him the ironworks!'

'No, Mariah. I think you will find that is not true. Women, generally, do not have money of their own. However,' he pronounced casually, 'your mother's father may have given her a dowry.'

Your mother? Mariah thought, not 'my mother' or even 'our mother'. She said pointedly, 'She was your mother, too.'

'Yes,' he sighed. 'Though Father did not wish me to be influenced by her. That is why he was so anxious for me to go away to be educated, and why he encouraged me to spend my time with young gentlemen from school, away from here.'

Well, thought Mariah angrily, go back to your expensive school and snobbish friends! She asked calmly, 'Then why have you chosen to stay at home now?'

'I would have thought that was obvious. Your mother is dead and soon you will be gone too. Father and I have plans. I shall not go to university, but become a partner in the iron-works when I am twenty-one.'

Mariah despaired. She had thought Henry might be her ally against Ezekiel's wishes in this matter. Her childhood memories were of austerity mixed with occasional cheer, but she and Henry had been friends as children playing in the attic or the garden. And she remembered how sad she had felt when Henry went first to a local day school and then, at eight years old, further afield as a boarding pupil.

15

He had visited them rarely since then and, when he did, had little time for her or her mother. Mariah had put his aloofness down to his new schooling. Mother said he was going to be a proper gentleman when he grew up. She had wondered at the time why Henry, who was a whole year younger than she was, went for lessons before her, and had asked innocently, 'When shall I go to school, Mother?'

'Heavens, my dear,' her mother had told her, 'Mr Bowes will not pay for you to go to school. You must stay at home with me and look after the house. I shall teach you how to cook and clean and sew. You do not need to go to school for that. I learned from my mother and you will learn from me.'

But her mother could not read or write so Mariah went to Sunday school and learned her letters and read Bible stories there. Mariah had often wondered why her mother spoke so little of her own mother. She presumed she had died young and so did not ask. Now that Amelia was dead it was too late and she wished she had questioned her more. All Mariah had now was a likeness of her that she had kept in her workroom. It was a drawing, well executed by a travelling artist who had visited the beast market, mounted in an old silver frame. The features were recognisable as her mother's and, indeed, a little like her own. It was all she had of her past now; her mother had said she must have it when she was gone.

Mariah shook her head slightly at Henry's lack of sentiment for his own mother. His father and his schooling had taken him away from both of them. Henry pushed back his chair and his napkin fell to the floor. He did not pick it up but wandered over to the windows where tall glass doors led into the garden. He fingered the material of the curtains and looked at the walls.

'Between the two of you,' he remarked, 'you have neglected

16

this house. Look at it! Dingy and unfashionable! What were you thinking of, letting it get into this state?'

Mariah had realised by now that her brother was not interested in replies to his questions. He did not want to hear about five years of illness and nursing and the small matter of her father's refusal to pay for paint or wallpaper, or even new fabric for window curtains. Father's usual response had been that all his profits were invested in raw iron for the furnace. Mariah thought this must have been true because Henry was right, the ironworks flourished while the house was run down.

It was a nice house to live in, though, and Mariah liked it. Situated, as it was, on the town side of the ironworks, it was convenient for the High Street and the market square at the top of the hill, and had enough garden around it to grow fruit and vegetables. There was a carriage house, too, where Father kept his haulage cart and heavy horses for transporting the bars of steel his furnace produced. Father had his own horse, too, a large spirited beast that Henry also rode.

The stable lad, who slept next to the hayloft over the tack room, looked after the garden as well, so they always had fresh greens and such like in the kitchen. But for years her father would not employ a housemaid and it was a large house to clean without a servant. Built of local stone, it stood four square to the roadway, with a large front door and wide entrance hall. They had a drawing room, dining room, morning room and a large kitchen with a roomy scullery at the back. Upstairs were four good bedchambers with two attics above them.

When her mother was well, they were able to keep down the dust from the coal fires, wax the floorboards and furniture and cook meals between them. But when she became ill, Mariah could not manage the house and nurse her mother. Reluctantly, her father had agreed to occasional help in the form of Emma, a ten-year-old girl from down by the canal on the other side of the ironworks. She was a willing and cheerful child, but not used to a large house, and Mariah had to teach her many things before she could become a real help.

Mariah knew Henry did not wish to know any of this and said, 'Well, if Father will open an account at the draper's in town, I'm sure I can make new curtains and—'

'Really, Mariah! What do you know of fashion for houses? You have never been anywhere grand enough to see what can be done.'

Henry began to pace about, looking up at the ceiling and turning to survey the whole room. His new leather boots squeaked on the floorboards. 'This furniture is too light,' he declared. 'I want mahogany from the East. And red velvet for the windows. Yes. Dark red, I think, with gold tassels. That is much more fitting for a gentleman's residence, don't you think?'

Mariah stayed silent. She recalled her mother telling her as a child, 'When Henry comes home from school he will be accepted in the very best circles, and so will his father.'

'And what about us?' Mariah had asked.

'Well, of course, we are part of this family so they must accept us as well. Perhaps Mr Bowes will give me an allowance to buy new dress material and ribbons.'

Perhaps not, Mariah had thought; he is happy for us to forage for used and damaged garments at the market. To afford the clothes for their backs, Amelia Bowes sold surplus garden produce to buy straw bonnets that she trimmed with bits of lace and ribbons, and then re-sold or traded for lengths of cloth. If ever her mother caught sight of a fashionable traveller passing through the South Riding, every detail of her dress would be noted, memorised and sketched out on a slate as soon as she returned home, then her cupboards would be searched for remnants and trimmings to enhance their workaday gowns.

Henry brought her back to the present. 'I shall open up the drawing room,' he declared grandly, 'and have a carpet from Persia on the floorboards. And perhaps a pianoforte for soirées.'

Mariah wondered if her father knew the extent of Henry's dreams for his house and whether his one furnace was enough to make that kind of money. She found it difficult to keep the doubt out of her voice. 'Soirées? Gracious, Henry,' she said, 'this will mean a lot more work for me in the house.'

'But you will not be here! You will be married and caring for your own family.'

'Really? And who will look after you and Father if I leave?'

'Emma will,' Henry responded. 'She is fifteen now, is she not? I am sure she has learned everything she needs. She will know what to do.'

'You mean Emma will be your housekeeper?'

'As soon as you marry. Before if you wish.'

'And you, Henry? What will you do?'

'I shall assist my father in his business matters, of course. What else should I do?'

What else indeed? Mariah wondered how he would survive in the ironworks with his father. She could not imagine Henry working for Ezekiel, hot and sweaty in dirty, greasy clothes, labouring at a fiery furnace during smelting.

Henry went on, 'Father and I have been planning these changes for a year now. We have been impatient for your mother to die.'

Mariah felt as if she had been punched in the stomach. Even though her mother's passing had been a release from her constant pain and suffering, Mariah had never wished to hasten her death. Henry's offhand remark appalled her and her voice was strangled as she said, 'How can you be so – so harsh and unfeeling!'

'Do not be so melodramatic, Mariah. It is not becoming in a woman of our standing. We all knew your mother was dying. I hope you will not behave like this should my friends, the Fitzkeppels, choose to visit, or I shall have to ask you to stay in the kitchen.'

Mariah stared at him. 'You are friendly with the Fitzkeppels? I am surprised you would wish to invite them here in the first place. This is a very small house compared to Fitzkeppel Hall.'

'Perhaps we shall move somewhere more gracious,' Henry mused. 'Father's investment in the works is paying off well for him now. Soon he will not have to oversee the men at all. He will be spending all his time with other ironmasters and men of substance at the lodge in town. You do see, don't you, Mariah, that neither your mother nor yourself could be a part of our future here?'

No, I do not see, Mariah thought angrily. It was her mother's dowry that had made all this possible! And she had been thanked with a position no better than a housekeeper. What kind of life had that been for her! Her workroom had been her only respite from the drudgery of being Ezekiel Bowes' unpaid servant. It had been Mariah's haven as well.

'But that does not mean I have to marry! I can run the household for Father and keep on Mother's workroom. She taught me everything she knew about garment making—'

'I want that room for a study. We shall need somewhere to discuss business affairs when gentlemen call at the house.'

'But we have an empty bedchamber I could use!'

'We do not! That is to be my dressing room. A gentleman needs space for his wardrobe and toilette. Oh, and would you

20

move your things to one of the attic rooms forthwith? Father's new works supervisor will be sleeping in the bedchamber that you are using.'

'I did not know Father was taking on a supervisor.'

'Why should you? It is of no consequence to you. But I shall tell you this: he is one of the best iron workers in the Riding. Father wants him to live here, next to the works, so he can take full responsibility for the furnace. And then Father and I shall be free to spend our time mixing with the right sort of Riding people.'

'So – so – this – this new works supervisor can live here, but I cannot!'

'You must realise how important he will be to our success. He comes to us from the Fitzkeppel works and understands all the modern processes. He knows how to make the very best steel for the cutlers of Sheffield. We shall be rich, Mariah! If you are sensible and marry the man Father chooses for you, you will be able to visit us when we are grand and take Sunday tea in the drawing room.'

'And you?' Mariah repeated, 'What will you do?'

Henry smiled. 'My education has not been wasted, Mariah: I shall help Father to become a gentleman. You will see how respectable we shall be now that I am home.'

'You are insufferable! You cannot order my life like this.'

'Of course I can. I do it on behalf of Father. You will move into the large attic. Emma will take the smaller one.'

'Emma? Emma is to live here in the small attic?'

'Of course. She may take over the running of the house immediately. Do not look at me like that. You will not be here much longer, for you will be marrying quite soon.'

Mariah swallowed hard and spoke slowly with an exaggerated patience, 'Henry, I am not yet betrothed to anyone.'

'Oh, but you will be! You must think of your future elsewhere now, Mariah. As a wife. Father is arranging a suitable husband for you.'

Suitable for whom? she wondered, but did not pursue the matter. 'I see. So when I marry, Emma will be living here with Father and you and – and – the new works supervisor? Henry, she is only fifteen, that is hardly respectable.'

'Mariah, do leave things like this to me. Father's new supervisor is Mr Thorpe, Emma's older brother. She can live here quite respectably if her brother is here, too.'

'And of course respectability is all that matters to Father! What will the ironmasters of the South Riding think if I refuse to marry his choice of husband, and he turns me out on the streets?'

'Do not be childish. Why should you not marry? I think you will find you will have no friends of consequence in the Riding if you disobey him.'

Mariah's anger turned to sarcasm. 'Well then, Henry, you must help me find a suitor. Do you know any gentlemen I could meet? They, perhaps, will be a little young, but I am sure that, if you are acquainted with them, they will be men of means.'

Henry answered her seriously. 'Be reasonable. My friends have their sights set on much higher prizes than you. No one of any consequence will want to marry *you*. You have nothing from your mother to take to a marriage, and no proper education at all. Certainly no talent for music or singing. All you can do is cook and sew.'

'Thank you for explaining that so clearly to me. With such paltry talents where should I set my sights? A coal miner's wife, maybe?'

But the irony in Mariah's voice was lost on Henry and he replied airily, 'Well, you have all you need to be a collier's wife.'

22

'I am to be a coal miner's wife, then,' she responded angrily. 'Is that how you see me? Would you come and visit your half-sister in her pithead cottage when she is a coal miner's wife?'

'Well no, of course not. If you marry a collier, our lives will part for good when you leave this house. But coal mining is a good living for a man. Emma's father was a collier before he got the – the – sickness that they get. I understand your own father was a pit man, too. You cannot set your expectations higher than that.'

'My expectations! What do you know of my expectations? Perhaps I'll marry Father's new works supervisor! I imagine that, if he is coming to live here, he does not have a wife. Have you met him yet? Will he do for me?'

'Do not be silly. You are, in reality, an orphan and you would do well to take your situation seriously. Now the funeral is over, you must clear the house of your mother's things and leave.'

Mariah was beside herself with anger. 'But who will have me? As you have so kindly pointed out, I have no dowry or talent.'

'Oh, do not fret yourself so. Father knows of somebody for you. There's a man at the lodge who lost his wife to the cholera. You might know him. He is an ironmonger with his own shop in the High Street. His trade is good and he already has grown children to help you in the house. He needs a strong, healthy woman like yourself to look after him in his old age. He would be a much better choice than a collier. He would do for you.'

'No, he would not! I know who you mean and I've seen him around his lady customers. He's a greasy old man and he makes my flesh creep. I shall not marry him and Father cannot make me!'

Chapter 3

'I don't know, Miss Mariah, this dun't seem right to me.'

Emma was standing in the middle of the large attic room. A good north light streamed in through two large skylights onto an old oak side table littered with bits and pieces of Mariah's sewing. A horsehair-stuffed calico mannequin draped in a brown woollen cape leaned against the old iron bedstead in the corner. Where the sloping ceilings met the floor, a line of limed wooden doors hid shelves storing travelling boxes and old clothes.

'What doesn't seem right, Emma?'

'Me moving in here to live and you going off, like. You should be 'ere with your family, not – not – where *are* you going to, Miss Mariah? Mr Bowes didn't say.'

'Well, I hear your brother is to run the works for my f–f—' Sometimes, Mariah found it difficult to call him Father. 'Er, for Mr Bowes and he needs to be here to do that. And you are more than capable of running this house as well as I or my mother ever did.'

'Oh yes, you've taught me well and I shall always be grateful. I shall get a proper wage, now. My mam and dad'll be right pleased about that.'

'And your brother's wage will be a help for them, too.'

'Oh yes, our Danny's money goes on rent and doctoring for me dad. He's got the miner's cough real bad now.'

'Your brother must be older than you, Emma.'

'Yes, Miss Mariah. He is.'

'And he does not have a wife yet?'

'Oh no, Miss Mariah. I had three brothers, you see. Only we lost two of 'em to the fever and then Dad got his cough and our Danny said he wouldn't wed and leave me mam with no money now only us girls is left. Mind, I know he's sweet on a young widow woman who lives near to us at home.'

'How many sisters do you have?'

'There are five of us now. The other four are all younger 'an me. My older sister went to the fever, an' all.'

'How on earth does your mother manage?'

'Oh, she's right clever me mam. She makes her own bread and brews beer for me dad and scrubs out for the butcher's wife so we get butcher's meat every week. She even weeds the garden for Dad now. Daniel does the digging, o' course.'

'It is no wonder you have turned out to be such a good housekeeper.'

'Thank you, Miss Mariah. Can I ask you something?'

'Of course you can.'

'Where are you going to? Nobody seems to know.'

'Oh, er – I – I – er – I haven't decided yet, Emma. I – I may have to go away from here altogether.'

'You wouldn't leave the South Riding, would you, Miss Mariah?'

No, I would not, Mariah thought, and why should I? The South Riding is the only home I know and I like it.

'I have not decided yet. But I would like to store my mother's belongings in here with mine until I'm settled. Mr Bowes never comes up to the attics so he need not know they are here.'

'I'll help you,' Emma volunteered. 'Are there still some things of yours in Mrs Bowes' workroom? Master Henry says it's got to be cleared as he going to change it into a gentleman's study, like.'

They worked together diligently until the downstairs rooms were empty of all signs of Amelia Bowes and her daughter. When they had finished, they flopped on the bed in the large attic and took off their boots until it was time to begin preparing supper.

'Emma, you have a split in the bodice of that gown.'

'Oh no,' she groaned, 'I'm growing outwards as well as upwards these days.'

'You are a young woman now, you can marry and have babies. Has your mother talked to you about that?'

'I'll say she 'as, miss! More about not having them, though! At least not until I'm wed.' She twisted round to examine the tear in the seam. 'Oh well, I can mend it and pass it on to one o' me sisters. I liked this one, though.' She fingered the material of the skirt. 'It's real good stuff, is this.'

'Yes, it was one my mother made for me. She had a good eye for cloth and never missed the beast market in case the traveller was there. When she could get the flannel she made shirts for the farmers' lads and exchanged them for all sorts of supplies.'

'She was real handy wi' a needle and thread, wasn't she?'

Mariah smiled to herself. Her mother had been the best seamstress in town and anyone who shopped in the market knew that.

26

'She was,' Mariah agreed proudly. 'Her mother taught her and she taught me.'

Mariah climbed off the bed and began to rummage in an old wooden chest. 'Look, Emma, take one of Mother's skirts for yourself and I'll cut that gown to fit one of your sisters. I have several bodices I have outgrown, why don't you choose a couple of them to wear with the skirt?' She began to lift the garments from their calico wrappings and hold them up to the light. 'These are hardly worn and the cloth is still strong.'

'Ee, Miss Mariah, I've never seen so many gowns all at once. Where did they all come from?'

'There used to be a travelling man from Leeds who came to the beast market from time to time. If my mother had money, she could not resist a bolt end of new cloth from him. We made it up together, mostly into skirts and capes to sell to the farmers' wives who came in for supplies. But sometimes we kept it for ourselves.'

Emma rolled to the edge of the bed and fingered the material of her newly acquired skirt. 'It's beautiful. But then you always look nice, Miss Mariah, even when you're in the kitchen.'

'Thank you, Emma. My mother said you had to start with good cloth. But it costs such a lot in the draper's shop. All ours was from the traveller.'

'I shall be the envy of my sisters.'

Mariah continued her rummaging. 'Why don't I cut them all down? I'll do one for each of your sisters.'

'Oh, I couldn't let you do all that needlework. If you show me, I'll do it.'

'I'll show you and help you as well. If you want we can make a shirt for your father and one for Daniel too.'

'Oooh, could we? I'd really like that.'

'We'll do the gowns first. I'll need to see your sisters. Oh dear, it's going to be difficult for them to come here now, without the workroom. Will you take me to meet them?'

'Oh – er – I don't know.'

'Emma?'

'Well, it's you I'm thinking of, Miss Mariah. It's only Canal Bank Cottages. It's not as nice as here, like.'

'You do not need to concern yourself with my sensibilities,' Mariah responded briskly. 'I am not at all like Master Henry with his airs and graces. Besides, I shall be leaving here soon to make my own way in life.' And heaven knows where I shall be, she thought. 'Does your mother have a sewing box with pins and chalk?'

'She 'as some things in a cupboard, I think.' Emma frowned.

'I'll take mine. Get my mother's old travelling box out and pack up these gowns for your sisters. They are all quite serviceable. And look at this one, it's really pretty. Mother liked a border or a frill, even on workaday skirts.'

As she sorted through the clothes, Mariah recalled how clever her mother had been at making trimmings from bits and pieces in her workroom. She made sure they looked their best when they went into town to market even though Ezekiel Bowes did not have an account at the draper's shop. She never complained that Ezekiel gave her no allowance and accepted that all his money was needed to pay the men's wages at the ironworks. But Ezekiel went to a good tailor for his own Sunday suits and now Henry did the same. Mariah and her mother had clothed themselves with what they could glean from good days at the market, while Ezekiel and his son had bespoke suits made of the very best wool.

If she stayed here much longer, she would begin to despise both of them for their selfishness. She knew her feelings would fester into hatred if she continued to live in the same house

28

as Ezekiel, and this would not be good for her. But she had no idea where to go, or indeed how to live without his support.

'There is one last thing I must collect,' she said at last. 'I shall not be long.'

Mariah hurried down the attic stairs to the spacious landing and then down the wide polished wooden staircase into the hall. She would miss this beautiful house with its well-proportioned rooms and large windows. Yes, it was shabby; she conceded that Henry was right in his assessment. But her mother had made it into a home although it was not the same now she had gone. Somehow, the warmth had disappeared and it was an empty shell. It no longer had a heart and she could not think of it as her home.

Since the funeral, Ezekiel had spent most of his time at his ironworks and Henry had taken charge of house refurbishments. Henry was growing more tiresome by the day. As Mariah nursed her grief, she tried desperately to make allowances for his youthful arrogance, born out of the expensive schooling that had given him such grand ideas about himself.

The morning room looked forlorn, its furniture stripped bare of any signs of her mother's presence. A few ornaments remained on the mantelpiece including her mother's likeness in its silver frame. She took it down and studied it. An attractive woman stared seriously back at her. Mariah could detect a family resemblance in her features, features that had passed to her. The ornate frame had become dusty and she rubbed it with her sleeve before pressing it to her bosom.

'What have you got there?'

She had not heard Henry's footfall in the hall. He stood in the open doorway, smartly dressed for town and sporting a new ebony cane with a silver top.

'What are you hiding, Mariah?' he repeated.

29

'I am not hiding anything. I am collecting my mother's things.'

'Let me see,' he demanded.

Mariah showed him the likeness. 'Our mother,' she explained. 'You must have noticed it.'

'Oh yes. That. Put it back, now you have looked at it.'

'Henry, this belonged to my mother!' Mariah protested.

'I ordered you to put it back.'

Shocked at his imperious tone, Mariah responded, 'I shall not. You told me yourself that – that Father said I may keep anything of my mother's.'

'Well, take the likeness out of the frame then and put the frame back. That belongs to Father. A rather fine frame it is, too.'

'Oh, Henry, why don't you just shut up and leave me alone! I am not taking the likeness out and I am certainly not leaving the frame.'

'I shall have to tell Father,' he warned.

'You may tell Father what you wish! I am sure he will think it is a small price to pay to be rid of us both!'

Mariah pushed past her brother and swept across the hall and up the stairs, bristling with anger. She could not wait to get away from the pair of them and in her anxiety ran all the way up to the attics, so she arrived out of breath and coughing.

'What on earth is the matter? You are shaking!'

'It's nothing. Only the dust from the fireplace.'

'Are you sure you are well?'

'Perfectly well, thank you,' she replied firmly, 'although I shall not be if I stay here much longer. I need something to take me away from this house. Would you ask your mother when it might be convenient to visit and meet your sisters so I may make an early start on their gowns?'

30

Chapter 4

Ezekiel watched Daniel Thorpe from his works office. High above his ironworks yard, he had a good view of everything that went on in the name of Bowes. Even so, he preferred to be down in the yard where the furnace was, packing raw bar iron and charcoal into the stone chests and shovelling coal for the firing. Making blister steel was an art Ezekiel had perfected over twenty years.

He liked nothing more than to take off his jacket, roll up his shirtsleeves and labour with his men. They were good men, hard working and willing, and he counted himself their friend. But they were wary of him; he was their gaffer. He knew they thought he should be up here in the office, paying his invoices and filling his order book, not sweating with them at the furnace face. He continued to survey them as they toiled in his yard.

He had been the same as them once: young, strong, willing, happy to be grafting with his mates. It was what men did,

31

what he did, what he wanted to do, until it had all fallen apart, until his young life shattered. Best not dwell on it, best the past was forgotten. He was a gaffer now and his future was here, in the South Riding, making blister steel, ready for the forge.

Daniel Thorpe was a piece younger than the other men who had applied for the supervisor's position. But his handwriting was good and he came with a top recommendation. He had been at the Fitzkeppel furnaces since he was a nipper and had nigh on fifteen years' experience of making iron and steel. He was a bright fellow who had been to the Mechanics Institute and knew all there was to know about smelting iron into steel.

Ezekiel watched him walk across the yard and nodded slightly to himself. That long leather waistcoat must have cost him a pretty penny. Hard wearing, though, and it set him apart from the rest. Thorpe had bettered himself, like he had as a young man. Well, maybe not in exactly the same way. Thorpe had more between his ears than most and you had to have brains as well as brawn these days to keep ahead in the iron-works business.

Aye, he was just what the works needed. Not wed yet, either. His mouth turned down at the corners into the smirk that signified approval. He listened for the young man's hobnailed boots ringing on the outside steps and knew he had made the right decision. Ezekiel straightened his necktie and stood up with his right hand outstretched.

'Welcome, Mr Thorpe. Welcome to Bowes Ironworks.'

Daniel took off his cap and shook his new gaffer's hand. 'Thank you, sir. Where do you want me to start?'

'All in good time. If you are to be my right hand here, we need to get to know each other a bit better first.'

My, he's a fine figure of a man, Ezekiel thought. Like I was at his age. He straightened his back and pulled in his gut. I've not worn too bad, he mused to himself. Hard graft never hurt nobody and I'm a testament to that.

He said, 'You're not married, are you?'

'No, sir.'

Ezekiel raised his eyebrows. 'Five and twenty and not yet wed? A fine handsome fellow like you? Have you plans?'

'I might have,' Daniel responded warily.

Again, Ezekiel remembered himself, twenty-odd year ago; younger than Thorpe and in deep trouble. His gaffer, the iron-master at the time, knew it. He gave him a way out of his trouble that Ezekiel was obliged to take. He was miserable for a time but it kept the law off his back. Who knows what might have happened to him if he had not been well in with his gaffer? It was who you knew that counted then. Still is, he thought. His son Henry was right. You had to have the right friends.

He said, 'A man needs a wife for respectability. I don't want any scandal at my works, d'you hear?'

'Yes, sir.'

'Do you get on with the men all right?'

'Well, I did at Fitzkeppel's. I don't know your gang yet, but I don't expect they'll be much different.'

'Did you know the Fitzkeppel men outside o' work?'

'A few of us with no wives to go home to sometimes shared a jug of ale at the Lion. Furnace work is thirsty work, sir.'

'Aye, well it's different now. Don't forget you're their gaffer. When you're outside the yard, stay away from the men.'

'If you say so, sir.'

'I do. Keep out of trouble.'

Daniel nodded. 'Sir.'

'Like I said, you'll lodge at my house next to the yard. My son Henry is seeing to the refurbishments and your bedchamber

33

will be ready for you next week. You know how important it is to keep the furnace temperature right and I shall be relying on you to deal with anything to do with the works, night or day. Do you understand?'

'Yes, sir.'

Ezekiel handed Daniel a heavy iron key. 'This is for this door here. Keep it on your person at all times. You can use this office as your own. I'll show you the billing. Make sure it's kept up to date because I check the books every week. I have the keys to the safe and I'll give the men their wages, but you'll do the book work. Understood?'

'Yes, sir.'

'Good. Now, I've been thinking over some of your ideas. Sit down, will you?'

The office was dusty and grubby, with piles of papers pushing open several wooden cupboard doors. Ezekiel's old oak desk had seen much better days but the worn leather chairs were comfortable enough, and Ezekiel watched Daniel's face as he settled in one by the fireplace. Ezekiel shovelled more coal on the fire, sat opposite him and said, 'We're a lot smaller than the Fitzkeppel set up.'

'Aye, sir, I know.'

'And I can sell all the blister steel I can make.'

'Aye, Mr Bowes, but for what price? Do you know what crucible steel fetches these days?'

'I'm listening to you.'

'Sheffield cutlers are crying out for the best steel. Crucible steel. Fitzkeppel's are building another bank of crucible furnaces to keep up supply.'

'Fitzkeppel's have got three cementation furnaces and word has it they're going to build more.'

'They'll always be the biggest smelters around these parts.

But there's plenty of room for others. Sheffield knives goes across the ocean to the Americas. Now we have the railway from Sheffield to Manchester and the docks—'

'Yes, I know all that. But building furnace pits for crucibles costs a lot o' brass.'

'I reckon a yard this size could keep half a dozen crucibles going,' Daniel stated, adding, 'With extra men, of course.'

Ezekiel noticed a wariness in his eyes, which he did not let pass. 'And?' he prompted.

Daniel fingered the band of his cap. 'Well, you can increase your blister steel output an' all. You've got some slack here, Mr Bowes.'

'What do you mean – slack?'

'With the men—'

'They're good men down there.'

'Aye, but they need organising, Mr Bowes. They need more discipline. You don't want to have to watch 'em every minute.'

'That's why you're here,' Ezekiel responded. 'If I do put in crucible furnaces – and I'm not saying I will, yet – but if I do, then you'll have to show the men how to work them.'

'Aye, I can do that. You'll have to up their pay, though. It's dangerous work lifting out red-hot crucibles and pouring molten steel into moulds.' Daniel went quiet, wondering if he had said too much too soon. He'd been lead man on the crucibles at Fitzkeppel's and knew what he was talking about. He could make the best steel in the Riding at Bowes, and he couldn't wait to get started.

'Right, then.' Ezekiel stood up. 'You increase my output of blister steel from the cementation furnace and I'll look into costing up a crucible shed.'

The younger man's face beamed as he got up to leave. 'You won't regret this, sir, I promise.'

'Don't you forget I haven't got a bottomless pocket.'

'No, sir. I thought I'd make a start in the warehouse. See what stock you have.'

Ezekiel gave a nod and waved him away saying, 'Get on with it, then.'

As soon as Thorpe left the office Ezekiel moved to the window overlooking the yard and watched him clatter down the stone steps and stride across the cobbles. After talking briefly to the foreman of his furnace gang, he made his way back to the warehouse beneath the office.

Ezekiel should have been watching his furnace workers to see how they reacted to their new gaffer, but he did not. He could not take his eyes off Daniel Thorpe and his confident swagger that reminded him of himself all those years ago.

It could be me, he thought. History repeating itself. If only Henry had turned out to be like him. There was too much of his mother in that lad. He was always thinking about the way he dressed these days. He was never going to make a proper ironmaster.

He swallowed a quick draught of whisky from his hip flask. This settled him down a little. He turned the key in the office door and went to the safe. The heavy door creaked as it swung open. He pushed aside his money bags and retrieved a thick packet of documents carefully folded and tied round with tape. He stared at it for a long time.

While he was alive the works would thrive. But how could he be sure they would do so after he had gone? He heard voices below, male voices, floating up from the warehouse beneath his office. Making steel was his life. He wanted his only son to reap the benefit of his labours. He had to find a way of keeping the works going after he had gone.

Chapter 5

'We have company for dinner today. What are we having?'

Mariah looked up from the pastry she was rolling out on the kitchen table. Ezekiel rarely came into the kitchen when she and Emma were cooking. 'The butcher sent beef this week,' she replied.

'Got any horseradish to go with it?'

'Emma is just digging up a root in the garden.'

'Grand. You'll eat in the dining room with us today. I don't want our visitor thinking you're a kitchen maid. Make yourself look nice for him.'

'I am still in mourning, Father, and I have only this one gown in black.' Mariah was careful to wear her largest apron over her gown when cooking to avoid any unnecessary splash marks.

He grunted his annoyance.

'Who is your visitor?' she asked.

'You'll see. Be sure we have plenty of cream for the pie.'

'Of course.'

Mariah guessed the company would be one of his lodge friends and hoped Ezekiel would take him to see the iron-works after dinner. She was looking forward to a free Sunday afternoon to get on with her sewing. Emma would be off to see her own family as soon as the table was cleared and the pots washed.

When everything was ready, Mariah carried an oven tin containing a large Yorkshire pudding through to the dining room and Emma followed with the gravy boat.

'By gum, that looks good,' Ezekiel commented.

She slid the crisp ballooning pudding from the tin onto a large oval meat plate in the centre of the table and stood back. Henry was pouring ale from a stoneware jug into a pewter tankard and handing it to the visitor. Mr Smith, from the hard-ware shop in town, looked up at Mariah and smiled at her. Mariah gave him a faltering nod in return.

'Take your pinny off and come and join us, lass,' Ezekiel ordered. 'Mr Smith wants to meet you.'

'I – I have to see to the joint and dish up the vegetables.'

'Nay, lass. We have Emma to do that now. It's Sunday and we have a visitor. Say good day to Mr Smith.'

Mariah bobbed a curtsey in his direction and muttered a greeting. He was a thin bony man with a lined face and knobbly hands. When she looked more closely at him, she thought he might have been almost handsome when he was younger, with a square jawline and eyes set well apart. But now, he looked like a crow, a carrion crow, perched at the dining table with his large hooked nose and his claw-like fingers on the white linen cloth ready to pounce on the food. A black coat, made of good cloth, hung loosely on his scrawny frame. She gave him a small smile. At least the black respected their mourning.

As she removed her apron and gave it to Emma to take back to the kitchen, she noticed his watery blue eyes dart over her, taking in her bright hair, pinned up in coils under a black lace cap. Up and down, his chin moved as he looked her all over until she thought there must have been a tear or something in her gown. His shrewd gaze made her feel uncomfortable as she walked around the table.

'Very pleased to meet you, my dear,' he said, adding with a nod to her father, 'Fine-looking lass, Ezekiel.'

'So I'm told,' Ezekiel answered shortly.

Mariah's heart sank. She wished she could say something similar about Mr Smith. His thinning hair was lank and long at the back. It should have been grey but he had blackened it with some oily substance that was rubbing off, making dirty smears on the collar of his white shirt. He smiled at her again, showing a gap in his tobacco-stained teeth.

Emma had disappeared to the kitchen and Mariah resigned herself to making polite conversation with a stepfather she despised, a half-brother she barely knew and a man whose appearance sent a cold chill down her spine. She knew why Mr Smith was here and she was having none of it! She would be obedient and civil over Sunday dinner, but that was all. They could not make her like him, so he was wasting his time!

All three men watched her as she took her place on her father's left opposite Mr Smith. She cut up the pudding and forked it onto plates. They ate silently for a few minutes, then Mr Smith spoke.

'Very nice, Ezekiel. Your daughter is a decent cook too.'

'Aye. Takes after her mother in a lot of ways.'

'I am sorry about your mother, Miss Bowes,' Mr Smith continued, looking directly at Mariah. 'You must miss her.'

'Yes I do, Mr Smith,' Mariah replied.

'My own daughters, too, have lost their beloved mother. But we have to go on with our lives, do we not?'

'Yes.'

Mr Smith turned to Ezekiel. 'And how are you getting along, my friend?'

'I am well, sir. Henry is home from school as you see. Isn't he a fine gentleman now? He is taking charge of my house refurbishments. I have a supervisor at my ironworks, too. You may have heard of him. He was at the Fitzkeppel works before and was one of their best furnace workers.'

Mariah concentrated on her Yorkshire pudding. She was hungry, having been up at five with Emma to get the kitchen range going for hot water and the Sunday joint. Besides, she was tired of hearing about all the changes at the ironworks and the wonderful Mr Thorpe who knew how to handle the men and was going to make them a fortune from crucible steel. He may be Emma's brother, but he was Ezekiel's underling and she knew very well where his loyalties would lie. Then Henry started on about his new furnishings for their house. Their house. A house bought and paid for with her mother's dowry.

Clearly she was no part of it any more. They had decided her future was with Mr Smith. Well, she was going to have a say in this. Father could not get rid of her so easily. But even as she thought it, Mariah knew he could, for he did not make idle threats. She could not let him sully her mother's reputation. No, the answer was to make sure Mr Smith did not like her. But she had no idea how to do that.

Emma came in and out, taking away the Yorkshires' plate and fetching the joint and vegetables.

'We always use the same plates for our meat, Mr Smith,' Ezekiel commented as he carved the ribs of beef.

'We do too. The gravy is too good to waste.' Mr Smith handed up his plate to receive several steaming slices of tender juicy meat.

Mariah leaned forward to pass Mr Smith a tablespoon for the vegetables.

'Did you cook this joint, Miss Bowes?' he asked.

'Yes, sir.'

'And everything else to go with it?'

'Emma helped me with the preparations.'

Mr Smith turned to Ezekiel. 'The late Mrs Bowes did a good job with this one.'

'I told you. She's nigh on twenty years of age and can look after you as good as any housekeeper to the gentry.'

'Father!' Mariah dropped the spoon.

'Steady on, Miss Bowes,' Mr Smith said. His gnarled bony fingers rescued the spoon and he brandished it at her in a friendly fashion. 'I'm looking for more than a housekeeper, y'know.' He paused. His watery eyes began to roam over her again. He added, 'That's a pretty gown you're wearing, even though it is black. A husband likes his wife to look nice when she goes with him to church.'

Mariah's mouth opened to respond but Ezekiel got there first. 'Sews them all herself, don't you, Mariah?'

'Yes, Father.' She resigned herself to being picked over like a heifer at the beast market. She wanted this meal and Mr Smith's visit to be over and done with as quickly as possible.

Henry added, 'Quite a fashionable gown too, Mr Smith. For the South Riding, anyway.'

Her father added, 'I've been telling Mr Smith how clever and thrifty you are. A man with several daughters needs a wife who can be of use to them.'

Mr Smith simply nodded quietly to himself and piled baked

41

potatoes and greens on his plate. Mariah stayed silent. She was inwardly fuming and could not trust herself to say anything civil. The conversation soon turned to how the Riding was prospering and how fortunate this was for their businesses and she was forgotten for a while. She tried to enjoy her dinner, for the meat was very good and the horseradish fresh and tangy. But every time she looked across at Mr Smith's lined and drooping face, large hooked nose and flaccid mouth chewing his food steadily, her stomach lurched and knotted.

Was Ezekiel serious about her marrying this man? He was well over twice her age, though that would not have bothered her quite so much if he had been personable and she had felt an attraction for him. As she grew older Mariah realised her mother had not known love in her own marriage. But Mariah could not imagine ever even liking Mr Smith, let alone loving him. He was creepy. He always stood too close to his lady customers, making them hot and flustered with embarrassment. The idea of him near her made her backbone go shivery and the food become dry and tasteless in her mouth. She sat back and took a swallow of her dinner ale, but did not feel any better.

Emma came in with pudding and cleared away their plates. Her father droned on about the price of coal and transport. Henry told them how an old farmhouse on the road out of town had been bought by a glass manufacturer and was being totally remodelled. They would soon need a larger meeting place for their lodge friends, now there were so many gentlemen of means moving into the Riding. Mr Smith drank and ate heartily, and looked at Mariah for a good deal of the time. She was more than ready to scrape back her chair after the apple pie and say, 'I'll leave you gentlemen to your cigars.'

'Where will you be, Mariah?' her father asked.

42

'In the scullery. Helping Emma with the washing-up.'

'Not today, it's Sunday. Bring us another jug of ale and then wait in the study for Mr Smith.'

Mariah nodded silently, stacked the plates and picked up the empty jug. She drew the ale from a barrel in the scullery. Emma would be off to see her family as soon as she was finished at the sink.

'Everything all right with you, Miss Mariah?' Emma asked.

'Yes, of course.'

'You look a bit pale and strained. Was the dinner all right?'

'Yes, Emma, you did very well. Don't forget to take that new bonnet for your mother.'

'No, I won't. Thank you, Miss Mariah. I'll be back just after dark.'

'There's no rush. I'll put out the tea later.'

She carried the ale to the dining room, leaving quickly to return to the kitchen and stack the dried crockery on the dresser. Then she riddled the kitchen fire before banking it up for the afternoon, delaying as long as possible the inevitable time when she would have to wait for Mr Smith in the study – the room which had once been her mother's special place. She rehearsed what she would say if he offered for her hand today: I thank you for your attentions, sir, but I am unable to return your affections and therefore, in fairness to your good self, I must decline your offer.

Short. Civil. She hoped he would accept her decision and not make a fuss with Ezekiel. There would be enough of that after he had left. Perhaps she would try and explain to her father that she was not against marriage, but that she wished to have a say in who her husband would be.

The study had a carpet on the floor now, a fancy one, imported from the Orient, with a beautiful pattern of exotic birds. The whitewashed walls, too, had been covered with embossed wallpaper giving the room a more sombre appearance and making it look smaller. A few pieces of drawing-room furniture had been moved in and although a fire had been lit, the room was distinctly chilly after the warmth of the kitchen.

Henry had arranged for a carpenter to make mahogany bookshelves and a large desk with a leather top, which would fill the remaining space. Mariah conceded that the room would look nice when it was finished. She sat in a comfortable leather chair by the fire and waited. When the door opened, her father came in first. He had his Sunday-best cloak about his shoulders, with his hat, gloves and cane in one hand. Henry hovered behind him, also dressed for outdoors. Mr Smith was directly behind them and came straight into the room.

Mariah stood up quickly. 'Where are you going?'

He ignored her question and said, 'Mr Smith wants to talk to you. You be nice to him, Mariah. Do you hear me?'

'Yes, Father.'

Ezekiel pursed his mouth and gave a very slight nod. She doesn't look too happy about this, he thought, and she can be stubborn, that girl, just like her mother. He'd never understand women. Mariah ought to be fawning at Mr Smith's feet. He was a well-set-up family man with money in the bank. His business was good, he had a decent house to live in and was not overly fond of the drink. Perhaps he *was* a bit old for her but, by all accounts, he could still keep her well satisfied in the bedchamber. Proud of himself in that department, Mr Smith was.

Ezekiel wondered if Mariah was like her mother in that respect as well. Amelia must have lusted after men, the bastard was testament to that. And she had wanted *him* in the bedchamber. At first, any road. Well, he was giving the bastard a better life than her mother ever had with regard to that. She should be grateful to him.

'Henry and I are taking a walk,' Ezekiel said, 'we'll be back for tea.' When he saw the alarm in Mariah's eyes, he added, 'You'll not come to any harm with Mr Smith. Will she, Mr Smith?'

'No, sir. I'll look after her for you.'

Ezekiel closed the study door as he left and a moment later Mariah heard the heavy thud of the front door slamming. She remained standing, acutely conscious that she was the only person left in the house with Mr Smith. He stood in front of her and held out a small object wrapped in calico.

'This is for you, Miss Bowes. Best that Sheffield makes and very popular with my ladies in the shop.' He spoke carefully, as he did to his best customers. It was an affected way of talking that did not help Mariah to like him.

Mariah's heart sank. She wished she could say she did not want any gift from him, but did not know how, and, anyway, her father would be angry if she refused it. His hand jutted out further.

'Go on, then. Take it.'

Reluctantly she did and unwrapped the calico carefully. It contained a pair of scissors, brand new, with long sharp blades. They were not fancy but well crafted and would be very useful for her sewing. She appreciated the thought. She hoped he would not take her refusal of matrimony too hard.

'D'you like them?' he demanded.

She nodded and put them on a side table. 'Yes, sir. Thank you, sir.'

He seemed to relax. He crossed the room to the fire, turning his back to it and lifting his long jacket to warm his rear.

45

Mariah felt the room become even cooler as he blocked out the heat.

'Well, sit thissen down, lass. We 'as ter get ter know each other proper like, now.'

Her eyes widened in alarm as he so readily made himself at home in their study. She had not detected such a strong local dialect when he spoke at dinner. But then, that was before he had drunk several tankards of ale. She backed away towards the door.

He raised his voice, 'We'll have no running away now, shall we? Where's there to go, any road? You heard what yer pa said. You 'as ter be nice ter me. So why don't yer sit down here, like the good lass you are, an' we can talk.'

Talk? Yes, talk. In a civilised way, and then he would see the nonsense of it all. She wondered if her father would give her a beating for turning down Mr Smith's offer. Her father had never thrashed her when she was growing up. Not a proper thrashing with a belt or a beating with his cane, though he had slapped her when she answered him back.

'Well?'

Slowly, she returned to her chair, pushing it back a little to increase the space between them.

After a short silence, Mr Smith remarked, 'That wa' a fine dinner you put on today, lass.'

'Emma did most of it. And we are a small family.' She paused. 'Not like yours, sir. I shouldn't fare very well in a large household, I'm sure.'

'Yer don't have ter put yerself down. What tha' dun't know, tha'll learn soon enough. Tha'll 'ave to, wi' my lot.'

'How many children do you have, Mr Smith?'

'Too many now their ma 'as gone.' He grunted sourly. Then he appeared to think better of his comment and added, 'But that dun't mean I'm against having any more. Young lass like you, there'd be no problem wi' that.' He stopped and coughed.

Mariah held her breath as her cheeks went hot; she did not know where to look. She kept her eyes on her hands folded in her lap and examined the signs of wear in her black mourning gown. It would soon be past repairing.

Mr Smith coughed again, loosening the phlegm in his throat, and then turned around to spit into the fire; the coals hissed and sizzled.

Mariah saw her chance. 'But I could not care for your family properly, Mr Smith. I have never looked after children or been a nursemaid or anything like that. I would be of no use to you, sir. You need a wife who has had her own infants and knows what to do.'

'Nay, lass. All mine are growing up now. The youngest is nigh on eight and the eldest lad is older than you. Got a lass, too, your age, so you'd have some company when me and my boys were at the shop all day. And the lasses'll help wi' the cooking an' the scrubbing.'

'But I wouldn't know what to do for such a lot of you! There were just the four of us and Henry was away at school for most of the time. I would be a disappointment to you, Mr Smith. Truly, I would not do for you.'

'Aye. Yer pa said you might need a bit o' persuading.'

Mariah's mind raced. What had she rehearsed in the kitchen? The words had flown from her mind, but her feelings had not: she did not like Mr Smith, let alone love him.

She inhaled deeply and looked up at him. 'Mr Smith, I am . . . er . . . privileged you should consider me in this way, but I do not return your compliment. I have no feelings for you, sir.'

'Feelings fo' me, is it, that yer lack?' He stared at her so intently she was obliged to return to examining her skirt. The silence lengthened until, eventually, he moved away from the fire and picked up the coal tongs.

'T' fire needs making up, lass.'

He stretched out his arm and handed the tongs to her.

He did not give her much room to get by him and her full skirts brushed against his legs as she moved towards the scuttle at the far end of the hearth. His head was on one side and he was smiling at her. She caught a whiff of the ale he had drunk and the cigar he had smoked at dinner.

She leaned over with one hand on the mantelshelf to pick up the coal. As she bent to her task, she was startled by the rough touch of a bony hand reaching up her skirts and over her stockings and garters. Quickly, his fingers moved upwards and under the leg of her drawers to grasp the soft exposed flesh of her thigh.

She dropped the tongs and coal in surprise and attempted to turn round. 'Mr Smith! What *do* you think you are doing?'

'What does that do fer yer feelings?'

She could barely believe this was happening to her. She struggled to break free, but he held her by her waist while his fingers continue to press into the naked skin of her leg. He was a surprisingly strong man and she was thrown off balance, only just saving herself from a nasty blow on the corner of the mantelshelf.

'Let go of me!'

He ignored her plea and tightened his arm about her waist, pressing her against him so she could feel his hot breath on the back of her neck. 'I can show you how ter 'ave feelings fer a man. You need have no worries there. A fine well-grown lass like you and not yet wed at nineteen years of age. It's not right, that.'

'Mr Smith! Take your hands off me this minute!'

'Oh, tha' 'as ter say that. All maids 'ave to say that. But I know better. I know tha' likes it all the same.' He made a soft grunting noise in his throat.

'No, I do not! I insist you let me go this instant!'

'Ee, fiery little thing, aren't yer? Don't you fret none, my little maid, I'll not hurt thee.'

Mariah raised her voice. 'I am not your little maid. Get away from me at once! At once, I say!'

'Yer won't be saying that if yer stop yer struggling. Yer got some pleasures to come wi' me, I can tell thee.'

'Lord, no!' she cried out desperately. 'Never! Take your hands away. You are too forward, sir, and you mistake my meaning. How can you ever think I should want you to . . .' She could feel the heat of the fire on her face and Mr Smith's thin hard body pressed up against her back as he held her so tight she thought she might faint. How dare Ezekiel leave her alone with this vile man? She coughed and choked in her anger and tried to kick his shins with the heel of her boot.

The groan in his throat turned into a chuckle. 'Tha's got a bit to learn yet, lass, if tha' gunna wed me.'

'Wed you? I haven't said I'll wed you!'

His voice took on a serious edge. 'Your father has, though, and that's good enough fer me. We don't want ter be wasting no time, do we?'

Ezekiel had already promised her to him? No, it was not possible, she had not agreed. She hated this horrible creepy man forcing himself against her and breathing down her neck. She tried again to push away his hand but his fingers continued to play with the skin of her thighs, stroking and squeezing as he said, 'Ee, lass, that dun't half feel good to an old widower like me, let me get me other hand round thee an' all.'

'Get off me! Help me someone! Get him off me!' She made a futile attempt to lean further away from him. The glow of the fire was beginning to burn her cheeks, but the heat was nothing compared to the hatred she felt for Ezekiel and this man. And Henry! He, too, had left her alone to endure this humiliation. She hated all of them!

'Steady on,' he muttered. 'We don't want yer falling in t' fire afore we're wed, do we? Come over 'ere where we got more room.' He pulled her away from the fire, removing his hand from her thigh, but he did not let her go. Roughly, he turned her around so she was backed against the study wall.

Her cap had come loose and her hair was beginning to fall from its fastenings. This man, truly, must have lost his senses and she feared what he would do next. She raised her voice. 'Mr Smith! You must not touch me. My father will be very angry! I have told you I am not going to marry you!'

Again he chuckled, a low growling sound. 'Ee, yer pa didn't say I'd 'ave a fight on me hands. We don't want ter be scrapping now, do we, lass?'

'No, we do not.' Mariah sighed thankfully. He stood squarely in front of her. He was so close she could feel his breath fanning her forehead.

'Well now, that's better, isn't it? I know what you young 'uns need. I'm not that old I can't remember what young lasses like you want.'

Mariah's breath was coming in shallow bursts. He had no idea what she wanted! Certainly not him. She had refused him clearly enough, so why could he not accept that and then all this would be over? Her father would be disappointed but, surely, *surely*, he never really believed that she would marry Mr Smith?

'Y-you said we should talk,' Mariah suggested. 'Shall we sit down?'

Mr Smith seemed to recover his composure a little, but he did not move away from her. He said, 'No, no. We're best off here. You thinks 'cos I'm an old man, I'm past it, don't you?'

'No, it's not that.' Flustered and embarrassed, Mariah said the first thing that came into her head, 'I do not love you, Mr Smith.'

'Not yet, you don't. And I understand that. A young maid like you needs a bit o' learning when it comes to love.'

'It is not your age, sir, it's just that—' Oh what is the use, she thought, he had made up his mind about her and would not listen to reason.

'If we are to be wed, it's on'y natural that yer wants ter know what yer getting.'

She was puzzled by his change of tone. 'Well, yes,' she answered, 'that is why we have to talk. But I have already given you my answer, sir.'

'Yer don't know me yet.' He smiled lopsidedly. Y'ought ter try out the goods, proper like. I promise yer, yer'll not be sorry.'

'I don't understand what you're talking about.'

'Oh, I think you do.'

As she caught the leer in his eyes, she suddenly did understand. Oh God, no. Was this what he meant by getting to know one another? Her mother had warned her that some gentlemen could be very persuasive and give all kinds of reasons why they should lie with you before they wed you. But Mariah had not been interested enough to ask her questions at the time.

It was now very clear to her what Mr Smith wanted. He wanted to lie with her to show her he would not fail her in the marriage bed. Dear heaven, she thought despairingly. If she were wed to him, his failure in that respect would be her only salvation! She could never give herself to a man she did not love, and she could never love Mr Smith.

Her rage and resentment simmered. How could Ezekiel do this to her! Did he know how Mr Smith would behave and had no care for her feelings at all?

'No, sir, you misunderstand me. I mean it when I say you must not touch me! Step away from me at once!'

'Just look at them eyes flashing at me. And that wild hair o' thine. By gum, I'll bet that looks a treat when it's spread across the pillows. Well, don't thee worry, lass, I can keep thee satisfied like a young 'un. An' if tha dun't believe me, I'll show thee.'

'No! Let me go!' she wailed desperately. 'What are you doing to me?'

But he was not listening to her. He hardly seemed aware that she protested. He was breathing heavily and there were beads of sweat on his brow. His words came out rushed and anxious, 'I'm on'y gunna show thee, lass. Don't fret theesenn so. Gi' us thee hand.'

'No!' She flung her arms above her head, but he forced one hand down to where the front of his breeches bulged with his need for her.

'Feel that, then,' he breathed 'as hard as a young 'un's and a grand big 'un, even though I do say it mesenn.'

His fingers began to fumble with the buttons on his flap. Shocked beyond belief she squeezed her eyes tight shut. She had to get away!

Trapping her with his arm, he pushed his body against her again and again and muttered incoherently under his breath. She squealed and then her voice sank to a grunt as she desperately tried to yank herself free from his grasp. Her stomach, full of Sunday dinner, knotted into a lump and she thought she was going to be sick all over him.

'Get away from me, Mr Smith. I do not want you near me and I shall not marry you!'

But he did not seem to hear her and, when she opened her eyes, his face had slumped into slackness and his eyes were half closed and glittery. His body ceased its rhythmic movements and he released his grip on her, but he was grasping at her skirts as though he were holding them for support. His breath was coming in short gasps and then, quite suddenly, he let out a strangled groaning sound and relaxed his hold.

Horrified and shocked into stillness, she held herself rigid as he fell flaccidly against her. He groaned again and then whispered, 'Tha'll not want for owt when tha weds me, lass.'

She struggled from his grasp and ran out of the room, through the kitchen and scullery, across the back yard and past the ironworks to the scrub land next to the canal until her legs were tired. She could still feel Mr Smith's breath fanning her face, hear his panting and smell the ale and tobacco on him. Exhausted, she slowed down and coughed. It was then that she noticed the sticky damp stain on her skirt and she retched on the rough grass.

She wished desperately her mother was here. She would never have let this happen. She would have spoken up for her, made Ezekiel understand. What on earth was she going to do? She could never marry Mr Smith. He was a coarse, vile man and she hated him. She shivered in the cold and wished she had snatched her shawl before she fled. She was determined not to return before Mr Smith had left.

She waited until daylight began to fade before going back home and crept in the back door. Hurriedly, she lit a lamp in the scullery and poured water from a ewer into a bowl. She had to get the stains out of her gown before anyone saw them. As she mopped at them with a cloth, a dark patch of water spread over her skirt. She prayed that the marks would be gone when it dried.

The house was quiet and she hastened through to the hallway. Her foot was on the bottom stair when the study door opened.

Ezekiel called out loudly, 'Get in here this minute, Mariah. I want an explanation.'

The fire was dying and he had already lit a lamp. His face was like thunder. Mariah breathed in raggedly. Best get this over with, she thought.

'What do you think you're doing? Mr Smith came here courting and you throw it in his face.'

'I do not want to marry him.'

'I'm not having this. I'll not have it round the town that my daughter disobeyed me, do you hear?'

She stood silently in front of him.

'Nothing more to say for yourself? Too ashamed, are you? I should think so, running off like that!'

She took a deep breath. 'Father, he tried to . . . that is he . . .' She started again. 'He showed me no respect.'

'Rubbish! He told me about that. He was courting you, that is all! Good God, woman, he will be your husband within the month. He has a right to court you!'

Mariah had no idea what Mr Smith had said about his approaches towards her, she simply replied, 'I cannot marry him. I cannot.'

'Don't talk daft! Silly woman! You'll want for nothing as his wife. And he is keen to have you, so you *will* wed him. You'll wed him as soon as the banns are read.'

'Don't make me do this, I do not love him,' she pleaded.

Ezekiel's anger simmered. 'Not love him? You will learn to love him. Besides, you don't know what love is!'

'I know you did not love my mother and she suffered from it.'

'What about me?' he yelled. 'Didn't I suffer too, from being manacled to that whore?'

'*Don't call her that!*'

'Why not? It's what she was! She came from a good family, well off they were, and she carried a *miner's* bastard.'

'You may call me what you will, but my mother was a faithful and dutiful wife to you and I think your own good name in this town would suffer if you sullied her memory with your accusations.'

His silence told her that she had scored a hit. Respect was everything to Ezekiel. He must realise that ruining his wife's reputation, or indeed his daughter's, would have a damaging effect on his own standing in the Riding. Mariah bit her lip and wondered if she had gone too far. She became nervous of his mounting rage and turned to leave the room.

'Don't you turn your back on me!' His heavy hand struck her across the head, knocking her sideways. 'I haven't finished with you yet,' he went on. 'You will do as I say and wed Mr Smith.'

She rubbed her stinging ear and scalp, but stood her ground. 'No, I shall not.'

He hit her across the face with the back of his hand. Her head spun. She stumbled and fell against the door, sinking to her knees. She felt a hot trickle of blood running down her cheek.

'Don't you dare disobey me! I'll not have it. I'll not be the laughing stock of the Riding. Get up on your feet and listen to me. You'll do as you're told and wed him or it'll be the belt for you until you agree. D'yer 'ear me?'

'Yes.'

'Good. Now get off up to bed and think on what I say.'

Mariah sat in the dark for a long time. The cut below her

eyebrow was small, but her face and head were smarting. The damp spot on her gown had dried but, in the light of a candle, the stain was still evident. She had to get it out before Emma saw it and asked her what it was. As she remembered how it got there, the corners of her mouth turned down and saliva ran into her mouth. She felt the vomit rise in her gullet. She could not face another moment in the company of Mr Smith. Nor could she continue to live in Ezekiel's house. He did not want her here and she had no wish to stay. If she left she was sure he would consider his own interests first and not spread the truth about her birth; he had too much to lose. She should leave before he locked her in and beat her into submission. Tonight perhaps. Or tomorrow. She had to go soon. But where could she go? And how would she survive?

Chapter 6

'But our Daniel is moving in today! Mr Bowes said he would be eating with the family and I'm making meat and 'tatie hash. I want you to meet him, Miss Mariah. You'll like him, everybody likes our Daniel.'

'I know, Emma, and I am sorry. I cannot stay. He may be your brother but he is Mr Bowes' works' supervisor. It would not do to draw him into my affairs, so it is best that I do not meet him.'

'You had a row with Mr Bowes last night, didn't you, Miss Mariah? I heard him shouting at you when you got back in from your walk. It doesn't mean you have to go, though, does it?'

'I am afraid it does. I shall stay up here until Mr Bowes has left for the works. Is he at breakfast now?'

'Yes. Master Henry was there, too, all dressed up to go out.'

'That's good. He is usually gone all day. I'll wait until they have both left and then carry my boxes downstairs. Are they coming back for dinner?'

'No, not until teatime. Mr Bowes said to take a jug of ale and two meat pies over to his office at dinner time.'

'Two meat pies?'

'One for our Daniel.'

'Oh yes, of course. Do you think you'll manage here on your own?'

'I should hope so! There's eight of us at home to look after.'

Mariah grasped one of the rope handles to test the weight of her mother's old travelling box. She had packed it, determined to move out immediately. 'We can manage this down the stairs between us. I'll leave it in the wash house and come back for it later.'

'What about the other one?'

'It's got those gowns in for your sisters. Perhaps Daniel could take it to your mother's on one of the carts?'

Emma tested the weight of the second box. 'We could carry it down home together. I'll make the pies first thing and take them to the works on our way. Then I can show you where I live and you can meet my sisters.'

'All right. I'll make the pastry for you.'

When they were putting on their cloaks to go out, Mariah stood for a moment in the kitchen, looked about her and said, 'I shall miss this house. But it is not a home for me any more. I cannot come back here.'

'Where will you go?'

'I shall take lodgings in the town. I have a little money from selling my baby linen. Mother made some beautiful things for me and Henry when we were infants. She was saving them for her grandchildren, but Henry did not want them and I, well, I am sure it will be a long time before I have any infants.' She added wistfully, 'If ever.'

As she said this, Mariah felt a pang of regret for her actions and vowed that if she did have any children, she would make new baby linen, just as beautiful as those tiny gowns she had been forced to sell.

Emma grimaced sheepishly. 'You don't have to leave today, Miss Mariah. You can creep back up to the attic. Mr Bowes won't know.'

'Henry would! His bedchamber is right underneath mine. No, Emma, I do not wish to stay here. I am no longer wanted as part of this family and Mr Bowes' ideas for my future are not to my taste. I'll find lodgings for tonight and look for a position somewhere.'

As Henry had so clearly pointed out to her, she could cook and sew. There must be suitable work for her somewhere. But her immediate problem would be finding lodgings that would take her in as an unmarried woman with no male companion and no obvious way of supporting herself. Word would soon spread that she was Ezekiel Bowes' daughter, so if she stayed in town he would, no doubt, drag her back to avoid a scandal. She might have to travel to Sheffield or even further. She began to feel anxious about the small amount of money she had.

'But where, Miss Mariah?' Emma repeated.

'Emma, I am no longer your mistress. You need not call me Miss Mariah now. Mariah will do. Just Mariah.'

'If you say so, Miss – if you say so, Mariah.'

The two young women smiled at each other, heaved up the tightly packed box by its strong rope handles and set off for Canal Bank Cottages. The Thorpe family lived in the middle of a terrace of little houses with long back gardens that went down as far as the towpath. They belonged to the canal company which leased them to the local pit owner for his colliers. They were situated next to a foundry that had prospered and expanded and was now surrounded by a high brick wall with iron gates opening onto the towpath.

The foundry had bought the land behind the cottages and built a large store for its heavy iron output, effectively cutting off the cottages from the town. The only way to market was through the narrow alley between the works and its warehouse. Mariah shivered in its dankness as they clattered down the slope. At the bottom of the alley lay the canal with its constant traffic of bar iron, coal and manufactured goods from furnaces and forges. On the opposite side of the water she could see scrubland, more ironworks and, in the distance, gentle hills that led to the Fitzkeppel and Grassebrough estates.

A soft breeze rippling the water surface cheered Mariah. It whirled playfully around rows of vegetables in the cottage gardens on her right. To her left, in front of the foundry, the towpath gave way to a stone cobbled wharf littered with spilled coal and pieces of rusting iron. The wharf provided good overnight mooring for any passing barge on its way upstream through the water meadows to Sheffield. A pair of huge cart horses plodded by, diligently drawing a tandem of laden vessels bound for the Tinsley basin.

The scattered spoil crunched under their boots as they walked and Emma explained that Mr Thorpe's bad cough had stopped him from working down the pit and he would have had notice to quit his cottage if the mine had needed men. But the thin coal seam was nearly worked out and the pit owner was laying workers off so, as long as they paid the rent, the Thorpes could stay.

They staggered through a squeaky gate and up a long brick path in the middle of a garden. The path widened into a yard outside a lean-to scullery at the back of the cottage. They stepped into a busy noisy kitchen that seemed to Mariah to be full of squabbling children. Mrs Thorpe stirred a blackened cooking pot over the fire. Mr Thorpe sat in a rocking chair by the fire, humming softly to a fractious infant who was wailing pitifully in his arms. The rest of the room was filled by pushing and shoving children.

Mariah, used to a much bigger house, was stunned by so much activity in such a small space. She realised quickly there were only three other girls apart from the baby, it just seemed like so many more as they crowded around the box wondering over its contents.

After very brief introductions Mrs Thorpe took charge of the chaos. 'Meg, help our Emma take their cloaks and that box through to the front room. There's no space in here for it. Liddy and Lizzy, you two set the table and no squabbling.' She turned to Mariah and smiled. 'You'll join us for some broth, will you?'

'Thank you. I'd like that.'

The front room was small, neat and tidy with a couch, an old polished table and a bed in one corner. The bed was covered with a counterpane that matched the window curtains. Emma and Mariah set the box on the fired-clay floor tiles in front of the hearth.

Meg took their cloaks and laid them over the couch. 'What's in the box?' she demanded impatiently.

'Meg, be quiet! It belongs to Miss Mariah.'

'Oh, but it concerns all your sisters, Emma,' Mariah responded. 'Shall we show them now?'

'Ooo, yes, yes,' Meg squealed.

They unpacked the gowns and draped them over the bed and table. Meg, who was just ten and growing fast, stared at them for a while and then approached warily and fingered the skirts. 'Are these all yours, Miss Mariah?' she asked quietly.

'They were. Which one do you favour?'

'This one, I think. No, this one. Or maybe that one over there, or . . .'

'Stand over by the window where I can see you properly.' Mariah looked steadily at Emma's younger sister for a minute. 'I think the red woollen one will need the least alteration and the colour will suit you. What do you say, Meg?'

'Really? For me?' She picked up the red gown, held it in front of her and danced around the room. 'Oh, thank you, Miss Mariah.'

'Mariah will do, Meg. Just Mariah.'

Meg stopped and looked at her older sister who gave her a nod.

The front-room door opened and Mrs Thorpe stood in the doorway with her hand on the knob. 'I wondered what was taking you so long.' She gazed at her front room as Liddy and Lizzy, who were close behind her, darted underneath her outstretched arm.

'Look, Mam!' Meg, still holding the red gown, twirled around.

'It's beautiful,' Mrs Thorpe commented, raising her eyebrows at Emma.

'I've been helping Mariah to clear her mother's workroom,' Emma began to explain.

Mrs Thorpe turned to Mariah. 'I was very sorry to hear about your mother, Miss Bowes. She was a kind and gracious lady. You must miss her very much.'

'I do.' Suddenly overcome by the warmth that pervaded

this household, Mariah's grief rose to the surface. Tears filled her eyes and she sank onto the edge of the bed. 'Did you know her?'

'I met her once, when I took Emma along to start work. And I saw her in the market place occasionally. You too. You were often admired for the cut of your gowns.'

Mariah's voice shook a little as she pulled herself together. 'Thank you, Mrs Thorpe. I – I thought these might be of some use to your daughters. One or two are hardly worn and I can easily alter them to fit.'

Mrs Thorpe looked around her front room again. Emma was already wearing one of the gowns and it really did suit her. Meg, clearly, had set her heart on the red one and Liddy and Lizzy were watching anxiously for their mother's re-action. She said, 'I usually make alterations myself—'

'As a gift, Mrs Thorpe,' Mariah added hastily. 'Emma has been such a help to me, I should like to give something in return.'

'Very well. Thank you, Miss Bowes. Your gowns are most welcome.'

'Perhaps you would care to choose ones for Liddy and Lizzy now, and then Emma can pack the rest away for another day?' Mariah suggested.

'You are very kind. I shall leave the choices to all of you. Dinner is almost ready.' Mrs Thorpe returned cheerfully to her kitchen.

Lizzy and Liddy, at seven and eight, were almost the same size and tussled over a checked cotton gown with pretty ribbon insets on the bodice until Mariah intervened.

'It's far too big for either of you,' she said. 'Besides, you need something warmer for the winter. The brown ones are much more serviceable.' She searched in the bottom of the

63

box. 'When I was little I put these lace collars and cuffs on for Sunday school.' She arranged them on the gowns and added, 'I'll show you how to attach them, if you like.'

This seemed to please the younger girls and they dashed off with their choices to show their father. Emma and Mariah exchanged a smile and re-packed the box, stowing it under the bed.

'Have you decided where you are going to sleep tonight?' Emma asked.

Mariah shrugged. 'I don't think a lodging house is a good idea.'

'Me neither. You get all sorts in them. Why don't you go back home? Make it up with Mr Bowes.'

'Never. I can't do that, Emma. Please don't ask me why.'

'But you'll be on the streets!'

'Who will be on the streets?' Mrs Thorpe was standing in the open doorway.

Emma jumped up. 'Mam! I didn't know you were there.'

'I came to tell you the broth is ready. Now, who will be on the streets?'

Emma gave Mariah a hurried glance, 'Mariah. She's got nowhere to sleep tonight.'

'Emma! Be quiet about it.'

'Is this true?' Mrs Thorpe asked.

'She's had a row with Mr Bowes and he's turned her out. That's right, isn't it?'

'Mrs Thorpe, please believe me, I did not know Emma was going to tell you this.'

'My Emma tells me everything, lass. Has he really turned you out?'

'Not exactly. But he has made it impossible for me to stay, I'm afraid.'

There was an awkward silence until Mrs Thorpe said, 'You'd better come through for your broth, now.'

As they walked past the bottom of the stairs to the kitchen, Emma said, 'I can't stop, Mam. I've got to get back and put the tea on for Mr Bowes. Mariah will stay, though, won't you?'

'Of course she will. She has already said so,' Mrs Thorpe responded. 'Sit down, dear.'

Emma left through the back door and Mariah joined the girls at the table. Mrs Thorpe ladled her meaty soup into earthenware bowls and handed them round.

Mr Thorpe, who had been gently rocking his youngest to sleep, got up and laid the infant on the chair to doze by the fire. 'Well, Miss Bowes,' he said, 'I'd like to thank you for your kindness. I've never seen my little girls so pleased with theirsenns.'

'It's a pleasure for me, Mr Thorpe.'

Mrs Thorpe finished serving and said, 'Arthur, things are difficult for Miss Bowes at home.'

'Oh aye? It's nowt to do wi' our Daniel, is it?' he responded.

'No, Mr Thorpe,' Mariah replied. 'It's between me and my father.'

'Well, we know about Mr Bowes and his ways, lass. Our Em 'as told us.'

'We'd like to help you if we can,' Mrs Thorpe added. 'I won't see you out on the streets.'

''Ave yer nowhere else ter go, lass?'

'Well, no, but—'

'That's settled then,' Mrs Thorpe concluded. 'You can have our front room. What do you say, Arthur?'

'You're more than welcome to stop with us, lass. We're only working folk, though. I were a coal miner afore the cough took me down.'

'I know, Mr Thorpe,' Mariah replied. 'My father was a coal miner, too.'

Mrs Thorpe's eyes widened. 'Mr Bowes was a miner? Oh! I didn't know.'

'No – er, I mean, er, I should explain . . .'

'Either he was or he wasn't.'

Mariah considered her position. She had left Ezekiel's house for good and there was no going back. He was glad to be rid of her, she was sure, and she reasoned that if she stayed silent, so would he in the interests of his own reputation. But she could not lie to these good people. Nor did she wish to compromise their livelihood, vested in their only son at Bowes Ironworks.

She said, 'I think everyone in town will know soon enough that Ezekiel Bowes and I have quarrelled. They will not know why and I am sure they will talk. If I am to stay here then you should know the truth about me. But only if you promise to keep it to yourselves. I mean that, Mrs Thorpe, because, well, it's about my mother and I do not want her memory sullied. I would rather folk think ill of me.'

A silence fell round the kitchen table. Mr Thorpe broke it by saying, 'That's a fine speech you made there, lass.'

Mrs Thorpe looked wary. 'We're good-living folk here, miss. We may be poor but we don't have no time for idle chit-chat.'

Mariah looked straight into Mrs Thorpe's eyes and said, 'Then you should know everything about me before you allow me into your home.'

Mrs Thorpe frowned slightly and addressed her daughters who were being unusually quiet and listening intently to the conversation. 'Liddy and Lizzy, if you've finished your broth, wash your hands and go with Meg into the front room to try on your new gowns. Arthur, why don't you take the little one upstairs to her crib?'

All three girls left dutifully and Mr Thorpe carried the sleeping child upstairs.

Mariah began. 'Ezekiel Bowes is not my true father. My true father died before I was born. My mother's family – er – persuaded him to marry her when she was carrying me to avoid a scandal. Now that Mother has passed on he no longer wishes to support me and I have nowhere to go.'

Mrs Thorpe sat down. 'Well, I'll be. Has he really told you to leave?'

'Not exactly. He has decided that I shall marry Mr Smith from the hardware shop in town. Mr Smith wishes that also, but I do not.'

'Mr Smith! Nay, lass, he's far too old for a young lady like you!'

'His age would not be such a great concern to me, if – if I cared for him. But I find his ways so – so repulsive.'

She saw Mrs Thorpe watching her intently as she said this and looked down into her empty bowl. Mrs Thorpe said, 'His ways around the womenfolk are well known hereabouts. I wouldn't wish him on any o' my girls.'

'Quite. My father has insisted that I obey him and marry Mr Smith so I have left his house. I would rather make my own way in life – if I can. But you do understand that, for the sake of my mother's memory, I do not want people asking too many questions?'

Mrs Thorpe nodded. 'Aye, I see that all right. But you've got your own reputation to think of as well. Folk round here can be spiteful, I can tell you.'

'I shall understand if you do not wish me to stay in your home.'

'Nay, lass, none o' this is your fault. Not your mother's neither, and I should know. I know how men like their way with womenfolk. I've had more babbies than I can count on me fingers and my Arthur still hasn't lost his liking for the bedchamber — if you know what I mean. Sorry, miss, if I've made you blush, but some men are like that. And I fall for a babby as easy as blinking. I'm lucky I've got my sister over at Keppel to put me right, else I'd have had even more. What happened to your real dad then?'

'He was killed in the pit.'

'Round here?'

'No. My mother came from the North Riding. Mr Bowes too.'

'Have you thought of going back there?'

'They made Mr Bowes swear not to return.'

'That's families for you. I couldn't do that to any of mine. Mind, as soon as they're old enough, I do drum into each o' my girls not to let any man near 'er afore she 'as a gold band on her finger.'

My mother said the same to me, Mariah thought. Though, apart from that dreadful Mr Smith, she had had little opportunity. Nursing her mother and looking after the house had been a full-time occupation and the only gentlemen she met were delivery boys from the butcher and grocer in town. Even her father's labourers were kept well away from the house nowadays. If Mariah went down to the works she was only allowed in his office, which was over the warehouse and away from the furnace. How could you start a courtship on that basis? Assuming that I wanted to, Mariah thought grimly.

She began to fret. She had no regular income and she could not impose herself on the Thorpes for more than a night or two. They were overcrowded as it was. She had a small amount of money that would pay for a few weeks in a decent lodging house. But when that ran out, she would need some kind of work to pay for rent and board or she would end up starving. Or in the poorhouse. Or, heaven forbid, really on the streets! She had seen it happen to other women who had become destitute through no fault of their own. For the first time in her life she realised why there were so many ladies of the night frequenting the ale houses in town. They had no other option. It didn't bear thinking about.

Mrs Thorpe watched her closely as she fretted. Miss Bowes was her mother's daughter, a good, kind woman who did not deserve the grief and unhappiness that she had suffered. She said, 'You are welcome in this house for as long as you wish, Miss Bowes.'

'I am most grateful. I should like to stay. Thank you.'

Chapter 7

'How do I look, Henry?'

Ezekiel Bowes stood quite still as his son walked around him slowly and silently.

'Well?' He ran a forefinger inside the stiff collar that cut into his neck. This was the most uncomfortable part of his evening dress. But the shoes, the dress shoes that Henry had insisted he wear, felt like a pair of slippers. Their shiny patent leather was featherweight in comparison to the heavy boots he wore at work.

Henry took his hand and examined it closely, turning it over and running his palm over the hardened skin and rough edges of the nails. He gave a sigh. Ezekiel snatched it away.

'What's up? They're clean, aren't they?'

'Keep your gloves on, Father.'

'I can't do that! Not to eat my dinner!'

'Then try and keep them out of sight. Bow your head to the ladies with your hands behind your back.'

'I know about that, lad. I have been to grand dinners before.'

'Not at Fitzkeppel Hall, you haven't.'

'No. I grant you that. I wasn't good enough for them when old Fitzkeppel was alive and this young 'un 'as never tekken an interest in local folk before now.'

'If you mean Master Nathaniel,' Henry responded stiffly, 'he is only just one and twenty. If this evening goes well, there will be other invitations to the Hall.'

'Aye, well I 'ope he knows there's nowt wrong wi' a bit of muck under your fingernails,' Ezekiel muttered sourly.

Henry sighed again and corrected him. 'Nothing wrong, Father. Nothing.'

'There'll be other ironmasters there? And engineers? I want to know more about these crucible furnaces.'

'You will be acquainted with some of them from the lodge. I expect you will be seated next to one of their ladies. Do remember to converse with the ladies on both sides of you at dinner.'

'Do I have to?'

'Yes, you do!' Henry sounded irritable. 'Speak to the one on your right for the first course and then the one on your left for the second and so on. And try not to talk about the ironworks. Ask them about their sons and daughters.'

Ezekiel groaned. 'I don't know why we have to have women-folk there at all. We don't have 'em there for dinners at our lodge meetings.'

'This is different. You can talk about the ironworks when the ladies have left us to our cigars and port.'

The evening wasn't the ordeal Ezekiel had anticipated. The first part wasn't, anyway. The men there were better placed in the Riding than his usual business friends. These were forge and factory owners, not the usual shopkeepers and dealers he

71

knew from the lodge. His lawyer was there, too; Abel Withers was chairman of the parish poorhouse board and Fitzkeppel was his major benefactor.

'Good evening, Mr Withers.'

'Mr Bowes! A very good evening to you, too. Is that young Henry over there?'

'It is, sir. He has finished with schooling now and is joining me in my ironworks, I am thinking of moving into crucibles.'

'Indeed? We should have a talk. Not here, of course.'

'A talk? What about, Mr Withers?'

'Your will, Mr Bowes. Henry is not of age, yet. You need a trust for him.'

'A trust? I don't know anything about trusts.'

'As I said, we should talk. Come into my office next week.'

Ezekiel nodded thoughtfully and moved on. Lawyers could be useful when you wanted 'em. There was a churchman there, too. That new one who had been at Amelia's deathbed. At her funeral as well.

'Good evening, Vicar,' Ezekiel said politely as he shook his hand and attempted to move on straightaway.

'Are you well, Mr Bowes?' he asked.

Ezekiel nodded

'We never see you in church on a Sunday, sir,' the vicar added, holding on to his hand.

Ezekiel's back went rigid and he pulled his hand free. Quickly, he took up a glass of sherry wine from a footman and walked to the other side of the anteroom. It was a small oval chamber, overcrowded and uncomfortably warm. He swallowed the wine, hoping to push down the memories with it. He saw the vicar watching him and hated him for it. He hated churches. He grew hot and angry as he remembered – it was all so long ago.

He took another glass of wine from a passing silver tray held aloft in a white gloved hand. He was hardly aware of going in to dinner. There was an old lady on his arm and they followed the procession. She seemed to know where to sit and he was next to her. He was glad to see the vicar was seated at the other end of the table and he calmed down.

My, he thought, the dinner table was laid out fit for a king. Well, I suppose you had to say fit for a queen now this young Victoria girl was on the throne. The polished mahogany glowed and the lead crystal sparkled. This is where young Henry was getting his ideas from. He caught his son's eye as another footman pulled out a chair for him, and smiled. Henry smiled back and settled nearer to young Mr Fitzkeppel at the top of the table.

Ezekiel was next to the hostess, *Miss* Fitzkeppel. She was Fitzkeppel's older sister, Henry had told him. Well, he couldn't ask *her* about her sons and daughters. She smiled at him and he gave her a stiff bow before he settled in his chair.

'Tell me about your ironworks, Mr Bowes,' she asked.

So he did and she seemed genuinely interested when he told her about his new supervisor and plans for expansion into crucible steel. He talked so much his soup went quite cold.

The old lady on his other side was Mrs Withers, the lawyer's wife. Her father had made his brass years ago through the Canal Company. He was dead now, though. Just as well, seeing as the railways were taking most of the canal transport. She prattled on all through the fish about her sons at university. Ezekiel did not care for the pike stuffed with chestnuts and he was glad when a footman took it away so he could turn back to Miss Fitzkeppel.

The wine was plentiful and strong. An elderly butler carried in a roast haunch of venison and carved it at the sideboard, layering steaming slices on plates that were hot to the touch. Ezekiel liked a good joint on his own table and he relished this feast. A footman served him currant jelly and gravy; the meat was well hung and tender, the best he had ever tasted. Henry was right. This is where they should be. Dining with the gentry.

After the ladies had left for the drawing room, he moved up the table to sit with the other gentlemen. The glossy wooden surface was littered with broken cobnut shells and smears of ripe Stilton. Fitzkeppel's old butler brought round a box of cigars and Ezekiel took one, passing it under his nose to inhale the aroma. The conversation became more interesting and he engaged with his companions about the price of coal and iron and how much money there was to be made in smelting steel.

Fitzkeppel and Henry looked bored and Ezekiel noticed them exchanging glances. He resigned himself to the fact that Henry would never have a real interest in his furnace. He wished he was more like young Thorpe in that respect. But his son's schooling had not been wasted; Henry was already making powerful friends in the Riding. Besides, the profitability of his ironworks was safe in Thorpe's hands.

The vicar was on the other side of the table and he tried several times to catch Ezekiel's attention. He managed to avoid his eye until the vicar stretched across with the decanter of port. Ezekiel fumbled as he took it. The churchman nodded briefly and smiled, making him feel hot and uncomfortable. After that he concentrated on his port and withdrew from the conversation. He had had enough of this. He wanted to go home.

Memories had been stirred and he struggled to suppress them. He was torn between wanting to remember and the pressure of needing to forget; to put it all behind him. He wished he was back in his works yard, labouring with his gang, not here, not dressed up like the butler, making polite conversation with the gentry and their womenfolk.

'You went very quiet in there, Father,' Henry murmured in his ear as they went upstairs to the drawing room. The ladies looked rich and beautiful all together in their silks and satins, drinking coffee out of tiny gilded cups.

'I'm tired, lad,' he explained. 'It's all a bit of a strain.'

'Take some of the coffee, then.'

'Aye. I think I will.'

Ezekiel hoped no one would notice him, alone by the window. He had to do this, to be here, to be part of Riding gentry. He was going on all right until that new vicar – oh no, he was coming over –

'Mr Bowes,' the vicar began, 'please allow me to apologise to you. I had no wish to upset you earlier. I was merely making conversation.'

'I am not upset,' he replied stiffly.

'Forgive me, sir, I believe you are. You are, perhaps, of a different persuasion.'

'I am of no persuasion, sir.'

Clearly, the vicar did not believe him. 'You are not comfortable with my Church I take it. Are you, perhaps, of the Jewish faith?'

'I was baptised in the Church of England.'

The vicar looked surprised. 'But you no longer worship with us? I should know if you did.'

'I do not wish to talk about it, if you do not mind.'

'But I think you should. Clearly, my presence here causes you much concern.'

'How would you know what concerns me?'

'It is my calling, sir. As making iron is yours.'

'Steel, actually.'

'I beg your pardon.'

Ezekiel stared at him uneasily. He wasn't gentry because he wasn't a rector. Old Fitzkeppel never had a brother or a second son, so there was a stipend available for a vicar. Ezekiel gave him a curt nod and turned away. His evening was ruined. He hated himself for allowing his past to intrude like this, for not being able to put it completely out of his mind. That vicar was shrewd, though. Shrewd enough to spot a troubled soul when he saw one.

He felt the man's eyes on him as he moved about the room and was thankful when the first carriages were announced. Henry had arranged for them to travel with a glassmaker who lived at the far side of the Riding and they talked of trade and politics during the ride home. But Ezekiel felt unsettled as he prepared for bed.

Long after the house was quiet he lay awake. That vicar knew something, he was sure. No, how could he? He had come here from the south of England and Ezekiel's past was in the North Riding. No, the past was dead and gone; it could not be revived. But as he lay in bed he realised he wanted to remember. He wanted to relive the agony, because there had been joy among the pain. Forbidden joy, wicked joy and some-times, just sometimes, he wanted to go back.

He turned restlessly in his bed, unable to sleep. Finally, he lit a candle and went downstairs for a sleeping draught, shivering in his nightshirt and felt slippers. He poured a few drops into a glass of port and tossed it to the back of his throat.

That should work, he thought. That should take away the memories and allow me to sleep.

★　　★　　★

76

'I'll take those in for you, Em.'

Daniel had come into the kitchen from the works yard as usual to wash and change into his jacket for breakfast. He had been living in the Bowes household for a few weeks now and had settled well. He carried the warmed platters of fried eggs and toast into the dining room and placed them on the sideboard next to a heated chafing dish of kidneys and mushrooms.

'Good morning, Mr Bowes. Henry.' He nodded in their direction. 'Shall I put some of this on a plate for you, sir?'

'Aye.' Ezekiel was dressed as he was, in tough moleskin trousers, flannel shirt and thick jacket, an indication that he planned a day in the yard.

'Two eggs?'

'Aye.'

'Henry? How about you?'

Henry was in his dressing robe. It was an ornate affair of heavy wool, edged in braid and with a gold embroidered crest on the breast pocket. He had tucked a linen scarf around his neck and throat.

'Not now,' he responded tetchily. 'Father and I are talking.'

Daniel handed Ezekiel his breakfast and sat down to his own. He was hungry. He had been up since six o'clock – over two hours ago. As he ate, he glanced at the papers on the table between father and son. They were invoices and not for coal or bar iron. He recognised the supplier's names. These were bills for the changes Henry had been making to the house, for new furniture and carpet for the study and Henry's dressing room.

Ezekiel gathered up the papers and brandished them at Henry. 'Well, if you say you have bought these things, then I'll pay for 'em. But it seems a lot o' brass to me.'

'You want the best, do you not, Father?'

'Aye. I do.'

Emma came in with a pot of coffee and poured them all a cup before placing it in the centre of the table.

'Where are my eggs?' Henry demanded.

Emma looked puzzled.

'Boiled eggs,' he added impatiently. 'I want boiled eggs this morning.'

'Very well, sir. They'll only take a few minutes.'

Daniel avoided her eye as she left the dining room. 'The blister steel will be ready today, Mr Bowes. We can start to cool down.'

'I thought it would be. I'll check it myself first, though.'

'Yes, Mr Bowes. Will Henry be with you?'

Ezekiel turned to his son. 'What do you say, Henry? Do you want to come and learn about what earns the brass to pay for all this?' He stuffed the bills into his jacket pocket and picked up his knife and fork.

'No, I do not. I have things to do here.'

'The works will be yours one day, son. At least find out what goes on down there.'

'You buy iron, make steel and sell it to the forges. There, you see. I know.'

Daniel ate silently. The field mushrooms were tasty and his kidney very fresh.

'You know there's more to it than that,' Ezekiel retaliated sharply. 'It won't do you any harm. Put on your outdoor clothes and come down to the furnace with us.'

'My outdoor dress is for riding or shooting. As yours ought to be. I really do not think we should have working clothes in the dining room. The kitchen is a more suitable place for your workmen to eat, surely?'

Daniel put down his knife and fork, picked up his coffee and sat back in his chair. If he had had any respect for Henry Bowes, he might have been offended. But he thought that the boy was an overeducated, underdeveloped excuse for a man and Ezekiel indulged him far too much. A couple of weeks at the furnace face would set him right, thought Daniel. But that was never going to happen.

'I am not wearing a good suit for the yard, Henry,' Ezekiel replied.

'I don't see why not. You don't have to shovel coal any more.'

'I am not a clerk. I am an ironmaster.'

'*He* isn't,' Henry said petulantly.

'If you are referring to Mr Thorpe, he is as good as. Mr Thorpe is my works supervisor and without him there is no way Bowes Ironworks can make enough steel to keep you in the style you require.'

Daniel reached for the butter and kept his eyes on his plate. He didn't want Ezekiel dragging him into this exchange. Neither did he want Henry Bowes anywhere near his furnace, distracting the men with his foppish manner. Besides, he thought Henry was more use doing what he preferred to do, dressing up and hobnobbing with the local gentry.

Emma came in with two boiled eggs and some thinly sliced bread and butter. She placed them on the table next to Henry and smiled at Daniel, who returned her silent greeting cheerfully.

Henry looked at the eggs disdainfully. 'I do not want them now,' he said. 'You have taken so long my hunger has passed. Father, do make haste and pay those bills. I wish to order more furnishings.'

'I shall call on my bankers *after* I have checked my steel,' Ezekiel responded.

Daniel sought to ease the tension between father and son and asked lightly, 'Will your daughter be returning home soon, sir?' A barely suppressed squeak from his sister made him look sharply in her direction and he noticed the alarm in her eyes.

'I have no daughter, Mr Thorpe, and I'll thank you to remember that.'

'Sorry, sir. I thought—' He saw Emma shake her head and stopped.

'She has shamed us both by refusing to marry the suitor that my father has chosen for her.' Henry smiled. 'We are glad she has gone, aren't we, Father?' He stood up, took two pieces of the bread and butter and left the room.

'Shall I pour you more coffee, Mr Bowes?' Emma asked, reaching for the pot.

Ezekiel nodded. 'Mr Thorpe, while I am down in the yard today, I'd appreciate your opinions on the siting for a crucible shed.'

'Right, sir. I have been thinking about that. We've got to leave space to get the drays round.'

They discussed the layout of the yard as they finished breakfast. Afterwards, Ezekiel went upstairs to fetch his outdoor coat and Daniel carried the coffee pot and eggs into the kitchen.

'You said the daughter was away visiting. What's going on, Em?' he asked.

'She's left. They had a terrible argument. It was after Mr Smith came for his dinner. Mr Bowes hit her. I saw the blood on her face.'

Daniel looked shocked. 'Why didn't you tell me?'

'I don't want to cause any trouble. You saw how he was about her.'

'Where has she gone, then?' His sister look pained and

pursed her lips. 'Come on, Em, I ought to know. I don't want to upset Mr Bowes again by saying the wrong thing.'

'Promise me you won't tell him.'

'Of course I won't.'

'You'll find out soon enough, anyway. She's staying with me mam.'

'What!'

'It's true! I took her down there. I knew Mam wouldn't turn her away.'

Daniel frowned. 'Her father would want to know she is safe, surely?'

'Don't say anything, Danny! If he finds out I helped her, I'll have to leave!'

'All right, I won't. But it doesn't seem right for father and daughter to argue like that.'

Chapter 8

'Daniel!' Mrs Thorpe was sitting on a kitchen chair outside the back door, nursing baby Victoria and enjoying the fresh air after a morning spent cooking Sunday dinner. She was delighted to see her only son striding along the towpath to their garden gate. Mr Thorpe was in the garden, too, showing Lizzy how to weed between the bean plants.

'Danny! Danny!' Meg and Liddy stopped what they were doing in the kitchen with Mariah and ran through the scullery into the yard.

Mariah watched them through the small kitchen window and thought what a happy close-knit family they were and how lucky she was they had welcomed her as a friend. She had been there for several weeks now and this was the first time Daniel had come home. Emma came down when she could, with money and a message that he was busy at the works learning his new job and would see them soon. She also carried messages for the widow in the end cottage, but no one else knew about those.

Mariah had settled well in these happy, homely surroundings. She slept and sewed in the front room, altering her outgrown gowns to fit the three older girls, and showed Emma, when she visited, how to make a shirt for her father. Today, all three girls still had on their new skirts and bodices, which they had worn that morning for Sunday school and which were now almost completely hidden by their calico pinafores. However, they still twirled around in the full skirts to show them off to their beloved brother.

Mariah went back to making pikelets for tea in the kitchen. She busied herself at the fire, dropping spoonfuls of batter onto an iron plate over the coals. But she could hear a chink of coins and subdued conversation through the open door.

'Take it, Mother. Get Father what he needs from the apothecary and some of that salve you like for your hands. Emma has sent the extra money for the girls, and here's a bag of spice for later. Mmm, something smells good.'

'It's the pikelets for tea. Can you stop?'

'Not for long. I've got people to see and Mr Bowes is expecting me back for supper. Emma says their Mariah is staying here. Is that right?'

'Aye. She's in the kitchen if you want a word with her.'

'I do.'

He stepped inside and peered into the darkness that contrasted sharply with the bright sun outside. 'Miss Bowes?'

'Yes.' Mariah straightened and turned to him. Her cap was pushed well back from her brow to prevent it scorching in the fire and her face was pink from the heat.

She had not expected him to be so striking. She had imagined him to be a dreary, serious kind of man who had worked hard at his studies to escape being an ordinary labourer and rise to the position of foreman and then works supervisor. She

83

had thought he would be younger, nearer to her own age. But, of course, she realised that a working man did not get to be a supervisor by nineteen or twenty, even of a small works like Ezekiel's.

No, Mr Thorpe was older than that, middle twenties, Mariah thought. Attractive too, she conceded, and not dreary at all! There must have been many a girl set her cap at this one. He was a well-built man dressed in his Sunday best of a brown jacket and trousers, clean white shirt with a high collar and a dark red necktie.

Mariah noticed that his shoulders filled out the jacket well and his dark curling hair grew thickly. In the small cottage kitchen his height and breadth blocked the daylight from the window.

'Daniel Thorpe. At your service, Miss Bowes.'

As he spoke his teeth flashed white against his skin and his deep voice resonated in the limited space. He stood quite straight and gave her a brief bow of the head. She thought it was an incongruous gesture from a working man in the informality of his mother's kitchen but realised he was rising in the world and learning the ways of his betters. She appreciated his civility; it made her feel valued and that was something she had not felt since her mother had died. That is, until she came to live with the Thorpes.

She returned his compliment with a smile. 'Sir.'

For a moment they simply stared at each other. Mariah wondered what it was about him that she found so attractive. He was handsome, to be sure, but then so was the traveller from Leeds who came to the market, and she did not find him particularly attractive. Mr Thorpe was different. He had an air about him she could not fathom. It was an air that appealed to her, and she warmed to his presence.

She still held the spoon and bowl, now empty of pikelet batter.

He stepped forward. 'Shall I take those?' He removed them and carried them into the adjoining scullery, reflecting on his surprise. So that is Mariah Bowes, he thought. He had expected her to be dark, like her father and brother, not – not this young woman with the remarkable colouring. He supposed that Emma or his mother must have mentioned her to him at some time. But he and his father were often discussing other things when his sisters chattered on and he probably had not listened.

He had first seen her years ago, when he had started his night-school studies at the Institute. A young girl, out with her mother at the end of the working day, seeking bargains from the market stalls. Who would not notice hair the colour of burnished copper? He did not see her often, for there was no reason why their paths should cross. But on rare occasions, when his eye caught a glimpse of flame beneath a bonnet, he took a second glance and recognised her features.

Latterly she had visited the market alone and now he knew why. Why had he never made the connection? He knew of Mariah Bowes' existence before he went to work for her father, but not that she was this fiery-haired girl he had noticed grow into a comely young woman.

'I'm afraid I have interrupted you,' he said.

Mariah glanced at the iron griddle over the hot coals. 'Oh, they're fine for a few minutes.' She wondered how much he knew about her. Since Henry had told her about Mr Thorpe's position in the works, she had asked Emma about him.

Daniel Thorpe had been spotted at an early age as a bright and enquiring boy, learning to read at Sunday school and, from there, invited to join a group of boys tutored by the preacher.

He had gone out to work at the age of ten, though he did not follow his father down the pit. His interest in natural sciences, mathematics and engineering led the preacher to recommend him for a job at the big Fitzkeppel ironworks, and more learning at the local Mechanics Institute where his potential was evident and quickly exploited.

His hard work and diligence impressed Mariah and she admired him for it. As she considered that this might be why she found him so attractive, she experienced a small shiver down her back. It was not an unpleasant feeling, but it was one that was unfamiliar to her.

'Are you comfortable here?' he asked.

'Oh, yes. Thank you.'

'I fear the bed is a little hard.' It had been his bed and it suited him. But he had discovered how much softer feather mattresses were since he had moved into the Bowes household.

'Yes. More than I am used to.'

'I am sorry. I prefer a firm—' He stopped as her face became pinker.

He had embarrassed her by reminding her he had previously slept there. He blinked as his imagination took over and in his mind's eye he saw her at rest in his bed, neatly tucked in with the sheets up to her chin and her brushed and burnished hair spread over his snowy-white pillow. For a moment it was an image he savoured until he mentally rebuked himself. He swallowed, trying desperately to think of something else to say.

Mariah felt herself blushing and raised the back of her hand to her brow. 'Oh, it's so hot by the fire. Shall we sit?'

'May I speak with you on a personal matter?' he asked as they pulled out chairs from the table.

'Of course.' Something about Emma, she guessed.

His expression became serious. 'I did not know that you had left your father's house until I asked Emma where you were. She told me you had quarrelled with him. I am sorry about that, Miss Bowes.'

'Oh!' She had not considered the conversation would be about her and became alarmed. 'Does my father know I am here?'

'I do not think so. He has not asked Emma about you and she has not told him.'

'Then he truly does not care what has happened to me.' Mariah got up and went back to her pikelets, testing them lightly with a knife.

'Oh, I'm sure that is not so!' Daniel responded with concern in his voice. 'He is a hard taskmaster, I know. And proud. No father would want his daughter to disobey him.'

'He has said that I disobeyed him?'

'No, he has not spoken of you at all. I – I heard about Mr Smith's visit from Emma.'

'What did she say to you?'

'Very little. Only that you argued with your father after Mr Smith left and that she brought you here.'

'She did not say why?'

'Henry mentioned you had refused a suitor. I can only guess it was Mr Smith.'

'It was,' she said over her shoulder.

Daniel blew out his cheeks. He wouldn't have wanted any of *his* sisters saddled with Mr Smith, no matter how prosperous he was. 'Perhaps Mr Bowes will relent when he has had time to consider your objections?'

Mariah remained silent.

'It is not unknown for fathers and daughters to disagree. Fathers and sons, too.'

Mariah heard a sigh in his voice as he spoke the last few words and glanced at him. Was he referring to Henry? Or to himself and Mr Thorpe? He was frowning at her, in a sympathetic, appealing way, as though he really cared for her welfare.

He added, 'I am sure your father will welcome you back if you can mend the differences between you—'

'No, sir, you are wrong. You do not know him.'

'He is your father. He wishes only the best for you.'

'Then why does he not seek my return? I shall tell you why. It is because the best for me – and him – is for us to stay far away from each other. He knows that and so do I.'

'Surely this is some misunderstanding?'

'No. He will not own me. Of that I am sure.' She took a thick cloth, moved the pikelets to a cooler spot on the range and returned to her chair.

'Miss Bowes, please reconsider,' he begged. 'I have your father's confidence. I believe he will listen to me and I can speak for you if you will let me.'

'Do not trouble yourself. It is of no consequence to me because I shall never return to that house while he lives there.'

This seemed to shock him and he responded quickly, 'Those are harsh words, Miss Bowes.'

'Ezekiel Bowes is a harsh man! I have told you he will not own me. He wanted rid of me and I have obliged him!'

It occurred to her that, although he was a Thorpe and the Thorpes had been good and kind to her, he was also Ezekiel Bowes' right-hand man. His first loyalty after his own family would be to his employer and therefore she could not count on Mr Thorpe as a friend.

She asked bluntly, 'Has he sent you to speak on his behalf?'

He answered her with an equal frankness. 'Of course not.'

She sensed she was annoying him with her forthright manner

and did not want to cause unpleasantness in this cheerful household. She had a sincere respect for Mr Thorpe's concern, but she did not wish to recall those last unpleasant days with Ezekiel. She felt an urgent need to close this conversation before she became more agitated.

'Do not be drawn into my affairs, Mr Thorpe. They are not of your doing and I am capable of dealing with them myself.' She would like to have felt as confident about the latter as she sounded.

She saw a flash of anger darken his grey eyes. He did not speak for a second or two. His mouth pursed slightly, then he nodded briefly. 'As you wish. I trust you will be safe and well here.'

'Thank you. I am sure I shall. Your family are good people.' Mariah returned to the fire and slid the cooked pikelets onto a warm metal plate.

The appetising smell brought the rest of the family in and they all sat around the table eating the still warm tea bread spread with honey Daniel had brought from town.

Shortly after tea, he stood up to leave. 'Miss Bowes, I am pleased to have met you at last. Should you change your mind about your father—'

'I shall not,' Mariah replied firmly. She saw Mr and Mrs Thorpe exchange a glance and added, 'But I thank you for your trouble.'

Mrs Thorpe put her hand on her son's. 'Do you have to go so soon?'

'I – I –' Daniel glanced at his father, 'I have some plans to read for tomorrow. Mr Bowes has already started to build new furnaces – crucibles, to make better steel – and you know how things are. I'll call next Sunday if I can.'

As he left, Mariah collected up the knives and plates and

took them into the scullery to wash up. Mr Thorpe began to wheeze and cough and Mrs Thorpe went to the cupboard by the range for his linctus. 'Calm yourself, Arthur. He's a grown man and can take care of himself.'

'It's still not right.'

'Arthur, be quiet! The girls are listening.' Mrs Thorpe waved a hand in their direction. 'Meg, take the little ones and give Mariah a hand with the pots.'

When they had gone she said, 'Leave it, Arthur. He is a single man and she is a widow.'

'Then he should wed her!'

'Perhaps he will one day.'

'Not while he can have his way wi'out. All that we drilled into our lasses about wedding afore bedding and he goes an'—'

'Keep your voice down. They'll hear you.'

But Arthur was not to be quietened. 'He lets hissen down when he goes there. I'm right proud of our Danny for everything he does apart from that.'

Meg had closed the door after her when she went into the scullery and the clattering of pots effectively prevented Mariah from hearing the details of this exchange.

'Take no notice,' Meg sighed, 'they're on'y going on about our Danny and Mrs Cluff in the end house.'

Mariah wondered who Mrs Cluff was and why his father was so upset by her. Was this what Daniel had meant earlier about fathers and sons disagreeing? Mariah tried to concentrate on her task. It was none of her business yet she wanted to know more and this irritated her.

Later, as she went through to the front room with Meg to do some sewing, she could not look at the bed without remembering Daniel's conversation earlier. She was unable to forget that this bed had been his. Where she slept, his body had also rested and her pillow had once supported his head. The image filled her mind and unsettled her. He was a man she could not ignore. He was an achiever, a man to be reckoned with and one she found attractive in spite of his allegiance to Ezekiel. She busied herself with shirt seams and pondered on this dilemma.

Chapter 9

Daniel Thorpe was in a pensive mood as he let himself out of the back door of his parents' cottage and turned towards the end house. The differences between Mr Bowes and his daughter ran much deeper than he had imagined. Emma's concern was justified. She, like him, hated arguments in the family. He had tried to help, but there was little he could do if Miss Bowes was unwilling to accept his support.

He reflected on her strong will, a quality he admired. She intrigued him with her forthright ways, but he considered she had acted foolishly. However, she was safe with his family; he felt easier in his mind about her when he remembered that. He feared she was right about her father. If Mr Bowes ignored her wishes so readily, then he did not hold his daughter in very high esteem. Coming from a close and loving family himself, Daniel found this difficult to comprehend. But if father and daughter were determined to oppose each other, he could not see a solution.

He walked down the garden along the towpath and through Mrs Cluff's untidy garden to her back door. How different Mariah was from Lily, he thought. Where Mariah was proud and independent, Lily was compliant and clinging. He could not imagine Mariah behaving towards him as Lily did, but he found himself imagining what she would be like if she did. He had to rein in his thinking sharply and compose himself before he rapped on Lily's back door. Lily would be waiting for him and, tonight, he wanted to talk about their future.

Now he was in charge of the old cementation furnace and looked forward to making crucible steel he knew Ezekiel Bowes would soon be a wealthy man. And Daniel knew, also, how much Ezekiel relied on him for that success. His son Henry was no use at the works, and never would be. Henry was more concerned with spending his father's money on fashionable clothes and buying new furniture for the house than with the price of bar iron and coal. Ezekiel was becoming more and more like his son now, dressing in fancy waistcoats and going to dinner with the gentry.

Daniel shook his head as he thought about his employer. Henry Bowes might be able to pass himself off as a gentleman, but Ezekiel had little chance. The man was too rough round the edges and had an abrasive nature. He was not happy with himself somehow, Daniel thought. Ezekiel was a man who was closed up to others, as though he was keeping himself on a short leash. Perhaps, he thought, he had a foul temper on him and had to control himself in front of others.

Still, a fine house, even one next to the ironworks was welcome when it came to impressing customers. New crucibles meant new trade and new money. And the more money Daniel could make for Ezekiel Bowes, the better he would be paid for his labours.

Strange, he thought, that Mariah Bowes was so different from her father and brother. She had no artificial airs and graces and possessed a kind of courage about her that was unusual in a woman. His mind slipped back easily to their meeting earlier that day. Interesting woman, Mariah Bowes, Daniel thought, I should like to know her better.

He grinned to himself. But perhaps not in the way he knew Lily! Mariah was not a bit like Lily. Soft, submissive Lily who had no hidden depths and whose mock surrenders he relished. He raised his clenched hand to knock on Lily's door and it opened in front of him.

'Danny! Oh Danny, I thought you would not visit me any more, now you are living over at Bowes.'

'And why would I not call on you?'

'I thought you would not have the time.'

He took her pretty face, framed by light brown curls and white lace, in his hands and kissed her on the lips. 'And leave my little Lily all alone on Sunday afternoons?' he asked, drawing out a parcel from his jacket pocket. 'Look, I've brought you some satin ribbons from town.'

Lily took the small package and opened it excitedly, dropping the frayed muslin wrapping on her kitchen floor. 'Oh,' she breathed, 'they are such a lovely blue.'

'To match your beautiful eyes.' He smiled. He looked into them and thought they were, indeed, the prettiest eyes in town.

Suddenly, he was hungry for her and stooped to kiss her again, this time more urgently. He felt her body open to him, curvaceous and yielding, and he wanted her. He gave a low growling noise in his throat, probing her sweet delicious mouth with his tongue.

She made a slight, squeaky noise in her throat, her own familiar, feminine protest that she knew excited him and he felt his arousal pushing inside his Sunday best trousers. Her delicate fingers crept around his neck and climbed through his thick dark hair, tangling and teasing it at the roots.

She pulled away from him tantalisingly. 'Oh!' she squealed softly. 'You are such a wicked man, tempting a poor defence-less widow woman with your charming ways!' She twirled across the room, her full skirts lifting slightly as she moved, so he caught a glimpse of a shapely ankle and a felt slipper. She wore no stockings and the sight of her naked white skin inflamed his passion further. Lily was such a perfect name, pure white and delicate, a flower waiting to be plucked and adored.

'Temptress,' he breathed, darting across the room and catching at her small hands.

Again, she twisted and swirled away from him, opening her china-blue eyes wide in mock fear and simpering, 'Oh, sir! You mean to have your wicked way with me!'

This always made Daniel smile, because they both knew she had been the one to seduce him on that sultry Sunday afternoon last summer when he had been stripped to the waist in the garden and she had called for his help to open an upstairs window. The window was warped and had been stuck fast for years, but he offered to return and repair it the following week and that was how it had all started.

He caught her again, pulling her hard against his body, taking her chin in one strong hand and capturing her mouth again. She slipped away from him through the door to the stairway dividing the two small cottage rooms. He knew when he climbed the stairs after her she would be waiting for him, her eyes as hungry as his.

The bedchamber was quiet, its window shut tight against the gathering dusk and the only sound was their laboured breathing as he peeled away her gown and she unbuttoned his

95

shirt. When he was naked, his muscled labourer's body tense with desire, Lily lifted her chemise over her head and stepped out of her drawers so they stood face to face, as naked as Adam and Eve in their own private paradise.

He marvelled that she understood his needs. He liked to wait, to prolong the pain of passion, until he could barely contain himself. It made their eventual union all the more pleasurable. She had taught him that, as she had taught him how her own body worked up to that same level of desire.

She stood before him, lily white with a skin as delicate as petals. Her full breasts drooped towards a small rounded belly, and, as she turned towards the bed, her plump behind made his fingers curl with the desire to grasp that soft white flesh.

He stretched out beside her on the wide bed and she fondled him, smoothing on the sheep's gut cundum for him. He kissed her breasts and belly and explored her hot wet hunger with practised fingers. He knew that when her arms or legs made those small involuntary jerks she was ready for him, and that, before long, she would abandon any control and be his to tease and tempt until neither could restrain their passion any longer.

His name came from her throat as a strangled cry, and her body convulsed in an arching spasm. He pulsed inside her, closing his eyes and relishing every second of exquisite pleasure, until they lay side by side, spent and sweating in the gloom. Her arm was flung across his body. He took her small left hand in his and fingered her slender gold band.

'Do you still miss him?' he asked.

'I used to. But not since I met you,' she murmured.

'How long were you wed before – before you lost him?'

She hesitated. 'Well, I were wed at sixteen so it must have bin twelve year.'

'That long? And no children?'

'He – he were away from me a lot of the time, wi' 'is brother and their lad. Working on the railway line took them all over.'

He kissed her lightly on the lips and asked, 'Do you love me, Lily?'

'What kind of question is that for a woman lying beside you in a bed?'

'No, I mean more than this. I know we are good for each other like this, but do you love me as a man as well?'

'Of course I do! What woman wouldn't? You are strong and handsome with a good job and a regular wage.'

He pushed her away playfully. 'So it's my good job and regular wage you love?'

'You know it's not!'

'What is it, then?'

She stroked his hard chest, roughened with hair and drew light fingers down over his firm flat stomach to fondle him gently. 'It's this,' she said quickly. 'It's being with you like this. I need you, Daniel.'

They were two of a kind, he thought. She craved the possession of his body as he did hers. He wondered whether it would be enough for them together.

'Could you live with me?' he asked.

Lily sat up promptly. 'What is this, Daniel? What do you mean, "live with you"?'

'Well, I'm earning good money now. And it's two years since you were widowed, you could wed again if you wanted.'

Lily looked surprised at first and then wary. 'Are you asking me?'

'Yes,' he replied firmly. 'Marry me, Lily. Make all this legal and respectable.'

'I couldn't! Er – that is –' Lily stuttered. She shook her head. 'I thought you just wanted – well – just wanted this.'

'We live in a small town. We cannot carry on as we are. People are beginning to talk.'

'Is that why you want to marry me? Because now you're a fledgling ironmaster people might talk about us?'

'I am worried about you,' he snapped. 'Folk round here know about us and they can be hard on women they see as sinful.'

Lily was quiet. All the other women in Canal Bank Cottages were wives and two of them were her age. But none of them spoke to her in the street and even Mrs Thorpe ignored her. But she did love Daniel.

'I didn't know you thought like that about me.'

'You know I love you.'

'Well, you say you do when we do this, but—'

'If you were prepared to walk out with me on a Sunday afternoon, others would see that I do!' He was becoming irritated with her. He was five and twenty. He had a future in this town and she was a childless widow. He had thought she would be pleased he was prepared to offer for her. But she was shaking her head.

'I can't do it. I can't marry you.'

'Why ever not?' he demanded.

She looked desperate, almost frightened, and he began to wonder what her husband had been like to her.

'It's – it's too soon after . . . It's just too soon. My brother would not approve.'

'You're thirty years old, for God's sake! Who is this brother of yours? Let me talk to him.'

'He's – he's my – my late husband's brother. He looks out for me.'

This was the first Daniel had heard of him and he became

alarmed. 'Is he some kind of benefactor to you? Or does he want you for himself? Do you have an understanding with him? Is that it?'

'No. Nothing like that. He has his own wife and grown-up son.'

'What then?'

'I told you, he looks out for me. He's family.'

'You're independent, Lily. You said your husband left you money.'

'A little. His brother looked after me at first but I – I had to get away from – from the memories.'

'So? I can look after you now. I can pay your rent. Why don't you let me do that for you?'

'Oh no! You can't do that!'

'Why not? If we love each other and we are going to wed—'

'But we're not. If you paid my rent I would be a—!'

If she could not bring herself to say the word, he would say it for her. He did not understand why she had rejected him and he was angry with her. If she did not love him she ought to say so. But he knew she did love him, so why wouldn't she marry him?

'Whore?' he finished for her. 'Is that what you mean? If I pay your rent, it makes you a whore? Well, let me tell you something, Lily. Every time I visit you I leave you money for food and coal! And if you don't love me, if you don't care for me, then that does make you a whore!'

'Stop it! I do care for you, I do love you. It's just that we can't – can't marry. Not just yet.'

'I don't understand. There is nothing to stop us. I have a good position at Bowes and it is difficult for me to keep coming down here like this.'

She rolled over and clung to him, her heavy breasts pushing against his chest. 'Don't leave me, Danny! Please say you won't leave me!'

'I don't want to, Lily. But you're making it tough for me.'

'I need you, Danny.' She began to whimper and her wide blue eyes glistened with unshed tears. 'I've done my best to please you. I do please you, don't I?'

'You do. You do. Oh, come here.' He began to kiss her tumbled hair and then her eyes and nose and lips. She had taught him such a lot and he thought she did love him really. Perhaps it *was* too soon for her to wed again? Perhaps her late husband's family felt she needed their protection? Perhaps he had been too hasty? He decided to talk to her brother before he mentioned marriage again.

He began to stroke her skin, tracing the shape of her breasts and waist and the roundness of her rump until she relaxed, then he fondled her between her thighs until she, once again, began the slow climb to abandonment.

It took her longer this time so he pulled her on top of him, watching the rising ecstasy in her face and her sheer pleasure as she controlled their movements. He hoped she would be quick because he wore no protection. She was, and she cried out as she rocked and then flopped back onto the bed, spent and exhausted. She was unaware she had left him unsatisfied but she had forgotten their quarrel and that made him happy.

He could not keep visiting her now he was working for Ezekiel Bowes. There was already too much gossip, and Mr Bowes would not tolerate any scandal. Daniel had a good position and did not wish to lose it.

Besides, he wanted to marry Lily. She was the first woman he had seriously courted. If what they had could be called courting, for she never let him take her anywhere they would be seen together. She was the only woman he had bedded. But she was true to him, he was sure. He would have found out if she had been with anyone else.

He had to wed Lily soon! He would not give her up.

Chapter 10

'That's him!'

Daniel heard the thud of heavy boots behind him as he cut through a narrow alley that led from the canal wharf past the forge. The weather was overcast and gloomy and the track was quiet as the works closed on the Sabbath. High iron gates secured the yard fronting the canal, and a blank brick wall formed the alley boundary.

'What the—!' Daniel turned and was met by two angry men, roughly dressed. They rushed at him with clenched fists, and started to throw random punches at his head and body.

Taken by surprise, he shielded his head with his arms until a well-placed fist in the middle of his body winded him and his knees buckled. The younger of the two men grabbed his arms and pinioned them behind him while the other positioned himself squarely for a further attack.

Daniel saw a consuming rage in the older man's eyes and felt a sudden sickening fear. The man drew a knife from the waistband of his trousers and approached Daniel slowly. Terror sent Daniel's pulses racing. These men were not just a couple of drunks looking for sport. They had a killing in mind. But why him? He did not know them. He had not seen them before in town.

'I'll teach you to mess with one o' the Cluff women,' the man growled menacingly. 'You'll be lucky if you can shove your cock in a greased pipe by the time I've finished with you.'

Daniel did not wait to reason with him, or to argue the mistaken identity he was sure this was. His woman was a widow and a willing mistress. Had one of their women been set upon and degraded in some way? Was the ruffian holding his arms a vengeful suitor? He could smell drink on both men and, mistake or not, they meant to do him harm.

He twisted round sharply, bending his strong back to throw his captor off balance, flinging him bodily against the other attacker, following through with a kick that made the younger man yelp with pain. Both men fell heavily on the cobbles and he heard one call, 'Mind the knife!'

Daniel used those few seconds to search around for a weapon, an old fence post, an iron bar, anything to even the odds of two against one. He found nothing and fear gripped his stomach as the ruffians untangled themselves. These were not men who gave in easily. They were a couple of thugs, toughened by the struggles of surviving the harsh world of industry.

Daniel was taller and broader than either of them and did not doubt he could lick each one soundly in a one on one fight. But two of them together? And one of them with a knife! He feared for his manhood if not his life.

He aimed a couple of kicks at both men as they struggled

to their feet, effectively flooring them again and shouting, 'You've got the wrong man, mate!' Then he ran for all he was worth along the alley and away from these snarling, snapping villains.

As he ran, he heard one of them call after him, 'We'll get you, Thorpe. We'll find a way. You see if we don't. No one fucks one o' the Cluff women and gets away with it!'

Daniel continued to run, up the hill and away from the canal, his breath coming in fits and starts as he darted across the square to the back of Bowes Yard. He slowed down, breathing heavily as he approached the gates. They knew who he was and they talked of Cluff women.

Lily's husband was a Cluff but he was dead, taken by the fever. The same fever that had robbed him of his own brothers a few years back. It had hit most of the industrial towns. Surely they could not mean Lily? She and her late husband came from Manchester. Besides, she had told him that there was no one else. He let out a sigh. It must be another Cluff. There were a few by that name down Mexton way and somebody had got it wrong.

As he unlocked the gate and let himself into the yard, he reflected that this was a nasty outcome of the gossip about him and Lily. The sooner she was Lily Thorpe the sooner they would still the wagging tongues. He reckoned he could persuade her to wed him eventually. Perhaps he would be firm about courting her more openly, walk out with her on the Sabbath and be proud of themselves as a couple.

He wondered again why she was so against wedding him. Emma constantly reminded him that he was quite a catch now for an ordinary working lass. Women! He was a slave to Lily's body, but he would never understand her reasoning! The thought of her delicious soft curves waiting for him at his next visit to her cheered him as he leaned against the warehouse door to recover his breath before he went into the house.

The following week Daniel had trouble with the old brick-work in the cementation furnace and had to let it cool right down so the fault could be repaired. He stayed at the works all weekend overseeing the repair. He was anxious to have the furnace ready to load again when the men arrived for work on Monday morning. Ezekiel and Henry were at the country-house home of the biggest ironmaster in the Riding and would not be back until after dark. Emma roasted a hand of pork for herself and Daniel and he came in from the works yard to eat it with her at the kitchen table.

'That was very good, little sister,' he said, as he finished off her rhubarb pie. 'As good as our mother's.' He got up from the table. 'Sorry I can't stay and talk. I have to get back to the furnace.'

'Will you be going home for tea?' Emma asked.

'Not today. Here, take this money for Mother and tell Father I'll try and get down to see him one evening after I've got the furnace going again.'

Emma washed the pots, then laid out some bread, cheese and pickles on the kitchen table for Daniel's tea. She saw to the fire, damping it down to keep it in until she got back. Then she cleaned herself up in the scullery and went up to her attic to put on the new gown Mariah had given her and helped her alter. It was made of lovely reddish brown cloth and fitted her perfectly. She twirled around the room making the full skirts flounce out about her, showing her brown boots and thick stockings and the frill on her drawers underneath.

The sky was cloudy again and she needed her shawl to walk down the hill to Canal Bank Cottages. They were all

105

pleased to see her and spent the afternoon talking and laughing in the kitchen. After tea, Emma and Mariah went through to the front room to work on the shirt Emma was making for her father. They wouldn't let the little ones in because they were using the best white linen from the market and wanted to keep it clean. They sewed by the window until dusk, when it became too dark to see the tiny stitches even by the oil lamp.

Emma got up and stretched. 'I must be getting back to put out a cold supper for . . .' She stopped, glancing at Mariah.

'It's all right, Emma. You can talk about my half-brother and his father without upsetting me. They are nothing to me now. I hope they are paying you well.'

'Ooh yes, Mariah, and Master Henry lets me have Meg in to help clean up while the alterations are being done.'

'Alterations?'

'Mr Bowes is having two big doors made leading from the dining room to the drawing room. And the bedchambers are having paper on the walls! Master Henry has been buying new furnishings and everything. I've never seen anything like it!'

'This is to entertain their new friends, I presume. How will you manage?'

'Oh, Master Henry said they would be getting in a proper cook and housekeeper and I would have to do what she says when she's there.'

'Their new friends must be quite important people in the Riding, then?'

'Oh, yes. They are visiting the Fitzkeppels again today. Fancy that, eh? The Fitzkeppels.'

'Yes, indeed,' Mariah responded wryly. Mr Fitzkeppel was the wealthiest ironmaster in the Riding and owned land with coal underneath it as well as the biggest ironworks in the area, located in a prime spot between the river and the canal. Henry must have worked hard to get such an invitation, for, most certainly, the Fitzkeppels would never have entertained his father.

'I should get back before it's pitch black. I hate going past the forge when it's dark.'

'I'll walk with you to as far as the square. You'll be safe from there.'

'But what about you? You'll have to come back along the towpath on your own!'

'Oh, I don't mind that. There's usually a barge moored with a lamp glowing on board and some wife taking in her washing off the bushes. It's just the alley by the works that's creepy. It's so dark.'

'We'd better get a move on, then. You'll need your shawl. It's chilly out.'

The cottages were quiet as families settled in for a Sunday evening around the kitchen fire, reading Bible stories and talking. The end house was different. The back door was open and there was a commotion going on. Two men and a woman were standing outside shouting at each other. The woman was crying.

Mariah slowed and put her hand on Emma's arm. 'Shall we go the long way round?'

Emma peered through the gloom as they passed the end of the garden. 'Ooh, what's going on there? It's not our Daniel, is it?'

'Isn't he at work today?'

'Aye, you're right.' The two girls stopped, unsure of which way to go. But the shouting went on. 'That's Mrs Cluff from the end cottage who's crying. He's sweet on her, you know, our Daniel.'

'We'd better get on. It's none of our business.'

'It might be our Daniel's business. I wonder who those men are? Can you see them?'

'Don't stare, Emma.'

'I can't make out their faces. I expect they're strangers 'cos Mrs Cluff's from Manchester. Our Daniel said she came here to stay with a cousin over Mexton way.'

'Mexton?'

'It's rough over there, isn't it? Danny said it was a distant cousin of her husband and she'd gone there to get over his death.'

'Shush, they might hear you.' Mariah tugged at Emma's shawl. 'We'll carry on this way. Hurry, it's getting dark.'

As they walked by the end cottage, the shouting stopped. Mariah began to feel uneasy. Mrs Cluff was still hiccupping and sniffing, but the men were silent. Mariah kept her head down and her eyes firmly fixed on the dirt path beneath her boots. But she was sure they were watching her. Her and Emma.

Emma's head turned towards the cottage when they passed the garden gate. 'I don't like the look of them at all,' she whispered.

'Just ignore them.'

They hurried along the towpath in silence. Mariah heard a garden gate creak and her heart began to beat a little faster. Then there was a crunch of heavy boots on loose stones behind them. She took Emma's hand in hers as they reached the high iron fencing and turned up the alley towards town.

Mariah thought she would not come back this way. There was another way round. It took longer and came out at the front of the cottages, but it avoided the alley.

'I think they're following us.' Emma moved closer and linked arms.

'No,' she reassured the younger girl, 'they're only taking the same way home, that's all.'

But Mariah's voice shook and, when she looked behind her, she saw the men were catching up quickly. They jostled Emma as they overtook the two women and then stopped, barring their way forward. The two girls backed away until they were hard up against the high brick wall.

'What do you want?' Mariah demanded. 'We don't have any money.'

They were full-grown men but one was thicker set and older than the other. Close up she saw they were ill-dressed ruffians with heavy boots on their feet. The older man bared his teeth and leered at her.

'Well, my lad, I think our luck is in tonight,' he said. 'We got two o' the Thorpe lasses together 'ere. D'y' think we can handle two on 'em?'

The younger man began to chuckle. 'Oh aye, Dad. One each, like.'

Mariah sensed Emma go rigid beside her. Her hand tightened on Mariah's arm and the younger girl said, 'Our Daniel is coming to meet us. He's on his way now.'

The older man stepped closer. 'Your Daniel! Oh aye, we know all about your Daniel. Thinks 'e can tek what 'e likes when 'e likes, 'e does.'

'What do you mean?' Mariah demanded. She sounded much more confident than she felt.

'Don't tell me y' don't know what your Daniel gets up to in t' end 'ouse on a Sunday a'ternoon.' The older man sneered.

His son added menacingly, 'An' we're gunna teach him not to tek what's not 'is. See how 'e feels when it 'appens to 'im!'

Fear stiffened Mariah's back as the men circled them, looking them up and down and moving closer. She released Emma's arm, took her hand and whispered, 'When I let go of your hand, run for your life and get Daniel. Run as fast as you can, Emma.'

The older man was taking a particular interest in Mariah. He was so close to her that she could smell the stale sweat and grease on his clothes and see his broken, blackened teeth as he threatened them.

'Think you're 'andsome, you Thorpe lasses, don't you? Living in a pit man's house and prancing about in your fancy frocks? Well, we'll make whores o' you like your Daniel's done ter our Lily. You see if we don't!'

Mariah's face froze in horror but she saw her chance as the younger man moved away from his father. She dropped Emma's hand and yelled, 'Run, Emma. Now!'

Emma darted between the two men and fled up the alley towards the square. Mariah, confident that their real quarry had escaped, faced the two men squarely and declared, 'You are wasting your time with me. I am not a Thorpe.'

Chapter 11

The younger man swivelled round to run after Emma but his father stilled his progress.

'Let 'er go, lad. This 'un'll do fer starters. We can gi' young Thorpe a warning, like, wi' this 'un.'

'I am not one of the Thorpe sisters,' Mariah said firmly.

'D'y' 'ear that? This 'un lies an' all.' He leered at her. 'We seen yer come out o' the Thorpe 'ouse. We knows yer lives there.' He grabbed her roughly by her arm and dragged her down the alley towards the canal.

Mariah pulled and struggled but was no match for the two of them. In fear of her life she opened her mouth to scream for help. A grimy hand stifled her and the older man breathed in her ear.

'We ain't gunna kill you. There's no fear o' that. We wants yer ter go back to yer jumped-up gaffer of a brother and tell 'im what's 'appened. We wants 'im ter know what's it's like to 'ave 'is sister turned inter a whore. Cos whoring is

111

all you'll be fit fer when we've done with thee.'

As soon as he removed his hand Mariah inhaled deeply and tried to scream again. But this time a corner of her shawl was stuffed roughly into her mouth until she almost choked on it, and then they wound it about her head so she could not see and could barely breathe. They took hold of her arms and hauled her bodily along the towpath away from the cottages.

The hard stone under the toes of her boots told her they were dragging her past the forge loading wharf. Their hands gripped her arms so tightly they hurt. She attempted to struggle free and shout for help but fragments of wool from her shawl caught in her nose and at the back of her throat making her cough.

They pulled her through the scrubby bushes bordering the towpath and she heard her skirts tear on the branches and thorns. Then the ground became softer as they lugged her across the hummocks of the water meadows. It seemed a long way across the bumpy grass until they stopped and she heard the older man say, 'This'll do. It's far enough away to let 'er scream to 'er 'eart's content and nob'dy'll 'ear.'

He sounded out of breath and both men loosened their hold. Mariah took her chance and tried to break free, tearing the shawl from around her head. It was a hopeless attempt. They grasped her skirts and the fabric ripped away further as she fell head first to the ground.

'Eh up, Dad, she's a bit of a fighter, i'n't she? D'yer think she fights dirty like her brother?'

'Maybe she does, maybe she doesn't, lad. Either way we can 'ave usselves a bit o' fun finding out. A man likes a bit o' fighting spirit in a wench.'

They rolled her over on to her back and bent over her, laughing at her cries and attempts to escape and pinning her easily to the cold damp ground. The moon had risen giving an eerie silver light that was reflected in her frightened eyes as she cowered there, terrified of what they might do.

'Handsome woman an' all, i'n't she, lad? A man likes a pretty face to look at when he's fucking 'er.'

'No, please, no,' she cried. 'You are mistaken. I'm not a Thorpe. I'm not.' She shook her head from side to side and lifted her feet off the ground to try and kick them as they leered at her. Both men grinned.

The younger one said, 'I'll wager she's a maid an' all. Word 'as it in the tavern that all the Thorpe lasses are maids and will be maids until they wed.'

'This 'un won't be.' The older man's voice had taken on a hard edge. 'An' she'll be lucky if any man wants to wed 'er after we've done wi' 'er. I'll teach that young Thorpe stallion to mess wi' one o' the Cluff women. Tek 'old of 'er arms and keep 'er still.'

'I'm Mariah Bowes. Bowes—' she wailed. But her throat was closing with fear so her voice weakened and they did not hear her. She struggled and kicked as the older man tore away her skirts and pulled down her drawers until she felt the cold night air on her naked thighs and stomach. Her strength to fight was sapping away. She clenched every muscle in her body, drawing up her insides as tight as she could and crossing her legs rigidly as he took off his jacket and unbuttoned his trousers.

His heavy body on hers squeezed her breath out of her lungs. She smelled the oil and grease on the coarse cloth of his waistcoat and the foulness of his breath so close to hers. He did not try to kiss her. He fumbled around his open trousers and then, with both his hands, gripped her thighs pulling them wide apart. Her sinews tightened against him. She tried to push her back into the ground to get away from him as he

113

jabbed at her until he found his way into her. Thorns and nettles scratched and stung her naked skin but it was nothing compared to the pain of his assault, stretching and tearing her virgin flesh as he shoved and grunted and, finally, pulsed inside her until he was spent. His sweating face, roughened with coarse stubble, fell against hers, smothering her cries, which were now reduced to feeble whimpers of protest and pleading with them to stop.

'Thy turn now, lad,' he mumbled.

The younger man tore away the tattered remains of her gown and chemise exposing the full extent of her skin to the elements. He had already rolled down his trousers and he knelt over her, his hands pinching at her breasts and then his teeth nipping at her until she yelped with pain.

He laughed. 'Tha likes it, really,' he said, and probed between her legs with his fingers before invading her as roughly as his father had done before him.

She was past struggling now, worn out by the effort, numb with shock and whimpering with pain. Lord, help me, she cried silently. Lord, where are you? Help me. Someone must be there. Anyone. Please help me. But no one was listening to her in that isolated ditch away from track and canal. No one came to rescue her as they invaded her body and humiliated her in the most brutal manner.

She began to pray they would kill her, for then it would be over. But they had said they would not do that. They wanted her to live, to tell Daniel Thorpe what they had done and why. But she would rather die and wished only for it to end, and for them to leave her alone so she could fade away. She would rather be dead than endure any more of this most personal of tortures.

But endure it she must. She realised they had not finished

with her and meant to continue to raid her body, forcing themselves into her, one after the other. The pain and despair brought on tears. She squeezed her eyes tight shut and held her breath. If she stopped breathing she would faint. She hoped, again, that she would die quickly. She did not know how long they were there with her, in that cold wet field, worrying and sporting with her as a terrier does with a frightened, cornered rabbit.

When she roused, she could feel nothing except the heavy weight of a man on top of her and the cold night air on her exposed skin. Her wide-open eyes stared straight up at the sky. There was a moon, bright and silvery, playing hide and seek behind fast-moving clouds. She thought she heard a distant voice calling her name. No, she was wrong. The voice was here, above her, rough and grunting, like a boar on heat. It was not a nightmare. It was real.

He climbed off her and she saw the older man's face, leering triumphantly in the moonlight. Vomit rose in her throat and she twisted her body to spew on the grass. She grasped at the tattered remnants of her gown to wipe her mouth as he bent down towards her.

'Listen 'ere, you little whore,' he breathed menacingly, 'tell that fuckin' brother o' thine that if he don't stay away from our Lily, next time it'll be his *little* sisters.' He buttoned up his trousers. 'Come on, lad. We're finished 'ere now.'

She was dimly aware of them crashing through the hedges, making their way further across the fields, away from the canal and town. The taste of vomit burned the back of her throat, her feet were icy in her boots and cold crept through her veins. Her last conscious thought, lying there alone and in that dark and freezing field, was that, soon, it would be all right, soon she would be dead, and then everything would be all right.

Chapter 12

As Emma ran away leaving Mariah to face the two thugs alone she heard her protest that she was not a Thorpe. Mariah could stick up for herself and if it was a Thorpe they were after, she would be all right. Even so, Emma was frightened and wondered what all the fuss was about. No matter. Daniel would sort it out. He always did. Since Father had come down with the miners' cough he had been the strength behind their family, able in mind and body. Emma relied on him to know what to do.

'Danny! Danny!' Emma ran across the works yard, past the half-built crucible shed to the old cementation furnace where two or three men were standing talking.

'Where's Danny?' she demanded.

'Danny? Who's Danny?'

'The supervisor here.'

'Oh, you mean Mr Thorpe? Sorry, miss, we don't work here, we're only masons doing the repairs.'

'Do you know where he is?'

'Inside t' furnace. Checking it out wi' our boss. Hey, steady on, you can't go in there. It's not for womenfolk.'

Emma ran to the base of the huge brick structure and yelled into the gloomy interior. Her voice echoed through the empty space. 'Danny. Come out here quick. It's Mariah, she needs your help.'

He loomed in front of her with a lamp. 'What is it, Emma?' he began irritably. 'I've told you before not to come down to the works.'

'It's these two men. They came after us for summat and Mariah told me to run and fetch you. They were rough-looking and said they knew you.'

'After you? Why? What did they want?'

'Summat about you and Mrs Cluff, I think.'

'Who were they?' An urgency began to run through his blood. He hoped they were not the same ruffians who had come after him, but he feared they might be.

'I don't know. Oh, please hurry, Danny. I left Mariah talking to them in the alley.'

'Men like that don't waste their time talking,' he said grimly. He turned to speak to the builder who had appeared behind him. 'I'd better go and sort this. I had a bit of trouble myself the other day. Mistook me for some other man.'

'Get yourself off, then,' the mason replied. 'We've done all we can here for the time being.'

'Right you are.'

Ned stepped forward from the dark interior. 'I'll come with you, Mr Thorpe.'

'Thanks, Ned. Follow me with a lantern. And hurry. Emma, go in the house and stay there. *Do as I say!*' Ned could be trusted. The Thorpes had known him since he was a nipper.

Daniel sprinted on ahead, out of the yard towards the alley, but when he got there he was met by a silent blackness in the narrow passage. He could not see or hear anybody. He slowed to a jog, clenching his fists in readiness. Ned caught up with him by the time he reached the end, where the alley met the towpath. Still they saw no one. The night was quiet apart from the scuffling of animals in the undergrowth and the occasional screech of an owl or a vixen.

'There's a barge moored over there, we'll try them.'

Daniel banged on the cockpit door and the bargeman's head appeared at the open flap. 'Clear off, will yer?' he said, angrily. 'We got youngsters asleep down 'ere.'

He was not one of the thugs and Daniel apologised. 'I'm looking for a young woman. Bright coppery hair. Maybe with two men.'

'None o' my concern,' he replied gruffly and shut the flap.

'Try the other way,' Ned suggested.

'The cottages are that way. Maybe she ran away from them and went home. We'll go there. Hurry.'

Daniel burst into the kitchen of his parents' house. 'Is Mariah here?' he demanded.

'Hey, steady on, lad,' his father replied, nursing baby Victoria by the fire. 'Calm yoursenn down.'

'Where is she?'

His mother replied, 'She went to see Emma up the alley.'

'Yes, I know that! But how long ago?'

'Quite a while, come to think of it. Afore it got dark. Should be back by now. I wonder what's happened to her? Who's that with you, Daniel?'

Daniel inhaled deeply to calm himself. There was no sense in worrying his mother. But he had a nasty feeling in his gut. 'It's Ned from the ironworks. You remember? The poorhouse sent him down the pit when Father was there? We can't stop now, we have to find Mariah. She can't be that far away.'

She was a sensible woman, he thought. But she had a tendency to speak her mind and to deal with things that faced her. If the thugs had threatened Emma because of him, Mariah was likely to have given them what for instead of running off. So where was she now? He hoped to high heaven she had got away from them. But an uneasy fear gripped his stomach. There was something not right about this business. Lily's name had been mentioned. Perhaps she knew what was going on? Perhaps those thugs had taken Mariah there?

Daniel turned to Ned. 'Those ruffians seem to have gone to ground, but I know where they might be and where I can find some answers. Follow me.' He went out of the kitchen door and headed for the end cottage.

It was a long time before Lily came to the door with a candle and when she did he could see why. Her face was bruised and there was bleeding about her mouth. Her delicate skin was blotchy from weeping and her pretty light brown hair was all over the place.

Daniel let out a cry. 'My God, Lily, what have they done to you?'

Lily fell into his arms and began sobbing hysterically. Behind him, Ned exclaimed. 'Did those men do this? They must be evil beasts to take it out on a defenceless woman!'

'We must find Mariah quickly! She may have got away from them and be hiding somewhere in fear of her life. Or—' Daniel stopped, unable to contemplate that they may have treated Mariah in the same way as Lily. 'Take the lantern, Ned, and search the towpath and the alley again. Go all the way back to the works. If you find her, take her to Emma and tell her to stay put until I get back. Make sure the yard gates are

119

locked up for the night. Mariah may have gone there for safety.' Even as he said it, he remembered Mariah's vow never to return to the Bowes' house, but she was sensible, he reminded himself. Clear thinking too. He desperately hoped she was safe. She had to be.

'You gonna be all right on your own, Mr Thorpe?'

'Aye. I think I've found the root of the problem.'

Poor Lily. She was all over him, clutching at his leather waistcoat, weeping and wailing and choking on her words. He held her close, smoothing her tumbled hair. He hoped that if Lily had been their target then Mariah must be safe and that made him feel better. Emma and Mariah had got away from their attackers and the men had come after Lily instead. He took hold of her shoulders gently and held her head away from him so he could see the extent of their beating. His teeth clenched in anger. 'Are they still here? Let me get my hands on them. I'll make them pay dearly for this.'

Lily shook her head, coughing and hiccupping through her sobs. 'Th-they've g-gone.'

'I'll get them back for this, don't you fret.' He pushed her away as carefully as he dare, grimacing at the angry bruising on her delicate features. 'Now tell me, who are these men?'

But he could get no sense out of her as she continued her weeping. He closed the door behind him and sat her down by the dying kitchen fire. He added a few coals and drew up a chair next to her. 'Is this your brother's doing? You have to tell me what's going on. They've been after my sister today.'

This news heightened Lily's weeping to hysteria level again. Daniel got up and rummaged in her kitchen cupboard until he found a small bottle of brandy she kept as a medicine. He poured some into a chipped cup and stood over her until she had drunk it.

120

When she had calmed he turned up the lamp and took a good look at her, wincing at what he saw. Those thugs had really given her a pasting. He said, 'I'll get some water and clean you up first.'

He took off his waistcoat and did his best with cold water and linen strips, but even the lightest touch on her face made her squeal and recoil with pain. What kind of men were they, for God's sake? he thought.

After giving her another gulp of brandy, he ventured, 'There were two of them, Lily. Two men. They came after me the other day. And now this. Who are they?'

'M-my brother, and – and his son.' She hiccupped shakily. Daniel frowned.

'He lives in Manchester. But he's – he's come over to – to stay with his cousin. He – he is my hus— late husband's brother. He – he d-does not like me seeing y-you.'

'But why not? You must tell me, Lily. Your husband has been dead for two years now.'

She began weeping again and he took her in his arms as tenderly as he could, for they had beaten her about the arms and body as well. These people were not men, they were no better than beasts of the fields! 'Hush now, Lily, my love. Do they want you to marry someone else? Is that it?'

She shook her head against his chest, snuffling wet tears on his flannel workshirt. 'I-I c-can't see you any more.'

Daniel frowned. 'Why not? You're a grown woman. If there is no one else, is it money that's the problem? Do they think I cannot look after you?'

She had finished the brandy so he fetched cold water from a ewer in the scullery for her to drink. 'You must tell me, Lily,' he insisted quietly.

She inhaled deeply, and let out a long juddering sigh,

burying her face in the folds of his shirt. Her muffled voice was soft and quiet. 'He's n-not d-dead. M-my husband is n-not d-dead. H-he's in gaol.'

Daniel's arms dropped away from her and he stepped back, horrified, astounded and shocked as a host of unanswered questions seethed through his mind.

'Tell me that is not true.'

She shook her head. 'I-I was lonely and – and I – I missed him.'

'You *missed* him! Your husband is in gaol and you missed him? While he languished in a prison cell, you used me to keep his bed warm? Lily? How could you?'

She flung herself at him, gripping the fabric of his shirt. 'Don't hate me, Danny. I love you. I do.'

'And what about your husband? Do you love him as well?'

'Not like I love you. Honest.'

'*Honest!* Honest? Do you know what that word means? You lied to me!'

'I had to! You would not have come to me otherwise! And we have such fun – we are good together, you and me. Oh Danny, you do still want me, don't you?'

He collapsed into a chair and held his head in his hands. 'Have you any idea what you have done?' he groaned.

No wonder those thugs came after him. And as they were no real match for him they had opted for a softer target in Emma. My God, thank goodness she was safe, for what kind of revenge would they have extracted from her? His anger rose and spilled out. 'You stupid, *stupid* woman!' he shouted.

'I am sorry. Truly I am. I had to have you. I need you—'
In the flickering firelight she caught sight of the contempt on his face and stopped mid sentence, adding in a small voice, 'Emma wasn't hurt, was she? Or your other sister?'

'What other sister?' he demanded roughly.

'There were two of them. Two Thorpe lasses, they said, who came out of your house and my brother and his lad followed them.'

Mariah! They thought Mariah was his sister, too. And Mariah had stayed behind to face them when Emma ran for help!

He stood up. A cold hand was gripping his heart. Emma had left Mariah with those thugs and they thought she was his sister. He did not know where she was. What if she had not escaped them and run after Emma? He made straight for the back door, stopping only to turn and say, 'I never want to see you again, Lily Cluff. Never. Go back to your husband's family and wait for his release. As any good wife should.'

He closed the door on her and did not look back. Mariah was out there somewhere and God only knows what had happened to her.

Chapter 13

Daniel did not need a light for his search as the moon was high and the clouds were clearing. There would be a frost on the ground before dawn. Was Mariah already lying beaten in a ditch somewhere? Or had they kidnapped her for sport? Had they taken her back to Mexton where they were staying?

His heart was thumping in his throat and his mouth was dry. Why had he gone running to Lily first? Why had he not realised sooner that they could have taken Mariah? That they *had* taken Mariah! Please God let her be all right!

Would the Lord listen to him? He regretted he no longer went to church to pray. Sunday school had taught him to read and write, and going to church with his parents had taught him right from wrong. He knew his regular visits to Lily were wrong. His father had always disapproved and told him no good would come of it. Why hadn't he listened? Daniel had ignored the warnings and now he was reaping the consequences.

He retraced his steps to where the barge was moored, then carried on searching the hedges frantically, expecting to find her, beaten up and discarded. He examined every broken twig and flattened stem until he saw the gap. A new break in the hedge, recently pushed aside and – and – his heart stopped in his breast. His body went cold all over. A strip of cloth torn from a dress, quite a long strip of woollen cloth and some shreds of lighter cotton. Further on he saw a trail of flattened grass through the meadow.

Daniel clutched the torn fabric in his fingers and hurried on. Please, Lord, he prayed, please let Mariah be safe. I have never asked much of you, but now I do. Keep Mariah safe. Please. Do this for me and I swear I shall repent my ways.

He searched every inch of the meadow, then the next one and the next until he found her. When he saw her, lying motionless on the wet grass, moonlight reflecting off her naked white skin, her gown and undergarments stripped from her body and in shreds about her, he realised this was not just a beating. This was worse, much, much worse. This was rape.

His anguished cry echoed through the night air. Daniel's face contorted in horror and despair. *He* had done wrong, not her! Why had the Lord not punished him? Why Mariah? But, as he sank to his knees beside her, he realised this *was* his punishment: to see an innocent woman, a *chaste* and respectable woman defiled in this way because of what he had done. This was his fault. He was as guilty as the men who had done this awful thing.

She was freezing cold. He tried to rouse her; he lifted her head and it flopped back like a broken doll's. Her bruised and battered body was limp but she was breathing. The moonlight revealed the bite marks and weals on her skin. He searched about for pieces of clothing to cover her. His jaw set rigid, twisting his features into a bitter grimace and saliva crept slowly into his mouth as he controlled the urge to vomit. Sickened by the sight and smell of this unholy deed he bowed his head, ashamed of being a man with a man's desires; tears filled his eyes.

'I am sorry, so sorry. It's all my fault. My fault. I am so, so sorry!'

He hugged her close to him, rocking her gently backwards and forwards. He would never forgive himself for this. He prayed for the Lord to punish him and let her live.

He did not know exactly when her eyes opened. Only that they stared. When he spoke to her to reassure her she was safe, she did not acknowledge him but continued to stare straight ahead, silent and unseeing.

He took off his thick leather waistcoat to cover and warm her, and then removed his shirt and vest. He did not feel the cold night air, he felt only the pain in his heart, a pain he had not known before. Guilt, despair and anger mingled with an overwhelming anxiety that she might die. He could not let that happen. This independent and courageous young woman was worth ten of Lily and she must live. He sat her up, supporting her back, easing her arms into his shirt, hardly daring to touch her damaged body.

He fashioned some drawers for her, gently wrapping her torn petticoats around her lower body and legs, and was forced to stop a moment, squeezing his eyes tight shut to stop the tears, when he saw the bruising on her thighs. And there was blood, fresh blood, sticky on her skin and on his hands as he tried to clothe her.

He buttoned his heavy waistcoat securely around her, protecting her from the night air and prying eyes of any prowler on the towpath. Then he lifted her up as gently as he could and carried her across the cold dark meadows, through the hummocks and hedges, and to home.

She grew heavy in his arms but he did not stop. He kicked open the garden gate and kicked again, hard, at the kitchen door. His father unlocked it, started and stared at the sight before him, then opened the door wide.

'Take her through to the front room. I'll get your mother.'

Daniel laid her on the bed that used to be his own. 'You are home, now, Mariah. Safe at home,' he whispered. Safe, he thought, but not sound. She was broken and bruised in mind as well as body. He felt her pain and anguish tearing through his own body and he wept. 'We'll look after you, Mariah, and make you well again. You will be well again, you will.'

But she only stared. And not at him. As he moved away her eyes did not follow him. They stayed, fixed on the ceiling, motionless and still.

The ceiling creaked. His young sisters had heard the noise downstairs and were curious. His father and mother came in to the room, anxious to help.

'She's in a bad way, Ma. What can we do?' They all heard the wooden stairs creak and Daniel continued, 'Keep the girls out of here. They should not see this – or know about what happened.'

Fanny Thorpe retreated, calling softly, 'Back to bed now. All of you. And quietly, I say.'

Arthur Thorpe looked at his son and asked, 'Did you see what happened?'

Daniel shook his head, choking on the words. 'She took a beating, and – and – oh, Father – they raped her. Those animals raped her – both of them and more than once, by the look of it.' He sank into a chair with his head in his hands, his broad shoulders shaking as he tried to repress the sobs. 'They thought she was my sister. It was me they were after. They wanted revenge on me and took it out on Mariah. Oh God, it's all my fault!'

'You'd better tell me what you did, son. Why did they want revenge on you?'

Daniel heaved a sigh and tried to control himself. 'I am to blame. I was too full of myself and vain. I believed a liar. I let a pretty face – and a – a pliant body – turn my head – and – never again will I allow that to happen. I won't ever get over this. I'm finished with women. Finished.'

'I take it the liar you speak of is the Cluff widow, then? What has she been telling you?'

'Sh-she is not a widow. Her husband is still alive. He's – he's in prison.'

'Good God, no!' Arthur Thorpe grimaced. 'So the man's brother came after you? And if not you, your sisters? An eye for an eye, eh?'

He was tempted to say, 'I told you no good would come of carrying on with that Mrs Cluff", but he did not. His son was suffering enough for the evil that had been done this night. The Lord had taught him a lesson. But even Arthur's faith was tested by what he had seen. Why choose Mariah for this deed? She did not deserve this.

Fanny Thorpe was standing at the front room door with a bowl of water and some strips of linen. 'I heard what you said, Daniel,' she whispered angrily. 'Does that mean no daughter of mine is safe because you could not keep your breeches buttoned? You are just like your father!'

'Fanny! That's enough!'

Daniel looked from his father to his mother in surprise. They were the closest of couples and this was the first crack in their loyalty to each other he had seen in all his years. From a young boy he had been aware of his parents' passion for each other. He was the eldest of nearly a dozen children and a regular birth in the family had been part of his childhood. This spat between his parents was caused by something he did not know about, he felt sure.

'Out of my way, both of you,' Fanny went on irritably, 'and let me see to Mariah.'

'I'll make her a toddy,' Arthur said and went off to the kitchen. 'And you, my lad, put some clothes on before you catch your death. We've enough with one invalid in the family.'

'What can I do?' Daniel pleaded. 'It was all my fault and I feel so helpless.'

'Nay, lad. You didn't do this damage to her. But for her sake you have to keep quiet about this, or the poor lass's life will truly be ruined. There is enough talk going on around her without adding to it.'

Daniel lifted his arms to encircle his head, as he paced frantically about the room. 'I feel so useless. There must be something I can do!'

'You can leave me alone with her, that's what you can do. Light me another lamp and go and help your father. Ask him to make some of that Indian tea. Here's the key to the bureau.' Fanny lifted her skirt to find the pocket in her drawers.

Daniel hovered, reluctant to leave until his mother said, 'Go on, then. Mariah does not want a man around for this.'

Fanny Thorpe set about tending to Mariah's injuries, removing her makeshift clothing as gently as she was able. She grimaced at the bruising on her face, and again as she uncovered her breasts. She almost choked when she removed Daniel's wrappings around her hips and legs, sticky with fresh blood.

'You're safe now, you'll be all right, Mariah,' she murmured as she worked. 'I am just going to wash you all over with this warm water and then put some salve on your cuts and bruises. Tell me where it hurts most.'

But Fanny could get no response from the young woman. She lay there, awake, eyes staring straight ahead and said nothing. Fanny thought it was like tending an infant's rag doll. Her limbs were compliant and moved, unresisting, as she washed them. But, when she had finished, they fell back, flaccid and lifeless. Lifeless, like her eyes.

Fanny began to frown as she worked. She padded and wrapped her like a baby, making her as comfortable as she could in the hard narrow bed. 'I am just going to get you a drink to help you sleep,' she murmured, before leaving to join her menfolk in the kitchen.

Daniel and his father busied themselves fetching fresh water from the pump at the end of the row, and stoking the fire to heat it.

'What was all that about?' Daniel asked.

'I don't know what you're talking about,' Arthur replied gruffly.

'Yes, you do. That spat between you and Mother.'

'It's nothing, son. It happened a long time ago, before you were born. But women never let you forget these things.'

'Who was she?'

'I said, it's all in the past!'

His father was angry and Daniel let the matter drop. It would only start his father coughing if he pursued it. His mother came through with the bowl of water, stained red with blood and both men grimaced.

'I'll empty that for you.' Daniel took the bowl from her. 'There's more water warming on the fire. How is she?'

'Not good. Not good at all.'

130

'Will she get better?'

Fanny let out a sigh. 'Who can tell? I've not seen anything like this before. I reckon her body will heal. Don't get me wrong, it's nasty all right. But Mariah is a strong young woman. No, it's not her body that I am worried about, it's – it's – oh, I don't know. She won't speak to me. Didn't say a word all the time I tended to her. She's been living here with me like a daughter for weeks now, and all I get from her is a blank stare.'

'She was the same with me,' Daniel added anxiously.

'It's the shock of it all,' Arthur said. 'I've seen it afore, when I was down t' pit. Remember that roof fall? One of the lads got a badly mangled leg and he went like that. He wouldn't talk to anybody for days on end.'

'Did he get better?' Daniel pressed.

'Depends what you mean by better. The surgeon took away most of his leg and it wa' months afore he wa' right in the head again.'

Daniel sagged into the nearest chair and covered his face with his hands. 'She needs looking after. Can you do that for her?'

'I'll do my best. But tomorrow is my day for the butcher's wife.'

'Meg or Liddy? You can tell them what to do.'

Fanny shook her head. 'I don't want any of my girls going in there, doing nursing duties and finding out what happened.'

'What about Aunty Dora?' suggested Daniel. 'You always go to her when one of the girls is ill.'

Daniel saw his parents exchange looks.

Arthur spoke. 'Can you have a lend of a cart from the works, Daniel, to take Mariah over there?'

'She can't travel all that way, Arthur,' Fanny argued. 'Not in her state. There's no proper road to speak of.'

131

'I don't want Dora over 'ere.' Arthur's voice was firm.

'I can't deal with this on my own. I need our Dora,' Fanny pleaded. 'She can help the lass, proper like.'

'Aye, I know. You allus go to her, though. She's out o' the way o' tittle-tattle over there.'

To hell with them, Daniel fumed silently. If Mariah needed Aunty Dora, he would fetch her himself! He stood up and said, 'Why can't she come here? Mariah needs her! She's mother's sister and she can sleep on the couch in the front room.'

But his father continued to grunt his objections.

Daniel grew angry with his father's stubbornness. 'Aunty Dora will know what to do with – well, with women's things like this. She's the best around here!'

His father swivelled round and challenged, 'And what do you know about your aunty's doings?'

'Oh come on, Dad. Men talk in the works. Mind, they always have something good to say about her. I don't let on she's my aunt, but if any of their wives or daughters needs that kind of help, they always send her out to Aunty Dora.'

This only served to make Arthur more angry. 'So Dora Barton's the talk of the works now, is she? Thank God the both o' you are Thorpes.'

Daniel's eyes rounded at this outburst and he was surprised his mother did not spring to her sister's defence and retaliate. Instead she put out a hand on her husband's and said quietly, 'Arthur, our Dora can help Mariah.'

Daniel lost his patience and stood up. 'I'm not listening to any more of this. I'm fetching her now. I'm going to saddle one of Mr Bowes' horses and go over there tonight.'

'Arthur?' Fanny Thorpe was looking intently at her husband.

'All right then. The lass needs her so you'd better fetch her,' he agreed.

Fanny jumped into action and went to a pile of clean laundry on a chair. 'Here you are, Danny. Put on one of your father's shirts, and your waistcoat. Your other things'll need a good wash before you can wear them again.'

As Daniel prepared to leave he heard his father say, 'I don't like having Dora in the house, Fanny.'

'I know you don't,' his mother responded, 'but it was twenty-five year ago. Things were different then.'

'I don't want to talk about it,' Arthur muttered.

'We're lucky to have her; she knows a lot about doctoring.'

'Aye, well, it isn't right for an unmarried woman to do what she does,' Arthur responded.

Fanny answered firmly, 'Mariah needs our Dora. Mariah has to come first for now.'

'I can see that,' Arthur agreed. 'Daniel'd best be off for her then.'

Daniel wondered about the family squabble his aunt had caused in the past. Whatever it was, they had to put it behind them and look to getting Mariah well again. He ran along the towpath and up the alley towards the stables behind the house, panting heavily as he roused the stable lad to saddle one of the lighter beasts. The lad came down from where he slept next to the hayloft with his breeches over his nightshirt. Before long Daniel was on his way.

Daniel liked his Aunty Dora and had looked forward to his childhood visits to her with his mother and younger brothers and sisters. Father was never with them. He was always working down the pit when they went. Daniel remembered it being a tiring walk for little legs, out of town and up past Keppel village, but the journey seemed much shorter on horseback.

Aunty Dora was in her nightgown, but not asleep. Daniel explained as best he could and helped pack a couple of

133

saddlebags for her while she dressed. She hitched up her skirts and rode astride the horse in front of him.

'Will you get word to Mr Shaw to feed and water my pig?' she asked.

'Don't you worry. I'll see he knows. You don't think it'll be too much for him?'

'He'll get one of the Home Farm lads to do it. He's kept an eye on my patch since your grandfather passed away. He promised him, you see. In return for the help I gave his wife when she was badly.'

'Do you mind if we go a bit faster, Aunty?'

'Ee, lad, I do. I'm not as young as I was. You'll make the horse nervous if you don't ease off those reins.'

Daniel swallowed and tried to relax. Maybe some of his aunty's tales would take his mind off Mariah. 'How old were you when Grandpa died?' he asked.

'Nineteen. Our Fanny was just one and twenty. And she, being the elder, decided she was in charge of me. I thought different, though. Ee, now I think back, I was a handful, all right. I wanted to know everything and do everything.'

'Is that why Father doesn't like you?'

'What has he been saying?'

'Nothing. He doesn't approve of what you do.'

'Well, it kept the home going when me and your mother were left on our own. And the vicar and his wife visited us regularly to see we were all right.'

'Weren't you lonely, though? Young women, stuck out here in the wilds with only old Mr Shaw next door for company?'

'We walked over to Keppel church on a Sunday, if the weather let us. Fanny was contented looking after the house and I was out and about tending to folk. They never had much money round here but they always paid me with something, a fowl or a brace of rabbits. I remember we used to save any silver I got in an old crock to pay for my boots. Fanny made sure I had good boots for turning out on a winter's night. Even so, it was touch and go that first winter after Father went. When he was alive we had logs from the estate and he kept the coalhouse topped up for us. We just about got through that winter, but we both knew we'd have to earn more in the following year.'

'So what did you do?'

'Well, the Fitzkeppel estate was losing its farm labourers to the works in town so the trustees went round the Dales offering work on the land, and these newcomers needed lodgings. We thought it would keep us off the parish and out of the poor-house if we took a lodger. We'd have help with chopping wood and digging the garden, too.'

'And did you?'

'Oh aye. That was when your father came along. He was twenty-three and a single man. Ee, do you know, Daniel, you're the image of him, as he was then.'

Daniel managed a smile in the darkness as the horse plodded on. 'We're nearly there.'

Dora stood alone by Mariah's bed.

'I'm right sorry this has happened to you, lass,' Dora began. 'Our Fanny's done her best, but she wants me to have a look at you. I won't hurt you, I promise. Just you relax and lie back on the pillow. There. Put your feet on these cushions . . .'

Mariah heard what she said but could not move. She had no control over her limbs. They were dead weights hanging from her body, a body that would not shift for her, no matter how hard she tried. She stared straight ahead, unable to form the words on her lips.

Dora continued, 'I'm Dora Barton, Fanny Thorpe's sister. You can call me Dora. You're Mariah, aren't you?' Dora frowned when she could draw no response from her patient. Still, the lass was compliant enough as she examined the bruising and bleeding, grimacing occasionally and tending to her wounds.

Mariah was dimly aware of stinging pain and the mingled smells of soap, wintergreen and camphor. Dora lifted her to a sitting position and she took the drink that was offered. Warmth seeped through her veins. Her eyelids drooped and closed. It was peaceful now and there was a warm glow in her head . . .

Dora waited until she was sure Mariah was asleep and went through to the kitchen where Daniel was hopping about impatiently.

'How is she?'

'Her body will mend given time and the right tending. But she needs rest and understanding more than ointments and salves. Do you know the men who did this to her? It's not right, Daniel. You should get the constable onto them.'

'They'll only deny it. Or even worse, say she was one of the street women from the tavern. Don't worry, I can find out who they are and they'll not get off lightly.'

Dora sat down in the rocking chair opposite her sister. 'Has Arthur gone to bed, Fanny?'

'Aye.'

'I still make him feel uncomfortable, don't I?'

'Aye, but don't you worry. It's him, not you. Do you want a drink of this Indian tea?'

'Don't mind if I do.' Dora took the cup gratefully. 'He's a fine lad, isn't he?'

'Our Daniel? Aye. A credit to the whole family.'

'I'm not a lad,' Daniel interrupted. 'I'm—'

'Five and twenty,' Dora finished for him. 'Aye, I know. But

136

you're still just a lad to me and your mother. This is nice tea, Fanny.'

'Will she get better? She's had a bad time. She's not long since lost her mother. And her father – well he just wants rid of her.'

'I don't know. She's still not said a word, and she turns away from all my questions. It's like she's blanked it all out of her mind. It might take her a while to come round.'

'What can I do to help her?'

Dora shook her head and grimaced. 'Nowt, really. But she needs a close eye kept on her. I'll stay until she's healed enough to travel and then take her back home with me. Country air'll do her good and there'll be no prying busybodies asking questions. Can you borrow a cart from work, Danny?'

'I think so. Just tell me when. I'll take you both back when Mariah's up to it.'

The two women nodded to each other in agreement.

Daniel added, 'I can ride out and see you both on a Sunday.'

'Best not, love,' his mother responded quickly. 'Your father wouldn't like that.'

'He's not still upset, is he?'

'Your mother's right,' Dora answered. 'Besides, Mariah won't want any men around her, reminding her of what happened.'

'Especially you, my lad,' his mother added. 'Your father knew that Mrs Cluff was trouble as soon as she moved into the end house. He told you to stay away from her.' She saw Daniel slump in the chair and stare at the floor. 'Why didn't you listen to your father?'

'How much does Mariah know about you and Mrs Cluff?' Dora asked.

Daniel shrugged. 'Just that we were sweethearts. Emma said she told her.'

'Sweethearts! Huh!' his mother exclaimed.

'All right, Fanny,' Dora said. 'Leave it for now. He's been through enough tonight.'

But Fanny was not to be put off. She turned to her son, leaning forward to reinforce her opinion. 'Don't be surprised if Mariah blames you and never wants to speak to you again!'

Again Dora soothed her anxious sister. 'It's not his doing, Fanny. He didn't do those horrible things to her.'

'Lily lied to me,' Daniel said quietly. 'She lied to everybody. She said she was a widow and I believed her. I'd even asked her to marry me,' he finished miserably.

Dora placed her hand on his arm. 'Your mother's right about Mariah, though. She won't want you around. You found her, you saw what happened to her and saw her as she was and she'll know that. It's best you stay away, like your mother says.'

'If you say so. As long as you let Mother know how she's getting on and send word to me and tell me as soon as she agrees to see me again.'

'*If* she agrees to see you again,' Dora added quietly.

Daniel looked shocked, but stayed silent.

Fanny said, 'Shall we all get some sleep, now? Daniel, you'd better get that horse back to its stable and make sure you are up for work on time tomorrow.'

After he had left, Dora said, 'Daniel has been asking me about the old days, when Father died.'

'What did you say?'

'Only how hard it was to manage before Arthur came along.'

'Aye it was. I remember that bad winter before he came down from the Dales after lambing. He said he was only staying the year to work on the Fitzkeppel estate.'

'It caused talk in the village, though, us being spinsters, like. He was a right handsome young fellow in those days.'

'There were the two of us! And Arthur was a good, God-fearing man. He went with us to Keppel church as regular as clockwork.'

Dora grimaced. 'Even so, the church folk didn't approve of him lodging with us.'

'Aye, if we'd have let it go on, we would have ruined our reputations for good.'

'Yours, maybe. I was a lost cause any road, doing what I did with the nursing and such like.'

'You were a lively young thing, weren't you?' Fanny reached across to take her sister's hand. 'Any regrets?'

Dora shook her head and gazed into the dying embers of the kitchen fire. She was remembering the old vicar and his wife, and how they had taken it upon themselves to invite the three young people to the vicarage one Sunday teatime before evensong. And while the reverend invited Arthur to talk in his study, Fanny and Dora drank tea and ate bread and butter and jam with his wife in their drawing room.

That afternoon visit had changed their lives for ever. The Reverend and Mrs Judd had decided that Arthur could not continue to lodge with them. He must marry one of them and they had chosen Fanny as his bride. Arthur was delighted. He worshipped her. Dora had not realised until then how much he truly cared for Fanny.

But Dora had loved Arthur. He knew it and Fanny did not. The banns were read for the following three Sundays and Fanny became Arthur's wife on the fourth. Dora was her bridal attendant. They wore their best Sunday dresses and put early primroses in their hair. Mrs Judd gave a small tea party for them in the vicarage drawing room.

139

Not long after that a new coal seam opened up near town and the pit owner was looking for men. There were cottages by the canal for men with wives and Arthur was taken on.

The sisters sat in silence with their memories of all those years ago as the fire grew cold. Eventually, Fanny said, 'Best get to bed now. Will you be all right on the couch?'

Dora nodded. 'I can keep an eye on the lass in there. Goodnight, love.'

Daniel stabled the horse himself and threw pebbles on the house roof to wake Emma to let him in. He fended off her questions. He was so full of remorse he could not trust himself to talk about Mariah without breaking down. He wondered whether he should tell Ezekiel about his daughter. But Ezekiel was determined to disown her and Mariah herself had begged him not to interfere.

He wrestled with this dilemma until he decided to keep silent. Mentally and physically exhausted, he fell onto his bed without undressing, but he could not sleep and was glad when the first streaks of dawn lit the morning sky so he could go down to the yard and make a start.

He could not get the sight of Mariah's damaged body out of his mind. Everywhere he looked he saw her still, ivory form, blemished by blood. What had he done to her? Even if she recovered, how was he going to live with this on his conscience?

Chapter 14

'Are you ready, Mariah?'

She nodded silently and pulled the hood of her dark winter cloak forward to shield her face. It was early and the morning air was chilled by mist. Dora had been away from her cottage for two weeks now. Fanny and Arthur stood at the open front door and the curious faces of their younger daughters peered out of an upstairs window.

'You go first.' Dora stood by while Mariah negotiated the step into the dog cart and sat facing her box and a basket of food on the opposite seat. Then she climbed in beside her and the horse whinnied and shied as she arranged herself on the seat beside Mariah.

'Steady, boy.' Daniel, in his best Sunday suit, held the horse's bridle and stroked his nose. 'All set?'

'Yes, love. Take it slowly.'

'Aye.' Daniel took the reins and climbed into the driver's seat. He looked behind him with a worried frown on his face.

Mariah buried her head deeper in the folds of her cloak. It was as though she were trying to make herself disappear, he thought. She had not said a word to him or looked at him since he had arrived with the cart.

His mother had warned him that Mariah was having a hard time getting over her attack. Anger and self-loathing bubbled through him. If only he could turn back the clock! Why had he ever allowed himself to be taken in by that whore Lily Cluff? That's all she was. A whore who had married into a family of rogues. By God, he was going to make those Cluff ruffians pay for what they did! He was going to give the pair of them the hiding of their lives!

The horse plodded on through the morning mist as Daniel tussled with his mounting rage. Before long the docile creature picked up his tension and began to whinny and fret.

'There, boy, calm yourself now.' Daniel spoke as much to himself as to the horse. This anger was no good to man or beast. He had to do something soon or he would burst with fury!

The sun's rays began to push through the morning mist. Daniel forced himself to relax his grip on the reins and make his voice sound normal. 'Nice day for a drive.'

'I hope my house is all right. I don't like leaving it empty for too long.'

'I looked in the other day. Didn't Emma tell you?'

'No. When was that?'

'Mr Bowes had some papers to go to Fitzkeppel Hall.'

'I thought you'd send Ned on errands like that?'

'They were important documents for his son to read. Master Henry is staying at the Hall and Mr Bowes said I had to deliver them personally. It didn't take long on horseback so I had time to call in and see if everything was in order.'

'And was it?'

'Aye. A bit chilly without the fire going, and the garden needs weeding. But everything was safe and sound as far as I could see.'

'Was my pig all right?'

'He seemed happy enough. I took him some stale bread from the house. But he had fresh greens and potatoes in his trough.'

'That'll be the lad from Home Farm. A good 'un, he is.'

'He still doesn't have a name, then?'

'Who? The lad?'

'No, Aunty. Your pig.'

'Oh no, no, no, no, no. How could I eat him if I gave him a name? He's just the pig.'

The first smile of the day crossed Daniel's face. 'That's a nice little house you've got.'

'Your granddad built it, you know.'

'Did he?'

'That's what your grandma told us before she died. He was a farm labourer on the Fitzkeppel estate. When he married, old Fitzkeppel gave him a plot of land on condition he built a house on it in a day. He did it for all his young farm hands when they wed. Saved building them himself, I suppose, cos he had to have the men there to work his fields. The other labourers helped my father build it, so they had their own house from the beginning. Old Fitzkeppel gave him stone from the quarry an' all. Mind you, your grandma said it only had the one room then.'

'On good land though. And near to a spring for water.'

'Your granddad had laid wooden boards between the roof trusses within a year, and put up a ladder so they didn't have to sleep on the earth floor.'

143

'You've got stone flags now, haven't you?'

'Nice, aren't they? Mr Shaw put them down for me after I'd looked after his son's wife when she . . .' Dora glanced at Mariah and changed the subject. 'Your granddad built the pigsty next and I reckon the Bartons have had a pig in there ever since. We never went short of a bit o' bacon.'

'Is Mariah all right back there?'

'Just the same. This fresh air will do her good, though. Ee, lad, I know there's brass to be made from them furnaces by the canal, but the smoke that comes out o' them chimneys fair makes your eyes water.'

'Aye, it gives Father a real bad cough on some days and nothing we get from the apothecary's can calm him.'

The small cart trundled on in silence. They left the works and terraces behind and slowly climbed a small hill on the Grasse Fell road, went through Keppel village with its neat rows of stone-built workers' cottages and an ale house at the end, and skirted the Fitzkeppel estate to the edge of the woods.

Daniel negotiated the horse and cart down the narrow lane leading to Dora's house. 'Nearly there. How is she?'

Dora peered at the tiny amount of Mariah's face visible under the hood of her cloak. 'Still too pale for my liking. Are you all right, Mariah?'

Mariah nodded silently.

'I laid a fire when I was there,' Daniel added. 'Just needs lighting. I'll chop some more wood for you before I go. How are you for coal?'

'Enough for me, but I reckon I'll need more with company to cook for.'

'I'll get Mr Bowes' carter to bring over a load. He can bill me for it at the works.'

'Thanks, love. You're a good lad.'

144

Daniel helped his two passengers out onto the overgrown track outside Dora's house. Mariah grasped his outstretched hand but still would not look at him. She took Dora's arm to walk down the garden path. Daniel grimaced silently and went ahead to open the front door. He led the way down to the back kitchen and continued his conversation with Dora.

'When was the front room and this hallway built on, then?' he asked.

'Just after old Fitzkeppel put up that folly to celebrate the end of Napoleon. His ironworks had made him a pile of money from the war and he paid his men well to build that monstrosity. There was plenty of stone left over. Good stone an' all. His labourers shared it out and your granddad bought timber for the stairs with his extra pay. Me and your mother were just little 'uns then.'

'I'd like to have known my granddad.'

'Aye. You're a lot like him in some ways. You get on with things.'

Daniel took off his coat and smiled. 'I'll fetch water from the spring first.'

'Let me do that. It's women's work.'

'No, you keep an eye on Mariah. I'll not be long.'

As soon as the fire was drawing, Dora boiled some water and made porridge for Daniel to ease his hunger. Mariah would not eat any. She sat silently at the table in her hooded cloak and prepared the vegetables that Dora put in front of her.

Daniel sat across from her and frowned, glancing from Dora to Mariah and back to Dora. Finally he pushed back his chair and said, 'I'll chop that wood and bring in more coal.'

Mariah did not even glance in his direction. When Daniel came back inside, his arms loaded with logs, she pulled her hood forward again and avoided looking at him. Then she got up silently and went down the garden to the privy.

'I'll just bring in some buckets of coal from the outhouse, Aunty, and then I'll get off.'

'Aren't you staying for some broth?'

'No. Thanks all the same, but I don't think Mariah likes me being around.'

'She needs time to herself, that's all.'

'She's had enough of that recently, but I suppose you're right. You usually are about these things.'

'She doesn't want you near her, Daniel.'

The strain of Daniel's pent-up feelings twisted his handsome features. 'She blames me, doesn't she?'

'I don't know. She might not be thinking about you at all. It's herself she's having trouble with.'

'I don't follow you.'

'It was an evil deed those men did to her that night. It was their doing but Mariah blames herself. She feels dirtied by it and is ashamed. She'll not forget it, you know.'

'But none of it was her fault!'

'That doesn't make any difference to the way she feels, love. She is going to need a lot of time to get over this. A lot of patient tending.'

'You will give her that, won't you?'

'I'll do my best, but I can't work miracles.' Dora's own heart was torn apart by the anguish on his face. He felt so guilty for his involvement in the attack on Mariah. But nobody could turn back time and he had to deal with his own part in this as Mariah was dealing with hers. 'Look to sorting yourself out, lad. You can't do anything for her, now.'

'Yes I can!' he yelled. 'I'll get my revenge on those Cluff bastards, if it's the last thing I do!'

146

Dora stared at him. She had never seen him so angry. 'Be quiet, will you? She'll hear you. I know how you feel—'

'No you don't! It was my fault. My fault! Mariah will never forgive me! Never!'

'She won't if you keep going on like this! She needs a bit of peace!' Dora retaliated sharply. 'All this shouting and blaming yourself will not do her any good at all! I think you'd better get off home now. Before she comes back inside.'

Daniel clenched and unclenched his fists. He wanted to make things right for Mariah, but he could not. He felt so useless. How was he going to live with himself? He pulled himself together and made an effort to calm down. 'I don't want to leave her. I want to help her get better. She will get better, won't she?'

Dora pursed her lips. 'Time will tell.'

'You send word to me if she needs anything. *Anything*.'

Dora reached up to give him a hug. 'I will, lad. I will. Look, it's a nice day out there. Why don't you go back home and help your father in the garden?'

He grimaced and Dora's heart ached for his anguish, but eventually he agreed with her and shrugged. 'If you think it is for the best. I'll call back next Sunday.'

'Best not. I'll let you know when she's ready to see folk from town.'

Mariah heard Ezekiel's cart rattle away down the track towards town and came in from the garden.

'There you are. You can come back inside. He'll not be back until I ask him. Why don't you take off your cloak? The fire's going well and it's warming up a treat in here now.'

Dora watched as Mariah obeyed. She hoped the fear in her eyes would go. It wasn't only when Daniel was around. Mariah shrank from looking at and talking to anybody except

147

her. Dora had seen it before. Mariah could not get over her disgrace.

She was such an attractive young woman, Dora thought, with that striking coppery hair and upright stance. A bit too thin now, though. That gown was hanging off her. The dark grey colour seemed appropriate for her sombre mood and it was very well made with a separate bodice and skirt. Dora had selected it from Mariah's box when she had been unable to salvage her tattered black mourning gown.

Dora persevered. 'There's a hook by the back door for your cloak. You'd better put a pinny on over that nice travelling outfit. Here's a clean one for you.'

Again, Mariah did as she was bid without a word. Dora continued, 'Sit yourself down. This broth won't be long. It's only vegetables today, but Fanny's given me a nice shin of beef for tomorrow.'

Dora was used to Mariah not speaking by now. She nodded and shook her head and, sometimes, her eyes lit with an expression that gave Dora hope for her recovery. But it never lasted. It was as though Mariah was climbing out of a deep pit. She took two steps up and one step back, and then, suddenly, for no apparent reason she dropped back into the abyss.

Dora resolved to carry on as normally as possible until she came round. She put some of Fanny's new bread to warm in the bake oven at the side of the fire. 'Ee, with the two of us here, it'll be just like when me and our Fanny were younger. Afore she wed Arthur and went to live in town. We had to fend for ourselves then, y' know, after our mother and father passed on.'

Dora watched Mariah's face carefully as she talked, looking for signs of what cheered her. Clearly mentioning their loss of parents was exactly the wrong thing to say. But Dora rallied valiantly and pressed on.

'Of course, we were grown women. But we had the garden and hens, as well as pigs in those days. Do you know, I might start keeping a few hens again, if the henhouse down the garden is still any use. I don't know why I stopped having them in the first place.'

Yes I do, Dora thought, the fox got in one winter and killed them all. But Mariah's face had brightened at her suggestion and she continued. 'I'll ask at Home Farm if they've got a few laying pullets to spare. They won't take too much feeding. What do you think, Mariah?'

Dora saw a vestige of a smile cross Mariah's face. She stirred the broth as it simmered in her blackened cauldron suspended over the kitchen fire. A large, similarly blackened kettle rested on the swing hob. She'd make some proper tea for them both later, and fry some of that black pudding Fanny had fetched her from the butcher's in town.

'Well now, lass. Why don't you take yourself off upstairs and unpack your box? I've put you in the front room. There's a nice little window that looks onto the lane.'

The broth was ready when Mariah came downstairs, her woollen shawl wrapped tightly about her. Dora ladled it into deep stoneware bowls and sawed at the warmed bread.

'This knife needs a sharpen,' she muttered with a tutting sound. 'Ee, when our Fanny and me were on our own, and Arthur came to lodge, he used to see to all that for us. Cleaned up our garden tools, tidied the outhouse, shovelled the coal – the lot.'

Silently, Mariah broke her bread and dropped the pieces into her broth.

'After we've had this,' Dora suggested cheerfully, 'we'll

walk down the garden and look at the old henhouse, if you like.'

Dora was relieved to see a light in Mariah's eyes and the hint of a nod. Poor lass, she thought, I'll just have to keep trying but it was going to be a long journey for both of them.

Mariah pulled a few weeds with her in the afternoon sun and then they went inside for their black pudding and potatoes, and drank tea by the fire as the daylight faded. Mariah clasped her mug in both hands and stared silently into the flames.

'It is nice having you to stay. I miss our Fanny sometimes. You couldn't separate us then. Not until Arthur came along.'

Mariah turned her head towards Dora, so she continued, 'We worked hard, o' course. There was money to be earned from helping out at the Hall. In those days there was always building work going on and the parkland being altered. And they had times when the Hall was full of visiting gentry for the hunting and the shooting. And sometimes there'd be a ball, with grand ladies and everything. We'd be up there for days on end, sleeping on straw pallets in the barns to save the walk there and back every day.'

But after the scandal with her ladyship, Dora thought to herself, the visitors stopped coming and the work dwindled away. Best not talk about that now. She leaned forward in her chair and picked up the brown teapot from the hearth. 'Would you like a drop more of this, Mariah, love?'

Mariah, sitting on the other side of the fireplace, held out her mug while Dora poured the hot liquid carefully. 'Thanks,' she said quietly.

Dora gave a half smile and nodded. That was the first word she had heard Mariah utter since Daniel had left. It was a start.

Tomorrow they'd have a nice walk over to Home Farm to see about the hens.

Daniel saw to the horse and cart himself when he got back to the Bowes' house. Being a Sunday, the stable lad had had his dinner and gone off to see his mother and father. Daniel cleaned up the cart and rubbed down the horse thinking all the time about Mariah. She was in the best place with the best person. Aunty Dora was the finest there was around here for tending to womenfolk.

Daniel remembered visiting as a nipper, not quite under-standing at first why they always went when his mother was swollen with child. He was sent to Mr and Mrs Shaw's house further down the lane when the baby started coming. And afterwards, they stayed on until Mother was strong enough to walk back to town. Aunty Dora came with them, but never stayed at the cottage. She'd have a bite to eat and a sit down until it was time for Father to get in from the pit, and then set off back on her own.

Daniel knew his father did not like his aunt coming to the house even though she was his wife's sister. He said she was ungodly. This shocked young Daniel because his parents had brought their family up to be decent church-going folk. All the children went to Sunday school and learned to read the Bible and write their letters.

As he grew older, he stopped going to church every Sunday and sometimes visited Dora instead if the weather was fine. She had told him about the cundums and even gave him some, making him promise not to tell his father who didn't hold with that sort of thing; he thought it was unnatural to use anything like that in his marriage bed. And his father liked the marriage bed. As the eldest child in a

151

small cottage, Daniel knew everything his parents did in their bedchamber.

He realised now how much he was like his father in that respect. He should have heeded his father's warnings about Lily. But she was a mature and comely woman and he had been unable to resist her advances. He did not need any persuasion to climb into her bed. Once he had tasted the pleasure of her soft body he could not get enough of her.

He had not talked to his parents about Lily. After their first disapproving row, they maintained an uneasy silence about her. But Dora was different; she did not discourage him. She said he was a grown man and he should not resist his urges. It was not good for men to contain their urges. She knew about these things.

Oh Lord, what had he done? He could not blame anyone else for his passion for Lily, or for what her menfolk had done to Mariah. He let out an anguished growl that startled the horse into a whinny. He meant to get his revenge on those evil men for Mariah's sake. He had made up his mind, and his anger simmered. He had to get it out of his system. He'd ask the men in the works about those Cluff thugs. Somebody would know where to find them. And when he did . . .

He shook out some fresh hay for the horse and then went indoors to the kitchen where Emma was clearing the remains of Sunday dinner.

'You're back early. I thought you were staying at Aunty Dora's for your dinner.'

He shook his head wordlessly, and reached for his leather waistcoat that he kept hanging by the back door.

'How's Mariah? Mam said she was on the mend when I called last week. She wouldn't let me see her, though.'

'Mariah has to rest. She be all right with Dora.'

'Those men beat her up, didn't they?'

'Who told you that?'

'Nobody. I was there, Daniel, when they came after us. I was scared stiff. I locked the kitchen door as soon as I got back. Ned told me they beat up Mrs Cluff.'

Daniel stared at his sister silently, desperately trying to suppress his mounting rage. His stomach knotted with anger. Why had he ever taken up with that whore?

'It shouldn't have been Mariah, should it? It should have been me,' Emma added quietly.

'It shouldn't have been either of you!' he yelled. 'It should have been me!'

'Don't shout. Sit down and have your dinner. There's some roast mutton still warm, and leftover 'taters.'

'I – can't eat. I can't.'

'I'll leave it on the hob for later. Shall I make a pot of tea?'

He shook his head again. 'I'm going down to the yard.'

'On a Sunday?'

'Yes, on a Sunday,' he replied sharply.

Emma turned back to her plates. He was very upset about Mariah. They all were. But Daniel seemed a different person these days. Not the big brother she knew and loved. He was always at work and no fun any more. Ever since that business with Mrs Cluff and Mariah. She heaved a sigh. She hoped he'd get over it soon.

Chapter 15

'You don't have to do this, Ned.'

'Yes, I do, Mr Thorpe. After what I saw they did to Mrs Cluff. They need some o' their own medicine.'

'It could be dangerous.'

'What? More dangerous than working down a coal mine? Or at the furnace face when the fire's at its height? I done both, Mr Thorpe, and look at me now!'

'Aye. Look at you, as tall as me and just as brawny. How old are you, Ned?'

'Seventeen. It's been seven year now since I left the poor-house and went down the pit wi' your dad.'

'Are you still lodging with Dad's mate?'

He nodded. 'We get on all right, we do. Let me come with you, Mr Thorpe. There'll be two o' them.'

'Saturday night, then. They're staying in a farm shed near their cousin in Mexton and going to the cock fight over that

154

way. I'll follow them afterwards and pick 'em off when they've split from the rest of their clan.'

'*We*, Mr Thorpe. *We'll* foller 'em and pick 'em off together.'

They took the towpath out of town, past Fordham down towards Mexton Lock. But before they reached the Navigator Inn, they cut across the fields to a tumbledown farmhouse outside one of the new pit villages. The farm had been one of the best around until the local landowner had discovered a coal seam running underneath it and now all the trappings of the pit dominated the land. The men worked under ground instead of on top of it and the farmhouse had decayed. A winding house and spoil heap scarred the pasture. But there were rows of new cottages nearby for the labourers, and an ale house, and even talk of a chapel.

Skirting the farmhouse, they followed the noise and glow of light from a broken shutter of the big old barn at the back. The fight was underway when they arrived. Daniel and Ned slipped unnoticed into a crowd of spirited men baying for blood.

The screeching and scrawing of fighting cocks as they flapped and scrabbled in the dust, pecking each other to near death, set Daniel's teeth on edge. But he understood the rivalry and it fired his own blood for revenge.

They climbed on an old cart, abandoned in the shadows, to get a better look and Daniel wished it were him and Cluff in that half circle enclosed by a brick pen against the back of the barn. He felt his pulse begin to beat and his fists clenched involuntarily. He had never been more ready than now to give Cluff his dues. The fighting pit was lit by oil lamps standing on straw bales and flares hoisted on poles sent grotesque shadows against the walls.

'Are they here?' Ned whispered.

Daniel scanned the jeering crowd of men enjoying their sport of a Saturday night after a week of grinding labour at the furnace or coal face. But they were not all working men swigging ale from stone jars. He recognised one or two, better dressed, friends of Mr Bowes, in a group around the bookie, flashing purses jingling with coins, and even banknotes, as they wagered. They drank spirits from small flasks and in the flickering light, their eyes and teeth flashed in their flushed sweating faces.

'We should've brought a nip to drink ourselves,' Ned said.

Daniel reached inside his jacket and drew out a small leather-covered metal flask. 'Try this.'

'You first.'

'I have no need of it.'

Daniel's blood was up already. He wanted no prop from any bottle. Cluff and his son were there, he recognised their wild eyes and harsh grinning faces showing rotten and crooked teeth. They called and sneered at the birds and their owners. The bookies pocketed their gains as the broken, bleeding cocks were packed away in wicker cages and fresh ones presented to the baying crowd.

The air was rank with the smell of old straw and horse droppings, fresh chicken blood and human sweat. Between bouts, a couple of rouged women with their bodices half open, crept around the back of the crowd, picking off men they knew were good for a tanner, and leading them away outside.

Daniel and Ned stayed in the shadows, watching, until there were no more cocks to fight and the noisy crowd began to disperse, some to carriages that loomed out of the darkness for their gentry owners. They followed the Mexton bunch until they saw the two Cluff men turn off the main cart track.

Then they cut across the scrubland and, a few hundred yards on, stepped out in front of them.

'What the—!'

'Ned, you take on the young 'un. Just a pasting. Understand?'

Ned was already laying into the surprised son, who took a few seconds to rally and give as good as he got. Daniel, confident that Ned could lick him, turned his back and faced the father, the instigator, the evil one. He saw a knife blade glint in the moonlight and heard him call out.

'Come on then. I know who you are and I'm ready fer yer. Think yer can fuck our Harry's missus and get away wi' it, do yer?'

Daniel ignored the taunts and leapt forward, kicking the knife from the other man's grasp. He heard it clatter as it fell on the rocky track. Cluff was surprised, but quick to respond and lashed out with both his fists. Daniel fended him off, taking the blows on his raised arms and then set about the man with a vengeance that had simmered in him for days.

One heavy punch after another, first to the man's head and then his body. He ducked and dodged Cluff's futile retaliation. Thump. Thump. The sickening thuds of fists on flesh sounded good to his ears, the tortured gasps and cries from his opponent were sweeter than music. Cluff was on his knees and still he hit him, lifting him by the collar to punch his jaw until he was nothing more than a bleeding, groaning heap on the rocky dirt track.

He felt a tug on his jacket sleeve. 'Mr Thorpe. Mr Thorpe. That's enough. You'll kill him.' Ned tugged harder, pulling him away.

Daniel straightened and tried to calm himself. Cluff's son was lying motionless on the ground. 'What about him?' he asked.

'Knocked out, that's all.'

He heard a groan and scrabbling noise behind him and turned to see the older man recovering, on his knees, the knife back in his hand. 'I'll get you back for this, Thorpe. I'll get you where it hurts. You see if I don't. You'd better watch them little sisters o' thine, cos I'll 'ave 'em afore I'm through wi' you. I'll 'ave 'em all.'

Cluff lunged forward, throwing the knife at Daniel. His swift reactions saved him from injury and the knife whistled by him and fell to the ground. Cluff tried to stagger to his feet but collapsed back into a heap on the track. 'I'll ruin 'em like I did that carrot top,' he croaked. 'They'll all be whores like 'er, afore I'm finished.'

Daniel caught sight of the knife, its glinting blade signalling, beckoning, no, summoning him to pick it up. And as he picked it up, it was Mariah's bruised body he saw through the red rage that engulfed him. Dear sweet Mariah, who was a friend to everyone and so misjudged by her own family.

'No, Mr Thorpe. That'll be murder. Chuck the knife away!'

Ignoring Ned's pleas, he slashed at Cluff's breeches, splitting them open at the front.

Cluff yelled and desperately struggled to roll over and scramble to his feet. He called over to his son who was stirring from his stupor. 'Gerron yer feet, lad!'

'Stop it, Mr Thorpe!' Ned pleaded. 'Just fists, you said. Fight fair. Man to man.'

'Do you think he fought fair with Mariah?' Daniel's voice cracked and broke into a hoarse whisper. 'Kind, innocent Mariah, who had no part in any of this.' He straddled Cluff as he tried to escape and pushed him back to the ground, tearing away the shreds of his clothing to expose his private parts.

Pinned on his back, Cluff struck out with his fists, finding strength through fear.

Daniel fended off the blows, keeping the knife well out of reach and breathed, 'This is for Mariah.' He angled the knife to slice.

He could not move his arm.

Ned had stilled his wrist with an iron fist as strong as his own.

'I thought this fight was about Lily Cluff,' Ned said quietly.

'Leave me be, Ned. He deserves this. You don't know the half of it.'

'I know you could end up in gaol or worse if you carry on like this.'

'It would be worth it!'

'And then what good will you be to this Mariah? Locked up wi' men no better than he is, and not able to help those who rely on you. You're not thinking straight, Mr Thorpe.'

Daniel wrenched his arm away. Ned was right. But, more than that, in his anger he had said too much about Mariah. He did not want Ned asking questions. What had happened to her was a secret Daniel would keep to his grave.

He had wanted to make Cluff suffer and by God, he had! He had frightened him half to death. Cluff really thought he meant to castrate him there and then. He was groaning as he squirmed, his punches weakening as Daniel's greater strength overcame him. ''Ow many sisters 'ave yer got?' Cluff goaded him hoarsely, and choked on his laughter.

'Shut up!' Daniel shouted. He bent over Cluff, grasping his chin in his hand and brandished the knife. 'If I ever see you or your vile clan around any woman again, I'll finish you. I'll cut off your scrawny balls and stuff them down your evil throat.' He flung the knife as far as could into the scrub. Then he marched over to the son and yelled, 'Let this be a lesson to the pair of you!'

He surveyed the scene in front of him. The Cluffs would recover; Mariah might not. He felt better for extracting this revenge but it did not assuage his guilt. It was his own greedy passion for that Cluff woman's body that was at the root of all this. He was as bad as they were and he hated himself for it! He stood there, breathing heavily, watching the men squirm on the ground and wondered what good he had done for Mariah by this deed.

'Come on, Mr Thorpe,' Ned said quietly. 'They'll not forget that in a hurry. Let's get off home.'

Wordlessly, Daniel followed Ned back to town.

Chapter 16

'What's been going on? Did that happen in my yard? Because if it did, my lad, you can leave right now. I'll not have fighting in my yard.'

'It was nothing to do with here, Mr Bowes. It was a private matter.'

Ezekiel looked more closely at Daniel Thorpe's face. A bit of swelling and bruising around the eyes and jaw. Not much. Just a scuffle probably. Then he caught sight of his hands. The knuckles were red raw. Thorpe was a strong man. He was tall and muscular and Ezekiel reckoned the other fellow had not fared so well. Poor sod, he thought. He remembered when he had been on the wrong end of fists like Thorpe's. It had only happened once and he hadn't deserved it. But he remembered it.

'You'll not do it again, Thorpe. Do you hear? I am not having my supervisor, who lives in my house, brawling in the streets. Now, who else was with you?'

'No one you know, sir.' Ned had had an easier time of it, seeing off Cluff's son in the fight. Men at the furnace face were often getting knocks and bruises, but to avoid any questioning Daniel had sent Ned off that morning with a delivery to Sheffield. 'It happened outside town.'

'Are you going to tell me what it was about?'

'No, sir.'

'I have a right to know!'

'It was over a woman, sir.'

This seemed to anger Ezekiel. 'Womenfolk!' he exclaimed. 'They always cause you trouble. Not your sister, lad! Not this one living in my house, I hope?'

Daniel's face was set in an angry grimace and he wanted to shout, 'No, it was your own daughter, you imbecile! The one you threw out because she would not marry that smarmy friend of yours!' But he knew the less Ezekiel knew about what happened to Mariah, the better. He simply said, 'No, sir.'

'This is not a good start, my lad, but this time – mind you, only this one time – I'll give you the benefit of the doubt.' He got to his feet and raised his voice. 'I mean it, though. If you bring any trouble to my yard, you're out!'

'I know that, Mr Bowes. It'll not happen again, I promise you.'

Ezekiel grunted. 'Sit yourself down a while. I have something to discuss with you.'

He watched Thorpe as he settled in one of the worn leather office chairs. He noticed the thick leather on his boots. It was worn and scuffed as he expected, but they were well-made, from the best cobbler in town – he recognised the workmanship. Thorpe had on tough moleskin trousers and a grey flannel shirt that was protected by his long leather waistcoat.

Thorpe wore that waistcoat every day and it carried the

scars of his trade. It set him apart from the rest of the men and gave him authority. Ezekiel wondered if Thorpe realised how much he did not want to row with him, or get rid of him from his yard. By heaven, he wished his son Henry was more like this fellow.

Ezekiel stood up and walked around his desk to sit opposite him by the fire. Thorpe was sitting rigidly upright, with a straight back and his shoulders squared. He was staring intently at Ezekiel, with a neutral expression on his face. He was his own man, this one was, Ezekiel thought. That's what makes him a good gaffer to the men. As long as he's on my side.

'You're a capable fellow, Thorpe. One of the best. Any man would be proud to have you as his son. You think on that when it comes to womenfolk.'

'Aye, Mr Bowes, I will.'

That seemed to relax him a bit, and Ezekiel felt better too. The last thing he wanted was any kind of scandal about his works supervisor. Although a fight over a woman might give Thorpe some credibility with his gang, so it was not such a bad thing. A bit of a reputation with the ladies would do him no harm as the works gaffer. It gave the men something to talk about as long as none of their own women were involved and Thorpe would know better than to cause that kind of trouble. Even so, Thorpe was five and twenty, too old to be a bachelor without causing talk.

'It's high time you got yourself a wife, man,' Ezekiel said. 'I run a respectable shop here and I'll not have any miner's son bringing us down. A fine well-set-up fellow like you should have no difficulty finding himself a good woman! You do have a lady friend, don't you? Didn't you tell me you were thinking of getting wed?'

'I said I might be.' Daniel did not care for the way this conversation was going. He felt uncomfortable, closeted in that small office with Mr Bowes. He had his own father to advise him without Mr Bowes pitching in as well. The fire radiated its heat onto his face. He did not want to lie to his employer, but he could not possibly tell him the truth, not about himself and Lily and his own daughter.

'She hasn't turned you down, has she? I don't know! Some o' these young lasses don't know when they're well off. Have you talked to her father?'

'It's not like that, Mr Bowes. My father has the miner's cough and I'm the only son left now, so most of my wages go to keep my mother and sisters.'

'I see,' Ezekiel responded. 'Well, that's right responsible of you, lad. They said you were a good 'un when I asked about you at the Fitzkeppel works. It saves the parish a shilling or two when families can look after their own.'

Daniel became more uneasy in Ezekiel's presence with each passing minute. He said, 'I thought you wanted to talk about the works, sir. I need to keep an eye on the furnace out there . . .'

'This won't take long.'

Daniel shifted his position in the worn office chair.

Ezekiel stood up but remained in front of Thorpe, with his back to the fire and said, 'What you need is a lass with a bit of dowry behind her. Don't you agree?'

'Well no. I . . .'

'Don't be daft, man. I reckon you could have your pick of one or two decent lasses round about here. What about one of Smith's daughters from the hardware shop in town?'

Ezekiel watched Thorpe's face closely. He had been trying to think of a way of getting back into Mr Smith's favour and this might be it. Mr Smith was powerful in the lodge and Mariah's behaviour towards him had caused Ezekiel a lot of embarrassment. By God, if she had been his own flesh and blood she would never have disobeyed him like that! He was glad to be shut of her and good riddance!

But it had not done his reputation at the lodge any good. Since then, he had been trying his damnedest to think of a way to make up the lost ground with Mr Smith. His young-sters were getting to be a real handful since his missus had passed away. Taking one of Smith's unruly lasses off his hands and marrying her to his ambitious young gaffer was the least he could do for him. By heaven, that would mend the rift between them, all right!

He went on, 'You know of Mr Smith, don't you? His eldest girl would do very well for you. He's got property, has Mr Smith. His late wife brought a row of houses with her when he wed her. In town they are, not far from here. His daughter'll be bound to come with one o' them to live in, and a dowry besides.'

Daniel swallowed. He knew about the Smith family. Everybody in town did because they were well off and Mr Smith's business was one of the best. But he had never met any of them, except in their shop. Nor had he any wish to. He was more than capable of finding his own bride when he was ready, and she would be of his own choosing.

When he did not reply, Ezekiel pressed on, 'I can arrange a meeting with Mr Smith, if you like. He's got five daughters to wed, you know.' After a further silence, he raised his voice, 'Well, man, I can do this for you. What do you say?'

Daniel stared at Mr Bowes uneasily, not sure what to make of this unsatisfactory exchange. He knew from the works gang that Mr Smith's eldest daughter had her eyes firmly set on the farrier's son from Keppel village.

165

That did not matter to Ezekiel Bowes, he thought. He was a harsh and unfeeling man when it came to women. After what he had heard about Mr Smith's visit to the Bowes household, he was in no doubt as to why Mariah had left home. Daniel began to realise the difficulty Mariah had faced with her father's wishes for her.

He said, 'No thank you, Mr Bowes. I have my own plans.' He wasn't even sure himself what they were, but he knew they did not involve one of the Smith girls. God, his life was in such a mess. How had he let it happen? How could he make things right again?

'What plans?' Ezekiel demanded irritably.

'I can't say. Not yet.'

'You think on about my offer, lad. It's a good one. And get yourself sorted out. I want no trouble sticking to my yard.'

'Right, sir.'

'Get back to work, then.'

'Yes, sir.'

Daniel was glad to escape from the office and back to the furnace. The last thing on his mind was getting wed. He'd had his fingers badly burned with Lily and he was damn sure he wasn't going to let that happen again. But he did not dwell too long on these thoughts. He'd produced a decent amount of blister steel from the furnace last week, and it was already sold. Once the new crucibles were installed he'd get an even better price for Mr Bowes and his fancy son. Now he was in charge, Daniel was going to make his name here. The men worked hard for him, and Mr Bowes, for all his faults, was not mean about paying his men, especially now the output was rising.

Daniel stopped as he went out of the office door. 'I thought that, when I've got the furnace loaded and going again, I'd show one of the men how to make the crucibles. I learned that before I did the teeming. We'll need a full-time potter when the new crucible shed is finished.'

'Aye. Do that.'

'When will the new furnace be ready, Mr Bowes?'

'You'll know in good time. Just concentrate on keeping the men working and yourself away from the fighting for now.'

'Yes, sir.' Daniel nodded, closed the door behind him and clattered down the stone steps.

Chapter 17

'I've collected some mushrooms for your breakfast.'

Dora Barton stopped stirring a pot of porridge on the hob and looked round. She smiled. 'Ee, Mariah love, I thought you were still in your bed. It's grand to see you up and about with a bit of colour in your cheeks. Come and sit by the fire.'

'It's your careful tending that's helped me, Dora.'

'I wish I could do more, lass. But it's really down to you to get over this now.'

Mariah gave a brief nod and chewed her lip. Dora Barton had looked after her as a mother does her own child, soothing her sleepless nights and talking to her. She could not remember the things Dora said, only that her words had been comforting and they had helped her recover a semblance of her self-respect and she would always be grateful.

She wished, oh, how she wished her own mother was still alive, to hold her and comfort her and tell her everything was fine. But she wasn't and everything was not fine. None of this would have happened if her mother had lived. A knot began to form in Mariah's stomach. She tried to ignore it and managed a smile for the woman whose unfailing kindness and generosity of spirit had helped her through. 'You have been so gentle and understanding towards me. I do not know what I would have done without you.'

'What happened was not your doing and I don't hold with womenfolk suffering like that. But it did happen and there's no turning the clock back,' Dora responded briskly. 'This porridge is ready if you're hungry.'

'Oooh, not just yet.'

'Shall I fry the mushrooms in a bit o' bacon fat instead?'

'Give me minute or two, Dora. I felt a bit queasy early on and it seems to have come back.'

'You need to eat more, lass. You've gone ever so thin since – well, these last few weeks.'

'I've lost track of how long it's been now. Just getting through one day at a time has been the best I could do.'

'Don't you fret about that, you take all the time you need,' Dora said soothingly. But a suspicion began to form in her mind. 'How do you feel in yourself?' she asked.

'I–I don't know. A bit strange, really.'

'You've healed well enough.' Dora frowned. 'You should be getting back to your normal self by now. I've some sweet milk fresh from the farm dairy, if you fancy that with your porridge.'

'Perhaps later.'

Dora's frown deepened and she went back to the fireplace.

Mariah made an effort to talk and said, 'The pig is looking nice and fat now. Did you get him some of the skimmed milk while you were over there?'

'It's in a bucket in the scullery. Why don't you take it down to him? You can pull some greens for the hens, while you're

169

at it. And see if there are any eggs to make a Yorkshire for dinner.'

Mariah tipped the bucket of milk into the pig's trough and stayed, leaning over the low stone wall of his sty to scratch his back with a stick while he sucked and lapped. Then he snuffled and grunted, searching for some of his favourite turnips in the corners of his trough. She scattered the greens and crumbled some stale-bread crusts under Dora's fruit trees at the end of the garden. Two of her hens had gone through the hedge into the woodland and she shooed them back to the orchard. The bread should keep them there now. You couldn't be too careful with foxes at this time of year.

Mariah took refuge in the isolation of Dora's cottage. The only living soul she had met since moving here was Mr Shaw, who had a bit of land on the edge of the wood. He had known Dora's father well, having worked with him on the land, but he was a very old man now. Mind you, he was still sprightly for his age, Mariah thought. In his younger days, when he was a labourer on the Fitzkeppel estate, he had kept a farrowing sow and a flock of geese as well as hens. And he'd had ferrets for flushing out rabbits in the hillsides.

She found a clutch of small pullet eggs and considered herself lucky now the days were getting shorter. There were plenty for one of Dora's Yorkshire puddings, to go with the stew she was making. They had meat today, scrag end of mutton with plenty of onion and barley. It ought to have smelled appetising to Mariah when she went indoors from the garden, but it did not. Something about her was still not right.

'How is Mr Shaw keeping?' she asked.

'He'll be all right as long as his cough doesn't come back this winter.'

'He has you to keep an eye on him.'

'We've allus looked out for each other.'

'You must have missed Fanny when she went to live in town.'

Dora looked wistful for a moment. 'You couldn't separate us until Arthur came along. He changed everything. We'd never had a man except our father living in our house before.'

Mariah raised her eyebrows. 'Mr Thorpe lived here with you?'

'He took lodgings with us one spring to work on the Fitzkeppel estate. We were glad of his help, I can tell you. But he was laid off after autumn ploughing with no hope of any more labouring until the following year. He had paid us rent at Michaelmas, but when it came to Candlemas he had nothing left. We didn't want to turn him out, so we asked him to do repairs on the sty and henhouse, and gardening and the like for us. Just like Father had done. That way we all got through the winter warm and well fed.'

'Even so, unmarried ladies living with an unmarried gentleman . . .'

'Oh, Reverend Judd kept a close eye on us. He took it upon himself to act as our guardian after Father died, and he made it his business to call on us regular. His wife too, if she was round this way on her visits to the sick.' Dora smiled and gave a chuckle. 'Good old Mrs Judd. She used to say she was only doing what our dear mother would have wanted when she asked to look over our housekeeping.'

'What, your account books and such like?'

'No, Mariah. The bedchambers. She would straighten the window drapes and run her finger over the mantelshelves for dust. But really she only wanted to see our sleeping arrangements, just in case we were not being truthful about our domestic activities.'

'I expect she was worried for your reputations,' Mariah suggested.

'Well, Fanny's anyway. I think I was beyond help by carrying on Mrs Shaw's work. Nursing and the like was not considered a fitting vocation for an unmarried lady, but I didn't care. Looking back now, I can see how they would be concerned. Arthur was a real handsome fellow and one or two of the maids at church had their heads turned by him.'

'Shall I mix the batter for the pudding today?' Mariah volunteered.

'Go on, then.' Dora sat at her kitchen table and chatted to Mariah as she measured and stirred. 'Mrs Shaw was the midwife round here. She did all the doctoring for the poorer folk as well.'

'What happened to Mrs Shaw?'

'She died the same winter as Father. There was a fever that year that took a lot of folk from round here.'

'That must have been hard for you and Fanny. And Mr Shaw.'

'We helped each other through. I had been going to see sick folk with Mrs Shaw, reg'lar, before she caught the fever. I knew all her doctoring ways. I still turn out when I'm called on, and I can get to the village quicker than anybody from town.'

'Don't you ever get lonely?'

'Not me, lass. I like it out here on my own, away from prying eyes and loose tongues.'

'Me, too.'

'Aye, I know,' Dora responded sympathetically.

'Did you never want to be married?'

'Oh, I did that! Mrs Shaw had told me I should get wed and have my own babbies if I was going to be of any use to others. But there weren't many suitors to choose from around here. Those we didn't lose to soldiering went off to ironstone pits or coal mines in other parts, or to the foundries in town. There were plenty of lasses for them to pick from in town.'

'Your sister seems happy with Mr Thorpe and their children.'

'Born to be a wife, she was, baking bread, salting down the pig, pickling vegetables.' Dora sighed and looked around her. 'The house always looked nice when she was here.'

Mariah glanced up from her mixing, at the framed samplers hanging on fresh whitewashed walls, and a mellowed wooden dresser stacked with pretty china. 'It looks nice now.'

'Not bad, I suppose. Mostly our Fanny's doing, though, when she visits. I have always been more interested in looking after the animals – and the doctoring and nursing, o' course.'

'That's lucky for me – and for a lot of other folk, I'm sure.'

'Me and Fanny helped out at the Hall from time to time. When they had their shooting parties to visit. But not long after Father died that stopped because her Ladyship upped and left and we had to find something else to make ends meet. When Father was alive he used to keep a sow and I lent a hand when she farrowed. Right from being little I was into all that. Not our Fanny, though. She liked the indoors, like our mother.'

Mariah smiled. It cheered her to listen to Dora talk about her younger days and her family. 'My mother was a good housekeeper, too,' she said, 'but she liked doing her sewing more than anything. She taught me all she knew.' Mariah lifted the spoon from her mixing bowl. 'This batter's ready now. Shall I put a tin in the oven?'

'Let it stand for a bit first.'

Dora bent over the fireplace to give her cauldron a stir and went on. 'I learned more from my father and Mrs Shaw. If there was a runt in the sow's litter, my father let me fetch it inside to see if I could rear it. Ee, I was full of questions in those days. I wanted to know everything about how the piglets got inside the sow and how she knew when they were ready to come out.' Dora laughed lightly. 'Mother told me it was God's doing and our Fanny knew no better. I never swallowed that, of course. I knew it was something to do with the season and the boar. But Father was really strict about us girls staying out of the way when the boar was here.'

'Did Mrs Shaw have any children?'

'Oh, aye. Three lasses and two lads.'

'And none of the girls wanted to follow their mother's calling?'

Dora grimaced and shook her head. 'They wanted better for themselves. Nursemaids and lady's maids to the gentry. No, it was left to me to go with Mrs Shaw when she had to turn out in the middle of the night in winter. Besides, after seeing to the sow and the lambing every spring, helping the midwife came natural to me.'

'Where are her girls now?'

'Long gone. All three. They went off into service in Derbyshire. Big house there, three times the size of the Hall. And very proper they were, too. They had royalty to visit and everything. Still do, but all the Shaw girls have left now, got themselves wed and settled over there.'

Mariah thought how wonderful it must be to have sisters. Like the Thorpes. They may be poor and living in a miner's cottage, but they had each other. Oh, how she missed her mother! She missed her so much, it hurt. 'Don't you miss your sister, Dora?' she asked.

'Yes, I do. But she has her Arthur and that's that.'

Dora's sharp tone made Mariah look up at her face and the older woman went quiet for a moment. But she recovered quickly and smiled. 'You look tired already, Mariah. Why don't you bring your mending and sit by the fire for an hour before dinner?'

Mariah sighed. She felt ill most of the time, she could not remember feeling this way before and her energy flagged easily. Dora said her flesh had healed well and she kept herself busy around the house and garden. But the feelings and images of that night were still strong in her mind and they ate away at her reason. Sometimes she felt so angry with those men she could not deal with it and wanted nothing more than to sweep all the pots off the table so they smashed on the floor. She never did, of course, and her resentment festered.

Sewing soothed her. It reminded her of happier times and helped her to think of other things and calmed her mind. But such calmness was usually temporary.

After a while Dora said, 'I think you can put that tin in the oven now. This stew is about ready and I'm feeling peckish.'

Mariah put aside her mending and got up. 'I'll set the table. I'm hungry, too.'

'That's a good sign.'

After dinner, when the washed pots were lined up on Dora's kitchen dresser and they had fetched fresh water from the spring, they sat by the fire for a rest, waiting for the kettle to boil on the hob.

'How are you feeling now?' Dora asked.

'Better. I just hope the queasiness doesn't come back.'

Dora pursed her lips, fearing it would. 'Shall I make some of my mint tea for you? It might settle your stomach a bit.'

'Thanks. I'll get the cups and you can tell me more about when you and Fanny were younger.'

When they were seated again, sipping the hot tangy liquor, sweetened with honey, Dora resumed her tale.

'The winter was the worst. The days were short, always overcast with heavy cloud, and the weather was bitter cold, so none of us ventured out much except for church. But we survived. Our Fanny always had a good fire to cook our dinner, and the washing and mending to fill her days. Arthur was there for the outdoor work. We'd killed the pig before the winter set in and it was salted down in a lead trough in the outhouse. He cleaned out the empty sty and whitewashed it ready for a new piglet in the spring. I was called out quite often, too, for my medicines, and usually came back with something for the table. Arthur built that big wooden cupboard in the back scullery for me to keep my lotions and potions in.'

That was the start of it for me, Dora thought. That was when I knew I had fallen for him. Best not talk to Mariah of courting and such like right now. It might upset her and set her back again.

Mariah pulled her shawl closer about her shoulders and thought how cosy this little house was and how lucky Dora and Fanny were to have each other. The fire warmed her face and her eyelids drooped.

Dora drank her cooling tea and thought she would let her doze a while. Mariah had eaten a good dinner today and it was clearly making her sleepy. It was nice to sit quiet by the fire and remember. As Mariah dozed, Dora thought back to earlier times, when she was Mariah's age, Fanny was one and twenty and Arthur just two years older, and those stolen times together.

Chapter 18

Dora watched her fire burn down. The flames flickered low and the glowing embers fell quietly. She decided not to add more wood. It might spit and crackle and wake Mariah. Besides, what had happened that winter was as clear to her now as though it were yesterday, and she might say too much if Mariah woke.

Dora did not plan it. It just happened. It was before Arthur had asked Fanny to be his wife. Dora had been out to see a sick child and, on the way back, called in to look up a treatment in one of Mrs Shaw's books. Arthur was there. He often went over to look after Mr Shaw and read the news sheets to him as his eyes weren't so good. When Dora saw Arthur tending quietly to the old man, in his waistcoat and shirt sleeves, she felt desire shoot through her like nothing she had experienced before.

She had some knowledge of men from Mrs Shaw's books and the widowers she had helped tend when they were dying and had no family to see to them. But this was different, an overwhelming need to explore Arthur's manliness and strength in a much more intimate and personal way. A way that was forbidden until a man and a woman were wed. In that isolated cottage, watching him move quietly about his tasks, she was overpowered by such a yearning for him she did not know what to do.

She wanted to lie with him.

She had seen the way he looked at her, sometimes covertly, in the kitchen at home. If she caught his eye, he turned away and went outside. Mrs Judd was right to be concerned about them living under the same roof. Men had these urges; Dora knew that Arthur had these urges.

But Mrs Judd had not warned her that she might have these urges too.

When it happened, it was all her own doing. Mr Shaw had taken to his bed early with a sleeping draught. Arthur and Dora were tidying round, damping down the fire and laying the breakfast table. They did not say much. But they kept bumping into each other as they moved about Mr Shaw's kitchen. Dora held onto Arthur's arm, first to steady herself, and then to stop him moving from her. She did not let go and, when he tried to pull away, she tugged at his sleeve.

'Arthur, I've seen the way you look at me.'

'Stop this at once, Dora.'

'Why?' Her hands reached around the back of his neck and she pulled his head towards hers and kissed him briefly on his lips, pressing her body against his, wanting him.

Taken by surprise, Arthur wiped the back of his hand across his mouth and exclaimed, 'Good God! What on earth do you think you are doing?'

'Kiss me, Arthur. Put your arms around me and kiss me. Please?'

'Certainly not! You shock me with this behaviour.'

'You want me, too! I know you do! Why do you deny it?'

'This is nonsense. Now, move aside so I can pass.'

'No. I love you. No one will ever know. Not even Mr Shaw. Come on, Arthur.' Her heavy winter shawl had suddenly become a hindrance and she pulled it away to reveal her throat.

'You must stop this now.'

But she had wanted this since the first day he had stepped over their threshold. 'I won't. And I won't let you run away from me.' She put her arms around him to hold him close.

His shoulders were sagging forward, his head bending to hers. She raised her mouth to his again, this time opening her lips and seeking his tongue with hers. Her knees buckled and she sank to the floor, pulling him down with her.

'Dora, Dora, what are you doing to me?'

But he no longer resisted her and her aching body melted for him.

'Hush. Here, come closer to the fire.' Hastily she bunched up her skirts and scrambled out of her drawers, discarding them on the rag rug by the hearth. She remembered her need at that time, her young, desperate need to know what it felt like to be possessed by him. No one had told her how much *she* would want this.

'This is what you want, isn't it? Say it is. Say it, Arthur.'

His voice came out a strangled, sorrowful moan. 'No, it's not right.'

But as he said it, his actions told a different story.

'Do it. Do it now,' she whispered urgently.

Her veins were throbbing in her head and her body opened up to him. He cried out, in a soft, throaty, satisfying moan that made her want to weep with joy. She felt so wonderfully fulfilled she thought nothing could spoil that moment.

But Arthur was distraught and angry. He scrambled quickly off her, pulling up his clothes and scolding her. 'Get up and dress yourself at once! You are a wanton woman, and you should be ashamed of yourself!'

'I love you.'

'Nonsense! You've behaved no better than a harlot. I can see you've been allowed far too much freedom since your father passed on. You know far too much for an unmarried lady of your young years. This will not do!'

'But you wanted me, too.'

'I am a man. It is different for a man. Did not Mrs Shaw tell you that? You seem to know all there is to be known about these things!'

'Please do not say that. Do not spoil it for me.'

'Spoil it! What are you talking about?' He shook his head and then held it in his hands. 'Oh God! What have I done? I have ruined you. What on God's earth shall I say to your sister?'

'Oh, you mustn't tell Fanny! Please don't tell Fanny. She'll send you away!'

'After this I am sure I should leave anyway.'

'No!'

They sat on the rag rug, in the darkness, dishevelled and silent, watching the fire burn low until Arthur took a deep breath and said, 'We must forget this happened. I am sorry, Dora. I have wronged you. The fault is all with me. The Lord presented me with temptation and I gave in to it. I shall pray to the Lord for forgiveness. We shall both pray for forgiveness.'

But all Dora could think about was that he had not told her he loved her.

180

'Whatever you do, you must not tell Fanny either. Promise me.'

Of course she promised. She did not want to have Arthur sent away. It was the first secret she had kept from her sister. Dora was not proud of what she had done but she did not regret it, whatever Arthur might think of her.

Arthur avoided being alone with her from then on. If they did find themselves in the same room without other company, he made excuses and left. He would not even look her in the eye and shortly afterwards, he and Fanny were betrothed.

As Dora watched Mariah dozing by the fire, she thought back to that stolen time with Arthur wistfully. Her illicit passion had been short lived but it caused repercussions for the rest of her life.

Mariah's eyes shot open suddenly. 'Did I fall asleep? I am so sorry, it must be the heat of the fire.'

'Do you good, dear. It's getting cold outside now. We'll shut up the hens early tonight and put bricks to warm for our beds. I don't want you catching a chill now you're on your feet again.'

'You were talking about your younger days, Dora. Tell me some more.'

'Oh, nothing really. Just that when Arthur came to lodge with us, I fell for him real bad.'

'But he married Fanny? He married your sister?'

'Aye, he did. Our Fanny was always more closed up than me, so you couldn't really tell what she was thinking, but I reckon she loved him more than I did. Mine was like many a young passion that flares out of control and then dies when – when it isn't returned.'

'Did Fanny know you had fallen for him?' Mariah asked.

'Not then. I thought when they were gone it would be an end to the matter.' But I was wrong, she thought. Arthur did not forget, or forgive, in spite of all his praying. Neither himself nor me. I think he would have got over it if Fanny had not found out.

'Did you tell her?'

Dora shook her head. 'Neither of us breathed a word at first. But she found out all right. She might be quiet, our Fanny, but she's clever with it.' Dora stood up and stretched. 'It caused a split between us for a while. Fanny and me made it up eventually, but Arthur will never forgive me.'

'That seems a bit harsh on you.'

'It's another story, Mariah my dear, another story.'

Besides, thought Dora, I don't want to let anything slip. Family secrets are best kept in the family. She got up and took the teapot through to the scullery.

'I'll go and shut up the hens and see to the pig before the light goes,' Mariah volunteered.

Dora watched her walk down the garden and sighed. She had told Mariah about her love for Arthur but not that she had lain with him, or the consequences. Mariah was not family. Dora must watch her tongue in future.

Chapter 19

The following morning Mariah sat on the edge of her bed holding her stomach as the nausea crept over her. Saliva trickled into her mouth and bile rose in her gullet.

'I'm going to be sick!' Her voice was strangled as she reached under the bed for the chamber pot and sank to her knees on the floor, helplessly retching and choking.

But there was nothing in her stomach and it was soon over. Dora came into her room and Mariah took the cup of water she had brought, pulling herself awkwardly to her feet and sinking gratefully onto the mattress.

'I had a bad dream,' Mariah explained. 'I saw those men again, they tried to—' She choked on the words.

'Don't get up too quickly. Take things slowly for a while.' Her own heart was sinking. She had seen women in this condition too often to mistake it. Oh Lord, she thought, I cannot tell her yet, not until she is stronger. It will be too much for her to bear. 'I'll mix you something to settle your stomach.

Then get a bit of fresh air, but don't stay out in the cold for too long.'

Half an hour later, Mariah dressed and, refreshed, carefully ate some porridge and said, 'I feel better now, thanks, Dora. A little walk might do me good this morning.'

'Good idea, lass. I'll come with you and show you the way. There's a footpath through the wood and over the fields to Keppel village. It goes across the parkland in front of Keppel Hall, but the present master doesn't mind village folk using it. Not like the old squire. He was a right tartar. His son's different though. Nice fellow. A bit of a dandy, but nice with it.'

Mariah wrapped a woollen shawl around her shoulders and put on her cloak. It was heavy on her thin body and it made her feel weaker than she was. She gritted her teeth and resolved to fight this decline! She must get well again!

She hated those men for what they had done to her and she would never be able to understand their actions, let alone find a scrap of forgiveness. Never. She could not. She could only believe, with Dora's wise counsel, that she had to get on with her life, a life that would be different now. She did not know how, just that it would, for she was a different person from the one who had lodged in Mrs Thorpe's front room.

Dora buttoned on a gentleman's long hunting coat over her dark brown working dress. It was made of thick waxed cotton and was old and worn. She tied a leather belt tightly around her waist and her skirts pushed out through the front opening and the back vent. It kept out the wind and the rain, and Mariah realised it was much more serviceable than a cloak against the brambles and undergrowth.

As they walked, an idea began to form in Mariah's head for a coat, a proper ladies' coat. If only she had some cloth. The more she thought about it, the more she liked her idea.

She would make a Sunday best coat for Dora, as a gift. The plan occupied her mind and cheered her.

The family resemblance between the sisters was strong. Both Dora and Fanny had large grey eyes, good cheekbones and healthy complexions. Arthur, too, had robust features with a straight nose and square jaw. Mariah realised, now, where Emma and Daniel got their strikingly handsome looks.

It was a bright, cold autumn day and Mariah inhaled its freshness, bringing a spot of colour to her pallid cheeks. They followed a pathway through the woods, and then a worn foot-path over the meadow past grazing sheep and rabbits. Eventually they crossed a wide track that led away from Keppel Hall to the distant park boundary. A rider was cantering along it, heading towards the gatehouse and onwards to the village. As he drew closer, he reined in his horse and slowed.

Mariah clutched at Dora's arm and whispered, 'Who is it? What does he want?'

'It's all right, love. It's only the master on his way to town.'

He waited for them to reach him, then lifted his tall hat and bowed his head, 'Good day to you, Mrs Barton.'

His hair, Mariah noticed, was fair and curly and his face had an aristocratic delicacy not weathered by outdoor labours. She looked down and pulled the hood of her cloak closely around her head, hiding her hair and most of her face.

'Good day to you, sir,' Dora replied. 'A fine morning for a ride.'

'Yes, indeed. And for walking too.' He looked at Mariah, raised his eyebrows and smiled. 'Why does your companion hide from me?'

Dora took her cue. 'Mr Fitzkeppel, may I present Miss Bowes, a – er – a friend of my niece. She is staying with me for the present.'

'Sir.' Mariah glanced up at him and dropped a curtsey. His skin was pale but not freckled like hers and his eyes pale blue. He had fine-boned features and sat tall and straight in the saddle carrying his dress well. They were garments that caught her attention. From the high polish on his chestnut boots and his soft doeskin breeches to the cut of his jacket and the frilled trim of his silken shirt. Mariah's expert eye recognised good tailoring when she saw it. A gentle approving smile lit her eyes.

Mr Fitzkeppel responded with a brief nod and murmured, 'Miss Bowes. Miss Bowes? A cousin, perhaps, of Henry Bowes? Of Bowes Ironworks in town?'

'We are related, sir.'

He replaced his high hat, a well-made hat with a cashmere finish if she were not mistaken, Mariah thought. 'Enjoy your walk, ladies.' He spurred his horse and rode on.

'So that is Mr Fitzkeppel,' Mariah murmured.

'Why? What do you know of him?'

'My half-brother, Henry, is acquainted with him. They went to the same school, though Mr Fitzkeppel is several years older than Henry, I believe.'

And now I know where Henry gets his notions of grandeur, Mariah thought. Henry would be very comfortable in the surroundings of Keppel Hall, with the friendship of its young master. But she wondered how Ezekiel would fit in there, away from his gang of labourers and his furnace. Oh well, it was none of her concern now, thank goodness.

She said, 'Back there, he called you Mrs Barton.'

'Every one does and most folk think I am a widow.'

'You had a husband?'

'I was never wed, lass. Mrs Shaw thought it was for the best if people thought I was a married woman. They don't

186

hold with their midwife being a maiden lady round here. So one day I said I was Mrs Barton instead of Miss Barton and I have been ever since. I wear my mother's wedding ring and none o' the younger folk question it. Not too many of the older ones who know different are still alive now. Mr Shaw does, and a few in the village.'

'What about the master?'

'No, he's too young to know about the Bartons.'

'Young, too, to be master of the Hall. But a fine-looking gentleman if I may say so,' Mariah commented.

Dora agreed, adding, 'His sister, too, is very pretty. Fair-skinned, like he is, and with hair the colour of honeycomb. They deserve better, poor mites.'

'Poor mites?' Mariah glanced around at the Hall and park-land. 'Is all this not theirs?'

'Oh yes. Master Nathaniel is one and twenty now and has just inherited. He is unmarried, so his sister Miss Christobel acts as mistress of the Hall.'

'They are not exactly poor, then.'

'No, I do not mean they lack wealth. Heavens, no! But they might as well have been orphans for most of their child-hood. The pair of them were brought up by schoolmasters and governesses, and latterly, the lawyers who were their guardians.'

'Yes, I remember hearing at the beast market when their father died.'

'Seven years ago, now. Master Nathaniel was fourteen and Christobel just sixteen. Old Fitzkeppel was in his seventies then and had been ailing for years. He was a crusty old bach-elor when he married and got steadily worse by all accounts.'

'I see. What about their mother?'

'Mrs Fitzkeppel? She ran off with her Italian lover. She came from the Dales. She was a pretty little thing when she arrived at the Hall. Barely nineteen and him in his fifties; he could have been her grandfather. When Fanny and I helped out at the Hall we heard tales of what went on, enough to make your hair curl!'

'What on earth do you mean? Did he beat her or something?'

Dora gave a low laugh. 'Ee, lass, no. Nothing like that. Antics in the bedchamber.' She stopped suddenly. 'I've said too much. Unmarried ladies are not supposed to know about such things.'

'No,' Mariah agreed quietly.

'I'm sorry, lass. I shouldn't have talked like that.'

'Of course you should. There is no sense in treating me as though I shall break in two every time I am reminded of what happened to me. I do not know why those evil men did what they did to me. But it is over and I am alive. Alive and – and I shall be strong again. One day. I shall.'

'Strong in body, I am sure. But you must look to purging the memories. I know they still plague you and that's not so good. You do not want that dreadful night haunting you for ever.'

'How do I stop it, Dora? I have tried to blank it from my mind but it is still there, as clear as yesterday. I don't believe I shall ever forget it.' Mariah added bitterly, 'Why are men so evil? Why?'

'Nay, they're not all like that, love.' Mariah was clutching tightly at her hand. 'You will have to put it all behind you, though, or else the memories will eat you up and spoil your chances of finding yourself a decent man to—'

'Decent man! *Decent man*,' Mariah retaliated scornfully. 'What decent man would look at me now?'

'No no, don't talk like that. You are still raw and hurting. But you will get over it. You will.' Dora wished she felt as confident as she sounded.

'I'll never get over it,' Mariah muttered.

Dora stayed silent. She kept a hold of her hand until they reached the boundary wall near the village and she suggested, 'Shall we sit and rest a while?'

Mariah nodded and leaned against the cold stone. 'Where is Mrs Fitzkeppel now?'

'Abroad somewhere. She has no contact with her children and even her own parents disowned her. Her husband didn't care about anything except his heir and the family name. She wanted to take Miss Christobel with her, but old Fitzkeppel was going to have her locked away in an asylum and she had to flee the country. So, you see, Miss Christobel and Master Nathaniel were more or less left on their own from a very young age.'

As I am now, Mariah thought. Poor things. Dora was right. No amount of wealth could be a substitute for your own mother. Mariah was aeons apart from the Fitzkeppels in her position in life but felt a bond of deprivation between them. Oh, how she missed her mother!

She thought of Arthur and Fanny Thorpe in their over-crowded cottage, a cottage that Daniel and Emma returned to at every opportunity. Mariah knew why. They didn't have land or wealth, but they had each other. Suddenly, Mariah felt very lonely.

She stretched out both her hands towards Dora and said, 'Thank you, again, for all you have done for me.'

Dora gave her a wry smile. 'You're a good lass. You never deserved what happened to you.'

The two women sat in silence for a moment each with their own thoughts, then got up to retrace their steps back to Dora's little house.

'My, it's turning chilly. We're in for a cold one this winter.'

'That coat is perfect for the rain, but you need something warmer when it's frosty. Shall I make a nice Sunday coat for you, Dora? A proper tailored one with a lining and a shoulder cape and everything.'

'Ee, lass, can you do that?'

'Oh yes, my mother taught me.'

'Where would I get the cloth, though? I can keep my little house warm and dry and put food on the table, but I couldn't run to buying that kind of cloth.'

'I've thought about that. I shall sell my silver picture frame. That will fetch enough.'

'And more besides, I should think. No, I can't let you do that for me.'

'But you have to let me do something to thank you.'

'Not your silver frame, though. It has your mother's likeness in it.'

'I shall keep the likeness, for that *is* important to me. But, truly, Dora, my mother would have approved of putting the frame to such good use. I shall have enough to buy cloth and notions for making other things, things I can sell at the market in town. I can begin to earn my keep. It is what I need to do, Dora, to get along. To get better. I need to do what I have always done when Mother was alive. And, eventually, pay my way with real money. If I may stay, of course.'

'Of course you may. Stay with me for as long as you wish. Are you sure about the frame?'

'Yes.'

'Well then, we can take the carrier into town next market day.'

Mariah inhaled sharply. 'Oh no, not me. Not yet. What if I see those men at the market? I am not ready to face that yet. Would you go for me, Dora? Take my frame to the silversmith

190

in the High Street and get as much as you can for it. Then go next door to the draper and choose some good woollen cloth, and some satin for the lining.'

'A satin lining? You'll be giving me airs.'

But Mariah was not listening. 'Oh, and I shall need my sewing things from your sister's house as well. It will be too much for you to carry on your own.'

'We-e-ell,' Dora began, 'I could ask our Daniel to bring them over on a Sunday.'

Mariah's heart lurched. 'D-Daniel? Over here? Oh no, I should be too ashamed to see him. He knows about the attack. He found me in that field—'

'I shan't ask him if you do not want him here,' Dora added hastily. 'It's just that he, well, he is always asking after you and he – he is so distressed about what happened to you.'

'I do not see why *he* should be so distressed. It was not Daniel who attacked me.'

'No, but he blames himself, you see, because he was carrying on with—' Dora stopped, unsure of what Mariah knew.

'With Mrs Cluff. I know. Emma said she was his sweetheart. Dora, she's a married lady! How could he?' Mariah's heart was beginning to pound in her breast. 'I am not stupid, Dora. I have been ill but I have not lost my wits. He must have lied about her to his parents!'

'But *he* did not lie! It was Lily who lied. She told him she was a widow and he believed her. We all believed her, even her neighbours at Canal Bank Cottages. Her husband is in gaol and she took some of the money he had stolen and moved to get away from his family. She lied to them as well. She told them she had to look after her dying cousin in the next county.'

'I didn't know about that,' Mariah said quietly.

'Her husband's family were suspicious and came looking

191

for her. They had heard rumours and when they demanded to know where her money was coming from if it wasn't her husband's, she told them our Daniel had given it to her.'

'He really did not know Lily was married?'

'No, he did not. Our Daniel is not a philanderer. He's a good lad. He could have wed any of the lasses from round here years ago and he did not. He worked hard and looked after his family. But he's like his fa—.' Dora faltered. 'He — well, he wanted his own woman. He had asked her to marry him, you know. When he got the supervisor's job with your father, he asked her to marry him.'

'Where is Mrs Cluff now?' Mariah asked.

'Went off back to Manchester. The end cottage is empty now. Good riddance if you ask me.'

'Yes, indeed,' Mariah echoed with a sigh. 'I expect that's what people think of me, now. A disgraced woman. Unworthy.'

'Why should they?'

'People talk about these things.'

'Only when they know about them.'

'Of course they know! Like everyone knows about Mrs Fitzkeppel!'

'No. The Fitzkeppels were different. Their servants talked, as servants do. Everyone thinks you were knocked sideways by a cart horse on the towpath!'

'Not quite everyone — there's your sister and her husband, and Daniel, and Lord knows who else.'

'I have not breathed a word to anyone, I swear.'

'And the others who know what really happened to me? What about them?'

'There's only Daniel, Fanny, Arthur and me. That's all.'

'Not Emma? Meg and Liddy?'

Dora shook her head. 'No. Fanny would not tell them. As

192

far as anyone else is concerned, you were thrown off your feet.'

'I see. I'm sorry, Dora. It's just that, oh, I don't know, it is all so dirty and humiliating. I feel soiled by it all. And worthless. I am – I am so ashamed.'

'I know. But you must try not to let it consume you like this. It was no fault of yours.'

Tears welled in Mariah's eyes. Dora noticed them and began, hurriedly, to talk of different things. 'Look, this sewing idea of yours is a good one. It will help to take your mind away from all this. Why don't we go into my front room when we get back and see if we can make space for you to sew in there? My mother's old oak dining table might be just the thing.'

Dora's table was a solid heavy piece, darkened by years of waxing, and it took pride of place under the window, graced by a white lace runner and burnished brass bowl.

'The only thing is,' Dora explained, 'it's got a rickety leg and it wobbles a bit, but I'm sure our Dan—' Dora stopped suddenly.

'It's perfect.' Mariah ran her fingers over its smooth polished surface and as she did it rocked noticeably. 'Apart from this corner,' she added. 'You were saying about the leg?'

'One of the legs is a bit loose. At the back. It has always been a bit wobbly there. Piece of soft wood gone rotten in the joint, I reckon. I . . .'

'Yes?'

'I was thinking of asking our Daniel to fix it. Will you mind?'

'Of course not. Why should I?'

'I mean, ask our Daniel to come round here. But not if you don't want to see him.'

How would she overcome her embarrassment? How could

193

she face a man who had seen her naked body? Who had touched her most intimate parts when he had wrapped her and carried her home? A man who knew she had been defiled by not one but two men? How could she face him knowing that, like her, he would be remembering that night?

Dora continued, 'If you really don't want him here, I'm sure I can wedge the joint somehow and stop the wobble.'

Mariah heaved a sigh. She would have to face him sooner or later. 'No, Dora, ask Daniel to come and mend it.'

'Not if he upsets you so much. When I go to market, I'll ask him to send Ned instead.'

'Daniel is your nephew, and he ought not to stay away on my account.' She straightened and inhaled sharply. 'I can keep out of his way for a day, I am sure.'

'You will eat your dinner with us, surely? It will seem strange if you do not.'

Mariah resigned herself to this. 'All right. I cannot hide for ever.'

Disgrace and shame weakened her resolve. It seeped into her heart, and she resented this enforced intrusion. She tried desperately to suppress her anger, but it would not leave her. Why did Daniel have to come here, reminding her again of that night and those despicable men?

She wished she could rid them from her mind, but she could not. She wished they were dead, but they were not. Sometimes she could smell their sweat and foul breath in her face, feel their hands holding down her arms and legs and worst of all, feel the scratching of their coarse hair on her vulnerable skin as they invaded her. God forgive her, but she wanted to kill them for what they had done to her. *She wanted to kill them.*

She took herself off to the copse and screamed as loudly as she could, long and hard until there was no breath left in her body and she fell into a crumpled heap on the damp leaves of the woodland floor and wept. She knew that Dora had followed her and was grateful she did not comment. She was thankful when Dora took her hand silently, led her back to a comfy chair by her kitchen fire and made her tea. Real Indian tea, with a splash of brandy.

Mariah pulled herself together, stood up and said she was well and occupied herself with mending. There was plenty of mending at Dora's. Dora was good with the sick and with women's ailments, but hopeless with a needle and some of her sewing efforts around the house raised a smile on Mariah's tear-stained face. She looked forward to making Dora a new warm coat for the winter.

Chapter 20

Ezekiel took off his hat and wiped his brow with the back of a grimy hand. 'That's a grand job done, lads. The fire's pulling a treat now. Thorpe, make sure you keep the heat up.'

'Aye, Mr Bowes. Steel'll be ready by next week, don't you worry.' Daniel surveyed the yard. His men were busy moving more coal in barrows, ready to be shovelled into the furnace.

Ezekiel sucked his teeth and gave his head a shake. 'Chimney'll be smoking on the Sabbath, though.'

'It won't be on its own in this town, sir.'

'No. I never kept the Sabbath meself. But many do. You'll have to keep an eye on it yerself.'

'I wanted to talk to you about that, Mr Bowes.'

'Oh aye? Let's get away from this heat, then.'

Daniel picked up Mr Bowes' jacket from the mounting stone near the office steps. 'I'd like some time off this Sunday, sir.'

'Going courting, eh?'

'No, sir. I've a few repair jobs to do at my aunty's cottage.'

'Can't be done, lad. I'll not be here. I'm invited out to dinner with Henry.'

'I've no need for you, sir. Young Ned over there is more than capable of watching the fire and keeping it hot. Look at him working, sir. Got a good head on his shoulders an' all.'

'Ned?'

'Aye, sir. He knows what to do. I'll see to everything before I go and be back before tea.'

Ezekiel thought for a minute. Thorpe was producing better steel than he ever had, and more of it. He was getting a good price, too. 'Are you sure you can trust him?' he asked.

'I wouldn't leave him with the furnace if I couldn't, sir.'

Ezekiel knew this was true. 'It's your responsibility. If owt goes wrong it'll be your fault.'

'I know. I'll be back even quicker with a horse,' Daniel ventured, and added, 'One of the cart horses.'

'Aye, I suppose you will. Don't you touch my hunter, though.'

'No, sir.' Daniel helped Mr Bowes into his jacket and watched him walk back to the house with a smile.

Aunty Dora wanted her table mending so Mariah could sew on it. He was to carry some cloth over at the same time. His heart lifted as he realised Mariah must be feeling better. Dora wouldn't have asked him over if she had thought it would upset her. He'd be able to see for himself how she was, and do something to help her. Something useful that would please her. It was only a small thing, but it was a start. He felt a pleasure coursing though his veins and looked forward to the Sabbath.

'He's here!'

The following Sunday, Dora was pulling grass from between the tansy and feverfew in her little front garden. She saw Daniel

197

leading one of Bowes' heavy draught horses up the lane. Laden with bundles and boxes and Daniel's carpentry tools, the gentle beast plodded slowly, as though enjoying his country outing. The weight of this burden was nothing compared with his usual haul of raw iron uphill from the canal to the ironworks furnace.

Mariah heard Dora call and jumped, startled into a sudden nervousness. She was in the kitchen, preparing vegetables for a Sunday dinner they would eat together when Daniel had finished mending the table. Quickly, she gathered up the corners of her jute apron and scraped the vegetable trimmings into this makeshift bag.

'Just taking these down to the pig,' she called and hurried out through the scullery to tip them over the sty wall. Mariah dawdled as long as she dared, until she heard Dora call her name from the door.

'All right.' She smoothed down her apron, straightened her back and forced herself to go into the kitchen.

Dora's face was a picture of pleasure. She was clearly so delighted to see Daniel that Mariah felt guilty about being there and the cause of their separation. She must try to behave normally, for Dora's sake. She would make conversation, be civil and polite, and not sink into one of the depressions that overcame her when she was reminded of that dreadful night.

It was easy to see why Daniel's family was so proud of him. Tall and straight with broad shoulders, strong arms and good features, he seemed to fill Dora's kitchen with his presence. He was not in his Sunday suit and looked ready for country work in a flannel shirt tucked into moleskin trousers under a riding jacket that had seen better days. His riding boots, too, were well worn and mud-splattered from leading the horse. He was smiling, easily, openly, naturally, at his aunty who he was so obviously pleased to see. Until he became aware of Mariah's presence.

Then he turned to her and his expression became more serious, his voice softer. 'Mariah. Dearest Mariah, how are you?'

'I – I am – I am quite well.' She swallowed, feeling a blush rise in her face. She resisted the urge to turn and run and added, 'Thank you. And you?'

'Very well, thanks.' He took a step forward. 'I am so happy you are up and about at last and that you are staying on here.' His arms moved towards her, just a fraction.

Mariah, instinctively, took a step backwards. She was relieved to see he let his hands drop to his sides and then put them behind his back. He was looking at her so intently she felt herself go hot all over. What was he searching for? Some outward sign that she was a defiled and disgraced woman? Was not her shame and degradation clear enough for all to see? Well, she would not stay to be stared at like the freak show from the travelling circus. She took off her jute apron, picked up her workbox and a pair of stockings from the line under the mantelshelf and said to Dora, 'I have finished the vegetables. I am just going upstairs with this darning.'

'Mariah?' She heard the query in Daniel's voice as she hurried from the room.

Dora put her hand on his arm. 'Leave her. It's hard for her to see you. It brings back the memories. She – she is an angry young woman.' Dora frowned as she saw the anguish contort his face, and suggested, 'Will you take a tankard of ale?'

Daniel grimaced at Dora's words. He had believed that Mariah was much improved, but what he saw told him otherwise. Lord help him, what should he do? How could he ever repair the damage he had done her? How could he ever make it up to her?

He said, 'I'll unload the horse and feed him first. I have a box of things for Mariah, from Mam's house. Emma packed it for me. And the new cloth you bought the other day. I hope I have brought everything Mariah needs . . .' He faltered. He had no idea what Mariah really needed to help her through her trouble. Except, perhaps, for him to leave.

'I'll come and help you unload,' Dora interrupted briskly. 'Fanny said she would send some butcher's meat for dinner.'

'Oh yes. A good piece of beef brisket for boiling. And some fresh suet for dumplings.'

'Best get it on then, if we want it done for dinner today.'

'This parcel from the draper's is heavy. He delivered it to Emma like you asked him to. Where shall I put it?'

The cloth, Dora thought suddenly, that will cheer Mariah. 'I'll take it upstairs while you're working in the front room.'

'Let me. It's too heavy for you.'

'No! You stay down here!'

Daniel slumped against the wall and lowered his voice. 'Does she hate me so much that I cannot even carry her boxes upstairs?'

'It's – it's not that she *hates* you.'

'But she won't talk to me! She won't even look at me!'

'Hush, she'll hear you.'

He groaned anxiously. 'What can I do? Tell me what I can do?'

'I don't know. Truly, I don't. But do not show you pity her. That will make her humiliation worse.'

Upstairs, Mariah listened to the sounds as Daniel carried in his tools. She realised this was going to be much more of an ordeal than she had imagined. It was not until after Daniel had finished unloading, and his horse was munching oats contentedly from a nose can, that Mariah moved to her chair by the window to do her darning.

A creak on the stairs made her stop and hold her breath. It was Dora.

'Daniel has brought over the cloth from the draper's. Will you come and unwrap it now?'

'When the table is mended. After dinner, perhaps.'

Dora sat on the edge of the bed and watched Mariah's nimble fingers as she mended her stockings. 'You will come down for your dinner, won't you?'

Mariah nodded. 'I said I would.'

'He means well, Mariah.'

'Does he? Then he should stay away from me. I do not wish to face him, knowing what he knows and − and what he saw.'

'He wants to help you.'

'There is nothing he can do! There is nothing anyone can do.'

Dora sighed. Mariah was right. But that did not help Daniel, and Dora was obliged to watch her beloved Daniel suffer as he tried to make amends for his part in Mariah's tragedy. Dinner time was a travesty of the friendly meals they had shared at her sister's house. They talked of the weather and the garden and the pig. Daniel was polite and Mariah was civil. They ate the last of the eating pears for pudding, with a wedge of crumbly cheese from the Dales, and then got up to clear away.

Mariah washed the pots in the scullery. Daniel went outside to chop wood in the back yard. Dora made some tea and began to wilt from the effort of keeping a smile on her face.

When Mariah came into the kitchen from the scullery with a stack of clean crockery, Dora commented, 'Daniel has finished my table.'

Mariah continued to arrange the china silently.

'Would you like to see it?'

Mariah nodded. 'Yes.'

'Why don't you ask Daniel to show you what he has done? He did it for you.'

Dora's comment made Mariah feel churlish at her truculence and she could not think of a reason why she should refuse the request. 'All right,' she said.

Although there was a chill in the air, he had taken off his shirt and under-shirt so she could see he was sweating freely as he swung the axe to split logs for the fire. She watched his muscles knot and flex as he worked and she became entranced for a second by his suppleness and strength. She remembered the admiration she had felt for him in his mother's kitchen, and how it had attracted her. What did she feel for him now? she wondered. Nothing? Only a numbness borne out of suffering? Was a void of affection within her to be the legacy of her ordeal?

Daniel concentrated on his task, trying to empty his mind of his grief and frustration. He did not notice Mariah watching him.

She hesitated, unsure of how to proceed, and hovered in the shadow of the house until he flung the axe with a final resounding thud to lodge in a tree stump. He walked over to the water butt and cupped his hands, drinking freely and then sluicing the cold water on his head and shoulders, smoothing it over his chest, arms and face.

Mariah frowned. Seeing him like this, he seemed unknown to her, a different man. She had not thought of him as a – a man like this, before. The earlier appeal she had felt for him had been for his achievements. And he was Dora's nephew, Emma's brother, Ezekiel's supervisor. Yes, that's who he was, Ezekiel's supervisor, not this strong, attractive man who was unsettling her fragile healing. She turned quickly and went back into the scullery.

'Mariah, is that you?' Dora called from the kitchen.

'Yes. I – I – er – I – Daniel needs a drying cloth.' She picked up a folded square of linen from by the sink and went outside again.

He was walking towards her. 'Just the thing,' he said, taking the towel and wiping it over his face and neck and shoulders and chest.

'Dora says you have finished her table,' she said. She felt strangely unsure of herself, stupid and shaky, and she wondered if he'd noticed.

He slowed his drying. She was too pale, he thought. Yet her pallor enhanced her beauty giving her delicate features a waiflike appearance. He wanted to stay around and help her recover. He wanted that so much it hurt and he frowned as he remembered his aunty's wise counsel to keep away.

She was looking in his direction and he tried to fathom her expression. But her eyes had a wariness in them and she did not meet his gaze. There was a brittleness about her that ate away at his heart. He understood why she was guarded in the company of men. But for her not to trust him? When his prime concern was for her well being? He replied gently, 'Yes, I have. I'll show you, shall I?'

'Please.'

'Let me get my shirt first.'

He turned away and so did she.

The three of them gathered in Dora's front room. As Daniel bent over the table, Mariah caught sight of damp patches from water or sweat darkening the shirt on his back. The seam of his sleeve strained as he stretched.

He pushed down hard on the surface of the table with his hands and said, 'There you are, ladies. As good as new. That joint will hold an ox.' He retrieved the heavy, calico-wrapped draper's parcel from the floor at the back of the room and placed it on the table.

'For you, Mariah.' He watched her and was rewarded by a light in her eyes that he had not seen since before the attack.

'My cloth! At last. Oh, thank you!'

Daniel stepped back as she untied the wrappings. He was so overjoyed to see her smile again that he hardly knew how to respond, and the sheer pleasure on his face brought a tear to Dora's eye.

'We'll have that drink of tea now,' she suggested.

'Good idea. And then I must get back and check on the furnace.'

'Shall I see you again soon, Daniel?'

'I don't know. My time is taken up by the ironworks and, well, Father does not like me to come over here too often.'

Dora smiled, a rueful curve of her mouth that made her look more sad than happy.

After tea, Mariah stood with her hands clasped in front of her and said goodbye to Daniel as he led away his horse down the lane. She was relieved his visit was over. His presence had disturbed her more than she cared to own. It had been an ordeal for her in a way she had not expected. His careful concern for her had stirred at the black hole within her and by doing so had caused her further anxiety. She had only begun to relax at the very end of his visit when she knew he would soon be leaving.

She gave herself a mental shake and turned to Dora. 'Will his father ever come round?' she asked.

Dora shook her head and thought, He'll not forgive himself, so how can he forgive me? She said, 'Our Fanny got over it years ago, but not Arthur. I hope our Daniel is not going to turn out to be as stubborn as his father.'

'I always thought there was a rift like that between my mother and Ezekiel. He never liked my mother. He despised her, and me even more. But she had actually lain with another man and I suppose I was a constant reminder of that.'

'Men are different creatures from women, that's for sure. Oh, enough of this self-pitying! It's the harvest supper in a few weeks and the Fitzkeppels are holding their usual barn dance. It's always a good do, that is. What will you wear?'

'Oh, I'll stay at home if you don't mind, Dora.'

'No! You need to get out and enjoy yourself. It'll cheer you up no end.'

Mariah shook her head. 'People may have heard rumours about me. They'll shun me and gossip about me in corners. I couldn't stand that.'

'Nonsense! They don't even know you.'

'I don't want to go out. Not yet.'

Dora didn't argue with her and waited a couple of days before raising the matter again. They had finished their household chores for the day and eaten a good dinner. Dora had given her kitchen table a scrub and was drinking tea by the fire.

'Will you help me get my gown ready for the barn dance?' she asked. 'It might need a stitch here and there.'

'Yes, of course. Bring it down. The table is nearly dry.'

Together, they examined the checked cotton gown and repaired weakened seams and loose bows.

'Are you going to let me go on my own, lass?' Dora ventured.

Mariah grimaced silently.

'People in the village know I have someone staying with me, and the master has met you already. What shall I say to them if you're not there?'

Mariah gazed out of the kitchen window. 'The light's going. We'd better finish this for now.'

'Well?'

'Tell them I'm ill.'

'I can't do that. They'd expect me to stay at home with you. They're good folk, Mariah. I won't lie to them. Master Fitzkeppel will be there in all his finery; at least, he will call in for a short time.'

Mariah brightened. 'Oh, he takes an interest in his village events, then?'

'Aye, he's not too bad as a landlord. But farming is not what it was now with all the pits and ironworks taking the labour. He leaves it all to his estate managers and legal people. Mind you, we still have the harvest festival in the village church, and he gives the best harvest supper around here at the barn dance. Everybody joins in. It's tradition.'

'Oh, all right! I'll go, then.'

Dora smiled. 'Champion. What will you wear?'

'This, of course.' Mariah looked down at her dark grey gown.

'I think you should wear something really pretty. You want to look your best for when I present you to the village.'

'I shan't be dancing, Dora. I am still in mourning. I shall stay by the wall and watch the others.'

'If you say so, dear.'

Dora cheered up. She wondered how Mariah would be in the company of other gentlemen. The barn dance would tell. A bit of dancing, a good supper and a cup of punch might be just what Mariah needed to get her back to rights again. She had been much better since she had started sewing and Dora had plenty of time to make sure she looked her best on the night. Her cheeks had a bit of colour in them now. Dora wondered if she had been wrong about her condition. If she was, it was a good job she had kept it to herself.

Chapter 21

But Dora's worst fears were realised when she heard Mariah being sick in the garden the next morning.

Mariah straightened up and looked directly into her eyes. 'Is this what I think it is?' she asked nervously.

'I'm afraid so, my dear. I guessed as much a few weeks ago. When did you last bleed?'

'I have not had any since – since the attack. Well, not my monthly bleeding, anyway.' Mariah sighed heavily and held her head in her hands. 'It cannot be so! I was a maid and it does not happen to maids, does it?'

Dora did not answer directly. She asked, 'Did you get a regular show before the attack?'

'Yes.'

'And definitely none since?'

'No.' Tears welled in Mariah's eyes. She began to feel afraid. 'I am not wed. I cannot be with child.'

'Yes, you can.' Dora nodded ruefully.

Mariah's felt her knees go weak. Her eyes grew wide and round as she contemplated Dora's answer. 'But what shall I do? Where shall I go?'

'Come back inside and sit down. I have suspected this for a while now.'

'Why didn't you say?'

'You were bruised and torn by the attack and I thought, well, there was a chance you might lose it early on.' Dora looked pained.

'Dear God, Dora, this is too much to bear. Have I not suffered enough? Do I have to carry a child as well?'

'Try not to distress yourself.'

But Mariah wasn't listening. She felt fear creep around her heart like the cold hand of winter. A child? A child resulting from that vile act? A child who would not even know which of those men was its father? This was indeed a cruel, cruel hand for the Lord to deal her.

She looked up at Dora and pleaded, 'How can I have a child conceived out of hatred and violence? How can I care for such a child? It does not feel like mine! It feels like – like the devil himself growing inside me! God is as cruel and evil as those beasts that did this to me!'

'Hush, Mariah. Do not blaspheme so. You must stay calm. Come inside and I'll make you an infusion to help with the sickness. You must get used to how you feel and think what you will do.'

'Do? Do? What can I do? I am ruined! I am an orphaned spinster with no means of support. A defiled woman whom no decent man would want for his wife. And now, with a bastard child growing inside me. Oh, Dora, I'm frightened!'

'There's no need to be. I shall look after you.'

'But I cannot stay here and bring more shame on you!'

'We are isolated here. No one need know.'

'Until the child is born! And then how shall I live? I cannot be a burden on you for the rest of my life!' Mariah felt desperate. What kind of life would it be anyway? One of more humiliation and disgrace? She had had enough of that already! She breathed quietly, 'I do not want a life with a child borne out of sin.'

'What do you mean?'

'My life is worth nothing now. I might as well end it.'

Dora took her by the shoulders and shook her. 'Stop talking like this, Mariah. Other women have suffered this fate and survived. We shall find a way for you.'

'How? I cannot stay here! I shall end up in the poorhouse and be condemned to a life in the laundry to pay for my keep!'

'Do calm yourself. It is not good for you to become so agitated. Your child will suffer.'

'What do I care for this child? I would as soon it was taken from me and brought up as a pauper. It is no child of mine. It is the devil's child.'

'Do not say such things. It is your child. When it is born you will surely love it?' Dora ventured gently.

'How can I? It is not possible! I shall not listen to you! What do you know of bearing an infant? You know only of others in this matter. You have had none of your own!'

'Yes, I have,' Dora replied quietly. 'I had a child.'

Mariah stopped and turned to her, wide eyed. 'You had a child?'

Dora nodded.

'You were married?'

Dora shook her head. 'I had Arthur's child.'

Mariah's eyes rounded and for a moment she forgot her own troubles.

'Oh Lord! I should not have told you. It happened before he and Fanny were betrothed. At Mr Shaw's house one evening. I loved him! At least, I thought I loved him then.'

'Did Fanny know?'

'Not at first. We did not see much of each other in the first months after they were wed. Arthur was working long hours at the pit and Fanny was busy with her new cottage. But she fell for a baby straightaway, I could tell as soon as I saw her. She was quite poorly with her first, so she came over here to rest in her final months and stayed for a while. Mine was well on the way by then and Fanny was quite overcome with shock.'

'What happened to your child, Dora?'

'My child? My – my—' She choked on the words, took a deep breath and steadied her voice. 'He was born too early, poor little mite, and I – I – I lost him. He's in the church-yard with my parents.'

'I am so, so sorry.'

'It was all a long time ago.' Dora sighed. 'But, you see, I do have some knowledge of your situation. You will love your child, Mariah. As soon as you hold it in your arms.'

'No! Never! My situation is different. This seed inside me is the devil's work! I could never care for a child borne out of such evil! Your child was conceived in love, at least on your part, but mine is not. It is made from revenge and hatred and every time I look at myself in the glass I am reminded of those unspeakable men and the unspeakable things they did to me. My growing belly will only serve to make it a hundredfold worse.'

Mariah began to sob, her tears spilling uncontrollably. 'I was getting better,' she wailed, 'and now this – this *thing* growing inside me. I cannot do this, Dora! Not a lifetime of reliving that night every time I looked at my child!

Saliva crept into her mouth and her stomach knotted. She

210

retched and dashed again for the garden, holding her stomach and weeping. She was on her knees among the grass and dock leaves, sobbing and shuddering, when Dora caught up with her.

'It is punishment enough for me to face the world as a defiled woman. But to be branded for ever as a whore! It will kill me,' she whispered. 'As sure as any cancer will. And if it does not, I shall surely kill myself. I cannot live with this.'

'You must not speak this way. It is a shock, I grant you. You need a little time, that's all.'

'Time for what?'

'To get used to the idea of a child. Your child.'

Mariah choked on her words. She covered her face with her hands. 'Their child, those evils thugs. Not mine.'

Dora's frown deepened. 'You are overwrought. Come inside. I'll make you something to calm you down.'

But her ministrations did not reassure Mariah and Dora was forced to watch her sink back into the depression she had fought so hard to overcome. She worried about leaving Mariah alone in this state, remembering girls before her who had harmed themselves. There was a limit to the number of knocks any woman could take and Dora believed this was one too many for Mariah.

She thought about it for three days, three whole days of anxiety and despair until, finally, she said, 'I can take it away, if that's what you want.'

Mariah had not slept properly. She had tossed and turned, dreading the future and wondering how she could end it all. She was exhausted, at the end of her tether and snapped, 'It will be taken from me anyway. The poorhouse will see to that.'

'I mean . . .' Dora inhaled deeply. 'Before it is born. I can take it away.'

'What!' Mariah was aghast. Surely she had misheard?

211

'I'm a midwife. I know how to do it.'

'But – but – you *can't* do that! You'll be damned in hell.'

Dora shrugged. 'I think God might understand.'

'But, Dora, you can go to prison!'

'Who will find out?'

'I – I . . .' Mariah did not reply. She was too stunned by the idea.

'I've often thought that if the men who made the laws had the babies, the laws would be different.'

Mariah pondered on this wearily. 'It's still a wicked thing to do.'

'I don't see it that way. The men who did this to you are the sinful ones. They get away with it and you have to suffer. You don't want to suffer for ever.'

'No,' she agreed. Dora could give me my life back, she thought. Instead of poverty and hatred in the poorhouse, I could have a life worth living. 'Would you really do it for me?'

Dora nodded. 'If that is what you want. Yes.'

Mariah tossed and turned for another long, sleepless night. There was no other way, she fretted. No other way.

'Have you finished that drink?'

'Yes. It was very bitter. What was it?' Mariah was sitting by the kitchen table dressed only in a muslin chemise that came down to her thighs. Her feet were cold on the stone flags, but her face felt the glow of the fire, banked high to heat water.

'A tincture of herbs.'

'What for?'

'To help you relax. You must keep very still.'

'I'm frightened.'

'I know.'

'What are you going to do?'

212

'I've already said. You'll be all right. I've done this before. Stand up now for me.'

'Will it hurt?'

Dora hesitated. 'Yes, it will. Afterwards. But not for long. And you'll have a nice hot bath by the kitchen fire.' She watched her, patiently, with a wise and practised eye. 'How do you feel now?'

'Kind of – kind of – floating.'

Dora smoothed the boiled calico covering her scrubbed kitchen table. 'Climb up on the table, now. That's right. Lie back and close your eyes.'

'Whass happening to me, Dora?'

'It's the poppy juice. It makes you dream. Close your eyes and dream, Mariah. Dream of nice things. Dream of trimming your gown for the harvest supper. I am just putting these pillows under your back.'

'Wha' for?'

'Bring your knees up. Both of them. Right up. Good girl. Now drop them to the side. Nice and wide. Try and relax, now, good girl.' Dora picked up her silver probe from the spirit and ran it back and forth through a candle flame.

'Whass that?'

'Close your eyes, I said. Go to sleep and dream. How is that gown coming on?'

A quiet strangled groan rumbled in Mariah's throat as Dora's gentle, cool fingers pushed aside her flesh. And then the probing, like the probing of her attackers, invading her, hurting her. This was different though, a deeper hurt, a dull uncomfortable hurt. Mariah's thoughts floated in the space above her head. It was not natural what those men had done to her. But neither was this . . . This was not natural . . . Her mind drifted as Dora probed.

213

She felt drunk and her eyelids were heavy. There was an uncomfortable feeling in the pit of her stomach. Through her sandy eyelashes she saw Dora standing by her head, watching her. 'Iss that it?' she slurred.

'No, my dear. It is not over yet. We must wait now.'

She did not know how long she waited, drifting in and out of sleep. Her discomfort escalated as she lay there, emerging from her dreamy stupor. But Mariah knew this was no dream and the ache spread into a sharp stabbing pain that made her cry out in agony, turn on her side and curl into a ball. Someone was carving away her insides, stripping them out, killing her! Someone was killing her!

She yelled and reached out, clutching at Dora's clothes with iron fingers that would not let go. 'Help! What have you done to me? I'm dying!'

'No, you are not dying.' Dora eased her arm underneath Mariah's shoulders. 'Try and sit up. Look, I have a nice hot bath for you by the fire. Let me help you down from the table.'

'Aarghh!' Every movement Mariah made seemed to make the pain much worse. Leaning on Dora she lifted one foot over the rim of Dora's tin bath. 'It's too hot! I can't!'

'You must. Slowly now.'

Mariah stood in the water, bending over double to support her aching innards. She rested her hands on the metal rim, watching her feet blush with the heat. Cautiously she lowered herself into the tub. The prickling of her skin as she sat in the hot water took her mind from the pain in her belly. The edge of her chemise floated to the surface and then sank as it soaked. There was a strong smell of wintergreen and the salve her mother had used on broken knees when she was a child.

Oh Lord! She wished her mother was here with her now.

214

Why did she have to die and leave her? If her mother had lived she would never have gone to the Thorpes' and been mistaken for one of them. She would never have suffered that degrading invasion of her body. She would never have lain with the devil! Where are you, Mother?

Her pain eased and the water cooled to a comfortable warmth. For a while she felt normal, soothed by the warm water, the banked-up fire radiated heat onto her face and muslin-clothed breasts. Dora busied herself refilling kettles for the bath and mixing another tincture which she offered to Mariah as she soaked.

Mariah shook her head. She knew it was laudanum and she had seen its effects on the street women who frequented the taverns in the market square.

'Drink it, Mariah.' Dora sounded stern. 'This is just the beginning. The pain will come back.'

'I don't want that stuff.' Mariah had made shirts as she sat with her dying mother and sold them to buy her laudanum for those last painful months of her illness. It had hastened her end she was sure. But for her mother that end had been a welcome release from her pain. 'Take it away,' she added.

Dora returned with a bottle of spirits. 'You do not have to suffer. I'll leave this here on the floor, it may help you.'

'I don't want that either. Save it for cleaning your ribbons.'

'At least take this.' Dora handed her a short rope of knotted linen. 'If the pain becomes too much for you, bite on the linen.'

'Thank you. You won't leave me, will you?'

'No, of course not. If you change your mind about the laudanum . . .'

'I shan't.'

When the pain returned it was worse than before, worse

215

than anything she had experienced in her short life, worse than the attack that had caused her to be like this. She screamed once, gritted her teeth and finally reached for the knotted linen.

She was sweating with heat and felt wearied by the pain. Her head flopped down to her breast and it was then she saw the red stain seeping through the water, spreading slowly and insidiously, at first making patterns between her legs and over her thighs, and then as she twisted in agony and the water became more bloodied she realised what she had done and screamed again.

'It is for the best,' Dora soothed. 'It will soon be over now.'

No, this will never be over, Mariah thought. This was not her life's blood that was ebbing away, it was her child's. A child that was part of her, her own flesh. Yes, a child conceived in brutality and rape but the child had done no wrong and yet it was the child's blood that darkened the water, spreading, swirling and soaking into her chemise.

She began to weep, silently at first and then with shuddering sobs she tried to repress but could not. Gradually her grief took over until she was crying vociferously and then hysterically, uncontrollably, her shoulders heaving with hiccups and coughs, her tears running down her face and falling into the water, mixing with the blood of her dead baby.

Her fingers tangled with her hair as she held her head in anguish. The pain was relentless. A tearing, searing pain that she deserved. She threw the knotted linen aside in contempt of herself. She had to suffer. She must suffer for her wickedness. This was an evil compounding evil. Her baby was innocent and her baby had died. She had murdered her own child and she screamed again. 'Murder! Murder! I am a murderess!'

Dora watched her silently. She had seen as many reactions

to this as she had the women that she helped. Some were simply grateful, glad to endure the pain and get back to normal. Some were mortified and secretive and took spirits or laudanum readily. Others, like Mariah, took it badly and these women worried Dora the most.

The worst would soon be over; the pain would ease and Mariah would stand and allow Dora to rinse off the blood with a ewer of clean, lavender-scented water, then dry her, wrap her and put her to bed.

Brutal rape was always the worst, women suffered in their heads as well as in their bodies. Now Mariah was grieving for the loss of her child on top of the loss of her mother. She was a strong lass, strong in mind as well as resilient in body. But, Dora wondered, was she strong enough to withstand all this?

Only time would tell. A good lass like Mariah deserved a better chance in life than the one she had been dealt. When this was over, the harvest supper would be a new start for her. New company and good food to build her strength. Her time of mourning would be over. It had to be. If Mariah was to come through this ordeal she had to have distraction. People and music and perhaps dancing to cheer her.

Dora fervently hoped she would pull through.

Chapter 22

Mariah cried every day for a fortnight. She went about her household chores silently and took solace only in her needle-work. Dora tended to her as best she could, but even she did not have lotions or potions to help this time.

Mariah worked away, fashioning Dora's Sunday coat on her mother's old mannequin. Dora helped with the seams, under Mariah's watchful eye. It was a beautiful coat and Dora thought she hardly deserved such luxury, but she looked forward to wearing it in the cold weather to come.

'Have you decided what to make with the remnants?' Dora asked as they sewed.

'Hand muffs for the winter. We have a flour sack full of wool-gatherings from the hedgerows for warm linings. The farmers at the beast market will buy them for their wives and daughters.'

'Will you take them into town and sell them yourself?'

'When I am ready.' Mariah heaved a sigh. 'At present I do

not think I shall ever want to go back there.' She put aside her sewing for a moment. 'Oh, Dora, what shall I do? I am ruined, totally ruined. How shall I look anyone in the face again?'

'You are not the only woman to have suffered what you have gone through,' Dora replied quietly.

'No,' Mariah responded bitingly. 'I suppose it happens to street women all the time. Is that what I have become? A woman fit only for work on the streets?'

'Do not compare yourself with them! It is unworthy of you.'

'*I feel unworthy.*'

'But you are not!'

'I let you take away my unborn child.'

'It was the right thing for you.'

'Fanny once said to me that she would have had more children if it hadn't been for you.'

The querying tone in Mariah's voice made Dora look up sharply. 'You don't think I do that for anyone who asks, do you?'

'I don't know. Do you?'

'No, I do not! Only for women like you, who had no say in the act. Never for a woman who is wed. When you get wed it is your duty to bear children, everybody knows that.'

'What? To have a child every year until you're too old and worn to care for them?'

'As a wife you have to give your husband his rights. And some of them are like our Fanny's Arthur. They never tire of wanting their wives in the bedchamber.' Dora looked at Mariah. 'Your family was different from mine and Fanny's. I suppose your mother did not speak of such things. Mrs Shaw told me.'

'What do you mean *such things*? I could tell *you* about men wanting – no – *taking* what they see as their dues!'

219

'Mariah, calm yourself. Those men had no rights as far as you were concerned. But it is possible to lie with a man and not make a child.'

'That is God's will. Sometimes you do and sometimes you don't. My mother told me the only way not to get with child was not to lie with a man.'

'Yes, well, try telling that to the menfolk around here. Besides, Mrs Shaw taught me it's not good for men if they do not lie with their wives when they have the urge. That's what wives are for. And rich men's wives know what to do to stop the babies coming.'

'I know. Separate bedchambers. Mother told me.'

'And more. I'll show you.' Dora put down her sewing and went to a polished oak chest in a corner of the room. She retrieved a key from a hidden pocket in her skirt and unlocked the top drawer. Carefully, she lifted out a plain wooden box. Dora placed it on the table and opened the lid.

'Before I show you what's in here, you must promise me you will not talk of this to anyone. There are folk around here who don't approve of these things and if the vicar's wife ever found out I had them, I can't think what she'd say. But I know for a fact that her ladyship at the Hall used them.'

Dora held up a piece of sea sponge, a very small piece of the kind Mariah used when bathing. It had a piece of narrow ribbon firmly attached at one end. 'I gave Fanny one of these to use.'

Mariah frowned. She had seen nothing like it before.

'Some folk make them out of folded muslin,' Dora explained. 'But the sea sponge is better. You soak it in vinegar and push it right up inside you before he comes to you in your bed. It has to be afore he is anywhere near you and you have to use strong vinegar. Mrs Shaw told me it stops the seed before it can make the child.'

220

Mariah's eyes rounded. 'I had no idea that there were such things. That means a woman could lie with her husband every night and – oh! Oh yes, I can see why the Church would not approve.'

'Some folk say it's all right and some folk don't. Mostly those who don't hold with these say they lead to wicked ways.' Dora glanced furtively at Mariah. 'Y'know, outside of wedlock. But I reckon folk around here have their wicked ways with each other any road.'

'Is that what I am, Dora? A wicked woman?' Mariah asked quietly.

'No, just the opposite. You are a good woman. You were an innocent, you *are* an innocent, and nobody can tell me otherwise.'

Dora noticed a frown gather on Mariah's forehead. Hastily, she closed the box and locked it away again.

'Are you still set on wearing that gown for the harvest supper?'

'I'm really not sure about going. After—'

'No one will know. Or even guess, if you act normally.'

Mariah fingered the cloth of her skirt. It had been her best gown, but she had worn it every day at Dora's house and the wear was beginning to show at the elbows and edge of the skirt. She would have to put a darn in it and re-stitch some of the seams. 'If I do go, I ought to wear black,' she commented.

Dora disagreed but did not say so. 'Have you got anything in black?'

Mariah shook her head.

Dora went on, 'Didn't I see a green one in your box? Dark green?'

'That one? That's was my mother's Sunday best when she was alive.'

'It's a nice, softly draped one and not too heavy. A bit formal for a barn dance but very cleverly cut, I thought, when I wrapped it to hang in the cupboard.'

'Oh, my mother looked really lovely in that gown. I used to try it on when I fancied myself grown up. I felt a proper lady in it.'

'It would suit you very well for your first outing.'

'It's beautiful cloth. Sewn from the end of a bolt used to make a ladies' afternoon dress.' Mariah thought about the gown. 'It needs another petticoat. And the bodice is a bit tight.'

'Why don't you cut in a new front like you did for Emma? Put in one of those low necklines? You can add a piece of muslin or lace for modesty and a trimming round the cuffs. It would be perfect for the harvest supper.'

'Yes, I might do that. I have some old lace that would suit. It's yellowed a little with age, but it would go well with the green.'

Dora nodded in agreement. 'And just right for a matching lace cap. You could dress your hair higher on your head to show off your features.'

Mariah shook her head. 'I don't want to go,' she repeated.

She thought about her mother's Sunday gown as she put the finishing touches to Dora's coat and wrapped it in calico to keep for her to wear at the harvest festival service in church. She looked forward to re-fashioning the dress even if she didn't go to the barn dance.

But she could not help thinking that Dora was right. She could not hide for ever. Dora often reminded her that her secrets were safe and she ought to face other people soon. Perhaps a festive supper and dance would give her a start? She took out her mother's gown from her cupboard, unwrapped it and laid it on the bed. Then she stood back from it for a long time with her head on one side before she picked up her scissors.

A neighbouring farmer collected them in his cart, which had straw bales and boxes for them to sit on. Dora looked cheerful wearing her brown plaid gown with a matching bow in her greying hair. Mariah, with Dora's encouragement, had made a special effort with her own hair, pinning it securely in coils at the back of her head and dressing it with a ribbon of lace to match the lace at her breast and elbows.

The barn was huge. Swept clean of farmyard debris, and lit by lanterns hanging from the wooden roof trusses, it was filled with people, noise and movement. In one corner, two fiddles and a flute were tuning their instruments and the ale-house keeper from Keppel village was preparing to call for the dancing. Servants from the Hall had set out chairs for the older people and furnished a long table they were covering with all kinds of delicious things to eat and drink.

Dora took a reluctant Mariah around to meet the people she knew from Keppel village, the butcher and his wife, the ale-house keeper and the farrier's family. They welcomed her among them. But when the dancing commenced Mariah lingered at the back, in the shadow of the barn walls, until she was dragged protesting, into one of the reels by the farrier's son whose boundless energy ensured he never missed a single dance.

After a second dance she began to enjoy herself. Who would not among such good people? Those solid, ruddy-faced country men, waistcoats unbuttoned and shirt necks wide open, flinging themselves about with wives and maids alike, restored a little of her faith in mankind.

The shouting and laughter continued after the music ceased

as men, women and children celebrated the end of long days working in the fields. Two barrels of ale had been set up and tapped to slake their thirsts. One of the cooks from the Hall carved at a roasted aitch bone of beef and several game pies, which were quickly devoured with pickled vegetables and marrow relish.

Mariah and Dora were talking with the farrier and his wife when the barn fell silent and everyone looked round. Mariah recognised Mr Fitzkeppel, but not his lady companion who was dressed in a very grand gown. He was flamboyantly dressed, too, in a long-coated suit of dark blue wool with gold braid trims that gave him the appearance of a naval man. His lady matched this opulence with a gown of rich maroon silk, its burgeoning skirts so full the villagers were forced to step back as she walked by them.

'How does she get her skirt to stay like that?' Dora whispered.

'Crin petticoats. They're filled with horse hair.'

'Not for dancing in, then?'

'Who is she?'

'His sister. Can't you detect a likeness?'

Mariah craned her neck, but her line of vision was blocked by others who had crowded forward to get a better view of their landlord and paymaster.

'Your lace looks better than hers,' Dora whispered.

'Can you see her? I can't.'

'Come over here.'

Mariah shuffled next to Dora as Mr Fitzkeppel and his sister walked around the barn, greeting and talking to the village folk. She ducked down to peer through a gap between two men. Yes, Mariah agreed, the lace was wrong for the gown. It was too heavy for silk and much of it was wrongly placed, detracting from the beautiful sheen. Mariah would have added flounces and frills in the same silk rather than this thick cotton lace.

She stepped back to allow the enormous skirt to pass. Mariah's sharp eye noticed a crooked seam in the bodice and escaping threads where the lace was attached. The sleeves, too, did not fit as closely as they should have. Goodness, Mariah thought, Mother would have been shocked that a lady's maid had allowed her mistress to go out like that! So am I, Mariah decided. She wanted to take this lady to one side, hitch up the sleeves and adjust the lace to make the neckline fit better.

It was then that Mariah realised how much she was like her mother in this respect, and thinking in exactly the same way when confronted with poor workmanship. She realised, also, that this was the first time she had thought about her mother without wanting to cry.

'A new face, I believe, brother dearest?' The people in front of Mariah had moved aside and Miss Fitzkeppel had not walked on.

Mr Fitzkeppel smiled at Mariah, a warm acknowledgement of their prior acquaintance, and Mariah thought he had an enchanting, almost ethereal, face. His hands too were smooth skinned and white with long fingers, and nails that were clean and tended. There was lace at his wrists, too, more subtle than that on his sister's gown and perfect against the fine weave of the wool. He was not much more than her own age and Mariah warmed to his friendly countenance.

'Christobel, my dear,' he said. 'May I present Miss Bowes. She is residing with Mrs Barton.'

Until that moment, Mariah's attention had been taken up by the details of Miss Fitzkeppel's opulent gown. She lowered gracefully into a curtsey with her head bowed. But when she looked up she was startled by Miss Fitzkeppel's arresting blue eyes, piercing Mariah's façade of gentility and seeming to reach into the dark recesses of her recent traumas. Mr Fitzkeppel's sister was, as local folk said, quite lovely. Her smooth milky complexion was lightly tinted on her cheeks with a mellow country glow rather than French rouge. Her thick fair hair was coiled high on the back of her head and dressed with peacock feathers and strings of jewels that matched a necklace at her throat.

Miss Fitzkeppel's keen eyes swept over Mariah and lingered on what she saw. She turned to Dora. 'Mrs Barton, would you call on me tomorrow afternoon?'

Surprised, Dora murmured, 'Of course, ma'am,' and dropped a small curtsey.

The Fitzkeppels moved on.

'What was all that about?' Mariah whispered.

'I have no idea. I'll find out tomorrow.'

'Do you think she's – you know – ill?'

'Heavens, no! She has a proper doctor from town to attend her. It may be for one of her servants.'

'She's not asking you about – er – what you did for me?'

'Lord, no! She doesn't know about that!'

'I thought for a second she knew about me – about what happened.'

Dora looked askance. 'Why should she?'

'That look of hers. It seemed to go right inside me.'

'It's those large eyes. They really are a brilliant blue. Everyone notices them. And they notice everything, mark my words. Miss Christobel is as clever as she is pretty.'

'Where is her husband tonight?'

'She doesn't have one. Don't look so surprised. I expect she is quite happy to remain as mistress of Fitzkeppel Hall for her brother. She is much more interested in the estate farms and livestock than he is. Mind you, *he* ought to be thinking about marriage and heirs even if she isn't.'

The interval was soon over. Brother and sister left, and the villagers quickly returned to the more serious business of enjoying themselves. Mariah, too, cheered immensely. She did not dance again, but talked with several village people, drank ale and ate well. That night, she slept soundly for the first time in weeks and woke the following day feeling refreshed.

She urged Dora to wear her new coat to visit Miss Fitzkeppel.

'I was saving it for the harvest festival in church next week.'

'You need to look your best for the Hall.'

'But I might catch it on twigs as I walk through the wood.'

'Then you will have to take great care not to,' Mariah insisted, as she helped Dora fasten the buttons down the front.

'It's beautiful,' Dora breathed. 'And it fits so well. How do I look?'

'Very handsome. Fit to be a lady's lady.'

'You are so clever, Mariah.'

'It helps to have the best woollen cloth.'

'But all those fastenings – they took you ages! And the matching braiding on the collar is beautiful. It has the look of, well, of a militia man's coat to me. Where did you find the braid?'

'I made it from the cloth,' Mariah commented absently as she stepped back with a critical eye. 'Yes, it fits you perfectly. Off you go. I'll make some nice broth for when you get back.'

But Dora did not return alone. Mariah was surprised to hear a carriage creaking and rattling down the bumpy track to the garden gate. Through the front-room window she saw a footman helping Dora and Miss Fitzkeppel onto the grassy

227

path to their front door. Quickly, Mariah removed her apron and smoothed her hair. Their visitor pushed her full skirts, protected by a large heavy cloak, through the front door of Dora's cottage and into the front room. It was tidy, but the table was clearly being used as Mariah's worktable and she stood in front of it to hide the mess. In the corner, Mariah's old mannequin carried the beginnings of another coat she was making for Emma.

Miss Fitzkeppel walked over to it and fingered the lovat green cloth. 'So it is true? You are more than a seamstress, Miss Bowes. Where did you learn all this?'

Mariah was proud of her heritage and answered, 'From my mother. She taught me everything.'

If this surprised Miss Fitzkeppel, she did not show it but went on, 'When I asked Mrs Barton who your dressmaker was, I did not believe her reply. She told me it was you who had fashioned the bodice of the gown you wore at the harvest supper – and also this coat that she wears today. I imagined them to have come from Leeds. Or London.'

'My mother's family were tailors from the North Riding, ma'am,' Mariah volunteered by way of explanation. She maintained a steady gaze, meeting Miss Fitzkeppel's searching expression calmly.

'And where is your mother now?'

'She is dead, ma'am.'

'I see. I am sorry.' She took a step forward and peered to one side. 'May I?'

Mariah moved aside to reveal her worktable. The visitor picked up an illustration, torn from a printed journal Mariah had used to guide her when making the coats. There were some light sketches in the margins and, on the table top, calico toiles that Mariah had made as models for herself, Dora and Emma.

228

Miss Fitzkeppel turned swiftly. 'I should like to discuss a commission with you, Miss Bowes. Will you come to the Hall on Tuesday? I shall send my carriage for you after luncheon.'

The excitement Mariah had felt during this visit threatened to bubble to the surface. Miss Fitzkeppel might be the most beautiful and powerful woman in this part of the Riding, but she was still a woman, and one who appreciated a well-made gown when she saw one. At that moment, Mariah felt herself to be Miss Fitzkeppel's equal and replied clearly, 'Of course, ma'am.'

'Very well. Good day to you.' She gave a brief nod in Dora's direction, adding, 'Good day, Mrs Barton,' and swept out as elegantly as she had entered.

Mariah stared at Dora with raised eyebrows. 'A commission? A commission! Dora did you hear that? A commission!'

'I did, indeed.' Dora's face softened as she saw the delight on Mariah's face.

'Just think! The lady at the Hall will wear something I have made! Mother would be so proud of me. Oh, Dora, I can do so much for her. Her shape is very womanly, like mine. I know how to fashion the cloth to improve her form, instead of detracting from it as her gown last night did.'

'Well, you have done it for me right enough. You should have seen the looks I got at the Hall!' Dora thought this could be Mariah's salvation. It could help her climb right out of the abyss of her despair. At last, Dora saw a glimmer of hope for Mariah's future.

Chapter 23

'A fine morning, Havers.'

'Oh! You startled me, Miss Christobel.'

Bel's eyes lingered on the patchwork fields which rolled away and disappeared into the valley in front of her. On the far side the hills rose again towards the high moor, obliterated by an early morning mist. She had walked through the kitchen wing of the Hall, and on past the stables to breathe in the fresh autumn air. 'We are indeed lucky to live in the South Riding, are we not?'

'If you say so, miss.'

'Do you not agree, Havers?'

'Depends which way the wind is blowing when the smoke rises from the furnaces in the valley.'

Bel laughed. 'Yes, indeed. You are quite right. But they are our future.'

'Aye, miss. Are you taking Chestnut out this morning?'

'I am. Is he ready?'

'Joe's bringing him round now.'

'Whoa, boy.' Joe held tight onto the bridle as Chestnut tossed his head and pranced across the stable yard, clattering his hooves on the cobbles. 'He's a bit frisky this morning, Miss Christobel. The farrier put new shoes on him yesterday and he likes the sound of 'em ringing on the stones.'

A cacophony of pheasants, spooked by the noise, rose from a nearby hedgerow and scattered over the fields. 'Your birds have bred well this year.'

'They have that. There'll be plenty for the larder this winter if I can keep away the poachers.'

'Do we lose many to the poachers?'

'Not if I can help it, miss. They take rabbit as a rule an' we've allus got plenty o' them.'

Joe held the bridle as Bel climbed the mounting stone and settled herself in the sidesaddle spreading her new riding skirt to cover her boots. She held herself well, head high and with a straight back, her fair hair hidden by a black snood and tall hat. She pulled at the cuffs of her gloves and took up the reins. Her new riding jacket fitted perfectly. It was the most comfortable she had ever worn. Miss Bowes certainly knew how to cut cloth to fit the female form. She must talk to Mrs Havers about further commissions for her.

Havers checked the buckles and smoothed the horse's neck. 'You'll soon ride that friskiness out of him this morning, miss.'

As Bel turned the horse's head towards a wooded hillside she had a sudden thought and called over her shoulder, 'Havers! Why don't we have a shoot sometime? Like Father used to have when I was a child? What do you say?'

She did not wait for his answer. The morning air beckoned and she urged Chestnut to a canter across the fields. At the top of the hill, Bel reined him in and he slowed, his nostrils

231

steaming in the crisp, fresh air. She pushed up her veil, inhaled deeply and marvelled at the early autumn colour of the woodland. In the valley, the chimneys were already smoking and she could hear the whine of winding gear at the pit head on Keppel Hill as a group of miners descended to their long day of toil at the coal face.

She wondered what it was like down there in the cold damp dark. Years ago she had asked her brother's trustees if she might see what a coal seam looked like and they had laughed at her, telling her that only men and boys went down the mines. She remembered that day when she had wished she was her brother. Not that she really wanted to be him, but she would have liked to be allowed to do some of the things he did, instead of spending her days with a governess learning to sing and play the pianoforte.

Her irritation with this state of affairs made her angry and the horse, sensing her tension, fretted under the reins. Why shouldn't she care about the estate and its mines and manufactories? She wanted to know about these things and no one would tell her! Why did people think this such an unsuitable, unladylike concern? It annoyed her that, as Nathan grew older, he became less interested in his estates and the industries that it supported. He spent his days reading poetry and painting and his only contribution to running the estate was to redesign the parkland to improve the view from drawing rooms – although she had to admit that the park was beautiful now. Even so, Bel looked forward to the day when she would leave the Hall as a bride.

She had hoped to find a suitor among her brother's university friends. But they shared Nathan's artistic tastes and none of them had really interested her. Besides, they showed no more than a passing politeness towards her and this vexed her.

232

She did not wish to be a spinster and spend her life playing second fiddle to whomsoever Nathan chose to be his wife and mistress of Fitzkeppel Hall.

'Come on, Chestnut,' Bel murmured to her mount, tugging at the reins. 'It is time I had a proper conversation with that brother of mine.'

She found Nathan in the north-facing conservatory where he had set up his easel and paints. He was dressed casually in an open-necked shirt and corduroy breeches, eating boiled eggs and bread at a small wickerwork table.

'Good morning, Nathan. Is Henry not taking breakfast with you?'

'No, he has ridden into town to meet his father. They have business at the bank.'

Excellent, thought Bel, we shall not be distracted by that boy. 'I wish to speak with you,' she began.

'What about, my dear?'

'About you, Nathan. About your plans for your future here at the Hall.'

Nathan put down the teaspoon he was using to tackle his second egg and looked at Bel with raised eyebrows. 'My plans? Why should I have any plans? Withers takes care of everything.'

'Then, are you and I to stay here together, like this, for the rest of our lives?'

'I don't see why not. Really, Bel, what on earth has got into you?'

'I am not getting any younger, brother dear. And the Hall is *your* home, not mine.'

'Bel, my dearest, darling sister, of course Fitzkeppel Hall is your home.'

'Only until you marry and bring your new wife as mistress to the Hall. Then I shall have to step aside.'

'When I marry? Why should I wish to marry?'

'Because that is what gentlemen in your position do! You have to marry. You need an heir for all this. If Father were still alive, I am sure he would insist upon it. Did your trustees not talk of this when you inherited?'

'They mentioned it once or twice, but they have not pressed me. Not yet, that is. I have only just turned one and twenty.'

'And I am three and twenty! Mama was married at nineteen. If she knew – or even cared – about me, she would be shocked.'

Nathan tipped back his head, looking down his nose at her, and responded. 'I am sure Mama does care about you. I am sure she cares about both of us and she would be shocked by the ruddiness of your complexion this morning, Bel. You are not a servant girl.'

'I have been out riding. Do not change the direction of our conversation. You must find yourself a suitable wife to run the Hall for you.'

Nathan seemed genuinely nonplussed by her suggestion. 'But – but why?'

Bel grew impatient with his languid responses. 'I have already told you why! I do not wish to remain a spinster for the rest of my days. I want to marry. If I do not marry soon I shall be the laughing stock of the Riding!'

'That does not mean that *I* have to marry.'

'Of course it does. The Hall needs a mistress.'

'But, Bel, this is *our* home. Yours and mine. We are happy here together, are we not? Why must we spoil everything by *marrying,* for heaven's sake?'

'Because that's what people do!'

'I have no intention of marrying,' he replied irritably.

'Then you should have! The Hall needs an heir!' After a pause, Bel added quietly, 'And I want a husband.'

'Really, Bel? You wish to go away and leave me?'

'No, no. Of course I do not wish to leave you. It's just that – well, why shouldn't I want to marry? If I had had a mama like other girls, I am sure she would have found someone for me.'

Bel felt her emotions rising in her throat. She really *did* want to marry. She wanted a gentleman to visit and court her, and then to wed her and give her children to care for. Most of all she wanted a husband who would cherish her and hold her close. When she was alone in her bed at night, she imagined how it might be with a husband. She would not be a shy bride, she would welcome his caresses on her tender flesh.

She knew what her body was for. One of her governesses had instructed her briefly and she knew it was being wasted as a spinster. She had learned much more by creeping from her room after dark and eavesdropping on servants as they gossiped into the night. The upstairs maids and footmen were always telling stories of things they had heard or seen in bed-chambers, including the most shocking tales of her own mama and the Italian artist. Bel often wondered if she was like her mama in this respect for sometimes her body ached to be held, her skin yearned to be stroked and her mouth became dry as her imagination ran riot.

Nathan's sympathetic eyes frowned. 'I thought you were happy as we are.'

'Well, I am not,' she pronounced. 'Oh Nathan, I shall soon be too old to marry. Who will look at me then?'

'Bel, my dear, if it means so much to you, I am sure I can find someone for you.'

'I do not want one of your insipid friends! I want a man with red blood in his veins! A man who shoots and enjoys the hunt and – and shows an interest in me!'

235

There was an awkward silence and Nathan went back to his eggs. 'I'll thank you not to be rude about my friends. Besides, Lord Stannic rides to hounds, and so does Warrender.' He paused for a moment and then repeated the name. 'Warrender. He has a large estate in the Dales that might suit you.'

Bel thought it wouldn't, but nonetheless her pretty blue eyes lit up. 'Then you'll do it?'

'Do what?'

'Have a house party, of course! Mrs Havers will open up the empty rooms and we shall invite the best families in the Riding. We'll have a banquet to welcome them. And a pheasant shoot. And a ball, perhaps, later. With gaming tables and – oh yes, a midnight supper and, oh, you will say yes, won't you, Nathan?'

'No, no, no! Never! All those dreadful, boring people who talk about the price of corn and coal and nothing else. It's bad enough having to listen to Withers and his worthy lawyer friends without inviting others of the same kind to my home.'

Surprised by his outburst, Christobel blinked and stepped back. 'But Nathan, dearest, they are Riding people like us.'

'Like you, Bel. Not me.'

'Nathan?'

'What do they know of art and literature? What interest do they have in the antiquities?'

'What – what interest do they need to keep their country estates going, or manage their mills and manufactories?'

Nathan clicked his tongue impatiently. 'You are so like Father. There is no wonder Mother ran away. *She* understood about art.'

'Just because she fell in love with an Italian artist doesn't mean she knew anything about his art! Really, Nathan, where did you get that idea from?'

'And what, pray, do you know of Mother's inclinations?'

'Well, more than you do about her appalling behaviour and the scandal it caused our family.'

In the silence that followed, Bel experienced one of those moments of clarity in her life that she remembered for years afterwards. As she said the words, she realised why it was so difficult for her to find a husband. She was tainted by her mother's reputation. No decent fellow who knew of that would risk her as a wife. Memories were long in Riding families and her mother had behaved wickedly and unforgivably. It wasn't fair! Why should she have to suffer as a result of her mother's indiscretions!

'I was here all the time, Nathan,' she added. 'She kept the servants' hall alive with rumours for weeks.'

'The servants were loyal to Father, I am sure.'

'Oh yes. And they said Mama knew where her duty lay. Do you know that one of the footmen used to listen at doors and then tell the maids? He was very popular with them. Sometimes he hid behind the curtains if he could and watched them in the bedchamber.'

'Bel! You should not listen to servants' gossip.'

'What else had I to do when you were away at school?'

Nathan sighed. 'I suppose Father should not have married her in the first place. Marriage does not suit everyone.'

'But there was no one to inherit!'

'No. He had lost both nephews and he needed an heir. So a healthy farmer's daughter was a good choice. He gave them land in exchange for her.'

'Really?'

'Withers told me. Her family could not have all the land until she produced a male heir.'

'The servants said it wasn't easy for – for Father – to – you

237

know, he was quite old on their wedding day. She must have been very disappointed in him. And with me as her firstborn. They said she cried when I was born. Is that why she did not take me with her when she left?'

'No, dearest. I am sure Mama loves us both. Father insisted we were looked after by nanny and her maids so she turned her attention to re-fashioning the Hall. I think she found her true self doing that. She had time on her hands and plenty of Father's money and – and she had a talent, a rare artistic talent for it. That's how she met him.'

'The Italian lover, you mean? How could she?'

'Withers said it was a meeting of minds. He was an artist who came over to paint the murals in the long gallery. They are beautiful, are they not, Bel?'

Bel expressed surprise. 'Withers has been talking to you about Mama?'

Nathan nodded. 'Since I inherited. There was such a huge scandal and I was away at school at the time. He thought I should know.'

'He thought you should know about a mother who abandoned her own children? Withers is losing his mind.' Bel felt tears welling at the back of her eyes. 'She deserted us. She left me to the mercy of others. What kind of mother does that?'

'She had no choice. Father would have locked her away.'

Bel held her head in her hands to stem the flow of tears that threatened. She recalled the twittering of the maids, all those years ago, and their chattering about the handsome young Italian and the mistress. They were gossiping about her mother! Her own mother! The whole of the South Riding knew how she had betrayed their father!

Nathan gazed through the glass conservatory wall at the

238

sheep grazing in the fields beyond the terrace. 'It wasn't all her fault, you know,' he commented.

'No, I do not know that,' Bel responded firmly. 'And neither do you.'

'Yes I do,' he said quietly.

Bel looked at him long and hard. He could be infuriatingly stubborn about some things, especially concerning his art, but, on the whole, since he had inherited he had been a good brother to her, never questioning any of her requests for gowns, horses or servants. She hoped her future husband would be as generous. Now, she realised, her brother was keeping something from her.

'What do you know?' she asked bluntly.

'She wrote letters to us. Every year on our birthdays.'

'What?' Bel sank into one of the cane chairs. 'Mama? Wrote letters to us?'

'Well, not exactly to us. To Withers. She knew Father would not allow us to receive anything from her. And neither could Withers until I came of age. He had to abide by Father's wishes as my trustee. But he has kept them all in his safe. I've read some of them.'

Bel was silent. All these years she had thought her mother did not care for her, there had been letters. Letters that her father and his lawyers had not let her see. She felt her tears threaten again.

'Nathan, is that coffee still hot?' she said at last.

'I'll ring for some more.'

'Ask for some brandy with it, would you? This is quite a shock.'

She felt better after hot coffee laced with brandy. Nathan told her Withers wanted to know what to do with the letters. Father had ordered them to be destroyed but Withers had counselled against that. Their father was elderly and Withers would soon be the children's guardian and trustee. So Withers had kept them until he could rightly hand them over to Nathan.

'Now they are mine,' Nathan explained. 'And I must decide what to do with them. They give Mama's side of events. She may not have been as wicked as we have been led to believe.'

At last she asked, 'Have you read any of the letters Mama wrote to me?'

'One or two.'

'And what do you propose to do with them?'

'They are yours if you wish. It might help you understand her.'

Understand her? Bel thought. Understand that her behaviour had ruined her childhood and was continuing to dominate her life by ruining her chances of finding a decent husband in the Riding? Understand that she might be an old maid because of her mother's scandalous behaviour when she was a child?

As Bel's silence continued, Nathan added, 'I'll ask Withers to bring them over if you wish.'

'No. I do not want to *understand* her. I do not want anything to do with her! She should have been here when I was a child, when I was growing up! She wasn't! She left me! She left us both! It is too late now.' Bel shook her head irritably. 'This is too much! After all these years! To have to wait until now to read letters sent to me as a child. I am so angry with her. It is all her fault. I blame her for the situation I find myself in now. You can do what you like with her letters – burn them for all I care. Mama's behaviour has ruined my chances of happiness and I shall never forgive her for that. Never!'

'I am sorry you feel like that about her, Bel.'

'It was all right for you! You had school and university and

240

the support of your friends! I was stuck here with only a succession of governesses for companionship. They were awful! Awful! Well-bred ladies, embittered by the bad fortune that had forced them into servitude. They despised me because I had money, dirty money from coal and iron, but no family title or breeding as they had. And they pitied me because I had no reputation! Not after the way Mama behaved. Is it any wonder I preferred horses and shooting?' She began to plead with him, 'Please, Nathan, please look for a wife. If you married, we should have another family. Your wife would have brothers and sisters and cousins for me to meet!'

'I have told you that I do not wish to marry. However, if marriage is so important to you, my friend Warrender has hinted to me he might have to find a wife soon. His father is insisting on it.'

'Not Warrender, for heaven's sake! He's like you. He hates our outdoor life here, and only rides to the hounds because his father orders him!'

'How do you know that?'

'Oh Nathan, do you not notice anything? Each time he has visited here I have tried my best to engage him in all manner of conversations and he is not interested in me. Everyone thinks I'll run off like Mama did. I'll never find a decent husband. Never!'

Nathan frowned. 'I am sure that is not the case. But maybe Warrender is not such a good choice for you. His father has curtailed his visits here, anyway.'

'I am sorry to hear that. You have been friends for a long time.'

'Yes.'

'Is that why Henry Bowes visits us such a great deal, now?'

Nathan shrugged silently.

'I cannot fathom what you see in Henry.'

'He has an artist's eye for colour and for shape.'

'But he is so much younger than you are. And, if I may say so, he shows it in his behaviour.'

'Yes, I find that rather charming, don't you?'

Bel did not, but refrained from saying so. Like herself, her brother had grown up without the care of parents who loved him. Friends were more precious in their circumstances as Bel knew only too well. If he was upset at losing his friend Warrender to the responsibilities of his estate, then she was happy for Nathan to have found a replacement in Henry Bowes. Nonetheless, she found Henry's 'charm' a little too brash for her tastes. She did not want her brother's good nature to be exploited.

'Well, he is several years younger than I am, so perhaps I cannot judge. But, forgive me, dearest, he is not really of our status.'

'He has no family of note, I agree. Henry's origins are humble, but his father is prospering as an ironmaster. Withers says the future of my estate, indeed the future of the Riding, is in manufacturing and not farming. Besides, Henry is a gentleman now, he is educated, he was at my school, the same one as our father. He understands my art and we share the same tastes.'

Bel nodded in agreement. Nathan knew more of London fashion than she did and Henry's dress, when she had seen him at the Hall, demonstrated that he did too. Well, perhaps she would surprise them both with her new gowns when they held a banquet or a ball at Fitzkeppel Hall! South Riding society may have had no interest in her at seventeen. But she would show them she was not to be ignored now!

She remembered the last chaperone Withers had found for

242

her when she was nineteen, a well-connected dowager who was employed to get her invitations further afield from the Riding, even into Derbyshire society. Bel had thought her dreadful. She had dressed her in the fashion that had been popular when she had been a young lady, in gowns she had decided were elegant and aristocratic. Bel remembered the stifled giggles from behind the fans of other young ladies at her first ball. No wonder she had not found a suitor! For a whole season Bel had trailed around house parties and balls with this lady, who insisted that she behaved like a silly young girl in an effort to attract the right sort of gentleman. Invariably they were gentlemen who were as stupid as the dowager and Bel grew impatient with their ways. Heavens, if she ever had the opportunity to launch her own daughters into society she would certainly do better than that!

Surely it was not too late for her? There must be other unmarried men like Warrender in the Riding and she would find one to suit her! Nathan must help her in this. He must!

She said, 'Then I am happy that you have found a new friend in Henry Bowes. But, Nathan dearest, do you not see that I have not had your advantages of school and university for my friends and that I am lonely?'

'You have me.'

'I cannot marry you. If I am to marry anyone at all, you have to do something about it. Now.'

Nathan heaved a great sigh. 'Must I have these parties in my own home?'

'Yes, you must. As you say, for the present it is my home, too. Do you not wish to show off your artistic tastes?'

Nathan sighed again.

Bel would not be put off. 'There will be new furnishings to buy and rooms to decorate for our guests. Perhaps Henry would like to help you?'

243

'You would not mind that?'

'I should be delighted for you. You can invite his father to our first house party. Please say yes, Nathan. Please.'

'If that is what you really want.'

'I do. It is as much for you. You really should look for a wife.'

'I have already told you I do not want a wife. Now go away, Bel, and plan your party.'

'There is one other thing.'

Nathan sighed and pushed aside his egg. 'This has gone quite cold now.'

'I shall need to spend much more of your money on myself: For gowns and extra maids, you know.'

'Yes, yes. I'll tell Withers when he calls. Have as much as you want.'

'Thank you, my darling brother.' She kissed him lightly on his forehead. 'You should not be so casual with your wealth. It may run out.'

'Withers says not. He says it's piling up and I should put more of it to good use.'

'Do your bankers not do that for you?'

'Yes, they do. But Withers wants me to build more furnaces and buy more machinery. He has a mission to get me interested in my coal mines and ironworks.'

Bel laughed. 'He never gives up on you, does he?'

Nathan smiled back at her and she bent to kiss him again. She wished he would behave more like the landowning industrialist that he was, but it was not in his nature. Perhaps if he married and had heirs, he would take his estate responsibilities more seriously. And not spend so much time with that boy Henry. But he seemed quite firmly set against the notion of finding a bride for himself.

Well, that was not going to stop Bel making a match for herself. There was much to be done. She gathered up her mud-splattered riding skirt and headed for the kitchen wing, calling, 'Mrs Havers! Mrs Havers! Where are you, Mrs Havers?'

Chapter 24

'Good God! What are you doing here?'

Mariah was waiting outside the housekeeper's private sitting room across the stone-flagged passage from the Hall kitchen. It was after luncheon and the servants were busy with their cleaning tasks. At the end of the passage the back door stood open, letting a shaft of light into the darkness.

'Henry!' Mariah recognised his affected vowels and looked up, as startled to see him as he was to see her. He was dressed for riding in a brown hacking jacket, moleskin breeches and brown leather boots, and carried a brown bowler hat in his gloved hands.

His clothes were new and he looked handsome in them. Mariah had felt confident in her appearance when she had left Dora's, in her dark grey gown and heavy outdoor cloak. But now, beside Henry, she knew she looked shabby.

'Is this what has become of you?' he demanded. 'A kitchen maid? Father is right when he says you are not worthy of our name.' He leaned forward and lowered his voice. 'I'll thank you not to mention our former relationship in these corridors. Just remember I know the truth about your birth.'

Mariah pursed her lips angrily. 'Go away, Henry. You need have no fear I shall own you as a brother, or Ezekiel as a father!'

Mrs Havers opened her sitting-room door. 'What is going on out here? Oh! Mr Bowes, sir! What are you doing in my kitchens?'

Henry stepped back. 'Taking a short cut to the stables, ma'am.' He turned to leave and then changed his mind, adding, 'I hope you are not giving employment to this person, Mrs Havers. I am sure your master would not approve. She is known to be wilful and disobedient.'

Mrs Havers knew better than to respond to this and simply explained, 'A visitor to the servants' hall, sir. That is all.'

'See that you check her pockets before she leaves.'

Humiliated, Mariah looked down at the flags and clenched her fists. She wondered what else he was going to say. No doubt Ezekiel had been quick to disassociate himself from her. She had caused him great embarrassment by her refusal to marry Mr Smith and she understood why he would not own her. Henry had agreed with his father about her marriage. But his main concern, she realised, was his reputation with the Fitzkeppels. Fortunately for her temper, Henry left as hastily as he had arrived without giving her another glance.

'Well, Miss Bowes?' Mrs Havers sat imperiously in her fireside chair and her chatelaine of keys rattled as she arranged her skirt. 'While you are here, working on Miss Christobel's new gowns, I shall be responsible for your conduct. I am waiting for an explanation.'

Mariah did not know what to say. She had no wish to be

connected with Henry or his father in any way. But he had acknowledged a familiarity with her.

After a short silence, Mrs Havers went on, 'You are Miss Bowes? He is Henry Bowes, of Bowes Ironworks. A cousin of yours perhaps?'

'No,' Mariah replied truthfully.

'Well? From where does he know you?'

Mariah inhaled deeply. She had hoped that Mrs Havers would ask no more questions.

'We are related, ma'am. But there has been a – a difference between us and I no longer – er – reside with them.'

'And why should he make that comment?' Mrs Havers had raised her voice.

Spite, probably, Mariah thought and replied defiantly, 'I really do not know, but it is not true!'

'Hmmm. He is right about you being wilful.'

'I am not a thief!' Mariah denied hotly.

'No, I do not believe you are. Mrs Barton would know if you were and she would not have you in her house. Her recommendation is enough for me. Nonetheless, I have enough to do looking after the Hall servants. Truman, our butler, is too old to cope now and the responsibility for them is left to me. I expect honesty and obedience at all times. Is that clear?'

'Yes, Mrs Havers.'

'Miss Christobel has insisted that only you will fashion her new gowns. Since you made that riding habit for her she has talked of nothing else. Nanny will help you with her sizings. Nanny has been looking after Miss Christobel since she was born. And we will find one of the servants to help you.'

'Yes, Mrs Havers.' Mariah was thrilled at this opportunity. To work at the Hall, with rich silks and satins, and to have a seamstress to help her – it was all she could wish for. 'I shall need somewhere to work,' she said. 'The laundry room—' Mariah stopped as Mrs Havers glared at her.

'It is in hand. My laundry mistress is fully aware of your requirements. Now what is all this she tells me about you wanting leftover silk and trimmings?'

'Only that I should like to purchase it out of my pay. Good wool and silk is so difficult to come by.' Mariah waited anxiously for Mrs Havers to reply. She planned to make shoulder capes and trim bonnets to sell at the market as her mother had done before her.

'Well, you can have them. On one condition.'

'Yes?'

'They are not to be made up into any garment for a whole year.'

'Oh.'

'Come now, Miss Christobel does not wish to see some village girl dressed in the same silk as herself, even if it is only a frill or a flounce! As soon as she has passed her outfits to her maids, you may make up the remnants into whatever you wish.'

'Thank you, Mrs Havers. When shall I start?'

'Today. Master Nathaniel's valet is run off his feet. Mr Bowes is a constant visitor and both gentlemen have extensive wardrobes. Their riding clothes will need sponging and pressing later today and you will take over the repairs.'

'Does Mr Bowes stay here, then?'

'He has his own bedchamber and dressing room.'

And Master Nathaniel's valet, thought Mariah. 'How pleasant for him,' she observed. 'I did not know that he was so well acquainted with Mr Fitzkeppel.'

'He is assisting the master with the Hall refurbishments.' After a pause, she added, 'They share the same tastes.'

Mariah pondered silently on this. She hardly knew Henry, but his early ideas for Ezekiel's house at the ironworks yard seemed, to her, to be far too grand for them. Mariah was sure that Bowes Ironworks was not prosperous enough to provide for the silk embossed wallpaper and carpets from the Orient that were to his taste. Clearly, he was more at home with a house the size of the Hall. And an income to match!

In the brief meetings that Mariah had had with Miss Fitzkeppel, she had found her to be most civil. She hoped Henry was not going to sully her name at the Hall. She thought he would not, for he would not wish to disclose that a close relative of his was working as a servant at the Hall. Why, Henry may even learn some of the Fitzkeppel civility while he stayed at the Hall!

'Miss Bowes, are you listening to me?'

'S-sorry, Mrs Havers. Yes. You were saying that I may wear my own gown and need not dress as a servant.'

'Quite so. The carrier from the village will bring you here each morning and you will take luncheon with myself and Truman. Now, I have to inspect the plate and china and after that I shall show you to your workroom.'

By the following week, Mariah had made a good start in her new workroom. Mrs Havers brought in the seamstress and then left to return quickly to her own duties. The girl hovered in the doorway.

'Come right in and tell me your name.'

'Maltby, Miss Bowes.'

The little girl took a step forward. She wore a dark brown housemaid's dress covered by a large calico pinafore and her hair was tucked out of sight beneath a close-fitting calico bonnet. She had bright eyes and was not timid in her manner.

'Maltby? That's the name of a village near town, is it not?'

'Yes, miss. It's where they found me when I was little. In a ditch by the turnpike.'

'I see.' Mariah inhaled. 'Do you have another name?'

'Sarah, miss. After the lady who found me. She took me to the poorhouse, miss.'

'Do you know how old you are?'

'Twelve, miss.'

'Mrs Havers tells me that your mending work in the laundry is very good.'

Sarah did not reply, but Mariah detected a flash of light in her eyes and slight upward movement of her head and neck. She guessed nobody had told her that before and asked, 'Do you know why you are here?'

'Mrs Havers said to go and work with you from now on and to do as you told me.'

Mariah noticed Sarah's eyes beginning to stray, taking in her huge worktable, cutting shears and threads, the new mannequin already padded with horsehair to Miss Christobel's shape and the pieces of calico Mariah was preparing for the toile she would use as a pattern for her outfits.

'Show me your hands.' Mariah examined the girl's nails and palms. 'Good. Keep them clean and smooth and never, *never* come in here with rough nails or salve on the skin. And never make up the fire. A footman will tend to that. Now, let me see what you can do with this calico.'

Mrs Havers had chosen the room well. It was on the first floor and had a large, north-facing window with inside shutters that folded back against the wall. There were no curtains and only a marble washstand remained to indicate it had once been a bedchamber. A large china bowl stood on the washstand, and a housemaid had brought up a ewer of hot water

251

and clean linen towels that she had hung neatly on the brass rails at either side.

The window looked out onto a walled fruit garden, and directly beneath it was a conservatory. Through the roof Mariah could see one or two large-leaved green plants, wicker furniture and an artist's easel with canvases stacked against the wall behind it.

Mariah sat at her sewing table, working at her creation and examining every detail of Sarah's stitching. She was determined not to be satisfied with anything less than excellence. But when a brewing storm darkened the sky she allowed herself to stand and stretch, walk about the room and linger by the window.

She took a minute to grimace at the dark clouds and then looked down at the conservatory roof. Lamps had already been lit and she was startled to see Mr Fitzkeppel there, standing by his easel. He must have sensed her eyes on him for he suddenly looked up and saw her watching. Mortified that she had been caught snooping, Mariah jumped back into the room with a cry.

'Oh, miss, you startled me. Oh dear, look, now I've drawn blood.' Sarah sucked at her stabbed finger.

'Come over here to the washstand.'

'What is it, miss? What did you see?'

'Oh nothing, nobody. Sarah, come away from the window.'

'There is somebody down there in the conservatory. Did that worry you, Miss Bowes? It's only the gardener tending to his plants, I expect, or the master doing his painting. Good at that, the master is, Mrs Havers says. He can draw a likeness as well as anybody.'

'Yes, I am sure he can. Let me look at your finger.'

'It's nothing. Just a needle prick.'

'Best stop for now. It must be nearly time for the servants' dinner. Off you go.'

Outdoor servants, housemaids and footmen, some of whom got up at 5 o'clock in the morning to get the fires going, had their dinner at half past eleven. Mariah ate later with Mrs Havers, her husband who was the estate's gamekeeper, and Truman, the Hall's ancient butler. The master's valet joined them as well as nanny who, to Mariah, appeared to be as elderly as Truman. Nanny's wits, however, had remained sharp and she questioned Mariah every day on aspects of her work to report back to her mistress.

Mariah fell easily into a routine. She welcomed such an orderly and regular existence. She felt safe working at the Hall, far away from the town and her stepfather, far away from the canal bank and her tortured memory of those horrible men. Even Henry seemed a distant relative to her now. She used the back staircase to get to her workroom and her path at the Hall rarely crossed his unless he chose to visit the kitchens.

She rose early at Dora's, dressed and walked down the lane where she met a horse and cart taking estate workers from Keppel village to the Hall. Mariah sat next to the driver and wrapped her cloak closely around her to keep out the cold.

When they reached the Hall there was hot porridge on the kitchen range for breakfast and, if it was raining or there was a hard frost on the ground, Cook laced their porridge with West Indian rum to warm them.

At the end of their working day, there was mulled ale in the kitchen before making the journey home. They were cheerful, friendly folk, from the same families she had met at the harvest supper, and Mariah began to feel as though she belonged.

Mariah was checking Sarah's seams after she had gone down-stairs for her dinner, when she was startled by an unexpected visitor. The door to her workroom opened, quite suddenly, and Mr Fitzkeppel walked into the room. She stood up hastily.

'So this is where Mrs Havers has hidden you?' he said. 'I remember you were at the harvest supper with Mrs Barton, and my sister told me you were here.'

He was casually dressed, looking more like an estate worker than a landowner, in corduroy breeches and a flannel shirt. But he wore a distinctive flamboyant waistcoat, made from an elaborate brocade. Mariah noticed smears of oil paint on his shirtsleeves.

'Good morning, Mr Fitzkeppel.' Mariah pushed aside Sarah's work and dropped a curtsey.

He approached her worktable and she jumped forward. 'Oh no, sir. I am so sorry, but you have oil paint on your clothes. I cannot allow you near to my worktable.'

He turned to her with a smile. 'Not even to look?'

'No, indeed.'

'You mean it, don't you?'

'Yes, sir.'

He gazed at her for a minute. 'Do you know you have the look of Henry when you are vexed like this?'

'I – er – that is . . . Henry, sir?'

'Henry Bowes. You are related to him, are you not?'

'Yes, sir. Distantly.'

'I think not, Miss Bowes. I shall ask him. Or will you tell me?'

Mariah guessed he already knew and resigned herself to the truth. 'He is my half-brother, sir. Since our mother passed on we have become estranged.'

'So I hear. He does not like you, does he? He became angry when I spoke of you. He says you are headstrong.'

'I have quarrelled with my stepfather, sir. I do not wish to speak of it.'

'Wilful, too. I have a sister just the same. Dear me, Miss

254

Bowes. Think on. At least you have a father to quarrel with. My sister and I have no such luxury.'

'No, sir.'

'I have painted a portrait of your brother. Has he told you?'

'We do not speak much.'

'I should like to paint a portrait of you as well.'

'Of me? Why?'

'I believe I can bring out the resemblance between you. Will you let me try?'

'I have work to do here. You know I have.'

He walked about the room from door to window and then turned. 'I shall sit quietly in this corner and draw sketches of you as you work and when I have my canvas ready on the easel I shall ask my sister if I may borrow you to sit for the final touches. Only if you agree, of course.' He raised eyebrows. 'Do you?'

'I believe you must ask your sister, sir.'

'And she will ask me if you are willing.' He sounded impatient.

'Very well. If Miss Fitzkeppel has no objections.'

'I shall speak to her today.'

Mariah sat and stared out of the window after he had left. Mr Fitzkeppel was indeed a charming man. Gentle too, and concerned for her wishes. He was so very different from the man she had grown up with. She began to understand why Henry came to the Hall so often and why he had formed an apparently strong bond of friendship here. Mr Fitzkeppel would be a good friend for anyone to have and Mariah felt a sense of relief that, for Henry, the attraction was not only the Fitzkeppel wealth and position.

Miss Fitzkeppel, on the other hand, did not echo her brother's gentle charm. She had a reputation in the servants'

hall for being more demanding and quite frightening sometimes, especially to very young maids who had known only
their own doting parents before they came into service.

She did not frighten Mariah. Nothing could frighten her
now, except perhaps her own anger if she ever met up with
those Cluffs again. In her dark moments she imagined facing
them in the street or market place and fearing they might
come after her. Rage bubbled through her to such an extent
she did not know what to do with herself. She no longer
wanted to scream at the memory, but she still wanted to kill
them.

'Miss Bowes? Mrs Havers is wondering if you have forgot
your dinner?' A young footman came into her workroom to
make up the fire.

'Is it that time already? Thank you.' She draped calico over
the fabric on her table. 'You will be careful with those ashes,
won't you?'

'Yes, Miss Bowes. I have my orders.'

Mariah smiled and thought how lucky she was to have
been given this commission at the Hall. She was comfortable
and safe here. And the fees Miss Fitzkeppel had agreed to pay
her meant that, for the first time in her life, she would have
real money in her pocket, money of her own. She inhaled
heartily and hurried down the back stairs for her dinner.

The following afternoon, Mrs Havers told Mariah that Miss
Christobel wished to see her in the small drawing room overlooking the west terrace. A weak sun silhouetted the distant
woods and brightened the parkland below.

'Miss Bowes. How are you finding your workroom? And
your seamstress, is she satisfactory?'

'Thank you, Miss Fitzkeppel. I am well suited and Maltby
is a good worker.'

'Mrs Barton told Mrs Havers you left town for the country air. You have suffered a recent bereavement and have been ill.'

'Yes, ma'am.'

'I am sorry. Are you quite well now?'

'Yes, ma'am.'

'I advise a walk every day, after luncheon.'

'Yes, ma'am, thank you. Mrs Havers has asked me to accompany her. Her husband will show us the glasshouses.'

Miss Fitzkeppel nodded as though satisfied with the arrangement. 'My brother wishes to make sketches of you at work. Did you know of this?'

'Yes, ma'am. He came to see me yesterday.'

'He told me that you are Henry Bowes' sister. Is this true?'

'Half-sister.'

'But you do not live with him? Or with your father?'

Mariah swallowed. If she did not explain, Miss Fitzkeppel would believe she had something to hide and be suspicious. She would rather any information came from her than from Henry via the master.

'He is my stepfather, ma'am. I do not live with them.' When she saw Miss Fitzkeppel was waiting patiently for her to continue, she went on, selecting her words carefully. 'My stepfather wished me to marry – someone – someone of his choosing. I did not care for his choice and we quarrelled.'

'You mean the gentleman he presented to you was not to your liking? Your stepfather is a successful ironmaster, I am sure he chose well for you.'

Mariah stayed silent.

Bel considered some of the suitors who had been selected for her at nineteen and did not press for further detail. She said, 'You are exceedingly lucky Mrs Barton took you in.'

'Her nephew and niece are employed at Bowes Ironworks. They were aware of my – my circumstances.'

'I see. You should have told Mrs Havers who you were.'

'I am sorry, ma'am. I did not know you were so well acquainted with my – with Mr Henry Bowes. And I have a settled situation in Keppel now with Mrs Barton.'

'Very well. Be seated. You will take tea?'

Mariah watched Miss Fitzkeppel as she poured and offered her milk and sugar. Poised and confident, she appeared to Mariah to have so many attributes desirable in a wife that she wondered why she was not yet married. Perhaps she was considered too strong-willed? Certainly, she had had no domineering stepfather to curb her behaviour and her trustees were, no doubt, only interested in preserving her brother's fortune.

Christobel's appearance was that of a woman older than she was. Her tea gown, in a soft dove grey with a darker braiding, did not fit as well as it should and Mariah was irritated that such good fabric had been wasted in this way. She was determined that Miss Fitzkeppel would look so much better in *her* gowns.

As she poured the tea and handed a cup and saucer to her visitor, Bel considered the independent nature of the woman in front of her. Miss Bowes appeared to be in improving health and was, indeed, very becoming to the eye and, most definitely, was the best needlewoman she had ever known. She was already using the tailoring methods the gentlemen were so taken by. And, since she first wore the riding habit Mariah fashioned for her, Bel realised the value of tailoring for ladies' outfits. What Henry Bowes had achieved with his suggestions for the Hall refurbishments, his sister was more than capable of echoing in Bel's wardrobe.

She said, 'You may spend the time with my brother that he requires for the painting. However, if the gown you are making is satisfactory, I shall require more for the winter season. And a shooting habit. So you may have another seamstress from the laundry. I shall instruct Mrs Havers that you may choose any girl you wish. Now, let us sit at the table and take a look at these illustrations.'

Bel opened a portfolio containing pages from a ladies' journal and some sketches of gowns, showing the form and detail of necklines and trims. Mariah almost fell on them with delight.

'Miss Fitzkeppel, are these the new fashions? They are magnificent. You will look very beautiful in them!'

'Do you think so? They appear splendid enough in the drawings but when they are made up and I see myself in the glass I am not so sure I shall.'

'May I suggest a solution, ma'am?'

'That is why you are here.'

Mariah held up two of the journal pages. 'Take the bodice from this gown and the skirt from that one.'

'Combine the two as one, you mean?'

'I can make the bodice separately from the skirt. That way the waist will fit more closely, as it does in the drawing.'

'Will it? Will it really? I do like the skirt on that one.'

Mariah nodded. 'With those flounces for extra fullness, oh yes. You will need more petticoats, though. They must be made with more crin to stand out like that.'

'You have worked with crin?'

'Of course. Mother used it for sleeve-heads.' Mariah was studying the pictures closely, noting how much lower the necklines were. 'Have you considered this one, ma'am?'

'I have. The bodice is very – er – revealing, don't you think?'

'Mmm,' Mariah murmured, 'the neckline is indeed wide. I do not see how you can move your arms if it is cut so low on your shoulders.'

Miss Fitzkeppel took the drawing from her and studied it. 'I shall not care for my comfort. Make it. I need a gown that ensures I am noticed.'

'You will certainly astonish your guests in that gown, ma'am. No other lady in the Riding would be so daring. If you choose a heavy silk I can tailor a waistcoat for your brother in the same colour.'

'A gentleman's waistcoat as well? You *are* clever!'

'What an entrance you two will make at your banquet!'

'Yes!' Miss Fitzkeppel's bright blue eyes shone. 'You will make the waistcoat in secret and I shall surprise him!'

Mariah smiled and nodded. She would have plenty of time to stare at Mr Fitzkeppel as he worked on her portrait. His valet would tell her which of his existing waistcoats was the best fit so she could fashion one to the same measure.

'I shall make you the envy of all other ladies, ma'am.'

'Yes!' Miss Fitzkeppel had taken her eyes off the sketches and was gazing out of the window. 'My brother and I will show the Riding that we are people to be reckoned with,' she said. 'We are ourselves, not our parents. We shall make a very fine entrance at our first Fitzkeppel ball, and we shall be the talk of the whole Riding.'

Mariah returned to her workroom elated. She was certain that, in her gowns, Miss Fitzkeppel would be a true belle. Every head would turn when she walked into the room. And every lady would surely wish to know who made her gowns! A shivering excitement began to run through Mariah. It was her responsibility to ensure Miss Fitzkeppel became the most beautiful woman in the Riding. She would not fail her. Long after Sarah had gone for her tea, Mariah studied the designs in the failing light. She brought the candle close and made sketches of her own. She could not wait to get started on the silk.

Chapter 25

'I told you I had completed one of Henry. Come and look.'

Mariah followed Mr Fitzkeppel to the back of his conservatory where his paintings were stacked against the wall. He reached down with his long white fingers, extracted a framed portrait and turned it to the light.

'Is your brother not a handsome fellow, Miss Bowes?'

Mariah stared at the picture. It was indeed a good likeness, but it was in a flattering light, making Henry look innocent and boyish, dressed as he was in a summer jacket and the necktie of his former school-house colours. She wondered what Henry thought of it now he preferred cashmere and velvet for his jackets. He had tried so hard of late to dress as a gentleman, to look the part of a man of means who rode in a carriage and conversed with gentry.

'It is as I remember him,' she replied. 'But I fear he has lost some of this young charm now he has left school.'

'How perceptive you are, Miss Bowes. Now come over to my easel and sit for me.'

He had made three visits to her workroom with his charcoal and paper, sitting quietly as he sketched, speaking to her only when Sarah left the room. He was so quiet that after a while Mariah forgot he was there and was able to concentrate as before. Sarah had shown herself to be an able and willing pupil and soon she would be joined by another young maid from the mending room.

Mariah was confident that her gowns for Miss Fitzkeppel would be the most stylish in the Riding. But she was unsure what Mr Fitzkeppel wanted from her as she arranged herself on an ornate gilt chair in the conservatory and stared at the back of his easel.

He walked over to her, examining her face closely. 'There is a furrow on your brow; this will not do,' he commented. 'You have no such expression when you are sitting at your worktable.'

'I am on familiar ground in my workroom, sir.'

'I see. So you are concerned when you are here. Not because of me, I hope, Miss Bowes?'

'I – I am not sure what you require of me, sir.'

'I require you to sit still, of course. Do you think you can do that?'

'Yes, sir.' Mariah made a supreme effort to relax. She was dressed in her dark grey gown, the one she wore to the Hall every day. It fitted her perfectly and she kept it very clean and in good repair. It was plain with a close-fitting bodice and sleeves. She had cut in a fashionably low neckline filled with a sprigged muslin, echoing this in a neat cap for her hair and the sleeve frills at her wrists. Since working at the Hall, she had added an extra crin petticoat to give the skirt more fullness.

He did not ask her to remove the muslin at her neckline as she had feared he might, or pull down the shoulder of her gown. But she was startled when he walked over to her and touched the skin of her face gently with his knuckles.

'And now the furrowing is worse. Really, Miss Bowes, I cannot paint you with lines on your face.'

Mariah inhaled deeply and forced a smile.

'I do not wish you to smile, either. I want the calmness you have when you are at work.'

'Then perhaps I should have some work to do?'

'Of course! An excellent suggestion!' He went out of the conservatory into the adjoining room and pulled on the bell sash by the fireplace. 'I shall send for some of your work,' he said.

Mariah was horrified. She wanted none of her sewing in here, picking up any of the strange-smelling pigments and spirits that Mr Fitzkeppel used. He might not care about a smear or two on his flannel shirts and corduroy breeches, but she did!

A footman came in and he said, 'Fetch the maid from Miss Bowes' workroom.'

When he had gone, Mr Fitzkeppel approached her again. 'This bright hair must be your mother's for Henry and your father are dark. Is that not so?' He removed her cap and began to unpin her hair so it fell about her shoulders.

He stood very close to her and she could smell the heavy musky scent that wafted from him. She did not recognise it, though she was certain it was not lavender or rose water. The gentle touch of his hands on her hair sent an unexpected shiver down her back. As he arranged it around her throat, his fingers stroked her skin, but she did not feel frightened or threatened in any way, and she was amazed that this was so. She marvelled

263

that his gentlemanly civility towards her helped her relax, instead of causing her the anxiety she had felt in the presence of any man after the attack.

She said, 'My mother's hair had the same colouring before it turned white due to her illness. She told me it came from her father's family.'

'Mmmm.' He stood back and considered her appearance. 'Do you have a riding habit?'

'No, sir.'

'I shall ask Bel to give you one.'

'I do not ride, sir.'

'For the painting, Miss Bowes,' he explained patiently. 'With white lace at your throat, Bel's black riding jacket will be a perfect foil for your hair. Such a colour. Such a challenge.'

Mariah had never met a gentleman like Mr Fitzkeppel before. He revered her appearance and when he was obliged to touch her for the purposes of his work, he handled her as though she were a piece of expensive porcelain. No man had ever treated her like that before and she felt cherished by his actions. She realised Dora was right. There were good men in this world and Mr Fitzkeppel was one of them.

The next afternoon Mariah was sitting in the same north-facing conservatory wearing Bel's jacket over her gown and with a white lace jabot at her throat. Her copper-coloured hair cascaded over one shoulder and she worked peacefully on a piece of embroidery. She felt at her most serene and continued to marvel that she was in the presence of a gentleman, a fine gentleman, who seemed to admire her appearance.

After a couple of hours a footman brought her refreshment in the form of a tiny cup of hot sweet chocolate. Eventually, Mr Fitzkeppel laid down his brushes and draped calico over his easel.

'Enough for today,' he said.

'Sir?'

'You may rest now, Miss Bowes. You are an excellent sitter and I thank you for that. Off you go, now.'

She removed the jacket and jabot and went back to her workroom, elated by such praise. The light was fading already and it was time to go down the back stairs to the kitchen for the cart back home.

Mariah was excited when she related the events to Dora that evening. 'He is such a kind and considerate gentleman. So civilised, so charming. I never thought I would feel this way in the presence of a man again.'

'He is not just any man, Mariah. He is the pinnacle of our local society.'

Mariah was not listening. She twisted round to look at the back of her skirt. 'Can you see any paint or spirits on my gown, Dora? Bring the lamp and look carefully.'

'There is a little mud around the lower part at the back. And on your boots, too. Wait until it dries before you brush it off. Well, I must say it is good to see you so cheerful.'

'The servants at the Hall are so kind to me. Although they do make fun of Mr Fitzkeppel's interest in me.'

'Do not forget his interest is only to paint your picture.'

'But he behaves in such a friendly manner towards me! He does not treat me like a servant.'

'I am pleased you find your situation so comfortable, but do take care with your affections for him. You are from a different position in life.'

'Surely most of the people in the Riding are? He is the biggest landowner around here, but Henry went to the same school as Mr Fitzkeppel and Ezekiel has visited him at the Hall for dinner. Mr Fitzkeppel told me so.'

'He has talked to you about your family?'

'I told you, he does not treat me as a servant.'

'I see. Then perhaps his interest in you is more than politeness. I do remember that he was quite taken by you that first time he saw you crossing the parkland.'

'I am to sit for him every day this week, in his conservatory. It is just below my workroom at the Hall. The light is good there. He is determined to capture my hair. That's another thing. He does not despise or make fun of my colouring. Ezekiel always hated it. And we speak of other things, just as you and I might.'

'You *do* seem to have made an impression on Mr Fitzkeppel.'

'Why are you so surprised, Dora? I am not a freak and he does not know of my – my recent misfortunes. He knows only that I have quarrelled with my stepfather.'

'I am very happy for you, Mariah. It appears that I am wrong and he has a genuine affection for you. Be careful you do not lose your heart to him.'

'Why not?'

'He is gentry and you are not.'

'You told me yourself that his mother was a farmer's daughter.'

'And her marriage was a disaster.'

'You mean they did not love each other? To know love in a marriage is a luxury, Dora. My mother did not know it and I do not expect to have that luxury in mine.'

'Then you should!'

'How can I? What gentleman could ever love me if he knew the truth about me?'

'I hope there will be forgiveness in the gentleman who loves you. If he truly loves you, he will understand and not love you any the less.'

'I think a knowledge of what happened to me and – and what I did would test even the strongest affection, don't you?'

'Yes, I suppose it might.'

'Well, it is my secret and a secret I shall keep to myself. I shall not let it stop me from accepting a proposal of marriage, should I ever receive one.'

Dora asked lightly, 'Do you suppose you could go forward into marriage without telling your betrothed the whole truth?'

Mariah fell silent. Perhaps not. How could she keep a secret like that from a husband? Besides, he would know she was not a maid on their wedding night. Dora was right. Dora was always right.

'I am not talking of *marriage* to Mr Fitzkeppel. Only friend-ship.'

'As long as you are sure about that, my dear.'

No one could deny he had a genuine and sincere interest in her, Mariah reflected. And she was becoming increasingly enchanted by him as she sat quietly assessing his shape and movement for the waistcoat, while he mixed pigments and oils to capture her colouring.

Nathan considered Mariah a good sitter. She was patient and good humoured and had a maturity her brother did not possess. She reminded him of Bel in that respect. He worried about Bel. Since her outburst about wanting a husband he realised that she was lonely. Perhaps marriage was a solution for her. It was certainly not for him. Although Withers had mentioned at their last meeting that he ought to be thinking about heirs.

As he studied and painted Miss Bowes, he thought she would make some ambitious artisan or worthy clerk a decent wife. She had attributes of energy and good sense, exceptional skill with a needle and was personable. Too wilful, though. Unless you wanted a lady like Bel to run your estate for you.

He realised, suddenly, that if Bel did marry and leave the Hall, he would need someone to take care of his domestic affairs. He toyed idly with the idea of marrying Miss Bowes. She was a comfortable companion, easy to talk to, and would be ideal for the task. He amused himself by imagining Withers' reaction to a match that was so obviously beneath him. Yet his father had done just that to produce his heirs. He sighed. Henry would be so distressed to know he had been thinking such thoughts.

'Thank you, Miss Bowes. I shall not need you to sit for me again. My painting is finished. You may look.'

She had thought his earlier sketches of her were a good likeness. But when, at last, she saw his canvas on the easel, she blinked at it with surprise. He had caught her features well, but it was her likeness as she had been before her mother died and before her ordeal. It was not a likeness of her as she was now, as a grown woman with maturity in her face. It was a portrait of her as an innocent maid. Her features were angular and undeveloped as they had been when she was younger. She looked more like a boy, a young boy.

She stared at it, swallowed and said, 'I had no idea I looked so much like Henry.'

'But of course you do. You have his bone structure if not his skin tone. The hair, too, is different. I have captured the colour, have I not?'

Mariah thought not. He had not secured the true copper colour. Rather, he had painted a paler version, and he had given her hair more waves than were actually there, so the portrait had a misty, dreamlike appearance. It was not unattractive. And it was clearly her. But not as she saw herself at all, or indeed as she believed others saw her.

He traced her features tenderly with the back of his knuckle and smiled at her gently and said, 'Ethereal, my dear Miss Bowes. That's what you are.'

In the painting, yes. Her skin was too pale and he had completely disregarded the freckling across her nose that was evident to any casual observer. In the painting, she was ghost-like in her appearance.

Well, she thought, I expect that is what ethereal is. But the sight of such fragility alarmed her. She may have looked like that when she first arrived at Dora's but not now, surely? She must take more exercise in the fresh air to improve her colour!

That evening as she sat in the cart home, she asked the driver to stop and let her down at the path that ran across the Hall parkland and led to the woods, so she could walk home.

'Are you sure about this, Miss Bowes?' the driver asked.

'My feet are quite cold from sitting, and my fingers are stiff. A brisk walk is exactly what I need.'

'If you say so. But I 'ave no lamp to lend you.'

'The moon is rising already and I know the way through the woods. Will you collect me from here in the morning?'

'Right you are, miss.'

When Mariah arrived at Dora's, she was slightly out of breath.

Dora frowned. 'Was somebody chasing you?'

'No, I came by the woods. Tell me, Dora. Are my cheeks a little pink?'

'Yes, they are. What on earth were you doing cutting through there in the dark and on your own?'

'I am familiar with the track now, and it's so much quicker than going round by the village and the lane.'

269

'Even so, after dusk and without a lamp? You could have easily taken the wrong path, or stumbled over a root.'

'There's a good moon tonight. I could see my way well enough and the leaves are soft underfoot.'

'But what if there were poachers about? If they heard you they might have shot you for a deer.'

'Oh, I thought I saw one or two, but they didn't have guns. They had ferrets and were flushing rabbits out of the warren on the long meadow. They were near to where the sheep graze, I think.'

'As long as they keep well away from the birds. Mr Havers doesn't miss a rabbit or two, but he won't stand for losing any pheasants or partridges. Mrs Havers should let you off before it gets dark now the nights are drawing in.'

'I sew as long as there is enough light. Besides, the cart for the villagers doesn't leave until their work is done, and there's so much to do now to get ready for the visitors. I know it's dark but it is still quite early and I am safe enough.'

'All the same,' Dora said, 'you should take care. What's all this about visitors?'

'The Hall servants and villagers talk of nothing else. It is Miss Fitzkeppel's wishes. She is to have a house party with a pheasant shoot and a ball. She has asked me to make her outdoor dress and a silk gown to impress her guests with two bodices. One of them has a very low neckline. And I am to make Mr Fitzkeppel a waistcoat in the same silk for him to wear at the banquet.'

'So I shall see less and less of you?'

'But we are going to be rich by Christmas, Dora! I have built Miss Fitzkeppel's mannequin and Sarah has made up the toiles. And Mrs Havers has given me another girl to train as a seamstress. A child from the laundry with good eyes and

270

nimble fingers who has already shown her uses in my workroom.' Mariah's eyes shone and her cheeks glowed as she hung up her cloak on the hook in the hall.

'I think this commission at the Hall may well give you a new direction in life,' Dora commented.

'Oh, I do hope so! I am so much recovered now, Dora! Miss Fitzkeppel has been very kind. I shall make certain she is the most beautiful lady at her gatherings. Her guests will not forget her gowns and there will be other commissions, I am sure.'

'So my front room will become a gown maker's workshop?'

For a moment Mariah closed her eyes and dreamed of that image. Her own workroom. As big as the one at the Hall, with seamstresses to work for her, and a pony and trap to visit clients. Dora's front room was only a beginning!

She opened her eyes and bit on her lower lip. 'Will you mind? I can give you proper lodging money now. Every week. Look.' Mariah hoisted up her skirt and fished inside the pocket of her drawers. 'A guinea. A whole guinea. Mrs Havers gave it to me for Miss Fitzkeppel's riding habit. She told her it was the best-fitting one she has ever had!'

'Like the coat you made for me. You really are very clever with a needle and thread.'

'My mother was the clever one. I shall always be grateful to her for teaching me. Here, take the guinea for coal and food. Are you going to the beast market in town next week?'

'Aye. We need flour and salt. I shall see the butcher there too, and ask him to call and stick the pig before he starts losing his fat to the cold weather.'

'You can pay the butcher with real money now instead of giving him one of the legs.'

'Yes, Fanny can have that. Salted down, it will be champion for her Christmas feast. I'll get the pickling trough ready in the outhouse.'

'I'll do it, Dora. I am leaving all the household tasks to you these days.'

'Aye, well, you do better with your sewing and I am happy for you to get on with that. Will you come to market with me?'

Mariah inhaled sharply. 'I cannot. I cannot take a whole day away from my workroom until Miss Fitzkeppel's new habit and gowns are finished. I'll meet the carrier at the end of the lane and help you carry the flour and salt.'

'All right, lass.' She hesitated. 'I'll be seeing our Daniel, I expect.'

There was an awkward silence.

'Shall I tell him you are on the mend?'

Mariah nodded. 'If he wants to know.'

'Of course he does!'

'Do you think he has said anything about me to Ezekiel?'

'Don't you trust him? He wouldn't say anything to anybody about what happened.'

'I'm sorry. It's just that, well, he is Ezekiel's supervisor and that is where his loyalties lie now.'

'Our Daniel is nobody's lackey. He is his own man. I realise you may blame him for your attack . . .'

'No, I don't blame *him*. He didn't know about Mrs Cluff's past. Those men are to blame. No one else. They should be hanged for what they did to me. What is it that makes men do those things?'

'Some men are just bad. Remember that.'

'I cannot imagine Mr Fitzkeppel behaving in that way. I suppose that's what wealth and education do for gentlemen.'

'He's different. It's the way he is. Do take care with him. It does not do to move out of your class.'

Mariah shrugged. 'Henry and Ezekiel have done. Why shouldn't I?'

When Dora did not respond, she let the matter drop and said, 'Fire's getting low and there's a clear sky. That means another frost tonight. I'll put a couple of bricks in the oven to warm for our beds.'

Chapter 26

The following week, Mariah stayed later than usual at the Hall. Miss Fitzkeppel's elderly maid had asked for help with cleaning and mending her day gowns. Nanny's eyes were too tired for detailed work, even though she did have spectacles. Mariah was feeling so much better now that, when she had finished, she declined the offer of a governess cart to take her round to the lane.

It was a fine night and Dora knew she would be late. There was a half moon, which gave a little light to her walk. She left the main driveway and cut across the fields on the now familiar path. As she neared the edge of the woods, she heard sheep bleating and their hooves beating as they scattered.

Mariah slowed her pace. Something had disturbed them. A fox, maybe? Unlikely, as it was not lambing time. Perhaps the flock had been spooked by a deer? One single sheep continued its plaintive bleating and Mariah guessed it had been caught up in brambles. Drawn towards the trouble, she strained her eyes in the darkness. The bleating stopped suddenly and as she crept closer she heard subdued voices, rough male voices, and she suddenly felt afraid.

Silently, she slipped into the cover of the trees, but she was drawn to the noises and by a sickening feeling that these men were not the usual rabbit poachers about their dubious business. They were sheep stealers. Instead of hurrying away along the path, she hesitated and strained her ears to listen.

The flickering of a lantern in the thick of the wood led her to their deed. One of them was dragging the dead animal with blood oozing from its throat into the trees and away from the chance sight of any passing rider. Mariah watched their movements in horror.

'Bring it round 'ere. Gerron with it, lad, we a'n't got all night.'

'A' tha gunna skin it first?'

'That'll tek too long. By the time I've gutted this 'un, t'others'll 'ave quietened and we'll fetch another.'

As soon as she heard the voices, Mariah became rigid as though frozen to the spot. There were two of them and they had a handcart, a small wooden affair stacked with old sacking and straw. The younger man held the lantern as the older man took his knife and slit the sheep's belly until its steaming sagging innards spilled out onto the leaf-littered ground.

'Keep that lamp high, I tell yer!'

'That's good money we're leaving behind, Dad. Yer can allus flog sheep's guts.'

'Aye, I know, lad. But it'll lighten our load. This lot'll be heavy enough ter push as it is.'

'Yer got a buyer, then?'

'A buyer? They've got labourers sleeping on clothes lines

275

over Sheffield way! We'll get a good price fo' this from some-body.'

As she crept a little closer and her eyes became used to the flickering lamplight her stomach sickened at what she saw. But it was not the sight of butchery that turned her, nor the stench of spilled guts – she recognised the Cluffs.

Mariah pushed her knuckles between her teeth to stifle her cries. Her recollection of her degradation was so clear it could have happened yesterday! As she watched them go about their foul deed, she re-lived that night of horror and her heart turned to stone. She knew exactly what she must do.

When they had loaded their first quarry onto the hand-cart, they would go back to the meadow for a second kill. She had time. She silently retraced her steps to the familiar track and then ran as fast as she could across the parkland and all the way to the Hall. She went straight to Mrs Havers' sitting room, and fell against the door, her heart racing and her breath coming in short urgent pants.

Mrs Havers herself answered her urgent thumping and calling. 'Miss Bowes! What on God's earth is wrong?'

Mariah leaned on the door jamb to steady her shaking body. 'Sh—sheep stealers. Got a handcart in the woods at the edge of the parkland. Two men. Ruffians, by the look of them.' She did not say their name, nor that she knew them.

'Go into my sitting room. Mr Havers is there.'

Mr Havers had been dozing with an empty ale tankard in his hand. As Mariah entered the room he was already on his feet and reaching for his gun in its resting place by the fire. 'I heard. Good work, Miss Bowes.'

'They said they were taking them over to Sheffield, to lodging houses there.'

'Mrs Havers, send one of the stable lads for the constable

right away. Jed and Joseph are just finishing their supper. I'll take them with me now.' He checked his pockets for gun cartridges.

'Take care, Mr Havers.' Mrs Havers stretched up to kiss him on the cheek.

He gave her a rueful smile and strode purposefully out of their small, cosy sitting room.

Mariah slumped down in a chair to recover her breath. 'Will he shoot them?'

'Only if they try to get away. Wait there until I get back from the stables.'

Mariah's breathing had subsided but she was still feeling nervous when Mrs Havers returned.

'Mr Havers will catch them, won't he?'

'He'd better! He has been losing too many of his sheep lately.'

'What if he doesn't, though?' Mariah asked anxiously.

'He'll get them, don't you fret. And he will have you to thank. He'll be right pleased, he will. Now, why not take a piece of shortbread and a glass of mulled wine to refresh you?'

'No, thank you. I'd better get off now, Mrs Barton will be worried and she might set out to meet me. I don't want her coming up against them.'

'Don't be daft! You can't go out there until Mr Havers has 'em handcuffed and taken away.'

'I can't let Dora—'

'Sit down and drink some wine. Jed's brother has taken our fastest horse to fetch the constable. I've told him to go to Mrs Barton's as well to tell her what's going on. When we know all is safe out there, he'll take you round in the trap. Now, lass, while we're waiting we can talk about this house party Miss Christobel is having. I am going to need as many hands as I can find when the guests arrive.'

Much later and safely home, Mariah related the events of the night to Dora over a cup of tea by the kitchen fire.

Dora said, 'Well, the judge won't have any trouble finding them guilty. You saw 'em and they were found with the sheep's blood on their hands and the carcasses in their handcart.'

A sudden fear gripped Mariah. 'Will I have to go to the assizes?'

'I shouldn't think so. Not if Havers and two of his men caught 'em at it and the constable's men took 'em away, sheep an' all.'

'Where? Where have they taken them?'

'Sheffield, I expect. They'll be locked up in the town hall until the magistrate decides what to do with them. He'll most likely send them to the gaol in York to wait for the next assizes. You've seen the last of them around here, Mariah.'

'I hope so, I really do. Will the judge hang them?'

'I can't say. He might favour transporting criminals to the Australias. They say the prisons here cost too much already and our colonies out there need the labour.'

'I heard that some buy their freedom and come back.'

'Not many, lass. Even when they're free, they are better off out there. The governor encourages them to stay. They can have a bit o' land if they want.'

Mariah did not like the idea of the Cluffs being free men again, even if they were on the other side of the world. She would prefer them to be incarcerated for life in a stinking gaol. However, either way, she would not see them again around here and that gave her a measure of redress. She sank back into her chair. 'I can't believe it. They're gone. Gone for good.'

'And we're all well rid if you ask me. Them woods'll be safe for the rest of the winter. As soon as news gets around about this, all the poachers'll stay well clear, you mark my words.'

At last Mariah felt a door close on her past. She could not undo what they had done to her, but she felt some satisfaction she had been able to play a part in their downfall. They were gone! Locked up. They would never threaten her or anyone else again. In time, she hoped their faces would become distant memories. She would never forget the ordeal they put her through, but she felt a kind of release from the torment that had lingered within her. For so long she had wanted punishment for those men and their wickedness. And now she had got it.

'It was them,' she said quietly.

'Them? Who?'

'Those men. Cluff and his son. Stealing the sheep.'

Dora glanced sharply at Mariah. 'The ones who attacked you?'

Mariah gazed into the fire. 'I recognised their voices and I saw their faces in the lamplight. I have never forgotten those faces, those evil mouths sneering at me. Or their hands, their hands and bodies doing unspeakable things to me. I hope they both hang. I'll go and watch them if they do.'

Chapter 27

'Come into town with me tomorrow, Mariah.'

'Yes, I will. It's time I put in an appearance, don't you think?'

'You have no idea how I have longed to hear you say that.'

They were in the outhouse, turning the flitches of bacon in their trough of brine. They would be ready to dry soon, though the hams needed a bit longer to cure. Autumn had been chilly and the ripening holly berries promised a cold winter. The ground froze early and their store of logs and coals had dwindled so quickly Dora had to order an extra cart load from the pit head.

Mariah took to wrapping a shawl around her head when she was sitting sewing by candlelight in the front room after tea. Her commissions at the Hall were finished and Miss Fitzkeppel had paid her well. She had money left over after paying Dora for food and fuel.

'I couldn't be sure until now that the Cluffs wouldn't show up again.'

'Well, you were right. They didn't stay in Manchester. There were too many rich pickings round here for them.'

Mariah straightened her back and heaved a sigh. 'Since they were put away, I feel I have turned a corner. I can hold my head up and face people again. If folk do shun me, I shall smile and turn the other cheek.'

'Why would they shun you?'

'Ezekiel will have blackened my name at the lodge to save his own.'

'Their womenfolk will understand. There's a beast market tomorrow. You can sell your hand muffs to the farmers' wives.'

Mariah heaved over the flitch, splashing her jute apron. 'Yes, I'd like that. If we go on the early carrier I'll get a good pitch.'

As well as muffs, Mariah had sewn rag dolls from scraps of fabric and stuffed them with soft wool gleaned from the hedgerows. She had also made several ladies' shoulder capes, woollen ones, fashioned with two layers of cloth for protection against the biting winds that whipped across the valley.

'We can go to our Fanny's for dinner. What do you say?'

'That would be nice. I'd love to see them all again. Won't Arthur mind you going there?'

'I've called once or twice since you came to stay and he's not been too bad about me. Fanny says he's going soft in his old age.'

'When I was there, I always thought he was good with baby Victoria.'

'He's a good man,' Dora said sincerely. 'Our Fanny's lucky.'

Mariah took her hands out of the icy brine and dried them on a cloth. Her fingers were shrivelled and red with cold and a graze on her skin was stinging. She did not complain. The salt in the water would help the healing.

'I'm looking forward to seeing your nieces again,' she said.

'Our Daniel might be there, as well. Will you mind?'

'About seeing Daniel? No, I don't think so. Not now.'

'He may have news from Sheffield about the assizes.'

'I'm not interested any more. It's over for me but I hope the Cluffs rot in hell.'

Dora nodded silently to herself.

They set off for the market before dawn, walking down the lane to catch the early carrier's cart, which soon filled to capacity as they trundled nearer to town. Dora and Mariah held her bundle between them sharing the precious space with village folk and squawking poultry in wicker baskets.

Dora helped Mariah spread out her square of calico on the cobbles and weight it down with stones. Then she went off to do her own marketing while Mariah arranged her dolls, muffs and capes to sell. She wrapped her cloak closely around her as a keen wind whipped up her appetite. She looked forward to going down the hill to the Thorpes for her dinner when she had done.

The wintry weather favoured her and she had sold everything long before dinner time. She folded up her pitch and went off with a spring in her step to spend some of her gains on a news sheet for Mr Thorpe, lavender water for Mrs Thorpe and spice for the girls, all of which she placed carefully in pockets on the inside of her cloak.

When she could not stand her hunger any longer she bought some hot chestnuts, roasted on a smoke-shrouded coal brazier. Her mother used to buy them for her when she had a copper to spare. Mariah blinked back a tear, blaming the smoke and thought her mother would be pleased she had found friendship with the Thorpe family. In those last few years of her life, her mother had taken to young Emma, and had often said what a good lass she was.

Mariah sat on a low stone wall waiting for her chestnuts to cool and thought how much stronger she was. She straightened her back and held her head high. Whatever Ezekiel had told his friends about her and whatever the town folk were saying she knew that she had been right to leave his house. The last few months and this morning had shown she could earn her keep by her own hand. Her mother would have been proud of her.

Despite the bitter weather, there was a general air of cheerfulness about the beast market as trade was good. Furnaces and forges were thriving, boosted by the new railways and talk of an empire across the seas. Yet another butcher's shop had opened in the town. The cobbled streets were familiar ground to Mariah and she scanned the bustling crowd for faces that she knew. One or two looked in her direction and gave her a nod, but did not stop to speak.

Across the square she spied the traveller from Leeds with his horse and cart and went over to see what he had for sale. He remembered her and was pleased to meet her again. She bought wool flannel for winter petticoats, cotton for new drawers and stockings for Dora and herself. He wrapped them up in her calico square and tied up the corners so she could sling the weighty bundle over her arm for the walk down to Canal Bank Cottages.

She felt confident at the top of the hill, but as she turned into the alley and the place where she had first encountered the Cluffs, her self-assurance deserted her. Her boots clattered on the cobbles as she began to hurry. She bent her head to her breast and pulled up the hood of her cloak.

The memory was not far below the surface of her mind

and it shoved itself forward, quickly and painfully. She pushed it away. I'm all right, she thought, it's daylight and there are people around. I passed two women back there. There is no need to panic.

'Oh!' Someone, a man, had overtaken her and was barring her way. She kept her eye on his boots. They were good boots, she noticed.

'Mariah?'

Her body went rigid and her voice rose to a squeak, 'Oh, it's you.' She relaxed a fraction and raised her head. Daniel Thorpe's serious face searched hers.

'I did not mean to startle you. Aunty Dora called in at the works. I am invited home for my dinner. She said you would be there too.'

Somehow, he was not as she remembered him when they had first met in his parents' kitchen. Since then, she had never really looked at his face properly, even when he came to mend Dora's table. She had been too distraught and embarrassed for her eyes to engage with his. But she recalled how shaken she had been by the sight of him chopping wood in Dora's back yard. And now she remembered that first meeting, and how she had thought then that he was a striking-looking man. She had warmed to his manner at first, until she had realised his mission was for her to do Ezekiel's bidding, return home and marry Mr Smith. He had been so very sure of himself. Too sure, she reflected, for her liking. His command of her affairs had reminded her of Ezekiel's ways.

She still found his manner and appearance striking. Dark hair and stormy-grey eyes, thick eyebrows and strong angular features like his father. But now there seemed to be an under-lying sadness shadowing his expression. It had not been there before and it belied the lightness of his voice when he spoke.

'Shall I carry your bundle?' he asked.

She thought there was an older, more worn look about his face now. He had fine lines around his eyes and mouth where before there had been none. Ezekiel was, no doubt, working him hard and he would be feeling the burden of his employer's domineering ways. But she knew he had spirit and backbone to carry such responsibility and wondered what else might be ailing him.

When Mariah made no move, he took the bundle from her, saying, 'You must be tired after a morning at the market in this weather.' He offered her a supportive arm which she ignored. After a few steps he added, 'A lesser person than you would stay indoors on a brisk day like today.'

'I have been indoors for long enough these past months,' she responded stiffly.

They walked on in silence until he asked, 'How are you, Mariah?'

He always asks me that, she thought, as if it mattered to him. She did not think it did. No, he felt the guilt of his complicity in her degradation, that is all. Well, let him suffer! If Daniel Thorpe chose to blame himself, it was his worry and not hers. She said simply, 'I am quite well.'

'I mean how are you – er – after your ordeal. Have you—'

'I know what you mean,' she interrupted sharply. 'And I have told you I am well.' After another awkward pause, she added, 'Thank you.'

'I am concerned for you.' He sounded superior, like Ezekiel used to be with her and she felt her anger rising. Heaven forbid that he should grow to be like Ezekiel! But, she conceded, Daniel Thorpe was not an angry man in the same way Ezekiel was. Ezekiel had a bitterness about him. But Daniel, well, Daniel carried guilt and pity for her, that was all. He felt sorry for himself and for her at the same time.

285

The silence lengthened as they walked and Mariah wrestled with her thoughts. Of course she was grateful to him for finding her that night. She may well have perished in that cold wet field if he had not. But there had been times during her recovery when she had wondered if it would not have been better to let her die, for what kind of life had she to look forward to now? A defiled and degraded woman with a guilty secret. A spinster's life like Dora's, with no husband and children. It was an existence of sorts, but Dora would never know the joy of a family like her sister Fanny, of the love of a husband and children. Mariah did not want Dora's life for herself.

When Ezekiel had insisted that she marry Mr Smith, she had been resolute in her refusal, but it was not because she was opposed to marriage itself. Indeed, she would welcome the opportunity if she met a gentleman she wished to marry. Though she could not, for the life of her, imagine any gentleman would ever wish to marry her now. How could he, if he knew the truth about her?

Mr Fitzkeppel had shown more than a passing interest in her. She was not of the same standing as he, of course, but that had not seemed to matter to him when she sat for the painting. And meeting him had helped to restore some of her faith in mankind. She did, however, wonder if Mr Fitzkeppel would have shown such interest in her if he had known everything about her.

Even some of the ladies in town, if they knew, would think she had brought her suffering on herself. Decent girls did not put themselves in the position of offering such temptation to men, for, as all women knew, men were men. And much, much worse than that, she had killed her unborn child. Deliberately. A conscious decision, made for her own sake, and she guessed she would suffer for that for the rest of her life.

The Lord had found His own way of dealing with her, she realised. He had made it impossible for any man to love or marry her, impossible for any man to want her to have his children. She would never have a husband and family now and that was the cross she must bear.

She grew angry as she walked, irrationally angry with the man who walked beside her and carried her bundle. Daniel Thorpe did not know what he was talking about when he said he was concerned for her! His concern was for himself and his own guilt, that was all! She found it difficult to talk to him.

However, when they reached the cottage, Mariah's irritation faded as she was drawn into the Thorpes' happy, noisy family. Meg and her younger sisters delighted in their small gifts from the market and Mr and Mrs Thorpe showed a genuine pleasure in seeing her again. Only Emma could not be with them as she was too busy looking after Ezekiel and Henry.

Fanny hugged her tightly. 'We have had news of you from Dora, but it is not the same as seeing you here in the flesh. Let me look at you.' She stepped back. 'Yes, I do believe that country air suits you better than the town. You look well, my dear. Very well indeed.'

'Your sister has cared for me like one of her own and I shall always be in her debt.'

Mariah realised that Dora did not have one of her own. Mariah wondered if all the family knew about her lost baby or if it was a secret shared only by Fanny and Dora. Did Arthur know he had had a child born out of wedlock, a child that had died?

Dora looked across at her sister, who was slicing a piece of boiled bacon at the table, and then down at the blackened iron pot she was tending on the fire. Arthur had not heard. He and his son were distracted by a headline from the news sheet. Mariah frowned at her mistake and then saw Dora smiling at her so she smiled back.

'Dinner's ready,' Dora announced. 'Everybody sit at the table and let me and your mother dish up.'

It was a good dinner. Fanny had boiled the bacon with barley and lots of vegetables. Only baby Victoria did not join them – sleeping soundly in a chair by the fire. They had tankards of Fanny's own ale to drink and hunks of fresh baked bread to mop up the gravy.

'Mariah has been working as a gown maker to the gentry,' Dora announced proudly, and described their meeting with Miss Fitzkeppel at the harvest supper.

Liddy and Lizzy clamoured for details of Mariah's visits to the Hall and demanded to know if the rooms were as big as everyone said. Meg was more interested in Miss Fitzkeppel and her brother.

Mariah obliged her. 'Well, Miss Fitzkeppel, being the elder, seems to take charge most of the time. She runs the household and even talks to the estate manager about the horses and the farms. She likes being outdoors and it was a new riding habit she wanted me to make at first. You know, for the hunting season. I have seen her up and about very early in the mornings when the servants from the village arrive for the day. Her brother is just the opposite. Very cultured and artistic. He occupies himself with paintings for the walls and curtains for the windows.'

Meg and Liddy giggled and Mariah sprang to his defence. 'He is very skilled himself at drawing and painting likenesses! What is wrong with that? He is fortunate in that he has the means to indulge his talent.'

288

Surprisingly, Mr Thorpe supported Mariah in this view. 'Aye, it's food for the mind, that sort o' stuff. I knew a miner who could draw good likenesses wi' on'y a bit o' chalk on a slate. And another who went to the Institute and wrote poetry that were printed up and sold.'

Dora added, 'Mariah has an artistic eye herself, so she recognises it in others. She can tell you more about Mr Fitzkeppel's own paintings. He was quite taken by you, wasn't he, Mariah?'

'He – he asked to paint a picture of me. He made sketches while I worked and then I sat for him in the conservatory.'

'Really?' Fanny responded.

'Oh yes,' Dora said, 'and I do believe that Mariah has fallen for him.'

'Dora!' Mariah glared at her across the table.

Dora was not to be put off. 'Well, you talked about him all the time when you were working at the Hall and you yourself told me that Miss Christobel allowed you time to sit for the painting. She gave you a second seamstress for your workroom to help out while you were sitting.'

'Is this true?' Daniel, who had been quiet so far, was quite demanding in his tone.

He had heard tales from his drinking companions at the Lion about Nathaniel Fitzkeppel, and they were not stories he could repeat in the presence of his family. They came from the footmen and the gardeners at the Hall and told of the antics the young master indulged in with his university friends. They played games that never included ladies, dangerous games that could land them in prison or worse. It was not for him to question the ways of the gentry. But what they did together was not right and he could not stand by and let Mariah believe that Fitzkeppel might ever care for her as a man ought to care for a woman.

289

'Well, is it?' he repeated.

'Why should it not be true?' Mariah exclaimed. 'He wished to capture my – my colouring – my hair. We talked about Miss Christobel's new gowns as well and we became quite friendly.'

'From what you said, my dear, he *was* interested in you. Take my word for it.'

'Aunty Dora,' Daniel said firmly, 'I do not think you should be encouraging Mariah like this. She is his sister's gown maker, that is all, and he was being kind to her, as I would expect of any gentleman.'

'Daniel?' Now it was Fanny's turn to query Daniel's high-handed tone.

But Daniel was not to be quietened in this matter. His concern for Mariah overrode any consideration for his parents' dining table. He continued, 'Mariah, do not lose your heart to Nathaniel Fitzkeppel. He would never be interested in you.'

'Daniel! Do not be so unkind!' his mother scolded.

'I – I meant that he, that is –' Lord, he thought! 'He – he is not interested in ordinary Riding folk.'

'And you think you know him better than the rest of us?' his father asked.

'Yes!' Daniel replied stubbornly, and then tried to think of a way to explain his outburst. He could not and added lamely, 'I am saying that he is gentry and Mariah is not.'

'No, she was a servant there, like me and Dora,' Mrs Thorpe added sharply.

'It's quite all right, Mrs Thorpe.' Mariah turned to face Daniel. 'I never suggested that I was losing my heart to Mr Fitzkeppel, as you say. Or that his interest in me was lasting. However, despite our differences in status, he has shown kindness and friendship towards me at a time when my own family, such as it was, has shunned me.'

'Mariah, you must not be fooled by his charm.' This time, Daniel's overbearing tone was stronger.

Arthur and Fanny looked at each other with raised eyebrows. The girls looked down at their plates.

'I am not fooled!' Mariah responded valiantly. 'Will you not allow me a little pleasure, Daniel? May I not indulge in an occasional fanciful dream as other young ladies do?'

'He will never return your affection.'

'Not even as an acquaintance?' Now Mariah grew angry. 'Neither Mr Fitzkeppel, nor his sister, are as rigid as you may think in their choice of companions. My brother Henry is a frequent visitor to the Hall. Why should I not be their friend also?'

Daniel despaired. She did not understand and why should she? Yet he could not see her hurt more than she already had been and felt he must warn her away from Fitzkeppel and his ways. Somehow. He said, 'Do you not see that his position in the Riding demands that his friends should be from a similar standing?'

'Of course I see! But I may have a little enjoyment, may I not? After all, my life so far has not been much fun.'

'I – I – I am sorry, Mariah. I did not mean to suggest . . .' Daniel hesitated and glanced at his younger sisters who, to a girl, had stopped their hungry chewing and were waiting, with their forks poised and their mouths open, for him to continue. 'I am concerned for you, that is all.'

'So you say,' Mariah responded dryly. Dear me, she thought, he *is* becoming like Ezekiel in his ways. He believes he knows what is best for all the womenfolk around him.

Dora acknowledged Daniel's sisters with a tilt of her head and said, 'Little pigs have big ears. If you two have more to say to each other, why don't you go for a walk after dinner? Have you enough time, Daniel?'

He nodded.

Mariah said, 'Oh, I should help Mrs Thorpe with the pots—'

'No need. I've plenty of hands today,' Fanny interrupted. 'You two need a proper talk.'

Daniel looked from his mother to his aunty and saw Dora give a tiny smile. He pursed his lips. 'We came down from the town together. Mariah may have had enough of my company already.'

Dora did not give up. She smiled at him and said, 'Why not ask her and be certain?'

He said stiffly, 'Will you walk with me after dinner, Mariah?'

Mariah felt obliged to agree. The Thorpes were such good people and she owed it to his parents and his aunty to try and clear the air. After their apple pudding, Daniel shrugged on his heavy coat and Mariah shrouded herself in her warm cloak.

It was overcast and cold outside, but, well wrapped and fortified by a good dinner, they walked down the towpath towards the wharf, their boots crunching on the spilled coal and iron. It was the first time Mariah had retraced those steps since — since that night.

She hesitated for a fraction, regained her resolve and continued. As they passed by the empty end cottage, she suddenly realised what was ailing Daniel and why his manner was so brusque. His heart was shattered. It had been broken by Mrs Cluff and he was pining for her. He must have loved her if he had asked her to marry him as Dora had said.

They walked in silence until Mariah heard him inhale deeply for a second time, so she said, 'I am sorry about Mrs Cluff. Dora told me that you thought she was free to court and marry.'

'It was all my fault! Can you ever forgive me, Mariah?'

The anguished tone of his reply startled her. 'But did she not lie to her husband's family as well? You cannot blame yourself for that!'

'They would not have extracted such revenge if I had not been . . .'

He faltered as though the words had failed him and Mariah frowned to herself. This did not sound like the Daniel she knew.

She continued, 'Your intentions were honourable. I do not blame you for her family's wicked actions. However, I do not, indeed I *cannot*, understand why they should have behaved in such a terrible way for what *you* did. It beggars belief. But it is over, over and done with. I do not hold you responsible for their evil deeds. I am only vexed by the means they used to take their revenge on you.'

She thought that would have eased his conscience, cheered him even, but the dismay on his face became more agonised until he stopped in his tracks and turned to face her.

'Mariah,' he began, 'you do not know everything. I cannot go on with this duplicity until you know the whole story. Lily and I were—'

'Sweethearts. I knew that, Daniel. Emma told me.'

'More than that! Oh, much more than that! I had been seeing Lily since the early summer. Every week. I visited her on Sunday afternoons. She was – is – older than me . . .' He hesitated again and Mariah's own heart shrivelled a little as she realised how deeply he had loved and had gone on loving Mrs Cluff. His voice lowered to a hoarse whisper. 'I knew what I was doing. When I visited her we were – we were as man and wife. I gave her money for coal and food. Her brother did not know at the time that I wished to marry her.'

Her head reeled as this revelation. 'You were as man and wife and you gave her money! Oh God, now I understand.'

She turned away from him, covered her face with her hands and remembered the argument at the door of Mrs Cluff's cottage. The dark alley where she sent Emma off to fetch Daniel. Their fingers on her arms like iron bands as they dragged her along the path, the crunch of the coal grit underfoot, the cold air on her thighs and breasts and . . .

We'll make a whore out of you like he has done our Lily.

Now she understood his crushing guilt. Now she understood why their revenge had been so personal.

He put out his hand and she flinched.

'No! Do not touch me.'

She did not know whether it was the taint of coal dust in her mouth or the pain she had in her heart that made her feel ill. The hurt was in her heart not in her stomach or her nether parts where the physical damage had been worst. This was a different kind of wound. A wretched aching despair for what she had lost because of what he had done.

While he had tasted the pleasures of marriage, she must forgo them! A normal existence with a husband, children, a happy dinner table, like the one they had just left, was not for her. How unfair life was! How desperately she wished she had someone to hold and care for her. Someone who did not know about her past grief and therefore did not feel sorry for her. Someone like Mr Fitzkeppel. Certainly not someone who pitied her or who needed to dispel his own guilt. Certainly not Daniel Thorpe. Never Daniel Thorpe.

She said, 'Well, the Cluffs will hang for sheep stealing, so I have justice of a kind. The matter is finished with now.'

'Is it, Mariah?' he asked.

His tone told her that he did not believe her.

'You really do not have to worry so on my behalf. I am not made of china. You heard Dora. I have started a new life

294

making gowns for the gentry.' As she said the words she thought, And though I cannot have marriage I can have freedom and independence from my own hands. She added, 'I shall gain more commissions when Miss Fitzkeppel wears my gowns at her parties.'

'Yes, indeed. She has become something of an icon to the Riding of late. She has grown into a beautiful lady. I have seen her out on horseback in the hills. Once, when I had to deliver papers to the Hall, I was quite close to her. She did not notice me in the shadows but I thought then that she was most hand-some.'

'Oh, did you?' Mariah's voice came out in a surprised squeak.

'The town is fortunate to have such a mistress at the Hall. She takes an interest in her brother's estates and will soon be acknowledged as the most elegant lady in the Riding.'

'Really? I did not know.' She wished she had thought to lower her voice.

'You sound surprised. Do you not agree?'

'Er, yes. I – I was not aware that you knew her.'

'I don't. But most gentlemen in the town who have seen her have a similar opinion of her beauty.'

Mariah did not reply. Miss Fitzkeppel had the same kind of attractive features Mrs Cluff had possessed: the tiny waist that was becoming so fashionable nowadays, and that enhanced her womanly proportions; fair hair that waved and curled in tiny tendrils around her face; wide blue eyes and a generous smile. Daniel sounded as though he was as smitten by Miss Fitzkeppel as he had been by Mrs Cluff. She felt an irrational irritation and, feeling an obligation to break the ensuing silence, changed the subject.

'It is such a pity Emma cannot be here with us today. How is she managing on her own in that large house?'

'As best she can. Henry wants a cook like the gentry have, but his father has refused.'

'I hope he's not too hard on her.'

'You have taught her well. Mr Bowes is pleased with her and she has Meg to help out on laundry days. Now that you are recovered, Mariah, will you not at least consider coming back to your proper home?'

'Oh you, too, would have me marry Mr Smith, then? For that is the price I should have to pay!'

From her furtive glance sideways, Mariah saw Daniel looked uncomfortable with her outburst.

'Surely it is your home as much as Henry's?' he said quietly. 'Your father—'

'I do not wish to discuss my father. Or my brother.' She heard him sigh again and added, 'Shall we walk back? Dora and I are catching the afternoon carrier.'

As Dora and Mariah bumped along the track out of town, muffled up in their shawls and cloaks, Dora said, 'You didn't stay out long with our Danny. I am sorry about what he said at dinner. He's a changed man lately. He's different somehow, so touchy about everything and high-handed in his ways. He used to be such fun and now he's not.'

'It must be Ezekiel's influence.'

She wondered how similar they really were and if Ezekiel had rejected her mother's affections because he had kept a lady like Mrs Cluff somewhere in the Riding. For as long as she could remember he and her mother hardly exchanged a word between them, let alone a kiss. They had separate bedchambers, separate mealtimes, and separate conversations with her.

Mariah's thoughts and feelings were jumbled. For despite his role in her misfortune, she had a grudging admiration for Daniel

296

Thorpe. He had had the courage to tell her the truth about his relationship with Mrs Cluff. He was not a man to flinch from duty and that was why he had achieved such a lot already in his life, and would, no doubt, go on to greater heights in the Riding.

She thought back to their first meeting and the feelings he had aroused in her. She had felt like a normal young woman then and had been charmed by his concern for her, even though she had been obliged to reject it. But he had been Ezekiel's supervisor for only a short while at the time and had already shown signs of his influence. She hoped he was not going to turn into a tyrant like Ezekiel.

She had come away from their short walk with a feeling that he was lonely without Mrs Cluff. Her father had also seemed to her to be an isolated man. Surely such a handsome and successful man as Daniel need not be alone? She guessed she had been right in her assumption and he was still pining for Mrs Cluff. Certainly, he had been unusually distressed when they had walked past her cottage. Well, he could not marry her now, that was for sure. But, Mariah reflected as the cart carried her away from him, despite their unsatisfactory exchange and her increased animosity towards him, she owned he had many good qualities. More, even, than Mr Fitzkeppel.

Mr Fitzkeppel did not have the strength that ran through Daniel's veins. A strength that was in his character as well as his body. Despite her anger and resentment, Mariah could see that whomsoever Daniel Thorpe chose to be his wife would be a very lucky woman indeed.

She wondered who that might be.

Chapter 28

'Now then, Thorpe. What's to do with this wages bill?'

It was Ezekiel's habit to visit the works office at the end of every day, and on Saturdays he paid his men their dues.

'I've put an extra man on at night, sir. That cementation furnace is old and without him the temperature was dropping and it was taking longer to cook the steel.' Daniel turned over the page of a ledger on the desk. 'If you look at the output, you'll see we need all the blister steel we can make to keep our customers supplied now that we have the crucibles as well.'

'That crucible shed cost me enough without all these extra wages.'

Ezekiel gazed out of the window to his new building across the yard with its flight of stone steps up to the crucibles and wide brick chimney that gave the updraught needed to draw the fires. He called it a shed but it was much more than that. Six crucible furnaces were dropped into the floor. By, when they were at full stretch, he'd be making a pretty penny and no mistake!

'I need another teemer as well, Mr Bowes. I can't do all the teeming and run the works for you. And he'll cost. Pouring red-hot steel from the crucibles into the moulds is dangerous and it takes practice. Young Ned is nowhere near ready for that kind of work yet.' Daniel waited patiently for his employer to reply.

Ezekiel had watched Thorpe teeming and knew he was right. The crucibles were heavy when they full of molten steel. They had to be gripped with great long tongs and tipped at arm's length. The heat was so fierce that Thorpe had to bite on an old rag to stop his lips burning as he poured. Mind, he'd got such a good price for his first load of ingots that Ezekiel would have tackled the teeming himself if he had been a younger man. But not now, not with his shoulder the way it was.

'Aye,' he agreed grudgingly. 'Don't forget I've the bank to pay too. If I don't pay them there'll be no house to live in and we'll be sleeping under the crucibles with the coal.'

Daniel was satisfied. He knew just the man at the Fitzkeppel works – steady and strong and looking for a gang-leader's job. He stepped aside so Ezekiel could inspect the ledger.

'When can I take him on, sir?'

Ezekiel grunted. 'I don't want to talk about that now. Have you heard they're having a pheasant shoot at the Hall? Big affair, with visiting gentry and the like.'

Daniel nodded. 'I knew there was work going on at Keppel Hall.'

'Aye well, Master Henry and me, we shall be there at the shoot. Master Henry has been invited by Mr Fitzkeppel himself. They are well acquainted, those two. They know each other from school.'

Daniel was aware that Henry often stayed at Keppel Hall and he thought it high time that Ezekiel stopped indulging his son and made him take a proper interest in his works. The furnaces would belong to Master Henry one day and he would not have the slightest idea what to do with them. But Daniel did not say any of this as he waited patiently for Mr Bowes to continue.

'Havers has asked for you to lead the beaters. He says you used to beat for them reg'lar when you were a lad and he wants a good man in charge.'

'I can't leave the works for a whole day, Mr Bowes.'

'You can if I say so. You're the gaffer down there now, so you see to it. I've told Havers you'll do it.'

'Right, sir.'

'That's settled, then. You'll answer to Havers on the day. Now, step aside, man, so I can get to the safe.'

Ezekiel knelt in front of the heavy iron box that sat in a corner of his office. It was decorated with an ornate brass plate on the door that carried the name of the manufacturer. He took two large keys out of his waistcoat pockets. The thick metal hinges creaked as he opened the safe and reached inside to extract his leather money pouches. One contained folded banknotes. The other, heavier one was more bulky and it grated with coins as he dropped it on the desk top. By gum, it took up a lot less time to pay the men their wages these days now he had Thorpe to make up the ledger and count out the coins.

The men's boots were already ringing on the stone steps outside as they lined up outside his office door. When he was ready, Ezekiel sat behind his old wooden desk and Daniel stood behind him holding the heavy ledger and calling out the names of his gang one by one, and the amount that he was due. Ezekiel picked up a pile of coins for each man and handed it over.

'Thank you, sir,' each one said, turned and pushed quickly past the men behind him to clatter down to the yard with his earnings.

Finally, Ezekiel gave Daniel his wages, inspected the household bills and added an amount for the butcher's boy and grocer's lad when they next called at the house.

'Anything else this week?'

'Just a dozen sacks of oats for the horses, sir. And your stable lad has asked for some more of that West Indian molasses to mix in their morning feed.'

'That's dear, that stuff is.'

'It gets 'em going of a morning, Mr Bowes. Especially if they do the Sheffield haul instead of us having to wait for a barge. Saves us time, sir.'

'Go on, then.'

'Thanks, Mr Bowes. I'll get off back to the warehouse now. We're loading for the next firing on Monday.'

'Aye.'

Alone in his office, Ezekiel placed his money bags back in the safe. He considered whether he could trust Thorpe with the keys to it yet. While he was on his knees he shuffled the papers, checking they were all there. His order book, bills of sale, a copy of his new will, and now the mortgage deed on the house. He wondered if he'd have to ask the bank for more to pay his next wages bill. At the rate young Henry was spending, it looked likely. He was going on about his own horse and carriage now and moving the heavy horses and cart from the stable at the back of the house down to the works yard.

His hand fell on some old papers. Damn! He would have to move them out of the safe if he gave Thorpe the keys! Where would he put them? He dare not risk Henry finding them if he took them into the house. But he could not give the safe keys to Thorpe until he had removed those papers. Should he destroy them? No, he would not, could not. However much he despised them, and himself for owning them, he coveted them and was not capable of burning them. Henry had suggested he purchase another safe for the house and put it in the study. One of the new models Mr Smith had in his shop. Perhaps he would.

Henry would never make an ironmaster like Thorpe. But he was his son and he thanked God for that blessing. Henry made all his grafting at the furnace face worth while. Everything he had worked for was for Henry. And, while Henry might not be good at the hard work needed to make steel, he would better the family name and become proper gentry. In fact he was virtually gentry, for he had been schooled with them and was invited to their houses and to the Fitzkeppel shoot and ball, securing invitations for them both.

With his new supervisor chosen for head beater, Ezekiel, too, was socially accepted. Respected. This was as it should be. As soon as Henry became of age he would find him a bride. He was a handsome lad with good manners and graces. There would be ladies at this party. Young ladies of breeding and charm just right for his Henry.

Ezekiel smoothed the sheets of thick paper lovingly and placed them carefully in the bottom of the safe, away from prying eyes. It was all for Henry. He had endured his silent sufferings for years now. He could continue to bear them when he thought of Henry and Henry's reputation. What did his own feelings matter now? Henry was his future.

Chapter 29

A flock of heavy birds squawked and flapped and broke cover from the trees. The air split and cracked and a few fell like stones to the meadow below. Blue smoke swirled from the butts and the stringency of gunpowder and hot metal assailed Mariah's nostrils. A second volley of shot brought down more birds and then there was quiet while the guns reloaded and the dogs were sent out to retrieve their prey, carrying the birds back in their soft mouths.

'Not many of the ladies here,' Dora commented. 'I suppose they are still in their beds after yesterday.'

'I reckon so. The servants were already busy with breakfast trays when I arrived at the Hall this morning. Apparently last night was pandemonium in the kitchens.'

'I heard about that too,' Dora said. 'Truman said some of the guests were dropping asleep at the dinner table because they were so tired from their journeys.'

'The maids and valets too. They were exhausted. It's too

cold to travel in carriages at this time of year. They were glad of my help.'

'You were very late back last night.'

'There was so much to do! All the unpacking and pressing of gowns and gentlemen's dress for dinner. We were all yawning by the time we'd finished!'

Mariah and Dora were well back from the butts, in a clearing Havers had prepared especially for this occasion. Mrs Havers had asked Dora to help Truman but, in spite of his advancing years, Truman was clearly in his element and had declined Dora's offer.

'Is that Lady Grassebrough over there?' Mariah asked.

'It looks like her,' Dora replied. 'But I can't see her maid around.'

'No. I'm standing in. She is helping the visiting maids to clean up all the travelling clothes and prepare the dinner gowns for tonight's ball. It's just as well not many of the ladies are here this morning or else they'd have all the shooting habits and walking boots to deal with as well.'

Mariah and Dora sat on the stump of a newly felled tree and watched as footmen set up wooden trestles and boards on a level piece of ground. They had a good view, too, of the woods and fields as the birds were flushed out into the open when the beaters closed in on them.

There was only one other lady shooting with Miss Fitzkeppel. Her brother was there, but he was not shooting. He was talking to Havers as he supervised the loaders and stewards. There were twelve butts and, Mariah noticed, Henry and Ezekiel were positioned at one of them. They were sharing a loader and quite obviously enjoying their sport.

Truman shook out a white cloth over the wooden boards. Then he tapped a barrel of ale on the cart and began filling metal tankards with the foamy brew. The footmen were busy setting up a shiny new spirit warmer under a large urn of soup that had been carried out from the kitchens. A group of kitchen maids began slicing an assortment of raised game pies and opening stoneware jars of pickle and chutney.

Although tired, the servants were cheerful and there was an air of festivity about the occasion. Mariah became caught up in this atmosphere. She relaxed and began to enjoy herself as the morning progressed towards luncheon.

Havers signalled the guns to cease and all went quiet as the dogs ran for the last of the birds, rushing back with wagging tails. He supervised his keepers as they checked the pheasants and tied them in braces on wooden racks for hanging in the outdoor larder at the Hall.

A straggle of beaters emerged from the undergrowth and trees, flushed and scratched, to join the loaders and keepers for pork pie and ale served from the cart. The clearing and beyond was soon filled with a noisy, hungry crowd, marvelling at the morning's bag as it was displayed for all to admire.

Truman was pouring tots of whisky, very carefully, into tiny thick glasses. He placed one on a silver salver and took it over to Mr Fitzkeppel who was stamping his feet in the cold and looking miserable.

Miss Fitzkeppel, in contrast, was talking and laughing with her guests. She was a good shot and her cheeks glowed with excitement. She helped herself to a tot of whisky, swallowed it in one and reached for another, not caring about sideways glances from some of the gentlemen.

'You're wanted, Dora.' Mariah saw a footman waving and gave her a nudge in the ribs. 'Over there. One of the maids has tripped up by the look of it. Shall I come with you?'

'No. You wait here in case Miss Christobel needs you.'

Mariah stayed at the back of the clearing, warming her mittened hands in the folds of her cloak, content to watch the activity. It was her first experience of a shoot and she was interested in the way masters and servants mingled and enjoyed the delights of the crisp outdoors.

She saw Mr Fitzkeppel pick up two whiskies and hand one to Henry. They wandered over to the wicker tables and chairs where a footman brought them soup and pie. She faltered as she caught sight of Ezekiel talking to a man of similar age to himself. Hobnobbing with the gentry! she thought irritably. It was all he wanted to do now her darling mother had gone. Her anger began to simmer and she tried to repress it. Her instinct was to hide in case he saw her and made a scene, for she would retaliate with as good as he gave and that would never do here. But if he had noticed her he did not acknowledge it and Mariah was grateful. She was enjoying the party and did not want him to spoil it for her. Dora returned from her task with two stoneware mugs of thick oxtail soup and they sat back to back on the tree stump to drink it.

'What happened?' Mariah asked.

'She fell in a rabbit hole and hurt her ankle. I had to take off her boot and stocking and wrap a wet flannel round it.'

'Poor girl.'

'She seemed cheerful enough. Two of the footmen are carrying her back to the kitchens.'

Mariah chuckled. A weak winter sun was beginning to push through the clouds. 'Look, Dora, one or two more ladies have walked out from the Hall for luncheon.'

'And there's our Daniel. Can you see him? Over there with the beaters.'

Mariah started and spilled her soup.

'Careful, lass. I should have warned you it was hot.'

'No harm done. Did you say your Daniel was here?'

'He's with young Ned from the works.'

'Has he seen us?'

'I don't think so,' Dora answered. 'Who's that handsome young fellow sitting with Master Nathan?'

'That's Henry Bowes. Ezekiel's here, too. I saw him earlier.' Mariah looked about her. 'Can't see him now. Oh, yes I can. That's him, Dora, over by the bird racks, talking with – do you know who that is?'

Dora strained her neck. 'Oh yes, he's the manager from Keppel pit. Useful man for him to know, I should think. Want some pie?'

'I'll fetch it. Mustard pickle or marrow chutney?'

As she pushed through the servants, milling around their dinner cart, Mariah glanced over to where she had last seen Daniel. He had a metal tankard of ale in one hand and a slice of pie in the other and he was laughing. Mariah had not seen him laughing like this before. She stared at him for a moment and her heart gave a flutter. He had a noticeable presence, even in a crowd. As he laughed he seemed to come alive and she thought how very attractive he was when he was not being serious and overbearing. She wondered what had made him laugh. Suddenly she really wanted to know what it was. She wanted very much to be a part of the small circle of people that stood around him and whose company he was enjoying.

'Miss Bowes, there you are.' Miss Fitzkeppel threaded her way through her guests towards her. Her face carried a healthy ruddiness, whether from the cold winter air or the whisky Mariah could not tell, but clearly she was thrilled that the shoot was going so well. 'Where is your workbox? Lady Grassebrough has torn her skirt with the heel of her boot.'

She followed the hostess over to one of the wicker tables

where her titled guest was twisting in her chair to examine the damage. She was relieved Henry had moved away. Mr Fitzkeppel, also, had gone. This did not surprise her for the two of them had always had their heads together, talking about something, when she saw them at the Hall.

Mariah knelt on the damp grass beside Lady Grassebrough. 'Nothing serious, your ladyship. The edging has broken free and is trailing as you walk. It will get worse if I do not stitch it now.'

Mariah's mittened fingers, warmed by her mug of soup, chilled again to the bone as she strained her eyes to insert tiny stitches into the dark wool. Her knees, also, felt the damp through her own woollen skirt and she was glad when she was finished and able to get up. She blew on her finger ends and wrapped them in the folds of her cloak.

Alarmed, she noticed Ezekiel moving towards them. His face had darkened and he looked angry. She did not want a scene with him here where she was surrounded by her new friends from Keppel village and the Hall staff. But he had reached them before she could move away.

She need not have worried; he ignored her and walked straight past. She felt an irrational hurt as he looked through her. They had lived as father and daughter for nineteen years and he behaved as though she did not exist! In spite of the traumas she had experienced since their quarrel, she would have acknowledged him with a bow of her head. Now she was glad she hadn't!

Yet she was impressed by his appearance. He certainly looked the part of a country gentleman out shooting, dressed in new woollen breeches and waistcoat with a smart tweed jacket and hat. He carried a polished gun over his arm and a new leather hunting bag across his shoulders.

'Miss Fitzkeppel,' he called as he swept by Mariah, 'I am looking for my son. Henry, my son, have you seen him?'

'He was here earlier. I believe he took luncheon with my brother.'

'Then where are they now?'

'I really have no idea, Mr Bowes. Would you excuse me?'

Miss Fitzkeppel moved away with Lady Grassebrough and Mariah followed them, checking her sewing had done its job.

Ezekiel was not happy. He was standing alone talking to the air around him. 'Where is that son of mine? Where has he gone?' He became more agitated as he moved among the guests. An acquaintance hailed him to talk but he would have none of it. He pushed him aside and strode off. 'He should be here with me. He is *my* son . . .'

Ezekiel noticed people looking at him and quietened. He had been enjoying the shoot until Henry had gone off to talk to their host. Fitzkeppel had so many others around him to talk to, without taking Henry away from him today. He needed Henry beside him on these occasions. He was beginning to think that perhaps Henry spent too much time at Fitzkeppel Hall. Henry's visits had served their purpose. They were now accepted in the upper circles of Riding society and invited to all the right gatherings. And Ezekiel was on good terms with several forge masters and pit owners. Their house too, was looking grander every month.

It was time for Henry to stop squandering his father's money so he could invest in more pig iron and men for his furnaces. That young Thorpe fellow was proving to be worth his weight in gold, and he had done an excellent job with the beaters today. All the guns had told Havers so.

Next time Thorpe would be a gun himself. Ezekiel would

see to that. He had influence now. Fine man, young Thorpe. He was going to make Bowes Ironworks sing with new steel.

That nice Fitzkeppel lady was here today, as well. Braving the cold, not like most of the other ladies. They were too nesh by half, were womenfolk. He had seen Amelia's girl with her needle and thread. Where she belonged. On her knees at the feet of the gentry. Silly woman, just like all the rest. She could have been mistress of her own house by now if only she'd done as she was told. She could have had Mr Smith's young daughters waiting on her hand and foot. Just like her mother; didn't know when she was well off. If the pair of them only knew what he had given up for them, for their sakes, for this life of respectability. He rebuked himself silently. Stop it, man! Don't think of what might have been. Not today. Not here.

But suppressing his memories and his desires was becoming more difficult since Amelia had passed on. Her presence had been enough to separate him from his past. But when he was alone, he often thought of those times before Amelia and her bastard and how much he wanted to go back there. And how he could not. Not now. He had spent twenty years of his life gaining respectability in this town and he meant to hold on to it.

Ezekiel became more agitated. He wanted Henry by his side. He marched about with his gun over his arm, asking after Henry until one of the beaters told him he had seen Mr Fitzkeppel with a well-dressed young gentleman go down the keeper's track through the trees. Ezekiel set off after them.

He came across the old keeper's hut in a small clearing and gazed at it uneasily, ignoring the thoughts tumbling through his mind. An assignation? He had heard tales of young gentry and the women who pleasured them. Was this why Henry was so attracted to the Hall? Were the two of them with some willing wench from the servants' quarters? The woodland was still, but there was a noise coming from the hut.

It was solidly built of rough timber with a stone chimney wall at the back and a heavy door at the front, slightly ajar. The hut was large enough for a gamekeeper to stay in for days and nights on end when chicks were hatching or poachers were about.

There was a shuttered window and, as Ezekiel crept closer, he recognised the sounds within. His heart began thumping in his chest. He had not heard grunts and groans such as these for many a year. He prayed it would not be Henry with some kitchen maid from the Hall. He wanted better for his only son. He crept to the door and listened. Whoever she was she was quiet about it. But it would not do. He would not have his son the object of any servants' gossip at the Hall. He must stop this now. He swallowed and pushed the door with the barrel of his gun. It swung wide open and banged against the wall.

Light flooded into the dusty, sparsely furnished room, illuminating two fused figures rutting on an ancient couch. Their boots and breeches were scattered over the table and chairs, their long white legs exposed to the chilled air. Both their heads turned as daylight streamed in and then was blocked by Ezekiel's figure looming in the doorway.

Henry's strangled, painful cry was muffled by the fusty couch under his face. Fitzkeppel yelped with surprise and slowed the rhythmic movements of his rump. Ezekiel stared at this horror before his eyes. No, this could not be. Not Henry. Not *his son* Henry, coupling with a man who called himself *gentry*. Not Henry, please not Henry, complicit in this shameful act.

Despair and torment engulfed Ezekiel.

Was this why Henry was always at the Hall? Nothing was

311

secret there. The servants knew everything and they gossiped. The single barrel of his shotgun clicked into place. 'Get off my son,' he growled.

Nathan Fitzkeppel heard rather than saw the gun. He peeled himself away from Henry's back, allowing his shirt to fall and cover his nakedness.

'Calm yourself, Father. Put down your gun.' Henry struggled to a sitting position on the couch.

'How long?' Ezekiel demanded through the mist that was clouding his eyes. 'How long has this been going on? *How long?*'

'Come, Father. You know how it is—'

'How long, I said?'

Henry inhaled deeply. 'Since school days. I was his fag.'

'No! No!' Ezekiel let out a long and anguished cry, like that of a dog in pain. Not Henry. Not his son. He felt as though he had been sliced in two and he doubled over, crying and groaning. He swung about, backwards and forwards, pointing his gun in all directions, hitting the barrel against the wooden walls and eventually aiming at Fitzkeppel.

Henry leapt to his feet. 'Give the gun to me, Father.'

But Ezekiel was not listening. He turned towards his son, then back to Fitzkeppel. His mind was in turmoil and a descending blackness was engulfing his reason. This could not be happening to him. Not his Henry. He had tried so hard, so hard to do things right by Henry and that – that *Fitzkeppel* had undone it all. He could not live with this, he could not . . .

Henry took a step forward. 'Father, stop this. You have to understand, I love Nathan. I was willing, am willing. I have loved him since—'

But the remaining words were lost to everyone's ears as the shot blasted through the air, a deafening crack that sent the birds flapping from their roosts, cawing and calling, disturbing the quiet afternoon sky.

Daniel detached himself from his group of friends to speak to Mariah who was standing alone by a felled log.

'Good day, Mariah. You are looking very well, if I may say so.'

'Thank you,' she said simply.

'Your father seems troubled. Is something wrong?'

'I believe he is missing Henry.'

Daniel surveyed the mix of guests and servants in the clearing. 'Henry is here somewhere.'

'Oh yes. I saw him earlier. He was at the luncheon tables with Mr Fitzkeppel. They are very good friends, you know.'

'Very good friends, did you say?' Daniel's body went rigid with alarm. Fitzkeppel and Henry? 'No, I did not know. I understood Henry visited the Hall for business, to cultivate trading contacts for his father.'

'Well, yes, that too. But they have known each other since their schooldays.'

'I see.' Daniel schooled his features into stillness, raised his head and, again, looked about. He must be calm about this, but a sickening feeling was spreading though his veins. 'Mr Fitzkeppel is not here either.'

'I expect they have gone back to the Hall. Mr Fitzkeppel hates shooting.'

'He is the host. He would not leave before the shoot is over.'

'Then perhaps they have gone for a walk?'

'Perhaps.'

'I am sure they will be back soon. Ezekiel has gone looking for them.'

Daniel's face remained expressionless as though it was of no consequence. He stared at her for a moment, then said calmly, 'Yes of course.' Without leave, he took her elbow. 'Aunty Dora is looking for you, Mariah.'

She drew away from his touch, startled at first, but nonetheless allowed him to steer her through the throng towards Dora who had collected small cups of steaming chocolate for them.

Daniel kissed his aunty on the cheek. 'Sorry I cannot linger, I – er – after the shoot there's a tea laid on for the beaters in the old barn. Why don't you two come and join us?' He did not wait for a reply but hastily withdrew and Mariah watched him disappear through the trees down the track Ezekiel had taken.

It must be something to do with the ironworks, she reasoned. She took the small cup gratefully and inhaled the rich aroma. 'Mmm, this is delicious. I've tried this before at the Hall, when I was sitting for the painting. Are you sure we're allowed to have it out here?'

'Truman ordered it to be sent out for the ladies. But there aren't many of them braving the cold today, and the footmen have refused to carry a full urn all the way back to the Hall.'

'At least they keep warm dashing backwards and forwards. This is fun, isn't it?'

'Oh aye. It's like in my younger days when old Fitzkeppel was alive. My father was a beater for him and I used to come along for the tea afterwards. All the beaters' families did if they could. There was always a good spread, and cake for the children. I used to love the cake, the cook put plenty of butter in it and eggs and sugar. Ee, lass, I never thought I'd see the day when I would be able to afford to make my own cake. That's because of you, Mariah, my love.'

'Nonsense. You managed very well on your own.'

314

'Aye, but much better now I get regular money from you as well.'

'I am very grateful for all the help you have given me. I think I would have sunk so low I would never have recovered if it had not been for you.'

'You're a strong lass. Strong in mind as well as body. You had the worst of it, though.'

'I don't dwell on it now if I can help it. Shall we talk of something else?'

'Of course, I— What was that?'

The air was shattered by the crack of a gun going off, quickly followed by a cacophony of birds flapping through the trees. Every person in the clearing stopped what they were doing and looked around.

'Someone gone down to shoot early?' a male voice asked.

'Surely they haven't started for the afternoon already? The beaters are still here and they haven't drawn for the butts yet.'

'Some young blood can't wait to get going again?'

There was an air of disquiet from the guns and their loaders punctuated by a shrill voice in its midst. 'Havers! Havers! What was that?'

'I'll just go and see, Miss Christobel.'

Havers had a face like thunder. If someone was fooling around at his shoot, they'd have him to reckon with and no mistake. These jumped-up ironmasters and factory owners didn't know the form. He raised his voice, 'Ladies and gentlemen, would you all stay where you are, if you please?'

Mariah's eyes widened. The shot had not come from the butts. 'It came from the woods,' she whispered. 'Daniel is in there, Dora. He went to look for Ezekiel.'

Dora looked frightened. 'Daniel didn't have a gun with him. I'm off to see what's going on.'

315

'You can't! You heard what Havers said!'

'Just watch me. Danny might be hurt.' Discreetly, she picked up her battered leather bag and followed Havers down the track into the wood.

'Do be careful, Dora. Oh heck, you're not going on your own. I'm coming with you.'

'There's a keeper's hut down here,' Dora said breathlessly over her shoulder. 'They sleep there when the chicks are hatching.'

Mariah hurried after her, holding her cloak and skirts tight to her legs to avoid the worst of the brambles. Her heart was thumping in her chest. As the trees thinned and they approached the old hut, they heard a male voice, a raised and anxious voice. There was a faint whiff of gun smoke pervading the air. Some of the trees blocked Mariah's view but she could see the side of the hut and two men standing in the open doorway. Havers appeared to be in a state of high agitation, and Daniel was leading him away, trying to calm him.

Daniel heard the women crashing through the undergrowth and looked round. He immediately left Havers, who slumped against an oak tree, and came to meet them.

'What's happened, Daniel?'

'Go back.' He stood in front of them with his arms outstretched as though to embrace them both. 'Go back to the party. Take Mariah with you.'

'Is Ezekiel here?' Mariah demanded.

'Mariah, do as I say. Go back now.'

'What is going on?' Mariah looked past Daniel to where Havers was sagging against the tree. His knees were giving way under him. He had dropped his gun to the floor and his hands covered his eyes.

Daniel was saying, 'Please take Mariah away.' His voice lowered with intensity, 'Do as I say. Please.'

But as he spoke Mariah darted past him saying, 'Is Havers injured, Daniel? Dora, come and help me.'

'No, Mariah, come back!'

Daniel turned rapidly and caught her arm. She snatched it away, so he grasped the fabric of her cloak and pulled her back sharply.

Mariah heard the stitching give and turned on him. 'What do you think you are doing? Can you not see that Havers is not well?'

'Mariah! Stop!' he called as she broke free again.

But by then it was too late. Mariah had crossed the front of the keeper's hut and had glanced through the open door. She had a clear view of the motionless figure lying on the earth floor inside. A man, half clothed, his pale legs and feet bare to the elements and his shirt, his once white shirt, darkened by torn flesh and congealed blood.

Mariah choked on a strangled cry of shock. The vomit rose in her throat and she could not stop it spilling forth on the ground. Her legs buckled beneath her.

Daniel caught up with her and his arms reached around her, supporting her. 'Come away, Mariah. Don't look.' He turned her to face him and held her close against the coarse wool of his jacket.

She wanted to stay there for ever, leaning against his solid body, embraced by arms so strong they had once carried her for a mile over rough ground to safety, arms that now held her firmly so she could not fall. She fumbled in her skirt pocket for a handkerchief to wipe her mouth as Daniel attempted to steer her away from the hut.

'Who – who is it?' Mariah choked.

No one answered.

'Who is it?' she cried.

Dora stood by the lifeless form. She had seen blood many times before. She was used to blood. Animal blood and human blood. But not blood like this, oozing from an inert body torn apart by shot. A close-range shot, if she was any judge.

She gazed at the wounds, shaking her head in disbelief. His face was peppered too. Contorted and peppered, but recognisable. She looked anxiously at Mariah and said, 'Come along, my dear. This is no place for you.'

'No!' Mariah struggled with Daniel until he was forced to release his hold or risk hurting her. She tore herself away from him and went into the hut.

She bent over the body, swallowing hard to keep down the bile rising in her throat. Dark blood spattered his still, pallid face.

Her voice was weak and small. 'No. Not Henry? This cannot be Henry.' She dropped to her knees, not caring about the blood, desperately trying to wipe away the spatters on his face. 'I know we quarrelled, but you were all I had left.'

Tears fell from her eyes and rolled down her face. She sat back on her heels. Her hands were smeared with blood. Her own brother's blood. Her head fell back and a prolonged low wail escaped from her throat.

Daniel picked her up and carried her out of the hut. He gently lowered her to the woodland floor, with a tree to support her back, and made her swallow some brandy from his hip flask. He called for Dora to fetch a blanket from the hut and laid it over her, tucking it around her back and legs. Two of his beaters had followed him to the hut.

Mariah's head began to swim and her mind became muddled. What was Henry doing, half clothed in the gamekeeper's hut? She had seen discarded breeches, fine gentlemen's breeches. Were they his? Mariah moved her lips to speak but no words came out.

Daniel handed Dora his flask. 'See she takes some more of this,' he directed. 'And keep her as warm as you can. I'll ask one of the beaters to bring round a dog cart and take you home. The other can fetch the constable.'

'Was it poachers again?' she asked. 'Revenge, perhaps, for the sheep-stealing business?'

'I doubt it. The Cluff clan never use guns. Knives are more their style. Besides, since that night, things have gone quiet over Mexton way.'

'Do you know what happened here?'

'No. Neither does Havers. But I have found a gun. Abandoned in the undergrowth.'

'Whose is it?'

Daniel glanced at Mariah. 'I don't know.' A straggle of Hall staff had appeared in the clearing and someone called his name. 'Look after Mariah.'

On hearing her name, Mariah looked up at Daniel. 'Don't go,' she whispered.

He did not hear her. He was already distracted by a beater asking him what he should do about Havers. Mariah stared after him. She didn't want him to leave her. Not now. Not ever.

Chapter 30

Bel was concerned for her party. 'Where is my brother? Where is he?' She circled around the clearing, surveying her guests. 'Has anyone seen him? He should be dealing with this. Not me.'

Their shooting party had been going very well until then. Now it was in danger of falling apart. Some young blood had fired off early, trying to impress one of the ladies, no doubt. But Havers would sort that out. If only Nathan were here to help her calm their guests.

A ripple of concern was spreading, as a result of that single wayward shot. A few of the gentlemen had detached themselves from the group and followed the track to see who it was. How tiresome! Impatiently, Bel stamped over to where the Hall servants and beaters were lounging, heads together in speculation. They ceased their murmurings as soon as she approached them.

She marched up to a man that she recognised as a gardener at the Hall. 'Find Havers for me. He went after that loose gun.'

The man scrambled to his feet and scurried away. She watched him go, then on impulse followed him down the track. Perhaps Nathaniel was with Havers dealing with the incident?

There were several gentlemen clustered around the game-keeper's hut when Bel arrived. Her head gardener was bending over a figure sitting propped against a tree. As she approached she realised it was Havers and his face was as white as a bedsheet. The gentlemen were standing about with serious expressions and murmuring to each other.

But it was the figure of the man who was commanding events that riveted Bel's attention. Who was he? She had not noticed him before. Judging by his dress he was not a guest. Not one of Havers' keepers either. She knew most of them by sight.

No, not one of the Hall's regular staff. He must be a beater. Had she seen him earlier, she wondered, having a drink with Havers? As she stared at him, taking charge and organising, she saw the kind of outdoor man she thought her brother should be, the man she hoped that, one day, he would become.

She could not take her eyes from him and became fascinated by his movements on the opposite side of the clearing. He was tall with dark hair and a well-built form. She could see he was a very capable man. A rugged man dressed in rugged clothes. She wanted to know who he was and why he had assumed command of the situation. She wished she could hear what he was saying.

Slowly she walked across the clearing until he noticed her. As soon as he did he came towards her, his arms outstretched to bar her progress.

'Miss Fitzkeppel! You should not be here. Please return to your party.'

Ignoring his request, she demanded, 'Who are you? What do you think you are doing?'

'Daniel Thorpe, miss. I am the supervisor at Bowes Ironworks. You really should be with your guests.'

She gazed at him. His clothes were scuffed and rumpled but they could not detract from his air of authority. He had a handsome face too, although his features were marred by a frown that darkened his eyes to the colour of smoke.

When she made no effort to respond, he continued, 'Your brother must cancel the afternoon shoot.'

'And who are you to tell my brother what he should do?' Bel demanded.

As she moved closer to converse with him, she examined the detail of his face, and wondered why she had not noticed him before. This curiosity distracted her from the surrounding disarray and an unfamiliar flutter began to spread through her veins. The murmurs and mutterings of bystanders faded in her ears as Mr Thorpe became the centre of her vision. This man was exciting to be near, she realised, and she had to try very hard to concentrate on his words.

'There has been an accident. A shooting,' he said.

'Yes, I heard the shot. We all did. Was it a poacher?'

'A guest, miss.'

'A guest? A loose gun? After one of the deer, no doubt. Is the quarry dead? Or has the poor thing fled to lick its wounds? We must find it quickly and put it out of its misery.'

He did not answer her but lifted his hands as though he were about to grasp her upper arms and hold her. Startled by his boldness, Bel's blue eyes widened, but she did not shrink back from him and was shocked to acknowledge a fleeting disappointment when his hands stopped short of her.

'Is your maid with you? You should have someone with you.'

'What are you talking about, Mr Thorpe?'

'There has been a shooting, miss.'

'Yes, yes. You said.'

'One of the guests has been shot.'

Bel's hand went immediately to her throat and her face contorted in horror. 'No! This cannot be? But who – how –?'

'An accident, I believe. Henry Bowes. My employer's son. He is dead, miss.'

'Dead? Henry, dead? No, surely not? Where is he? Let me see!' Bel moved to walk around him, but he stepped smartly to one side to stop her.

'No, Miss Fitzkeppel. Stay where you are, I beg of you. We shall be taking him away from here as soon as the constable arrives.'

'We?'

Daniel nodded in the direction of Havers, still slumped by a tree trunk. 'Havers asked me to take charge. As you can see, he is not well.'

Bel's eyes narrowed and she assessed the scene in front of her. The gamekeeper's hut with its door swinging open. One or two gentlemen were standing about, avoiding looking at her and speaking in low voices. Havers was clearly unable to answer any of her questions. She chewed her bottom lip. Whatever the explanation, Havers would blame himself for this accident.

Her expression deepened to a frown. 'I do not understand. Who shot him?'

'We do not know.' Daniel kept his hands hovering by her shoulders as though to protect her from the surrounding air. He took a deep breath. 'We must find your brother, Miss Fitzkeppel. No one knows where he is.'

'Nathaniel? You don't think he did this, do you? No, he would never – not Henry, never. You do not understand, they were friends, the very best of friends . . .' Then the implication of what she was saying overwhelmed her. Hysteria began to bubble up in her throat. 'But Nathan may be injured and dying somewhere!' She swayed. Not her beloved Nathan! No!

Mr Thorpe's hands supported her, held her. She felt their power through the close-fitted jacket of her shooting outfit. She was thankful he was there, solid and strong and keeping her steady as a nervous panic began to spread over her. 'I must find him. I must!' She began to struggle out of his grip, but he held her firm.

'Please calm yourself, Miss Fitzkeppel. I am sure he is not seriously injured. There was only one shot and poor Henry Bowes took the full force of that. But your brother may have been peppered and, like yourself, miss, he may well be very agitated and shocked. We need to find him quickly.'

His commanding tone sounded confident and she slowed her struggle. She stood face to face with him, acutely aware of his hands on her arms. The steely determination in his eyes made her blink.

No gentleman had ever looked at her like that before. In fact, if one had she would have been offended by his audacity, and told him so! But Mr Thorpe was different. And she felt different, too. An unfamiliar tingle coursed through her. She felt it spreading, making her insides tremble. Her mouth became parched and her vision became hazy. Try as she might, she could not move her limbs. She was going to faint! Here, in the woods. In front of her guests and the servants. Her eyes rounded and she appealed to him, mouthing the words, 'Help me.'

He gave her a gentle shake. 'Are you all right, Miss Fitzkeppel? Do you feel unwell? Will you sit a while?'

The movement revived her and her faintness ebbed. But she struggled to regain her composure. In a daze she answered mechanically, 'Quite well. Nathaniel, my brother, where is he?'

'We shall find him, have no fear. Indeed, he may have returned to the Hall already, and be waiting for you. Why don't you take your guests to the warmth of your drawing room? Let me call one of the gentlemen to walk you back to your party.'

Bel allowed herself to be steered away by Mr Thorpe's guiding arm. 'He was with Henry,' she muttered absently. 'I saw them together, at luncheon. He is all right, isn't he, Mr Thorpe?'

Daniel did not respond. Ezekiel Bowes had disappeared as well, and this worried him greatly. In the short time he had worked for him, Daniel had come to realise that Ezekiel Bowes, underneath his tough exterior, was a very troubled man.

Bel clutched at Daniel's thick, coarse jacket. 'You must find him, Mr Thorpe! You must find Nathan!'

Daniel managed a smile. 'I am sure he is not far away.' He gently removed her gloved hand. 'We shall search for him all afternoon.'

'Then you will come to the Hall this evening and tell me what you know.'

'I am afraid Mr Ezekiel Bowes will need me tonight.'

'Tomorrow then. After breakfast.'

'I have a furnace to fire up tomorrow. Your man Havers, I am sure, will be fully recovered by then.'

'Oh, look.' Bel heaved a great sigh. 'He is on his feet already.'

'He will be needing orders, miss, for the remainder of the day. Until we find your brother, you will have to talk to him.'

'Oh, oh yes, of course. I do that anyway. Nathan does not involve himself greatly in estate matters.' Bel turned on Daniel and clutched at his coat again. 'You will find him quickly, won't you? He is all I have in this world.'

Again, Daniel carefully detached her strong grasp from his clothes. 'Come along, Miss Fitzkeppel,' he said gently, 'your guests will be waiting for you.'

Across the clearing, the brandy spread through Mariah's veins and revived her. She watched this meeting between Daniel and Miss Fitzkeppel. She saw a robust man take charge of a difficult situation, and a beautiful lady clutch at him for support. A lady who seemed unwilling to let him go. A lady who looked as attractive as she did because of her new shooting outfit, an outfit that she, Mariah, had fashioned for her to accentuate her womanly contours. She noticed how Daniel stared after Miss Fitzkeppel as she was led back to her party and, at that moment, Mariah envied her beauty.

A pony and trap trundled into the clearing accompanied by the constable on horseback and Daniel's attention was distracted.

Mariah staggered to her feet. 'I want to go home. Will Daniel take us?'

'I don't think he can until he's spoken to the constable,' Dora replied. 'I'll ask the driver.'

Mariah clambered into the trap. She watched Daniel talk to the constable and hand over a shotgun, the gun that had killed Henry. He came over to the driver and stood by the pony's head while Dora climbed in beside her. Then he retrieved the blanket and handed it up to them.

As he did, Mariah asked, 'Where is Ezekiel? Have you seen him?'

Daniel shook his head ruefully. He wished he knew.

'Try not to worry,' he said. 'I'll be round to see you later.'

He signalled to the driver to move on and frowned deeply as he watched them trundle away.

By nightfall, Bel was exhausted. She had stood on the front steps of the Hall as the carriages, one by one, had taken her anxious guests away. She would not see them here again. Her plans were ruined. Fitzkeppel Hall would not recover from this. No wonder Nathaniel had fled. What vestige of a reputation she had tried to salvage for herself and her brother had disappeared with the smoke from that gun.

Havers was devastated. She did not blame him, though most of her guests did and, for that reason, would never visit the Hall again to hunt or shoot. Forlorn and rejected, Bel retreated to her bedchamber, where her luxurious new gown was laid out for the evening ball.

She sat there, too tired to climb into bed. She tied the ribbon fastenings on her nightgown and stared at her image in the glass. Her old nanny had unpinned her hair and brushed it for her until, after a second stifled yawn, Bel had sent her to her bed. The candles on either side of her looking glass were burning low. In the flickering light, she took a long, critical look at herself and shook her head slightly. Her party was over before it had begun.

But it was not all bad news. Nathan was alive. In shock, perhaps, and probably with friends by now, she guessed. She had not spoken with him herself. One of the grooms at the stables had seen him, blood-spattered and agitated, but not bleeding so much that he was unable to ride. He asked for a saddle on his best mount and left as soon as the horse was ready. He had many friends across Lincolnshire and Derbyshire from his school and university days.

Bel could not believe that Nathan had shot Henry, though

others did, she knew. Talk was rife, especially among the gentlemen, who became silent as soon as she approached them. Nathan had disappeared without leaving a message for her. Perhaps he would write a note to her when he was recovered.

She would not get any answers from him for a while, so Ezekiel Bowes was her only hope to throw some light on the incident but he was nowhere to be found. Did he know his son was dead? Or was he dead himself? Shot by the same gun as his son? The gun that had been hastily discarded at the scene. By whom? she wondered. She sighed. Poor Henry. She did not wholly approve of him as her brother's confidant, but they were the closest of friends and she grieved for that loss.

She hugged herself and closed her eyes. How she wished she had someone dear to hold her now! Mr Thorpe's image swam under her eyelids. A proper man, like Mr Thorpe, to hold her in his arms and soothe her agitation, a man she could cling to for support.

She wondered where she might find a man such as he to marry her. Certainly not among the suitors her chaperones had found! Or, indeed, at her shoot. Those who had shown an interest in her were already settled with wives and children. Was waiting for a widower all she could hope for now?

She wished Mr Thorpe were here, comforting her as he had done earlier. She had never met a man such as him before, so strong and so capable, and with eyes the colour of a leaden winter sky. She wanted his arms instead of her own around her.

She remembered how sturdy he had felt beneath his rough clothes and wondered how his firm body would feel beside her, dressed only in his nightshirt and she in her nightgown. She blew out the candles and removed the warming pan from her bed, placing it carefully in the hearth. The room would grow chilly quite soon as the fire was low. In the light of its embers she noted the sleeping draught left beside the bed by her physician.

She imagined Mr Thorpe climbing into bed beside her, his fine body, hard and strong. Perhaps he had a scar or two from his labours? He would lean over and kiss her on the lips, then cover her body with his. She imagined his weight pressing her into the feathers of her mattress. And then what? What came next? She was three and twenty and did not know. Perhaps she would never know? But her body yearned to be touched by Daniel Thorpe, to be adored by him, caressed by him. To be loved by him.

With a small, anguished cry she rolled over, picked up her draught and swallowed it in one.

Chapter 31

'It's only me, Aunty Dora.'

Mariah and Dora were sipping hot ale by the kitchen fire when Daniel came in through the scullery door.

Mariah was on her feet straightaway. 'Have you found out what happened?'

He shook his head. 'Ezekiel has not shown himself since the shooting. We must wait for the constable to speak with him.'

'I am sure it was an accident. I cannot believe that either he or Mr Fitzkeppel would have shot Henry,' Mariah declared. 'Do you think he had an assignation with a girl?'

'Possibly.'

'Does that mean the girl's father may have shot him – and the others as well?'

Daniel shook his head. 'The constable thinks not. There was no trail of blood and, apparently, Fitzkeppel was well enough to ride, but there has been no sign of Ezekiel apart from—' He stopped and looked uncomfortable.

'What? Tell me, Daniel.'

'It was his gun that was fired.'

'*Ezekiel's* gun?'

Daniel's discomfort continued. 'I am worried about him, Mariah.'

'I am sure you need not be. He is tough and—'

'He is a troubled man!'

'What do you mean?'

'Something ails him. I cannot explain it, but I know he is not at ease with himself.'

'Well, yes, he was a difficult person to live with. For me, anyway, because Henry was always his main concern.'

'That is why he will need you now.'

Mariah laughed harshly. 'You do not know him as I do! I am the last person he wants.'

'Can you not forget your quarrel with him? You are his daughter.'

'No, I am not.'

'I don't understand.'

Dora, who had been listening quietly until now added, 'Neither do I.'

Mariah inhaled deeply. 'I told your mother when I moved in with your family. I am not his child. My real father died before my mother could become his wife and she wed Ezekiel instead.'

'Does he know you are not his?'

'Oh yes. He was paid by her family to marry my mother. He never really wanted her. I have often thought his true love must lie elsewhere. But he chose money. Perhaps that is why he is so troubled.'

'Perhaps,' Daniel conceded.

Dora looked across to her nephew. 'What do you mean by troubled?'

Daniel shrugged. 'Tense and agitated all the time. He tries hard to suppress it, but then he becomes angry for no obvious reason.'

'Yes, that's him, all right,' Mariah responded dryly. 'I am really, truly sorry about Henry. Of course Ezekiel will be devastated by his death. But I am sure you will find him in his office at the ironworks. That is where he always goes when he is – er – troubled, as you say.'

'Will you not, at least, attempt a reconciliation?' Daniel pleaded. 'You carry his name.'

'A name he wishes me to be rid of! That is why he arranged for me to marry Mr Smith. He wants me off his hands and so I have obliged him. He cares only for Henry and his profits from the ironworks!'

'And now there is no Henry, will his profits from the ironworks matter to him?'

Mariah did not answer him. Without Henry, Ezekiel would have no one to leave the ironworks to and his lifetime of labour would have been in vain.

'You are his only kin now,' Daniel added gently.

Mariah shook her head. 'He has disowned me.'

'But the – the shooting has changed everything.'

There was a weariness in Daniel's voice that reached Mariah's heart. She met his eyes with sadness in her own. Why did circumstances between them have to be so difficult? She wanted to accept his help but did not know how.

Dora interceded. 'I do not think you should be pressing Mariah in this way, Daniel. She has just lost her half-brother.'

Daniel saw the anguish on Mariah's face and immediately regretted his actions. In desperation, he shook his head wordlessly.

'It's all right, Dora,' Mariah responded. 'Daniel is right.

Ezekiel is a wealthy man because of my mother's money. I have some questions of my own to ask him. If Ezekiel is willing to speak to me I shall come to his office.'

Daniel heaved a sigh. 'I shall send word as soon as he returns.'

'Will you have some warmed ale?' Dora asked.

'I cannot stay. There is too much on at the works.' He embraced his aunty and without thinking did the same to Mariah.

Surprised, Mariah allowed herself to be taken into his arms and let her hands creep around him, feeling the roughness of his jacket on her face and inhaling an unfamiliar masculine smell that quickened her pulse. She lingered, welcoming the solid strength of his body against hers. His hug tightened as though he did not want to let her go.

She did not know how long she stayed there, only that it felt right. Eventually he stepped back and when she looked at his face his eyes were brighter and searched hers with an enquiry she could not fathom.

And then he was gone and she wondered if she had imagined the warmth she had felt for those few seconds in his arms.

'Enter.'

The foreman at last, thought Daniel. He was in Ezekiel's office, completing the billing for the week and anxious to keep the furnaces going until Ezekiel decided to show his face at the ironworks again. He was sure to return by Saturday. For the men had to be paid on that day and the keys to the safe were always with Ezekiel.

The rustle of silk made him look up sharply. He closed the heavy ledger with a snap and hastily scraped back the chair to stand up.

'Miss Fitzkeppel! I was not expecting you!'

'Mr Thorpe.'

She stood motionless on the threshold, framed by the light from the open door. Her full skirts, partly covered by a plush velvet cloak, filled the doorway. He walked around the desk, repeating, 'Miss Fitzkeppel!' then adding, 'I am sorry, but Mr Bowes is not here.'

She stepped forward. 'I have come to see you, Mr Thorpe. May I come in?'

'Of course. Sit by the fire. It is a frosty morning. Will you take a little wine to warm you?'

'Thank you, yes.'

She sank into Ezekiel's buttoned leather armchair while Daniel closed the door against the cold and asked, 'Is there news of your brother?'

'I believe he is unharmed, thank God.'

Daniel took the cork out of Ezekiel's sherry wine and poured some into a pewter goblet. 'Then he is safe?'

'I can only assume so. He was well enough to ride.'

'Does he know where Mr Bowes has gone?'

'I have not seen my brother, Mr Thorpe, or spoken to him. I – he . . .' He saw her swallow and take a deep breath. 'On the afternoon of the shoot, he took one of the best horses from our stables and left.' She paused. 'I expect to hear from him – eventually – but,' she turned her pretty face upwards, 'I have to know what happened, Mr Thorpe. Why did my brother leave so hastily? You must tell me.'

He listened to her silently, noticing a few tendrils of fair hair escaping from her fine velvet bonnet. Her delicate skin glowed from the cold air, enhancing her features with youth-fulness rather than coarseness. Beside her, he felt very much an artisan in his working clothes. He poured himself a goblet of Ezekiel's wine and sat opposite her by the fire.

334

'Miss Fitzkeppel, I do not know any more than your man Havers. I cannot help you.'

'You do, you do! You must know something. It was something between the three of them, I am sure! You lived with Henry. You live with his father—'

'I work for Mr Bowes and I am here at the works more than I am in their house. I hardly knew Henry and he spent much of his time with you at the Hall, I believe.'

'Not with me. With my brother. Do you know of a quarrel, Mr Thorpe?'

Daniel covered his eyes with his hands for a moment and then faced her.

'I do not *know* anything, Miss Fitzkeppel. Except that Henry is dead and your brother has disappeared.'

'But Mr Bowes was there! He must know what happened!' she responded shrilly. 'Where is he?'

'Mr Bowes has not yet returned home. He may have witnessed the shooting. He may have—' Daniel stopped. Speculation was of no use here. The less Miss Fitzkeppel knew of this sad and sorry business the better. There were enough stories about Henry and Fitzkeppel going around the works already. He stood up and continued, 'I would like to help you, but I have to keep the ironworks going, and I—'

He stopped again as she rose and crossed the hearth to stand close to him. In the heat from the fire a female scent assailed his nose, a nostalgic mixture of womanliness and lavender. Not since Lily had he inhaled such an aroma.

She placed her gloved hands on his forearm. 'Mr Thorpe, I have no one else to turn to. At the shoot you were so – so – *capable*. Please help me. Please.'

He stared at her wide blue eyes, glistening with unshed

tears, and frowned. 'Very well. I shall do what I can for you, Miss Fitzkeppel. Please do not distress yourself.'

'Will you really? I shall be so very grateful.'

'I am sure Mr Bowes will return to his ironworks soon. If he witnessed the accident, he will be in some distress himself. Henry meant everything to him. He had such plans for him.'

'An accident, you say? You are sure this was an accident?'

'The constable would like to speak to Mr Bowes and your brother to assure himself it was so.'

'I am sure it was. Nathan would never harm Henry!'

'No, of course not.'

He watched her pretty face darken as she considered that he may have. Eventually she said, 'May I have a little more wine, Mr Thorpe?'

When she took the goblet from him, he noticed she was watching him carefully. She grasped the cup with both hands and held on to his fingers. Their heads were close together and she looked directly into his eyes. He gazed back evenly, his face expressionless and unemotional. But he felt stirrings that reminded him forcefully that he was a man, stirrings he had not experienced for some time.

For a fleeting moment he remembered the indulgence of those Sunday afternoons with Lily. Miss Fitzkeppel had a similar look about her, with hair the colour of honey, finely boned features and delicate skin. The soft kidskin of her gloved fingers rested lightly on his hand and he did not wish to withdraw it from her touch. It had been so long since he had considered a woman in this way that he had almost forgotten the desire. Until now.

Miss Fitzkeppel broke the lengthening silence. 'You will bring me news when you have it, Mr Thorpe? You will come to the Hall yourself?'

'I cannot leave the ironworks.'

'Then, may I visit you? I hear so little out at the Hall. The servants know more than I do. Please allow me to visit your office, sir.'

'That would be a little unorthodox, if I may say so, Miss Fitzkeppel.'

'At the least until I have news from my brother?'

'Very well.' He stepped back and gave a short bow. 'If you would excuse me, I have my duties to attend to.'

'Of course, Mr Thorpe. Thank you.' She took her leave gracefully, leaving a cloud of feminine scent that was hitherto unknown in Ezekiel Bowes' office.

Mariah arrived at the ironworks in time to see Miss Fitzkeppel walk carefully down the outside steps from the office to her waiting carriage. Her rich blue velvet cloak and matching bonnet were as incongruous with the grimy surroundings of the yard as were her elegant coach and matched pair of well-groomed horses. Mariah stayed outside the gates until the visitor had left. She guessed that Miss Fitzkeppel had wanted answers from Ezekiel too.

Inside the yard, Mariah was taken aback by the sight of the new crucible furnace and its wide brick chimney already smoking. She realised how long she had been away and wondered briefly if Daniel was working there, labouring and sweating in the heat. But as she looked up at the office window she saw his face, and not Ezekiel's, staring down. He had, no doubt, been watching Miss Fitzkeppel leave and she was reminded uncomfortably of the intimate exchange between this elegant lady and Daniel she had witnessed after the shooting.

He clattered down the stone steps to meet her. She wore

337

her good green gown with flannel petticoats underneath for it had been cold on the morning carrier cart. But her bonnet was plain and her cloak was old and worn. Its shabbiness would not have concerned her so much if the vision of Miss Fitzkeppel's blue velvet was not still clear in her mind.

She remembered Daniel's warm embrace and wondered if he did too. She thought not for he seemed agitated. 'Ezekiel has not returned,' he said. 'Where do you suppose he is?'

'I have no idea. Unless he has gone to one of his friends.'

'Of course! He may be with Mr Smith.'

'Or Mr Withers, his lawyer,' Mariah suggested.

'I'll send Ned to find out.'

'No, you need him here. I'll go.'

'Try Mr Withers first. He knows everything that goes on in this town.'

They stood for a moment staring at each other. Mariah realised this was the first time that she had felt a true bond with Daniel. They were united in their task. She was glad he was her friend in this respect but it was a strange feeling. She hurried out of the yard to the lawyer's office on the High Street.

'Wait there, Miss Bowes.'

The outer office of Mr Withers' High Street chambers was filled with very old, heavy oak furniture and piles of documents. Two young gentlemen, dressed in dark jackets and high-collared white shirts, were seated at tall tables by the window carefully copying documents with quill pens and ink. They looked up at her as she waited, then exchanged murmurs and smirks until Mr Withers' clerk came to fetch her. He led her upstairs to a large chamber overlooking the street. The furniture here was newer, polished and lighter in colour and form, and there were cupboards around the walls instead of open shelves.

'Please be seated.' Mr Withers took off his pince-nez and stared at her from across his desk. 'May I offer you my condolences, Miss Bowes. Master Henry was a fine young man.'

'Thank you, sir. Have you spoken to the constable? Do you know how he died?'

'I cannot say.'

Mariah felt her patience dwindling. 'What do you mean? You do not know or you will not tell me?'

'I cannot say.'

'Then perhaps you can say something about my father, Mr Withers? Mr Bowes has not returned home since the incident. Have you knowledge of his whereabouts?'

'Do not travel this road, Miss Bowes. I cannot tell you anything about your father's affairs.'

'We both know he has disowned me.'

'Do not press me! Would you have me break a client confidence?'

She half rose from her chair. 'Henry was my brother!'

Mr Withers looked uncomfortable. He must know she had lost her last blood relation in the Riding. However, she had not meant to become so agitated and sank slowly back into her seat.

He said, 'Are you destitute, Miss Bowes? Is that why you are here? I believe you have a comfortable home outside town and – and have obtained work at the Hall? Besides, your father did his duty and found a gentleman of means for you. You could have married Mr Smith, my dear.'

'Just as my father married a woman of means! I know it was my mother's dowry that bought him the furnace in the first place! Please tell me where I can find him.'

'I have given you my answer.'

'But you do know where he is?' she persisted.

Mr Withers heaved a sigh. 'No, I do not. I should like to speak with him as much as you do. Now, if that is all, would you kindly leave me to my work?'

Annoyed and frustrated, Mariah got up and walked to the door. As she opened it, he added, 'If ever you do find yourself destitute, Miss Bowes, you will come to these offices and speak to me.'

Surprised and puzzled, she shook her head irritably and left the building. She imagined herself making gowns for stout Mrs Withers to earn her keep and thought she might earn herself a good living doing so. If only she had premises! A room as large as her former workroom at the Hall. It would not take much of Ezekiel's money to purchase a lease. It galled her to think her mother had provided him with the means to prosper and she could not reap the benefit. She became even more determined to ask him about his plans for the future of the ironworks.

The warehouse man told her Daniel was in the crucible shed when she got back to the yard. She stood at the bottom of the steep stone steps as the bright glow of molten metal lit the interior. A nipper appeared from the coal store underneath the floor. His task was to keep the flues clear and make sure there was a good updraught for the furnaces. He was as black as the soot he swept.

'I must speak to Mr Thorpe.'

'Don't go up there, now, miss,' he advised. 'It's too dangerous.'

'But he is in there?'

'Aye. But 'e's big and strong and knows what 'e's doing.'

She caught a glimpse of Daniel through the doorway as he stepped back and carefully lowered the empty crucible to the floor. He wore a long leather apron and had a rag stuffed in his mouth. His face was darkened and reddened with the smoke and heat. He did not notice her.

'Don't distract him, miss. Not right now.'

'No, of course not. Would you give him a message from me? Tell him I could find out nothing. He'll understand.'

Mariah bought provisions before she went back to Dora's, a sack of flour, a cone of sugar and some sewing notions from the draper's shop. She heaved the sack onto her back to wait for the carrier. Dora would be pleased with the sugar and Mariah planned how she would decorate her plain bonnet with ribbons for her next visit to town, and make braiding to smarten up her cloak. She would be back. Ezekiel would have to show himself sooner or later and she could wait.

Chapter 32

When the gun had fired in that fetid hut, Ezekiel had seen only a cold blackness descending on him, enclosing him in its own private cage. He had thrown the gun away from him as though it were a serpent, and had lumbered away, his mind filled with the sights and sounds of his own private hell. He had not known where he was going, only that he must get away from that hut. He ran, stumbled and walked blindly, crashing through trees and brambles, unable to feel, hear or even think of the world around him.

Where had he gone wrong with Henry? He had tried so hard to leave his past behind and make something of himself for Henry's sake, to provide a way of life to be proud of. And now that life had crumbled before him. He had no son to be proud of any more, no future in the Riding. He should never have married Amelia, should never have been tempted by the money. He was just a boy then, obeying his elders and betters who knew what was best for him . . .

★ ★ ★

As a youth, Ezekiel had been a strong, handsome lad – everyone said so. A natural son whose mother had died in childbirth. She had been a servant in an ironmaster's house in the North Riding and never told a soul who his father was. But he had been lucky. His mother had been a good worker, a favourite in the servants' hall, so she had not been sent to the poor-house as others in her unfortunate position had been. She bore a healthy, robust lad, and lads were always useful in the quarry or the foundry. He was brought up in the servants' hall, spoiled by attention from young maids and older matrons alike.

Well fed and properly shod, he grew straight and sturdy and at the age of ten was sent to work in the quarry, extracting the sandstone that was used in foundry work for iron-casting moulds. On Sundays, he went to school with other young-sters from the families who worked for the ironmaster and learned to read and write. When he was fourteen he was moved to the foundry, working on the steam hammers, forging the iron into cannon to fight the Frenchies. He was a good lad, loyal and willing, and he was favoured. On Wednesdays and Saturdays he was allowed to join the ironmaster's own chil-dren at their lessons with the rector.

The rector was one of the gentry, the second son of their local landowner, and he took his church responsibilities seri-ously. An educated man, he encouraged learning for all the children in his care. Ezekiel learned the Bible, right from wrong and the way of things. Most of all, he learned his place. He had no right to anything, he was a natural son, a bastard the men at the foundry called him, and he must be grateful to his masters, the ironmaster, the quarry master, the foundry master and the schoolmaster. Ezekiel *was* grateful and he felt proud to be allowed to learn. He was able and earned praise from his masters.

The rector gave lessons in the church vestry and the iron-master's children scampered off for their tea as soon as they were finished, but Ezekiel was a servant and stayed to clear away the books. He became the rector's right-hand help in the classroom, setting out the books and cleaning up the vestry afterwards.

At sixteen the rector trusted him enough to leave him with the keys to the vestry when he went back to the rectory for his supper. Ezekiel polished the table and swept the floor before returning the keys.

One evening the rector asked Ezekiel to join him for supper and conversation. He cut him a generous slice of pie, offering him pickles and relish and sliced the bread himself. There was cheese, too, and ripe pears in a bowl. And wine. The rector kept Ezekiel's glass topped up with wine until its warmth spread through his veins down to his toes and he smiled and relaxed. He gazed at the polished wood of the table, littered with crumbs and debris from the meal, and thought how much he could enjoy the life the gentry led. He felt special. He watched the red and yellow flames leaping from the coals in the fire and felt an affinity for their destiny. Burning, yearning, reaching through the blackness of the unknown for their freedom. The rector's arm crept around Ezekiel's shoulders and his fingers probed the muscles of his arm.

'So young and so strong,' the rector murmured. 'Take off your jacket.'

Ezekiel's private flames searched through their darkness. His heart began beating strongly in his breast. He obeyed.

'And your waistcoat.'

Ezekiel did so, then loosened his tie.

The rector's hand stilled his. 'No. Allow me to do that.'

The desire racing through his young body was almost

344

unbearable. He was aroused in a way he had not known possible. His skin felt alive as the rector removed his shirt and under-shirt and caressed his chest. The rector led him to the rug before the fire and kissed him. Their mouths joined and he tasted wine and mustard as their tongues entwined and his arousal pushed inside his breeches.

He was overtaken by a rising urgency as the rector's hands and mouth moved downwards. Kissing and caressing until Ezekiel thought he would burst. He had suppressed this desire for so long, telling himself it was wrong. How could this be wrong? They were as one, united in their fervour. In all his young life Ezekiel had never felt so happy, so fulfilled, and so loved.

He hardly remembered what happened afterwards, except that the rector had said, 'We shall not talk of this. You will tell your master I wish to give you extra tuition, so you may help me with lessons in the schoolroom. Every Wednesday and Saturday. Do you understand?'

'Yes, sir.' Ezekiel felt his excitement rise again. The rector wanted his body as much as he coveted the rector's. There would be a next time. And another after that.

He was in love.

How could Ezekiel imagine it would last? The other youths at the foundry, already jealous of his favoured treatment, began to push him around and call him names. Encouraged by older men in the works they set about him one night, beating him viciously until he lay senseless on the ground. The ironmaster found him and sent for his own surgeon. While Ezekiel lay, barely conscious, in his bed, the ironmaster made his own enquiries among his men.

'You listen to me, lad,' the ironmaster said later. 'You've been a good 'un so far and I reckon you've been led astray by them who should know better.' For a moment his face softened. 'Aye, you've been led astray like your ma was afore you. Any road, you're going away from 'ere.'

Going away? From everyone and everything he knew and loved?

'I'll set you up with a wife and child and enough to buy a share in your own concern.'

A wife and child? He did not want a wife and child.

'There's one condition.'

When he did not respond, the ironmaster went on, 'You never show your face or theirs around here again. Never visit, never write, never ask for nowt else.'

'I don't want to go away,' he protested miserably.

'There'll be no argument. You'll not go near my children, or the schoolroom again. And you won't be safe at the foundry or the quarry either. You'll pack a box and marry this lass as soon as I can arrange it.'

'What lass?' he muttered.

'It just so happens that my wife 'as a cousin who 'as a problem she needs sorting. The lass is not wed and she already 'as a bairn in her belly. So you won't have to touch her if she's not to your taste. With any luck the bairn'll be a lad to inherit your works, but you'll have to take that chance. You're to go over to her parish and be wed, then take the stagecoach south.'

'And never come back here?' he asked quietly.

'Never! You were not an innocent in this. If you had not been willing, none of this evil would have happened.'

Tears welled in Ezekiel's eyes.

'And don't look so miserable. You're a lucky devil, that's what you are! Without my connections you'd be on the gallows for what you've done!'

It was twenty years ago now. As Ezekiel prospered, he tried

346

to forget about those earlier times. Amelia was no help to him. If his firstborn had been a son, his life would have been more tolerable. But Amelia's baby was a girl.

'A girl!' He had shouted when Mariah was born. He had wanted a son so much. A son would have given him a proper reason for marrying Amelia, but he was tied to her now. It was God's punishment for his sins. He hated the Church for what it had done to him! He managed to lay with her the once and she bore him Henry. After that she had served her purpose and he wanted nothing more to do with her.

The ironmaster had been a man of his word, and gave him papers including a banker's promissory note that had bought him a share in a rundown cementation furnace. He was too young to hold the stake himself and it was held by a legal man, until he was twenty-one. He and Amelia lived with one of the partners in the house by the furnace yard and Ezekiel worked hard.

He laboured every waking hour at the furnace to make the best blister steel in the South Riding. He bought good Swedish iron and cooked it long and slow with charcoal, checking the fires himself until it was ready. His steel was reliable and his reputation grew. He sold it to big forges with contracts for the new railways.

His partners were old men and the one he lived with was already dying when he arrived. He planned to buy them out one day with a mortgage from the bank. It was a decent house to live in, built for an ironmaster and he settled well. He had insisted on separate bedchambers when he wed Amelia as she was with child. Anyway, he knew the gentry lived like that, and he was going to live like the gentry. One day . . .

Ezekiel forced his way through the undergrowth of Keppel wood, the brambles tearing at his smart new tweeds. He could not go on like this. He had tried. Lord, how he had tried! He had tried to bury his sinful ways when he had left that forge in the North Riding. He had not tolerated any such behaviour or inclination in his men. He had kept away from temptation and had rid his works of anyone who might test his resolution.

But his befuddled mind was overcome by how he had felt when he had opened the door of the gamekeeper's hut. He had faced a scene of manly love within, a love he had rejected. No one knew how desperately he had battled with his desires.

He had had such plans for Henry. And that – that, oh God, that *fop* of a man who called himself *gentry*, had used his son in the same way that the rector had used him. Not Henry! Please, not Henry! What had he done? What had he done to Henry? Without Henry, his life was empty, a deep, dark void of hollowness and sorrow.

Ezekiel stumbled on, in blackness and despair, until he came to the cut, the narrow waterway from Keppel pit to the canal and ironworks in the town. He sank to his knees by the silent brown water and grieved. He grieved for his son and for himself. He grieved for the way he was – a sinner who could not repent and who had to pay the price for his sin.

When he came to his very own Rubicon he knew what he must do and he did not flinch. The devil spawns devils. He would be welcome in hell.

Chapter 33

'I thought I heard a horse in the lane, Dora?' Mariah continued to knead her bread dough.

Dora looked up from plucking a fowl in the scullery. The hen had been a good layer, but was past it now and she would make a rich stew with some barley and field mushrooms. 'I'll go and look.' She put aside the half-plucked hen and went to peer out of the front-room window.

'It's our Daniel!' she exclaimed, as she hurried back to the kitchen. 'Very smart he looks too. On a black hunter. Is that Ezekiel's horse?' She took off her apron. 'Have I got any feathers in my hair, Mariah?'

'Come here.' Mariah took a damp cloth from the scullery and wiped away the down from Dora's bodice. 'There. Shall I get him some refreshment?'

'Please. It's a cold morning so you'd best mull some of that ale to warm him through.'

Mariah quickly took off her pinny, dusted the flour from

her grey gown and straightened her cap. When Daniel followed Dora into the kitchen she was heating ale over the fire.

'You'd better let me finish that,' Dora said, elbowing her out of the way, 'it's you he wants to see.'

Mariah turned around with an enquiring expression. She thought he looked very handsome in his brown riding boots and hacking jacket and guessed Ezekiel had lent him his hunter to come over here. So her stepfather had returned home at last! Her hopeful air faltered when she saw his face, serious, unsmiling, sombre even. She became alarmed.

'What is it? What news have you?'

'Sit down, Mariah. I am afraid it is not good.'

'Is this about Ezekiel? Henry's death *was* an accident, wasn't it?'

His composure wavered and the silence lay heavy in the air as he tried to find the words. Mariah sat down by the kitchen table, frowning, and said quietly, 'Tell me what has happened.'

He inhaled deeply. 'There is no easy way to say this. Ezekiel is dead.'

'Dead? No! But how? When?' Mariah rested her brow on her hand. Not Ezekiel! He was a strong man, hard working and always in good health. She had not expected him to die. Had he been injured himself in the shooting? Her shoulders sagged. Even in her quarrel with Ezekiel and in her condemnation of his ways, she had never wished him *dead*. Her head felt hot but tears did not threaten. A dull emptiness crept over her. He had been a hard man but he had been the only father she had known and now he was gone.

'How?' she repeated. 'How did he die?'

'He was drowned. In the Keppel cut.'

'I do not understand,' she frowned. 'He was a man of sober ways. How could that happen?'

Daniel half rose to his feet and stretched out a hand towards hers. When she made no similar move he thought better of his actions and sank back into his chair. 'You must be strong about this, Mariah. He – he was found downstream, caught up in the lock where the cut meets the canal. He – he had—' Daniel stopped and inhaled again. 'He had filled his pockets with rocks.'

'No! Surely not? Ezekiel would not have done such a thing! I do not understand,' she repeated. 'Ezekiel was strong in mind and body. How could this be so? Why would he *do* that?'

Daniel went on, 'Of course, we cannot be sure. But the constable believes he was, somehow, to blame for his son's death. It was his gun, you see, that fired the shot. And – and now, now, this.' Daniel exchanged a grimace with his aunty. 'The constable has concluded your brother's death was an accident, but one that he, your stepfather, had caused and – and he could not live with his guilt.'

'Then he has spoken, also, with Mr Fitzkeppel? Did *he* see what happened?'

'Mr Fitzkeppel has left the Riding. He is with friends in Lincolnshire.'

'Oh.' He has run away, Mariah thought. Why would he do that if he was not to blame in some way? He was Henry's friend. He should have stayed and talked to the constable.

'Mr Withers has sent a message asking him to return.'

Dora poured the hot ale into a tankard for Daniel and said, 'I'll fetch Mariah a drop of brandy. I could do with one as well.'

Mariah felt a weariness take over her. Now she could never ask Ezekiel about the future of the ironworks. Mr Withers was her only hope and his lips were firmly sealed. What would happen to the works now?

Mariah gazed at Daniel. The furrows in his brow and the downturn of his mouth aged him. But he was watching her closely and she thought that his anxiety, now, was not for himself; it was for her. She was grateful he had taken the trouble to ride over here, even though this news was so dreadful, and managed a small rueful smile of gratitude. A light came into his eyes that seem to burn right through her and, somehow, it gave her strength.

Dora returned with the brandy and the moment was lost.

But Mariah did not forget it and she knew she was fortunate to count Daniel as her ally. 'What will happen to the ironworks?' she asked.

'I am to see Mr Withers in his offices this afternoon.' He stood up and as she raised her head she saw again, for a brief moment, the fire in his eyes. 'You will think about coming home, Mariah?' he said.

'It is not my home,' she answered dismally, 'and whoever is fortunate enough to inherit it will not want me there.'

'Who will inherit?' Dora queried.

'I have no idea.' Mariah shrugged. 'I am sure Mr Withers will tell Daniel later, and I am certain that, whoever he is, he will not wish to know me.'

'It should be yours,' Daniel said quietly.

'Yes, it should!' Mariah suddenly felt angry. 'Without my mother and the child she was carrying, there would have been no Bowes Ironworks!'

'I am so sorry—'

'Don't be! My mother may not have had an income of her own to leave me, but she left me a far greater gift and one that nobody can take away! Miss Fitzkeppel continues to give me commissions. Only last week she sent over a length of woollen cloth and a plain bonnet for me to make a shoulder

352

cape and bonnet trimmed with matching ruches and bows. It is to be a gift to Mrs Havers from her mistress. Others will follow her example and I shall earn my keep quite well here in Dora's front room. I am happy living with Dora.'

Daniel pursed his lips and nodded. He left shortly afterwards to keep his appointment with Mr Withers. Dora followed him to the front door and spent several minutes talking to him before he rode away. When she returned to her kitchen, Mariah's cheeks were bright spots of pink and her eyes were bright.

'It does help to weep at times like this,' Dora suggested.

'I wept for my mother and for Henry, but I cannot weep for him. Let his friends lay Ezekiel Bowes to rest and remember him at his wake,' she said.

'A funeral is no place for a woman anyway, so they'll not expect you.' She poured Mariah more brandy and added, 'Do not make any hasty decisions, though. Mourning is a useful retreat for reflection.'

Mariah drank quickly and set down her glass. 'I have had enough of mourning. I have spent too many months grieving. The bread will be ready for the oven and I have Mrs Havers' cape and bonnet to finish.'

As Mariah busied herself with these tasks, her anger simmered. Why should some distant cousin or local worthy be given what was rightly her own inheritance? It was not unheard of for women to inherit when there were no male descendants. But, she reflected, those ladies were, no doubt, good-living wives and daughters who had not been disowned or discredited in any way. It was ironic, she fumed, that obedience was the price a woman had to pay for such independence.

Mariah found it difficult to concentrate on her tasks. Daniel's words echoed in her head. She had a right to know what would happen to the ironworks! Surely Mr Withers could not refuse to impart his knowledge of Ezekiel's affairs now. He may have disowned her during his life, but whether he liked it or not she was his daughter in the eyes of the law.

After two days of useless fretting, her patience gave way and she took the carrier into town to call on Mr Withers again.

He was not at his offices. He had just left to call on Mr Thorpe who was reluctant to leave the yard while the new crucible furnaces were firing. If she hurried she might catch him there. She was out of breath when she reached the top of the steps outside the warehouse at Bowes Ironworks. She opened the heavy door and almost fell into the office, her cloak half off her back, her cheeks pink from running and her bonnet and hair awry.

'Mr Withers! I must speak with you,' she gasped.

'Mariah, what is the matter?' Daniel was standing by Ezekiel's desk. His face was sooty and his hair dishevelled as though he had just left his furnaces. Mr Withers was handing him some keys, the ones Ezekiel had always carried with him. Daniel put the keys onto the desk and came towards her. 'Calm yourself. Come, sit by the fire and catch your breath.'

She shrugged away his proffered hand and approached the older gentleman.

Mr Withers smiled at her. 'You have saved me a journey, Miss Bowes, for I was coming to see you this afternoon.' He steered her towards a chair by the fire.

'Are those my father's keys?' she asked as she untied her cloak.

Daniel answered. 'Yes. They were on his body when he was found and the constable has just released them. I need them urgently to pay the men's wages, and – and the bank is calling for payment.'

Withers addressed Daniel, 'Are you able to deal with that?'

'Yes, sir. Mr Bowes gave me full responsibility for the accounts.'

Withers turned his attention back to Mariah. 'Miss Bowes, you should know that I have your father's will in my possession and he has appointed me as one of the trustees for his estate. I was about to explain this to Mr Thorpe when you burst in on us.'

'Please continue, sir,' Daniel asked, 'I have no secrets from Miss Bowes.'

Mariah flashed him a grateful smile.

Mr Withers continued, 'Mr Bowes' intention was to leave a thriving ironworks to his son in the hope that he would wish to continue to make steel and, eventually, pass on the works to his grandsons. But Henry, God rest his soul, did not have the makings of an ironmaster and Mr Bowes harboured concerns about his future. With this in mind, he added a clause to his will after he employed Mr Thorpe. Should Mr Bowes be taken from this world before Henry came of age, he appointed Daniel Thorpe as a second trustee for the ironworks, as long as Mr Thorpe remained employed as supervisor at his works.'

'Daniel! Did you know this?' Mariah exclaimed.

'No. It is as big a surprise to me as it is to you. Mr Withers, is there provision for Mariah?'

'He believed Miss Bowes would be married,' Mr Withers answered warily.

'I did not care for his choice of suitor.'

Withers shook his head slowly and Mariah sighed. Ezekiel's legacy to her had been Mr Smith. Mr Withers would view

355

marriage to a well-set-up widower like Mr Smith a good match for the daughter of a man with no background or connections.

'Yes, he told me you were headstrong,' Mr Withers added, as though it explained her misfortune.

'Well, I am not destitute, sir. I can provide for myself and I shall not be a drain on the parish.' But even as she said the words, Mariah realised how close she had come to the poor-house. She had known what it was like to see it as her only solution. Without Dora, she would have had to go there, in her degradation and shame. She stared into the fire.

Mr Withers arranged to return and talk further with Daniel after he had been to see Ezekiel's bankers. Before he left he said, 'Miss Bowes, as you are in town, I should be obliged if you would call on me at my offices later. Good day to you both.'

When he had gone, Daniel picked up the keys. 'This does not seem right to me. You should have these. Here, take them and open the safe.'

'No.' Mariah was emphatic. 'Please do not taunt me with what could never be. It was Mr Smith or nothing for me, and I chose nothing.' She held her head high but there were tears in her eyes.

Daniel's face took on a hurt and haunted expression. 'Tell me how I can help you, Mariah?' he pleaded.

He could take me in his arms and hold me as he had done at Dora's, she thought. That would help, but it was not what he meant. There was nothing he could do for her now. She had made her choice and she must live with it. She said, 'You are not responsible for me. Your duty is to the ironworks and the new owner.'

He became impatient with her and demanded, 'Why do you always reject my friendship so?'

Mariah frowned. Is that what he thought? Perhaps she had in the past because she did not want his pity. But she, no *they*, were through that now. The past was gone. She welcomed his friendship. She wanted to reach out her hand and touch him and say so. But she feared that she wanted more from his friendship than he was prepared to give and hesitated.

'Forgive me,' she said, 'I am overwrought by these events.'

He took a step forward. 'Of course. I understand.'

He reached towards her with his hands. She looked at them. Large, capable hands, grimy from his morning's work. His shirt-sleeves were rolled back and his forearms were sooty. She thought that, more than anything, she wanted those arms around her, holding her close to him, so close she would be able to feel the beating of his heart against hers.

But he would never want to hold her so, knowing what he did about her shame. Friendship was all that she could hope for and her face fell. She shrank from his touch and he noticed.

He gave a nervous laugh and stepped back. 'I am forgetting my manners. You do not want soot on your gown.'

Would he have taken her in his arms? She would never know. But she thought even if she were dressed in one of Christobel Fitzkeppel's silken ball gowns she would not have been bothered by a little soot. The image in her head excited and shocked her at the same time. She wanted to feel the strength of his back under her exploring hands, and to kiss him. She wanted so much more from him than he would give her and she was stupid even to contemplate the idea.

She said, 'I shall detain you no longer. I came here on impulse and it was foolish of me. There is nothing here for me now. Except . . .'

'Yes?'

She thought of Henry's patronising ideas about her, of Ezekiel's domineering ways and of Mr Smith and said, 'Except bad memories.'

'Does that include Emma?'

'No, of course not.'

'Then stay for your dinner. Emma would be pleased to see you.'

'Thank you.' She looked around the office, with its cupboards full of ledgers and its battered furniture. 'I wonder who will inherit,' she murmured.

He said abruptly, 'Whoever it is, you are always welcome here while I am employed as supervisor.'

He was being kind, and Mariah felt her emotions threaten to overcome her. Daniel and his family were everything Ezekiel and Henry had not been to her. They had taken her into their home and into their hearts without question. She took her leave quickly and went to the house to see Emma.

The kitchen was warm and smelled deliciously of a simmering stew. A wave of sadness swept over her as she remembered her childhood days, kneeling on a stool at the table and helping her beloved mother cook the dinner.

Emma was washing up her mixing bowl in the scullery. 'Mariah, how are you? Such dreadful news about Mr Bowes, I am so sorry.' She came through the open door drying her hands. 'This is all too much for you. Take off that cloak and sit by the fire. Will you have some dinner with me? There's mutton stew nearly ready. Daniel will have his later. He's staying in the yard today. That new crucible shed takes up all his waking hours nowadays.'

Mariah told Emma about the will. 'There is to be a new owner. Mr Withers is calling back after his visit to the bank and I am to go to his offices later.'

'Perhaps Mr Bowes remembered you after all?'

'I doubt it. Mr Withers did not give me any hope.'

Mariah draped her cloak over a chair and sat on the fender warming her hands. The kitchen had not changed much since she had left. Unlike the rest of the house. After they had eaten, she toured the rooms with Emma and marvelled at the beauty and craftsmanship of the new furnishings. She recognised the influence of Fitzkeppel Hall in Henry's choice of carpets and curtaining. The ironworks must be making much more than she realised to afford all this.

'What happened to the old furniture?'

Emma grinned at her. 'The attics are filled with it. Do you want to see them?'

'Not today. I've got to meet Mr Withers and do some marketing before the carrier leaves.'

Mariah collected her cloak and set out for the High Street.

Mr Withers saw her approaching through his upstairs window, and called down the stairs when she opened the outer door. 'Come straight up, Miss Bowes.'

A formal document was spread out on his polished desk and a second glance told Mariah it was Ezekiel's will. She sat opposite Mr Withers, composed herself as best she could, and waited for him to speak.

'Your father made changes to his will after your mother died,' he began. 'He provided for a trust in Henry's favour. He came to see me when Henry finished his schooling as it was clear his son did not aspire to be an ironmaster. He wanted to be sure Henry would inherit a profitable concern and Mr Thorpe was essential to that end. Hence his trusteeship. Do you understand this, Miss Bowes?'

'Yes, sir. Though I do not see any relevance to me.'

'A gentleman of Mr Bowes' standing would not have wished for you to become a burden on the parish and an embarrassment to his son. Your father took my advice and allowed for the trust to provide for you, should you become destitute.'

'I see. However, as you know, sir, I am not destitute.'

'No, Miss Bowes. But the will acknowledges you as his daughter. So you were not disowned in the end.'

She shrugged. It was small comfort to her if the ironworks went to someone else.

'You are therefore his heir, Miss Bowes.'

'I beg your pardon?' The surprise was evident in Mariah's voice.

'You are his only surviving relative.'

'There – there's no one else? No cousins in the North Riding?'

'No one, I assure you.'

'Do you mean I shall inherit the house and yard?'

He nodded.

Her mother's dowry had not been in vain! The ironworks were hers. She would make sure they thrived. With Daniel's help she would make the best steel in the Riding. She could hardly believe it! 'Surely Ezekiel would not have wanted that?' she ventured.

Mr Withers got up and crossed the room to a small table. 'I tried to explain that Henry could die first, but he would not even contemplate it. Will you take a glass of sherry wine, Miss Bowes?'

'Thank you. Is this true? Bowes Ironworks really do belong to me?'

'Not exactly. I am afraid it is not all good news.' He handed her a small glass half full of amber liquid. 'It is, of course, in trust until you are one and twenty.'

'Yes, I understand that. Mr Thorpe and your good self are my trustees. Does he know I am to inherit?'

Mr Withers nodded. 'I spoke to him first.'

She wondered how Daniel felt about this. She guessed his new responsibility would change his attitude towards her. His dutiful concern for her would likely make him even more paternal. Just as she thought they might have become closer; the fancy evaporated. That's all it was, she thought sadly, a fancy.

She did not want Daniel as her trustee, being a dutiful guardian and watching over her. She wanted to be his equal. She wanted to be a part of the ironworks with him. She could not make the steel as he did with his labourers, but she could work with him in the countless other things he did to keep their output flowing.

Their output. Hers and Daniel's.

She looked up at Mr Withers as she took the wine. His face was sombre and she realised this was not a celebration.

'You have more to tell me, sir.' She frowned.

'I am afraid so. I visited your late father's bankers today. He borrowed heavily to build his new furnace and has not been making any repayments. Unless cash is forthcoming immediately, the bank will foreclose on the mortgage. Your ironworks are bankrupt, Miss Bowes. I am sorry, but, as your trustee, I shall be selling them, and the house, at the earliest opportunity.'

Mariah's heart sank into her boots. She had come so close to her dream. 'But there must be a way to keep them! Can you not sell the house? The furnishings alone will surely—'

'I have considered all the options. Many of the new fittings have not been paid for and will be removed by the suppliers immediately.'

'The house?'

'It is of little value without the works. I agree it is a fine house, but who would live there unless they had an interest in the adjoining yard? Mr Thorpe has said he will stay on without wages and keep the furnaces firing in the hope we can find a buyer soon.'

'But he cannot work without pay! He supports a sick father! He has a mother and sisters—'

'Do try and stay calm, Miss Bowes. I am optimistic about a sale. If all goes well, the works will continue to make steel and there will be monies over to provide you with a small annuity.'

'I don't want an annuity. I want the ironworks,' she said stubbornly.

And Daniel, she thought. I want Daniel as well. This realisation surprised her. But the more she thought about it, the more determined she became that he must be a part of her future.

Mariah hardly remembered buying soap and beeswax for Dora, or her ride home. Her head was too full of tumbling thoughts. She could not, *would not,* let her trustees sell the works that had begun with the wealth her mother had brought to the Riding. It was her birthright and she wanted them. She had to find a way to keep them. And Daniel.

Chapter 34

'Fetch the horses, Ned. Have you got the harnesses?' Daniel was supervising the men as they loaded a shipment of crucible steel onto a dray for the start of the journey to Sheffield. The rain that had begun before noon had persisted and it was already growing dark.

'Right you are. The stable lad is just on his way. But Miss Emma called me over and sent me to tell you there's someone to see you at the house. A lady.'

'Who is it? Did Emma say?'

'Only that she wished to see you personally.'

Mariah, he guessed, come to talk about the future of the works.

'All right, Ned. I'm relying on you to keep that canvas in place and get those ingots loaded onto the barge. See you get a signature on the docket when the bargeman takes delivery at the wharf. Do you hear me, lad?'

'Yes, Mr Thorpe.'

'And don't forget to lock the warehouse.'

'No, Mr Thorpe.'

Daniel surveyed the scene in front of him. His steel was as good as any man could get from crucibles, and his output, though low, was reliable. But he had seen the figures and Mr Withers was right. Ezekiel had overstretched his credit. He had borrowed to fund Henry's ambitious plans as well as the new furnace. Bankruptcy was looming.

He feared for the future of the yard and the livelihoods of the men he supervised. With his present output, he could pay the bank or pay the men but not both. He was trapped. He could not afford enough men to work the crucibles to full capacity. Damn Ezekiel and his social-climbing son! If no buyer for the works came forward soon, he'd have to lay off his gang.

'Emma said not to keep the lady waiting, Mr Thorpe.'

'Right you are. Get yourself off, then.'

Daniel sprinted across the ironworks yard, past the warehouse and office and through the gate in the wall to the garden. He stopped in the scullery to take off his waistcoat and wash his face and neck. He kept a jacket for the house on a peg behind the door and shrugged into it, raking his fingers through wet hair and smoothing down his damp trousers. Emma was slicing cabbage at the kitchen table.

'Where is she, Em?'

'In the study. There's a good fire. She said you were expecting her.'

'Did she?' He stopped outside the door to draw breath and then opened it with a flourish.

For a second, he was speechless. 'Miss Fitzkeppel! I – er – I had not expected *you*.'

She rose to her feet in a rustle of blue silk and petticoats. 'You agreed that I may call on you?'

364

'In my office. I agreed to see you in my office, at the works.'

'I recall, sir, that you found my presence there a little uncomfortable.'

'I am a busy man, miss. What do you want of me?'

'Mr Thorpe, please do not vex me. My servants were whispering in corners this morning. I understand there is news of Mr Bowes. What have you to tell me?'

Daniel sighed. Emma had taken her cloak and Miss Fitzkeppel swished restlessly around the small study, fingering her silken cape and bonnet. 'Please sit down, Miss Fitzkeppel. I am sure Mr Withers will tell you all you need to know.'

'That is my point, Mr Thorpe. Withers communicates only with my brother. Who is in Lincolnshire, if you please. He does not think *I* need to know anything.'

'Your brother would be very wise to stay there until this sorry affair is forgotten,' he snapped. He regretted it the moment he had said it, having no desire to increase Miss Fitzkeppel's agitation. 'However,' he added, 'I believe his reputation is safe. The body of Ezekiel Bowes was found in – in your cut, and the constable has concluded that he was responsible for the accident to Henry.'

Miss Fitzkeppel seemed to shrink before his eyes. She sank into one of the chairs and whispered, 'So it is true, then? Henry's father really is dead?'

'Yes. And your brother, apparently, is cleared of any involvement.'

This seemed to cheer her a little and she murmured, half to herself, 'Perhaps Nathan will come home now.'

Daniel had no more to say to her and hoped she would leave. But, after an awkward pause, she inhaled deeply and continued, 'So, what will you do, Mr Thorpe? Will you continue at Bowes Ironworks?'

365

'Why should I not?'

'Why, because, without Henry to take over, I imagine it will be sold, of course!'

So that was why she was here. He watched the flames licking and cracking round fresh coals. He said, 'Well, I am sure that Bowes Ironworks is too small to be of interest to your brother.'

'I have not come to see you about the ironworks.' She began to loosen the ties on her cape. 'It is warm in here. Do you not find it warm?' She took off her blue silk and white lace cape to reveal a matching bodice, close fitted and decorated with pleats and lace trims. The neckline was cut very low and she wore no lace to cover the swell of her breasts. Neither had she adorned herself with a necklace and her smooth ivory throat moved slightly as she swallowed. She leaned forward to stand up and, for a moment, Daniel was captivated by the fluidity of her body.

Her bonnet carried the same pleating and white lace as her bodice and slowly she undid its ribbon fastenings until they fell softly onto her white skin, skin that trembled gently as she moved towards him in a warm haze of womanly scent.

He hoped he was mistaken by her demeanour, but when he noticed a gentle smile playing around her lips he knew he was not. The heat was rising in his cheeks and he held his breath.

'The fire is high. Are you not warm, sir?' she said again.

Daniel did not respond. He was momentarily mesmerised by the pale velvet of her throat, the swell of her breasts and the dark valley between them that descended beneath her gown.

'May I call you Daniel?' she suggested softly. 'I do hope so because I have a proposition I believe will interest you. Shall we sit down?'

Her wide blue eyes reminded him of Lily. He had never experienced such behaviour in a woman of her standing.

'What do you want of me, Miss Fitzkeppel?'

'You are so formal, Daniel. Will you not at least address me as Miss Christobel?'

'Do you have business to discuss with me or not?'

'I do. Daniel, I am sure you are ambitious for success as an ironmaster. I can help you achieve that and become a very rich man.' She chose the couch to sit on and extended a graceful hand towards him. 'Come, sit by me and listen to what I have to say.'

She was so near him he could see the sweep of her lashes against her skin and a tiny scar on her temple. He wondered how she had come by it. The last time they had been this close he had hardly noticed anything about her, but now he saw everything.

As she settled by the fire and arranged her silken skirts he caught a glimpse of soft kid, buttoned boots, tailored neatly round her narrow ankles. He wanted to kneel at her feet, take off those boots and peel away the white stockings that lay beneath them. He wanted to touch her legs, stroke the skin, gently, upwards. She was a woman any man would covet and he did.

Bel saw the light awaken in his eyes and felt a thrill of triumph. She was right. This man was no milksop around a lady, as so many of her brother's friends were. He had red blood in his veins and a hard strong body. She tried to imagine its contours beneath his clothes, but she had only stylised pictures, painted by artists, to guide her. How long would it take for her to know his body properly, to feel his hands exploring her as his eyes now did?

She patted the couch beside her but he settled in a chair,

stretching out his legs and watching her closely. She leaned forward a fraction to accentuate the swell of her breasts, and smiled again.

'Daniel, you are an unmarried man of five and twenty, I am told. Handsome, clever and ready to become an ironmaster in your own right.'

'If you say so, Miss Fitzkeppel.'

'Bel. Do please call me Bel. We are not so far removed in status that we cannot be friends.'

'Yes, we are, *Miss Fitzkeppel*. Your father was a landowner. My father was a coal miner.'

'But we are in the middle of the nineteenth century! There has been a revolution. I am told that coal and iron, and not land, will be our future.'

'Your brother has both in abundance.'

'And I have none. Like you, sir, I have none. I have nothing save what my brother chooses to give me.'

'Make your point.'

'Very well. My brother will not marry. He has told me so. We have no uncles, no cousins that we can trace. Therefore it is left to me to provide heirs for the Fitzkeppel estates.'

'Will that be such a hardship for you?'

She detected a mild sneer in his voice and panicked. She did not wish to lose his sympathy. Those who did not have land and wealth thought it a blessing. They did not know the responsibilities that it entailed.

'Of course not. I know my duty. However, I had been brought up to believe that I would leave Fitzkeppel Hall when I married. But my brother seems so set against his own marriage I feel it is my duty to stay.'

She detected a slight nod from Daniel and hoped she had regained his respect. She so desperately wanted him to like her.

'And – and to marry,' she added. 'I plan to marry quite soon.'

His face relaxed a little. He seemed relieved and genuinely pleased for her. 'I had not heard this news. May I wish you every happiness, Miss Fitzkeppel.'

'Do you not wish to know whom I shall marry?'

'I am sure I shall not know the gentleman – unless he was at the shoot?'

'Indeed he was.' She took a very deep breath. 'I plan to marry you.'

'What!' He rose to his feet and Bel prayed she had not alienated him with her boldness.

'You are being quite ridiculous! I believed you wished to have a serious conversation with me. But if all you want is to play parlour games at my expense, you are wasting my valuable time. I have an ironworks to run.'

'Please sit down. I do not play games. Truly. I mean what I say. You will be a great asset to the Fitzkeppel iron and steel works and . . . and to our . . . our blood line.' She watched him absorb these words and hoped she had not shocked him.

He sank back onto his chair and muttered, 'You really mean this, don't you?'

'Yes, I do. Of course, my brother will always own the estate, but he is not interested in its future. I am. And I believe you are too. Between us we can ensure the pits and the ironworks thrive.' She saw this had impressed him and carried on recklessly. 'And – and produce Fitzkeppel heirs to carry on.'

'Fitzkeppel heirs? Heirs called Thorpe?' He laughed and, again, she detected the derision in his voice. 'I think not.'

'No, of course not. I have not come here on a whim, sir. I have thought about that. You will change your name to

Fitzkeppel. Withers will do that for us. It is not unheard of in well-born families.'

She hesitated. His face was a picture of disbelief. This plan was not being received as well as she had thought it would. Anxiously, she added, 'And our firstborn son will be called Thorpe.' After a moment she put her head on one side and said softly, 'Thorpe Fitzkeppel. That has rather a nice ring about it, do you not think?'

'Out of the question. Your brother would never consent to such a match.'

'He would if I asked him. He knows I wish to marry and he cares for my happiness. I am three and twenty and time is running out for me. My brother is not a tyrant. He will welcome my marriage, I am sure. He will increase my income, as well. You have not said no, Daniel. You have only found practical difficulties to our union. May I assume then, that you are considering my offer? Think of it, wealth and position in the South Riding and making the best steel in the world. Think also of the advantages for your own family. You have sisters, I understand? They will need husbands. Imagine the choices they will have when they are my sisters too.'

Daniel thought all right. All his ambitions would be fulfilled by one single word. He would be a fool to turn away such an opportunity. But he would also be a fool if he did not consider the difficulties they would both have to face.

'It won't work,' he said. 'Gentry needs to marry gentry. Your own mother's conduct should have taught you that.'

'But that is precisely my point. I am only half gentry. My mother was a farmer's daughter.'

'Aye, and look at the trouble she caused. Working folk are best wedded to other working folk.'

'But do you not see? *I* come from yeoman stock. My

370

grandfather was a Dales man, a sheep farmer. I have money from my brother's estate, yes. But everyone in the Riding knows I do not have the breeding to be welcome as the wife of a baronet or lord.' She looked directly into his eyes. 'Or, indeed, the inclination.'

His expression stilled as he waited for her to continue.

'Daniel, I am sincere in this proposal. I am my mother's daughter and I have her desire to make the best of my life.' Her voice dropped to a murmur. 'And I have her needs as a woman. Do I not please you as a woman should please a man? Would you not care for me as your wife?' She fingered her throat and then very quietly added, 'In your bed?'

She saw his eyes darken as he contemplated this. He would have no misgivings about her wayward mother, or any scandal associated with her. She had no doubts about him. He was a strong, ambitious man. He would not allow her to stray from the marriage bed as her father had her mother. And she was sure she would never wish to, for, judging by the look in his eyes, he was already contemplating the experience. As she was. Imagining their first coupling. She could not wait and her body twitched with anticipation.

She swallowed nervously. 'You – you would be willing to take me to your bed? It – it would not be an – an ordeal for you?'

'No, it would not be an ordeal.'

It was what she desired more than anything. Her heart began to beat quickly and she became hot and damp under her skirts. She fidgeted nervously on the couch, but did not lose her courage. 'I believe it is the custom among the working classes for the future bride to – to prove her value in the marriage bed before the ceremony. Sh-should you wish that of me, I – I shall not resist.'

371

She stared at her hands folded on her lap and tried to keep them still. She had gone too far. He would be scandalised. But how else was she to ensure their union? If she became with child, his child, he would marry her. His sense of honour and responsibility would not let him do otherwise. Suddenly she felt an excitement surge through her. She wanted that more than anything. A baby. Daniel Thorpe's baby.

His silence made her uneasy and she dared not look at him, but she was unrepentant. What if she had shocked him? She had no reputation to lose, her mama had seen to that, and she had much to gain from this handsome and capable man. She wanted his flesh against hers, his body entwined with hers. She would learn what to do so he would enjoy her so much he would want her over and over again. Her insides began to melt at the prospect. When she found the courage to meet his eyes, she was startled by their dark intensity.

Finally, he spoke, slowly and deliberately, 'Miss Fitzkeppel – Bel – I—'

'No, do not say anything now. I know I have astonished you with my forwardness.' She bit her lip and frowned. 'You must think me wanton and I hope you will forgive me. Please, take time to reflect on what I have said. Come to luncheon at the Hall after church on Sunday and give me your answer then. Mr Withers will be there with his wife. But afterwards – after they have left we shall be alone. Most of the indoor staff have a half day and go out. If – if it is your wish, we may really get to know each other. Properly. In private.' She continued to look directly into his eyes and knew he had not mistaken her meaning. 'You will join me at luncheon on Sunday?' she repeated.

Such an invitation! The temptation stirred his desires. He had been celibate for so long – too long. If he visited her as she asked him to, he doubted he would be able to say no to her. And why should he? He had no wish to refuse her; he had an awakening hunger to satisfy. But the outcome of his previous carnal attraction towards Lily was still raw in his mind.

'I think it will be wise for you to go now,' he said.

'But you will visit me on Sunday?' she pressed anxiously. 'I shall not leave until you promise to be there.'

'Yes, Bel. I shall be there,' he replied.

Neither said another word.

When she had gone, he went to the stable at the back of the house and saddled a horse, the large black one Ezekiel had kept for himself and that was fretting from lack of exercise.

He rode the hunter hard, out of town and up onto the Keppel hills. From there he could see the Hall and its lands across the valley and smoke from the ironworks and forge chimneys down by the navigation. Most of what he saw was Fitzkeppel land.

He guessed Nathan Fitzkeppel would never marry. His inclinations were not towards ladies. He knew why Henry Bowes and Fitzkeppel had gone to that keeper's hut in the woods, and it sickened his stomach to think of what they did together. Over the years, the Fitzkeppels had been a sorry lot, to be sure. Except for Miss Fitzkeppel. She was a bold and determined woman. And clever. She knew if the estate was to thrive it would need a sure hand directing its manufacturing affairs.

He could do it and he would welcome the challenge. He could make crucible steel in abundance, go to all the lectures he wanted and learn about new processes, visit Manchester, London even, and meet great men like Stephenson and Brunel. And – and possess a pretty, intelligent wife who understood the ways of the industrial world. All this in front of him would belong to his sons. Any man of sense would not hesitate.

As he sat alone on that bleak and windy hillside, holding on to the reins of Ezekiel's horse, he tried to imagine a future living at the Hall with Bel as his wife. He would have to give up his job and all that it entailed. Mr Withers would probably sell it to the Fitzkeppels anyway and it would be absorbed into their estate. An estate he would be able to treat as his own. An involuntary cry escaped from his throat and reverberated across the valley, causing the horse to whinny and shy away. He soothed the animal and rode him less urgently back to his stable.

Chapter 35

After her Sunday dinner Mariah wrapped the finished bonnet and cape and placed them carefully in a box. 'Dora,' she called from the front room, 'I'm going to walk over to the Hall with this. Will you come with me?'

'No thanks, love. I'm taking that mutton pie over to Mr Shaw in a minute.'

'How is he keeping these days?'

'Not too good. The vicar has a place for him in the almshouse. He's moving quite soon.'

Mariah had walked through to the kitchen. 'Oh? I didn't know. What will happen to his house?'

'One of his sons will live there with his family. He needs the land for storing the stone and such like he uses in his building work.'

As she walked across the parkland in her hooded cloak, enjoying the crisp cold air, Mariah passed Mr and Mrs Withers in their pony and trap heading for the gatehouse and village.

They acknowledged her as they clattered by. Mariah thought they appeared quite jolly and guessed they had eaten and drunk well at the Hall.

Since Mr Withers had told her about the financial plight of the ironworks she had racked her brains to think of a way to save them. Daniel was the best steel maker in the Riding. There must be an answer somewhere!

Miss Fitzkeppel had instructed her to bring the cape and bonnet directly to her when they were finished, so she could present the gift herself. Mariah hoped Mrs Havers would be taking a nap in her sitting room.

Everywhere was unusually quiet. Mariah found a footman, a young lad, without his livery jacket, sitting on the floor eating a piece of cold Yorkshire pudding.

'Where is everyone?' she asked, pushing back her hood.

'Mrs Havers gave most of 'em the afternoon off. They've all gone out in one of the farm carts to listen to a travelling preacher. There's on'y a few of us 'ere. Can I help you, miss?'

'I have this box for Miss Fitzkeppel.'

'I'll keep it safe, miss. I'll give it to Mrs Havers when she comes in.'

'No, you can't do that. Is Miss Fitzkeppel here?'

'In the drawing room, miss.'

'Well, would you go and ask if she'll see me?'

'Oo, I couldn't do that, miss. Not until she rings for me. She was very firm about it. I was not to disturb her.'

'Tell her it's Miss Bowes.'

'I know who you are. You used to make the gowns here. Sarah's always going on about you. But I daren't go in there, miss. She 'as a visitor, y'see. She'll ring for tea when she wants it. I'll ask her then.'

'All right.' Mariah was reluctant to leave the cape and bonnet with such a young servant and decided to wait until the visitor left. 'Would you fetch me a chair from the servants' hall?'

'Right you are, miss.'

Mariah settled in the wide flagged passageway that ran between the kitchens and storerooms and connected the front of the Hall to the stable yard at the back. A solid, but worn, oak door separated the servants from the gentry. The door edge was so knocked about that there was a gap where it closed. As she sat, Mariah wondered what it was like to live on the other side of that door.

The unusual silence lengthened. But after a while she heard a door open and voices in the hallway. They were muffled at first, and then they became more distinct as they moved closer to the servants' door. There were two voices, a gentleman and a lady talking urgently to each other in a heated, passionate way, and they were getting louder.

Mariah instinctively rose to her feet as the door half opened, pushed by the man's shoulder. She heard him clearly.

'I have given you my answer, and I must make haste to return. If I do not make steel to sell, my men will have no wages.'

Mariah recognised Daniel's voice immediately. He was Miss Fitzkeppel's visitor! The door opened wider. He had his back to her and beyond him she caught a glimpse of Miss Fitzkeppel's face, shiny eyes and pink cheeks.

'Do not go! Stay with me, Daniel, and I shall show you how much I love you.'

Mariah had never seen Miss Fitzkeppel so agitated. She pressed her back against the wall as the door opened wider and Daniel turned to walk down the passage. He was very smartly dressed and held a riding hat and crop in his hand.

'Mariah!' He stopped abruptly and stared at her.

She saw him look from her to Miss Fitzkeppel and back again. There was an anguish in his face, a despairing anguish she had seen before but now it tore at her heart. She wanted to smooth it from his brow and take away his pain, no matter what it was. He started to say something to her, then must have thought better of it, for he stopped and turned back to Miss Fitzkeppel.

'Good afternoon, Bel,' he said. He gave the briefest of nods to Mariah and marched off down the passage towards the stables.

Bel? He had called Miss Fitzkeppel, Bel! A name she had previously heard only from the lips of Miss Fitzkeppel's own brother. She had no idea Daniel and Miss Fitzkeppel were so close. Miss Fitzkeppel was standing in the open doorway. Although she appeared vexed and was frowning, Mariah thought she looked quite beautiful in her blue silk gown with the delicate lace trims. She appeared not to have noticed Mariah and her voice dropped to a whisper as though the words were only for herself. 'He *is* going to marry me. He *is*!'

Mariah's eyes widened and she sat down again with a thud. Daniel and Miss Fitzkeppel? She was speechless. This could not be! Her heart was pumping loudly in her throat and her head began to spin.

'Miss Bowes? I did not see you there.'

Mariah rose to her feet instantly. 'I – I – er—'

'What is it, Miss Bowes?' Miss Fitzkeppel demanded irritably.

'The – the bonnet and cape for Mrs Havers. They're finished.' She picked up the box from the floor.

'Oh that. Yes. Where is my footman?'

'Here, miss.'

The young lad loomed out of the shadows buttoning on his jacket.

'Take this to the small drawing room.'

He grabbed the box and scuttled past her, leaving the two ladies alone.

'Was there anything else?'

'No, Miss Fitzkeppel,' Mariah answered.

Without another word, Miss Fitzkeppel walked away in a rustle of silken skirts and Mariah was left staring at the open door. She closed it gently and made her own escape to the stable yard, in time to hear the hooves of a horse galloping away. She broke into a run herself, in a different direction, across the parkland until she was forced to slow down, catch her breath and re-pin her loosening hair.

Miss Fitzkeppel and *Daniel*? It defied credibility. Surely Dora would have known of his affections? Unless it was a secret? Had she unwittingly stumbled on a covert liaison between Daniel and Miss Fitzkeppel? Mariah did not want to believe what her own eyes and ears had told her.

This would change everything for her. Mariah leaned against the stump of a recently felled tree. She had harboured ideas of keeping her ironworks afloat with Daniel's help but all was truly lost now. Marriage to Miss Fitzkeppel would bring him comfort, wealth, respectability in the Riding, and a grand house to live in with his pretty, clever wife. Why should he not marry Miss Fitzkeppel if she desired him? And desire him she did. Mariah had seen the passion in her eyes.

She did not know why she felt so angry. She kicked so hard at the felled tree trunk that she hurt her toes, and she was obliged to sit until the pain eased. How could he marry Miss Fitzkeppel when *she* needed him so badly? When her ironworks needed him so badly? Without him she had no hope of rescuing them from bankruptcy. She would lose everything: her mother's inheritance; a house she could make into her home; a man who, somehow, for her, made everything possible by his very presence.

She sat for a long time, growing chilly in the weak afternoon sun, until the sound of a horse galloping towards the Hall roused her from her thoughts. She was quite a distance from the drive, but as the rider levelled with her he slowed, turned the horse's head towards her, and cantered across the grassland. She recognised the elegant dress style and fine-boned features of Mr Fitzkeppel.

Nathan had been tired when he spurred his mount through the lodge gates. He had suffered a great shock at Henry's death and continued to grieve for his loss. He acknowledged that he had not loved Henry in the same way he had loved Warrender, but their friendship had been constant and he mourned his passing deeply.

The letter he received from Withers gave news of Bowes' death and the constable's decision. And it urged him to return. But Withers warned that there was talk about his friendship with Henry. If he came back to the Riding he must marry and staunch the rumour. He must assure the respectability of his family name and produce heirs for the estate. It was his duty.

Nathan had reluctantly agreed. He did not want to end up in gaol, or worse, for the life he led, so he resigned himself to this fate. He could surely find *someone* to be his wife? He wanted to be home, to be with Bel and to be painting again. The sight of Fitzkeppel Hall raised his spirits, as did the figure sitting alone on a tree stump in the middle of his parkland, her copper-coloured hair making her so easy for him to identify.

He dismounted, holding lightly onto the reins. 'Good afternoon, Miss Bowes.'

'Good afternoon, sir.'

She sounded forlorn. He stood in front of her and thought how much she reminded him of Henry. 'I heard about your father,' he said, 'may I offer you my condolences? So soon after Henry, too.' His voice cracked a little and he swallowed. When she raised her head he saw the sadness in her eyes, and added, 'I am truly sorry, Miss Bowes.'

'What happened that day, sir? Please tell me.'

'It was an accident, as the constable said.' After a short silence, he asked, 'What will you do?'

'I do not know. The ironworks are mine, but they are almost bankrupt. I have to find a way of keeping them going.'

He gazed at her and recalled his idle musings about her when she sat for him. A good match for an ambitious artisan, he thought. But that was before she became an ironmistress in her own right. The Bowes were far beneath him in status, to be sure. But Henry had been accepted as his friend, and Henry's father by the Riding's other factory owners. Why not the daughter? This might be a way forward for both of them.

She had a look of Henry about her that he coveted. She was personable and would be polite in civilised society. Bel spoke highly of her character. He wondered if it would work? And if it did not, would that really matter as long as she agreed to his terms?

'I could help you,' he said. 'I could pay off your creditors.'

'Why would you do that?'

'For a favour in return.'

'Sir?'

'From you. A favour from you.'

He saw a guarded expression cross her features. 'What would be the nature of this favour?' she enquired warily.

'Nothing immoral, I assure you. Just the opposite. Would you, by any chance, consider becoming my wife?'

'Your *wife*?' She sounded as taken aback as she looked. 'I do not understand, sir. Why would you wish to marry *me*? I can bring nothing to a marriage, no dowry, no connections.'

He remembered how well she had adjusted to sitting for him and how pleased Bel had been with the gowns and habits she had fashioned. 'My sister would approve of you,' he said. 'She would welcome you to the Hall.'

'And what of *your* feelings, sir?'

'We are comfortable in each other's presence, are we not?'

'I do not love you.'

'Nor I you. I have my art. You have your ironworks. We shall manage quite well without love.' She looked doubtful, so he added, 'I am sure your bankers are insisting you pay your debts immediately. Give me your promise and I shall instruct Withers to settle them.'

Until then, she had responded to him out of politeness without taking his proposal seriously, but now he saw a light in her eyes as she considered the possibilities.

'I see,' she said. 'And after our marriage my ironworks would become yours and you would have the best steel maker in the Riding working for you again.'

He had not anticipated this response and hastened to re-assure her. 'I have no hidden motive for my proposal, Miss Bowes. I do not want your ironworks. I want a wife because I need heirs.'

'And you think I will do for you?'

'I think you will do very well. Why else should I ask you? You are resourceful and intelligent. If you are so attached to your ironworks, you may continue to treat them as your own and put them in trust for – for any daughters of our union.'

The light in her eyes intensified as she gazed at him steadily. 'Do you want my answer now?' she asked.

'Do you think you might get a better offer, Miss Bowes?' he responded impatiently. He prepared to remount. 'You may have a week to consider.'

She watched him ride away, hardly believing that he had proposed *marriage* to her. But he *had* meant it and it *was* a way out of her troubles. She could keep the ironworks, take on more men and have both furnaces going all the time. She would be a woman to be reckoned with in the Riding!

But she would not have Daniel by her side and it was he who stirred her passion, a passion that was more than equal to Bel's. She would not give him up to her! Not until Daniel himself said he would marry her. Only then could she be certain she had lost him and would accept Mr Fitzkeppel's offer. And, like her mother before her, she would not know love within her marriage.

As she hurried through the woods she thought also of her workroom at the Hall. No one in the Riding made gowns as well as she did and she wondered if Mr Fitzkeppel would consider that a suitable occupation for his wife. He must care for her. He did not love her, but gentlemen in his position did not offer marriage lightly. This was more than, as Daniel had warned previously, 'only being kind to her'.

When she reached Dora's she could not settle. She flung aside her cloak and paced back and forth across the kitchen.

'What *is* the matter?' Dora asked, mixing her pikelet batter at the table.

'Daniel was at the Hall,' she said. 'He was visiting Miss Fitzkeppel.'

'Really?'

'Did you know that they were friends?'

'No. Are they? I think he might have mentioned it to me.'

'They are more than friends.'

'Are you sure? I can't see our Daniel—'

'I saw them together! Oh!' Mariah's elbow caught on the dresser and the china rattled.

'Will you please sit down, Mariah! I expect our Daniel was there on ironworks business.'

Bel's behaviour had indicated otherwise. She said, 'I – I don't want him to sell my ironworks.'

Dora put down her spoon and heaved a sigh. 'Then why don't you go into town and tell him.'

'I think I might. I shall stay for a few days. I'll go now.'

Dora put her head on one side and stared hard. The relationship between Mariah and Daniel had changed since the shooting. She said, 'Go tomorrow, dear. There's no cart on a Sunday.'

Mariah sat up front with the driver, the hood of her cloak thrown back to show off her new bonnet of ruches and bows. When he set her down, she hired a boy with a barrow to carry her box and walked home with her head held high. She no longer had time for self-pity and she stood proudly on the front doorstep of the house she was determined to keep. She reached up and dropped the heavy brass knocker against the door with a satisfying thud.

Later, as she was helping Emma prepare a tea of hot boiled ox tongue and greens from the garden, she asked casually, 'When will Daniel be in? I want to talk to him.'

'I haven't seen him all day. He went down to the furnaces straight after breakfast with some snap for his dinner. When he comes back tonight, I'll take hot water up to his chamber for his wash, and then he'll come down for tea in the kitchen.'

'What does he do after tea?'

'Sometimes he goes back down to the yard, or out to a meeting or a lecture at the Institute. He reads a lot as well. That new study is full of books now.'

'Is he going out tonight?'

'No. I'll make some of that coffee stuff for him. I don't like it, but our Daniel has a taste for it. I generally take a pot into the study.'

'Will you make enough for us both tonight?'

'Are you having tea in here with us, then?'

'No, I had a good dinner with Dora before I set off here. I shall unpack my box instead and come down afterwards.'

She had travelled in her green gown that so enhanced her colouring. This, she had decided, was to be her day dress and she would make a new Sunday gown with a matching bonnet and cape as soon as she could. Now she had made up her mind to talk to Daniel, she was determined to be strong, whatever the outcome. She had to know if he would be leaving the works to marry Miss Fitzkeppel, and she continued to wonder what she would do without him.

As the time to speak to him drew near, Mariah fretted about the outcome of their conversation. The last time she had been in the study had been for that embarrassing interview with Mr Smith. It seemed long ago now and she had suffered much worse since then.

He was not sitting by the fire reading, as she had expected, but standing by the window, drinking out of a tiny cup. When she opened the door, he turned swiftly. 'Mariah! Emma tells me you are staying?'

'Yes,' she answered coolly. 'Though not for long, I expect. Have you spoken to Mr Withers again?'

He nodded. 'We shall keep going while we can.' He moved to the centre of the room, to the desk where candles burned, and set down his cup. 'I shall make immediate plans to move out.'

Her coolness began to evaporate. He could not wait to get away from her and into Miss Fitzkeppel's waiting arms. Her teeth clenched as her irritation grated. 'You will do no such thing!' she replied. 'The men need you here.'

He looked surprised at her agitation. 'People will talk. I cannot stay and be the reason for that.'

'Of course, I should have realised,' she answered tightly. 'Now you move in grander circles you must guard your own reputation.' She stopped suddenly, embarrassed by her outburst.

'Mariah?' His voice was soft and full of concern. 'I am thinking only of *your* reputation.'

'My reputation? My *reputation*! You of all people should know that I have no reputation in this town.'

'That is not true. Town folk know of your misfortunes, and many have a good deal of sympathy for you. They, as I, will be pleased to see you return to your home.'

'Oh yes, so they can continue to entertain themselves with idle chatter and—'

'Stop this at once! I shall not listen to you speak like this. I was talking of your bereavements. Folk know nothing of other events.'

But you do. You know almost everything. She said, 'Well, I shall not insist that you stay. You have less than one year to serve as my trustee and then you may sever all connections with me.'

'Sever all connections? Why should I wish to do that?'

'To marry Miss Fitzkeppel, of course!'

His face darkened. In the candlelight he looked angry. The

coffee was forgotten and hopes for a pleasant evening were shattered. 'So you have decided how I shall live my future life?'

'I recall you were once just as sure I should not marry her brother!'

'I had my reasons!'

'Oh yes, I remember. It would never do for working folk to marry above themselves. Does that not apply to you also?'

He sighed. 'You are quite worn out and are acting like a petulant child. You are overwrought by events and – and, somehow, spoiling for a fight. I shall not continue this conversation with you. We may talk tomorrow after you have rested. Come over to the works, to your father's office, after breakfast. There is much for you to learn there.' He handed her one of the candles from the desk and said pointedly, 'Goodnight, Mariah.'

She took the candle from him ungraciously and demanded, 'When are you going to marry her?'

He sighed again and said firmly, 'Go to bed.'

She left, knowing she had behaved badly. She had not been able to help herself. She wanted him to stay here. With her. To be by her side, making steel instead of living at the Hall with *her*. She could not imagine the ironworks without him. She understood, now, what her mother meant when she had talked of love. She loved Daniel. Miss Fitzkeppel might be fair and pretty with wealth and position, but she was not right for Daniel. Miss Fitzkeppel did not, *could not*, love Daniel as she did.

Emma had gone to her bed, leaving hot water on the wash-stand in Ezekiel's room, where the stable lad had put her box. It was the largest bedchamber, furnished with an ornate wrought-iron bedstead. The quilt was new, she noticed, made in a heavy dark red satin and there were matching curtains at

387

the window. Henry's influence, she guessed. She did not want to sleep here, in Ezekiel's bed. She took her nightgown, neatly folded on the carved oak chest, undressed and washed, then picked up the candle and crossed the landing to her old bedchamber.

The number of books around the room told her this was where Daniel still slept and, for some reason that she could not fathom, she wanted to weep. She wanted to fall into the feather mattress and pour out her heart to him.

It was the first time since her attack she had wanted to be this close to a man, lying together, her body against his. Mr Fitzkeppel's kind and gentle ways had not aroused such feelings in her. But Daniel did and this made her want to cry.

She heard a door open downstairs and retreated to her mother's former sickroom. This had been Henry's dressing room until recently. It still contained some of his things. There was a couch against the wall. Mariah dragged the feather quilt from the bedchamber next door, wrapped herself in it and lay down. She remained awake for ages listening to Daniel's movements downstairs, checking locks and bolts, raking and damping down fires. He belongs *here,* she thought. Not at the Hall. He belongs here with me.

Her ears strained for his heavy footsteps on the stair treads, but none came. Perhaps like her he could not sleep. She heard again the squeak of a door hinge. Perhaps he was reading. He read a lot. That was why he knew so much, she thought. Eventually, she drifted into a restless sleep imagining Daniel, his long legs stretched out in front of a dying fire, a candle by his head, turning the pages of a book.

Chapter 36

It was dark when she woke, but the noises from downstairs told her it was morning. She dressed carefully, spending more time than usual with a candle in front of Henry's looking glass smoothing her coiled hair. Her hands and feet had become quite chilly when she went down to the kitchen.

Emma was standing at the kitchen table, rubbing dripping into some flour in a bowl. 'Oh, you're up early. Fire's drawing well, I was just waiting for the water to heat.'

'I'm going over to the works this morning. What time does Daniel leave the house?'

'He's gone already. Wi'out 'is breakfast, an' all.'

'But it's not properly light yet!'

'He likes to make sure the fires are going for the crucible steel. He makes that every day now.'

'I'll go over there straightaway,' Mariah said.

'Can you wait while the kettle boils and take a can o' tea for him? I'll cut some bacon and bread too.'

Mariah carried the basket of food and drink into the yard. There was smoke curling from the wide brick chimney of the crucible furnace and the men were already working, loading the cementation furnace for the next firing. The sky was overcast and the air was cold, but it was fully light. She hovered by the warehouse until Daniel saw her and came over, striding across the cobbles, his waistcoat flapping in the crisp morning breeze.

He stopped a few paces from her, taking in her gown and hair and how they complemented each other. Her clear, hazel eyes were challenging.

'It was a bad start last night,' he said. 'We ought not to quarrel.'

'Quite so,' she replied. 'What have you to tell me?'

He detached the keys from his belt. 'Come into the office.'

Mariah followed him up the outside stone steps. 'I've brought you some breakfast,' she said.

'Champion. The fire should be going well by now.'

The office was tidier than she remembered. The hearth was swept and the worn desk top cleared and polished.

Daniel poured hot tea into two metal tankards. 'Will you share this with me?'

'Thank you.' She handed him some bread and bacon in a cloth and took a piece herself.

'Did you sleep well?' he asked.

She shrugged, her mouth full of food.

He looked sympathetic. 'You have been through too much of late. The worst is over now.'

'Is it? I have inherited debts and this yard is a millstone around my neck.'

'I shall salvage what I can for you. Mr Withers will get a good price for the house and yard. The furnaces are sound. Ezekiel had plans to expand once the new crucible shed was finished. We talked of taking on more men. Even now we need a manager to replace Ezekiel.'

'But surely you are that person?'

'I am the only teemer for the crucibles and if I do not keep up output we cannot pay the men's wages. They have wives and children to feed.'

'Can you not employ another teemer?'

'I know of such a man eager to join us.'

'Then why do you not proceed?'

'I have no funds to pay him. Ezekiel borrowed too much to build the new shed.'

'But surely there is money for the men's wages? Ezekiel always had banknotes in his safe.'

'That was before Henry came home from school and started spending on the house and his new carriage.'

'*New carriage?*'

'It's in the stable at present. Henry had chosen a pair of matching horses to draw it. They are in the stables too.'

'But he was not gentry! He did not have the income for a carriage! Or indeed a life that demanded such an extravagance!'

'He had other ideas.'

'I suppose he wanted it for travelling to the Hall and Ezekiel indulged him. Have I any money at all?'

Daniel shook his head. 'Not after paying for bar iron and coal.'

'Is there any way you can keep going?'

He heaved a sigh. 'The bank is taking everything.'

'What does Mr Withers say?'

'The same as I do. We must sell up to pay off your creditors.'

'But if you did not have that burden, could you take on more men and increase your output?'

'Oh yes. Bowes Ironworks would be making the best steel

in the Riding! It would have a future. The price of crucible steel is rising all the time.'

Mariah thought she saw a glow in his eyes for a moment as he spoke. Then it disappeared as he added quickly, 'I am afraid it is not a possibility. Mr Withers and I have racked our brains to find a way.'

She gave a rueful smile. 'Is Henry's carriage paid for?'

Daniel nodded.

'Sell it. And the horses. And anything else we don't need. Will that pay the men's wages?'

'For a while.'

'With enough for another teemer?'

Now he shook his head and gave a harsh laugh. 'I would not take a man from another yard only to have to lay him off when the money runs out.'

She tipped the rest of the cooling tea into his tankard. 'Then I must find a solution. Bankrupt or not, these are my works, after all.'

'Do not be fanciful, Mariah. We cannot play games with men's livelihoods.'

'Mr Fitzkeppel has offered to pay off my debts.'

'Fitzkeppel? Is he not in Lincolnshire?'

'He returned to the Hall yesterday. After you left. Mr Withers has kept him informed of events. He wishes to marry.'

'Is that what he told you? I do not believe it.'

Mariah was startled by the scorn in his voice and she retaliated sharply. 'Well you had better believe it. He wishes to marry me.'

Daniel stood up, knocking back his chair. His voice resonated around the office like a clap of thunder. 'No!' He repeated the word twice, loudly and with anger, adding, 'Do not do this, Mariah. It will bring you only grief and unhappiness.'

Mariah stood up to challenge him. 'How dare you? How dare you presume to tell me what to do? Mr Fitzkeppel's generosity will allow these works to continue to employ men and make steel. They will be mine, in trust for my children, my daughters. My daughters will not have to suffer the humility of dependence that my mother and myself endured.'

'He will never love you.'

'Now who is being fanciful! Is love such a prerequisite of happiness? We are friends. We shall grow to love each other.'

He was shaking his head and his eyes had taken on that haunted, anguished look that tore her heart. He leaned over the desk, resting both his hands on its surface and stared at her. 'I forbid it. I am your trustee and I forbid it.'

For a moment she was dumbfounded. How had she ever considered she could have had a future with this man? She had thought he would be pleased. She pursed her lips and frowned. She would just as soon have Ezekiel back, ordering her life than this – this tyrant that Daniel had become. She said, 'I am sure Mr Withers will not share your view.'

'You do not understand.'

'I think I do. I think you have lived and worked for so long with Ezekiel that you have grown to be too much like him.'

'No!' he roared.

She gazed at him. Had he lost his mind? 'I shall give Mr Fitzkeppel my answer tomorrow. You may tell the men that Bowes Ironworks are safe from their creditors. I shall rename them Bowes Steelworks as soon as I can.'

She would have left that minute if he had not caught her arm. 'Stay,' he demanded of her. 'There is something you should know.' He stepped back, breathing heavily as though attempting

393

to compose himself and then went to the safe and drew out a sheaf of thick papers that he placed on the desk.

'What are these? Are they the drawings for the new crucible shed?'

'No. They are nothing to do with the works.'

'What are they, then?'

Daniel did not reply.

'Well, are you going to show them to me?'

He covered his face with his hands. 'You must prepare yourself, Mariah. These are not for – I mean, they are only for – they are meant for gentlemen.'

'Yet they do not concern the furnaces?'

He hesitated, picked them up again and shook his head. 'I cannot do this. I have made a mistake. I shall return them to the safe.'

'Daniel? What intrigue is this?'

'I am sorry. This is wrong. Please do not press me.'

'But I do. What secrets do you have that you must keep them in the safe?'

'They are not my secrets. They were there before I came here.'

'Then they were Ezekiel's?'

'Yes. They are – were – his.'

'Where did they come from?'

'Who knows?' he shrugged. 'Do you understand what I am saying? They are for – for gentlemen.'

'Ezekiel kept these drawings in his safe? No, I do not understand. Show them to me.'

He shook his head again. 'I should have removed them and destroyed them when I found them.'

'But they belong to me now.'

'Let me burn them in the fire, They are not for your eyes.'

'Nonsense. I am a grown woman. And I, of all people, know that men have these needs.'

Daniel shook his head emphatically. 'No, you do not know about this. You cannot see them.'

'But they are mine.'

'And I am your trustee.'

They stared at each other silently for several seconds.

'Do you think I cannot deal with these things now? Do you think I am some weak and whimpering woman who will faint at the sight of unclothed bodies? Do not misjudge me so.'

'I don't. I—'

'No, Daniel. Let me speak. My mother was an unhappy woman as Ezekiel's wife. I need to see the kind of woman Ezekiel wished my mother was. I have to try and understand why Ezekiel behaved towards her as he did. He treated my mother and myself abominably. He was successful but you believe he was a troubled man. Did you not say as much when you came to tell me of his death? For heaven's sake, he died by his own hand! Please Daniel, don't you understand? I need to know!'

She was half crying now, hiccupping with anger and frustration. Her voice had risen to a squeak. She had never understood Ezekiel, but she hoped some answers might lie in the drawings. Sobbing slightly she beseeched him, 'Let me look on them once, Daniel, and then you may destroy them.'

Daniel wrestled with her need to understand Ezekiel and her brother's friendship with Fitzkeppel, and his desire to protect her from the truth.

She was whispering to herself, 'Why? Why? Why was Ezekiel always so angry with Mother?'

Agitated, he ran his fingers through his hair and muttered, 'Very well, I'll show them to you.'

395

He cleared the top of the desk and laid out the drawings. He grimaced as he stepped to one side, gesturing for her to inspect them. 'I shall pour you a brandy. You are going to need it.'

The only sound was that of Mariah's skirts rustling as she walked around the desk and gazed at the papers. At first she was puzzled. She had expected ladies, foreign ladies, from the Orient or the West Indies, showing off their breasts and bottoms. As she studied the drawings incredulity crept over her.

Mariah choked and coughed, and then began to shake. She took the brandy that appeared in front of her and sank, speechless, into Ezekiel's battered old office chair. 'But – but these are young gentlemen.'

'You did not know about this, did you?' Daniel asked quietly. 'You did not know that there are men who prefer to look on other men?'

She shook her head wordlessly and drank. 'Did he – did Ezekiel . . . ?'

Daniel grimaced. 'He hid his preference well. He had to. The men would have found out and they would have talked. It is my belief he suppressed his inclinations and these drawings were his substitute.'

Mariah shook her head and spoke very softly. 'It's – it's – it's . . .' at last she got out her words, 'it's not natural.'

'Not to you or I, but it happens. I have seen it among farm animals.'

'What do you mean?'

'It's not unknown that sometimes a boar or a stallion won't do his duty at stud and prefers to run with other males.'

'You mean, it's not only that they prefer to look on gentlemen, but they do not have urges for ladies?'

He nodded.

'Mother told me Ezekiel did not love her. Now I know why. He was not able to. They had Henry though, didn't they?'

'Perhaps he tried to be a dutiful husband and found it too difficult. He lived the life he wanted through Henry and, I guess, when he found him with Fitzkeppel in that old keeper's hut—'

'Henry? Henry and Mr Fitzkeppel?'

'Fitzkeppel will never love you in the way he loved Henry. In time, he will find a substitute for Henry, but it will never be you, Mariah. Never. You must not marry him.'

'No, I see that now. Do other folk know about them?'

'There have been stories going round the works about those two for a while now, but not about Ezekiel. He buried his nature well and that was his trouble. I suppose he felt he could not go on.'

'Poor Ezekiel.'

Daniel began to scoop up the offensive papers. 'Ezekiel would not have wanted anyone to know about these. I'll burn them, as I should have done when I found them.'

'Thank you. I understand now why he was such a difficult man. It must have been impossible to reconcile this part of him with his ambitions to be so well-respected.'

She watched Daniel tear up the sheets one by one and feed them to the burning coals. She stared across the room at him, and thought what a fine gentleman he was. He had wanted to protect her from this knowledge for the very best of reasons. She finished her brandy and realised how very, very special he was to her.

She glanced at the open safe. 'What else is in there?'

'Well, no money, I am sorry to say. But I have paid the men for last week. The title deeds to the house and ironworks are with your bankers. The papers in there are orders, bills of

397

sale and ledgers, just the usual.' He took the poker and broke the burned drawings into ash that fell among the glowing coals. 'And something of yours,' he added.

'Mine?' She did not leave any of her possessions with Ezekiel.

He crossed to the safe, reached inside and retrieved a small package wrapped in calico.

'For you,' he said, handing it over.

The wrapping fell away to reveal a silver frame, the silver frame that had held her mother's likeness, that Dora had sold for her in town and bought woollen cloth to make a winter coat. The silver frame that had also given her money to buy notions and fabric to make the things she sold in the market.

Mariah gave a small laugh, her mouth widened into a smile and her eyes lit up with delight, a delight that lifted Daniel's heart more than he could tell.

'But how did you know? Where did you get it?' Mariah burbled, as she stroked the figured surface and turned it over and over in her hands.

'Dora came to see me when she brought it into town to sell. So I knew all about your plans. I would have bought it from her then if I had had the money. Instead, I went with her to the silversmith on the High Street and secured it with a payment and a promise to buy it over the following months. I took him the final sum last week and placed it in the safe for you.'

'Oh Daniel, it's the most wonderful thing you could have done for me. I still have my mother's likeness, between the pages of my Bible. Now it can resume its rightful place on the mantelshelf in the morning room.'

'I shall move my books out of there as soon as I can.'

'No, it is better as your library and study.' A plan was

beginning to form in her mind. A plan to keep her steelworks going. If only Daniel would stay.

'When will you marry her?' she asked quietly.

He did not answer and look pained.

'I saw you together. She says you will marry her.'

'Does she? She presumes too much.'

Mariah's heart turned over in her breast. 'You are not betrothed? You won't be leaving here, then?'

He gave her a long level stare. 'No.'

The word hung in the air and Mariah could hardly contain her joy. But she dare not hope for too much. Not yet. Her mind raced. 'We must find money for the men's wages every week.'

'If I could make more crucible steel, I could make more profits.'

'And you need another teemer to do that?'

'I *need* to be sure I can pay him.'

'I may have a solution. I have been thinking about this since I worked at the Hall. I shall make gowns. Fashionable silken gowns for the wives of manufacturing and professional gentlemen in this town. I shall need needlewomen, of course. If Emma is comfortable in the small attic, there is room for two girls in the large attic. Will that help?' Even as she said it, she was to planning how to use Henry's bedchamber for her workroom, and the adjoining dressing room to receive her clients.

'You mean in the house?'

'Do you think Meg would join me in this venture? I shall ask her. I shall be set up in no time, and surely make enough to pay for your teemer.' She wondered if she could persuade Mrs Havers to let Sarah Maltby go from the Hall and become a seamstress alongside Meg.

Daniel's eyes widened and met her steady gaze. 'I think it might. In fact, I do believe it would. I'll talk to Mr Withers tomorrow.'

Mariah began to pack the basket with the debris from their breakfast. He would stay at the works and give them a future. Give her a future, too. They would be together. She had hope. She noticed him watching her silently with his head on one side, the way Dora did sometimes. She was glad she wore her green gown and had spent time on her hair this morning.

'Will you ever truly forgive me?' he asked quietly.

She did not pretend she did not know what he was talking about. 'There is nothing to forgive.'

'It was my fault it happened.'

'No. The fault lies with others.'

'But, don't you see, it was because of my actions, my weakness for—'

'For Mrs Cluff. I know. You told me.'

'I was such a fool. I believed her.'

'But why should you not believe the woman you loved?'

'Because I did not love her. I know now that I did not love her. It was a physical craving for her, that is all. Love is more, it means more.'

'Did you love Miss Fitzkeppel?'

He shook his head slowly and deliberately.

'But you craved her in the same way as you did Lily?'

'I did. Briefly, yes I did. What do you want me to say, Mariah? That I am not a man with a man's desires?'

'I am sorry. I did not mean to cause you anger.'

'I am not angry!'

Clearly he was.

'I wanted the truth, that is all.' She shrugged.

'Truth? The truth is that no amount of wealth or position will take me away from here. Away from you.'

'Do not say that!' It was what she wished to hear. But, now, she had to tell *him* the truth. 'You do not know everything about – about what those men did to me that night.'

His anguish etched the fine lines on his face deeper. He looked haggard and grey in the pale morning light. For weeks he had despaired about Mariah's future, until he realised that her future was with him. It was not blame or guilt that drove him. He wanted her by his side. His woman. He was fired with a desire for her stronger than anything he had experienced. And yes, part of it was for the bedchamber, but he realised that he must proceed with caution at her pace.

He said, 'It is the past. To be forgotten. If you can.'

Quietly, Mariah replied, 'Some things may not be forgotten.'

The naked pain in his eyes was distressing for Mariah to witness. He turned to face her, his voice low and intense. 'Why do you torture me so? Do you not know that I would give my *life* for it never to have happened?'

The hopeless despair on his beautiful, strong face brought tears of sadness welling in Mariah's eyes. They stood, silent and still, facing each other.

Mariah's voice came out in whisper, 'And if you did, my life would not be worth living. Without you I have nothing, I have no strength, no desire, no passion. Without you I *am* nothing.'

There was no need for further words as they stepped closer and clung together in a mutual possession that wanted no kiss or passionate searching to satiate their unfulfilled desires. Daniel had wanted this for so long and had not dared hope she could ever return his feelings. It was an embrace that swelled his heart and told him they were as one, united in their need for each other and in their satisfaction that they had found each other.

But for Mariah, there remained one last truth that would test all her strength. She put him away from her, stepping back and swallowing hard before she continued.

'You do not know everything about me and you must.' She swallowed again. 'There was a child. After the attack I was with child.'

'A child? You had a child?' Yes, he agreed. A child may not be forgotten. 'Where is he?' he asked, spreading his arms to hold her again.

'No, please don't touch me. Let me finish. You must know everything.' She sank into a nearby chair. 'You see, I did not know which of those two men—' She stopped and choked on the words. 'I could not live with the fruit of their evil seed inside me. It felt as though the devil had invaded my body and was growing within me, corrupting me. I wanted to die.'

Mariah looked at Daniel's face, searching for his rejection of her. But all she saw was sadness and hurt in his eyes, eyes that were shiny with unshed tears. 'I – I would have killed myself, if Dora had not helped me – helped me rid my body of their wickedness. But when the deed was done I knew, too late, that a part of me had died with my unborn child.' She stopped and inhaled deeply and shakily. 'That is my punishment, you see, my suffering for condemning my child, my innocent child, and I cry every day for the life I took. I have sinned, Daniel. I am unchaste, and tainted for ever by my own actions. I am not worthy of you. Go to Bel instead, live at the Hall and be a wealthy gentleman. For if you stay with me you will become tainted too.'

'No. Never. We have both made mistakes we cannot undo

402

and we must live with them as best we can. But don't you see, Mariah? If we have each other we can survive.'

'You still want me, knowing this?'

'I love you. Do you love me?'

'Yes.'

'Then we can face the future together. When we marry, our vows to each other will be stronger because of what we know about each other.'

'It will always be there. Coming between us.'

'Only if we let it. You will have more children, *our* children, and they will bring you the joy and happiness you deserve. The bad memories will fade. I shall look after you and protect you so no one in this world will ever hurt you again.'

He held her so close and kissed her with such a passion she could barely breathe. She could taste fresh tea in his mouth. She could smell the smoke of the furnace on his skin, mingling with the leather of his waistcoat. Her arms crept underneath it and around his firm strong back. She wanted to tug away his shirt and kiss the naked skin of his chest. His hands roamed the surface of her bodice, exploring her contours hungrily, her waist and breasts, her shoulders, neck and head, tangling and disturbing the smooth coils of her hair.

When they pulled apart, breathless and eager for more of each other, he whispered, 'You *will* marry me soon, won't you?'

'I will. Yes, I will.'

Chapter 37

Bel sat alone in her small sitting room and stared out of the window. Even on this grey and overcast day, the parkland looked lovely. Nathan had been right to plant more trees. She had missed him so much after the shooting. Mrs Withers had suggested as much when she had come to luncheon with her husband. Bel remembered her surprise at Mr Thorpe's presence. The two gentlemen had conversed well. When the ladies left them to their port and cigars, Mrs Withers had made another suggestion to Bel, which she had taken seriously and to which Nathan had agreed. The door opened, bringing her back to the present.

'You wish to speak to me, Miss Christobel?'

Bel turned and pasted a smile on her face. 'Yes, Mrs Havers. The master and I are quitting the Hall for the remainder of the winter. Perhaps for longer.' Saying it made it seem more real. She would feel the loss of her horses and her morning rides more than anything. But, no doubt, there would be compensations where she was going. She added, 'We shall be in Italy with our – our mother.'

'Yes, miss.' Mrs Havers hid her surprise well.

'You may close up the main rooms. You will not need all the servants when we are gone, but do try and keep them gainfully occupied. If any of them wish to leave us, I should be grateful if you would help them find suitable positions elsewhere.'

'Yes, miss.' The older woman hesitated a moment, then continued, 'Forgive my boldness, Miss Christobel, but I shall miss you both. Very much.'

'Yes.' Bel sighed. 'We shall miss you too, Mrs Havers. You have been a loyal and faithful servant to us. However, it is for the best. Withers will keep you informed. We may decide to lease the Hall.'

'Yes, miss.'

When Mrs Havers had left, Bel returned to the window. She knew she had made a fool of herself in front of Daniel Thorpe and he would never marry her. She really would have relished him as her husband. But now there were other matters to occupy her thoughts. Withers had presented her with her mothers' letters last Sunday. She hadn't read them yet. She would do so on the journey. It was going to be a long journey for her, but one she must make.

Later that month, Fanny went to visit Dora and they walked over to Keppel village.

'She's a grand lass, isn't she?' Fanny said.

'Mariah? Oh aye. The longer she stayed with me, the longer I thought of her as the daughter I never had.' Dora took her sister's arm. Neither needed the physical support, but the unspoken bond between them had not broken. It had been tested over the years, twisted and strained by events that had served only to strengthen it. 'I'm really glad they are going to wed, aren't you?'

Fanny nodded. 'Arthur's as fussy as a dog with two tails. He says she's just what our Daniel needs to steady him down.'

They walked through the wet grass, towards Keppel church-yard where it bordered the woodland, and stopped in front of a mossy headstone. The chiselled names of their mother and father were already weathered. But the names of Fanny's children, Thorpe children taken before their time, were still sharp, and reading them brought tears to the eyes of both women. One name, the first of the children, had been there longer than the others and the edges were wearing just as their parents' names were.

Also Matthew Barton, aged two weeks, grandson.

'Poor little Matthew.'

Tears welled in Fanny's eyes and ran down her cheeks. She bent down and laid a posy of winter jasmine on the grassy mound. When she straightened, Dora began to cry as well. She put her arm around Fanny's shoulders and said, 'He was a little fighter and I did my best for him, but he was born too early.'

'Did we do a wicked thing?' Fanny asked.

'No. It was for the best.'

'Do you think Arthur ought to know about him?'

'He does know. He thinks, like everyone else, that Matthew was my child,' Dora replied. 'Why? Do you want to tell him otherwise?'

'No. It would upset him. I can't tell him now, he would never forgive me for deceiving him so. When I lied to him and told him your baby had died, he shed a tear, you know. He cried! I had not seen a man cry before. But he said it was God's will and asked if you were all right. And after that he said we should not speak of it again.'

Dora gave Fanny a brief hug. 'He was right. Is right. Daniel has a mother and father who love him and that is all he needs to know.'

'But what about you, Dora, love? Yours was the greater sacrifice. You gave me your healthy baby when mine died. I'll never forget what you did for me.'

'I had to. It was the only way I could make good the wrong I had done you. And Daniel has a proper name and family. I could not have given him that.'

'Even so,' Fanny insisted, 'it doesn't seem right not to tell him.'

'Some secrets are best kept for ever.'

'From Arthur, yes. But not from Daniel,' Fanny replied. 'He should be told you are his true mother. He should know what you did for Arthur and me.'

'If you tell Daniel, you'll have to tell Arthur as well. Don't do it, Fanny.'

'You know as well as I do that Arthur does not have many more winters on this earth. If God spares me and Arthur goes first, I shall tell Daniel the truth. So I want you to promise me something, Dora.'

'Yes, of course.'

'Promise me that if I go before you, you will tell Daniel you are his real mother. You will not take this secret to your grave.'

'Yes, I'll promise you that, Fanny. It will be a shock for him, though.'

'He'll be all right. He has Mariah, now.'

407

'Aye, you're right. I'm glad they're together. I knew they cared for each other. I could tell that from the beginning,' Dora added.

'Yes, I do believe he loves Mariah more than us at home.'

'Our Daniel has a big heart. There's enough to go round. And look what a lovely new daughter you will have in Mariah.'

The sisters bent down together to pull out a few weeds from the grassy mound.

Fanny added, 'I think they could spend more time with you from now on. A lot more time.'

'I should like that very much.'

WOMEN OF IRON

To the memory of Edmund Humphrey King

I should like to thank the staff of Rotherham Archives for enabling me to find the inspiration for this story, and my friend the novelist Elizabeth Gill for her encouragement and support in the writing. Thanks, also, to my agent Judith Murdoch and editor Rosie de Courcy for their advice and direction in its completion.

Chapter 1

1830

'My God, this child will be born with or without its mother's help! I swear it will! Push, I said!' the doctor urged her. 'You must push when I say so. You must.' He turned his tired, lined face to Grace. 'Help her, woman! Tell her what she must do. She will listen to you!'

The girl let out an anguished protracted scream as another wave of grinding torture seared through her body. She clutched at Grace's hand and begged her to stop the pain, to stop the infant, to stop her life. The bed, once smooth and white, was now tumbled, stained and rank with the smell of childbirth. Grace supported the young mother's shoulders and mopped her flushed, damp face with a torn piece of linen. The coals, banked as high as possible in the grate, gave out a fierce heat and a flickering light that danced shadows across the girl's frightened eyes.

'Keep breathing like I told you, miss,' Grace murmured

soothingly, 'and do as the doctor says. It will all be over soon. First timers always take longer.'

'Not this long,' the doctor commented grimly. 'Both of them are growing weak.'

Grace looked up sharply at the concern in his voice. She had seen difficult births like this before, both mother and baby worn out by the ordeal. If they were lucky and the doctor was good, he might save one of them. Best tend to the mother, she thought. She can always have another child, next time inside wedlock.

The girl screamed again, an agonising wail that tore at Grace's heart. The girl did not deserve this. She had brought shame on her family, but, Lord in Heaven, the poor girl did not deserve this.

'Let the baby go,' she muttered quietly to the doctor. 'Save the mother.'

The doctor, if he heard her, did not respond except to say hurriedly, 'Fetch a parson. As quick as you can, woman.'

Grace picked up a storm lantern and scurried away, snatching her heavy winter cloak from its hook by the back kitchen door and stopping only to bark at the timid maidservant, 'Keep this fire banked up and fill another scuttle for upstairs. I shall take it up when I return. You stay down here, do you hear me? You stay down here tonight and make hot toddies for the men.'

She would go herself for a parson. Young servants were unreliable. Also, servants gossiped. Grace knew that because she was one herself. The less the other servants knew the better. She pulled up her hood and bent her head against icy driving rain.

The parsonage was set near to the church, a little way up the hill in this tiny coastal village, far away from London Town. An onshore gale helped her with the climb, but coming back, accompanied by a sleepy dishevelled clergyman, it took her breath clean away. She paused only once, before they entered the bedchamber, to hand the parson a coin and plea for his discretion.

The doctor had removed his waistcoat and rolled up his shirtsleeves. His hands and forearms were smeared and bloody, and, miraculously, the mother's screams had quietened. Had the doctor eventually given her some laudanum?

'Ah, you're back at last,' he said. 'Get over here, woman. I need your assistance.'

The baby was finally coming, its head was through and the mother had fallen back on the pillows in a faint, tired out by her ordeal. The infant, too, was exhausted when, eventually, she slid into this world, a lifeless skinny thing with long limbs and black hair.

Grace held out her arms for the baby. 'Shall I take her, sir?'

The doctor shook his head. 'Do what you can for her mother.'

She pulled a sheet over the bloodied bed and offered some brandy to the girl's lips, already drained of any colour. Leaning very close she whispered urgently in her ear. 'Come on, miss. It's all over now and you have a baby girl. What will you call her? You must give her a name.' Grace thought that even if the infant died, at least she would get a Christian burial if the parson baptised her now. 'What will you call her, miss?' she repeated.

'Mama, Mama,' the girl breathed. She did not, or could not, open her eyes.

'A name, you must give her a name,' Grace insisted.

''Liss. 'Liss.' The first syllable was lost as the name came out in a fading sigh and her head fell sideways.

Grace smoothed her sticky, tangled hair. Now she could sleep. Maybe by morning she would be stronger. But the infant . . . ? Through the lamp's yellow glow she watched the doctor tending the babe. There was no sound from her yet. Perhaps she had already gone. Hopefully not stillborn, but the parson wouldn't know that unless the doctor told him. He would need a name for the infant. Liss? Aliss, was it? No, it couldn't be Aliss. That was her mama's name, a name for one of the gentry and not for one born out of wedlock and shunned by her family.

A thin wail emerged from the babe. She was alive! Not for long, no doubt, if a baptism was nigh. But, if she did survive, she was likely to end up as a servant. Best not call her Aliss and cause raised eyebrows. Aliss – 'Liss – Lissie – yes, Lissie would be better. Yes, Lissie would do. Grace glanced at the infant's mother. There was not a movement from her as the child's wail developed into a cry. The doctor had given her too much laudanum to quieten her screams. He had been tending her for eight hours now. Poor man, he looked all in, as if he were ready to sleep on his feet.

She took the crying baby from him and wrapped her up for the parson. He baptised her quickly, by the flickering embers of the fire, using a chipped kitchen bowl as the font. The child was skinny all right, but long limbed, like her mama and her mama's father. Maybe she was a fighter like him. Maybe she stood a chance.

A male voice interrupted Grace's thoughts. 'Parson! Over here. Quickly! You are not here for the child. The mother's need is greater. You should have tended to the mother first. I believe you will be too late.'

The exhausting, painful struggle had been too great for the girl. Her brief life ended during that stormy winter night in a soiled and bloodied bedchamber, far away from her family home. Grace held the young life that she had helped bring into the world and contemplated this unexpected turn of events. If anyone had to die this night, why should it be the mother? The mother was young and pretty and could have married and had more children. Why had the babe not died instead?

What hope was there for a babe-in-arms with no father to speak of, and now no mother to look after her? Her ladyship's orders had been clear. The girl's family wanted nothing to do with a bastard child. The infant must be farmed out to some worthy farmer who would pocket a purse of gold and not ask any questions in return for an extra pair of working hands when the child grew older.

The doctor interrupted her thoughts. 'You will be in need of a wet nurse. I attended a young woman two days ago who can provide. She's healthy enough. You have money?'

Grace nodded. Oh, yes, she thought. For the first time in my life I have money. She had been well paid to hide and care for her pregnant charge in this isolated fishing village on the windswept Yorkshire coast.

'I'll see to it then. Give the babe to me,' the doctor went on briskly as he dried his hands on a square of linen and rolled down his shirtsleeves. 'You know what to do with the body.' It was a statement rather than a question.

Grace nodded again. 'There's meat and drink in the kitchen and a maidservant to wait on you. I'll be with you when I have — when I have finished here.'

As soon as the room was empty but for her and her charge's lifeless form, Grace carefully removed the locket and chain that also carried the casket keys from around her neck, then began the process of laying her out. The girl had kept her jewels in the casket. And money. Grace needed money.

Less than one week later, Lissie whimpered and grizzled in the biting east wind as her mother was laid to rest in a bleak and barren churchyard. It was a discreet occasion. Grace had seen to that. Only the two of them and the parson stood by to watch a plain wooden coffin being lowered into the ground. Nearby, a worn and mossy stone covered a vault that guarded the decaying remains of distant cousins on her mother's side of the family. The parson had no objections to another departed soul joining those already laid to rest in this neglected corner of his graveyard. Grace had paid him well, with enough for a local mason to add another name on the ancient stone slab.

She stamped her feet to warm them as the wind whipped round her ears. The baby in her arms began to wail. No doubt hungry again, poor mite. No one from the girl's family came to the funeral just as no one had visited her while the child grew in her belly. Why should they? She was a family disgrace. They had done their duty. They had leased an empty house for her, far away on the Yorkshire coast. She had an elderly distant cousin, a childless bachelor, living on the other side of the moor who might have attended. But the weather was evil for travelling at this time of year.

It was God's will, and for the best, thought Grace, shrugging her new wool shawl closely around herself and the little one. By gum, she thought, these local fishermen's wives knew how to fashion a warm shawl. The rain began to fall in icy drops that stung her eyes and spiked her cheeks. It would turn to snow on the moors. She should get the infant home quickly now the deed was done.

Grace would have to send a letter to the girl's family in London, telling of recent events. She sighed. Poor, wretched girl. Not fifteen years on this earth. The scandal of it all had brought her low and a putrid fever did the rest. But the infant, well, the infant was a bonny, healthy lass with a fine appetite and a strong pair of lungs. Did the family want to know about the infant? Did they *need* to know? Lissie grew heavy in her arms as Grace walked away from the churchyard.

Any barren farmer's wife would pay well for such a child and be thankful, even if she was a girl. Girls made good dairymaids and, if they were handsome, made good marriages too. Grace had no need for a purse of sovereigns to farm out this little mite and she wondered if she might keep her to herself. She wrote to the family that the child was a puny boy who might not thrive and would be hard to place unless he grew stronger. She reasoned to herself that a bastard boy with a claim to the family name would be better dead as far as the family were concerned. They would want no scandal attached to them. She finished the letter by saying that she would stay in Yorkshire and do her best by him. Grace needed time to think about how she could get far away from the family.

The doctor had been as good as his word and a wet nurse had arrived promptly. She was a ruddy-faced, hungry fisherman's wife whose latest baby had sickened and died within the first few days of life. Little Lissie, having survived her fight for life at birth, carried on her demanding ways, took to a stranger's breast well and thrived.

Grace, for her part, had weathered the northern winter in a pleasant haze of warm fires and French brandy, courtesy of the grateful suppliers of her household needs. She had kept a good table for Lissie's mother, and continued to patronise the local tradesmen for herself and the baby and her wet nurse.

She needed to consider her future. If she kept the baby and the gold in the dead mother's casket, where would she go and what would she do? She could travel a long way with all that gold, but not so far at her age with an infant in tow. There was no hurry; this coastal house was comfortable and it would be madness to travel anywhere before the spring. Grace bided her time while Lissie ate, slept and grew.

It was Ruth, the wet nurse, who gave her the idea. Lissie was suckling contentedly at Ruth's breast and,

already, her skinny limbs were filling out. She had lost
the shock of black hair she was born with soon after
birth. Now it was growing back, just as black, but her
skin was not olive as Grace had expected. It was pale,
almost translucent, lightly tinged with a baby pink, and
her eyes were turning a smoky shade of green.

Ruth heaved Lissie over to her other breast. 'Blooming
'eck, she's getting heavy. I think she puts on weight every
day. And eat! Look at her, still going at it! Shall we try
her wi' some bread and milk tomorrer? 'Ave you thought
what you're going to do with 'er, Grace?'

Grace was mulling a tankard of ale for each of them
by a good fire in the upstairs drawing room. She had
cut two thick slices of bread and speared one to the end
of a long-handled brass fork. 'I don't know yet. I can't
keep her with me, whatever I do.'

'Do you want to go back down south?'

'No, I don't.' Grace shrugged, and then thought for a
moment. 'Well, it doesn't matter where I am really, only
I don't want to go back into service with the gentry.
I've had enough of running round after them and I've
done a good job here without having to take orders
from any gentry.'

'Oh aye, you 'ave that. Everybody says so. You've had
this place all cleaned up and cosy for the winter. Where
did you learn how to do it all?'

'In the poor house when I was a nipper. Over in the
South Riding. I was born there, you see. The Admiral's
family used to come up to Yorkshire every year for the
shooting and I was sent from the poor house to help
out at the lodge.' Grace became thoughtful for a moment,

shaking her head gently. 'I wouldn't wish the poor house on this little mite.' Then she brightened. 'I was good with the children and in the sickroom too, and, one year, they took me back to London Town with them. The master was a captain in the navy then and lived in a mansion near the Thames.'

'You were lucky to get out o' the poor house like that.'

'Not so lucky with my husband though. I married a sailor and he was always at sea. I had to get used to being on my own.'

'Didn't he come home ever?'

'Oh, aye! But when he did, he spent all his money, an' most of his time, in alehouses!' Grace became thoughtful again and sighed. 'He didn't come back from Trafalgar though. That was twenty-five years ago. I went to work for the Admiral again. He was a hero by then, and he knew the Regent and the old King and everybody.'

'Will you go back there?'

Grace curled her lip and shook her head. 'They don't want anything to do with the little 'un. They're too grand now, with all their fancy ways. No, after a lifetime of that I've had my bellyful o' the gentry. I'll move out of here in springtime. I shall find somewhere for the babe to keep her out of the poor house and will look for a little lodging house of my own.'

'A lodging house? There i'n't much call for them around here, or up on the moors. You will 'ave to go to t' big towns for that.'

'A town would suit me. I'm used to London Town.'

Lissie was slowing down now, snuffling at Ruth's breast and becoming sleepy. 'Best put her down,' Grace suggested, 'and come and get yourself something to eat.'

Ruth laid Lissie on the sofa, sat by the fire with Grace, and continued, 'There are ports down the coast, all around the river Humber. Always money from sea-going ships and canal barges down there, my Joseph says.' She took some toasted bread and butter and sank her teeth into it with relish. The butter ran down her chin and she wiped it away with the back of her hand. 'My Joseph says you can make a good living from the Humber. It's rough though, wi' all the sailors and gangs o' thugs about.'

Grace knew from her days on the Thames what it was like to live near docks. She was familiar with the comings and goings on wharfs, and the ways of sailors, whether they sailed with merchant ships or the King's navy, and she wanted none of it. No longer young, she wanted something easier for herself. 'Aye,' she replied, 'I know about living in ports well enough. And I know I've had enough of sea-going men.'

'Well,' Ruth added, 'they have plenty o' trade in the South Riding. There's coal and iron and they say they'll soon have railways as well. They'll be all over the Riding one day, my Joseph says. Three of the fishermen have already left their boats to work down the pits or on the furnaces.'

Grace's memories of the South Riding were grim. Brought up on the parish, her young life had been one of humility and hardship, constantly scrubbing away the ashes and soot belched out by the ironworks chimneys. Men and women worked hard, they sweated hard and drank hard. Her escape to London Town had been a welcome release from this at first. But she quickly realised that emptying slops and cleaning grates for the gentry was no different from the poor house, except that she wore cotton aprons instead of sacking.

The Admiral did not travel to Yorkshire for the shooting any more. Since Trafalgar he had suffered from an injured leg that pained him constantly and tried his patience. But the wealthy Riding ironmasters he knew from previous journeys often visited him in his elegant London house. And they brought their sons with them.

Lissie's father was one of those sons. A young gentleman he was, full of his own importance, based on his father's money and his university education. Lissie's mother was the Admiral's youngest child, fourteen at the time and a wild, wilful girl who was taken in by the young gentleman's charm. Some gentleman! Grace had heard them at it regularly, like a pair of rabbits, in the old attic nursery and was not surprised a few months later when she was asked to take the girl away somewhere and farm out the child. The young gentleman did not even know and nobody considered telling him.

The towns of the South Riding were grimy, and the gentry lived on the surrounding hills away from the smoke and dirt of the manufactories in the river valleys. But Grace remembered the soft wind and rain, sheltered as it was from driving westerly gales by the Pennine chain. Years ago the woollen trade had thrived there, but now the hills were scattered with ironstone pits and coal mines to feed the greedy furnaces of ironworks by the river.

The South Riding was prosperous, Grace considered. It had plenty of trade and men with money to spend on good lodgings. A woman could make herself a living there, she decided. She took another piece of toasted bread and spread it generously with fresh butter.

'Well, you were born in Yorkshire, so why not come back for good?' Ruth suggested. 'As you're on your own, like. Unless you think you'll wed again, o' course? You'd have no trouble wi' that, you being such a good cook an' all.'

As Ruth chattered on, between mouthfuls of toasted bread and warm, spiced ale, Grace's thoughts wandered. What about the babe though? She would not be able to run a lodging house with a babe in arms, and it would be years before the infant would be old enough to work. Grace went to sit by her on the sofa. She did not want the child to end up in the poor house. What would the poor house do for her? Work her hard and then place her as a servant when she was ten years old? The poor house did not look after its destitute folk for no reward. They expected, and they got, payment for the years their inmates had lived on the parish. Most of the payment never went back to the parish either, but into the pocket of the poor house master and his wife, if he had one.

Little Lissie already showed promise of becoming a real beauty with her large eyes and pretty mouth. She was too lovely for the poor house and a life as a drudge or a farm servant. Grace could do better than that for her. She owed it to her and her poor ma, if nothing else. There must be many a body who would pay well for such a beautiful, healthy infant. Then, Grace calculated, she would have her ladyship's purse from the casket, and more besides for her trouble. With all that gold and silver she could make a nice life for herself somewhere else, and she wouldn't have to go back to the beck and call of the gentry ever again.

Grace gave a rare smile and swallowed another mouthful of mulled ale. 'What did you say, Ruth? You think she is ready to take some bread and milk? Well, I'm sure you're right. We'll start her on that tomorrow. Your time with her is nearly done.'

As soon as the days began to lengthen and the weather turned warmer, Grace planned her departure from the Yorkshire coast. She told all those who asked that she was going back down south, from where she came with the infant. She would take the same route out that had brought her and the girl here at the beginning of winter, by turnpike south to the Humber and then she would take a coastal vessel to London. The first part was true. She would take little Lissie with her to the estuary. And then, who knows where she might go.

Travelling with a babe in arms in a coach and four was hard work for Grace now that she was no longer agile. Her joints were stiffened by sitting and ached when she moved. But her fellow passengers were entranced by Lissie's infant beauty and ready smile, and they were more than willing to hold her while Grace took a nap or ate her bread and cheese. And while she travelled, she thought about her plan and her future.

A babe like this might grow into a fine young woman, maybe catch the eye of a rich husband. She had breeding too. The blood in her veins was gentry. If Grace had been a younger woman she would have considered keeping her. But the exhausting carriage journey made her realise that she no longer had the energy to look after a little one as well as herself. And a child would cost her a good deal of money until she was old enough to work.

No, she would have to move her on and a healthy little beauty, as Lissie was, would fetch a good price from the right buyer. Besides, with all that gold she could take a house in a nice part of town, and provide lodgings for gentlemen to earn her daily bread. Once the babe was off her hands, she decided, she would transfer to the cheaper canal barges to reach her destination. Until then, she would stay in a respectable inn and she asked her fellow travellers to recommend one.

The North Star, near to the coaching inn where the horses were changed, was suitable. It was away from the squalor and noise of the docks, yet within easy reach of the waterways for those travelling on. Night had fallen when Grace arrived, followed by a boy and handcart with her luggage. The saloon was alive with drinkers and the landlord carried her boxes upstairs while an exhausted Grace wrestled with a tired and fractious Lissie.

Grace surveyed her room. 'I'll have my dinner in here, as soon as you can. Bring me some warm milk and toasted bread for the babe. You got a crib somewhere for her?' The landlord nodded and muttered something about his wife finding one. 'Good,' she continued, now well used to dealing with tradesmen and the like. 'Have you got a girl who can give me a helping hand with her? I think the poor mite's got her first tooth coming through.'

The landlord disappeared quickly, anxious to get back to the familiar territory of his saloon. Babbies, he thought, were women's work. However, a short while later a young woman knocked on Grace's door and offered her services as nursemaid. By the time Grace had eaten her dinner and Lissie had been quietened with a teaspoon of French brandy in some milk and honey, Grace had learned from her gossiping helper all she needed to know about the inn's regular visitors.

She waited until late, when most of the inn's drinkers had gone to their homes and wives, before going down for a tankard of porter. It was dark outside and the nights were cold, so the only people remaining were, like her, staying at the North Star. She took her drink to a seat by the fire, next to a genial-looking fellow in a respectable tweed jacket, with a round face and a belly to match. The nursemaid had described him well.

He looked up and gave a nod. 'Evening.'

Grace nodded in return.

'Saw you arrive earlier,' he said. 'With a babe in arms. Have you come far?'

'North Riding,' Grace answered, swallowing the greater part of her drink with relish.

She didn't want him knowing too much of her business, even if she was going to move on. The gentry all knew each other round these parts and it would never do for any word to get back to the Admiral's family about the child. Her mind began to race as she made up a story of the child's origins.

Her new companion leaned forward, threw a couple of logs on to the dying embers of the fire and shouted over his shoulder, 'Landlord! More whisky for me – and another of whatever the lady is drinking.' He raised his eyebrows in Grace's direction.

'Ta very much,' she replied, emptying her tankard. 'The name's Grace, Grace Beighton.'

'Luther Dearne. Pleased to meet you.'

They carried on exchanging pleasantries until Grace was satisfied she could talk business with Luther. He was a rogue and a crook, she didn't doubt, but he sported a fine wool waistcoat with a gold watch and chain across his ample belly. The nursemaid told her that he was known for being a soft touch with the landlord's children, having none of his own. For her part, Grace concentrated on covering her tracks regarding Lissie's story. She needed to have the story straight in her own head before she told anybody else.

The child, she decided, was a foundling and would have died of exposure if Grace hadn't rescued her, and she was such a beautiful child she deserved better than the poor house and a menial life as a laundry girl or scullery maid. But Grace herself was a widow, which was true, and no longer young, which was also true, and she needed help to look after a baby as she had very little money of her own. What she was seeking was someone with a need for a lovely, healthy child for their own. They had to have means to compensate Grace for the trouble and expense of rescuing the infant. And she was such a pretty lass, you only had to set eyes on her to take to her . . .

Luther interrupted her thoughts. 'How long are you staying here?'

'Just till I've completed my little bit of business,' Grace replied.

Luther stared at her. She was nothing special to look at, he thought, but she seemed respectable enough. Plain dress though, the sort of thing a housekeeper to the gentry might wear. 'And what line of business is that then?'

Grace lowered her voice and leaned forward. 'I've got something to place that needs a special kind of buyer.'

Luther drew his chair closer to Grace's. 'Tell me more. I do a bit of dealing myself.'

Grace told him her brief story about the 'foundling' child and before long she could see that he was interested.

'That was the child?' he asked. 'The one you brought with you? Can I 'ave a look?'

She faked a yawn to stall him. 'I've been travelling all day, my friend, and I need to rest. Tomorrow is time enough for that. I'll bid you goodnight for now.' She took a candle and retreated upstairs to where Lissie, soothed by her teaspoonful of brandy, slept soundly in an old and battered wooden crib. Lowering the light to see her better, Grace was pleased with the way the nurse-maid had washed and changed her before tucking a clean blanket around her. In the yellow glow, her skin looked as soft as down and her tiny lips like rose petals. Her silky black hair poked out of the pretty white night bonnet her mother had lovingly sewn for her.

Grace stroked Lissie's cheek with the back of her

knuckle. 'Little beauty, aren't you? And eyes so green, a smoky green like I've never seen before. You'll fetch me a good price, I'll wager. Enough for old Grace to set up her own little place and see out her days in a bit o' comfort. And well away from your poor ma's family and their prying eyes. Sleep tight, my little one. Your old Grace has a nice big fat fish on a hook for you.'

Chapter 2

Luther Dearne loitered on the dockside, thinking about the woman at the inn last night who called herself Grace. He wondered if she was wed and what kind of deal she would strike with him.

Pity she was so plain though, for he did like a pretty face to look at over a tankard of ale. Not that he had a particularly roving eye for the women.

Not like his mate Mickey from the Navigator Inn back home. Mickey just could not keep his hands off anything in a skirt when he was a young man. He had mellowed a bit of late, but even nowadays nobody's daughter was safe when Mickey was around!

No, it wasn't the woman herself who had caught Luther's attention. Truth to tell she was a bit of an old trout. It was seeing her when she arrived, carrying that babby up the stairs, that had pulled at his heart.

It was the way of things, he knew. Mickey and his missus had three lads and a lass now, while he and Edie had none. He stood watching that Svenson fellow who had come in on the clipper with iron to sell. There he was with his woman and their little lad, arm in arm and happy, talking together with the kid playing round his mam's skirts, and Luther knew he was missing out on something.

He should have realised on his wedding night that Edie was going to be no good to him in the bedchamber. He thought, then, that she was young and not experienced in these things and that excited him because he looked forward to teaching her a few tricks to help things along.

'Give us a kiss, lass,' he had said as he got into bed. Luther was proud of his manhood and it had not let him down that night, so he had left off his nightshirt to show off his strength. Edie did not seem impressed and was clothed up to her ears. He put his hand up her nightgown and played around between her legs with his fingers, but she was as dry as old sticks.

'You're not frightened o' me, are you, lass?' he asked.

'No. Me mam said to keep still and let yer get on wi' it. She said it do'n't last long.'

'Your mam 'a'n't seen my cock. Put yer hand on it, lass. You want to know what you're getting, don't you?'

'What do you mean, Luther?'

He pushed her nightgown further up and rolled towards her so that she could feel his hardness on her thigh. 'What do yo' think o' that, then?'

Edie did not know what to think and stayed silent. Her mam had said if she did not like what he did it was best just to lie there quiet until he'd finished.

Luther continued to probe around between her legs, but his heart was sinking fast. 'Bloody 'ell, Edie, the tarts on the cut would be begging me by now.'

'Well go an' find one o' them, then,' she retaliated, fed up with all this playing around.

Luther gave up his attempted foreplay and snapped, 'Oh shurrup then and oppen yer legs.'

She always let him do it, whenever he wanted. But she didn't rave on like the other women he'd been with. Maybe she'd be better when she had a babby, he thought. And they did it that often, he'd been sure he'd get her with child soon. But he had been wrong.

If only his Edie would give him a son, or even a daughter, their life would be better. But, no matter how much he tried, he couldn't get Edie with child. Now, even the sweat of all that trying was beginning to pall and this vexed him even more. Edie had lost her youthful bloom and he, too, was well past his prime, so it was hard work these days.

He'd really loved Edie when they were first wed, but she still never did anything for him in the marriage bed to help things along. Not that Edie ever complained about her duties in bed. She was a good wife to him in that respect. But he'd known from that first night, and her weary sighs when she rolled over for him, that he wasn't really welcome. Still, she always did her duty. Though it was nigh on ten years since they had wed and no sign of any babbies at all.

Oh my, he thought, Edie had been such a pretty little thing when he married her, like a china doll with brown ringlets and pink cheeks that dimpled when she smiled.

Now she seemed just like dried-out skin and bone. She could do with fattening up a bit, he reckoned, if she was ever to bear him a healthy babby. Yes, that's what she wanted! A fine ham or a joint of salt beef might set Edie to rights.

He stroked his ample chins and wandered over to where the barges and Yorkshire keels were unloading their cargo of fire grates and ranges for that foreigner Svenson to ship down the coast to London. He knew the bargeman well.

'Leave those till last,' he muttered to him under his breath as he was about to move the first of the ornate fire surrounds and mantelshelves. He slipped a half sovereign into the bargeman's palm and added, 'Wait until the foreigner has gone and then hire a wagon and a couple of hefty lads. Keep what's left o' this for yourself and there'll be the other half and a good dinner wi' a flagon of ale for you if you get a couple of those fireplaces safely to the stable yard behind the North Star after nightfall.'

Luther reckoned that Svenson wouldn't miss a few pieces from his payload, and a stylish fire grate and surround for the best room at the North Star should easily take care of what he owed the landlord at the inn. The other would take care of his winter larder at home with no questions asked and a bottle or two of gin for Edie to keep her sweet.

That Svenson fellow, the foreigner, had driven a hard bargain for his cargo. But Luther knew ironmasters who would take all he could get of Swedish bar iron for their furnaces and forges in the South Riding, and he had finally secured some at a fair price. It was not cheap by any means. This Swedish iron was the best there was, and Svenson knew it, by God. Luther also knew that a barge-load of new cast-iron cooking ranges to ship down the coast to London would be good business for Svenson too. He could strike a deal with any man, dealing was in his blood, and the foreigner had seemed satisfied.

The bargemen were under pressure to keep their transporting prices down, now that they had a bit of competition from railways. Their Yorkshire keels, when they were empty of fire grates and ranges, would be loaded with bar iron to carry back through the canals and cuts to the South Riding to be forged into wheels, axles and beams for steam engines and railways. The new cut went right up to Tinsley now, making it easy to get the heavy stuff right into the heart of the South Riding.

Even so, the bargemen were uneasy about their future. There was a lot of talk of the success of the railways in the North Riding, and of how the waterways had had their day. They feared for their livelihoods on the barges, and that of their families. Luther knew this and used it to get the lowest prices he could for transporting the iron. With his contacts on the wharfs and in the coal-field manufactories, he could guarantee barges had full payloads both ways. This kind of dealing meant that there was always a bargeman who owed Luther a favour, and who would give him free passage back home when his business was done.

Luther spent the next couple of hours bartering the remaining cast-iron fireplace with its fashionable brass trimmings. He had trading cronies near the docks who

knew a bargain when they saw one and asked no questions. His blood was up when he got back to the North
Star at the end of the day. Doing deals always fired him
up in this way, it was what he lived for. Some good ale
and a hot dinner was what he wanted now. If only he
could sort Edie out with a babby, his life would be
perfect.

It was late when he finally sat down to some hot
food, but the old trout was still there at the inn. She was
in the same place by the fire with her tankard of dark
stout, which she raised to salute him as he strolled into
the saloon. Luther tried to keep calm but he was bubbling
underneath. His day had gone well and it wasn't over
yet. He hoped the old woman was not spinning him a
line about the babby.

He played for time by eating his dinner first. But he
wolfed down the roast mutton and greens and gulped
his ale. Finally, he wandered over to the fire. 'Evening,
ma'am,' he began. 'Had a good day?'

'Fair.' Grace was in fine fettle, having spent her day
recovering from yesterday's journey and arranging her
onward passage. 'You?'

'Usual.' Through a haze of wood smoke, he thought
she didn't look too bad in the flickering light of the fire.
He drew up a chair and stretched out his legs. 'You still
got your bit o' business to finish?'

'If you mean the business we talked of last night –
aye, I have.'

Luther's spirits soared. 'You still got hold o' the goods
then?'

Grace raised her eyes to the ceiling. 'Still up there. I

want a good price, mind. You'll see for yourself that she's a little beauty and I know she's from good stock.'

'It's a girl then.'

'Didn't I say? Are you looking for a boy?'

'Might be.' A girl, Luther thought. A girl would do. A little beauty, the woman said. When she grew up, she'd be like Edie was as a young girl. A little beauty! Edie would be bound to love her, like Mickey's wife loved their little Miriam. He tried to calm himself. 'Good stock, you say? I thought you said she was a foundling.'

'Take my word for it, she's gentry.'

'How do you know?'

'I know because I brought her into this world. I looked after her ma and her ma was a lady.'

Luther persisted. 'Last night you said she was a foundling.'

'Aye, well, she is. Her ma died and there was no other family to take her in. She was destined for the poor house.'

'What about her pa?'

'Nobody knows who he was,' she lied. 'Born the wrong side of the blanket, y' see.'

Luther believed the woman. 'Let's have a look then.'

Grace rose to her feet. 'Bring a lamp and follow me.'

Luther knocked back his drink and went upstairs to the bedchamber. As he approached the battered crib in the darkest corner of Grace's room he felt the excitement rising in his chest until it nearly choked him. This little babby was everything the old woman had said. Here was his future with Edie! A child. A beautiful child. Their very own child. He couldn't believe his luck! He almost forgot he was a dealer in his haste to talk terms. Almost.

'Well, well, yes, she is a little beauty, just like you say. Does she 'ave a name?'

Grace shrugged. 'When she's yours you can call her what you want.'

'Nay, I know nowt about girls' names.' And Edie knows even less, he thought.

'What did her ma call her?'

'Lissie.'

'Lissie? Not heard o' that one afore. Pretty, though. I like it.'

'It's short for Aliss. Her ma called her that afore she went. But we baptised her Lissie.'

'She's baptised then?'

'The . . . I . . . I thought she was going to die as well as her ma, so I fetched a parson.'

'Parsons cost money.'

'There was a bit of money from her ma. It's all gone now and I can't afford to keep her.'

The air was silent while Luther absorbed this information, then he asked, 'Are there any papers or letters?'

'Nothing, I swear it,' Grace lied. 'If you buy her, she'll be yours, don't you fret.'

Grace reckoned that even if the girl's family knew about her they wouldn't want her. No, she was best dead as far as they were concerned. She had found some trinkets and papers in the locked casket with the gold. These keepsakes were too good to throw away but she'd probably burn the papers when the babe had gone. Grace began to get restless. She wanted this business over and done with and demanded impatiently, 'Do you want her or not?'

Luther thought he had better cover his tracks, just in case somebody came after her. 'Oh aye, I want her all right. Not for me, you understand. It just so happens that I know of a couple looking for a babby to bring up as their own. They're not gentry but they have means and good connections.'

'What sort o' connections?' Grace demanded. The last thing she wanted was any gentry poking their noses into this deal.

'They're in trade,' he answered, 'and they live a long way from here.'

'Whereabouts and how far?' Grace wanted to know. It wouldn't do for the babe to go back to the North Riding, even if her cousins there were distant ones.

'Nigh on middle o' the country if you're going coast to coast. They are good folk though, and they live away from the 'factories. Cordwainers they are. Folks allus want boots so the little 'un will never want for owt.'

Luther never had any trouble in enlarging on the truth. He was well-practised in the art, and he continued, 'Of course, there'd be my expenses in getting her there, but I'll take full responsibility for that. If they don't like the look of her I wouldn't bring her back to you. I'd find somebody else for her. Mind you, a girl is harder to place than a boy. But, no matter, I can take her off your hands for good if you want – at the right price, o' course. What do you say to a deal?'

He was good, Grace thought, at pretending the babe was for someone else. But she knew that he had fallen

for her, and the gleam in his eye told Grace he wanted
this baby, and he wanted her badly. Maybe he was telling
the truth and maybe he wanted to sell her on when she
was a bit more grown. But she could see that he'd set
his heart on her, and Grace was not going to let this
one off the hook. She named her price, adding, 'In gold,
if you please.'

Luther eyes rolled. 'That's a bit steep.' He offered a
smaller sum, like he did with his dealing, expecting to
agree a lower price.

Grace walked over to the door and opened it pointedly. 'No deal. That's her price. It's what she's worth. Take
it or leave it. I've got another body interested if you've
changed your mind.'

He thought for a minute. He could not let this chance
slip through his fingers. If he walked out now and offered
a higher price in the morning, he might be too late; she
might be gone. Oh what a pretty little babby she was,
wrapped up in shawls and slumbering in her battered
old crib.

As far as Luther was concerned she was his already.
He said, 'For that money, I'll want all her clothes and
everything – and your silence.'

'That goes without saying. Her things are in the crib
for you.'

'And I want to take her with me now. Tonight.'

'You got the gold here?'

'I 'ave that.'

'All of it?'

'Aye.'

'Done, then.' Grace spat on her hand and held it out.

Luther did the same and he grasped hers briefly as
he did with the canal traders. Then he began to pat his
tweed coat and breeches to locate the small leather
pouches of gold and silver he kept secreted about his
person. He counted out the coins on to the marble slab
of Grace's washstand and put the remaining loose coins
in his waistcoat pockets.

Grace watched him closely then picked up the money.
She turned her back on him and hoisted up her skirts
to reach the leather belt and purse around the waist of
her under-drawers. When she had hidden the money
from his view she turned back and asked, 'Have you
looked after a babe before?'

'The landlord's girl has been helping you, hasn't she?
Send her along to me.' With that closing remark, Luther
picked up the crib with the babe asleep in it, and left.
Lissie was his, all his. He had a daughter, a little beauty
of a daughter and he couldn't wait to get her home to
Edie.

'Edie! Edie, lass, look what I've got 'ere for yer!'

Edie Dearne jumped when she heard Luther's voice
outside. She did not particularly like being married to
Luther, but she reckoned it was better than being a
pithead lass or a farm girl. Or a mill girl. Edie had heard
terrible tales of working in the big mills hereabouts. She
had never gone after the boys much, not like the other
village lasses, so when Luther took a shine to her her
mam had made sure he took her to the altar. But Edie
never thought that being married was up to much and
it suited her for Luther to go off for weeks at a time

doing his deals. He was generous with the money he
made and she could do exactly as she pleased all day
and every day when he was away.

She was in the front room trying to get a fire going
so that Luther could sit in there with a jar of ale after
his dinner. He was fussy about that when he came home,
and had sent word ahead with one of the bargemen that
he was on his way. He liked things to be ready for him,
a good dinner, some strong ale and a comfy chair by a
roaring fire. And Edie looking pretty.

She patted her ringlets and took off her pinny. It was
hard to keep looking nice all the time. Her mam used
to help her afore she was married, and afterwards until
she died. But Edie found it tiresome to curl her hair on
her own. Luther was strict with her as well, about her
not going over to the Navigator when he was off down
the canal doing his dealing. He said she had enough to
do keeping up with the house and garden when he was
away.

She stared out of the front-room window. Luther was
striding across the clearing in the trees with a sack over
his shoulder. And behind him was a woman carrying a
bundle. No, not a bundle, a babby. The woman had a
babby in her arms. What was going on?

Fear clutched at Edie's stomach. Luther was *her*
husband! What was he doing with another woman and
a babby? She hurried through to the back kitchen and
opened the scullery door to let him in.

'Ee, lass,' Luther said, 'you'll be right pleased about
this.' He turned to the woman behind him. 'Ta, love.
Step inside a minute.'

The woman nodded at Edie and laid her bundle on the kitchen table, then loosened a pack strapped to her back, dropped it to the floor and held out her hand. Luther counted out a few coins, murmured, 'Much obliged,' and the woman left as silently as she had arrived.

'Who was that?' Edie demanded, looking aghast at her departing back.

But Luther, excited to have Lissie home at last, was focused on the sleeping child. 'Isn't she a beauty?' He smiled.

'She looks like any other barge gypsy to me,' Edie responded sourly.

'Not 'er. The babby. I've fetched us a babby, Edie.'

Edie felt herself go rigid all over. 'I can see that. Whose is it and what do we want wi' it?'

'It's ours. O' course we want it. It's a little lass, just like Annie Jackson's Miriam. All 'er things are 'ere an' all. She's ours, Edie, love. All ours.'

Edie thought Luther had lost his wits and said, 'Well she's not mine and I don't want owt to do wi' 'er.'

'Course you do, Edie. We've been wed ten year now. That's a long time to wait for a babby and you're not a young lass any more.'

'You don't have to tell me that, Luther Dearne,' Edie scowled. ''Ave you been carrying on wi' that barge whore who brought 'er? Is she 'ers?'

Luther didn't like the way Edie was talking. He thought she'd be as pleased as he was to have a babby at last. But she was not taking to the little 'un at all. 'I told you,' he said firmly. 'She's ours.'

'Oh aye? Are you 'er dad, then?'

Now he was getting impatient with Edie. She had no right to question him like this. She was his wife and she'd damn well do as he told her. 'What if I am?' he answered angrily. 'You 'a'n't given me any, 'ave yer?'

'Well,'it i'n't fo' want o' trying,' Edie snapped sullenly. She di'n't want any babbies anyway, spoiling it between her and Luther. If she allus did as Luther said she never went short o' coal or food on t' table. An' he brought her snuff and gin when he was flushed wi' money. An' she could do what she pleased when he was away, as long as she stayed this side o' the canal.

'I don't want 'er round 'ere, Luther,' Edie continued. 'Why can't her own mam look after 'er?'

'You're her mam now, Edie. Look at 'er, she's lovely.'

But Edie was stubborn. 'I don't know how to look after a babby.'

'Yes you do. You're a woman, aren't you? Empty one o' them cupboard drawers to put 'er in for now. I've got some more of her things waiting on the wharf.'

Edie began to whine. 'Tek 'er back where she came from while you're down there. And bring me me snuff. You 'ave got some snuff for me, Luther, 'a'n't you? You allus brings me some snuff.'

But Edie's pleading fell on deaf ears. Luther walloped 'er one if she didn't get on wi' things. 'E spent all 'is money on things for the babby and left Edie on 'er own to do the extra washing and feeding. She got fed up wi' 'im allus cooing an' gurgling at the little 'un so as 'e 'ad no time for 'er any more. She 'ad no snuff neither. And when Luther said 'e'd on'y fetch her some from the Navvy if she looked after the babby right, Edie realised that she had moved to second place in Luther's affections.

In contrast, Grace was satisfied with her deal. Luther Dearne was soft about the babby and the landlord's girl had said he had a wife and a house and money in his pocket. She was sad to part with the infant, but she had already booked a passage on a Yorkshire keel heading for the South Riding. She planned to find a position to keep her while she looked for a house of her own.

She obtained a place as a housekeeper and nurse to a merchant and his dying wife. Mr Sowden, a successful grain dealer, had acquired two stepdaughters when he had married their widowed mother. The elder girl had packed her box and gone before Grace moved in. But the younger daughter, Clara, would not leave her dying mother.

They were reasonably well-to-do, though the house was small and inconvenient and they did not keep a pony and trap. Only Mr Sowden went out, alone and on horseback. Grace did not like him, but she reckoned that his wife would not live much longer and then her position would come to an end. She spent three months of her life trying to organise his dilapidated household while cleaning up the soiled bed and washing the decaying body of his dying wife.

On the day Mrs Sowden died, Grace stood in the open door of his study and informed him. 'Your wife has passed on, sir,' she said.

He was unemotional. 'Do what you have to,' he said dismissively.

'Shall I arrange the funeral as well, sir?'

'Yes, yes!' he replied irritably. 'And do not bother me with this matter again.'

'As you wish, sir.' Grace bobbed a curtsey. 'I'll lay out her body in the sickroom.'

Mr Sowden, she thought, was a harsh, mean-spirited man. His cold grey eyes became flinty in their bony sockets. Grace left the study quickly.

He called after her. 'Wait,' he barked. 'Come back here.'

'Sir?'

'Send my daughter to me.'

'Yes, sir.'

Miss Clara was a grown woman, but her stepfather treated her like a servant. Paid servants, Grace realised, did not stay long and now she understood why. But the position, located as it was on the edge of the South Riding, had suited her until she got to know the Riding better. Although the house was cold and dank and dirty, she had done her best for mother and daughter in the time she had been there. She hurried to the kitchen where Clara was helping with supper.

Clara had been crying and Grace's hardened heart melted a little. 'I am so sorry, Miss Clara. I did all I could for your mother.'

Clara wiped her eyes with a soggy handkerchief. 'I know you did, Mrs Beighton. You have been a great support for me too. You are a good woman. Do you think Father will keep you on?'

Grace had no intention of staying. But she frowned at the idea of leaving Miss Clara with her stepfather. He was a nasty man.

'I cannot say. He wants to see you in his study.'

Grace noticed the alarm in her eyes. Such a pity her life was so miserable for she was quite lovely to look at, Grace thought. Just as she imagined her little Lissie would be when she grew up, with fair skin and grey-green eyes, and glossy black hair dressed in coils at the back of her head. Lissie's eyes had been green, whereas Clara's were blue. She hoped that Luther was being kind to Lissie.

Grace Beighton did not shed tears easily. She had lost a few when she heard of her husband's death at sea, and when Luther Dearne left the North Star with Lissie. And now, as she saw the grief and fear in Clara's eyes, she allowed herself a few more. Since Clara's sister had left the household, all Mr Sowden's bidding fell to her.

'It's going to be awful here without you,' Clara said. 'Just me and him, and no one else to turn his anger on.'

Her sorrow was heart-breaking for Grace to see. Despite her position as servant, she walked around the kitchen table and took Clara's hand in hers.

Clara did not snatch it away. She held on to it, took a deep breath and said, 'You are such a help for me.'

Grace nodded slightly. Life was hard for women when the master was cruel, she thought, even in a well-to-do merchant's house like this one. And this master was cruel. Grace was uncomfortable in his presence, recognising, as she did, a man of dubious appetites. He had married an older woman for her property, yet preferred the pleasures of younger flesh, which he sometimes brought back to the house. Clara's mother's second marriage had been ill-judged and poor Clara was now alone with this brute of a stepfather.

'Best not keep him waiting,' Grace advised.

Clara dried her eyes and remembered just in time to take off her apron and smooth down her hair before she entered her stepfather's dusty study. He was a thin, bony man with greying hair and copious whiskers around thin lips and a receding chin. Her mother had told her he had been a charming young gentleman fifteen years ago when they had married. And a successful shopkeeper.

Clara stood in the middle of a worn square of carpet, gritty with spilled ashes from his warm study fire. Her stepfather stood up and examined her appearance in detail before he spoke.

'You are the lady of this house now. If you attempt to run off like your sister I shall find you and flog you. Do you understand?'

'Yes, Father.'

'And be sure that you do not fall ill and die on me as your mother has done.'

'She only became ill because you treated her so badly,' Clara muttered.

'What did you say?' he breathed angrily.

'It's true!' she cried. 'You treated my mother like a servant and insulted her by bringing your . . . your women into her house!'

'How dare you speak to me like that!' he shouted.

'This was my mother's house, *her* house, left to her by my own dear father, and you defiled it with your . . . your whores!'

The back of his hand across her face sent her reeling to the floor. 'This is *my* house. *Mine*. Your mother was *my* wife. Everything here belongs to *me*.' His flinty glare swept over her again and he added, 'Including you.'

'Well, I shall be twenty-one soon,' Clara replied, 'and then you cannot own me.'

He grabbed her by her hair and hauled her to her feet. 'We shall see about that. Go to your chamber. Now.'

Grace had heard the argument from the kitchen and hurried to the study, opening the door without knocking.

The master was furious. 'Leave this instant, Beighton. I did not call for you.'

'But, your daughter, sir, she has a cut on her face.'

'I ordered you to leave!'

'Yes, sir.' Grace retreated to the kitchen. She glanced at Clara as she left and saw the fear in her eyes.

Clara's fear was justified. Her stepfather was unpredictable and he was a frightening sight when he was angry. He had taken out his temper first on her mother and then on her elder sister. Now they were both gone and Clara remembered the last rational words her mother had spoken before she died. She had pleaded with her to leave this house.

'Do not let him break you as he has me,' she had begged. 'Follow your sister. I am finished now. He can hurt me no more.'

'Daughter.' Her stepfather never used her name. 'You will go to your chamber. I shall deal with you presently.'

Clara hurried away. Her face was stinging where he had struck her. She sat on the edge of her feather bed and nursed her swollen cheek. He would beat her for this outburst. The long wait for her punishment made her nervous. She wondered how many lashes from his strap she would have to endure this time, and whether they would be across her hands or her back.

Eventually the stairs creaked and she stood up, swallowing anxiously. He came into her bedchamber and closed the door behind him, turning the key in the lock.

'You are not in your nightgown,' he observed.

She remained silent, not wishing to annoy him further.

'Why are you not in your nightgown?' he demanded

'It is early in the day, Father, and we have not yet eaten our supper.'

'But I sent you to your chamber, Daughter.'

'I . . . er . . . I thought, that is, I . . . I am twenty years of age, Father.'

He stepped close to her and glowered. 'Then it is high time you learned how to behave in my house. When I send you to your chamber you put on your nightgown.'

'Yes, Father.'

'Do it then.'

Clara frowned and looked about her. 'I do not have a screen. If you would leave my bedchamber . . .'

He sat down on the only chair in the room and stated baldly, 'I am your father.'

Clara's fingers shook as she fumbled with the buttons of her bodice. He was going to thrash her back without the protection of her chemise and corset to dull the pain. He watched her impassively as she took her long white nightgown from the chest in the corner and draped it over her body while she removed her corset and stepped out of her drawers. Then he got up and walked slowly around her as she stood silently with bare feet in the middle of the room.

He had his cane with him, the one he used to beat off street urchins and dogs. Would he use the cane instead of the strap today? She could not see his strap anywhere.

'Are you sorry for what you said?' he demanded suddenly.

Clara stared at the bare wooden floor in silence.

His voice lowered threateningly and he poked the cane painfully into her stomach. 'I asked you if you were sorry . . .'

'Yes, Father. I am sorry,' she answered quickly.

'Will you speak to me like that again?'

'No, Father, I shall not.'

'No, Father, I shall not,' he repeated softly. 'That is good. You wish to please me, do you not, Daughter?'

'I . . . er . . . I—'

'Do you wish to please me?' he demanded loudly, pushing the cane harder into her flesh.

'Of course I do, Father.'

He looked satisfied. 'Very good. Now you may kneel by your bed and say your prayers.'

Shakily, she lowered herself to her knees. He was going to beat her back with his cane as she knelt, she thought. The worn floorboards were hard and cold but the soft edge of her familiar satin quilt provided comfort. She clasped her hands together, squeezed her eyes tight shut and waited for the pain to start.

She heard him moving about and imagined him taking off his jacket, flexing his arms and testing his cane for strength. He would be smiling, she thought. Her step-father enjoyed beating people.

'I cannot hear your prayers,' he snapped. 'Speak up.'

'Please God, forgive me for the sins I have committed. I have been disrespectful to my dear father who has looked after me and my mama. Take care of my dear mama and receive her into the Kingdom of Heaven. Bless my father and his house for my father is a good man . . .'

She choked on the words and her voice dwindled to a whisper. The bedstead creaked as he sat down beside her. She kept her eyes tight shut and tensed her body, waiting for the blows. If she held her breath she might faint and not feel the pain. A draught came in under the door, making her legs and feet feel icy cold. How long would it take to faint? She could smell him close to her. He smelled of strong drink and stale tobacco, with an underlying sourness of wet dogs and his chamber pot.

She let out a small, surprised squeal as he grasped her clasped hands in his. Her eyes opened smartly. He was sitting on the bed in his shirt and with his breeches opened and pushed down around his ankles. He yanked her hands across to his lap and shoved them down towards his private parts.

'No!' Horrified, she tried to pull her hands away, but his hold on them was firm.

'Yes,' he growled. 'This is your punishment. Look.'

A vile sight confronted her as his shirt parted to reveal a brown quivering arch of flesh struggling to raise its head.

'Look!' he ordered harshly. 'You see this. This is your punishment. Kiss it.'

'I . . . I c-cannot,' she whispered hoarsely.

'Kiss it!' he demanded. 'And hold it. Like this.' He

pulled her clasped hands apart and folded them around his trembling flesh.

It felt hot to her chilled hands and as he pushed her face towards it it seemed to shrink beneath them. But when her lips collided with its smelly brown skin it grew again and raised itself strongly in her hands.

'Aaaaah.' A low growl came from her stepfather's throat. 'Yessss. Move your hands. Like this.' He covered her hands with his and moved them up and down his hot, rigid flesh.

'You do it,' he snapped.

'I . . . I cannot. Please don't—'

'Do it! *Do as I say, you whore!*'

Sick with loathing and fear of this vindictive man, she obeyed as best she could until her wrists were tired and her body ached with tension. The gruesome sight before her sickened her further and she shut her eyes to blank out her ordeal. But it did not take away the disgusting smell and feel of him. Or the bark of his voice when she slowed.

'Faster, whore, faster!' At some moment during her nightmare he took his own hands away. The growl in his throat became a louder and more frequent pulsating groan as he threw back his head and cried out, a strangled animal-like snarl that made her open her eyes in fright.

His flesh pulsed and throbbed in her fingers, and quite suddenly her face and hands were covered in a sticky white mess that shot out of him, first as a dribble and then as a prolonged spurt that clung to her skin and tasted salty on her lips. His snarling quickened and then faded as he fell backwards on her quilt. The pulses slowed and his flesh went limp in her hands. Numb with shock and hatred, she stared at it, a soft crumpled heap of wrinkled brown skin and sticky, greying hair.

The vomit rose in her throat and she choked it back, overwhelmed by disgust. He revolted her, lying there helpless and groaning, with his eyes closed and a lick of spittle leaking from the corner of his mouth. She did not think that she could hate her stepfather any more than she already did. But now she knew she could. She despised him for living.

Was this the reason her elder sister had left? She had thought it was the beatings, just the beatings, and they were used to those. Beatings tore at your body but your body healed. This – this assault on her sensibilities had poisoned her mind. She wanted to kill him. A knife – a kitchen knife – would suffice. If she had one with her she would do it now. She knew that if she stayed with him she would surely kill him. She knew that this was why her sister had left and she must do the same.

Calmly, she wiped her face and hands on the bedcover, staining the beautiful satin sheen with his poison. She kept her eyes on the damp smears as her stepfather recovered, sat up and said, 'Your duty, Daughter, is to please me. If you please me I shall not beat you. When you are finished in your duty you must ask if you have pleased me. Do you understand?'

'Yes, Father,' she answered meekly.

'Ask me, then!'

She swallowed wearily. 'Did I please you, Father?'

'For the present, Daughter. For the present.' He grasped

a handful of her skirts and wiped away the stickiness from his own flesh, then pulled up his breeches and left her bedchamber, taking the key and locking the door behind him.

Grace had eavesdropped outside the door without shame. She had heard Mr Sowden's groans inside Clara's bedchamber and knew them for what they were. Now she darted along the landing to hide in the sickroom where her mistress's dead body rested. As soon as the master was downstairs she returned to Clara's door.

'Clara,' Grace whispered. 'Are you all right?'

'No I am not!'

Grace thought she sounded angry rather than weepy. 'Come to the door so we can talk,' she urged.

'What is it?' Clara demanded.

'I heard what he did to you. You don't have to stay here. You can leave with me.'

'Where would we go?'

'Anywhere. Away from him.'

There was a short silence, then Clara asked through the door, 'When are you leaving?'

'Tonight. I'll add some spirits to his ale at supper. When he's sound asleep, I'll take his keys and let you out. Do you have a travelling box?'

'Yes.'

'Put some clothes in it. Not too many because you must carry it yourself.'

The two women, shadowy figures wrapped and hooded in long dark cloaks, set off after midnight. They trudged steadily along the road, hardly uttering a word to each other until Grace, worried by the younger woman's silence, asked if she was all right.

'Yes, thank you,' Clara responded firmly. 'I was just thinking that I had learned something today.'

'What do you mean?' Grace asked.

'I learned that men have a weakness – even the strongest of tormenters.' She turned to Grace and added, 'That's useful for a gentlewoman to know, isn't it?'

They reached the turnpike as the first streaks of dawn appeared in the eastern sky.

'Let's rest a while and wait for an early-morning carrier,' Grace suggested. 'It'll take us to the far side of the Riding and away from your stepfather.'

Clara remained subdued as they sat on a mounting stone by the horse trough. 'I wanted to kill him, you know,' she muttered. 'I would have done so if I had stayed with him.'

'And ended up on the gallows for your trouble? No, Miss Clara. It is best you leave him to his dubious pleasures. You can make your own way in life now.'

'How? I have no money and only a little education.'

'Do you have nothing left of your mother's?'

'Some jewellery and a few silver coins that Mama kept back for us. She gave half to my sister and half to me.'

'Does he know about that?'

'I do not think so. Why?'

'Well, he may come after you for it, as you are not yet twenty-one.'

'Oh, Grace, I shall kill myself before I go back to him.'

'Then we must plan for your future. Or our future, if you wish it.'

Clara looked surprised and Grace continued. 'I have enough gold to take a house with bedchambers for lodgings. Times are changing in the South Riding. When I was your age there were only the gentry and their servants. Now, with all these manufactories there are more men like – well, in trade like your stepfather. They do not have land but they have money, money from ironworks and mills, from haulage and other callings. They travel and they buy from each other. They come from all over, from Manchester, even from London Town. So they need lodgings. Good ones, like their own homes. And wholesome food to eat at the end of their working day.' Grace paused for breath. 'I . . . I can't do it on my own, Miss Clara. But, if you wish, together we can make a decent living providing for them.'

'What if Father finds out and comes looking for me?'

'You have to take that risk. But I shall say that you are my niece. With any luck you'll be turned twenty-one before he catches up with us.'

Clara thought for a moment. 'I haven't run a household before, only helped Mama, then my sister, and now you.'

'I know what to do in the kitchen and laundry. Your manners and charm are all we need to impress our guests and gain a reputation.'

Clara was doubtful. 'I don't know whether I can do it.'

'I shall do all the housekeeping and as soon as we can afford it, we'll get a girl to help with the work. You are beautiful, Clara. You will make a fine mistress of the house, welcoming the guests, seeing that the rooms are as comfortable as their own homes, and that they have good fires and hot water for their shaves.'

'Yes, I could do that.'

'Then we could be equals in this venture?' Grace asked hopefully.

Clara nodded, warming to the idea and feeling an inner excitement welling. She would be independent, with money of her own, free of her stepfather and his evil ways. 'Equals,' she repeated. 'I like the sound of that.'

Grace smiled. 'We shall look for a house together and you can choose the furnishings.'

The sun's rays streaked across the early-morning sky, and in the distance a carrier cart plodded slowly towards them and their new life in the South Riding.

Chapter 3

One year later Grace and Clara had furnished three bedchambers for guests in a sturdy, stone-built house on the road to the moor just outside a busy Riding town. They had heard from the butcher's boy that Clara's step-father had come looking for her, but no one in this part of the Riding knew Clara's real identity and he soon moved on to Sheffield in his search. And now she was twenty-one and free of him for ever.

It was almost the end of their working day. Grace had cooked a roast beef dinner that Clara had served to their three guests in their elegant dining room. Clara carried a tray of dirty china back to their spacious kitchen.

'Mr Hardcastle said the roast beef was especially good tonight, Grace.'

Grace was helping their scullery maid, Mary, to wash the pots. She called from the sink, 'This is his third visit to us. We shall soon be able to afford to mend the roof.'

'But what we really need is enough money to furnish another bedchamber so that we can take on extra help,' Clara stated wearily.

Grace wiped her hands and came through to the kitchen. 'I am sorry, Clara. I should have realised you would not be as used to hard work as I am. Sit down and I'll make you some tea.'

'Heavens no, Grace! I am thinking of you. I can keep going. But you are more than twice my age and I know how your bones pain you, especially in the mornings. You must let me do more in the kitchen and laundry. It is too much for you with only a girl to help.'

'No, Clara. You are the lady of the house. You need to look elegant for our guests, and to call on tradesmen in town. It is important for our reputation and our credit with the bank.'

'I suppose you are right. But the work is too much for you! I know it is!'

Grace sighed and sank on to a rickety kitchen chair. 'I manage. But you are right. We need another pair of hands.'

Clara picked up the heavy blackened kettle from the hob. 'A girl to do the laundry, as soon as we can afford it,' she said firmly. 'Do you want a hot toddy? Mr Hardcastle has asked for Scotch whisky for his nightcap.'

'Don't mind if I do,' Grace replied. 'Shall I take his drink upstairs for you?'

'No you shall not. You have done far too much today.' Clara mixed their best Scotch whisky with hot water, honey and spices in a jug, then poured it into a small pewter tankard. She pushed it across the table to Grace.

'Take this to bed and rest. Mary will turn down the lamps. I'll see you in the morning.'

'Good night, then.'

'Good night, Grace.'

Grace and Clara had small bedchambers on the second floor that was reached by the back stairs. There were attics further up where servants had slept in the past when the house was built. But the attics were damp and Mary slept downstairs in an anteroom that had once been the butler's pantry and now housed cupboards of china and plate for the dining room.

Clara placed Mr Hardcastle's nightcap together with a lighted candle on a silver tray. She flexed her aching shoulders and massaged the back of her neck before calling good night to Mary and going through a heavy, brass-studded door to the spacious square hall at the front of the house.

Clara was tired and her back hurt, but she thought that her life here with Grace was perfect. She was mistress of a fine house, finer than her own dear father's house, and without her cruel and vicious stepfather to dominate her. She was weary but she was content. Well, almost content. As she climbed the front stairs she thought how much pleasanter life would be with a little more income from the lodgings.

'Your nightcap, sir.' She tapped on Mr Hardcastle's door. He had asked for this chamber. It was one of their best, with a large bay window that looked out on to a village in the distance and the moor beyond. She had furnished it well, with a comfortable bed and a carpet on the waxed floorboards.

'Come in, Clara, my dear.' He was in his shirtsleeves, sitting at the side table reading documents by the light of an oil lamp.

'Over here.' His voice sounded heavy as he moved his papers aside to make room for the salver.

But as she put down the tray, his left arm snaked around her back to encircle her waist.

'Stay a while,' he said.

She was startled, but not frightened. 'I beg your pardon, sir?' she responded.

'Sit down and talk to me. Your work is finished and I am in need of company tonight.' He put down his writing pen and turned to face her.

Clara thought that he looked as exhausted as she felt. His days were taken up visiting ironworks and forges on behalf of the railway company that employed him.

'I . . . I don't know that I should, sir.'

'Oh, Clara, some distraction from this boring task of mine is long overdue. And the South Riding has very little to offer a weary traveller.'

'There are inns and taverns in town, sir,' she suggested.

'They are hardly to my taste,' he muttered. 'Not like you.' He raised his bushy, greying eyebrows and she did not mistake his meaning.

She took his arm from around her waist and said clearly, 'I think not, sir.'

'Why not? A man has needs when he is away from his wife. A woman can help him with his needs. Especially a beautiful woman like you.'

She stepped away from him and said, 'Drink your whisky, Mr Hardcastle.'

'Oh please, Clara. I need you to be a woman for me, not just a servant.'

'No, sir, I shall not oblige you.'

'Come along, my dear. You must crave a little distraction yourself at the end of your working day,' he persisted.

'No, sir, it is not distraction I crave,' she pronounced briskly. 'Rather, some well-earned rest.'

'Are we gentlemen too much work for you?' he asked lightly.

'Of course not! No, Mr Hardcastle. It is my Aunt Grace who causes me concern.'

'She is quite well, I trust?'

'She . . . she is getting old, I think.'

'Then she needs another servant,' he explained patiently. 'In the kitchen perhaps?'

'The laundry, actually . . .' she began. She stopped as she realised that he was simply humouring her.

He gave her a gentle smile. 'I believe we can help each other, Clara.' He reached under the table for a small leather travelling box that he opened with a key on his timepiece chain. He took out a small stack of gold sovereigns and placed them on the salver.

'How much extra help do you need?' he asked.

Clara stared at the coins. She was speechless and her heart began to thump in her throat. She knew what he meant. She knew the kind of proposition he was suggesting. Her mouth opened but no sound came out. But neither did she flounce from his chamber as she had imagined she might.

'I can see that you are tempted,' he persisted calmly. 'You need have no fear of me. I shall not harm you.'

Clara thought of her stepfather and shuddered. But Mr Hardcastle was not like her stepfather. Mr Hardcastle was a cultured man, kind, well-educated and from a good family in Manchester. Clara thought also of Grace, who had rescued her from an intolerable future and provided everything to set them up here. She would always be in Grace's debt for that. Perhaps it was now her turn to provide for Grace? Her heart continued to thump.

'What . . . what do you want of me?' she asked nervously.

'I want nothing that you are not prepared to give,' he said, then added, 'I promise you that. But I would like to see you without your gown — if you are willing?' Again he used his small, gentle smile to entice her.

She should have talked to Grace first. But Grace would have said no. Definitely no. And Clara felt a frisson of excitement run through her. She was frightened, but she felt a strange thrill at the same time. She had never lain with a man, but she knew of their weakness, even though her only knowledge was that of her stepfather's needs.

She wondered again what she would have to do, and in the next moment she realised that she did not care. Men may be powerful and dominant in life, but they all had this weakness in the bedchamber. Mr Hardcastle was being honest with her about his. He was a businessman and, to him, this was a business deal.

She took a deep breath and nodded. 'All right,' she said.

She began to remove her bodice, skirts and boots until she was down to her corsets, drawers and stockings. He watched her silently, then asked her to help him take off his own clothes. He stood there impassively as she undid buttons and peeled away the layers. He was so passive she had to ask him to assist her, murmuring, 'Lift your arms, sir. Step out of your breeches, sir.'

'Call me Master Henry,' he asked.

She did not question him. 'Of course, Master Henry.'

'Now my under-drawers.'

She swallowed and knelt on the floor, rolling them down to his feet, not having the courage to raise her eyes.

'Is it time for bed now?' he asked quietly.

'Yes, Master Henry.'

He walked over to the bed and she dared to look at him. He was a pale, skinny man, but unclothed she could see that he was capable of physical work. His arms and legs were sinewy and his shoulders and chest, though narrow, were muscled. His greying hair had once been black and he had a small amount on his chest, and more between his legs where a fleshy projection hung, limp and forlorn. It flopped to one side as he lay on the bed, resting his head on his hand.

'Walk around the chamber for me,' he asked.

She obeyed tentatively, her nervousness showing at first, and then as her confidence grew she straightened her back and held her head high. He seemed to approve of this because he began to smile at her. But she noticed that he did not stir with any desire for her.

'I do not please you, do I?' she uttered at last.

'On the contrary,' he sighed, 'you please me greatly. You remind me of my first boyhood passion. She was a handsome woman who valued her freedom.'

Clara thought that he was shrewder than he looked. His unassuming manner concealed a wealth of knowledge about the world and its people. She stood before him, her legs slightly apart and her hands resting lightly on her hips where her corsets met her calico drawers. She had no idea what to do next.

'You have not done this before, have you?' he smiled. 'Or you would know that an older man such as myself needs a little more persuasion.'

Her smile faltered a little as her mind raced. Her stepfather had been an older man. Should she touch him? Of course, yes, that's what he wanted. Nervously she knelt by the bed, pushing all memories of her stepfather aside. Mr Hardcastle was different. He was kind and cultured and he smelled clean and wholesome, of real soap and the cologne he used when he dressed. Tentatively, she began to stroke his thighs and his stomach.

He closed his eyes as she progressed towards his private parts, but still there was no reaction from him and she began to despair. Would she have to kiss it to make it stir? She glanced at his face and saw a tiny glitter of eye through his lashes.

'Do not look so worried,' he murmured. 'This is only a game.'

For you, maybe, she thought irritably. If she could not succeed at this, what was she doing even trying? Game, was it, Master Henry? She rose to her feet and gave him a sharp slap with the flat of her hand on his naked rump. 'Well, wake up and start playing!' she muttered desperately.

'Yesss,' he said softly and she heard him sigh. 'Again.'

Again, he'd said. So this was part of Master Henry's boyhood passion? She hit him again on his behind, hard, leaving red marks where her fingers had struck. He gave a little whimper in his throat and she could not tell whether it was from pain or pleasure. But he did not protest or ask her to stop and she hit him again, this time saying, 'Wake up, you naughty boy!'

Clara did not know why she said that, except that she was growing impatient with him and he had told her it was a game. But it was then that she noticed the first stirrings of his male desire. Her eyes widened and she swallowed. Her thoughts tumbled around her head as he continued the whimpering in his throat.

'Naughty, *naughty* boy,' she repeated. 'What are you?'

'Naughty boy, Nurse,' he whined.

Good heavens! she thought. His nurse was his boyhood passion! And this is what he *wants*!

'And what does Nurse do to naughty Master Henry?' she asked imperiously.

His voice had raised an octave to that of his childhood. 'Nurse beats him with the rule,' he replied.

Clara's mind raced. Beats him. Beats him with the rule? Ah yes, there was a wooden rule on his writing table that he used for making drawings. Quick as a flash, she crossed the room to collect the rule and a folded linen towel from the washstand.

'And where does Nurse beat him?' she asked, placing the linen carefully beneath him.

She did not need an answer as she saw the bead of moisture pushing out of his enlarged arousal. It was bigger than she'd realised, she thought absently as she rapped the wooden rule across his buttocks and heard him groan.

To her surprise it was all over quite quickly. The folded linen served its purpose and he was flaccid again. Gently, she cleaned him up with the towel and dropped it by the door. She stood watching him in the lamplight for a moment. He had rolled on to his back and his eyes were closed. Well, almost closed. She detected that tiny glitter between his lashes again.

'Can I put on my nightshirt now, Nurse?' he asked in a small voice.

Clara thought quickly and wondered what she should do next. Perhaps he expected more of her? She stood in front of him, still holding the rule in her hand.

'Is Master Henry going to be naughty again?'

'No, Nurse. Not tonight.'

'Then you may.'

She handed him the nightshirt that was folded on the wooden blanket chest at the foot of the bed. As he pulled it over his head he seemed to become his normal adult self again.

Was that it? she thought, and asked, 'M-may I get dressed now, sir?'

He nodded, giving her that small, secretive smile of his. 'Do you want help with your gown?'

Clara shook her head. The buttons were at the front and she fumbled with them, wondering if that was all she would have to do for a guinea.

He gave her two and said, 'You are good. I know other men who would pay you just as well. As much

for your discretion as your services. It's a lucrative business, Clara. Think about it.'

Her hand was shaking as she took the money, knowing
what she had become. But this was not how she had
imagined it when she saw women loitering in the streets
at night. She picked up the soiled linen and the candle
and left. Once on the landing, she leaned against the
waxed, wooden-panelled walls until she regained her
composure.

What had she done? She felt a kind of fluttering
excitement in her breast. She had been so nervous with
him, but that had added a frisson of danger to her
encounter. She realised that she had enjoyed the experience. And it had been easy! She did not deceive
herself that it would always be this easy. But for the first
time in her life she felt powerful.

The coins chinked in her hand and she thought about
a laundry maid for Grace. Clara went to her bed
wondering how she would approach talking to Grace
about a new direction for their business. She fell asleep
rehearsing the words.

The next morning, Grace and Clara were sitting at
the dining-room table finishing their coffee while Mary
stacked the breakfast dishes on a wooden tray.

'Oooh, they've left some kidneys this morning,' Mary
squealed.

'Would you like them for your breakfast?' Clara asked,
ignoring Grace's raised eyebrows.

'Ooh, yes please, Miss Clara.'

'Take them through to the kitchen then, and eat them
while they're hot.'

When Mary had left, Grace chided Clara lightly. 'I could have put them in a pie for dinner,' she pointed out.

'I know, I know.' Clara took a deep breath. 'I need to talk to you.' She retrieved the gold coins from a small pocket in her overskirt and placed them on the polished tabletop.

'Where did they come from?' Grace asked.

'Mr Hardcastle. Last night.'

Grace raised her eyebrows again. 'Clara?'

'I didn't have to do much. Truly, Grace. Just hit him, really.'

Grace's eyes rounded. 'I warned you they might ask. Oh Clara, I told you not to get involved with any of the guests—'

Clara interrupted. 'But look how much he gave me for – for just beating him on his behind. That's all it took.'

Grace gave a short dry laugh. 'Well, well. That's what the Admiral used to like too.'

Now it was Clara's turn to be surprised. 'Did you do that for him?'

'And more. It started when he got the gout and I had to help him in and out of bed. He said it took his mind off his bad foot.'

'Mr Hardcastle wanted me to be his nurse.'

The two women stared at each other across the table.

'We can mend the roof,' Clara began, 'and get a laundry maid and—'

'No, stop. You're not doing this. You don't know what it can lead to.'

'Oh, Grace. Mr Hardcastle is a respectable man. He knows others like him. I can be very discreet. Anyway, I shan't need many if they pay this well.'

'I said no.'

'Why not?' Clara demanded. 'It will be on my terms, at my price. My choice, Grace. My choice.'

Grace laughed harshly again. 'When you're a servant you don't have any choice. I got myself out of service so I could have choice. But not this, Clara. Not this.'

'You said yourself that times are changing. There's a different way of life emerging in the Riding. I can provide a different kind of service here.'

Grace stared at her. 'You are determined, aren't you?'

Clara nodded.

'Carriage trade only?' Grace queried.

'Of course.'

Still Grace hesitated. 'No, Clara. You don't know anything about this kind of business.'

'But you do, don't you?' Clara suddenly knew that she was right. 'And I can learn.'

Grace stared out of the large dining-room window. It was raining again. She loved to watch the soft gentle rain washing the heather on the moor. But today it meant more damp in the attic and more coal for the fire to dry the laundry. The gold coins glinted among the break-fast-table debris.

'Are you really sure about this, Clara?'

Clara smiled. 'Then you agree. You will not regret it, I promise.'

Chapter 4

1833

Down at Mexton Lock one year later, Edie Dearne was becoming thoroughly fed up with her lively inquisitive toddler. When Luther came home, it was all 'Lissie wants this' and 'Lissie wants that' with no thought for Edie who was doing all the work. *He just plays wi' 'er*, she moaned to herself, *talking at 'er like 'e were slow in the 'ead.* And Edie didn't get 'er snuff if the house wasn't clean or there was no dinner on the table. Now he'd told her he was going on another trip down the canal.

'Don't go and leave me wi' 'er again, Luther!' she pleaded.

'And what are we going to live off, if I don't? Where am I going to get t' money for your snuff, tell me that?'

'Can't yer tek 'er wi' yer?'

'Don't be daft, Edie.'

'I thought you'd want 'er along, you're that soft wi' 'er all the time.'

'You know I can't take 'er on the canals wi' me. She's a good little lass fo' you now, i'n't she?'

'No! She's into everything now she's toddling!'

'She sits on t' po' for yer, do'n't she?'

Edie looked down at Lissie sitting on Luther's lap and playing with the chain on his timepiece. Luther was the one that was daft. He was that daft with the little 'un, it made Edie want to spit. A grown man gurgling and cooing at her, and bouncing her on his knees. Then he'd pick 'er up so that she could dance her feet on his legs and he'd go on and on about how big she was growing. But it was Edie who had to wash her mucky clothes and curl her hair and all sorts when he was home.

Edie put on her wheedling, whining tone and said, 'I don't know what to do wi' 'er on me own.'

'Not that again! It's time you grew up a bit, Edie lass. You just 'ave to get on wi' it, like all mams do for their little 'uns.'

'But I'm not 'er mam.'

'Don't start all that either!' Luther gave Lissie a last big hug and said, 'Now you be a good little lass fo' yer mam, and yer dad'll bring you summat back wi' 'im. Some spice or summat.' He gave her big sloppy kisses all over her face and added, 'Ee, lass, I could eat you.' He put her down on the rag rug in front of the hearth and turned on Edie. 'Now, you do as you're told when I'm away, else you'll get what for when I get back. I'll find out, y' know, if you go over ter Navigator or owt.'

'Well, bring me back some more snuff this time,' Edie cried as the back door slammed shut. 'It's allus summat for 'er these days.'

But Luther was already on his way, striding across the clearing towards the lock and thinking about a bargeman he'd heard was on his uppers. Might get some cargo at a good price to sell on, he thought, whistling cheerily to himself.

Edie turned her petulance on the child. 'It's all your fault! I didn't get owt from him this time, it were all stuff fer you that he brought! I may as well not be 'ere when 'e comes home now!'

Lissie grasped a piece of coal that had fallen out the bucket and lifted it up to show her mam, making a gurgling noise in her throat. But her pretty smile was wasted on Edie, who continued to scowl and mutter to herself.

'Well, I don't care what Luther says about me not going down to the canal wi' yer. I gotta 'ave summat ter keep me going. Put that coal down and get on yer feet.' She yanked at Lissie's arm and dragged her across the kitchen. 'Now sit there on yer po' while I get me shawl.'

Edie waited until she was sure Luther would be gone from the lock before she yanked again on Lissie's little arm. She let out a noisy sigh through her lips as a smell rose to meet her nostrils. 'Pooh, you mucky little gypsy. Stand still while I wrap this shawl round yer. We're off to see Rosa.'

Leaving the smelly po' in the kitchen, she went out of the back door dragging a whimpering Lissie behind her, following in Luther's footsteps across the clearing and down the track through the trees.

The main work on this side of the canal was timber

from the woodland. There was a big warehouse in which to store it and a permanent crane on the wharf for loading it into barges. The familiar smell of sawn wood mixed with an oily metallic stink from pulleys and chains that screeched and rattled endlessly.

Luther had said that trade had got steadily worse since he brought Lissie home, but folk always needed timber. And coal. There was plenty of coal heaped up that year as the ironworks were not taking much for the furnaces now some of the melting shops had closed.

Edie slowed as she reached the canal, not wanting anyone to see her, then hurried to the end cottage in Woodmill Row and rapped on Rosa's door.

'It's me, Rosa. 'Ave yer got any o' that snuff mixture? Luther's gone, but he's left me a few coins.'

The door opened. 'Aye, I saw 'im go. Come in outta t' cold. What's she crying fer?'

'I don't know, do I?'

'Is she wet?'

'Don't think so, she's been on the po' half the morning.'

Rosa bent down and lifted the hem of Lissie's skirt. 'Edie, she 'a'n't got any drawers or owt on. And she smells a bit.'

'I told you. She's been on the po'.'

'You 'aven't washed her though. You should gi' 'er a wash, Edie.'

'Oh, I don't know, Rosa, she's nowt but trouble. I wish 'e'd never brought 'er home. I liked it better wi'out 'er. Just Luther and me. He a'n't got any time fer me any more. It's all Lissie this and Lissie that, I could crack 'er one just thinking about it, I really could.'

'Here, try this, love.'

Rosa tipped a small amount of brown powder on to the back of Edie's hand. Edie sniffed it hard up her nostrils and held out her hand for more.

Rosa obliged then said, 'Come and sit down while I clean up the little 'un for you.'

'Oh ta, Rosa. I can't stand to touch her sometimes when I think where she's come from. I swear he's been wi' some tinker's whore. And I get lumbered wi' looking after her! It's not fair!'

'Di'n't Luther tell you her ma died?'

'Aye, but yer never know wi' Luther whether to believe all he says.'

'Well, you sit there while I gi' 'er a wash.' Rosa lifted the snivelling Lissie into the stone scullery sink and cleaned between her legs with a cold wet cloth wrung out from a tin bowl on the wooden draining board. She called through the open door. 'Fetch me that pot of salve from the table, Edie, she's a bit sore. 'A'n't yer got any drawers fer 'er?'

'There might be some in that pile of stuff that Luther brought on his last trip.'

Rosa placed Lissie on her horsehair couch by the kitchen fire and lifted down a stone bottle from her cupboard in the alcove. 'Try some o' this, Edie. It'll make you feel better.'

'What is it?'

'A drop o' gin.'

'Ooh lovely, I don't mind that.'

The two women sipped contentedly out of tin mugs.

'Don't you miss Luther when he's away?' Rosa asked.

'Not now. When he's home 'e 'as me running around all the time, dolling her up, I'm glad when 'e's gone these days.'

'You must be lonely at night though?'

'Not as long as I got me snuff.'

'Not even in the bedchamber?'

'Especially not there! I'm glad of a break from all that. Always at it, 'e is. I'm that fed up wi' 'im heaving and sweating like a pig all o'er me. I put up wi' it when we were first wed, and now I 'as ter do it when he asks, 'cos if I say no he wallops me one.'

'Don't you like it, then?'

'I've never liked it wi' 'im! It's the worst bit of 'im coming home. I allus gives 'im plenty of ale wi' 'is dinner now and then 'e goes straight off to sleep after 'e's done it ter me once.'

Rosa was looking at her with a little smile on her face. 'I never liked it wi' mine either. He cleared off and left me years ago.'

'D'you miss 'im?'

'On'y the money, when me rent is due.'

Edie took another sip of gin and thought how much nicer it would be if she lived here with Rosa, instead of up in the woods with Luther. She gave Rosa a shy smile in return. 'Well then,' she said, 'my Luther's generous to a fault when 'e's got summat in his purse, so we can share it when 'e's gone away.'

Rosa poured more gin into Edie's tin mug. 'Well, you can come down 'ere any time you like, Edie, m' love. D'you think the little 'un'll 'ave a sleep now?'

Edie shrugged. 'Don't know.'

'I'll put 'er over 'ere on the rocker then we can both sit on the couch, together like.'

'Go on, then.' Edie helped herself to another pinch of Rosa's snuff mixture and sat back with her gin. She thought how nice it was here with Rosa. She'd come down here more often when Luther was away. She liked Rosa much more than she liked Luther.

Chapter 5

1839

'Lissie Dearne, you get back here this minute, do y' hear me.'

Lissie heard all right and put her hands to her ears to shut out the screech of her mother's high-pitched voice. Her head ached from the rags that her mam had tied into her hair the night before, and her toes hurt as her feet squeezed into boots that were too small. She swung her legs, banging the heels against the boarded front of the privy seat. If she pointed her toes, they touched the ground now. The wooden seat felt safe and comforting against her bottom and, compared with the harsh icy weather outside, was smooth and warm.

'Lissie, I won't tell you again! If I have to come down there for you, I'll clip your ear 'ole!'

She would too, Lissie thought, rubbing her ears to warm them up. Her mother's hands were claw-like and bony and the back of her hand could easily knock Lissie sideways, and frequently did. She shuffled to the edge of

the privy seat and slid off the end, pulling up long calico
drawers under her woollen smocked dress as she scampered up the frozen mud path to the house. She was
nearly nine and growing fast.

'My boots are too tight, Mam,' she complained, 'and
my feet hurt.'

Edie pushed a dusty and battered tin bucket at her.
'Shut up and rake the ashes from the kitchen and the
front room grates, then get on with cleaning 'em. And
don't forget to put on your old pinny.'

'Can I have a drink of tea, Mam?'

The older woman bent down to Lissie and glared at
her. 'We 'a'n't got any tea till yer dad gets 'ome, and
anyroad, nobody can have a drink of owt until the fire's
going, halfwit.' She gave the child a sharp clip on the
back of her head. 'Now shut up, I said, and get on with
what you're told.'

Lissie hated the scratchy rasp of dry cinders in her
fingers, and the dust made her nose all itchy and twitchy
when she heaped them into the bucket. Although it was
heavy for her little arms, she managed to lug it down
the garden to the dump behind the apple trees, and found
a small juicy eater hidden under the criss-crossed
branches as her reward.

Blackleading the grates was harder on her small hands
as the blacking got into her sore skin and hurt even
more, but at least she warmed up a bit while rubbing
at the ironwork. The kitchen grate was worst because it
was so fiddly with its bars and swing hob that held the
sooty kettle. Then there was the bit o' brass on the oven
door at the side to shine up.

Her dad was proud o' the new grate he had fitted in the kitchen chimney place. 'You look after it, Edie,' he had said. 'It were made for t' gentry.' Lissie thought it would have been best rubbed up last night while it was still warm from the fire; it was so much harder to get a shine on it now it was cold. She tried to say this to her mam but she only shouted back at her, yelling, 'Well, you were asleep in bed when the fire died down last night. Did you want me to wake you and make you clean it in your night-gown? No, I thought not. Get on with it now and make sure you rub it until you can see your face in it.'

Lissie finished the grates and laid both fires, then went outside again, this time to the woodshed for kindling wood to replace the sticks that had been drying in the bottom oven next to the grate. She was shivering with cold and very hungry by this time. Her mam had left a bucket of coals in front of the kitchen grate, as well as a flint and some old rags smeared in musty cooking grease to make sure the fire caught first time. Lissie could hear her next door in the scullery, pumping water to fill the kettle. The greasy rags crackled and spat at her but soon the flames were licking round the coals and giving out some heat.

'I've done it, Mam. Fire's going,' Lissie said proudly. 'Shall I do the one in the front room next?'

Her mother dumped a kettle full of water on the hearth and picked up an empty one. 'No, leave the front 'un till later. Just look at the mess you've made of the rug. Get out of it, you little toerag. You'll have to give it a shake now.' She landed another clip on the side of Lissie's head. 'Go on, roll it up and take it outside.'

'Ow!' Lissie held her ear where her mother's hand had caught her and looked at the rug. She had been extra careful not to spill any ash or coal dust on the rug and couldn't see anything that wasn't there before she started. Lissie tried ever so hard to please her mam, but she was so difficult, especially when Dad was due back from one of his trips.

It didn't matter what Lissie did, or how much she tried, it was always wrong and more often than not she'd get a clip round the ear for her trouble. Her lower lip trembled and she frowned as she gathered up the rug and went out once more into the cold. She hoped the first kettle to boil would be to pour on some oats for breakfast, and not for the pots. The dirty stone sink was piled high with greasy pots and she hated the cold draughty scullery in winter.

But Lissie was out of luck that morning and all she got to eat was some bread and dripping, and a mug of chilly dusty water that had been standing out all night, before she had to climb up on the old milking stool to wash the pots.

'Now get on with those and mind you don't break anything. Your dad will be coming home soon and you don't want me telling 'im you're a slovenly little brat, do you? When I get back I want all them pots washed and drying on the draining board.'

Dad! Her dad was coming home soon? Lissie drew in her breath sharply and asked, 'When will he be here, Mam?'

'When 'e's made enough money, that's when!'

What on God's earth possessed Luther to bring home

a *babby* all those years ago, she would never know. It must be eight or nine summers now that they'd had that little toerag causing rows and too much extra work for Edie's liking. Still, she had grown up fast and was becoming a good little help to Edie round the house. Edie thought that that was the only good part about keeping her instead of sending her out into service.

Well, she had heard that the ice on the canal was cracked and the barges were moving again, so she had better get in some bread and taters. She took a thick wool shawl from a hook behind the scullery door and slung it round her skinny shoulders.

'Where are you going, Mam?' Lissie ventured.

'Never you mind, nosy little madam.'

Edie slammed the door behind her. Lissie jumped and the old milking stool wobbled on the uneven bricks of the scullery floor. She grasped the rough rim of the stone sink to steady herself. Her hands were still filthy from blackleading the grates even though she had tried washing them under the pump. The water was icy cold this morning and didn't make any difference on its own. But Lissie knew from doing this in the past that scrubbing a sink full of pots and cooking pans would do the trick.

The soda in the water hurt her hands and made the skin red raw, but at least the blacklead had gone by the time she had finished. Then she took off her coarse jute apron and scrubbed some more to get the soot and blacking out of it. She looked forward to rubbing some salve on her hands and sitting by the fire while it soaked in.

Spreading the cold wet apron over a hedge to dry, Lissie lingered in the morning rays of an early winter sunrise. Night frosts had blackened the last of the flower heads and the beanpoles were falling over. When her dad came home he would straighten everything out, and Lissie would help him. She prayed for her dad to come home ever so soon. Her mam never made her do all the dirty jobs in the house when her dad was here.

As long as Dad made no complaints about the mess, they left all the worst chores until he went away again, when her mam asked him for extra money to get a girl in to clean up. Lissie was excited by this the first time she understood what her mam was asking for, as she thought it would be like having company and Mam might buy a cake from the inn by the lock. But when she asked her mam about 'the girl to clean up' all she got was another clip round the ear, told not to be so cheeky, and the scullery floor to scrub.

The frost had melted under the sun's rays and Lissie looked for some dock leaves to wrap round her chapped hands. Her mam was gone a long time so she went inside and wandered round the house for something to do. Better not light the front-room fire. She lifted the empty kettle from the brick floor and heaved it up into the scullery sink. She could pump the water to fill it but then it was too heavy for her to lift it down again. She climbed on to the old milking stool and played with the pots and pans on the wooden draining board for a while. Bored with that, Lissie remembered where her mam kept the old papers that dad brought in with him and sat turning the yellowing pages, looking at the patterns the words made and wondering what they meant. Hurriedly, she put them away when she heard her mam coming round the side of the house.

'Get the door open, Lissie. Look sharp, will you, these are heavy.'

Edie deposited a tin can of milk and an old sack filled with bread and vegetables on the scullery floor. The wholesome smell of fresh-baked bread filled her nostrils. Mam never went to so much trouble for just the two of them and Lissie's eyes lit up.

'Ooh, Mam! Is Dad coming home today?'

'Aye, lass, he is that. There's been some ice down-stream but the ice-breakers 'ave got through it and the barges'll be here later on.' Edie spotted the kettle in the sink and immediately lugged it through to the hob that swung over the kitchen fire. 'I'm parched after all that carrying. The sooner you're big enough to do this for me the better.'

'I can go to the lock for you if you want, Mam. I can.'

'And there'd be hell to pay from your dad if you did. You know he says you haven't to go down there on your own. One o' the Jacksons 'd see you and tell him. Then there'd be no nothing for either of us, so shut your trap.'

'But I'm big enough, aren't I?' Lissie stood on tiptoe, squashing her cramped toes, and stretched as tall as she could.

'Aye, you are that. And you cost me a fortune to feed when your dad's away.'

I didn't believe him when he said she was six months old when he found her, Edie mused, and I still don't believe it. She looks more than eight to me. Anyway, if she was a foundling, how did he know how old she was?

'Will Dad be home soon, Mam?'

'Oh, give over, will yer!' A bastard, that's what she is, a filthy little bastard that he's lumbered me with! Probably his own, an' all, Edie thought, with that cheap floozy from the docks. My God, I hate the sight of 'er.

As Edie lifted her hand to give her a crack on the head, Lissie ducked and disappeared fast into the pantry, dragging the damp sack of potatoes and carrots and saying, 'I'll put these away for you, Mam.' She closed the door behind her and sat on a piece of old wood on the floor until the clattering in the scullery had died down and her little bottom was frozen stiff.

When everything went quiet Lissie knew it would be safe to go back with the empty sack. The door to the kitchen was open and her mam was sitting dozing by the fire with a mug of tea. Her nose was brown where she had been taking her snuff, and there was a bottle of spirits falling from her hand into her lap.

Lissie climbed on to a wooden chair and carefully poured herself some lukewarm tea from the big brown pot on the table. There was still only bread and dripping to eat, but when Dad got home there would be a feast! Dad always brought good things to eat when he came home. She wished she could go down to the lock to meet him, instead of having to wait here. P'raps he'd bring her some new boots this time, and a thick wool shawl like her mam's.

She scrambled down from the table and sat on the hearth rug by the fire to warm her chilled feet and legs.

She wondered why her mam was always so cross. She often grumbled that she didn't know what Luther was thinking of when he'd brought home a little gypsy. And when Lissie had been running around the garden in bare feet in the summer, with her long black hair flowing behind her, her mam had often called her 'a dirty little gypsy', and threatened to 'take her back to them and swap her for a pony and trap'.

Lissie leaned against the brass-buttoned leather of her dad's favourite chair by the fire. She hoped her mam would wake up soon and take the rags out of her hair as her head was hurting something cruel. Mam always twisted her hair really tight and when Lissie had asked her not to, she'd pulled it more and made it worse, snapping, 'Yer dad likes you wi' ringlets. I don't care if you look as if you've been pulled through a hedge back'ards! If it were left to me I'd cut the whole lot off.'

The glowing pile of coals in the grate fell, causing a few sparks to dance in front of the sooty fireback. Mam had put the new bread on top of the oven to keep warm and the blackened kettle was just beginning to grumble on its hob. Suddenly, Mam woke up and wiped her nose with the back of her hand. She put the empty mug and her spirit bottle down and roughly pulled Lissie towards her.

'Come here, thee. Let's get these rags out.' She tugged at the fraying strips of linen, catching and pulling strands of Lissie's long black hair.

'Ow, ouch, ooh stop, Mam, it hurts!'

'Oh, shut up whining. Your dad'll be here soon and you'd better look your best.' She grabbed the freed ringlets with her bony hand and tied them back with a piece of faded ribbon saved from an old petticoat. Then she opened a drawer under the alcove cupboard next to the fire. 'Here. Put this clean pinny on and no going into t' garden, d'you hear?'

'Ah, Mam,' Lissie pleaded, 'can't I go out and watch for Dad coming up the path?'

'No you can't. Go an' put a light to the front-room fire. You can watch from there. And as soon as you see him, you come straight in here and tell me. Straight away, d'you hear?'

'Yes, Mam.'

Lissie stood on the horsehair cushion of one of the high-backed front-room chairs and pressed her nose against the window. The house stood on the site of an old charcoal burner's cottage in a wooded area that stretched for about half a mile to the canal. It had been rebuilt in brick with a slate roof years ago by a young engineer working on the cuts and locks in the area. However, it was out of the way and not a handy place to live as there was no proper village nearby.

When the waterway was finished, the engineer and his new wife had gone overseas and the house had lain empty for several years. It was too dear for a farmer to buy to house one of his workers, having a front door and staircase leading up to the bedchambers. Workers' cottages had stairs in the kitchen and no front doors. Not that there were many farm workers around any more. Most had gone to work in the manufactories or collieries in the heart of the South Riding. Furnaces and forges that belched out smoke and grime crowded into the Riding towns. They were some way upstream from Mexton Lock where Lissie lived. But few folk from Mexton ventured that far even though they were easier to get to now, with the canal completed to Tinsley.

Luther Dearne had heard about the empty house as a young barge hand grafting a living on the waterways that linked the rivers Humber and Trent with the South Riding, and he knew a bargain when he saw one. It was perfect for him, far enough away from the merchants near the coast and the factory owners in the Riding for him to disappear quickly when his shady dealings went sour.

The barge owner that Luther worked for as a young man was a cussed old bugger who lived alone on his barge. When he took sick one winter and died, Luther tipped him overboard into the Humber and sold the barge as his own. This was all he needed to be able to set up home in the engineer's house with his new bride Edie. He was able to stop working on the barges after that, and rely solely on the gains from his dealings to keep body and soul together.

That was nearly twenty years ago and trading had been good at first. The ironworks and foundries had their ups and their downs but there were always deals to be made in coals and bar iron. He bought and sold materials on the coast and manufactured goods from the town and arranged the transport of them in and out.

Nowadays, with regular business so unreliable, he tried to deal for other people as much as he could because there was less risk to his own money that way. Being a broker meant that he had plenty of opportunity to cream off more than his dues and that was something Luther could not resist. The traders never found out and, as they were all better off than he was, he reckoned that there was enough to go round.

Manufacturing in the South Riding expanded, water traffic increased and bargemen demanded a source of refreshment for themselves while they waited their turn to go through Mexton Lock. There had always been an inn at the lock, since the days when numerous thirsty labourers had cut the canal through farmland near the river Don.

The Navigator did a good trade and Mickey Jackson, with his wife Annie, worked hard. Annie kept clean rooms and cooked good food for travellers. Mickey, a burly, rough-and-ready man who spoke with his fists, preferred to keep the company of his regular ale drinkers in his saloon, one of whom was Luther. Mickey could always rely on Luther for extra muscle when he needed it.

Over the years, Mickey had added stables and livery to the inn for the workhorses that drew the heavy vessels through the oily black water. The youngest of Mickey's lads had recently set up as a horse marine for this stretch of the canal and the eldest was nearing the end of his apprentice bond with the blacksmith. The middle brother had taken over ale brewing from his father, who was now more interested in drinking it. A thriving community was developing on the bankside and there was a regular trade at Mexton wharf in timber and coal from a local land owner.

While Mickey's business grew, Luther was beginning to find work hard to come by. His reputation was not

good with respectable traders and big transport companies took the best trade. Luther had to confine his dealings to newcomers who had no knowledge of his past.
As his trade dwindled, he relied more and more on what
he could purloin from his deals. When challenged he
always blamed the other party's short supply, and if things
got really hot he simply disappeared until they had cooled
down.

Edie had turned out to be a disappointment to Luther,
but he easily found solace on his travels. There was many
a young widow or neglected wife in town or port with
a warm bed to offer in exchange for a piece of good
linen, a cooking pot or a brace of rabbits. And the child
was a joy to behold. Meeting that old trout in the North
Star all those years ago and buying little Lissie when she
was but a few months old had been the best deal he had
ever made.

As Luther lumbered through the woodland track, a
bulky sack bouncing over his shoulder, his heart lifted
at the thought of seeing his lovely little Lissie. She was
all that kept him with Edie now. He beamed at the sight
of her little white face and bouncy black ringlets peering
out of the front-room window. He saw her disappear
from view, guessing she was dashing through to the
kitchen.

Lissie squealed when she saw her dad striding up the
mud and cinder path that emerged from the wood into
the clearing that formed their front yard. Dressed in his
usual brown moleskin trousers and thick tweed jacket
that refused to stay buttoned, he sported a fancy new
waistcoat straining across his ample belly. She jumped

down from the chair and hurried through to the back
kitchen.

'He's here, Mam! Dad's home!'

Edie leaped to her feet and smoothed down her apron,
hissing at Lissie to behave herself and only speak when
she was spoken to. Luther burst in through the scullery
door shouting, 'Get the fire banked up, woman, I've got
yer favourite leg o' mutton in here for you to bake wi'
some 'taters!' He threw the heavy sack on to the wooden
table in the kitchen, picked Lissie up by her elbows and
balanced her against his corpulent belly. 'How's my little
trooper today? My God, I believe you've grown some
in only a month. You're so heavy now. Wait till you see
what I've got for you.'

She was as pretty as a picture with her hair as black
and shiny as wet coal. It was done up with a ribbon that
bounced with her curls as she moved. She wore a white
pinafore over her dark winter dress and black lace-up
boots on her feet. Luther wondered again, as he had
done many times before, what he had done to deserve
a little lass that was such a vision of loveliness. He was
never a church-going man but he reckoned he must
have done something right in his dubious life for Him
up in Heaven to bless him with Lissie.

Lissie jumped up and down on the spot. 'Where is it,
Dad? What you brought me?'

'Wait on, lass. The barge is unloading as I speak. I've
borrered Mickey's cart this time. Do you want to come
down to the lock with your dad, and ride back with
me? Do you?'

'Oh yes, Dad. I do, I do,' Lissie squeaked in excitement.

Her smoky green eyes shone and she forgot how much her boots pinched her toes, or how her hands felt sore and stinging. The recognisable warm smell of old tweed and tobacco filled her nostrils and comforted her.

Dad took her small hand in his large first. 'Off we go then.' He led her through the scullery, shouting at Edie over his shoulder, 'And cut one o' them cabbages from the garden, Edie. We can have a right good dinner tonight.' He turned to Lissie. ''Ave you missed me, lass? 'Ave you missed your old dad, then?'

'Oh yes, Dad. I have.' Lissie turned to say 'ta-ra' to her mam, who met her with such a scowl of spite and hatred that she recoiled in silence. What had she done now to upset her mam? Why did she hate her so and what, oh what, could she do to put things right? Her dad tugged at her arm, jolting her out of her stillness. But the edge was taken off her happiness as she wondered what her mam would do to her when her dad was gone again.

Chapter 6

Erik Svenson had struggled for eight years to establish his reputation in England. Dealers like Luther Dearne, who had no time for foreigners, didn't help him. But with the assistance of his wife, Ingrid, he had survived and prospered enough to employ a clerk to run his warehouse on the Humber. His son, Blake, now thirteen, was growing fast and Ingrid had found them a decent house in Goole, well away from the rats and diseases of the coastal ports. One of his buyers had recommended a good school in the South Riding to complete his boy's education, and Erik thought that he now had a future in England.

Blake jumped out of the family horse and trap leaving his neatly stacked boxes behind him and ran the last few yards to the red-brick villa that was his home. He scrambled through the damp, dripping shrubbery surrounding the building to reach the kitchen at the back of the house and darted inside, picking up a slice of fruit bun on the way.

'Papa! Mama! I'm home again!' Bursting into the drawing room he collided straight into the tall, upright figure of Mr Ephraim, his papa's clerk. 'S–So sorry, sir, I didn't see you there.'

'Evidently not.' Mr Ephraim was a serious man with curly dark hair and a greying straggly beard. He was dressed as always in dark sober clothes and carried a black felt hat with a low crown and wide brim. Blake's mama said that he kept Papa's manifests in good order and could remember the smallest detail when asked. Blake never saw him laugh, but his mama said he was a good man who was steadfast and loyal and they were lucky to have him in the business.

His papa was on his feet and walking across the thick Persian carpet that furnished their drawing-room floor. 'No need to call the maid, Ingrid, I'll see Ephraim out.' He turned to address his clerk. 'Thank you. I'll be at the warehouse first thing tomorrow to go through those documents.'

As Papa followed his trusted employee into the spacious hall they continued their conversation in hushed voices. Blake's mama remained seated as she gently chastised her son. 'Blake, you will behave more quietly in the house, please? Now come here and give your mama a kiss, then sit down. Your papa wishes to talk to you about your new school and Lucy will bring tea in a few minutes.'

Blake quickly swallowed the last of his bun and wrapped his arms around his mama. He kissed her on both cheeks. 'Mama, you look beautiful in that dress. The blue is the colour of your eyes.'

'Thank you, my dear. How was school?'

'Dull, I'm sorry to tell you, Mama. When can I leave?'

'Blake! How can you say such a thing?'

School had bored him a lot lately and it was good to be home. He was restless to be outdoors, to find his young friends in the town, or perhaps go with his papa on one of the keels down the Humber to their warehouse. But he settled reluctantly in one of the damask upholstered chairs that furnished their drawing room.

He answered dutifully while his mama quizzed him about his stagecoach journey to the post in town where their own horse and trap had collected him and his luggage. He had had a seat inside the coach but it was still freezing cold all the way and he hated sitting still. Maybe his papa would let him work in the warehouse after Christmas so he would not have to go back to school. He had had too much of school already!

'My boy! At last! Stand up and let me see how you have grown!' His papa strode back into the drawing room, filling it with his presence. He was a big man, broad-shouldered and strong. He was Blake's hero, and his mama's too. In Sweden he had sawn timber, mined coal and forged iron, before buying a share in a sailing ship to cross the North Sea and set up a trade with England.

Erik had heard that Swedish iron was always in demand with the ironmasters of the South Riding. There they had good coal and good men who knew how to forge iron. Yes, he conceded, they really knew how to forge iron in the South Riding! Trade had been steady, even in the bad times when some of the factories had closed.

Blake listened to his father telling his mother that closures were often due to poor handling of business and profits, for there was always a need for good iron in peace as well as wartime.

Erik Svenson was an outgoing, sociable man who drove a hard bargain but always dealt fair. In contrast, Blake's mother was quieter. But she was strong in her own way, listening and commenting in her unassuming manner. Often when his father discussed business with his mother over a glass of schnapps, she would simply listen as he talked and talked until he had decided what he would do next. Sometimes, his mother made a suggestion, but always, they talked it over together.

Mama had worked as hard as Papa in their early days of trading. She still kept her interest in the warehouse even now that they had Ephraim to help with the work. She liked England and the English way of life and they stayed, at first renting a small house in Goole, a pleasant town, well upstream of the brackish, estuarine waters and away from the lawlessness and smells of the Humberside docks. After a few years, with his wholesale trade established, Papa sold his share of the ship that had brought them over and bought this villa with its own carriage house and stabling, spacious cellars and attics for the servants.

Blake saw the pride in his father's eyes as he spoke. 'You are taller for sure, but you're pale and too thin. It is time you filled out a bit, I think. School is all book learning and not good for a growing boy.'

'He's only thirteen, Erik, and book learning is so good for his future,' his mama argued. 'You have the letter from his headmaster? He says Blake will go to the university if he wishes.'

Papa ruffled Blake's bright golden hair. 'You have your mama's wits, my boy,' he said, adding with a touch of regret, 'which is just as well, for I have no brain to speak of.'

Mama protested. 'Now that is nonsense, Erik, and you know it.'

'Oh, Ingrid, Ingrid. I should have known there were thieves about. You only need to look at the manifests to see—'

'Well, Ephraim has been right through the papers. We shall know the worst tomorrow.'

Blake's curiosity got the better of him. 'What is it, Papa? Have we been robbed?' One of his best friends had had to leave school because his father had been robbed of all their money. 'Papa, Papa, are we going to lose everything?'

'No, my son, we are not. But, but . . . well . . . we have been cheated and . . . and . . . robbed by an unscrupulous dealer.'

'Is it very serious, Papa?'

'Yes, it is. We have lost some of our goods and the profits from them.'

'If you want, Papa, I could give up school and work for you. Please let me give up school. I'll work with Mr Ephraim in the warehouse.'

His father gave him a benign smile. 'You are a good son and you can work in the warehouse when you're older. Your mama is right about school. This is a foreign land for us and you need to learn its ways as much as you can. We have found a better school for you, now you are a grown boy. It is further to travel – inland in the South Riding – but there will be other boys like you there, sons of professional men and factory owners. It will be better for you, I am sure. And if you want you can go to university.'

'But school is so dull, Papa! I want to be with you and Mr Ephraim at the warehouse—'

'You will be. You will. When you have finished your schooling. How about you come with me and Ephraim to get our stolen money back?'

'Erik, no! I do not think that is wise. He's just a boy.'

'And he'll soon be a man, Ingrid. He needs to know of the world outside school. Then he will be ready to handle himself with the bigger boys at school.'

'Yes, yes, Papa!' Blake jumped up and down with excitement. 'Can I come with you? Can I?'

'I have business in Doncaster to attend to first, but then we can travel on the waterways into the Riding towns.'

Mama continued her protest. 'But those towns are so smoky and dirty now. It will not be good for him.'

'Ingrid, I shall look after Blake. He is my son and I love him. We shall lodge outside of the towns and I shall not let anything happen to him.' Papa walked over to where Mama was sitting primly in a blue full-skirted gown, with her hands folded in her lap, and kissed the top of her head. 'Do not worry, my dear wife. He will be safe with me, I promise. I shall find an inn away from the manufactories. Ephraim has done all the work and we have letters from merchants in the Riding.'

He paused, stroking her hair gently. 'You know I have to do this, my love. Luther Dearne has cheated both me and the merchants who supply me and I must challenge him about his thieving ways.'

'Won't you go to the constables first?'

'I am a fair man. I shall give him a chance to own up. And pay up, of course. As soon as he sees the papers that Ephraim has prepared, he will know that his crooked little game is over. He will have to repay us, all of us, or his fraud will be exposed and he will most likely end up in the debtors' prison. I am sure he will not wish for that.'

Blake watched this exchange of views between his parents, his bright blue eyes dancing with excitement. Papa always listened to Mama where Blake was concerned, and he so wanted to go with Papa on this trip. His father had frequently taken him on to the estuary waters of the Humber where the sea was choppy and the keels had sails that agile sailors hauled up and down to catch the keen coastal breezes.

He pleaded with his mother. 'Let me go, Mama! Please let me go. Mr Ephraim will be with us too,' he cried.

'Mr Ephraim is older than your papa. He cannot help if ruffians and the like set upon you and rob you!'

'And why should that happen?' Papa argued.

'You know that bargemen can be very rough. They drink so much and they fight – and Blake is so young,' Mama complained.

'Ingrid! Do not judge too quickly. *Ja*, some of them are bad but I have my friends also among the bargemen. They are good men and they work hard. Besides, we shall travel by stagecoach as far as Doncaster and from there with a carrier that I know and trust.'

There was a silence before Mama said, 'Then if it is so safe, I shall come with you too.'

'No. This is men's work.' Papa's voice was firm.

Blake stared at his mother with wide pleading eyes. 'Mama?'

Ingrid sighed heavily. 'Bah! Blake, you are your father's son. What can I, a mere woman, say? Go! Go! Leave your mama to look after the warehouse. But you must take care. We – you – are foreigners in this land and so you will count for nothing if it all goes wrong. Promise me, Erik, that you will take very great care.'

Papa kissed her again. 'I promise. What do you say, my son, will you come along with your papa?'

'Yes, yes, yes! Oh yes, Papa, yes!' Blake jumped around the drawing room almost knocking over Lucy as she came in with the tea tray. He took some bread and butter in his hand and ran outside to help unload his boxes from the carriage.

Blake, his papa and Mr Ephraim took the stagecoach as planned from Goole to Doncaster. The weather was miserable, so cold and wet that the coach felt as damp inside as it did for those riding on top. At least the rutted turnpike was not frozen solid and they reached their destination mud-spattered, but without any mishap.

From there they were to travel on a feed barge taking oats and bran, and bales of hay for the horse marines along the navigation. Most of the barges carried heavy forged iron for recasting, or coal for the furnaces. They were long and wide, carrying a hundred tons or more and needing two horses to tow them. In winter, this meant a lot of feed for the animals and frequent changes at the horse marines to keep the cargo moving.

There was some delay in Doncaster as a biting and persistent east wind had brought a keen and lingering frost that had frozen the canals. Barges were backed up at the lock basins until teams of heavy horses hauled the icebreakers through. The local inns were doing a good trade in spiced, mulled ale for the stranded bargemen.

For Blake, the experience of travelling on the feed barge filled him with excitement. The bargeman allowed him to drive the fine Cleveland Bay along on the towpath. He showed him how to walk behind the horse, holding the long reins loosely, and he learned how to crack the whip to warn other canal users of their approach at bridge holes and tunnels. His special task was to re-fill the horse's nose can when it was empty, and to make sure he had fresh water at the stopping places.

The feed barge had a warm cabin below deck at the stern, with a stove where they could mull ale to keep out the cold and dry their muddy boots and breeches. The bargeman told Blake stories of how he and his wife used to live on board before he had made enough money to buy a cottage near the wharf in Doncaster. Now he could take paying passengers and was glad of the extra for his growing family.

While his papa and Mr Ephraim talked of business and the fraud, Blake darted about at locks and basins, heaving sacks of oats, holding mooring ropes and winding sluices up and down at lock gates. During quieter moments, he thought to himself that travelling on a canal barge was the best thing he had ever done and much more fun than going to school. Oh, why did it take so long to grow up? This adventure was over much too soon for him as the feed barge reached Mexton Lock, just outside the iron towns, where it changed horses and they reached their destination.

A weak winter sun was already low in the sky ahead of them. The barge emerged from under a stone bridge into a wider basin where the bargeman waited for his turn to go through the lock ahead of them upstream. On the north side of the canal lay a timber yard with a few cottages nearby. Stark bare branches of woodland trees in winter gave a bleak backdrop to the cottages. In the yard, piles of lumber and coal waited to be loaded into barges for hauling away to the towns.

In contrast, the south side of the canal was alive with activity, for there was an inn and other buildings serving the canal trade. A horse marine with barns and stables stood next to the inn, and beyond that was a blacksmith and forge. Further upstream a small, whitewashed house stood nearer the water than the other buildings, where the lock keeper stood guard to make sure all dues were paid.

Blake heaved their boxes on to the towpath and held out a helping hand for Mr Ephraim to climb ashore. Although Mr Ephraim lived by the tidal waters of the Humber he never sailed on them if he could avoid it. This was the first time he had climbed off the barge during the whole of their journey, being afraid of the water and the moving gap between the barge and bank.

They had been travelling since dawn and Blake was hungry and tired. His papa climbed ashore last and surveyed the scene around him. Soon the light would be fading and he was anxious to find where Dearne lived so that he could talk to him before nightfall. He buttoned up his warm overcoat and caught up with the others.

'Ephraim, you're looking pale! You need a brandy, man!'

'Yes, I do believe that would help. I hope the land-lord keeps a good fire.'

The small party hurried inside and arranged for their boxes to be brought in. Ephraim headed straight for the fireside and took off his thick winter gloves to warm his hands. Blake stayed near to his father and sat on a narrow bench next to the counter.

'Landlord, two glasses of brandy and a hot toddy for the boy, if you please,' Blake's papa called. 'We also need a good dinner and rooms – two rooms – and my companion needs a lively fire in his. See to it.'

Mickey Jackson, the landlord of the Navigator, reluc-tantly turned his florid face away from his regular customers. His expression was surly, but he recognised good custom when he saw it. He shouted over his shoulder to an unseen person through a door into the back, 'Miriam, get your ma!' then turned back to the travellers. 'Right away, sir. Come far have you?'

'Doncaster.'

Mickey Jackson also recognised foreigners when he heard them. 'Donnie, eh? And afore then?'

'What do you mean?' Papa sounded stern.

'On'y that I meant you're from foreign parts like, from over the sea.'

Papa nodded silently then added pleasantly, 'The brandy, landlord?'

'Aye, sir. Coming up. I were on'y thinking there's bin a bit o' ice Donnie way.'

'Yes, indeed. It has caused us some delay.'

'Aye. How long will you be wanting the rooms, then?'

'One or two nights. Perhaps more, for it depends on how long my business takes.'

'What kind of business might that be, sir?' He put the drinks on the worn wooden counter and nodded to a young girl who had appeared in the bar. 'Hot water and honey for the lad,' he barked and she disappeared as fast as she had arrived. When Blake's papa stayed silent, the landlord persisted. 'It's on'y that I know the folk round these parts if it's directions you need.'

Papa must have decided that a little information would keep the landlord quiet. 'Iron,' he volunteered. 'Bar iron, ready for the forge.'

Mickey Jackson was satisfied and noticeably impressed.

The girl brought Blake's toddy to the bench where he was sitting. He took it gratefully, savouring the warmth as it seeped down his throat and through his veins. She lingered, batting a wooden tray against her long skirts and blinking at him. He smiled at her and she stared back, pushing her lower lip forward. With her free hand, she twisted loose curls of hair round her fingers and swayed a little. Surprised, Blake stopped drinking.

She was just a young girl, he noticed, but she was

enticing him, making him look at her in a different way. She pulled a curl down on to her chest so that it trailed away to the lace that covered the tiny swell of her budding breasts. Blake felt a stirring inside him, and he began to look at her more closely. She was pretty, in a little girl way, with her honey-coloured hair and hazel eyes. He guessed that she was a few years younger than he was and wondered, briefly, if she behaved like this with the local boys.

He liked the feeling she aroused in him, the adolescent thrill that bubbled through his veins. It was a new kind of excitement and he relished it. He wanted more. He smiled at her, gulped down the rest of his toddy and shuffled along the bench to make room for her to sit with him. She sat very close and placed the tray across her lap. It jutted over his thigh and she moved it very slightly, backwards and forwards. He looked at her again and saw that she was smiling at him.

'Miriam!' The landlord's bark shattered their brief contact. 'Get in the back kitchen! Now! Go and help your ma with the dinners!'

Miriam rounded her eyes and looked towards the ceiling, then scuttled off leaving Blake wondering what she would have done next. He stood up and joined his papa at the wooden counter.

'Well, landlord,' his papa was saying, 'you may be able to help me. I am looking for a dealer called Dearne. I'm told he lives at Mexton Lock.'

'Dearne, eh? You got business with him, then?'

Papa ignored the question. 'This is Mexton Lock, isn't it? He lives around here, in the woodland I believe. Where might that be?'

'You done business with Dearne in the past, 'ave you?'

Papa leaned forward and breathed, 'If I had, my good man, it would be my business and not yours.'

Mickey Jackson scowled. He liked to know everything that went on around Mexton Lock. It was his patch, his manor. Luther was his crony. But he knew better than to upset a good spending customer. 'Pardon me, sir. The woodland is on t' other side o' the canal. You go over t' stone bridge downstream o' the lock, or you can walk across t' lock gates if you've a head for the deep water. Follow the track up through the wood and you'll come to Dearne's house. Only house there, in a clearing where the old charcoal burner's hut used to be.'

'Thank you, landlord. Do you know if he is home? I plan to visit him tonight.'

'Tonight?' He turned and yelled, 'Miriam! Miriam, answer me when I'm talking to you! Is Mr Dearne back yet?'

'Yes, Father. He came through on the icebreaker. He's just been over to borrow the horse and cart for his supplies.'

Mickey Jackson turned his attention back to his customers. 'There's your answer, sir. Will you take a lantern with you? It will be a cold 'un tonight for sure. You'll get a bit o' moonlight later on if you're lucky.'

'Good. We'll have dinner now. Over by the fire if you please.' His papa crossed the inn saloon to join Ephraim by the fire and Blake followed him. 'Are you warmed through yet, Ephraim?'

'Much better now, thank you, Erik. Wouldn't you rather wait until morning to confront Dearne?'

'I want to get this over with and also give the man time to think overnight. If he cannot see sense now, he might by the morning. I'll take the papers with me.'

'I've written out copies to show him. You can leave them with him so he knows how much you have on him.'

'You're a good man, Ephraim. You always think of everything.'

'Do you want me to come with you?'

'No, you need to rest after dinner. The journey has been long and cold and you need to keep yourself warm. If Dearne proves to be stubborn and difficult we'll move on to the magistrate in town tomorrow.'

'They are sure to send a constable for him with all this evidence.'

'I am a fair man. I shall give him a chance to pay back what he owes me first.'

'Be careful, Erik. You do not know this man.'

Blake, who had been listening closely to the conversation, echoed Ephraim's concern and urged, 'Don't go alone, Papa. I'll come with you.'

'There is no danger. I am going to talk business with this man, and that is all. But, my son, you can come along too if you wish. It is good for you to learn that business is not all profit and plenty. We shall have our dinner first, yes? I hope they will not be much longer with our food.'

Blake wandered outside to look at the lock, glad of his thick coat and good boots. There were a few children working on the other side of the canal, picking over a coal heap for slack and carrying it in buckets to a separate pile. They looked thin and chilled to him, and filthy with coal dust, but called cheerfully to each other and chased around, throwing about the slack they were supposed to be sorting.

A pair of heavy draught horses being led to the stables for the night got wind of the feed barge and whinnied and snorted, ignoring the stable lad's entreaties to move on. As daylight faded, Blake watched the huge animals with their fluffy white fetlocks eventually clomp slowly towards their own feed cans and a good rub down. The stable lad was not much older than he was, but he had a kind and calming manner as he coaxed them inside to the shelter of their warm, straw-filled stalls.

Then Blake noticed more activity on the other side of the oily dark water and shrank back into the shadow of the buildings. Keeping close to the rough stone wall of the inn, he watched quietly and covertly. There was a timber-built sawmill on the other side, as well as a row of stone cottages. The nearest cottage had its front window open and a plank set up outside it displaying small wares for sale. Daylight was fading fast and the progress of laden barges through the lock was slow. Someone lit a couple of flaring torches and Blake moved from the inn's protective shadow to the water's edge to get a closer look.

There was a man over the other side, a man he had seen before, just last summer when he had been helping Ephraim at Papa's warehouse on the Humber. The man had talked business with Papa and now Blake recognised him. He was striding around holding a lighted flare that caused flickering shadows on the muddy ground.

This must be Dearne! The man his papa said was a crooked dealer and a thief. He was a short, stocky man with a big round belly and a loud voice as he shouted at a couple of lads who were loading an untidy heap of sacks and boxes on to a cart.

When he had finished loading his cart and hitching up the horse, Dearne walked towards a row of cottages where a group of small children were playing around a stray log from the wood yard. The raucous squeals of their game of tag were savage, and by the light of the flare the laden barges transformed into monstrous shapes patrolling a deep dark crevice. He took one of the children back to the cart and prepared to leave.

Shadowy figures moving between piles of coals and timber seemed ghoulish and unreal. Lock gates creaked, and the winding machinery screeched. The sound of water rushing through open sluices caused an involuntary shiver to snake its way down Blake's back. In the darkness there was a malevolence about this place that scared him.

Undeterred, Blake walked right up to the water's edge and strained his neck for a closer look. But it was no good, the light had faded and the flare was almost spent. The horse and cart became a shadowy spectre as it trundled its way along a rutted track towards the woodland. As it passed the wood mill, where more flares were burning, the driver looked back at his load.

Blake could not see his face, only a fleeting picture of the man who had brought them on this cold dark journey to Mexton Lock. Already the injustice Dearne had caused his papa had insinuated itself into his head and etched itself in his mind. Papa was right. This man must pay for his double dealing! He watched until the cart disappeared through the trees and he heard his papa calling him back to the inn for dinner.

'He's here, Papa!' Blake exclaimed. 'I've seen him – the thief we have come to find!'

'Hush, boy, the landlord will hear you and he is a friend of Dearne. We do not wish to make the landlord our enemy as well. Now be quiet and eat your dinner.'

The food was good and wholesome, prepared that day by the landlord's wife. Erik and Ephraim dallied by the fire afterwards, and for the price of a few jugs of ale were able to question a few regulars about the Navigator Inn and its inhabitants.

They heard that Mickey Jackson was as tough as he looked and that he knew how to fight for what he wanted. Anyone who drank regularly in the Navigator learned very quickly to stay on the right side of the landlord and his two eldest sons, who were both from the same mould. The three of them were nothing but thugs, they were told, who would knock you down as soon as speak to you. Between them they saw to it that there was never any trouble at the inn save for the disturbances caused by the landlord himself.

Mickey Jackson finished most working days with a skinful of strong ale downed in the company of his sons and their cronies. More often than not, he slept it off by the fire in the saloon when all those with lesser constitutions had gone to their beds. All too frequently though, he caught the eye of one of the women who came in for the company of working men, women who knew by the end of the night which of the menfolk would have money left in their pockets to pay for a little more pleasure.

Mickey had a liking for women and his position and means in the thriving lockside community gave him his pick of them. A knowing look and a brief word would secure him some late-night company from any one of them who would be happy to indulge him in return for a coin. If she was especially pleasing to him she might acquire a length of dress cloth purloined from a passing barge, or a pair of fancy shoes bound for some merchant's wife in the Riding, before being sent off home in the middle of the night.

Mickey's wife Ann knew of his dalliances, of course, and had little choice but to ignore them. She gave her attention to the travellers staying at the inn, and spent her time in the kitchen rather than the saloon. Her daughter Miriam was her main consolation from being married to a bully and a thug. Miriam was her youngest child and her only girl. She had indulged her since birth, which made the boys jealous. If Ann wanted anything for Miriam, she could usually persuade Mickey to provide it.

Only their youngest lad, Peter, showed any kind of sensitivity or feelings. His two older brothers tormented him routinely, so from a very young age he had found solace in caring for animals. Horses were his passion, and already he was earning himself a good reputation with the horse marine next door to the inn.

Mickey's eldest lad would soon be a blacksmith and there was talk of him taking over the Mexton forge. He shared with his father the same controlling manner and liking for women and drink. The middle brother was fast learning these ways too, but for now had turned his strength to the brewing and heavy cellar work at the inn.

Blake watched and listened as he ate his dinner with his papa and Mr Ephraim by the fire in the Navigator saloon. He quickly realised that Mexton Lock, or at least much of the business on the Navigator side of the canal, had a Jackson's hand in it one way or another. The Jacksons were friends of Dearne. Papa was right. It was wise to keep your own counsel in these parts.

Chapter 7

During the years since Luther Dearne had first set eyes on Erik Svenson, Lissie had thrived. But she knew little of the world beyond Mexton Lock. Her young life had been spent mostly doing what her mam said and waiting for her dad to come home. Her only journeys were down the woodland trail to the canal to help with fetching and carrying.

For her those walks were exciting adventures and the constant activities on the wharf fascinated her. She loved to watch the heavy docile horses, heads down, straining their ropes, or waiting patiently on the towpath for the lock to fill or empty. When they stopped to feed, she stroked their huge noses and admired their chestnut leather collars and harnesses, decorated with polished brasses.

There was always plenty to see at the lock, and usually a convenient log to sit on while Dad went over to the Navigator or picked up a sack from one of the barges.

Her dad did not allow her to go over the canal, especially by the lock gates, for although they were wide
enough to walk on, there was no rail to stop you falling
in.

'When you're a bit older, lass,' her dad said, 'you can
walk downstream an' go over t' bridge.'

The stone bridge was a hundred yards away and had
been built to take timber and coal wagons out to local
farms. Once over the bridge, the track went past the
'Navvy' and on through farmland, coalfields and pit
villages before it reached the outskirts of town.

Dad always ordered her to stay on the woodland side
of the canal until he came back from the Navigator.
Sometimes, when he did return, he staggered over the
lock gates carrying a can of ale to take home for dinner
and Lissie was scared he would fall in the canal, but he
never did.

There were times when he stayed a long time in the
Navigator and Lissie went to see Rosa. Rosa's house was
on the same side of the canal as the woodland. It was
the end one of a row, built for labourers at the wood
mill. The stone cottages faced the canal and they all had
long gardens that backed on to the trees.

Rosa's husband had worked at the mill for years until
one day he had suddenly cleared off and left her. Since
then, Rosa had scratched a living from her garden and
her kitchen. She kept a beehive and grew strong-smelling
plants that she used to cook up all kinds of healing cures
and salves to sell from the front door of her cottage.

Once, a bargeman's wife had taken most of her stock
and paid her well in flour and lard, and a whole skirt of

beef. So Rosa made meat pies and when they were done, she opened her kitchen window to sell them hot from the oven.

On rare occasions, when she got hold of a cone of sugar, Rosa boiled it up with liquorice to make a spice that she called pomfret cakes, which she kept for her favourite customers. Lissie was always sure of some spice from Rosa, if she could remember a bit of gossip to repeat. So she learned to become a good listener when her dad stopped to talk to the woodcutters or lock keeper.

'Mr Jackson's bought the stables, me dad says,' she related to Rosa, 'and he's going to set up his youngest lad, Peter, as the horse marine. Just as soon as he has rid of the one already there. He's going to put the rent up to make him go.'

'Ee, lass,' Rosa sighed, handing her a nib of pomfret. 'There'll soon be no room for nob'dy else but the Jacksons over there. Tell yer mam to come down to see me as soon as yer dad's gone off again.'

Dad didn't much like Rosa, but Lissie's mam was very friendly with her and when her dad was away they often visited her small, weird house full of dried herbs and stale air that made Lissie's head spin. Her mam liked Rosa and was always in a hurry when they went there.

'Pick yer feet up, girl,' she snapped, as her bony hand gripped Lissie's tightly and pulled at her tiny arm, dragging her down the woodland track. 'We're going to Rosa's,' her mam told her firmly, 'to buy a pie for dinner because we haven't got no coal to keep the fire going.'

This puzzled Lissie because when they eventually got

back home with the pie, the fire was still in and Mam
would put the pie in the oven at the side to heat through.
She remembered the visits well as she was usually left
on her own in Rosa's kitchen to play. At first, the ugly
bunches of drying plants and the odd smells frightened
her. But eventually Lissie became fascinated by the tiny
pots and corked bottles that Rosa kept on her kitchen
shelves.

When they reached the cottage Rosa poured spirits
from a bottle into two tankards and her mam sat with
Rosa on her horsehair sofa, their heads close together,
whispering and laughing.

Lissie knew that if she behaved herself and was quiet
she would be given a drink of new milk, bought from
the Navvy in a tin can, and a pomfret cake out of the
locked cupboard by the fireplace. She sat on the carpet
and played with some old pots and pans as her toys.
Then her mam gave her another cake and told her to
be a good little girl while she helped Rosa turn the
mattresses. Rosa and her mam were giggly when they
went upstairs, leaving her alone on a rag rug covering
the stone flagged floor of the empty kitchen.

There was one visit when Rosa and her mam were
upstairs for ages. Lissie climbed on to the window ledge
to catch a glimpse of the barges with their cargoes of
coal or iron queuing up to go through the lock, or watch
timber or coal being loaded to take onwards to the towns
in the Riding. But the canal was frozen, and she got
bored as the floor was too cold to play on.

She listened at the door to the stairs and heard the
creaking bedsprings and the groans and squeals of Rosa

and her mam as they turned the beds. Lissie knew her mam did not like doing this at home, but with Rosa she never got bad-tempered like she did at home and she was always cheerful on days spent at Rosa's.

When they came downstairs she got another spice because she hadn't wet her drawers and cried. This was easier for Lissie now she had grown up, now she was tall enough to reach the back-door latch and go out to the privy down the garden.

Rosa mashed some tea and put in 'something to keep the cold out'. Lissie had a drink of it out of a saucer and fell asleep by the fire.

'Quiet kid, i'n't she?' Rosa commented.

'Good job too,' her mam replied. 'I never wanted her in the first place, you know. It was Luther's idea to have 'er. "To keep me company," he said, when he was away down the canals doing his deals and such like. That was afore he knew about you, like. Still, he doesn't mind me coming here when 'e's away, as long as I bring the lass wi' me.'

'She's a little beauty though. That black hair looks a bit foreign-like, to me.'

'Gypsy blood, I've allus thought.'

'Is she his?' Rosa asked.

''E says not, but I don't believe him. 'E's had some floozy down the Humber, I'm sure of it.'

Rosa gave her a sly smile. 'We-ell, you don't mind that, do you, Edie?'

Edie shook her head and giggled. 'Suits me and you, do'n't it?'

'Where's she from, the mother, like?'

'Down south, I think. Luther's got some trinkets and stuff from her, locked away in the old casement clock. 'E says she died and she was away from her own folk. There was a nurse wi' her, but she couldn't take her back to her family, the little 'un being a bastard, like.'

'Nurse, eh? They were well-to-do, then?'

'Oh, aye. Just born the wrong side o' the blanket.'

'Aye, well, there's plenty o' them about. We 'ad some Londoners through the lock two summers ago and they said t' old king had bastards all o'er t' place but he still couldn't manage to produce one for t' throne. And now we have a woman on t' throne. Whatever next?'

'Just a slip of a girl, I heard. Fancy that, Rosa. I don't s'pose it'll make any difference to us, anyroad.'

'She'll still 'ave a 'usband who'll tell her what to do, an' gi' 'er a tribe o' kids like this 'un. You're lucky Luther on'y brought home the one.'

'Oh aye, and she 'as her uses,' her mam declared. 'Luther, well, he fair dotes on her, and it keeps him off my back. She's right quick on the uptake and she's making a good little housekeeper now she's growing up.'

The two women exchanged smiles and finished their mugs of tea and gin.

At the other side of town, Grace's new business was thriving, and Clara was choosing fabrics and trimmings for new dresses. The dressmaker came to visit their home now, with her samples and drawings, and they all took tea in the small study before she left. And cakes. They ate cake every day now. They could afford it.

'Such a lovely house you have here, Mrs Beighton,'

the dressmaker sighed. 'Just the right distance from town, I've always thought.'

Grace smiled benignly at her visitor. 'It suits us to be away from the smoke and grime of the furnaces.' She stretched her hand, covered in a long, black lace mitten, to pat Clara's knee. 'My niece must have clean air to breathe.'

'But you are also away from the businesses, for your gentlemen – er – lodgers.'

'Guests,' Grace corrected her. 'As gentlemen, you understand, they have their own horses.'

'Or they hire carriages,' Clara added. 'Our guests are always gentlemen of means.'

The dressmaker, mindful of the cost of her own hired trap for the journey, took her leave. Clara showed her to the front door and wished her a safe journey home. She was a good needlewoman and, as such, important to Grace's household. After saying goodbye, Clara returned to the study. The furnishings were fashionably heavy and dark and it was a million miles away from the dirty smelly study she had left behind eight years ago.

'More tea?' Grace topped up the silver teapot from an ornate matching kettle keeping warm over an oil flame.

'Thanks. Do you think she knows?'

'Oh yes. I'm sure she does. She has the same customers as we do. Well, their wives and daughters anyway.'

'I suppose the wives know about us too,' Clara shrugged.

'And some of them are grateful to us. So don't you go fretting about that.'

'Do you mind all the changes we have made here, Grace? I mean, not taking lodgers any more?'

'Never! This is a far better use for the place. Well away from prying eyes and town gossips. Do you have regrets? It was your idea.'

'Yes it was, wasn't it? Well, Mr Hardcastle's actually,' Clara conceded. 'The lodging house was fine to begin with, but there was a lot more money to be made from my special services to the gentlemen. I had no idea there would be so much demand though. Or that we would need one or two other girls to help.'

'Me neither. But we must continue to be discreet. I am past fifty now, and I don't want to be run out of town before I'm ready to go.'

'You have no fears there, Grace. Not with Sir William as my personal client. And his private physician advising us.'

'And one of our new regulars is an alderman, I hear.'

'There you are, then. As long as we only take recommended clients.'

They sipped their tea and finished the cake. The coals fell in the fireplace, sending a few sparks on to the brass hearth rail.

Grace thought for a minute. 'You know, Clara, you are a very pretty girl, and not yet thirty. You don't have to do this. You could marry and get out of here if you want — I shan't mind if you do.'

'I don't,' Clara replied flatly. 'Any more than you wanted to wed that innkeeper who took a fancy to you when we first arrived here.'

'But I'm just a plain old widow—'

'A wealthy one though,' Clara reminded her.

'You could be proper rich,' Grace persisted. 'Sir William worships you—'

'Sir William has a wife.'

'You could be his mistress, set up in a house of your own, with servants.'

'That's just the same as being married. No, I vowed when I left my stepfather that no man would ever own me and I meant it.'

'You were distraught then. You—'

'Besides, I'd never leave you, Grace,' Clara interrupted. She got up and kissed Grace's brow. 'I owe everything to you.'

Grace squeezed Clara's hand. They were two of a kind, she thought.

That day, the day the foreigners came to Mexton Lock, Lissie was excited. Her dad was home again. With Christmas not far off, trade had picked up a bit and there was a lot of talk of a new era with the new Queen. Dad had brought clothes as well as extra food to see them through the worst of the winter. He was loading coal on to a borrowed cart to keep the kitchen fire going. He liked it kept in all day when he was home. When he was away, Mam was always letting it go out because she would forget to bring in the coals from the coal house next to the scullery. And then Lissie would get the blame and a clip round the ear.

Now she sat outside Rosa's cottage on one of the hewn logs that lay around, and watched, fascinated, as a long barge heaped with coals disappeared from view when the lock emptied as water drained away. Then, ages later, another rose from the depths as the lock filled again. She couldn't see what was in this one as it was covered in oily wet canvas. She would have liked a closer look but Dad had forbidden her to move from her seat until he returned.

The evening air was damp, and filled with a smell of horse droppings and the thick grease that kept the lock machinery moving. Huge, heavy wooden lock gates creaked and groaned as they were moved by strong young lads who leaned backwards against the wide levers to walk the gates open and closed. They shouted to each other across the canal, and to the bargemen who stayed aboard while their valuable craft went through.

Then she saw him. On the other side of the canal. A new face. As tall as Mickey's boys but not as thickset. Not quite as old as them, she thought, but better dressed in a neat dark overcoat with a thick shoulder cape. His boots were polished and clean, not even dusty from the towpath. He was wearing a proper cap made out of tweed, which he took off briefly, and when he did his bright fair hair glinted in the light from a window. He ran his fingers through that hair, combing it straight back from his brow in a quick fluid movement, then replaced his cap firmly on top of his head.

Lissie's attention was riveted by him. His clothes alone set him apart from the other boys playing around the lock. He didn't join in their games either, or help with the lock gates and winding the sluices. He just stood there, watching, as the canal folk went about their work.

Lissie stared, straining her eyes to see as much as she

could in the fading daylight, wondering who he was, where he came from and most of all, where he was going. With his cap pulled down to cover up that striking fair hair, he looked the same as any of the other better-off boys that sometimes came with their fathers to do business at the lock. But he wasn't from round here, she was sure.

Suddenly, and annoyingly, she was distracted.

'How's my little Lissie, then? Are you being a good girl?' Her dad stood with his sturdy legs wide apart and his arms behind his back, blocking her view.

She leaned to one side to peer round and catch another glimpse of the stranger on the further side of the canal. The boy was still there, he had not moved. He watched silently as a bargeman finished loading the cart.

'No peeking,' her dad chided, 'or it won't be a surprise, will it? Guess what I've got for you?'

Lissie's concentration was diverted as she jumped down from the log and squealed, 'Spice! Ooh, is it toffee, Dad? Oh, can I have it now, Dad? Please can I have it now?'

'Aye, lass, you can that. It'll be a while before tea's ready with the size o' the joint your mam's roasting for tonight. Don't tell her what you've been eating, mind. Y'know what she's like.'

Lissie unscrewed the top of the paper cone and placed one of the lumps of toffee in her mouth. Ann Jackson at the Navigator bought it in slabs from a traveller every Christmas, and sold it on to passing barges and keels. Sometimes Dad bought a small slab to take home. Then he would make a great ceremony of breaking it up in a cloth with his hammer and sharing it out. Lissie sucked and chewed with relish, thinking that it was the nicest thing that she had ever tasted in her life.

As soon as the wagon was loaded, her dad paid off the bargeman, who took one of the flares over the lock gates and went straight into the inn to spend his wind-fall. As the light flickered by him, Lissie noticed the boy was still there, keeping to the shady side of the inn and watching everything that was going on.

He was definitely one of the bigger boys, and one that Lissie would normally avoid – especially if he was in a gang. Big boys threw stones at the girls and pulled your hair if they got a chance. Her dad got really mad if big boys came anywhere near her when he was around. But she was safe from them this side of the lock. And anyway, this boy wasn't in a gang.

Dad lifted Lissie up and swung her round into the cart. 'You sit on the boxes there, lass, and don't go near the coal. Hold on to the side when it gets bumpy.'

'Yes, Dad.' Lissie pushed the last piece of toffee into her mouth. Dad led the horse and wagon up the dirt track through the trees, keeping to the well-worn ruts. She took one last look back but she could not see the boy. Where had he gone? she wondered. And why?

Chapter 8

Tea was very late that day, partly because it took Dad so long to get the coal loaded at the wharf and then to shovel it from the cart into the coalhouse next to the scullery. Then he had to take the horse and cart back to Mickey's and fetch a quart of ale for dinner. Mam had taken ages to cook the meat and Lissie was starving by the time it was ready.

It smelled so good she could hardly wait, and Dad kept calling from wherever he was in the house or garden to ask if it was ready yet. Only her mam seemed un-impressed and bored by all the fuss. But then, Lissie knew, she didn't like cooking and never ate that much anyway, preferring her bottle of spirits and pinch o' snuff to keep her going.

Dad often laughed at Mam saying, 'No wonder you're as skinny as a bird, you eat like one.' And then he'd tweak Lissie's nose and add, 'Not like my little Lissie, who knows how to enjoy a decent dinner.'

A clear sky promised another frost that night, but it was warm and cosy inside the house. Dad had dug some parsnips to roast with the potatoes and Mam had made a Yorkshire pudding with flour and eggs, baked in some of the drippings from the meat. They ate the pudding first, with lots of rich gravy, and after that Lissie had so much meat and vegetables that she could hardly get down from the table, she was so full.

Dad beamed at her as he helped himself to more slices of the roast mutton. 'I don't think you've eaten at all while I've been away. Either that or you've got hollow legs!' He looked under the table to where she had kicked off her boots. 'What do you say, Mam? Has she got hollow legs?'

Her mam picked at what she had left on her plate. 'She eats enough for two, that's for sure.'

'She's a growing lass, Edie. Why has she got her boots off?'

Lissie piped up straight away, 'They hurt me toes, Dad.'

Mam snapped at her just as fast, 'Speak when you're spoken to!'

Lissie shut her mouth and concentrated on her plate, but her dad continued, 'Edie, why didn't you say she needed some new boots? I could have brought some in with me.'

'There's plenty of wear left in them yet,' Edie muttered sullenly.

'Take 'em down to the wharf and swap 'em for some that fit tomorrow.'

'If you say so, Luther.'

'Yes, I bloody do. Are you sure she's getting enough t' eat?'

'She eats all right. You saw the way she scoffed her way through that little lot. God bless her belly, that's all I can say.'

Lissie's ears stayed alert as her dad persisted, 'But there's no spare flesh on her anywhere. What does she do all day when I'm away?'

'Not much, I can tell you! Always getting under my feet, so I can't get on with my work. And if I give her owt to do, I have to watch her like a hawk! She 'as to be shown everything.'

'She's not full grown yet, Edie.'

'Aye, Luther, don't I know it. The sooner she learns 'ow to 'elp in t' house proper, the better.'

Lissie kept her eyes focused on her plate and wondered if her mam was going to tell her dad how useless she had been, and if Dad would get cross with her and not give her the nice woolly shawl waiting in the front room. But Mam didn't, and Dad took another gulp from his tankard and settled back in his chair.

He said, 'Well, Edie, you might have a bit o' luck there.'

'Oh, aye? How come?'

'Mickey Jackson was telling me about a dame school up at Fordham.'

Lissie looked up quickly. 'What's a school, Dad?'

'I told you to speak when you're spoken to,' Mam snapped.

Dad ignored her and continued, 'Fordham is not too far upstream and Ann is sending their lass there after Christmas.'

'What? Their Miriam? I'n't she working wi' 'er ma at the Navvy?'

'Mickey says her ma wants her to do some learning.'

'What sort o' idea is that? A school is no place for a lass. School is for lads. I'd 'ave thought Miriam would be more use to her ma in t' kitchen.'

'Mickey thought it'd be a good idea for the two of 'em to go together.'

'What? Their Miriam and our Lissie? What for?' Mam argued. 'Waste o' good money if you ask me.'

'I've got a few pennies put by.'

'Aye and we'll need them if t' winter goes on like this.'

'It'll be good for her to learn to read and write, Edie.'

'Why? I never did. What use is reading to a girl? She has to learn how to clean and cook. And do sewing. Will they teach her that?'

''Course they will. They do all kinds of things. And there'll be other girls for her to learn with.'

Lissie saw that her mam was getting really het up about this and thought that whatever school was, she didn't want it if it made her mam any more cross with her than she was already.

'I need her here with me,' Mam said bluntly.

Dad persisted. 'She'll still be here with you, Edie. She won't have to live there. Mickey's lass is just going for the day.'

'What? There and back every day?'

'Aye.'

'Well, how far is it? Think of all the boot leather she'll need!'

'Edie.' Dad sounded stern. 'It'll be good for her.'

'Well, it won't be good for me. I don't want her to go. I want 'er 'ere wi' me.'

'I thought you said she was a nuisance to you?'

Lissie watched the talking between her mam and dad nervously. Her mam was always upset when Dad changed things at home, but Dad usually kept calm enough when he'd made up his mind. Though now she could see he was getting angry with Mam. She began to think about where she would hide if they started shouting at each other.

Mam must have also realised that Dad was angry, because she went quiet, got up from the table and said, 'I've done an apple pudding if you've still got some room left.'

Dad ate a plateful, and as Lissie's dinner had gone down a bit she managed to squeeze a bit more steaming food into her little tummy. Mam liked apple puddings sweetened with some of Rosa's honey more than anything, and did justice to her plateful as well. But neither of them had finished with the talk of school.

'I don't know, Luther. Going there and back every day? What about the big lads on the way? You know what they can be like with the little 'uns.'

'They'll be all right wi' two of 'em together. Anyroad, most o' the big lads know me and they'll have to answer to me if there's any trouble. Mickey says the same. And his eldest lad's got a fine pair o' fists on him nowadays.'

'She'll have to have a new dress and some more pinnies.'

'Yes, yes.' Dad sounded irritable now. 'They'll make the pinnies there. But she will need boots that fit her for walking. Ee, woman, why didn't you realise she'd grown out of her boots?'

Mam was getting mad now and she spat, 'I can't do everything when you're away! I never wanted a babby in the first place. Bringing her 'ere was all your idea.'

Dad retaliated sharply. 'We're not going through all that again!'

Lissie looked from her mam to her dad with some alarm. She did not want to be around if they started fighting.

Her mam was really cross and whined, 'Well, you spend more on her than you do on me! And now a fancy school, if you please! You 'ave better things to do wi' your money, Luther.'

Dad got to his feet and raised his voice. 'That's more than enough lip from you. I don't keep you short, do I? The lass is going to school wi' Miriam after Christmastide and that's it. Now mull some more o' that ale and bring it through to t' front room wi' another bucket of coal.'

Mam did as Dad had asked without further comment and Lissie, feeling sleepy after so much food, wandered after her mam and dad into the front room. A whole load of questions about school were beginning to crowd her mind. What was a school? Where was it and what would she be doing there? It was definitely something her dad wanted for her and Mam didn't, but she knew better than to keep on asking about it if Dad's temper was up.

Things calmed down once he had settled himself by the front-room fire with his ale and a pipe of tobacco. Mam cheered up a treat when Dad gave her a bottle of spirits and Lissie was more than pleased with her snug wool shawl. It was just like her mam's and she wrapped it round herself and waltzed about the front room.

'I've got summat else fo' thee, lass. Nip upstairs and fetch it down. It's on t' top o' me box in t' bedroom.'

Lissie looked quickly at her mam who scowled but said nothing, so Lissie scampered upstairs. On top of Dad's box, neatly folded, Lissie found a heavy wool cloak, a proper cloak with a hood! She ran downstairs, squealing with joy.

'Look, Mam, look what Dad's bought me!'

'Filched, more like,' Mam muttered through her gin.

Dad swallowed more ale and grinned. 'It's not new, lass, and it'll be too big fo' you now. But the rate you grow, you'll soon fill it up.'

Lissie flung it on and put up the hood. Her small shape was totally swamped and the hem trailed on the floor as she paraded across it, feeling like the new queen.

She saw Dad glance sternly at Mam as he added, 'It's just what she wants for walking to school in t' winter.'

Lissie had learned in the past not to start chattering on about something when Mam and Dad had a row, otherwise they would send her upstairs to bed. Wrapped in her woolly shawl, she took off her boots and curled up quiet as a mouse in the horsehair chair. She was as warm as could be with her new cloak draped over her as well and soon fell fast asleep. Tonight was no different from usual when Dad got home from his travels. Except that usually, while she was asleep, Mam and Dad put Dad's old shooting coat over her and left her there all night by the warmth of the fire.

But tonight *was* different. Something was going on. Roused from a deep slumber by all the noise, Lissie sat bolt upright clutching her cloak. The fire in the front room was low and the candles had burned out. Although Mam had closed the door to the hallway, the sound of raised voices came through it clearly. Dad was shouting and somebody else was shouting back at him. But it wasn't Mam. It was another man, and they were really mad at each other.

She heard her dad yell, 'Who d'you think you are? Coming round to my house like this? We finished our business weeks ago and I owe you nowt! Nowt, I say! Do y'hear me?'

A voice replied angrily in strange clipped tones, 'You are nothing but a common thief, Dearne. You have been stealing from me and others like me for years, and now it is time to pay!'

'Just you clear off out o' here,' Dad answered. 'I don't know what you're talking about. You're all the same you foreigners. I tell you, I don't owe nobody nothing!'

'You will pay me what you owe me! I swear I'll make you pay for your crooked deals!'

'You want to watch your tongue, saying things like that round 'ere! I got friends, y'know.'

Lissie scrambled to her feet on the high-backed chair to look out of the front-room window. The moon had risen high and it bathed the yard and clearing in a bluish hue. That boy was there! He was standing near to the house but he wasn't the one doing the shouting. He was watching, just watching everything that was going on. Lissie recognised his coat and cap straight away, and, closer to, she thought he was the most handsome lad she had ever seen. As she pressed her nose against the glass, he looked in her direction.

Lissie ducked down quickly, out of sight. She could not see the man he was with; he must have been right up close to the front door. Who were they and what did he want? She heard her mam's high-pitched whine join the row.

'Leave it be, Luther, it's freezing out there tonight. Come in and shut the door. He won't hang around long in this weather.'

'You are wrong, madam,' she heard the stranger say. 'I shall not go away. I have travelled a great distance to catch up with this man and I shall have the money he owes me.'

Lissie slid off the chair and leaned against the door to listen. The stranger talked in an odd way without the soft burrs of Yorkshire that Lissie knew. She was desperate to open the door and look at him, but knew it was more than her life was worth with Dad in such a mood. He shouted, 'Stay outa' here, Edie. This is men's business.'

But her mam was having none of that, having spent most of her day cooking, which, Lissie knew, always put her in a bad mood. 'I will not. I want ter know what's been going on.' An evening with the gin bottle had heightened her courage and she raised her voice even more. 'I want ter know what you been up to on the canal!'

Lissie's eyes rounded at her dad's angry response. 'Shut your mouth, you daft old witch! Get back upstairs and close t' door behind you!'

'Don't you speak to me like that, Luther Dearne. I told you, I want to know what all this is about.'

Lissie, by now riveted to the spot, concentrated hard to hear the stranger's response. Her smoky green eyes darkened with a mixture of fear and excitement as his strong voice came through the door. 'You will not like what you find out, madam. This man is a liar and a cheat and I can prove it!'

'Like 'ell you can! You're bluffing,' Dad argued.

'I have papers, sir. I have ship's manifests, invoices and loading notes. What do you say to that?'

'I say you're the liar and the cheat, trying to get more than your dues for that creaking tub you call a ship. Why don't you clear off back to wherever you come from!'

The stranger lowered his tone and paused before he replied in a slow deliberate manner. 'Because, as you well know, the manufactories in the South Riding need my best Swedish iron so that they can keep their furnaces and forges working. I am sure the magistrates will want to know that you are cheating your own countrymen as well as me.'

'Why you . . . you . . . bloody . . .' Dad sounded as though he was going to blow up. 'You . . . you wouldn't have the front.' He stopped for a second then added in a quieter tone, 'They won't believe you anyway, you're just a foreigner round here.'

The foreign voice responded, 'They don't have to believe me. I shall show them the papers.'

Dad yelled, 'Why you—'

'Luther! No!' Mam squealed.

They were fighting! Lissie heard the thuds and stran-gled cries as the two men struggled with each other on the front door step.

'Papa! Papa! Stop it!'

That must be the boy! Was he joining in too? Lissie scuttled across to the high-backed chair by the window and peered through the glass. She could now see her dad and the other man wrestling in the front yard, trying to thump each other as they staggered around. Then the foreigner broke free and hit her dad so hard in the stomach that he was winded and went down. The ground was solid with frost. Patches of ice crunched and cracked as he fell heavily and rolled in the rutted track.

The foreigner stood with hunched shoulders and clenched fists, ready for her dad to get up and fight back. He did, picking up an old piece of timber that he waved backwards and forwards in the air as he staggered to his feet.

The boy moved quickly, retrieving a similar weapon from the woodland floor and handing it to his father, who had not taken his eyes off her dad as he ducked and weaved to avoid the weapon. Lissie knew her dad would win though. He was big and strong and always said nobody had ever knocked him down in a fight.

But the boy's dad was big in a different way. He was taller, and not as round as her dad. The two men clashed and recoiled, holding the heavy timbers with both hands as swords and cudgels. As her dad drew back his weapon, the stranger swung in from his right and caught him a slamming body blow that knocked him down again.

This time he couldn't pick himself up off the ground

quite so fast and the stranger moved in and stood over him, brandishing the timber. Mam was out there now, carrying the oil lamp, getting all excited and shouting at Dad to get up and thump him one and show him what for. Lissie had to press her knuckles into her mouth to stop herself crying out as well. If Mam knew she was watching she'd soon get a thump herself and be sent straight upstairs to bed.

'Come on, Luther,' Mam cried. 'Get up on your feet, man!'

But Dad didn't. He raised himself on one elbow and wiped a trickle of blood from his face with the back of his hand. He was breathing heavily and had split open the armhole of his tweed jacket.

The foreigner towered over him. He kicked the wood out of her dad's hands and then threw his own aside. Stepping back, he dusted his clothes down and reached inside his jacket to take out a sheaf of papers that he threw down, scattering them over her dad's heaving body.

'Read these, Dearne. Read them carefully. You have until midnight tonight to bring the money you owe me to the Navigator Inn. Otherwise, you'll be finished,' he said. 'Tomorrow I go to the magistrate with these papers.' He nodded, as though confirming the decision with himself. 'This is your last chance.' He turned to the boy, who had stayed close to his father throughout the fight. 'Come along, Blake. Our business here is done.'

Blake. Lissie held her breath and kept as still as she could. Blake? She didn't know any local lads called that, but she liked it. Even if his dad was a foreigner, he had a nice name. Blake. In the lamplight she saw him remove his cap and comb his floppy fair hair back with his fingers. He replaced the cap firmly, pulling it down over his brow. She noticed he had done that before when he was outside the inn. She wondered where he came from and whether she'd dare to ask her dad in the morning. Better not, she decided. She didn't want Dad to find out she'd been watching him fight.

Mam was all over Dad now. 'Luther, Luther, are you all right, husband? Get on your feet and come in the house. Your face is bleeding, let me wash it for you.'

But Dad was angry with her and he pushed Mam off, shouting, 'Get away from me.' He was shuffling through the scattered papers, cursing and crumpling them but not tossing them away. 'Go inside yourself, woman,' he growled. 'Get back in there and see if the lass's all right. Ask her if she heard owt.'

Lissie's eyes stretched wide open with alarm and she shot off the chair and under her new cloak on the horse-hair chair in a trice. The coarse tapestry of its upholstery was rough against her face and she pulled the cloak right up over her head. Her feet were sticking out from under the hem and they were icy cold, but she dared not move them. It seemed as if she held her breath for ages, and she only remembered to let it out and breathe normally when her mam opened the front-room door.

Mam walked a couple of steps into the room and her dad must have been right behind because Lissie heard him say, 'She's fast on. Slept through it all, thank God. Leave her be, Edie, and gerroff to bed.'

'Aren't you coming up, Luther?'

Lissie heard the rustling of the papers. 'No. I have to

do some thinking. I'll go through to t' back kitchen and smoke another pipe.'

'Shall I mull you some more ale?'

'I said clear off, Edie,' her dad retaliated irritably. 'I've got to be on me own to think.'

Lissie did not move a muscle until she heard the top stair creak as her mam went to bed, and then her dad in the next room raking the kitchen fire and throwing on more coal. She rolled over on to her back and stared at the darkness, too keyed up and wide awake to sleep. Why had that foreigner come to see her dad and what was it all about? After a while, her eyes began to close, but the next thing she knew she was being wakened by the sound of her dad's keys jangling in the dark.

She stayed absolutely still and opened her eyes slowly. As she got used to the moonlight coming in through the small window, Lissie made out the bulky figure of her father. He was unlocking the front of the old casement clock that didn't work. It stood in the back corner of the front room and Dad kept things in it that he never allowed her to see. He put some of those things in his pockets and then took out his big shotgun that he used for killing rabbits and wood pigeons in the back garden.

Lissie was puzzled. What was her dad doing, going out to shoot pigeons in the middle of the night? They didn't want any pigeons anyway. Dad only went out for pigeons when there was nothing else in to eat. And they still had loads of mutton left on the joint! Something was up. Something to do with that foreigner and Blake, his son. She crept back to the window and watched her dad walk down to the track. He had his gun under his arm and the barrels were set, ready to shoot.

Chapter 9

As Lissie watched her father disappear down the frozen woodland track, Blake and his father had reached the stone bridge over the canal. The moon was high and shone brightly through black leafless twigs, picking up sparkles of frost and the wing of a barn owl hunting for food. A single flare still burned by the lock gates and lamps glowed through the windows of the Navigator. Sensible cottagers had banked up their fires and shut their doors tightly against the promise of another freezing night.

'Dearne will not wait until midnight, I am sure. He, like me, will want this matter dealt with now,' Blake's father said to him. 'Go back to the inn. I shall stay here, on the edge of the woods. I do not want everyone at the Navigator knowing my business.'

'I want to be with you, Papa.'

'No, Blake. You saw how I handled him and you have no need to worry about your papa. I learned to fight well in the timber forests back home and I can beat a fat old man like Dearne any time. Tell Ephraim not to worry. I'll be back at the Navigator before midnight.'

Blake thought that Mr Ephraim might persuade his papa against this idea and said, 'At least come back with me to warm through, Papa. It is a cold night and you may have a long wait.'

But Papa was adamant. 'I know men like Dearne. He will not wait until morning. Besides, I need to cool my anger and the Navigator is not the place for me to do that. Do as I say and tell Ephraim everything is going well.'

'Leave it until the morning, Papa,' Blake pleaded. 'You'll freeze out here.'

His papa laughed. 'Not me, boy. I've endured worse than this in the Baltic. When Blake hesitated, he repeated firmly, 'Do as I say, Blake. Go back to the inn and tell Ephraim to go to his bed.'

Reluctantly, Blake did as his papa asked of him. He dawdled by the canal, watching the moonlight reflecting on shards of broken ice floating in the dark oily water. He strained his eyes to catch sight of the moving shadow of his papa as he retraced his steps to the woodland. The Navigator Inn was noisy with drinkers and the singing suddenly became louder when a door opened and two men fell out, hurrying through the icy air, home to their wives and beds.

Ale was flowing freely in the saloon as working men forgot how tired they were and thought only of their next drink. They clustered around the counter, talking and laughing loudly with the landlord, breaking into raucous singing and casting an occasional glance at the painted smiles and loosened bodices of the women who lingered with them.

Mr Ephraim was dozing alone by the fire. He ordered another brandy and a hot toddy for Blake.

'Your papa is a brave man,' he said. 'I hope he gets his money tonight. This is not a place for staying longer than we need to.'

Blake agreed. 'Why don't you take your brandy to your chamber?' he suggested.

'I cannot leave you alone down here.'

'Of course you can! No one will notice me in this dark corner. You are tired and should get some proper sleep.'

'Perhaps you are right. Your papa will not be long. I have seen him deal with strong young men, two at a time, on the dockside. He will be safe, I am sure.'

Mr Ephraim stood up and stretched. 'I need to rest.'

'I shall wait here for Papa,' Blake reassured him.

The burned-out logs on the fire fell with a hiss and Mickey Jackson came to replenish them. 'Your pa gone to his bed? Why don't you have a drop o' rum in your toddy?'

Blake shook his head and yawned, so Mickey returned to his cronies at the counter. Blake went out to the privy, next to the brew house across the backyard. The moon was high and frost already sparkled on the hard ground. As he came out of the privy, he saw Mickey Jackson leading a woman to a shadowy spot in the yard. He heard Mickey's rough voice and her girlish giggles.

Blake skirted the yard to avoid them. He heard muffled

protests from the girl, the tearing of fabric and then the rutting grunts of Mickey satisfying his lusts. He drew the collar of his coat up around his ears and shunned the warmth of the inn fireside to wait for his papa by the bridge.

The deep waters of the lock were still, the gates and sluices quiet. The silence unnerved Blake as he crossed the stone bridge. The only light was from the moon and a tiny glow that burned in the end-cottage window as he passed. Instinctively, Blake knew that something was wrong. The woodland was too quiet, as though all its creatures had gone to ground. There was no screech of a vixen or hoot of an owl, no scurrying of hedgehogs. The only sound was of his boots as he crunched through the ice and frozen leaves.

Halfway up the track, he heard the cracking of twigs and a weak human cry from among the trees. He stopped quite still and listened, following the sounds. He found his papa slumped against a fallen log, on the freezing ground. His right hand clutched at his thigh. Blake could smell the blood as he approached.

'Papa! Papa! What happened?'

'Blake! Is that you? Thank God, you are here. Help me – it's my leg – I can't stop the bleeding . . .' His voice trailed away and his face twisted in pain as he tried to shift his position.

'What happened? Who did this to you?'

His papa spoke breathlessly, 'He came after me as I guessed he would and we faced each other on the track. But when I saw he had a gun I had to run for it. I dodged into the trees, but he came after me.'

'Luther Dearne did this?'

'He was yelling at me, that I'd never get him and he'd kill me first. He meant it, son. He meant it.'

Blake had taken off his coat and jacket and was now removing his shirt and tearing it into broad strips. His hands shook as he bound the strips tightly around his papa's thigh.

'He's winged me, son, that's all. Caught me in the leg. I rolled into a ditch and under bracken. I had to bite on a twig to stop myself crying out with pain.'

Blake's hands were sticky with blood. He wiped them on the frozen bracken and shrugged into his jacket and coat. 'Where is Dearne now?'

'Gone. I heard him thrashing around until he gave up looking for me.'

There was blood everywhere. It had seeped through his papa's thick clothes and Blake could see the stain already spreading on his makeshift bindings. His papa tried to sit up but yelped with the pain. Gasping for breath, he went on, 'He walked right by me. But the gunshot had scattered the birds and foxes. The fool was distracted by their noises.'

'Hush, Papa. Be calm. How did you get to here?'

'I crawled out of the ditch. But I fear I have made the bleeding worse.' Exhausted, his head flopped forward.

'I must get you inside. You will die out here. Do you think you can stand? Here, Papa, put your arm round my shoulders.'

Blake gritted his teeth as he felt the heavy weight of his papa bearing down on his smaller frame. His father suppressed a cry and hobbled forward, uttering, 'You are stronger than you look, my boy. With you, I think I can make it to the inn.'

Blake almost collapsed himself as he half-carried, half-dragged his papa down the woodland towards the lock and the inn. 'We cannot cross the lock gates like this, they're not wide enough,' he muttered. Blake was exhausted but thinking fast. His papa was leaving a trail of blood and weakening by the minute. The bridge was fifty yards downstream. He might not make it to the inn. 'There is someone at home in the end cottage. I can see a light through the window.'

His papa nodded silently and his pasty face contorted as they fell with a thud against the cottage door.

Rosa was working by the light of her kitchen fire, melting beeswax with goose grease and eucalyptus oil to make green ointment. This salve was very popular with bargemen's wives for soothing cuts and burns. She hummed a tune quietly to herself as she stirred the mixture in a small saucepan. The thump at her door made her jump and she placed the pan carefully on the hearth before crossing the room to look out of the window.

'It's late,' she called. 'What do you want?'

'Help. Please help us. My papa is injured.'

Rosa opened her door a crack to see who it was. But the weight of Erik Svenson against it pushed it open wide. As soon as she smelled the blood, she stood back. Blake and his papa fell into her kitchen. 'What happened?' she demanded.

'Sh-shot. In . . . leg . . .' Erik groaned.

Rosa immediately pulled out a pallet from under her

dresser. Blake moved away a chair and between them they dragged his papa on to the makeshift bed.

'He isn't bound tight enough,' Rosa observed. 'The blood still flows. Fetch me that clean linen from under the mantelshelf.'

Blake obeyed instantly, shivering in spite of the warm fire. Rosa picked up a kitchen knife and began cutting through the blood-sodden wool of Erik's breeches. As she exposed his torn and bleeding flesh she realised that no amount of salve would heal this wound. Blood was seeping out in pulses and it showed no signs of abating. This man needed a surgeon. Even a surgeon might not save his leg, but he could at least save the man's life.

'Fetch me that pail of cold water from t' scullery, lad. I'll do what I can to stem the blood, but you'll have to go fer t' doctor from over Fordham.'

'Where's that?'

'Two mile upstream from t' lock. Get a horse from t' livery at t' inn. The marine sleeps over the stables.'

Blake nodded and Rosa continued, 'Light me that lamp first, and then hurry. When you come to t' next bridge, you'll see t' houses. The doctor's house is end-on to t' road an' built o' stone. Big 'un. Can't miss it, it has a brass plate on t' front wall. Tell him Rosa sent you.'

Blake stared anxiously at his papa's shredded, bleeding thigh. 'Papa, I don't want to leave you like this.'

His papa weakly waved an arm to dismiss him and croaked, 'Go.'

Blake dashed out into the frozen night. The stables by the Navigator were quiet, though a dim glow was visible through a crack in the wooden door. A lad of about his own age answered the thumping of his fists.

'I need a horse. A good one with a saddle.'

'Who . . . who are you?'

'I'm staying at the inn. My papa is badly hurt and needs a doctor.'

'Come inside. What's your name?'

'Blake.'

'I'm Peter. You're lucky I'm still awake. My horses are usually down for the night by now.'

'Quickly. My papa is bleeding.'

Peter Jackson crossed to one of his stalls. 'Take this one. He's the lightest and fastest I have — a thorough-bred carriage horse.'

Between them they saddled the horse and led him out into the cold night air.

Peter said, 'I'll wait up. It's not far. Follow the towpath to the next bridge. Good luck!' He slapped the horse on its rear and Blake galloped into the frosty darkness.

The doctor's house was in darkness but his rapping on the door was soon answered by a woman in her nightclothes. 'He's not here, lad,' she said. 'He's up at the Hall tending her Ladyship.'

'The Hall? Where? Where is it?' he demanded breathlessly.

'Nay, it's miles away from here, lad. Anyway, it's no good going for him. He won't leave her Ladyship, not in her condition.'

Blake was frantic. 'Is there another doctor?'

'Not round here, lad. But there's a woman who's good at tending t' sick down at t' lock.'

'Who? Where?'

'She lives in one of them woodmen's cottages down by Mexton Lock. Goes by the name of Rosa, I believe.'

Blake's shoulders sagged. 'Papa is with her now.'

'Then he's in the best hands round here.'

'But she says he needs a surgeon.'

'Been shot, you say? Step inside, lad. I'll give you some of the doctor's dressings for her. You can't do no better for him this night.'

The woman disappeared for a few minutes and returned with a package wrapped in calico. Blake offered her a coin.

'Nay, lad. T' doctor doesn't need that. Give it to Rosa. Not many folk have much time for her down at Mexton Lock, but if summat's up she'll allus do what she 'as to to help, like.'

'Thank you.'

The woman nodded. 'Best get off back now. Good luck.'

Papa was barely conscious when Blake returned. Rosa had built up the fire and lit more lamps. His leg was propped up with a bed bolster and Rosa was supporting his head as she tried to get him to drink.

Blake looked at the fresh wide binding on his leg and the red stain that continued to seep and spread. 'The . . . the doctor wasn't there. He's at the Hall somewhere.'

'Swinborough Hall, that'll be. 'Er Ladyship's with child. Must be 'aving trouble again,' Rosa observed.

'His housekeeper sent you these.' Blake dropped the calico parcel on Rosa's kitchen table.

'Well, I've done my best for 'im, lad.'

He stood in the centre of the room, watching help-lessly. 'What can I do?'

'Here. Try and get him to drink. I'll fetch another blanket.'

Blake took over from Rosa and cradled his papa's head while he sipped a little more water.

'Blake? Is that you?' he breathed.

'Yes, Papa. It's me.'

'It's bad, my boy. Bad. The bleeding won't stop.'

'No, Papa, it will, it will. You'll get well again. You're strong. Your leg will heal.'

His papa moved his head very slightly from side to side. 'Dearne,' he whispered. 'It was Luther Dearne.' His eyes closed but a moment later he opened them and murmured, 'Look after your mama for me.' Then his eyes closed again and his head fell sideways.

Despair overtook Blake and he pleaded with Rosa. 'Help him! Rosa, for God's sake, help him!'

She covered his papa with another blanket. 'I can't do no more for 'im. The shot goes deep and his flesh is badly torn. I don't know if the surgeon could have done anything, anyroad. Let him sleep for now. We can only wait and see.'

Blake gently lowered his papa's head. 'He won't die, will he, Rosa?'

'Hush, boy. Morning will tell. Here, come and sit by the fire. I'll brew a concoction to calm us both down.'

It was a long night for Blake. He sat and watched his papa's breathing become slower and more laboured until it rattled weakly in his throat. He did not move a muscle

as he watched. His mind and body were frozen, not from
cold, but numb with shock.

This could not be happening. It was a nightmare, a
demonic dream that he would soon wake from and all
would be well. His papa would be whole and strong and
– and – Luther Dearne would be dead. Luther Dearne
dead, instead of his papa.

Rosa dozed in her chair by the fire. At daybreak, when
the first barges came through, she went outside to pump
fresh water. When she returned, Blake was still sitting in
the exact same position that he had held all night, staring
at the motionless body of his father.

Rosa placed a hand on Blake's shoulder and said
quietly, 'I'm sorry, lad. I did all I could.'

Tears coursed down his tired, young face as he held
his papa's large cold hand. 'No, Papa, no. Don't leave us.
We need you. Mama and I need you.'

'You must try and be strong now, lad. For your mama's
sake. Is she staying with you at the Navigator?'

'No, we – I have a friend there. Mr Ephraim's there.'

'You'd best go to 'im now, lad. You'll have to tell 'im.
Make arrangements, like.'

Blake stared at the newly carved headstone and seethed
through clenched teeth. 'He was murdered, Mama. He
was not armed and he was shot!' His face was grim as
he tried to control his simmering rage. His grief and
anger had festered in the weeks since his papa's death.
Neither his mama nor he wanted any of the lovely goose
that Lucy had prepared for their Christmas dinner. Instead,
they had walked together in silence to the churchyard.

'I know, my son, and I grieve for my beloved Erik as you do. Our lives will never be the same again, not for either of us.'

'Will you go back to Sweden, Mama?'

'Do you want to, Blake?'

'I shall go with you, Mama, if you wish.'

'I'd like to see my cousins again. But, you know, I like it here. It is not so cold in the winter. We have a lovely home and we still have our warehouse. You will soon be a man, Blake. Where do you want to make your future?'

'Without Papa, I don't know.'

'The warehouse will be yours when you are twenty-one. Ephraim and I can look after it until then, if you want.'

Blake nodded slowly. 'Can I leave school and work with Ephraim in the warehouse now?'

'You have to go to school for a few more years. There is still much for you to learn.'

'Schoolwork is boring, Mama. I want to be doing something more.'

He thought about the confines of the classroom. He could do the book work easily enough but preferred practical things and being outdoors. And he wanted to get even with Dearne!

'You will, Blake. When you are older.'

'Always it is when I am older, Mama!'

'Be patient—'

'How can I? When my father's murderer is free?'

'It is hard for me as well, Blake.'

'I'm sorry. It's just that I feel so . . . so helpless.'

He tidied away the last of the funeral tributes that lay

around the headstone and his mama laid a fresh wreath of evergreens and berries from their garden. She hooked her arm through his and leaned against him.

'If we stay,' he remarked, 'I would have to become part of life here, learn to be a Yorkshire man, live like one, ride and shoot, go hunting on the moors.'

'Your papa has found you a school where you can learn all those things. He understood you, Blake. You are like him.'

'And fight,' Blake continued. 'I want to learn to fight with my fists as Papa could. Real fighting, Mama. Like Papa did, like the prize-fighters do for money.'

His mama stumbled a little and he held her elbow until she recovered. Blake knew that she would not want this for him. But he was his father's son, and his mama knew that when he made his mind up to do something, he would do it.

'Would you leave me alone for a moment, Mama?'

'Of course.' She walked away towards the church.

Blake stood facing his father's grave and made him a promise. 'I shan't let him get away with this, Papa. You can rely on me.' And to himself, he vowed, 'You won't escape me, Luther Dearne. I'll kill you for this. I swear, I'll kill you.'

Chapter 10

Luther Dearne kept Lissie and her mam away from the lock after the fight. Lissie knew that something serious had gone on that night, something that had unsettled her dad. He was mad at the foreigners and the next morning was flushed and agitated. He had forbidden Lissie and her mam to go down to the lock until he said they could. The day after that, a stranger in a tall hat and dark coat with shiny buttons done up to the neck had come to see Dad and they went to talk in the front room.

The stranger wasn't expected, Lissie knew, because it was chilly outside and her mam hadn't told her to light the front-room fire. Mam went upstairs to put on her good dress and told Lissie to wear a clean apron and run a rag over her boots. Then Mam did something she'd never seen her do before. She stood on a chair to reach the top shelf of the kitchen cupboard and got down some little glasses that she rubbed up with a piece of old linen. Then she put them on the wooden tray with the bottle of sherry wine that her dad had brought back from Hull.

'Listen, you,' her mam hissed. 'We're going in there wi' this and you're not to say a word. Not one word or I'll thrash you wi'in an inch of your life. If 'e says owt to you, you just bob a curtsey and say "sir". And look down at your feet, d'you hear me?'

'Yes, Mam. Who is he? What's going on?'

Lissie's answer was a clip across her ear as her mam snapped, 'I said be quiet, di'n't I? Now open t' door for me.'

It was cold in the front room and the gentleman sat on the sofa with his hat beside him. He seemed very glad to have the wine and Mam refilled his glass twice. Lissie perched on the footstool by her mam who had settled in one of the high-backed chairs.

Her dad was in the other chair and he was saying, 'Aye, a foreigner did come to see me about putting some trade my way but I didn't know the gent and you can't be too careful wi' foreigners.' Dad gestured towards Lissie and her mam as he went on, 'I've got a wife and little girl to think of, so I sent him off sharpish, like.'

The visitor asked if there'd been a fight.

Her dad shook his head. 'Not wi' me, there weren't. I were too busy, I 'ad to get some supper in for the family. Just a few wood pigeons, like. You can see 'em roosting when the moon's up and the squire don't mind. He says shooting 'em keeps 'em off his corn.'

Everyone went quiet for a few minutes and then her dad took a deep breath and continued, 'If this foreigner

were shot in the woods as you say, what was 'e doing
creeping around that time o' night, I'd like to know? Up
to no good, that's for sure. Well, I don't know nothing
about no shooting, apart from the wood pigeons. And I
bagged enough wi' just the one blast. Just the one.' He
turned to Mam. 'They made a good supper, didn't they,
Mrs Dearne?'

Mam nodded vigorously. 'They did that, Mr Dearne.'
She put a bony hand across Lissie's shoulders and looked
at the visitor. 'He's a good husband, sir. Always takes good
care of us both. He came back real early and stayed in
all night.'

The visitor sipped his sherry wine and looked around
them. Their front room, he thought, was perishing cold
without a fire this weather, but it was clean and tidy and
he had been let in the house through the front door.
Dearne, he decided, was a bit above your average canal
trader, and he believed his story about the wood pigeons.
More likely the foreigner had got into a fight with one
of the rogues from the barges and they'd done him in.
He got up, making comments about being satisfied, then
took his leave. The landlord at the inn had told him that
some travelling folk had followed the foreigner. He'd had
trouble with them before and they must have shot him.
Decent man, that landlord. He'd asked him back for his
dinner. The visitor put on his tall hat and looked forward
to some roast beef.

But Lissie noticed there were no smiles from anybody
and she knew better than to ask any more questions.
After the man had gone, Dad was very jumpy and short
tempered and instead of going over to the Navigator, he

spent quite a lot of time in the garden clearing out the brambles and ferns. Lissie wasn't allowed to go and see Miriam about school and even her mam couldn't go to Rosa's. Dad had forbidden it until all the tittle-tattle had stopped.

Lissie liked having her dad home all day and she helped him with tidying up their unruly garden. Even Mam pitched in with piling up the rubbish. Dad set light to it one afternoon and Lissie stayed outside until dusk watching the flames and warming her hands.

Not long after that, Mexton Lock was abuzz with tales of a bad accident where people had got killed on the new railway line yon side o' the Riding. The shooting was forgotten as canal folk nodded knowingly to each other and said that waterways were still the best way to get around. As the days grew shorter and Christmas was nigh, Dad started going to the Navigator again for his ale. They had a ham to eat that winter. Dad brought it in one night and hung it on the hook from the wooden cross beam in the scullery.

The shooting was forgotten and after Christmas he fetched Lissie some new boots to wear for going to school. Well, he swapped them for an iron cooking pot down by the canal wharf. They were not really new, but her dad rubbed beeswax in them until they were so shiny that they squeaked when she skipped about the house in them. They were too big for her now but she had her thick winter stockings to go inside them and she had put some screwed up rags in the toes to fill the space for this winter.

On her first morning at school, she laced them up

tightly and wrapped herself in her new cloak then scampered over the rough ground towards the lock. For the first week Dad had walked down with her and hung about the Navigator waiting for a free ride to the coast. He wanted to be off, away from here as soon as he could, he said.

He told Mam to take her to meet Miriam for school, but Lissie knew her mam never wanted to get up in the morning to go with her. She was glad to get away from Mam when Dad wasn't there. Anyroad, she had to rush. Lissie had to get to the Navigator early because Miriam wouldn't wait for her if she was late.

'It's bad enough 'aving to play nursemaid to you wi'out you slowing me down,' Miriam complained as they picked their way around the muddy puddles on the towpath.

Lissie knew they were supposed to walk together. Her sharp ears picked up most things in her mam and dad's conversations when they thought she was asleep by the fire. Miriam's dad didn't want her walking on the towpath on her own either. 'I'm not late,' Lissie protested. 'Anyroad, your dad says you have to wait for me and if you're not there I have to go into the Navvy and find you.'

Miriam grabbed her arm roughly and gave her a push. 'If you ever do that, I'll shove you in the water an' you'll die. You can catch me up, that's what you can do.'

Lissie stayed silent. Miriam was eleven, two years older than she was, and much bigger. The older girl wasn't a lot taller, but she had grown rounder this last year and was heavier. Lissie knew Miriam could and would carry

out her threat, so she took to walking on the hedge side
of the towpath. Miriam then took delight in stepping
sideways and elbowing her into the brambles when she
felt like it. Oh well, Lissie reasoned silently when she had
to disentangle herself from the thorny branches, a few
scratches were better than drowning. Luckily, she was
faster on her feet than the older girl and was able to run
ahead and avoid the worst. Miriam, she noticed, didn't
chase her, and Lissie quickly learned how she could avoid
the worst of Miriam's little tricks.

'Got any spice today?' Miriam asked her.

'No,' Lissie lied. She had a piece of pomfret cake
wrapped up in a scrap of old muslin that she was saving
until it was time to begin the walk back home at the
end of the day. It was in a little pocket in her calico
drawers and it would be nice and sticky and chewy when
she sucked on it later in the day.

'Don't believe you.' Miriam gave her shove into the
wet hedge. 'Your dad allus gives you some spice. Give it
'ere.'

'I 'aven't got any, I tell you!'

'You're a liar, Lissie Dearne. That's what you are!
Where've you hidden it?'

Rain or no rain, the mud wouldn't stop Miriam
knocking her to the ground and pulling up her skirts
to search for the liquorice. She darted ahead, skipping
with an agile grace over the smaller puddles. But the
bigger, deeper ones slowed her down as they had to be
negotiated right next to the deep water to avoid the wet
hedges at the other side. Miriam caught her up easily.

'Give it 'ere or I'll push you in.'

Lissie really believed she would. She had watched Miriam's two older brothers dangle a young lad by his feet over the side of the lock and threaten to drop him in the water head first if he didn't give them the coppers he earned from running messages.

Well, Lissie thought, that was two against one and this is just me and her. The constant housework Lissie did every day for her mam when she got home from school had made her a strong little girl, a fact that was belied by her skinny appearance. She darted ahead again and waited further up the towpath for Miriam to reach her and carry on with her threats and demands. Then, quick as a flash, she pulled at the older girl's right arm, twisting it behind her back and pushing up the loose sleeve.

She grasped Miriam's wrist in her strong little hands and with a grip like tight iron bands twisted her hands in opposite directions as if she were wringing out a wet cloth. 'You're goin' to stop pushing me about, Miriam Jackson, d' you hear?'

'Ow! Ouch! Stop that, Lissie, stop it, it hurts!'

'It's meant to. Swear to me you'll stop.'

'All right, all right. I'll stop.'

Lissie loosened her grip but held on to the wrist. 'You 'ave to promise.'

Miriam scowled and stayed silent until Lissie tightened her grip again.

'Give over, Lissie. You're hurting me!' Miriam squealed.

Lissie gritted her teeth and doubled her effort. 'Not until you promise me you'll stop your little tricks. Just because you're bigger 'an me, doesn't mean I can't get you back!'

'Don't! It's burning me! Give over!'

'Promise me you'll stop! Promise?'

'I've already said I'll stop, 'aven't I?'

'Swear to me.'

'I swear on the Holy Bible.'

'Cross your heart and hope to die?'

'Cross my heart and hope to die,' Miriam replied miserably.

Lissie dropped Miriam's wrist abruptly. Miriam rubbed at the reddened skin on her forearm. 'I were on'y larking about. That hurt. Where'd you learn to do that?'

'Off your big brothers. I watched 'em try it on wi' one of the farm lads who came over looking for work. Soon sent 'im on his way, that did. And they tried it on wi' me once. But your mam saw 'em and stopped 'em. Gave 'em a right telling off, she did.'

'Yes, well, you wait till I tell 'em about this, they'll be after your blood again.'

Lissie frowned for a second, worried that Miriam might be right. But she knew that Miriam's mam could be as fiery as her dad and there was always hell to pay if the boys went anywhere near the two of them when they were playing by the lock.

'They wouldn't dare,' Lissie stated flatly. 'Your mam'd have their guts for garters.' Lissie had decided that she was no longer frightened of Miriam or her bullying brothers and her green eyes smouldered in defiance. The two girls stood face to face on the muddy towpath, neither sure whether they were friends or enemies.

Miriam pouted petulantly, thinking that this little gypsy from the woods was turning out to be more than she'd bargained for. But their dads were good mates so she supposed they'd better be as well. She said, 'Well, if you really 'a'n't got any spice you can 'ave one o' mine. They're barley sugar from the sweet shop in town.'

'Ta.' Lissie took the peace offering graciously and vowed to break her pomfret cake into two pieces to share on the way home. She'd have to save face with Miriam by 'finding' it in her things at school later though.

Miriam began to be much nicer to her from that day. She could be very nice when she wanted to be, Lissie realised, as they progressed through that first year walking the towpath together. At school, in her dad's inn and especially talking to the canal boatmen that summer, Miriam could be really nice to people when she wanted.

Lissie was at her happiest during those few years she spent at Miss Kirby's dame school. After two years, at eleven and thirteen, Lissie and Miriam were the oldest in the school, and they could mend and sew, cook and clean, and look after the little ones like their mothers did.

They spent hardly any time at all on letters and numbers, which pleased Miriam and disappointed Lissie. She liked reading and doing sums, and quickly progressed in both where her friend became bored. It was a long walk to school but one that Lissie would have done in bare feet in winter just to be able to read one of Miss Kirby's books! Sometimes she was allowed to read passages from the Bible to the whole class, or asked to write words and figures in Miss Kirby's big heavy accounting book that was kept locked away in a cupboard. She dreaded the day when she would have to leave school and go back to helping Mam in the house all week.

Mam seemed to despise her even more now that she went to school. When Dad was home Mam had to cook a tea every day and keep the house tidy without Lissie to help, so she was always in a bad temper by the end of the day. Even when Dad was back, Lissie dreaded going home from school and having to face her mam. But she was lithe and quick on her feet and, even as she grew taller, managed to dodge most of the cuffs and clips from Edie.

Dad didn't bring back many supplies when he came home these days as trade was going through a bad patch. This happened every now and then when one of the ironworks or foundries he dealt with went bankrupt, or a ship foundered at sea. On top of that, a new railway line had put a number of barges out of business. Lately, when Dad was home his days were passed more at the inn than at their house.

Mam snapped and sniped at Lissie all the time when she wasn't full of gin, and lashed out with her bony hands when she was. If Dad wasn't in when she got home from school Lissie disappeared fast to put on her old dress and weed the garden or clean up the scullery to keep out of Mam's way. And she always got up early, before Mam and Dad, so she had plenty of time to see to the fire, pump the water and set a kettle to boil before she went to meet Miriam at the Navigator.

That morning, Miriam's dad knew the boatman on a barge going upstream and he agreed to take them the two miles to Fordham, where their school was situated. It was a fine day and Miriam sat on the cabin roof, spread out her skirts and lifted her face to the sun. Lissie preferred to walk with the horse while the bargeman's son took a break. She loved the strong docile animal with his leather harnesses and polished brasses. But they dawdled and were late in arriving at school. They hurried into the dingy back rooms where Miss Kirby ran her dame school in the house that she shared with her brother.

'Line up!' Miss Kirby called in her high, trembling voice.

Her pupils scurried around until they stood shoulder to shoulder in front of her high wooden desk. Boys were on the right and girls on the left, with tall ones at the ends. Miss Kirby allocated tasks to her pupils according to their height. Quickly, the girls pushed their hair out of sight under bonnets and dusted down their pinafores with their hands. Miss Kirby walked up and down the row moving their positions until she was satisfied.

'Silence now,' she demanded, clapping her hands. 'Mr Kirby! We are ready for you.'

Miss Kirby's brother came down the dark passage from his study. He was dressed for town in a long coat and polished boots, with a proper top hat and a walking cane that he tapped on the brick floor as he inspected them.

'Boys! Outside!' he ordered.

'All of them, brother dear?' Miss Kirby asked timidly.

'Are you questioning my decision?'

You could have heard a pin drop, Lissie thought.

Miss Kirby stuttered a little. 'Th-the t-two new ones are very small. They cannot reach the workbench.'

He peered down at the smallest pupils in the middle of the row. 'Are they boys? Really, sister, why are they not wearing brown smocks?'

'Th-the g-girls will make them today.'

Mr Kirby ignored his sister and addressed the boys. 'George is waiting with the cart outside.'

They walked out silently, in single file, and climbed aboard the open farm cart that would take them to local workshops for the day.

Mr Kirby turned his attention to the girls, clothed in calico pinafores that covered their dresses and fastened at the back. Their bonnets were plain white and tied with tape under their chins. Mr Kirby was very strict about their pinnies and bonnets. The girls shuffled their feet and spread out so that he could walk round and inspect each one of them individually.

Lissie had some difficulty in keeping her thick black hair out of sight now that it had grown so long. She sensibly plaited it and wound it round her head to fit under her bonnet. Miriam just twisted and pinned hers into a loose knot so that honey-blonde tendrils kept escaping to frame her face.

Mr Kirby stood in front of the two of them with a stern expression on his long thin face. 'Sister, these girls are vain.' He glared at Lissie and Miriam. 'Vanity is a sin,' he declared. 'It leads us into temptation. You will both do extra Bible readings today. Sister, you will give these girls readings on the wages of sin.'

He lingered in front of Lissie and stared at her intently. 'This one, especially, is in grave danger of moral decay. You will see that she learns her Bible passages by heart. I shall listen to her recite them tomorrow at inspection.'

'Yes, brother dear,' Miss Kirby responded.

When he had gone, Miriam exploded. 'I'm glad that was you and not me! I'm hopeless at learning by heart.'

'Oh, I don't mind,' Lissie sighed, resigned to her task. 'He does pick on me though, doesn't he?'

Miriam shrugged. Lissie was growing up to look really pretty, but she wouldn't dream of telling her that. Mr Kirby was a regular chapel-goer and thought all pretty girls were 'in danger of moral decay'. He thought they should all look as plain and dull as his poor old sister!

'Where does he go all day?' Lissie asked as they set about organising the day's sewing.

'Business,' Miriam said importantly.

'My dad said the Kirby works had closed down.'

'They did, but he still goes into town every day.'

'What for?' asked Lissie.

'He wants to start the works up again, and—'

'And what?'

Miriam took on an air of superiority. 'I can't tell you. You're not old enough.'

'You always say that and I'm nearly as old as you.'

'No, you're not!'

Miss Kirby stood up at her high desk. 'Be quiet, you two, and get on with your work! Lissie, how dare you waste time chattering when you have Bible passages to learn for Mr Kirby.'

'Sorry, Miss Kirby.'

Miriam lowered her voice to a whisper. 'My mam says Mr Kirby's got a lady friend in town, and he goes

to see her every afternoon. You think on that when
you're reciting your Bible to him.'

Lissie didn't reckon there was anything wrong with
Mr Kirby having a lady to court, but clearly Miriam
thought otherwise. She wondered if he'd marry her and
bring her to live here. Miss Kirby wouldn't like that, for
sure!

The Kirbys' home was one in a collection of elegant
houses in a small village, that had grown up around a
track linking the turnpike to the canal. It was about three
miles downstream from the Riding town and situated
on the edge of a large landed estate, rich in coal and
iron ore. The surrounding farmland was an attractive
place to settle for enterprising men who had made their
money from the manufactories of the South Riding, and
who wanted their families to live away from the smoke
and grime of the works.

Originally the turnpike had provided the only way
into town, but later the canal and its tributary cuts opened
up new transport links. Now there was talk of a railway
to follow the waterways and keep the townsfolk of the
South Riding supplied with all their needs.

Miss Kirby's dame school paid for the upkeep of the
once elegant, but now run-down house that was her
home. When her father and her dear mama were alive,
her father's ironworks in the town had done well and
her mama had employed an upstairs maid to help them
dress in the morning and go to bed at night. It was such
a trial for Miss Kirby now the ironworks had closed and
she could no longer afford her own maid.

But her brother had kept on the elderly couple who

lived in the coach house at the far end of the garden. They slept in the upstairs room next to the hayloft and came into the kitchen for their meals. George had been her father's coachman and his wife Hannah her mama's cook. Now that Miss Kirby's brother kept only a pony and trap, as he could no longer afford a carriage, George did the gardening, looked after the orchard and fetched in the coals, while his wife stayed on as Miss Kirby's housekeeper.

It was a pleasant house to look at from the road, with large sash windows either side of a wide, panelled front door that carried a heavy brass knocker. Built at the end of the last century, before the days of the Regent, by Miss Kirby's uncle, it had been bequeathed first to Miss Kirby's father and then to her brother. In less than ten years, young Mr Kirby had shown that he was no iron master like his father or uncle, and had managed to bank-rupt the small South Riding ironworks that his father had left to him.

He had kept the house, which had large rooms on two floors, spacious attics and a collection of store places and outhouses at the back. But it was too much work for one elderly housekeeper, even with help from one of the local village girls, and Miss Kirby was not gifted in any of the domestic arts.

She had been taught by her dear mama to read and write and do numbers but, unfortunately, did not care to pass her time with any of those pursuits. She could, however, play the piano and sing, and speak a little French, not that they were much use in her school. The parents of her pupils were not interested in their chil-dren learning those skills.

Miss Kirby was frequently irritated by her school but she tolerated it. It allowed her to buy silk for her Sunday dress and keep a good table for her brother. She looked after the young sons and daughters of local folk who had the means to pay her brother a small fee, called them her pupils, and had a ready supply of help for Hannah in the kitchen.

She relied heavily on bright energetic children like Lissie, who already knew how to clean and mend and could show the others for her. Without a talent for learning herself, Miss Kirby struggled hard to teach the children their letters and numbers and expected the older ones to learn more about housekeeping and cooking from the books and papers she kept in the house.

The schoolrooms were not proper living rooms but had been stores and pantries near to the kitchen at the back of the house. The windows were tiny which made the rooms dark, and the brick floors were damp and chilly in winter. When the weather was really cold Miss Kirby allowed her pupils to crowd into the warm kitchen across the passage. The older girls were usually baking bread and cooking broth for dinner and the smell was tantalising for hungry children who never seemed to get enough to eat.

Now it was summer, at least the schoolrooms were cool, but they were stuffy unless all the windows and doors stood open. The little ones were always restless and Miss Kirby kept discipline with a small leather horse-whip that she carried in her right hand all the time. Lissie had an advantage when she started school as she had already learned from living with her mam how to avoid grown-ups when they were angry, and Miss Kirby was no different.

But other pupils didn't fare so well and frequently sobbed into their mending. If their tiny fingers couldn't manage needles and threads they would be given cleaning to do, and Lissie knew from her own experience how depressingly awful scrubbing the brick floors could be.

One sunny morning, Lissie found the schoolrooms suffocating and oppressive. Miss Kirby came downstairs in her best sprigged muslin gown and in a bad mood. Lissie had heard raised voices from Miss Kirby and her brother in the adjoining room when the other pupils arrived for school that morning. She whispered to the young ones to get on with darning sheets and keep their heads well down. She waited until Miss Kirby had settled in her high chair at the front before venturing a question.

'Please, Miss Kirby, I was wondering if I could take the little ones outside today?'

'What on earth for, child?'

'They can start on their letters. If I take the slates we can sit in the orchard.'

'Nonsense! They're far too young for letters.'

'But some of them—'

'Do not answer back! Really! Why are you always so . . . so . . . argumentative?'

'Sorry, Miss Kirby. I thought—'

'Well don't! Sometimes I think you are too clever for your own good.'

The room fell silent. Only the sound of flies buzzing round the children could be heard until Miss Kirby continued, 'Miriam is my oldest pupil and therefore she will take the younger children today.'

Miss Kirby turned to her senior pupil and managed a smile. At thirteen years of age, it was high time the Jackson girl was off into service. A few months as a scullery maid in one of the big houses would soon knock some sense into her. But the girl's mother wanted better for her only daughter and life as a downstairs maid was not part of her future.

Neither was it to be back at the Navigator Inn helping her mother, which was just as well as the girl was useless in the kitchen. Fortunately, her father had money and had been persuaded that some extra learning and looking after the younger pupils might eventually get her a better position in service.

Lissie glanced at Miriam who preened her escaping tendrils of hair and smiled silently. Miriam taking the younger children for Miss Kirby? She had no patience with them at all, and poked them in the back if they didn't do things right. Lissie couldn't let it happen and exclaimed without thinking, 'But everyone knows Miriam hates looking after the little ones!'

'Lissie! I shall not tell you again.' Miss Kirby lashed her horsewhip against the chair leg. 'Sit down at once and hold your tongue.'

'Yes, Miss Kirby.' Dejected, Lissie resumed her place on a low wooden bench beside Miriam, who immediately stuck out her tongue at Lissie.

Miss Kirby clapped her hands together. 'Now, pupils. Miriam is in charge today while I accompany Mr Kirby into town. Everyone must do as she says and she will give me the name of anyone who disobeys.' She handed Miriam the horsewhip and swept out of the room.

Miriam stood in front of the group of wide-eyed children and smirked. As soon as she heard Mr Kirby's pony and trap outside, she took off her bonnet and pinny. Miss Kirby kept a small looking glass in her teacher's cupboard and she opened the door to search for it. The little children began to whisper and fidget on their wooden benches.

'Be quiet!' Miriam shouted with her head in the cupboard.

Lissie stood up and suggested, 'Why don't I get them started on the sewing?'

Miriam straightened up with the looking glass in her hand. 'Good idea. Right then, Lissie is taking the class and no one is to move from this room.'

'Where are you going, Miriam?' Lissie asked.

'For a look round upstairs, where do you think?' She twisted strands of hair around her finger and smiled at her image.

'What if Miss Kirby comes back?'

'She won't be back for ages. They've gone to see the manager at the bank in town. My dad says Mr Kirby's in queer street and Miss Kirby's on'y too pleased for me to stay on here as long as my dad pays up. Yours an' all.' She smoothed down her dress and went on, 'If old Hannah comes nosing, tell her I've gone to the privy.'

Lissie stared in disbelief. It didn't matter what Miriam did, she always seemed to get away with it. Fancy going in Miss Kirby's private rooms! No one was ever allowed to do that! Well, at least she would be out of the classroom and out of Lissie's hair. Lissie really looked forward to helping the little ones with their mending. And there would be time for the bigger ones to learn some letters.

'All right,' she replied. 'And I'll send two of them to the kitchen to help Hannah when she's ready.'

When Miriam had gone from the schoolroom with the looking glass in her hand, Lissie looked at the little faces in her class. They were smiling at her, some quite shyly and others more broadly. She heaved a sigh of relief and beamed back.

'Now, if you'll all get on quietly with your sewing, I'll read you a story.' As she turned to the cupboard to fetch a reading book she heard a whisper of pleasure ripple through the room and thought how much she enjoyed being there, helping the little ones, helping Miss Kirby, even helping Miriam with school work. Life was looking up for Lissie at last and she hoped her dad would let her stay.

Chapter 11

1842

'Do you have a name, boy?' Sir William demanded.

'Svenson, sir. Blake Svenson.'

Sir William raised his eyebrows slightly but did not comment as most South Riding folk did when they heard his family name. 'So you are young Svenson. Dan Sanders speaks highly of you,' he said and handed Blake his silver hip flask. 'Do you want to try some of this?'

Blake glanced at Dan and tipped the brandy to his lips, gagging slightly as it burned his throat.

Sir William watched, mildly amused. 'Well, Blake, you look like a boy who can take care of himself.'

'Thank you, sir.'

Blake flexed his shoulders, pleased with Sir William's observation. After two years at Grasse Fell school in the South Riding, he could shoot and ride as well as any of the other young gentlemen there. He attended his lessons and pleased his tutors, but the classroom stifled him and he lived for the outdoor life and sporting pursuits. Cross-country running and washing in ice-cold water from the pump were part of the school week, but on Wednesday afternoons a tutor came to help with extra sporting activities.

Dan Sanders was a burly, grizzled man of about forty years. He had Negro blood in him that showed in his large frame, broad nose and frizzy grey hair. His dark-brown skin and black eyes were unusual in the South Riding and he was well known among sporting men for his success in bare-knuckle fights when he was a younger man.

He worked the boys of Grasse Fell hard. In good weather they raced on the school field, lifting logs and running with them across their shoulders. On rainy days he taught them fist-fighting in the old buttery and they sparred with each other in a makeshift ring, protecting their young hands with mufflers brought in by Dan. Dan's visits quickly became the most important part of Blake's school week.

Blake had grown tall and broad with a long reach that gave him an advantage over boys his own age and Dan quickly noticed his potential. He gave Blake a series of exhausting tasks to build him up, most of which he repeated on his own when lessons were finished, using discarded logs on the cinder track outside the school stables. From there it had been a short step to persuade the headmaster and his mama to let him go to Dan's gymnastic rooms in town for extra coaching on Saturdays.

Blake had not seen Sir William there before. But then he was usually packed off back to school on the evening carrier, before the men arrived for their evening's entertainment. Tonight was different.

Sir William continued, 'Are you one of Dan's new fist-fighters?'

'No, sir,' he replied truthfully. 'I am at Grasse Fell.'

'Is that so? I know the headmaster there.'

'He knows that I am here, sir,' Blake explained.

Sir William laughed. 'Then he'll know you are in good company. Come and meet my friends.'

Dan's rooms were in a disused mill in a run-down part of town. He rented a storage house and loading area of Kirby's closed ironworks. Every Saturday after breakfast, Blake clambered into the back of a farm cart on its way to market to spend the day at Dan's. He had extra lessons from Dan, helped him set up his practice ring, and sparred with fist-fighters as they limbered up for their manly art of boxing.

He was matched with men his own size and sometimes heavier and stronger. His reaction to a beating was to learn to move faster and to ask Dan for more coaching. And with every winning punch he landed, he imagined his opponent was Luther Dearne. The more accurate he became with his fists, the more he planned his revenge.

Dan's Saturday-night fights had a small but regular following that included men from all classes of South Riding society. His orders from the headmaster were to make sure Blake returned to Grasse Fell on the afternoon carrier. This he did until one particular night, a week after Blake's fifteenth birthday, when he had arranged a fist-fight between one of his own men and a contester from the next town.

Blake was helping Dan set up the ring for the fighters and their handlers when Sir William and his party strolled in. They were well dressed and, to Blake, did not seem to be working men. He put down the water bucket and watched.

Sir William carried a silver-topped black cane that he waved as he came forward. 'Sanders, my man, how are you?'

'Good evening, Sir William. Have you come to watch the fight?'

'Depends. Is it London Prize Rules?'

Dan stood up straight in the large, double-roped square that was his ring. 'All my fights are London Rules now.'

'Excellent! Well, whatever your purse is, I'll double it.'

'That's very generous of you, Sir William,' Dan responded. 'I take it you've had a win at the races today?'

'You could say that,' he replied with a grin.

'Then, thank you. A good purse is sure to add more – er – interest. I expect you and your friends would like some refreshment?' Dan turned to Blake. 'Look after Sir William and his friends, lad. Get them anything they want from the back.' Dan gave him the key to the store cupboard in the room he called his office.

'Here, lad. Fill these.' Sir William and his friends handed Blake their pewter and silver hip flasks. He took them through to the back room and topped them up from a flagon of French brandy.

Sir William's friends were older than Blake, though not all gentry as Sir William was. One managed a local colliery and another worked his own forge. But he hoped they all shared Blake's liking for riding, hunting and fist-fighting. He grew excited by the prospect of an evening in their company and wondered what they were like.

The fight promised to be vicious and bloody, and the watching crowd was emotionally charged and loud. Dan's fighter and his contestant were well matched and each had brought in followers, mostly working men exhausted at the end of a day of physical labour but restored by ale or porter. Blake shinned up tall poles to set torches that lit the ring and threw the crowd into shadow. Then he joined his new friends to watch as the fighting began.

It started slowly. The fighters circled each other warily, throwing jabs punctuated by jeers from the floor. Then the blows came faster and heavier and the fighters began to sweat freely, their bare chests and backs glistening in the flickering light. Blood trickled down the face of Dan's fighter and smeared the knuckles of his opponent. From his privileged ring-side position, Blake could feel the heat radiating from their sweating, muscled bodies.

Blake joined in the chants and shouts with a racing heart. His face was flushed, his fists were clenched and his shoulders hunched as his body leaned and ducked, mimicking the blows, urging on the fighters. He glanced at Sir William, who seemed more controlled, and then at the others, whose blood was up as his was. Sir William smiled at him briefly then returned his attention to the fight.

The men from the next town cheered when their fighter knocked down Dan's man. The cheer rose to a roar as he staggered to his feet and retaliated with a vengeance, urged on by Dan and his supporters, raining blow after blow on his adversary. Both men were showing signs of exhaustion now, their knuckles skinned, their faces cut, swollen and bloody. Then Dan's fighter landed a strong, right-handed punch to his opponent's head and the man went down heavily with a thud, momentarily senseless.

Blake threw both his arms in the air, yelling as loud as he could. Someone grabbed him and hugged him, shouting in his ear. The noise was deafening as the local man was declared the winner. Supporters rushed to attend their precious injured fighters, the crowd cheered and jeered at the same time, coins and banknotes changed hands and arguments developed. Dan called Sir William into the ring to present the purse and raise the arm of the victor. He gave the loser, now back on his feet, words of encouragement and shook Dan's hand congratulating him on a good fight.

Blake watched with interest. Nobody commented to see a member of the local gentry shake a Negro's hand in front of a crowd. In this arena, where men were united by their shared passion for the sport, it seemed natural and he felt proud to be part of it. The crowd began to drift away, continuing their loud arguments as they re-enacted, indeed relived, every blow. Dan was beaming, clearly high on the success of the evening. He caught Blake's eye and called over, 'Good fight, eh, lad?'

'The best,' he replied. 'Shall I start to clear up?'

'No' tonight, lad. I've plenty of hands. You go off with Sir William and his party to celebrate. I've sent word to the school that you're with him. He'll make sure you're back by morning.'

'Morning? Where does he go to all night?'

'You'll find out, lad. Off you go now.'

'See you next week, then.' Blake shrugged and thought, Why not? Then joined his new friends in the cold night air.

The noise and arguments spilled out on to the street and into a nearby alehouse, disturbing the quiet stillness of the dark street. Sir William was in a good humour and he hailed Blake across the heads of his drinking companions.

'Are you coming with us, boy?'

Blake sprinted across the cobbles and clambered into the carriage with Sir William and two of his friends for the short journey to nearby supper rooms where they joined others from the fight to dine on Yorkshire puddings with roast beef and strong ale. As the hour grew late, Blake became caught up in the high spirits of his companions and he joined in their loud exchanges and laughter. A portfolio appeared from apparently nowhere and was given to Sir William to untie ceremoniously. The contents were passed around the table for all to see.

Blake was familiar with paintings of women in fine dresses and elaborate hats; he had seen them hanging on the walls at Grasse Fell and in the grand houses of school friends that he had visited. But he had not seen drawings like these before. These were Italian drawings, drawings of real women, women without their finery, showing the full curves of their bodies without dressing or cover. He stared at the likenesses, appreciating the skill of the artist, and listened to the comments of those around him.

The women in the drawings were beautiful, with handsome faces and voluptuous bodies. Simply looking at them stirred a masculine excitement in his groin and Blake understood the attraction of owning such likenesses, though, he acknowledged, they were not portraits to hang on the walls at home.

Sir William goaded him lightly. 'What do you think of these, Blake, my boy?'

Blake thought for a moment, aware that he was the youngest man in the party. 'Well, sir, I do not know the ladies so I cannot say whether they are good likenesses or not.'

A ripple of laughter ensued. 'But would you want to meet them, boy, to get to know them? Or maybe some – er – other ladies like them?' Sir William pressed.

'Yes, sir,' he replied smartly.

'Ha!' Sir William laughed. 'I knew it! Our young friend is one of us! Tell me, Blake, have you been with a woman yet?'

Blake knew what he meant but feigned an innocence. 'I'm not sure what you mean, sir.'

A voice from the end of the table called, 'I'll wager he hasn't. A guinea says he hasn't.'

'Keep your money for a real wager, Mr Kirby,' Sir William parried. 'The boy is just fifteen.'

'Time he tasted the real thing then,' someone else called.

A deeper voice added, 'A visit to Grace's, I think.'

There was a slight hush until someone said, 'Ask the lad, then.'

Sir William turned to Blake and said, 'Well? Are you

ready to learn about real pleasure from one of the ladies at Grace's, or do I send you back to school now?'

Blake had not heard of 'Grace's' before, but he had gained some knowledge of the kind of place it was sure to be from talking with other boys at school. He did not take any persuading. He was ready.

'Grace's,' he replied firmly.

There was more laughter and banter as the party began to split up. Some left for their homes and others went out to their carriages with Sir William and Blake. As Blake pulled on his cap, Sir William faced him squarely, tipped the brim back with the silver top of his cane and asked, 'Are you sure about this?'

In the light of the carriage lamp, Blake's clear blue eyes darkened and gleamed at the notion. 'Yes, sir.' He relished the thought of the pleasures to come. 'I am.'

Sir William gave him a brief nod. 'Yes, I do believe you are.'

Blake knew something of Sir William Swinborough as he was the biggest landowner in the Riding. A baronet of some forty years of age, his family held, and had held for generations, vast tracts of the South Riding. The land was good for farming and sheep thrived well on the wintry hills. Frequent rain produced soft spring water for making woollen cloth. But there were greater riches beneath the Riding soil. Ironstone and, especially, coal had made wealthy men of Sir William's father and grand-father. And Sir William had shouldered the responsibility of these new industries well. He was a fair landlord to the tenants and workers that tilled his soil, mined his coal and forged his iron.

Blake sat quietly in one corner of Sir William's carriage as it rattled its way through the dark cobbled streets. This would be the first time he had stayed in town past supper. Even with the backing of Sir William he would be in deep trouble at school. But he was finished with school now. In his heart he knew that he wanted to be out of it. Book work and a future at university rubbing shoulders with the sons of the English aristocracy was not for him.

Real life was what he wanted and he was about to start living it. His groin tingled with anticipation of a real woman, a proper woman, not a portrait or a drawing. He became nervous at the thought of experiencing real intimacy. What would he do? How would he do? A hand clutching a silver flask jutted in front of his face. He took it gratefully and swigged a mouthful quickly down his throat.

The carriage took them out of town, up the hill where a successful ironmaster was building a new home of local stone and best Welsh slate. Beyond lay farmland, and in the next valley a village by the river crossing. Before that was Grace's, the former home of a gentleman farmer, with its mellow stone walls and tall chimneys. The carriage stopped and, save for the snorting of the horses, there was silence. After the rowdiness of the fight and ensuing arguments over supper, Grace's seemed as hushed as a church.

Blake had expected an inn, or something resembling an inn. Once inside, he realised with a start that it reminded him of his own home, with an entrance hallway furnished as his mama's was. He saw a low table supporting an oil lamp with a tall glass chimney, two upholstered chairs and a looking glass in an ornate gilt frame on the wall. They stood on a turkey carpet as Grace appeared from the back of the house to greet them. She seemed to be expecting Sir William and knew his friends by name.

Sir William called him forward to meet her and he saw that she was quite an old woman, with a worn, lined face. She was dressed in grey silk with a lot of black lace at her wrists and throat and a jet comb in her grey hair.

'We have a novice for you, Grace,' Sir William told her lightly. 'He needs a lesson or two, don't y' know.'

Grace raised her pince-nez to her eyes and peered closely at Blake. 'Handsome fellow, isn't he?' she mused. 'First timer, you say?'

Blake began to feel uncomfortable as he was scrutinised by this older woman. She moved closer and addressed him directly. 'Tell me, sir, what are you looking for? Dark or fair? Or maybe—'

Sir William interrupted. 'How about a bit of a show, Grace? We've not had one of those in a while.' A purse of coins passed from Sir William to Grace and the older man said to his companions, 'What d'you say to giving the boy first pick? Just this once.'

Grace led the way into a large room, furnished and lit like a private drawing room. She waved her arm towards a decanter of port wine and glasses that stood on the sideboard. 'Help yourselves, gentlemen, while I organise my ladies.'

Blake declined the wine. He had drunk ale with his supper and taken brandy in the carriage. His courage

was high and his nerves were already tingling in anticipation. The men settled comfortably in upholstered chairs
and sofas and waited.

Grace came back with a sheet of music and began
to play on a harpsichord. Her ladies entered the room
one by one, parading and twirling around the elegant
furniture. They were lovely, all of them, each one handsome in her own way. Soon they filled the room in
their fine, billowing silk dresses of pinks and reds and
greens. The air in the room was charged with desire.
The men became restless and moved about in their seats,
forgetting their wine and undoing the buttons of their
jackets.

And then the women began to, gradually, slowly, take
off their finery, helping each other with tapes and buttons
until their copious gowns and lace-edged petticoats were
abandoned, draped over sofas and tables, and they were
clad in only their stiffly boned corsets and ribbon-
trimmed under-drawers. There were six or seven of them,
smiling, twirling, bending forward to show the swelling
of their breasts and the roundness of their rumps. Blake
stared in awe. His heart was throbbing in his throat and
his body fired by an animal desire. Furtively, he glanced
at the other men and saw that, like him, they were
mesmerised by this show.

Blake had never in his life felt so excited. Never. Not
like this. These women were so desirable, so arousing, so
ready. His eager pulse raced and his immediate need to
possess one of them overwhelmed him. There were two
that he found especially irresistible. Both were mature,
rounded women of good stature. Their womanly curves

bulged from beneath their corsets. How he coveted an exploration of those curves!

Each had glossy dark hair dressed smoothly around her head in braids and swathes arranged to complement her smiling face. But, whereas one was from a southern climate with olive skin, abundant curls and smouldering brown eyes, the other had a northern pallor with ivory skin and light eyes, her long black hair coiled smoothly around her elegant head. When she circled in front of him for the second time he could barely restrain himself and his breeches bulged with desire. She looked straight into his eyes for a few seconds and they exchanged a steady level gaze.

And from that moment he was lost to her. He stood up and caught her hand to stop her moving on. She hesitated and looked about her. Blake saw her eyes meet Sir William's and watched as he rose to his feet quickly. The woman pulled at her hand to loosen it from Blake's grip, but he would not let her go. The music slowed and stopped as Sir William picked up his glass of port wine and crossed the room.

'Hah!' Sir William said. 'You have chosen Clara. You have good taste, my boy.' He swung round to face Clara squarely and asked, with an ironic twist to his lips, 'Tell me, Clara, do you choose him?'

Blake watched Clara frown silently and realised he had chosen badly. He had displeased Sir William. He let go of Clara's hand and stepped back, deferring to the older man. But Sir William surprised him by taking Clara's hand, kissing it lightly and handing it back to him, saying, 'Now, Clara, you take very good care of my young friend. I put my trust in you to teach him well.'

Clara looked mildly surprised but led Blake silently out of the drawing room and up the stairs.

Blake had seen a woman naked before, the only woman before this one to have stirred his sexual desires. That woman had been a relative of the school's head-master, a distant cousin of some sort who had stayed as a guest of his wife for several months. The summer that year was hot and he had seen her bathing in the forest stream as he crashed his way through the trees on a cross-country run.

He had slowed when he noticed the empty donkey-cart on the forest track, and crept through the undergrowth to where the stream fell into a wide rock pool before meandering on its way. She was a young woman with large drooping breasts and a round belly that other pupils had also noticed swelling under her skirts.

Her condition was the source of much dormitory snorting and giggling among the boys. When he had looked at her then, he thought she was beautiful. Her fair hair had been loosened from its pinning and she sat on a rock leaning back on her hands as though proud of her growing bulging belly.

Blake had crept away, aware of the masculine desires it had stirred in him, desires that were now repeated and burgeoning tenfold as he followed Clara up the wide, carpeted staircase. This was no hole-in-the-corner whorehouse as he might have expected, but quiet and well-furnished, as his own home was. With a shock, Blake realised that this familiarity added to the frisson of his arousal. The girl, no, the woman, closed the bedroom door and stood motionless in front of him, unashamed by her scant covering of frilled corset and drawers.

He realised now what he wanted in a woman, of all the women he'd seen that night and before. A woman of good proportions. Not a dainty and pretty little girl, but a handsome and comely woman with soft round curves. Like this woman. With light skin, like his and his people across the North Sea, yes, but with the drama of dark hair that made her skin look alabaster in contrast.

The room was lit by a subdued yellow glow from an oil lamp placed on a small table. A large bed made up with white linen and a red satin cover dominated the room and he began to feel nervous with anticipation. He pulled at his already loosened necktie and threw it to the floor, then began to fumble excitedly with the buttons on his shirt.

Clara came forward and stilled his hands. 'Wait. Wait a little. What shall I call you?'

'Blake. Blake Svenson.' Noticing her slightly raised eyebrows he added, 'It's Swedish.'

'Is that so? Yes, I see – the flaxen hair and blue eyes. Blue, like mine.' Clara's voice was soft and she spoke slowly. 'You must tell me more about your home country. But not now. Afterwards. We can talk afterwards. First, Blake, come closer to me and help me take off my corset.'

His fingers shook as he untied laces and ribbons and peeled down stockings to reveal soft white flesh that was cool and smooth and lightly scented. Her breasts were pale soft cushions, her belly gently curving and her rear as round and plump as a pudding. He wanted to devour her, to dominate her and to possess her whole body with his. But when her delicious body was fully exposed to him and he could not stop himself from exploring the contours of her velvet skin, she took his hands in hers, telling him, again, to slow down and enjoy the waiting.

Yet, as she moved away from him she swayed and pouted, and her smouldering eyes were sending Blake a far different message. He growled, an unfamiliar low groan, deep in his throat that he had not heard himself utter before. He was, he realised, totally bewitched by her. How long would she play this game with him?

Now she moved in closer to him, so that he could feel her softness through his shirt, and began to unbutton his breeches. With a practised skill she looked into his eyes and smiled as she helped him with the fastenings and peeled away his garments. She kissed his cheek and whispered into his ear, 'Now your under-drawers, put them over there on that chair and let me see what you're really made of.'

When he turned back to face her she was stretched out on the bed, completely naked, with her arms above her head and her legs gently moving and swishing on the shiny red cover. Her long black hair, now unpinned, tumbled across the white linen pillow shams. She gazed at him as he moved, naked, towards the bed, gave a gentle nod, a tiny smile and she murmured softly, 'Well, now, Blake, what do you want to do next?'

He could not contain himself. His throat closed as every sinew in his body strained to take her for his own. Involuntarily, he shook his head slightly, trying to deny the power she held over him, the strength of this brutal animal desire within him. Clara continued to smile gently, and now her whole body was moving and squirming over the slippery, sensuous satin. 'Blake,' she whispered, 'why do you hesitate? What are you waiting—'

Her whispers were stifled as his body covered hers and he drove relentlessly into hers, loosening his caged passions and giving himself up to his adolescent instincts and desires. Clara was the most beautiful creature he had ever seen. Her naked body, soft and white and yielding, was a symphony for all his senses. She smelled of a rose garden in full flower and tasted of fine French wine. Her soft murmurings, intent on soothing and calming his desperate passions, only served to inflame them further, and her velvet skin, moving in harmony with his urgent hunger, drove him wild with desire.

Young, strong and virile, he could not have enough of Clara's seductive body, he could not sate his passion. Once spent, he was quick to recover and take her again. And again. And when he was finally, finally exhausted, he slept.

But not for long. For Clara woke him and took his hands in hers again. 'Now, my young stallion, let me teach you a little about a woman's body. Let me show you how to tease and tempt a wife so that she will never look for pleasure outside your marriage bed. Such strong hands and searching lips must learn how to be gentle . . .'

That smile again and those wide bewitching eyes! How could he resist her? Slowly she guided his exploration and further discovery of her body into an adventure he found amazing and wondrous until – he did not know why or how or when exactly – he was aware that it was he and not Clara in control. She was lost in a writhing, whimpering submission, moving her body with his in a rhythmic joining together that enhanced the wonder of his newly discovered power.

Then Clara was panting, no, not panting, but giving out small harsh cries from the back of her throat, pulling her knees high and clasping her ankles around his sweating back. Her hands snaked over his damp skin, nails digging into his flesh, then her flat palms pressed against his muscled rump to urge him on to drive deeper into this most exquisite captivity.

Her body arched beneath him, surprising him with her strength. A prolonged strangled cry made him slow. Then she subsided and sank back on to the bed, sighing deeply. He stopped and rolled off her, seeing her face and body relax and flop. He lay beside and watched her in the lamp-light. She became tranquil and the lines of age etched about her eyes and mouth were softened and less obvious.

Her eyes opened suddenly and surprise creased her forehead. 'That should not have happened. My job is to . . .' Quickly, she glanced at him, lying full length on his side, his head resting on one hand. 'You didn't – finish. You must – you must carry on.' She reached out to pull him back across her, but he resisted.

'No. No, I said! Leave me be.' His desire for her was already subsiding. She had been a good teacher for him and had done her job well. And she was lovely, very lovely. But, he thought, she did this all the time, for Sir William, for other men perhaps, for her living. He sat up on the side of the bed and turned up the lamp.

'Why do you do this, Clara?' he asked.

'Why? Why?' She sounded irritated by his question. 'Why do you think?'

'But you are a beautiful woman and you have some wealthy and well-connected clients. Couldn't you get out of this and marry one of them? I'm sure you must have had offers.'

She sat up quickly, supporting her full breasts with an arm. 'You wouldn't understand. You're just a boy still.'

Blake twisted to face her and placed his hand between her thighs. 'Just a boy, am I?' He did not resist when she moved his hand away.

She answered, 'Well no, not now, maybe. You're a man and marriage is for men. They get the best deal out of any marriage.' She thought for a moment and added as an afterthought, 'Unless they are very lucky.'

'Has no one ever offered for you?'

'A few.'

'Well then?' He got up, passed her a shawl and pulled on his under-drawers.

Clara hugged the fine lacy wool about her shoulders and said bluntly, 'You don't know what marriage can mean for women – to – to be owned like a slave by some man. My father was a kind and gentle man but he died young when my sister and I were small children. And Mama had no means to carry on alone.'

'Ah, I see. Did your father not leave anything for her?'

'Our house and a small income; the reason why my stepfather married her.' She gave an involuntary shudder. 'He was a brutish man who beat us when we did not do as he demanded.'

Blake covered his eyes with his hand. He could never imagine beating a woman for any reason whatsoever. 'And you had no choice but to stay with him,' he stated quietly. 'I'm sorry.'

'Yes. So were we. Mama was older than he was, but he married her and then treated her as his housekeeper, and me and my sister as his – his servants.' Her voice faltered. 'He had women too, who visited the house to share his bed.'

'Oh, Clara, how awful for you.'

'It was so much worse for Mama,' she whispered. 'She challenged him one day and he beat her so badly that she never recovered. Her spirit was broken. She just took to her bed. And then, of course, without Mama to protect us, he began to take a carnal interest in my sister . . .' Clara choked on the words.

'You mean he violated her? His own stepdaughter?' Blake felt sick with anger.

Clara nodded briefly, biting her lower lip. 'When my turn came, I knew that I must leave him and Grace helped me. She had nursed my mother and when Mother died we both left. I would have starved if it hadn't been for Grace. Grace is good to her girls and being here is better than being a laundry-girl in the workhouse.'

'But what happened to your poor sister?'

'She escaped before I did, with a local farm hand. They married and took a sailing ship to the Americas.' Clara held her head high and continued, 'I am – now – quite alone in this world, and being here with Grace is my choice.'

'I see.'

'No, I do not think you do because you are a man. When women marry they become a chattel of their husbands, like a cooking pot or a plough.' Suddenly her frowning face relaxed and she smiled. 'Enough of this, I am beginning to sound like Grace.' She ran her fingers lightly down his naked spine. 'You are a fine young man, Blake. And I am sure you will find a lovely girl to marry and you will be kind to her.' She added lightly, 'If I were younger and if you asked me, I should marry you myself!'

He twisted round to kiss her perfumed hair. 'Can I come back and see you?'

'Can you pay my price?'

'I don't mean for this. I am planning on getting my own girl to love and marry one day. I mean to talk, as a friend.'

'A friend? Not likely, lad! Grace would soon see you off!'

'Then I shall just have to become Grace's friend too, shan't I?'

'Away with you! You have too much charm for your own good. Go on. Get dressed now. I have given you too much of my time. Sir William and his friends will be waiting for you downstairs.'

Blake kissed her again, this time on the cheek. 'Thank you, Clara. Thank you for everything.'

Dawn was breaking when Sir William and his party finally left Grace's. Blake gazed out of the carriage window for the first half-hour then slept soundly as it rattled its way across countryside and moor. The school was quiet as he climbed in through the buttery window

and took a piece of cold pie from the pantry on his way
to his cold, hard, dormitory bed.

In the weak morning light he looked about the
building. It was too small, too confined a place for him
now. He wanted to be out of it. He wanted freedom
from book learning and neat suits of clothes. He wanted
the open air, hard physical work and a girl of his own
to love. Yes, a girl of his own to love. That's exactly what
he wanted now.

'Mama.' He bent to kiss her on both cheeks and she
looked up, momentarily startled.

'Blake! You're home so soon! The stagecoaches get
faster and faster these days.'

'They do, Mama. We had a fine team of horses for
most of the way, thank Heaven. It was hellish dusty and
crowded.'

'Blake, your language! What have you been learning
at that expensive school?'

Blake smiled to himself and was glad his mama did
not know. 'How are you, Mama?'

School had finished for the summer and Blake knew
that this was the last time he would be taking the stage
home. The July sun was warm and his mother was sitting
in the garden under the shade of a leafy walnut tree. As
he'd walked across the grass to join her he'd thought
how attractive she looked in a light printed–cotton dress
trimmed with white lace.

Suddenly he felt fiercely protective of her. Somehow
he would find Luther Dearne and make him pay for the
murder of his father. He would see justice done, he

would! If the constables and magistrates could not help him, then he must do it for himself, for himself and for his mama.

'Me? Bah! I am in fine health,' his mama replied. She was sitting at a small wickerwork table going through a substantial ledger and sipping a tall glass of iced tea. 'But let me look at you. It seems so long since I saw you last.' She tilted her head back to take in his full height, and studied him shrewdly for a moment. 'You are taller. And no longer a boy. No. You have grown manly like your papa in these past months.' She stood up to get the measure of him and lifted her arms to place her hands on his shoulders. 'My! What a fine man you have become. So tall and broad and strong – your father would be very proud of you.'

Blake took off his linen jacket and wide-brimmed straw hat and sat down, glancing at the open pages on the wicker table. 'What's this you're doing?'

'I'm looking after your papa's business for you.'

'Doesn't Mr Ephraim do that for us?'

'*Ja.* He manages the warehouse and office in Hull. And he does that very well. As good as when Papa was here.'

'So why do you have this ledger here?'

'Ah yes, the ledgers. I do as much for Ephraim as I did for your papa. Together we make sure we have no more fraud, *ja*? I look after the business for you.'

Blake laughed. 'The business belongs to you, Mama.'

'Only until you are twenty-one, and then it is yours. That is what your papa wished. By then you will have a university education and be a proper English gentlemen. *Ja*?'

Blake was silent for a while until his mama prompted him with another '*Ja?*'

'*Yes*, Mama. *Yes*. We are English now.'

Ingrid Svenson knew her only son, indeed her only child, well. 'What is it, Blake? You are not happy with what I have said? Shall I call Lucy for more tea?'

'No, Mama. No tea.' He flung himself down on the grass and looked up at her with a heavy sigh. 'I don't want to go to university. I want to – hell, I don't know what I want to do for sure yet, but I know it is not more studying. Book work is not for me, Mama.' There was a pleading tone in his voice. He knew this was going to be difficult.

'But you are so good at it. Your headmaster says so in his letters!'

'It isn't what I want to do, Mama,' he said simply.

'Oh, Blake, no. It would be such a waste.' His mama sounded disappointed at first but then she brightened. 'So, do you want to work in the warehouse? With Ephraim? That is good also, he will teach you instead of your schoolmasters. That is good.'

'Maybe,' he conceded, 'but later, when I'm older. I . . . I have things to do first.'

'What – things to do? What are you talking about?'

'I . . . I don't know, yet. Perhaps work on the keels in the Humber as I have done in the school holidays.' He paused before adding slowly, 'And go upstream, follow the canals through to the industrial towns in the South Riding. I have friends there now. Friends from school.'

'Upstream? Inland!' His mama raised her voice. 'You mean the towns near Mexton Lock, don't you? Where your papa was killed. Bah! Now I understand what you are saying. You wish for revenge. This is for revenge, isn't it?'

Blake grimaced. His mama was so perceptive. 'I have unfinished business there, Mama.'

'No, Blake, no! I will not allow you to do this. The waterways are dangerous. And that part of the canal is notorious for crime. There are so many thieves and vagabonds. That . . . that Dearne man had – has – many friends. They will kill you as well. No, I will not let you do this! I do not wish to lose my son as well as my husband.'

'And you won't, Mama. I promise. Look at me! I am a man now. I can take care of myself.'

'You are still a boy of sixteen even though you look like a man.'

They were both silent for a moment, then Blake spoke quietly. 'I have to do this, Mama,' he said.

She shook her head wearily. 'You are your father's son. But I worry so much for you.'

'You don't have to, Mama. I am strong and I can fight.'

'Blake! Blake! Please! No more fighting, please! I could not bear to lose you!'

'You won't lose me, Mama. I promise. Dearne may have his cronies at Mexton Lock but I too have my friends now. I have to find out what really happened to Papa and – and – and make Dearne pay for his crimes – one way or another.'

Ingrid groaned in despair. 'But we have tried! Ephraim did all he could. The constable would not listen to us. We are strangers, we are foreigners. They would not – will not – help us!'

Blake kept his voice low but the steeliness of his tone was evident as he responded, 'Then we shall have to help ourselves, shan't we?'

'Blake, do not do this! We cannot change the past now!'

His mama's anguish made him hesitate, and for a moment his shoulders sagged as he ran his hands through his thick fair hair. 'I have to know what really happened that night.'

His mama shook her head. 'I know. But it will do no good to anyone. I miss your father every waking minute of my life. But nothing is going to bring him back to us.'

Blake sprang to his feet, fired by the anger he felt every time he revisited the memory. 'He was murdered, Mama, and the constable did nothing. Nothing!'

'Blake, you cannot take the law into your own hands.'

'Why not? Dearne did!'

'It makes you as bad as – as he was.'

The anguish on his mama's face tore at his heart. 'Maybe I am, maybe I'm not, but Papa's death was no accident and we both know that. Yes, I want to kill that murderer Dearne for what he did to Papa. But first I want him to admit the truth about what happened that night – about the fraud and his fight with Papa and . . . and . . . yes, the shooting. I want him to admit to shooting Papa, and, by the devil, he shall!' He slammed his clenched fist on to the table, making the tea cup jump and rattle.

His mama stared at him silently for a long time. She knew now that she could not stop him. Finally, she spoke, choosing her words carefully. 'Then, my dearest son, my only son, you must do what you have to do. But I do not want to see you die like your father or be imprisoned because you could not control this anger of yours. Yes, I have anger like you have, but the years have helped me to deal with it and I have had the warehouse to occupy my thoughts. Your sporting activities in school have done the same for you, I know. Yes, you are strong and you can fight. But you must also have control. How will you control your anger, Blake, when you meet with Dearne face to face?'

'I don't know, Mama. But until then I'll labour like a man. Hard work will help to numb my pain. Try not to worry. Look at me! I am tall and strong and I know how to look after myself.' His voice took on a pleading tone. 'I have to do this. I owe it to Papa.'

'Yes, I know, and for that I love you dearly. But promise me that you will talk with Ephraim first. He hears news from the barges all the time.'

'I'll talk to Ephraim tomorrow. There is plenty of work on the canals. And in the South Riding there are coalfields and ironworks—'

'Blake, does it have to be the South Riding? You do not have the safety of your school now. Look at you! You will stand out in the crowd. You are not one of them. The people there – they will remember you. They will ask about you and they will find out whose son you are. Bah! I have a bad feeling about this notion of yours!'

'Mama, calm yourself. No one will remember *me*—'

'They will! Your hair is so fair and your name—!'

'I was a skinny boy when Papa died and I am a grown

man now. My hair is not so flaxen. My skin will soon be as brown as a Negro's and I shall grow whiskers.'

'Bah!' Mama put her head on one side and studied his handsome, chiselled features. 'You have been thinking about this for a long time, haven't you?'

He nodded silently.

'So you really mean to go and find him?'

'Yes, Mama. I do.'

'And there's nothing more I can say to you to change your mind?'

'I'm sorry, Mama.'

'I am a mother and I have a son so I have to suffer. I have to let you go some time and watch you get yourself injured or worse. You promise me, Blake, you promise me that you will take care of yourself and that you won't forget about your dear mama?'

'As if I could! Mama, I am not crossing the sea. But this is something I . . . I have to do. I have to. I love you dearly, Mama, but now that I am grown I am my own man, and I have to make my own way in life.'

Chapter 12

Blake picked up a keel from the wharf at Goole. It was heading for Kingston upon Hull with a cargo of heavy metal axles for railway engines to be shipped down the east coast of England. The docks were busy, even busier than he remembered as a boy. He dodged and darted around mechanical hoists, wagons and horses, and heaps of coal and timber until he came to their warehouse and office.

Mr Ephraim was standing outside the wide open doors of their huge timber building, checking out a wagonload of raw pig iron that was to be loaded on to barges and hauled inland along the canals. He wore his usual sober suiting and polished black shoes, dusty from the warehouse floor, and carried, as always, a sheaf of papers. But as soon as he saw Blake approach, he waved away the wagon and a broad smile appeared from the depths of his straggly grey beard.

'How are you, Mr Ephraim?' Blake asked as the two

men shook hands cordially. 'And your dear wife and family, how are they?'

'I am well, my wife and family are healthy. The business is good. I am a happy man. And you – you are bigger than I am. A grown man. You must call me Ephraim now, like your mama does.'

'Thank you, I shall. Are you very busy? I'd like to talk if you can.'

'About the business? Of course! Come into the office.'

Blake followed him into a small room with a window that looked out on to the warehouse floor and two mahogany roll-top desks, one open for work and the other closed and locked. The walls were covered with mahogany cupboards which, Blake knew, contained shelves of precisely kept ledgers. They sat in leather upholstered, round-backed office chairs and Blake opened the conversation.

'I've decided not to go back to school, Ephraim.'

'Hah! And your mama does not approve so you have come to me to persuade her.'

'Not exactly. But you are right, Mama is not happy about it, although she accepts that there are other things I want to do.'

Ephraim nodded. 'You want to work in the business with me. Or perhaps instead of me?'

Blake laughed gently and shook his head. 'No, no. Never. I could never run it as well as you and Mama. But I do want to work.'

'Then work here. This is a good business, Blake, and it will need you one day.'

'I know, I know. And Mama is angry with me for not

wanting to do that. But this was Papa's dream. Not mine.
I have my own dreams to follow.'

'Making your way in life is not a dream.' Ephraim
sounded quite severe. 'In the future you will appreciate
the fruits of your labour here.'

'Not my labour. Papa's labour, your labour, your fruits.
And now Mama's. I want something different, something
new.'

'And what is it that you want?'

'I don't know yet. That's why I need to go off and
find out.' He turned suddenly to look out of the small
window. The wharf was busy with men going about their
business, unloading cargo, trading goods, shouting, sometimes fighting, but above all else they were living. Living.
And his papa was not out there with them. He slammed
his fist against the wooden panelling that lined their
crowded office.

Ephraim nodded slowly. 'Ah, young Blake. My dear
boy, you have this anger deep down. You need to work
it out of your system, don't you?'

'Something like that, I suppose.'

'Yes, I see. You do not need my permission though.'

'No. But I need you to understand. Do you?'

'Yes, I do.'

'And I need your help to find work on the Humber.'

'Does your mama agree to this?'

Blake grimaced. 'Not exactly. I've tried to make her
understand. I've tried, Ephraim, I've really tried!' He
shrugged and his shoulders sagged. 'But she's my mama
and I'm still her little boy.'

'Children! They always make us despair for them.'

There was a silence and then the older man asked quietly, 'You have made up your mind, haven't you?'

Blake looked directly into Ephraim's wise brown eyes and nodded, stating briefly, 'I have to do it.'

Ephraim thought for a moment. 'You could try the fly boats. They go by Thorne to the South Riding. A new carrier has set up taking fish and fresh vegetables from Lincolnshire through to the markets there. They haul non-stop for twenty-four hours and take two crews. It's hard work but as you can ride, the wages will be good—'

'Ride? Barges use heavy horses, don't they?'

'Not these! Fly boats are smaller and lighter than barges and they use Yorkshire Carriage horses. Thoroughbreds or near, fine bloodstock, I'm told, that haul for ten or twelve miles without stopping. The company keeps its own changes at horse marines on the way.'

'Yorkshire Carriages, you say? The same as those that pull the stagecoaches?'

'They're the best ones to keep up the pace. You drive them at a trot most of the time. But at night when the canal traffic stops you can ride them even faster. So they need men who can ride as well as being strong enough to labour.'

'A little different from the usual rough types on the barges, I'll wager,' Blake observed.

'Do not underestimate them, Blake. They are tough men who know their business. Manufacturing in the South Riding is expanding fast and the people there are hungry.'

A gleam came into Blake's eyes. Fly boats through to the busy towns in the South Riding! Fast, quiet and travelling at night. It would be a perfect cover for him to find out the lie of the land around Mexton Lock, to find out more about Luther Dearne and to work out how best to corner him and challenge him.

This is fate for me, Blake thought. Fate has presented me a way of confronting Dearne with my father's death and dealing with him once and for all. Luther Dearne is going to pay for what he did, and I shall not rest until he has.

Ephraim was right about the crews. They were strong men who rode well and worked hard and they expected the same from others in their teams. He passed easily for a local man now, thanks to his South Riding schooling. He knew the local dialect and geography. However, his arresting good looks ensured that he continued to stand out in any crowd.

Although his hair was no longer the flaxen blond of his boyhood, it had grown into a striking golden colour that took on lighter streaks in the summer sun. And it was still thick and silky so that it flopped over his brow if he didn't keep it cut. He covered it most of the time with a workman's cap. Now in his seventeenth year, he could labour as well as any man, and that summer he joined a crew of four that worked non-stop, two on, two off, through day and night carrying documents and cargo along the canal routes in the South Riding.

Sometimes they carried fresh fish rushed in from the North Sea, or picked up baskets of summer vegetables and salads that fetched a good price if they could get them into the early-morning markets. Return payloads were often small, honed-edge tools made by the Riding's numerous little mesters and bound for ships going to London or Newcastle.

His stamina was good, but not the same as the older, more experienced men who made up the crew. The hours were long and the work arduous and so for that first summer when he was not at the rudder or riding the horse, he was often sleeping in the small cabin off the rear cockpit. Timetables ruled his life and there was no respite for social visits to his friends.

They passed through Mexton Lock at night on the way into the towns, and it was often late evening before their return. The older men saw to changing the horse while he stayed at the rudder and there was little time to talk to anyone except the lock keeper. But he had not forgotten his quest and he watched and listened, biding his time as summer turned to autumn, and waiting for his chance.

Winter came early that year and a bout of fiercely cold weather well before Christmas froze several stretches of canal. The flyers were suspended and the company offered Blake work on coal barges for the winter. He would have taken it if he had not received a message from Ephraim, asking him to go home to see his mama.

He arrived in Goole expecting to hear bad news and feared the worst. His mama was in the kitchen helping Lucy make festive puddings for boiling. She was wearing a large white apron over her brown woollen day dress. He threw his hat and canvas kitbag on a nearby chair and hugged her, getting flour all over his jacket. She looked well, he thought, so what was wrong?

'Lucy,' Mama asked, 'would you make a start on plucking that goose in the scullery?'

Blake smiled at her as she bobbed a curtsey and disappeared. 'What is it, Mama?'

'Can we sit down first, Blake? Do you want some tea?'

He shook his head. 'I want to know what all this is about. Is something wrong?'

'Of course not! I just wanted to talk to you. I have made a decision.' She sat in the chair that Blake had pulled out for her.

'Well?'

She looked up into his eyes, narrowed by his furrowed brow. 'Don't be so worried, my dear. I have decided to go back to Sweden.'

Blake's jaw dropped and his eyes widened. 'I thought you liked it here?'

'I do, I do. But I want to see my cousins again. And their babies.'

Blake understood her need and his mind was in turmoil. This must be partly his fault. If he had been with her instead of following some crazed idea of his own, perhaps she would not feel the need to return to her distant relatives. 'Of course you do,' he said. 'I am so sorry, Mama. I should have stayed here with you, I didn't think—'

'Nonsense, Blake. You are young. You do not want to be looking after your mama.'

'You miss Papa very much, don't you?'

'Yes, I do.'

'So do I. Do you want me to go to Sweden with you?'

His mama shook her head slowly. 'No. Not unless you want to, dear. You have your life here.'

'You cannot travel all that way alone, Mama. I shall go with you.'

'I shall not be alone. Lucy will come with me.'

This was another surprise for Blake. 'Lucy is going to live in Sweden?'

'Oh, Blake! No, of course not. I am only going to *visit* my cousins. My home is here now and I shall come back.' She stretched out her hand to pat his comfortingly. 'You must stay in England and do what you have to do. But we have to talk about the warehouse, and what to do with this house while I am gone.'

'Will you be gone for long?'

'I do not know, dear. I will write to you from Sweden.'

'Have you spoken with Ephraim?'

She nodded. 'He manages our business so well now, and his eldest boy is a great help to him. We have no worries about that. But I want to know if you will be living here while I am away.'

'I . . . I wasn't planning on that, Mama,' he said cautiously.

She smiled. 'Just as I thought. I do not want to leave the house empty for so long a time. So, if you don't want to live here, I will make arrangements to let it. And if you do want to come back this way to work, you can lodge with Ephraim and his family until I return.'

Blake nodded in agreement. 'You have thought of everything, Mama.'

'Yes, I have been thinking of this visit since – well, since your papa died. You will promise to write to me, Blake?'

Blake got to his feet and bent to put his arms around her and kiss her. 'Of course I shall.'

So, early in the following spring, Ingrid Svenson and her maid Lucy sailed from Hull across the North Sea to Sweden. The flyer service on the canals started up again as soon as the hard frosts were over and Blake rejoined his old team as an experienced crew member. The waterways of the South Riding became his home and he came off the barge only when it was laid up for repairs, or a cargo had been delayed. Blake Svenson became a part of canal life; hard working, sometimes hard drinking, but all the time blending easily with others who made their living on the waterways of the South Riding.

Chapter 13

1844

Lissie Dearne, in her fourteenth year, feared she would have to leave Miss Kirby's soon to go and work all day in the kitchen of the Navigator Inn. Already, her evenings and Saturdays were spent there as a kitchen maid, leaving Sunday to clean up their own house for her mam.

Dad said Mickey Jackson paid part of Miss Kirby's school fee for Lissie so that she could work at the Navvy. She didn't mind. She knew her dad could not get much work nowadays and that money was short. But she did like going to school and would do anything to stay.

Miriam liked Lissie going to school as well because she helped her with the duties Miss Kirby gave her in the schoolroom. As the elder of her two senior pupils, Miriam was often asked to take over the schoolroom to give Miss Kirby a break. While Miriam enjoyed being left in charge, she needed Lissie to keep the children occupied, so their uneasy friendship continued.

As the days lengthened, they often dawdled along the

towpath, lingering at bridges, watching the water traffic and chattering to each other. They were enjoying the early morning sun on a farm bridge near to Fordham when they saw the flyer approaching fast.

'That's late today,' Lissie commented. 'It should be in town for the market by now.'

'Let's stay and watch,' Miriam decided, and leaned over the low stone wall, holding her bonnet on with her hand.

The rider was crouching over the neck of his horse, with his head well down as he slowed to a canter towards the bridge. Just before he disappeared underneath, he looked up at them and smiled.

'Did you see that?' Miriam said.

Both girls dashed across to the other side in time to see him emerge, sit up straight in his saddle, let go of the reins and raise his cap to them in salute. He raked back his floppy fair hair with his fingers and replaced his cap before urging on the horse. The small barge whooshed after him leaving a turbulent wake on the glassy brown water.

'I've not seen him before, 'ave you?' Miriam commented with wide eyes. 'He's younger than the others. Handsome too, from what I could see.'

Lissie stood rigidly beside her friend, staring after him. 'He's on'y a bargeman like all the others,' she managed to say at last.

He wore the same type of cap, with a soft crown and a peak to shade his eyes. Underneath it, his hair was the lightest she had seen in the South Riding, even at the front where it was darkened by sweat from his brow. But most of all she remembered the way he combed it with his fingers, taking it straight back from his forehead and replacing his cap firmly on top of it.

The memory jarred in her mind. She had been much younger then but she remembered that night. The night when her dad had seen his dad off. Well, his dad had knocked hers down, but he'd cleared off all the same.

He had been a boy then, one of the bigger boys, a stranger who had watched everything, as she had, Lissie recalled. She remembered that the constable had called at their house and Mam had given him sherry wine. And Dad stayed home so they had a bonfire in the garden and a ham for Christmas that had lasted to Twelfth Night.

Miriam's elbow in her back brought Lissie back to the present. 'Well? Don't you?'

'Don't I what?'

Miriam sighed irritably. 'Don't you think 'e's 'andsome?'

'Oh aye,' Lissie replied. 'He's handsome all right.'

It was that same lad, that foreigner she was sure, except that the lad was now a man. But he had the same features, like his dad had, noble-like, looking like one of those Greek statues pictured in Miss Kirby's books. And his skin wasn't pockmarked or craggy, it was smooth and a glowing light brown, not the mahogany wood colour usually found among the other barge folk on the canal.

'But 'e's not from round here,' Lissie added.

'Could be from one o' the ports on the coast,' Miriam conceded.

'Why don't you ask your brother about him?' Lissie suggested. 'He'll know. He knows all the horsemen on the canal.'

'No fear! My dad would skin me alive if he found out I'd been asking about one o' the bargemen.'

'We were only watching from the bridge. That's not doing any harm, is it?'

'You don't know my dad. He thinks all men are the same and he's not soft like yours.'

'My dad's not soft,' Lissie protested.

'He is – he's daft with you anyway. 'E thinks the sun shines out o' your backside.'

'Well 'e's me dad, isn't he?'

'That's all you know,' Miriam said archly.

'What d'you mean by that?'

Unusually for Miriam, she didn't snap back at her with a smarting reply. Instead, she took her eyes off the fly boat stern receding into the distance and turned round to face Lissie. 'They 'aven't told you, 'ave they?'

'Told me what? What are you going on about?'

'Not for me to say.'

Lissie stepped closer to her so-called friend. Although she was two years younger, she was as tall as Miriam now, though not as heavily built, because Miriam was buxom like her mam and at fifteen already looked like she was a proper woman.

Lissie was 'filling out nicely' as Miriam's dad had commented that morning, but her body was fine-boned and slender, so her budding breasts and rounding bottom were more noticeable. But although the heavy house-work she did for her mam after school had made her

strong, Lissie knew there were other ways to influence
her lazy friend.

'You'd better tell me, or else.'

'Or else what?' Miriam laughed.

'Or else I shan't help you with the little 'uns at school
and you'll have to do it all on your own.'

'Oh, Lissie, you wouldn't! You know I'm no good
with the little 'uns wi'out you.'

'Only because you're bone idle, Miriam Jackson! I've
showed you what you can do and you just can't be bothered.'

'Well, you do it better than me.'

'Why don't you tell Miss Kirby that then, and we can
do different jobs for a change?'

'Oh, I'd be even worse in the kitchen and I hate
cooking even more than I hate the little 'uns!'

'So tell me what you meant and I'll keep on helping
you,' Lissie answered sharply.

'All right, all right.' Miriam looked uncomfortable.

'Go on then, tell.'

'It's nothing. Well, everyone knows anyway. And you've
only got to look at you to see—'

'See what?' There was a threatening tone in Lissie's
voice. 'Tell me or I'll give you a Chinese burn again!'

Quickly Miriam said, 'Everybody says the gypsies left
you on your mam and dad's doorstep.'

Lissie dropped her jaw, astounded. 'What?'

'You heard.'

'It's not true. I don't believe you.'

'Look in the glass, Lissie, at that black hair o' yours.'

Lissie knew her mam didn't like her black hair. It

was thick and glossy whereas Mam's was sparse and mousy-looking. Mam often called her a little gypsy when she was cross. She didn't look anything like her mam, either. Her mam had thin lips and a bump in her nose. Lissie was already taller than her mam, and Mam had really little hands and feet. Lissie's fingers were long and she was always needing new boots for her growing feet.

She shook her head, confused and angry. She was Lissie Dearne from Mexton Lock and nobody could say otherwise. 'I'm not a gypsy,' she protested. 'I'm not! I . . . I . . . I haven't got black eyes, have I? Or dark skin?'

Miriam shrugged. It was the only thing about Lissie that she envied. That delicate, pale complexion and those large, almond-shaped, smoky-green eyes were lovely by anybody's standards. Not that she'd ever tell her that. She grimaced and muttered, 'Maybe only half gypsy then.'

Maybe she could be, Lissie thought. Maybe her mam wasn't her real mam and her real mam had been a gypsy. That would explain why her mam never liked her. But Miriam had been talking about her dad. Her dad was her real dad. He had to be! She was his little darling, not his little gypsy. She wondered if she dared ask him about it. She thought not. Dad didn't hold with her asking questions like that. 'Be seen and not heard', was his usual reply.

Lissie looked silently at Miriam trying to be superior and putting her down all the time. It was all right for her, she was the spit of her mam and with her dad's hazel eyes. Everybody said so. Her two big brothers were just like their dad as well, though Peter, the youngest,

was different. It was all very confusing! Even Miss Kirby
and her brother had the same nose! And what a conk
that was! It was just the same as the ones in the oil paintings on their stairway.

Lissie put her hand over her nose. It didn't have a
bump and it was a lot smaller than her dad's nose. Well,
she thought, you couldn't expect a girl to look like her
dad anyway, could you?

She stated firmly, 'My dad is my dad and don't you
say no different!'

'Suit yourself,' Miriam sneered. 'But you'd better learn
summat more than a Chinese burn trick, because that
won't save you when the gypsies come and get you. You
want to watch your back, Lissie Dearne.'

This alarmed Lissie. If her mam wasn't her real mam,
what if her real mam came back for her? She shrugged
bravely and moved on from the bridge, saying, 'Gypsies
don't come out this way. They camp near the towns
where they can get tinkering work and sell their pegs
in the streets. They couldn't have left me on the step, so
there!' She was pleased with this and it seemed to quieten
Miriam. Anyroad, she thought, even if Mam was not her
real mam, her dad was definitely her dad and he loved
her.

They watched the waves washing at the canal bank
subside as the fly boat disappeared out of sight, but not
out of Miriam's mind. She soon forgot her taunting game
with Lissie in favour of a new interest in her life. 'That
fly boat rider was 'andsome though, wasn't he? Don't
you think so, Lissie?'

'Yes he was,' Lissie agreed. 'Very.'

She saw Miriam's head turn quickly to look at her. 'Well don't you go getting no ideas about him, Lissie Dearne, because I saw 'im first.'

No, you didn't, Lissie thought, but wisely kept silent.

'And anyway,' Miriam continued, 'you're not old enough yet.'

'Old enough for what?'

'Y'know. Courting. And getting wed.'

'I'm nearly fourteen!' Lissie protested. 'Eliza at the farm was wed at twelve!'

'On'y 'cos the farmer wanted a good dairymaid that didn't cost 'im owt.'

'Who told you that?'

'It's what me mam says. And she says fifteen is plenty soon enough for having babbies.'

When Lissie didn't reply, Miriam explained, 'You 'ave babbies when you get wed.'

'You don't allus have to have babbies. My mam on'y had me.'

'Aye, well, everybody knows about her. Sometimes it's like that. 'As yer mam told you about kissing yet?'

'Kissing? No, why should she?'

''Cos if you let a lad kiss you, you have a babby, that's why!'

'Don't be daft. Your dad is always kissing girls at the inn.'

'You watch your tongue, Lissie Dearne, or I'll thump you one.'

'Well, I've seen him do it! And they don't always have babbies.'

'That's different. I'm talking about the lads on the

canal. He kisses you and then he sticks 'is thing in you and then you 'ave a babby.'

'His thing?'

'You know – his thing.'

'What thing?'

'Oh, you know,' Miriam replied irritably. Then she paused. 'Well p'r'aps you don't 'cos you 'an't got any brothers like me. Miss Kirby's got a book about it. She keeps it in her top cupboard. I'll show you when we get to school, it's got long words in it and weird drawings and everything. You're good at reading so you can tell me what it says.'

'Why don't you just ask your mam?'

'She says I'll find out when I get wed. That's when you do it.'

'Do what?'

'Y'know. Like when we 'ave the stallion to the mares in the stable.'

'Oh, that.' Lissie blushed. If she accidentally caught sight of any of the animals coupling, her dad dragged her away and told her not to look. Maybe she would get down that book Miriam had seen and find out more.

From that day, Miriam was always anxious to get down to the towpath quickly after school, hoping to catch sight of the fly boat on its way downstream back to Thorne. Lissie was more wary. She remembered the night of the fight with her dad and thought that the lad might be a bad lot like his dad. But he was handsome all right, tall and straight-backed with muscled thighs you could see outlined through his riding breeches.

On one such day, a fine summer afternoon, there was

a bit of a commotion by the bridge and both girls gath-ered up their long skirts and broke into a run to see what was going on. The horse reins were slack and the fly boat was floating idly on the water. Two men were on the bankside, their attention taken up completely by their horse.

'What's up?' demanded Miriam as soon as they were close enough to be heard.

The elder of the two men looked up. 'Mind your own business,' he snapped, 'and clear off.'

Lissie hung back. The foreigner was there, half-hidden by the front of the horse as he examined one of its hooves. She heard his voice as he called to his mate.

'It's no good. He's lost a shoe. I'll have to walk him on to the smithy at Mexton Lock. It's not far.'

His mate replied, 'You get off then. I'll wake the others and we'll tow the boat after you.'

Miriam stepped forward importantly. 'My brother's the smithy at Mexton.'

'I told you two to clear off,' the older man growled.

'Come on, Miriam, let's go,' Lissie begged, anxious to avoid any trouble.

The foreigner straightened, patting the horse's neck and whispering soothing words to him. Then he said to Miriam, 'Walk with me, if you like.' He gave her a wide smile and Miriam immediately swayed up to him and replied, 'I don't mind if I do.'

Then he looked past her to Lissie and added, 'And your friend? Will you walk with me too?'

Lissie hesitated. He hadn't seen her at all on the night of the fight so he didn't even know she existed, but at the same time her dad had told her not to talk to the bargemen. 'I . . . I don't know,' she hesitated.

'Oh come on, Lissie,' Miriam whined. 'It's on our way 'ome, i'n't it?'

'I . . . we . . . don't know him,' she hedged.

The foreigner smiled again and, keeping hold of the reins, took a couple of steps towards her. 'My name's Blake. And yours is Lissie. We're all walking the same way so why don't we keep each other company?'

Blake? Yes, she remembered that. His other name was foreign though. I expect that's why he doesn't say it, she thought. But he certainly didn't sound like a bargeman. He sounded more like Miss Kirby's brother. More like the gentry.

'You can lead the horse if you want,' he offered.

Lissie nodded her thanks. He seemed respectable enough, but you couldn't be too careful with bargemen, her dad had said. 'All right,' she agreed, taking hold of the long reins. She threw them over her back so she could walk closer to the horse's head. He was a fine beast, well groomed and strong but not as big as some of the old cart horses that hauled barges on the canal. 'What's his name?' she asked.

'Atlas.'

Blake was walking a few yards behind and Miriam fell into step with him and said, 'That's a funny sort o' name for a horse. My other brother's the horse marine at Mexton and I 'a'n't heard o' that one before,' she said.

'Oh, Miriam, don't you know anything?' Lissie replied over her shoulder. 'Atlas holds up the sky on his shoulders. I've seen it in one of Miss Kirby's books.'

'Books! Huh, that's all you think about. Wait till you're *fifteen* like me. You won't be reading books all the time then.' She turned her smiling face to her handsome companion and fingered the curls of hair escaping from her bonnet. Then she made a show of lifting the hem of her skirts away from the ground so that Blake could see her shapely, stockinged leg above her dusty boots. 'How old are you, Blake?'

'Older than you, miss,' he replied gravely.

Miriam persisted. 'You can call me Miriam, if you like. Can I ride Atlas?'

'Miriam!' Lissie held her breath while she waited for his reply. That girl had the cheek of the devil!

'I don't think so. Not today,' Blake said.

'Ah, go on,' Lissie heard Miriam's wheedling voice. 'You can lift me on to his back.'

'I said no.'

Good, thought Lissie. Miriam should know better than to ask, when the horse had lost one of its shoes. 'You can come and help me lead, if you want,' she offered. But her friend wasn't really interested in the horse. She was only interested in Blake.

Lissie wondered why he worked the fly boats. It was clear to her that he belonged more with people like the Kirbys or even landed folk. Miriam pranced around and prattled on about the Navigator and her brothers, and how Miss Kirby had put her in charge of the little ones at school. Blake said very little in response. In fact he was so quiet that Lissie thought he had dropped back to the barge for some reason and turned her head to look.

She was surprised at how close he was walking behind her, and for a few seconds her smoky-green eyes met his. His eyes were blue, a bright clear blue like the sky in summer, and she recoiled at the intensity of his stare. He smiled at her, a friendly grin that showed a set of good teeth. Lissie thought, for a fleeting moment, that he was the most beautiful man she had ever seen in her short life.

'Are you tired yet?' he asked her. 'Shall I take over?'

'No, thank you. I can handle him. He's a quiet beast and no trouble at all.' Lissie reached up to pat his neck as Atlas plodded on down the towpath. Glancing over to her friend, she noticed Miriam scowling, no doubt because Blake's attention was diverted from her. She turned her concentration back to the horse, not wanting to upset Miriam too much by encouraging Blake, but it made no difference.

He drew level with her and nodded in the direction of Atlas. 'He is obviously very happy with you leading him. Do you like him?'

'Oh yes, I love all the canal boat horses. They're so big and strong, but gentle at the same time.' She thought for a moment. 'Actually, your fly boat horses aren't that big, are they? What are they like to ride?'

'They're not racehorses, that's for sure. But they're fast for their size, and they have amazing stamina. That's why we use them.'

Miriam was not going to be left out of a conversation about horses and caught up with them, interrupting shrilly, 'My brother says they're carriage horses really, and pure bred, and that the fly boat company won't use any others.'

'That's right. He's a good horse marine, your brother. One of the best. Do you want a turn leading the horse?'

'No, ta. The reins'll dirty my dress.'

'Well, you could run ahead and ask your brother to get the fire hot in his forge. We haven't got time to waste.'

Miriam seized her chance. 'Lissie, why don't you do that? You're better at running than me.'

'Your ma says we should never leave each other on our own.'

'I won't be on my own. I'll be with Blake.'

'And your dad says you haven't to talk to any bargemen, 'cept the ones he knows.'

Miriam became irritated. 'Well my brother knows him, doesn't he? 'Cos he shoes the horses. That's just the same and—'

'You're doing just fine as you are, Lissie,' Blake interrupted. 'Unless you'd rather run on ahead.'

'No, thank you. This is fun.' Lissie continued with her task and smiled to herself as she imagined the scowl returning to Miriam's face. Do her good not to get her own way for a change, she thought. If she had offered to lead the horse, Lissie might have gone on ahead as she'd suggested.

But then, maybe not. She was beginning to like this foreigner. She liked the way he spoke now he was fully grown up. She liked the way he presented himself. He was a proper gentleman and he knew how to handle Miriam and her manipulative ways.

Yes, Lissie thought, she really liked him now. Well, she would always like the way he looked when he was riding a horse. Commanding. Yes, that was it. As though he was in charge of everything and gave the orders. And close up he looked even better. He was obviously tough and strong, all the fly boat men were. But he was tall with it, not like the stocky, thickset miners from around Mexton. He had a kind of presence in the way he walked, like he was proud of who he was, even if he was a foreigner, and he'd challenge any man who crossed his path. Looking at him gave her an unusual kind of thrill that she had not experienced before in all her thirteen and a half years.

'That's settled then,' Blake concluded. 'We'll all walk Atlas together. It's not much further now anyway.'

When they arrived at the smithy Miriam's brother yelled at her to stay out of the way and get inside the inn to help her ma. Petulantly she did as she was bid, pushing Lissie ahead of her. Lissie's dad was away on the canals at the time and had been gone for more than a week now, so her mam would be at Rosa's cottage. At least she would be in a good mood when she arrived home later today, Lissie thought.

'Thank you kindly for your help,' Blake said with a gentlemanly bow before the two girls walked on. He watched them hurrying towards the Navigator Inn and disappear round the back. Perhaps Lissie lodged at the inn with Miriam's family? Nice girl, he thought. A pleasant, uncomplicated country girl with the finest green eyes he had ever seen. And black hair too. He had noticed how dark her hair was as it escaped from her white cotton bonnet to frame her pretty face.

She was a few years younger than he was but he

hoped he'd see her again. That was something to look forward to, he thought, as he held on to Atlas's head, whispering gently to him while the new shoe was hammered into his hoof.

Miriam, the older girl, was a saucy young madam, he thought. Too pushy for her own good. Nothing like her young friend Lissie. Lissie was going to be a cracking woman when she was grown a bit more. She was a beautiful girl now, and one that greatly interested him. Her manner intrigued him. With her sharp wit and a wisdom beyond her years, she would be a woman to be reckoned with, he thought. He wanted to know her better. And he would, he decided. He had not worked out how he could accomplish this aim yet, but such practical details never worried Blake Svenson. He would find a way.

The fly boat, hauled by its crew, arrived shortly afterwards and they were soon on their way down to Thorne and the Trent, leaving the South Riding behind them until the next trip. Blake took a lasting image with him, an image of a young girl, with black hair, alabaster skin and an arresting pair of almond-shaped, smoky-green eyes.

He felt a thrill rising in his loins as he thought of her and he wondered how long it would be before he saw her again. She was young still, and so was he. But how much time did he have? She could be wed to some miner by this time next year! He could not, would not, let that happen!

Yet he had unfinished business to complete first. Business that must be dealt with before he could let any girl into his life to distract and cloud his judgement.

Business that would keep him working on this waterway until he had finished it, and finished with Dearne. Blake grew restless with impatience. He was eager to move on, to set himself up in the South Riding and be part of it. He knew where Dearne lived even though he was often away. Silently, he vowed to find out where Dearne was working and confront him soon, so that he could get on with his life.

Chapter 14

Quickly and quietly Blake slid down from the horse's back, released it from the harness and led it through the open door of the livery stable.

The horse marine was already waiting with a fresh horse. 'Where's Thomas?' he asked.

'Taking the rudder for a change. My name's Blake.'

The horse marine held out his hand. 'Peter Jackson. Call me Pete.'

Blake shook his hand. 'Do you live here?'

Pete nodded and raised his eyes to look at the ceiling. 'I sleep up there, next to the hayloft. My father owns the inn and my brother's the blacksmith.'

Blake nodded and yawned. The hours before dawn were the worst for staying awake, but he had volunteered to ride this stretch so that he would be the one to change the horse at Mexton. 'Pleased to meet you at last,' he said, yawning again. 'I am usually sleeping as we pass here.'

Pete grinned. 'You'll get used to it. I'll walk your fresh horse up the towpath if you like. You'll soon be through – the lock's emptying already.'

'Thanks.' Blake stroked and slapped the horse's glossy coat as they walked. 'Nice beast. Does he have a name?'

'This one's Titan. He'll see you right on to town and they'll look after him well there. Are you from these parts?'

'Further up-country. You?'

'Father's had the inn here since I were a nipper.'

So, thought Blake, this was the stable lad who had helped him on the night his papa was shot. He was the son of the landlord at the Navigator. But he did not appear to be a surly rogue like his father. Pete obviously loved his horses and didn't like them ill-treated or starved.

He stayed silent as Pete walked with him and talked about his stables, leading the horse, apparently relaxed in the stillness of the cool night air. He was not anything like his father, Blake decided, and wondered how much he knew about Dearne.

The gushing water escaping through the sluices of the lock gates slowed as they reached the far end, and Blake asked, 'Do you know anybody by the name of Dearne around here?'

'Luther Dearne? Aye, I know him. He lives yon side in the woods. What do you want with him?'

'I heard he does a bit of dealing up and down the canal.'

'I'd stay away from him if I were you. He's a bad lot.'

'Do you know where he is now?' Blake persisted.

'No idea. I don't think I'd tell you if I did. He's an out and out rogue, that man, even though he is a mate of my father's.'

'So, he's not there now then.'

Pete shook his head. 'He used to go downstream to the Humber a lot, but he gave that up a while back. He had a bit o' trouble wi' 'is dealers down that way. Now he goes upstream Sheffield way, I believe. I allus know the minute he's back though, because he calls in at the school on his way home. My sister's there and he brings them bolt ends of cloth for the sewing.'

'Your sister, eh? Where is this school, Pete?'

'I'm not sure I should tell you that. All those young girls and you such a virile young man . . .' Pete was grinning but he changed the subject and asked, 'Are you riding or Thomas?'

'I am, but only to the next village. There's a dairy there where we generally pick up some fresh milk and butter for the boat. Then we swap crews and I get some sleep.'

'That sounds like Fordham. Not far then.'

'Is there anything interesting at Fordham?'

'Nowt really, just a farm, a chapel and a collection of houses. Nice ones though. A doctor lives in one . . .'

I know, thought Blake, I even know which house. You told me all those years ago and you don't remember.

'. . . and that's where the school is,' Pete went on with a smile. 'It's a dame school at t' far end. A cut from the Swinborough estate joins the canal just past there. It carries coal from Sir William's mines down to the main canal for his ironworks in town. There's an alehouse too.

Started with a brewer selling to bargemen from his back door—'

Blake interrupted him. 'Sir William, did you say? Would that be Sir William Swinborough?'

'The same. You heard of him?'

Blake nodded and Pete went on, 'He's got coal and iron right under his feet. So 'e's got money, plenty o' money – the lucky bugger.' Pete fitted the heavy neck collar around Titan's thick neck. 'Whoa, fella. Steady now.'

Between them they tightened up the harness and saddle. 'There, Blake, he's ready. Thomas is just opening the lock gates. I'll pick up the tow ropes if you like.' Pete returned quickly and fixed the twin ropes to Titan's harness. He gave Blake a leg up into the saddle and the horse a friendly slap on his rear. 'Away you go.'

'Thanks. See you on the way back?'

'Not me. One o' my brothers, mebbe. I've 'ad enough o' working fo' me dad around here. I'm off to some stables near Donny to groom racehorses for the track. No more heavy horses for me,' Pete grinned.

Blake saw the excitement in his eyes and felt elated for him. 'Good luck, Pete,' he said. 'You deserve the best and I hope good fortune comes your way.' He flexed his shoulders and took up the reins, thinking that Pete was right to move on. He didn't fit in with the thuggish ways of his father and brothers. But he had given Blake some vital information about Dearne. Dearne had moved his crooked trading from the coast to the towns, and he had a customer at Fordham.

He rode on. They were behind schedule on this trip. Their milk and butter were in the shade of the small bridge at Fordham, waiting to be exchanged for a coin. But the farmer had taken his cows back to the fields after morning milking and the village was quiet. Blake's mind was full of plans as the sun crept into the cloudy sky in the east behind him. He kept riding. He was past his tiredness now and his mind was racing.

The waterways of the South Riding were full of contrasts, cutting through rural farms one minute then passing pit heads and furnaces the next. Dawn mists from the meadows swirled and mixed with smoke from the factory chimneys. Drystone walling and hedges gave way to rows and rows of brick cottages that housed miners and ironworkers and their families.

There was a future here for him, he thought. Furnaces and forges excited him and he wanted to be part of it. He could live here. He could mine the coal, or smelt the iron or hone the tools. This was more exciting than loading notes and ships' manifests. This was his future. But a future that could only be his after he had dealt with Dearne. First he had to confront his father's murderer. Fordham was where he needed to be. He had to find a way to get there.

As the sun rose on his back, canal traffic thickened and slowed until the flyer was forced to idle downstream of Tinsley for the morning. Bargemen were gathered in small groups on the bank and word spread quickly of a breakdown up ahead. A winching crane had jammed the previous day and the wharf was thick with heavy barges waiting to unload. Blake moored the boat, fed Titan, then joined the others already slaking their thirsts at a nearby alehouse.

Thomas shoved a tankard in his direction. 'No point in waiting. That lot in front'll be all day an' we got fish on board. We got t' get the fish off to market.'

'Can't we get through at all?' asked Blake. 'We don't need winches to unload.'

'It's chaos down there today. I've bin talking to t' land-lord here and 'e's got us a couple o' carrier carts. We'll leave the boat 'ere and take what we can by road.'

'What about the return load?'

'I dunno what it is till we get to the Tinsley office.'

Thomas, a brawny ex-sailor with a wife and family back home in Hull, had already finished his ale. 'Blake, you come wi' me, lad, and you two tek t'other cart. Mek sure you tek plenty o' ice wi' t' fish. If we've got good 'osses we'll get it to market in time.'

Blake gulped down his tankard of ale and followed. After loading the carts, he took the reins of a pair of heavy draught horses.

'Want some o' this, lad?' Thomas offered him some tobacco to chew.

He shook his head. 'D'you know around these parts, Tom?'

'Aye, a bit. What you looking for?'

'I came to a fight here once. Big crowd.'

'Oh aye, they likes their fights round here.' He gave Blake a searching look. 'You done any fighting yerssen?'

'A bit. Sparring, mainly. For Dan Sanders.'

'I've 'eard of 'im. Negro, i'n't 'e? Used to t' be a prize fighter hissen.'

'That's him.' Blake paused. 'We went on to a – a country house after. You know, men only.'

'Whorehouse, you mean?'

'Yes, I suppose it was. For men of means though. You know, gentry and the like.'

'Did it have a name?'

'Grace's. They just called it Grace's.'

'Never 'eard of it. Ask in the office, it's not far now. Keep them 'osses going – we don't want t' sun on this fish.'

The wharf side was in as much chaos as the canal. Loads coming in by the new railway for shipping to the coast by barge were already queuing and they were turning away all smaller traffic until the following day.

Tom came out of the company office with a smile on his face. 'No payload until t' morrer. I'm back to the flyer to get some sleep. The rest on yer can do what yer like as long as y're back 'ere by six in t' morning.'

Blake set off to explore some old haunts. He hitched a lift on a carrier heading towards the fringe of town and from there walked to Grace's. The terrain became familiar and he recognised landmarks from his previous visit when he made an early morning exit with Sir William in his carriage.

He grinned, as he had done before, when he caught a glimpse of Swinborough Folly, a tall stone tower standing proud in the landscape, built to celebrate the defeat of Napoleon. It was not that long ago he'd been here, but it seemed a lifetime. He was just a schoolboy then, but now he was a working man.

There were not many factories out here and the houses were bigger. They were quite close together but some had tracks around them, leading to carriage houses. It was after lunch when he arrived at Grace's. The canvas bag slung over his shoulder was heavy and ice-cold water was dripping from it down his back. Grace's would be quiet, he reckoned, but somebody would be up and about. He whistled cheerily as he went round to the back door.

'Who are you? What d'you want?' A young girl, wearing an old work dress and grubby cotton smock, was carrying a bucket of ashes across the backyard.

'Urgent delivery for Grace. It won't keep. I've got to get it in some cold water.'

'There's a pump at the sink in the scullery.' The girl tossed her head in the direction of an open door.

Blake tipped the slippery fish out of his bag and into the deep stone sink. Some of the ice was still there under its calico wrapping. Huge chunks of it had been packed around the boxes in the hold of the flyer. It had stayed cold enough down there during the journey but under the hot sun it had melted fast.

The young girl returned with an empty bucket. 'Pooh! What's that when it's at 'ome?'

'Cod. Best fish in the sea. Ever tasted it?'

She shook her head and peered in the sink. 'Don't think so. Ugly, i'n't it?'

Blake began to pump fresh cold water over it. The sound of leather shoes on the flags behind him made him stop.

'What is going on in here? I heard a man's voice.'

'Clara?' He didn't have to look round. He remembered her soft husky tones.

'Yes. Who are you?'

He turned. She was wearing a light-grey print cotton dress and a white lace cap. Just as handsome as before, but in the light of day through the open doorway he was reminded sharply of the age gap between them.

'Blake? Blake!' she laughed. 'Yes, it is you, isn't it? Well, I don't believe my eyes! You're so much bigger, and broader – and – and – well, you're a full-grown man now, aren't you?'

He grinned. 'I am. I'd give you a hug but I'm a bit – er . . .'

Clara wrinkled her nose. 'Yes, you are. What is that smell?'

'This fellow.' He gestured towards the sink. 'It's a present for Grace. Is she well?'

Before Clara could reply, another, older voice interrupted. 'Yes she is, thank you. Quite well.' All three turned to see Grace who had joined them in the scullery. She was wearing a plain black silk afternoon dress that rustled as she moved. Her gnarled hands were covered by black lace mittens and she held a gold framed pince-nez that she used to peer into the sink.

'Is that a cod? A whole cod? I haven't seen a whole one o' those since . . .' Grace paused for a moment, remembering younger days on the east coast of Yorkshire when – well, it must be nigh on fifteen years ago – when little Lissie was born. 'Is it for us?'

'For you, ma'am,' Blake replied smartly.

'From whom?' she demanded.

'From me, of course.'

'And who, young man, are you?'

Clara exchanged glances with Blake and explained,

'He's a friend, Grace. He came to – er – see us with Sir William two years ago and – er – since then he's—'

'Do you mean he is a client?' Grace's voice had risen an octave. 'What is he doing in the scullery and why do I not know him, Clara? What has been going on?'

'Nothing, ma'am,' Blake broke in. 'Truly. I used to be at Grasse Fell school.'

Grace gave him a cold silent stare.

Clara added, 'He came to us with Sir William once. Just the once—'

'And Clara, well, Clara's was – is – we're just friends. Almost a sister to me, aren't you, Clara?' he added hastily.

'A sister, eh?' Grace examined Blake closely through her pince-nez. 'What is your name, sir?'

When Grace was satisfied he was telling her the truth, she thanked him, quite sincerely, for the cod and retreated to her upstairs parlour. Clara breathed a sigh of relief and took Blake's hand in hers.

'I warned you not to call. Grace doesn't allow gentlemen callers if they're not clients. She's very strict about it. But it is good to see you. I want to know everything you have been doing since you left Grasse Fell. Come into the kitchen, there's some game pie left over from luncheon.'

They sat at the corner of a large pinewood kitchen table and talked while the kitchen maid put on a clean apron and prepared tea for Grace's household. Blake told her about leaving school and starting on the fly boats. He also talked of his mama going to Sweden and that led to questions about his papa. So, after some hesitation on his part, and persuasion from Clara, he told her about the murder and the injustice of it all.

'You're very angry, aren't you?' Clara commented when he stopped talking to draw breath.

'Wouldn't you be?'

'Well yes, I would. But try not to let it eat at your heart so. You cannot bring him back and you have to put this search for vengeance behind you.'

'I cannot. Not until I have confronted Dearne and got the truth out of him.'

Grace's kitchen maid slid a tray across the table carrying tea to drink, sandwiches and scones. Clara poured the strong brown liquid into china cups with matching saucers. 'Do you know where he is?'

'Around here somewhere. Have you heard of a place called Fordham?'

'Of course. It's on the edge of Sir William's estates.'

'Who lives there?'

'I don't know exactly. There's a dairy farm and a chapel. The old doctor lives there and there's a dame school . . .'

'Do you know anything about the school?' Blake asked.

'The house belongs to an ironmaster who went bankrupt. Kirby Ironworks, if I remember rightly. He rented out some of his factory storerooms when the furnaces closed. His sister runs the school and he – er – he comes into town quite frequently.' Clara stopped talking abruptly.

Blake raised his eyebrows. 'I remember Kirby! From that night?'

Clara's face remained expressionless.

Realisation dawned on Blake and he laughed. 'No! Do you mean he comes here?'

'Regularly. Most afternoons. He has quite an appetite, I am told. He sits on the management board of the Mechanics Institute and he spends his mornings there.'

'The Institute? Where's that?'

'In town. It's very popular with all the furnace workers and forge masters round here. Sir William's a trustee of the Institute, I believe.'

An idea began to germinate in Blake's mind. An idea for his future. 'Clara, you're a wonderful woman and I love you,' he exclaimed.

'That's what they all say,' she replied with a grin and sat back to drink her tea. She watched him eating and drinking for a few minutes then asked, 'Have you found yourself a girl yet?'

Blake thought of Lissie and how she had often been in his mind since he met her on the towpath when the flyer's horse lost a shoe. 'Maybe,' he murmured.

'Only maybe? If it's only maybe, she's not the one—'

'She is!' he interrupted fiercely. Then added more calmly, 'She is young, that's all. I should wait until she's older.'

'Well, don't wait too long. If she's caught your eye, she will have others interested as well.'

'You're right, she will,' he realised. 'She is a real beauty and might not wait, and I have things to do first.'

They both heard the casement clock out in the front hall strike the hour and Clara stood up abruptly. 'So have I,' she exclaimed. 'I must go and help the others get ready.' She stood up to face him and added, 'Come and visit us again soon and do take good care of yourself, Blake.'

'Don't worry about me.' He grinned and kissed Clara's cheek. 'You make sure you keep yourself well. Grace too.'

She walked with him through the back door and round to the front of the house, then waved as he took his leave. He strode away, fortified by friendship and food, and planning the downfall of Luther Dearne, his courtship of Lissie and his future.

Chapter 15

'I've got a secret,' Miriam announced. She licked a finger and curled a strand of hair around it.

Lissie followed her along the path from the canal to school, swinging her bonnet by its tapes. It was summer and silky red poppies were blossoming in the surrounding cornfields. Lissie trailed her free hand through the long grass by the path and said, 'Knowing you, you won't have it for long. Are you going to tell us?'

'I can tell you — er — *part* of it,' Miriam decided.

'Go on then, tell. We'll be at school soon.'

'It's about Miss Kirby's. Of course, you know, I should have left school by now for a *po-sition*.' Miriam's emphasis made it sound very important.

Lissie shrugged. Miss Kirby did not want either of them to leave because they did all the work in the school-room while she was 'at home' in her drawing room or returning the visits. But pupils left all the time if they were needed in their own families or could get a job in service. 'So what?' she asked. 'Is that all?'

'Don't you want to know what's going to happen?'

Lissie resigned herself to Miriam's game. 'Are you leaving then?' she ventured. 'To help your mam and dad at the inn?'

'No, no, no! My mam and dad say they won't have me working at the inn. I've got to do something more befitting.'

'Befitting what?' Lissie asked.

'Just befitting,' explained Miriam. 'My dad's got money, you know, so I can do what I want.'

'What d'you mean, do what you want?'

'Well.' Miriam took a deep breath and launched into a speech. 'My mam says she doesn't want me to marry any of the lads from round here and that I'd be better off doing a ladylike kind of job until somebody suitable for me comes along. She doesn't want me to go back and work at the Navigator. She says I can do better than that, I can.'

'Get you, Miriam Jackson! You mean you're going into service!'

'Better than that and it costs a lot of money, Miss Kirby says! Your mam and dad 'as to be able to buy the stuff to make your dresses. You have to 'ave dresses for winter and summer, with collars and cuffs and caps to match. Three of everything, Miss Kirby says, one on, one in the wash and one ironed and waiting.'

Lissie was impressed. This sounded more exciting than blackleading coal grates and scrubbing cooking pots at the Navigator all day. 'What are you going to do then?' she asked.

'Can't tell you.'

'Don't you know?'

'I told you – it's a secret.'

'Well, where are you going then?' Lissie persisted.

'That's a secret an' all.'

Lissie kicked at loose stones on the dusty path. If Miriam left school she'd most likely have to go as well. Her dad had said as much to Mam the other night. Money was short and now she was nearly fourteen she'd have to start earning her keep. Most girls her age had been earning for two years or more. Oh, but she did like going to school. Not that she'd ever let Miriam Jackson know how she felt about it. 'Well I don't care,' she lied, with a shrug of her slender shoulders.

'Oh, you will when you hear. I'm fifteen now and I'm going to have a proper *po-sition*. You'll find out soon enough. I won't have to wear a pinafore or take a turn in the kitchen like you. And my mam says I can have a new gown for Sundays, after the harvest is in, Mam says.' Miriam looked sideways at Lissie and gave a smirk. 'Then you'll have to be nice to me all the time, Lissie Dearne.'

Only if you're nice back to me, Lissie thought. But she wondered what was going on. Her dad had already said that there was no more money for school and that they were lucky the railways were not built on this side of the Riding yet so he could still pick up a bit of work from the canal trade.

'Well, I don't suppose I'll be at Miss Kirby's much longer, either,' Lissie responded defiantly. 'I'll be leaving school an' all soon. My dad says it's time I went out to work, but my mam says she doesn't want me to go away because she likes me at home with her.'

'Well, my mam'll be wanting more help at the Navvy when I'm not at home. You can go and work there,' suggested Miriam. 'Come on, let's run. We're goin' t' be late!'

But Lissie didn't run. She jammed her bonnet down over the thick black braids coiled around her head and kicked the loose stones on the path angrily. It wasn't fair that she'd have to leave school. Miss Kirby was a mean old maid but she let Lissie read her books and always asked her to help with the accounting in the big ledger. A life of scrubbing pots and floors at the Navvy and living with her mam just didn't bear thinking about.

'I tell yer, trade's bad, Mickey.' Luther leaned on the counter at the Navigator and nursed his tankard of ale. 'If it's not them canal companies it's the railways tekking it all. There's not much left over for me these days.'

'Aye, well, that's not my fault and I can't do nowt about it.' Mickey's eyes hardened. 'You owe me, Luther, and I wants paying.'

'I 'a'n't got no money.'

'Well, you'll 'ave ter get some. I wants me dues. My Annie's got her heart set on some o' that fancy satin stuff for our Miriam's new Sunday doings.'

'That costs a lot, that does.'

'Aye, I know. Tell you what – you get me some of it and we'll call it quits. Decent stuff, mind. Fit for a lady.'

Luther considered Mickey's offer. It would be easy enough for him to filch a bolt end of calico. There was so much of it about that warehouse place, it would hardly be missed. But fancy stuff was different. He looked across the counter at Mickey's face, staring at him, hard like. Mickey had offered him a deal because they were mates. He'd be setting his lads on anybody else.

Luther took a swallow of his ale. 'I'll 'ave ter go over to Sheffield fer that.' He could go and see that widow woman he had met. She knew where the best stock from Manchester went and she did not mind a bit of knocked-off stuff for herself. This cheered him and he finished his tankard. 'You're on, Mickey.'

'See to it then,' Mickey growled, and added, 'Your Edie gunna stay away from 'ere while you're gone?'

'She bin mekking a nuisance of herssenn again?'

'Not right in the 'ead, if yer ask me. Allus round 'ere asking folk for gin. Our Annie 'ad to fetch that Rosa woman to tek her home last time.'

'I'll gi' 'er another belting. Don't seem to make no difference though.'

'You want ter try some o' that tincture from the 'pothecary. That'll calm 'er down.'

Luther thought about this and murmured, 'Aye. I might do that.'

He'd have to do something about Edie. He did not have the money to keep buying her gin these days. He relied on Lissie to cook him a dinner and keep the house straight. She was a good little lass, but she would have to start earning proper now. He did not want her working here at the Navvy. Not with Mickey and his lads around. Maybe he could get her a place in service? Edie would just have to put up with it if she did not like it. She spent most of her time with Rosa when he was gone anyway.

He had a good idea what they got up to in that smelly little cottage down by the wood mill, but did not really care any more. Edie did nothing for him now and he couldn't even rise to her in the bedchamber. He got all he wanted from that widow woman over Sheffield way. Bit of all right, she was. Knew what to do to him and enjoyed it as much as he did. The first time she'd sat on top of him in her bed and done all the work he nearly cried. All those years he'd wasted on Edie! He washed his hands of her. Rosa could have her for all he cared!

Lissie's school routine went on as usual for another month. When they arrived, Miriam, as Miss Kirby's oldest pupil, was asked to supervise the little ones for morning sewing. Lissie loved to look after the little ones because she liked showing them how to do different stitches, whereas Miriam simply prodded them with the blackboard pointer when they stopped to rest their little fingers.

But Miriam's news, when she thought about it, cheered Lissie. If Miriam was leaving to go into service, then Miss Kirby might ask her to take over! Oh, that would be lovely! She'd like nothing more than to be able to take over teaching the little ones, instead of being sent to help Hannah in the kitchen!

'Miriam,' whispered Lissie before they went into their groups, 'tell her you don't want to take the little 'uns today.'

'Why should I?'

'Because you don't! You haven't got any patience with them. And I have. You know I have.'

'That's where you're wrong,' replied Miriam smugly. 'I'm going to be taking them every day from now on.'

'What? You? Give over, you can't stand them.'

Miss Kirby interrupted their hurried conversation. 'What are you two girls whispering about?'

Miriam got in first. 'Nothing, Miss Kirby. Lissie was saying how much she will miss my help with her lessons. When I start my *po-sition*.'

Lissie gave Miriam a sharp kick under the desk as Miss Kirby smiled benignly at her eldest pupil and said, 'Yes, indeed, I'm sure *all* the older pupils will miss your help. But you are old enough now to move on and you are very fortunate that your father has seen fit to let you learn by my example. Most girls . . .' Miss Kirby gave her class a pitiful look '. . . most girls would have left home and been in service for several years by your age, so think Miriam, how lucky you are to be able to stay near to your dear mother and father and find an occupation here.'

'What!' Lissie's jaw dropped open and there were mutterings among other girls in the class.

'Silence!' Miss Kirby snapped the class to attention by striking a heavy book on her high teacher's desk. 'Your mothers and fathers already know this, so it is fitting that I tell you all now. The school will be expanding from Michaelmas. I shall be taking boarding pupils and Miriam will be my new pupil teacher for the younger ones. I, of course, shall continue to be in charge.'

'What?' Lissie repeated, flabbergasted and wondering

what would happen to her. Her dad couldn't afford to pay Miss Kirby for any more schooling, let alone any bond as a pupil teacher or anything else for that matter. So that was Miriam's secret! She was bound to be even more superior in her ways now, going on and on about her new *po-sition*.

'Lissie,' Miss Kirby snapped again, 'do stop saying "what". You heard perfectly well. Now, on your feet, girl. Hannah is not at all well today and she needs you in the kitchen. Take two of the others with you and start the broth for dinner.'

Lissie's heart sank. No one would want to work in the kitchen on a hot day like today and whoever she chose would be sullen and fractious. She thought quickly and, with one eye on the horsewhip, asked, 'Miss Kirby, can we fetch the vegetables in ourselves? Save old George's back a bit?'

The older woman levelled a glare at Lissie, who kept a lively enquiring expression on her face. 'Very well, Lissie. Tell George I sent you and ask him to chop some wood and bring more coals in for the kitchen fire. Now, who wants to help Lissie this morning?'

Six hands shot up which Miss Kirby ignored and instead she chose two who would have preferred to stay and sew.

Lissie fixed a blackened cauldron over the kitchen fire and set the bones to boil. Not much meat on them today. She'd have to crack them and get the marrow out to get any kind of nourishment into the broth. There was no sign of Hannah so Lissie put the flour and barm for the bread in a crock under a cloth by the hearth to

warm and found a couple of garden baskets for her
helpers.

The old man that Miss Kirby's brother kept to help
with their outside work was well past it now, she thought.
Time they got someone younger to do the garden.

In Miss Kirby's father's day they could afford their
own coach and four, as well as indoor and outdoor
servants. But George did everything now and he was
probably very glad of the home and few shillings that
Mr Kirby paid him to do the outside jobs and look after
the pony and trap.

His wife, Hannah, was as ancient as he was, and with
a back just as bent. She had to do all the work round
the house, including the cooking, and Miss Kirby never
volunteered any assistance. Mind, Lissie thought, it was
going to be different now, what with boarders and everything. It was going to be far too much work for old
Hannah.

The Kirbys had an outside pump for water, and a
trough big enough for the horses to drink. Lissie organised her helpers into washing the onions, potatoes and
carrots, then carrying fresh water into the kitchen. The
pump water was cold and crystal clear and she drank a
tankard of it while she kneaded the bread dough. Miss
Kirby came through to check up on them as she usually
did, but this time, instead of walking briskly around and
poking her nose into all the pots and pans, she sat in
one of the kitchen chairs and watched Lissie at work.

'Lissie.'

Lissie jumped. What now, she thought?

'Yes, Miss Kirby.'

'Has your father spoken to you?'

'What about, Miss Kirby?'

'A position, girl!' Miss Kirby sounded irritable and raised her voice, repeating, 'A position for you.'

'Oh that.' Lissie guessed that she'd have to leave, especially now that Miriam was starting as pupil teacher.

'Well?'

'He hasn't said for definite. But he told me he couldn't pay you any more. And I do like coming here, Miss Kirby.'

'Of course you do, child. Any girl of your background would be very grateful for the schooling that your father has provided for you.'

Miss Kirby paused and thought. Mr Dearne was a rough one to be sure. He didn't have access to the means that his friend Mr Jackson did, but he brought her good calico on a regular basis and for a knock-down price. Both the men were of dubious character though and she fervently hoped that her new boarders would come from better families.

But of the two men, she preferred Mr Dearne. She didn't like the way Mr Jackson looked at the older girls on the occasions when he called at her school. It sent a shiver right down her back. Nevertheless, he was prepared to pay for a bond for his daughter to learn to be a teacher, which meant less time in the classroom for herself.

Mr Dearne was not a man of means and he had driven a much harder bargain. But Lissie was by far the brightest and most hardworking of the two girls and Miss Kirby did not want to lose her. Mr Kirby was very pleased with his plans for the school expansion, but she was not very happy about all the extra work. Thank goodness she had been able to strike a deal for both girls.

She managed a smile at her young pupil and said, 'Well, now you are nearly fourteen and quite full grown, your father has decided you must leave school this summer.'

'Yes, Miss Kirby.' Lissie had thought this might happen. But she wished she could stay on like Miriam and learn how to teach the little ones.

Miss Kirby became agitated as she talked. 'I don't know what will become of us all, I'm sure.' Lissie resigned herself to a lecture as Miss Kirby went off on one of her rants. 'Taking boarders is Mr Kirby's idea. He says there are lots of these new tradespeople in the towns who want their boys and girls away from the manufactories. Can't say I blame them. The smoke and grime from the ironworks in these parts is too thick even to breathe. A bit of country air will be very good for their young girls.' Miss Kirby shook her head and sucked her teeth in disapproval. 'But these new railways will be everywhere before long, bringing more smoke and grime.'

Lissie hadn't seen any railways yet but she thought they sounded exciting and something to look forward to. The railways were making changes to trading all over the Riding, she'd heard her dad say, but they hadn't come as far as this side of town yet, and the Kirbys, like all the folk down at Mexton Lock, still relied on the canal and the turnpike for getting around.

Wisely, Lissie kept quiet about her views and

continued to pound the bread dough. The Kirbys had nothing to complain about, she thought. They had this big house and more money to spend than most folk round here. But Mr Kirby was known for being mean with his money and Lissie had heard them arguing earlier in the morning room, so she guessed it was about Miss Kirby's allowance and the new boarders. And, no doubt, about who was going to do all the work!

'So you see, Lissie,' Miss Kirby continued, 'I shall be turning the attics into dormitories for the extra pupils and it will be far too much work for my housekeeper.'

Housekeeper? Lissie thought. She meant Hannah of course, already bent double from a life of toiling for the Kirbys. Poor dear, how would she cope with an attic full of school pupils? Perhaps Miriam would be living in to keep an eye on them?

'I am taking on a maid of all work to help my house-keeper and,' Miss Kirby seemed quite proud of her next statement as she gave that simpering little smile she normally saved for other gentry like herself, 'and,' she continued, 'I shall have a laundry woman to come in once a month.'

No laundry maid job for me, then, thought Lissie, as she cut up her bread dough into even-sized lumps. That would have suited her, tucked away in the wash house out the back, away from Miss Kirby's prying eyes and her little horsewhip. She'd often been sent to help Hannah in the wash house.

'Of course,' Miss Kirby went on, 'I shall have plenty of pupils to keep the schoolroom clean and cook their food, but my dear brother and I shall need someone to

do the cooking and cleaning for us, as well as supervise
the pupils when they are doing their domestic training.'
Miss Kirby stopped talking, then added, 'Well?'

Lissie eyes widened. Well, what? She hadn't been
listening properly. What should she say in reply? She
repeated the word, adding a slightly incredulous note
and brief shrug.

Miss Kirby's eyes narrowed. 'Aren't you pleased, girl?
That your father has agreed to this? That you will be
that lucky girl?'

Lissie's jaw dropped in amazement. *She* was going to
be the Kirbys' maid of all work? Her! All she could think
of was that she wouldn't have to work at the Navvy and
have Miriam's dad and brothers leering at her scrubbing
the kitchen floor.

She said, 'Oh! Oh yes, Miss Kirby, I am very pleased.'

Fortunately Miss Kirby took the surprise in her voice
for delight. But Lissie wasn't surprised that Dad had
agreed to it, because he'd already told her she would
have to leave school. She was surprised that Miss Kirby
wanted her of all people. Miss Kirby always favoured
the girls who came from better-off families than she
did.

She continued shaping dough into bread cakes for the
oven and added in her most humble voice, 'Thank you,
Miss Kirby. Does that mean I shall be living here?'

'Yes it does. And you will do well to remember how
very fortunate you are that I have chosen *you* from all
my pupils. You have shown great promise in your
domestic ability, and Mr Kirby prefers your bread to
anyone else's.' She stood and put on her sternest glare.

'But you must learn to curb your tongue. And you will learn, Lissie. You will learn to curb that tongue of yours.'

Miss Kirby swished her horsewhip against the table leg to emphasise her point and continued, 'Your father will receive a remuneration for your services and he has promised to provide you with new boots. Board and lodging will be deducted from your wages, of course, and,' Miss Kirby hesitated as though she found the words hard to say, 'and I shall provide the stuff for your aprons and caps.'

Lissie suppressed a smile and kept her head down, pretending to concentrate on the bread cakes so Miss Kirby wouldn't see her mouth twitch. Good old Dad! He must have driven a really hard bargain with mean old Miss Kirby to get her to pay for the uniforms. Dad would know that the cheap calico cloth he brought her from town was sold at a profit to her pupils for their smocks and pinafores.

This news, and the realisation that she wouldn't have to live at home with Mam any more, or suffer her drunken tantrums and frequent clips round her ears, cheered Lissie. Of course she'd miss her dad. Though knowing him, he'd stop off to see her at Miss Kirby's every time he passed by on the canal.

She wondered what it would be like living here with the Kirbys all the time. It was a nice house, she thought, with big airy rooms at the front, and it had a lovely garden that grew scented roses in the summer. There was also a big vegetable patch with gooseberry bushes and an apple and pear orchard right at the bottom next to the coach house. Fordham was nice too. It wasn't rough like Mexton Lock and it had a chapel that everybody went to on a Sunday. She might not be a pupil teacher like Miriam, but this was definitely better than being at the Navvy.

Lissie remained composed as she made the last of the bread into a cottage loaf and pushed a floured finger down the middle to stick the small ball of dough on top of the big one. 'Thank you, Miss Kirby,' she repeated. 'When do you want me to start?'

'Why, right this minute, girl! My pupils will be off to help out on the farms soon and you have the attics to get ready as well as your uniforms to make. Mr Kirby has a man coming in to clear out the old storerooms at the back for a new schoolroom. There will be plenty of cleaning for you to do. Oh, and remember, from today you are no longer a pupil here. You are a servant in this house so you must address me as "ma'am" and Mr Kirby as "sir".'

'Yes, Miss K— I mean, yes, ma'am,' Lissie replied dutifully.

Miss Kirby gave her an approving look, adding, 'And of course, you will address Miriam as Miss Jackson in front of the pupils.'

Lissie groaned inwardly. Miriam would treat her like a servant now. Still, her friend had told her she wouldn't be starting as pupil teacher until Michaelmas and there was the rest of the summer between now and then. Her cheer was short-lived though as Miss Kirby added, 'Miss Jackson will be here after the harvest, helping me to get the new schoolroom ready.'

'Will she be moving in as well, then?'

'Er – er – well no, she will be lodging in the village. There is not enough space in the attics as you will be sleeping on the landing up there.'

'With the new pupils, ma'am?'

'From Michaelmas, yes. Hurry up with that bread. Then find yourself an old smock to wear because it's very dusty up there and you need to get a bed ready for yourself for tonight.'

'Tonight?'

'Of course tonight, girl. You have a position now. You father will bring your box tomorrow.'

And so Lissie did not go back into the schoolroom that day, but spent the afternoon scrubbing out the landing at the very top of the house and searching the dark cobwebby attics for something to sleep on. She found an old feather mattress stuffed into an even older wooden box and some pieces of rough woollen fabric for blankets. By the time it grew dark she was very grubby and very hungry, having missed her tea as no one thought to call her to come and eat. She crept down to the kitchen. No one was there and the house was quiet. The Kirbys were probably in the drawing room or their bedchambers and she had not seen Hannah all day.

She cleaned herself up under the outside pump making her dress very wet in the process and then tackled the pile of dirty pots and pans left, obviously for her, in the scullery sink. All the food had been locked away in the pantry except for a tin plate on the kitchen table with some bread and cheese.

Lissie scrubbed down the table and fetched herself a

tankard of fresh cool water from the pump to wash down her simple, but very welcome, meal. She found a stub of candle in the cupboard by the range and lit it from the dying fire with a taper.

She didn't like the attic landing. Isolated at the top of the narrow back stairs, she felt cut off from the rest of the house. There were draughts from the skylight over her head and scuffling noises of mice − or rats − from the closed doors to the attic rooms. But she cheered herself up by thinking of her dad who would be coming to see her the next day. Tired out from all the work, Lissie blew out the candle and was soon fast asleep in her makeshift bed.

Chapter 16

'Why don't you let me do that for you?' Lissie asked.

Hannah continued to cough – a cough that made Lissie grimace with distaste. Lissie took the heavy breakfast tray from her and put it back on the kitchen table. She led Hannah to a chair and sat her down, rubbing her bent old back. The coughing eased and was replaced by hoarse, wheezing breaths. Lissie measured a spoonful of doctor's linctus and tipped it down her throat.

'You sit there for a few minutes and I'll take Mr Kirby's tray in.'

Hannah did not protest as Lissie carried the kidneys and bacon, and freshly made coffee, down the passage to Miss Kirby's morning room. Her boots left footprints in the lime dust and Lissie looked forward to another day of washing floors. Raking ashes and cleaning fire grates was nothing compared with the muck in the new schoolroom from Mr Kirby's builder!

Mr Kirby was alone in the morning room. His sister

had decamped to stay with cousins as she could not abide the upset in her household. Before she left she had supervised Lissie as she covered all the furniture in her dining and drawing rooms at the front of the house. Then she had locked them up and departed. The only downstairs rooms in use were Mr Kirby's study and the morning room, apart from all the domestic offices and schoolrooms down the passage at the back.

'Where is Hannah?' Mr Kirby demanded. He was sitting at the small table reading a newspaper.

'Hannah is not at all well, sir,' Lissie explained as she finished serving his breakfast. 'It's the dust, sir. It makes her cough.'

It makes us all cough, she thought. It got everywhere and it was difficult to shift, leaving grey smears all over despite her scrubbing. Every day it floated up the back stairs to the attics that she was trying to clean up for the new pupils. And it made her hands so sore! She had taken to smearing lard on them at night and sleeping in old gloves.

He was watching her again. Lissie didn't dare look at Mr Kirby, but she knew he was. She felt his beady brown eyes on her every move and his stare made her nervous. She had thought at first her cap was skew-whiff or her apron had a mark on it. But he was always the same. Normally she didn't see much of him as she spent most of her time in the back rooms. She didn't go into the front rooms to clean until after he had left for town.

'Will that be all, sir?'

'Tell Hannah she must serve lunch. I do not want to see you in here again.'

'Sir.' She bobbed a curtsey and left.

Hannah had recovered from her coughing, but she was still sitting on the kitchen chair, with a vacant look in her rheumy old eyes.

'I'll do the cooking today,' Lissie volunteered. 'You just sit at the table and do the fruit and vegetables.'

While the builder was knocking down walls in the old stores, Mr Kirby stayed at home. But he never set foot in the kitchen. He spent the morning in his study or outside giving orders to his builder and to George.

Lissie raced around doing as much as she could of the cleaning and laid the table in the morning room for lunch. She placed the tureen of vegetable soup on a tray and said, 'Can you take this in, Hannah? Mr Kirby wants you to serve him, not me.'

Lissie held open the passage door for her then hurried to the scullery to make a start on the pots. She was heaving up a pitcher of hot water when she heard the crash. She dashed through to the passage and found Hannah sprawled on the flags, surrounded by broken china and a pool of steaming vegetable soup. Mr Kirby stood at the open door of the morning room.

'You clumsy woman! You will pay for the china out of your wages.' He glared at Lissie as though it was her fault. 'Fetch me some more soup.'

'I think she has fainted, sir,' Lissie said.

He stepped forward and peered down at the still form of his housekeeper.

'Find George,' he ordered, adding, 'Get my soup first.'

Lissie scurried away to change her apron and serve up more soup. She tried to make Hannah more comfortable with her shawl and some kitchen cloths, then went out for George who carried his wife down the garden to their bedroom over the stables.

Fortunately, summer pudding was Mr Kirby's favourite and he brightened when Lissie presented it to him. 'Is Hannah not recovered yet?' he asked.

'No, sir. George has put her to bed.'

'This is not good enough. My sister would soon have her to rights.'

Lissie bit her tongue to prevent herself shouting at him that Hannah was very old and very poorly and did he want to work her to death? She was resigned to thinking that, yes, he probably did.

'I have no instructions for supper, sir.'

Mr Kirby tutted and shook his head. 'Really, I should not have to speak to a kitchen maid,' he answered irritably. 'I shall dine at the Manse tonight.'

Lissie cleaned up the passage and washed the cooking pots and china, then cleared and cleaned the morning room and Mr Kirby's study and bedchamber, emptied his chamber pot and swept down the stairs, scrubbed the front steps and polished the brass doorknocker, emptied the ashes from the kitchen range and scrubbed the kitchen table and floor, then thought about tea for George and Hannah – and herself.

She prepared beef tea with toasted bread for Hannah, and cold cuts and pickles for George. Exhausted and thirsty, she quaffed a tankard of ale left over from lunch and immediately felt better. More lime dust was beginning to settle as she heard the builder stop his bashing at the old brick walls and go home.

She felt sticky, dirty and tired. After George had taken their tea to the coach house, she was alone in the house. So she banked up the kitchen fire, shifted the damper to heat water in the side boiler and took down the tin bath in the scullery.

It was bliss, sheer bliss! She wallowed in hot water scented with refreshing sprigs of rosemary and washed herself with her own soft soap that she had made over the kitchen fire. Her dusty dress had had a beating on the line outside and her chemise, bodice and drawers were rinsed out and pegged alongside it.

She poured another jug of water over her head and began to pull a comb through her long black hair. It was dark in the windowless scullery and dusk had closed in while she bathed. She began to hum a tune to herself and sing the words of hymns that she knew.

As the water cooled she climbed out and reached for a square of linen to dry herself. A sharp intake of breath caused a soft scream in her throat. Mr Kirby was standing in the doorway to the kitchen.

'Sir!' She held the linen cloth in front of her.

He was finely dressed in evening clothes with a starched white shirt and a silk tie around his neck. He had a silver hip flask in his gloved hand and he tipped it to his lips.

'Sir?'

'Carry on.' He waved the hip flask in her direction, took another swig and swayed against the door jamb.

'I shall not, sir. You will be good enough to leave.'

He gave a low laugh. 'Wilful little trollop, aren't you? I said carry on.'

'No.'

He strolled towards her and snatched away the cloth. She slouched forward to cover herself with her hands and arms.

'Stand up straight when I'm talking to you!'

Reluctantly, she dropped her arms to her sides and straightened her back and shoulders. She stood stock still, tense and frightened, an ivory statue lit by a rising moon coming through the kitchen windows and doorway.

He walked all around her, inspecting her as he used to when she was a pupil. He was very close to her and she could hear his heavy laboured breathing and smell strong drink on his breath. He stood behind her and leaned forward to whisper in her ear. She felt his suiting brush against her damp skin.

'Harlot,' he whispered.

She heard him take another drink and then felt a gloved finger trail over her bottom and around her waist to the soft swell of her young breasts. As he circled each breast in turn she winced and tried to think of a way out. Duck and run up to the attic? No, there were no locks on the attic doors. Down the garden to the coach house? Yes, she would be safer with George and Hannah. But she had no clothes or boots to hand. Perhaps she would have time to drag them off the line before he caught up with her? Perhaps not, she realised.

'Harlot,' he repeated. He pushed one of her breasts upwards with his hand.

Evil man, she thought, he had no shame. She said, 'I'm sure Miss Kirby would not want to know of this.'

He stopped and removed his hand abruptly. 'And who would believe a cheap little slut from Mexton Lock?'

But he must have thought better of his actions for he hit her sharply across the face, just once, and barked, 'You will not speak of this.' She fell sideways against the stone sink and when she had recovered he was gone. She heard him shouting at George to harness the pony and trap as he was going into town.

'Well now, Lissie,' Miss Kirby said, in the New Year. 'You are fourteen and quite a grown woman. How would you like to be my housekeeper?' She did not wait for, or expect, an answer, and went on, 'I shall hold the keys to the pantries and as soon as Mr Kirby has left for town each morning you will give me your list for the day.'

Considering she had been doing the work of house-keeper since Hannah collapsed last summer, Lissie thought she would like the position very much. Hannah had died before Michaelmas and Lissie had coped single-handed until the pupils returned from the harvest. Now she had as many willing helpers as she needed and those that cared for domestic work took to Lissie easily.

The folk in Fordham had done well this year because the harvest was good. But Lissie knew that her dad had hardly done any work this winter and her mam couldn't get out of bed without her gin, so money was still short down at Mexton. She considered Miss Kirby's offer silently.

'Well? Have you nothing to say?' Miss Kirby demanded.

'Er – Miss Kirby, ma'am. Will I be getting more pay?' Lissie asked. There. She had said it.

Miss Kirby frowned at her angrily. 'It is not your place to ask for such things.'

Lissie kept a bright smile on her lips and responded quickly, 'What did my father say when you discussed it with him?' Dad had not said anything to her about this last time he visited.

Miss Kirby shuddered. The idea of *discussing* anything with that dreadful ruffian from Mexton Lock made her skin crawl. 'Oh, you are such a tiresome girl,' she muttered.

Lissie drove home her point. 'I am only paid as a kitchen maid, ma'am.' And, she thought, You've been getting a housekeeper on the cheap for nearly half a year. I deserve more wages and my dad needs the money at home.

Lissie was worried about home. Her mam didn't do anything to look after Dad and spent most of her day sleeping off the drink, or whining at Dad to get her more of her gin. Dad had started taking her a tincture instead. It calmed her down, he said, and the apothecary in town had said that a lot of women took it.

Lissie only saw her on her half-day, which was one Sunday afternoon a month. But she thought better of asking Miss Kirby for more time off as well. This was a good position and she needed it.

The only regular money going into home was her wage. Miss Kirby paid it quarterly to Dad, but it never lasted the quarter and, if he didn't get any work, there was nothing else when it had gone. At least this position gave Lissie food and shelter and a supply of calico to make her drawers!

Miss Kirby tutted and muttered indecisively until she said, 'Well, I suppose you do the domestic training for my pupils too.' She heaved a sigh and finished, 'I . . . I shall talk to your father next time he visits. Now put on your bonnet, it is time for chapel. Have you laid out the sherry wine in my morning room?'

'Yes, ma'am.'

She added water to the stew for the pupils and checked on the joint of beef for Miss Kirby and her brother. It was roasting on an iron grid in the big oven by the fire, with a dish of potatoes underneath to bake in the drippings.

'Come on, Lissie,' Miriam called from the passage. 'We're waiting for you.'

She grabbed her wool shawl and filed out with the pupils, following Miss Kirby and her brother to the chapel. Lissie avoided Mr Kirby these days and when they did come face to face he gazed straight through her as if she did not exist.

No one from Mexton Lock ever went to chapel but Fordham folk gathered there on a Sunday. The Kirbys sat in the front pew with the old doctor and two local farmers. Other families sat together behind them. Miriam and Lissie with Miss Kirby's boarding pupils in their clean caps and pinnies were at the back.

'I see the alehouse keeper and his wife are not here again,' Miriam smirked.

'And a few of the farm labourers, keeping him company in the tap room,' Lissie giggled. 'Oh good, here's Eliza. Move up so she can sit by me.

'Where's Job?' Lissie whispered to Eliza.

'One of his cows is off-colour, so he's stayed with her. He's not fond of chapel anyroad.'

'Shame,' Lissie responded, disappointed. 'We'll miss him singing.'

'We can make up for him, can't we?' Eliza smiled.

The three girls and dozen pupils sang their hymns gustily. The louder the organ played, the louder they sang. Miss Kirby looked round once at them and Lissie beamed back at her. Her pupils were enjoying the freedom and Miriam was there to shush them up during prayers.

'What's he going on about?' Eliza whispered once the sermon had started.

'Search me!' Lissie answered. 'But I like watching him, don't you?'

Eliza nodded and grinned. The preacher became red in the face, waved his arms around and his voice rose to a crescendo. Lissie recognised his Bible references but was lost when he alluded to goings-on nowadays. It was interesting to watch, though, especially when she noticed the back of Mr Kirby's neck go red.

Lissie was flattered that Eliza had made a friend of her. Eliza was eighteen and married to a dairyman with his own land and herd. He was a lot older than she was but they rubbed along well enough, as far as Lissie could make out. Eliza was well known as the best dairymaid in this part of the Riding. Her butter tasted better than any that came from the market in town.

After the service they spilled out into the chilly damp graveyard that surrounded the chapel building.

'I wish we had more time to chat,' Eliza said.

'Me too. But you know what Miss Kirby's like. No slacking!'

Eliza giggled. 'My Job has just arranged to supply your school with butter and cheese. And fresh milk, if you collect it.'

'Ooh, that'll be nice.'

'I'll put a pailful aside from the morning milking. What time do you get up?'

'Oh, early. I have to get the range going for hot water and for cooking breakfast.'

'Come down while it's drawing. There'll be nobody about then and we can have a chinwag.'

'You're on!'

Early morning was Lissie's favourite time of day. As winter receded and streaks of dawn lit the bridge and canal, she watched the countryside emerge from its hibernation. She carried the empty pail down to Eliza's dairy just in time to see Job herding his cows over the little bridge to taste the first juicy grass of spring. Eliza met her on the bridge with two tankards of rich, creamy milk, still warm from the cow.

A tandem of narrow boats laden with coal came down the private Swinborough cut and glided into the main navigation. They were hauled by a yoked pair of carthorses that plodded diligently on towards the ironworks in town.

Lissie looked back down the canal towards Mexton. 'I think the flyers have started up again,' she commented. 'There's one coming up fast now.'

'Well, he'll 'ave to look out, the coal's not straightened up yet.'

Lissie's heart began to thump as the flyer approached. The horse rider was a man she didn't recognise, dark skinned and swarthy-looking. The helmsman, too, was unfamiliar. She wondered if Blake was still working on this flyer and imagined, if he was, that he was sleeping below, his eyes closed and his floppy fair hair tangled.

His features were still vivid in her mind and she thought how much she would like to see him again. She hoped the coal barges would get stuck on the turn and slow down the flyer. But they didn't and the flyer was soon on its way and overtaking the slower tandem.

'Come on, Lissie,' Eliza reminded her. 'Time to get back to work.'

The following week there was an unseasonable warm spell of weather that caused early morning mist to rise from the fields by the canal.

'Shall we walk a little this morning?' Eliza suggested when Lissie called for the milk.

'I like sitting on the bridge,' Lissie responded, and thought, I might see the flyer again.

Eliza put her head on one side. 'All right then.'

They sat on the low stone wall in silence while they drank their milk.

'Here it comes,' Eliza said suddenly.

'What?'

'The flyer, of course. What else are we here for?'

Lissie twisted her head. Her heart turned over. The rider was approaching fast and she realised, with a start that, this time, she recognised him. She stood up, flustered. The rider slowed down to go under the bridge and stopped altogether when the barge was past them.

Blake swung down from the saddle, fixed a nose can on his horse, and called to Thomas at the helm who passed him a tin jug, a plate and a coin.

Lissie stood rooted to the spot on the bridge.

Eliza commented. 'It looks as though they want something. I hope it's a regular order like last year.'

Blake sprinted down the towpath and on to the bridge. He gave them both a smile and a short bow and Lissie felt a strange nervousness course through her veins.

'A fine morning, ladies,' he said, handing over the containers to Eliza. 'A quart of milk, if you please, and some butter.'

Eliza took the utensils and money and went off in the direction of her dairy. 'I won't be long,' she called to Lissie. 'Wait for me.'

He turned to Lissie. 'Well, this is a pleasant turn of events. How are you?'

Momentarily tongue-tied, she acknowledged him with a brief nod of her head. It must be nigh on a year since she saw him last. He looked tired. There were dark shadows under his eyes and his face appeared strained. He wore riding boots that came up to his knees and they were worn and scuffed and dusty. As were his mole-skin breeches and dark riding jacket.

But she still thought he was the tallest, strongest, handsomest man that she had ever seen. He took off his jacket and flexed his neck and shoulders. If anything, his shoulders were broader than she remembered. His forearms, visible below rolled up shirtsleeves, were tanned and sinewy and his hands looked strong and capable.

She found her voice eventually, but 'I am very well,

thank you' was all that she could think of to say. After a brief silence she added, 'And you, are you well?'

'In excellent health, I am pleased to say, Lissie.'

He remembered my name! With an inner thrill, she thought: He remembered my name, and gave him a small smile.

Blake suddenly felt weak all over. He put it down to a hard night's riding. But he thought, She is so lovely, I want to hold her and kiss her and . . . He felt a stirring in his loins and pulled himself together quickly, trying to control this most basic of instincts that he felt for her at that moment.

Lissie marvelled at how white his teeth looked against his tanned skin. He had a good growth of beard around his chin, she noticed. It gave him an untidy, ravaged appearance that she found surprisingly attractive. She was aware of a new sensation, a kind of yearning that she felt low down in her stomach. She tensed to make it go away.

After a pause, he added, 'Canal life suits me.' He continued to gaze at her, taking in her increased height and developed figure. Under her dark shawl she wore a plain grey cotton dress with lace edged collar and cuffs. Most of her full skirt was covered by a starched white apron and her beautiful black hair was tucked away out of sight under a white mob cap. He saw a clean, fresh and very lovely young woman with alabaster skin and wide green eyes, and he coveted what he saw.

'Shall we walk awhile?' he suggested, gesturing to the footpath by the field. 'Tell me what you have been doing this past year.'

Lissie hesitated for a moment. He began to loosen his neckerchief and undo a few of his shirt buttons to wipe away the sweat from his throat. She was mesmerised by these movements and the glimpse of his chest beneath his clothes. A small amount of springy hair, darkened and dampened by sweat, appeared and then disappeared as he re-buttoned his shirt.

When she didn't move he raised his eyebrows and asked, 'Shall we sit then? Are you working at the dairy?'

She shook her head. 'Oh no. I just came down for the morning milk.'

He sat on the wall, stretched out his long legs and yawned. 'Well, I'm just finishing my night's riding, so I don't mind if we sit. Will you not join me?'

Lissie felt the odd stirring in her nether parts again. She wanted to move closer to him, to sit beside him, but her instinctive caution would not let her.

This man was a bargeman, on the elite flyers, yes, and he spoke well – like a gentleman – but he was still a bargeman and, therefore, one to be avoided. Yet at the same time he had this manly presence that thrilled and attracted her.

'I . . . er . . . I . . . yes, of course.' She backed away and sat on the opposite wall, facing him. Sitting primly upright, she straightened her long skirts around her, allowing her shawl to fall away from her shoulders.

Blake felt his heart begin to beat faster. He realised that she was totally unaware of how perfect she looked to him, and of how much he wanted to kiss her pretty mouth. Indeed he had been unaware of how strong these feelings were himself until now. He had conceded from their last meeting on the towpath that he was attracted to her, and convinced himself that it was her good nature and pleasant disposition that he liked.

But that was a whole year ago and she had grown into a handsome woman since then. As he sat there in the early morning light watching the mist burn off the surrounding meadows, he forgot what he was doing on that stretch of the canal. His mind filled with thoughts of the beautiful creature in front of him, who had been too young for his serious interest when he last saw her, and who had now blossomed into a fine young woman and was sitting just a few feet away from him.

He swallowed and took a breath. 'You have a position here?' he asked.

Lissie began to relax a little and nodded. 'At the school.' She sat up even straighter, and, proud of her new title, added, 'I am the housekeeper.' It was the first time she had described herself as such and she took pleasure in it, raising a smile and placing her hands, neatly clasped, on her lap.

It was her innocent pride that fired him and how he controlled himself at that moment he would never know. Blake had had a long arduous night on the canal and was all but dead on his feet. He had been doing most of the riding as they were missing one of their crew until they reached Tinsley. Yet he could have taken her in his arms and ravished her right there on the bridge, tired as he was. He managed to keep his voice steady and asked, 'Is the school far from here?'

Lissie nodded towards the main street. 'Oh no, not far. It's the big house at the end.'

'Do you like it there?'

'Oh yes, the pupils are always nice to me.'

'And so they should be! What is the name of this school of yours?'

'Oh it's not mine, it's Miss Kirby's . . .' Lissie stopped as she blushed and looked down, feeling foolish.

He was so – so strong, she thought, and his natural easiness was drawing her closer to him. She wanted to touch his face to see if it was real. Her heart began to beat in her throat and her stomach felt a little queasy.

Blake would have liked that moment to go on for ever. He had a desperate urge to take her in his arms and to love her with a passion. At eighteen, he thought of himself as a man. Lissie, he saw, was a woman now, no longer too young to court. And he wanted to claim her as his own, before any local miner or farmer's boy turned her head.

With a sudden nervous gesture, he took off his cap, ran his fingers through his damp sweaty hair and tried to stay rational. 'Ah yes,' he replied. 'I know Mr Kirby. He gives talks at the Institute in town.'

Lissie had seen him rake back his hair like that before and watching him do it again only served to remind her of those times. Down by the lock that night, at the fight between his dad and hers, riding by on the flyer and then during that walk along the towpath last year. He remembered her from the latter but she remembered them all. Who was he really? She took a deep breath to calm her churning stomach and said conversationally, 'Miss Kirby is his sister.'

'And do you help to teach the younger ones? I should

imagine you would be very good with them, very patient.'

Lissie thought again how much she would have liked to do that. But Miriam had been the lucky one there. 'Oh no,' she said. 'My friend Miriam does that. She is a pupil teacher now.'

Blake, desperately trying to retrieve his normal composure, picked up this line of conversation. 'That would be Miriam from the Navigator at Mexton Lock? Her brother, Peter, used to be the horse marine there . . .'

As he talked of Peter and the smithy at Mexton, Blake began to feel in control of himself again. Soon he would be free of company timetables and living properly in the South Riding. He was getting closer to Fordham, closer to the school and closer to that scoundrel Dearne.

He was near to catching up with him and then he could get on with his life. A life, he realised with some satisfaction, that would include this delightful young woman sitting sedately on a small stone bridge by an English meadow.

Lissie was aware that something in the conversation had changed his countenance and inwardly groaned. It was when she mentioned Miriam. Miriam! It was always Miriam! She seemed to have this effect on grown men. They were always interested in her and her coquettish ways. Even the preacher in chapel was taken in by her preening and twittering. And here was another one just like him!

Lissie sighed, gathered up the folds of her skirt and stood up. 'There's Eliza with the milk. The pupils will be wanting their breakfast.'

'No, wait! Don't go yet, Lissie. Stay and talk a little longer. Please?'

Lissie was shaking her head and muttering 'I can't, I have to get back' when a loud voice from the water interrupted them both.

'Hey! Blake! What a' you playing at there? Get back 'ere wi' that milk.' Thomas had mounted the horse and was ready to move on. 'You don't get paid to go courting, lad. You'll 'ave plenty o' time for that when we gets to Tinsley.'

Blake grimaced and got to his feet. 'It seems I cannot stay either. I must say goodbye for now, Lissie, but I'll look out for you as we pass. Shall you look out for me?' He raised an eyebrow in query before replacing his cap, turning towards the canal and calling, 'I hear you well enough, Thomas, I hear you.

'Until the next time we meet?' He gave her a friendly salute and hurried away, collecting the milk and butter from Eliza before sprinting back over the bridge.

'When will that be, I wonder,' Lissie whispered softly to herself, watching him stride down the towpath. He scrambled aboard and took the helm as Thomas urged the horse forward. She watched the flyer gliding slowly through the water, gathering speed until it disappeared from her sight, hidden by a curve in the bank and the bushes lining the fields.

'D'you want this milk for the school today or not?' Eliza called from the track.

Lissie jumped and turned round. 'Yes. Yes, thank you, Eliza. I was just enjoying the morning air.'

'Mmm, if you say so. I saw you from the dairy. Found yourself a sweetheart, have you?'

'No, I have not,' Lissie protested with a blush.

'Well, if you haven't, I reckon he has. Believe me, Lissie, that one has taken a bit of a fancy to you. You want to watch them bargeboys. They don't call 'em fly-by-nights for nothing. You'd better not let Miss Kirby see you wi' a follower or she'll have you out on your ear as soon as look at you.'

'We were only talking, Eliza,' Lissie said.

Eliza smiled knowingly. 'And I were only watching you,' she said archly.

Nonplussed by this reply, Lissie simply shrugged and picked up the heavy pail. 'Thanks for the milk, Eliza. See you tomorrow, then.'

Eliza grinned and shook her head as Lissie walked away. But Lissie was thinking, It wasn't me that he was interested in. It's never me. It's always Miriam where men are concerned. Lissie grew angry as she stomped back up the dirt road to Miss Kirby's. Miriam didn't deserve him! And he deserved better than Miriam! She was saucy and flighty with every man she met and Blake would be no different. Well, if he was taken in by her wily ways she could have him, and good luck to him!

Chapter 17

'Dad! Dad!' Lissie waved her cloth at him as he walked up the road with a package under his arm. It was after luncheon and she was washing the half-landing window that looked out over the front door. She finished the window quickly and hurried down to the kitchen.

'Come in, Dad. Oh, it is nice to see you.'

He was puffing and panting and immediately sat down to get his breath back. The kitchen chair creaked under his weight and he said, 'It's a bit of a pull up that hill for me now.'

'I'll get you some water,' Lissie volunteered.

''A'n't you got any ale, lass?'

Lissie went to the pantry and drew a jug of George's brew from the barrel. She poured them each a tankardful. 'What have you got there?'

He winked at her and unwrapped two or three layers of muslin to reveal the end of a bolt of cream-coloured silk.

Lissie fingered the fabric gently. 'Oh, that's beautiful, Dad. Where did you get it?'

He took another swig of ale. 'Well, Lissie, lass, there's this widder over Sheffield way and she's a right good seamstress—'

'Dad!'

'You don't mind, do you, lass? Me and yer mam, well, yo' know what she's like. She's gone from me now, and a man needs his comforts.'

Lissie had suspected that this was going on and sighed. 'I know, Dad. I wish I could get home more to help.'

'Nay, lass. You're better off 'ere. You've got a good carry on 'ere. Anyroad, this widder, like, she's got her own workshop, but no fella to look out for 'er, and she 'as some right good customers. Rich folk from the manu-factories, not wi' a lot o' land like round 'ere, but they live in big 'ouses all the same.'

Lissie was still fingering the silk. 'She gave you this?'

'I done a few jobs for 'er, round the 'ouse, like. It were left over from a bride's doings.'

'A trousseau?'

'Aye, that were it.'

'Ooh, Dad, it's lovely. Is some of it for me?'

Her dad grimaced and took some more ale. 'There's on'y a few yards left and I reckon Miss Kirby'll give me a good price for that, lass. I need the money for the . . . for yer mam's medicine, see.'

Lissie was disappointed but understood about the money. 'Miss Kirby's having one of her quiet rests in the drawing room. I'll tell her you're here when I take her tea in.'

'You 'a'n't got owt t' eat, 'ave yer, lass?'

Lissie cut him some bread and the end of a collar of bacon that she had boiled. She knew it was his favourite. She placed a jar of mustard pickle on the table and he helped himself, topping up his ale at the same time.

Later that day, after her dad had left with his profits, Lissie was sitting in the back garden shelling peas for supper when she heard the trap arrive and saw old George lumbering up the drive to see to the horse. Miss Kirby, flushed and excited, called Lissie into the kitchen.

'There will be three for supper tonight,' she said, inspecting the dinner already simmering on the hob. 'Put out the best table linen and make sure you have a clean apron. I shall need you to serve.'

'What's going on?' Miriam asked when she brought the pots back from the boarders' tea in the schoolroom.

'A guest. You will have to watch the pupils doing the washing up tonight. I'm busy.'

'There's no need to go all lah-de-dah on me just because you've been made up to housekeeper,' Miriam responded loftily.

'Oh, Miriam,' Lissie sighed, 'just watch that they don't break anything.'

Lissie tied a fresh, lace-trimmed apron over her grey afternoon dress and put on a matching cap. She took a tureen of pea soup to the dining room, where she left it on the mahogany table next to a cottage loaf. After standing back to satisfy herself that the silver and china settings looked their best, she went to the drawing room to announce supper.

Three heads turned towards her. She opened her

mouth to speak but nothing came out. He was here. Blake was here. In Miss Kirby's drawing room. His long, booted legs were stretched out across the hearth. His black coat looked new and he was wearing a neck tie, a proper neck tie, over a white shirt.

If he was surprised to see her he did not show it. Perhaps he wasn't, for he knew she was the housekeeper here. He sat there and smiled at her, making her knees go weak and shaky. They all waited for her to say something. She swallowed but still no sound came out.

'Yes? What is it, Lissie?' Miss Kirby said eventually.

She found her voice at last. 'Supper, ma'am. It's ready.'

Her hands were shaking as she dished up jugged hare, greens and carrots. She sat on a kitchen chair waiting for the dining-room bell. Blake! Here! He certainly looked different from when she had last seen him by the canal. In fact, he looked quite the gentleman in light-coloured breeches and polished leather riding boots. What was he doing here, of all places? She hoped fervently that he had not told Miss Kirby that he knew her, otherwise she would be in trouble.

She jumped when the little brass bell high on the kitchen wall jangled. Usually, Lissie removed the soup dishes, took in the meat course and went straight back to the kitchen. But when they had visitors, she stayed to serve, taking round the plates and then offering the vegetables.

As she approached Blake's chair, she thought she would drop the dish, her hands were shaking so much. Only when he had taken his vegetables did he turn his head and look directly at her. His face was expressionless apart from the eyes, which were like the clear blue sky on a summer day. His eyes smiled, briefly, at her, but that was all. She moved on to Miss Kirby and the gentlemen resumed their conversation.

Blake had been warned by Kirby not to talk about Sir William's parties. As far as his sister was concerned, they had met at the Institute.

'I tell you, Mr Kirby,' Blake said, 'the future is steel – carbon steel. It's more versatile for all manner of things.'

'Not as strong as iron though,' the older man pondered. 'It's no use for the railways.'

'No. I grant you that. It's a different metal for a different job. You can roll it thinner and make all manner of things that are lighter and cheaper to transport.'

Lissie shrank back against the wall behind him. His broad shoulders strained the seams of his jacket as he stretched to pass the breadboard to his host.

'Have you been in Yorkshire for long, Mr Svenson?' Miss Kirby asked.

'A few years now.' He hesitated. 'I was at Grasse Fell school.'

This information impressed Miss Kirby. 'Does your family come from the South Riding?' she asked.

'East Coast, ma'am. The Humber. My late father had business there.'

'Late father, eh?' Miss Kirby murmured. 'And your mother? Does she still live there?'

'She is in her home country at present.'

'Oh? Home country? Where—?'

'Sister, dear,' Mr Kirby interrupted. 'Do stop quizzing our guest like this. Why don't you tell us about your own little school?' Mr Kirby gave his sister one of his glares.

Miss Kirby took a deep breath. 'My school? Yes. I . . . I have two classes now, you know, and my own pupil teacher for the little ones. Her name is – er – Miss Jackson. You . . . you must meet her, Mr Svenson—'

'Sister,' Mr Kirby warned.

Miss Kirby blushed. 'Oh! Of course I did not mean to say – er – only that all my pupils adore her, and . . . and, well, brother dearest, she *is* one of the prettiest girls in the parish.'

Mr Kirby took over the conversation. 'Do you have brothers and sisters, Mr Svenson?'

Lissie quietly collected the empty dishes and returned to the haven of her kitchen. She sat at the table and stared at her gooseberry flummery for a long time. She had made little almond biscuits to go with the flummery and she arranged them prettily on a porcelain plate. An extra batch was finishing off in the oven.

Why was it that Miriam always cropped up in the conversation? she thought. Perhaps that's why he was here? To meet Miriam. Well, that wouldn't be tonight because she had already sent the pupils to bed and left for her lodgings in the village.

The bell went for pudding and Lissie carried it through. She tried not to look at him, and when she furtively glanced in his direction his eyes were firmly fixed on the tablecloth. She stacked the plates and tureens wondering how much longer he could pretend that he did not know her.

As she carried a pile of dishes out of the room, she

heard Blake raise his voice and say, 'This is really a very delicious meal, Miss Kirby. You have an excellent cook and I can see that I shall enjoy my stay here.'

His stay here? *Here?* Perhaps she had heard wrongly. Surely he was not *staying* here? The Kirbys entertained guests for supper quite often these days and occasionally, they did not go back to town until the following morning. Lissie kept the two spare bedrooms at the back clean and aired for just such occasions. But they didn't *stay*.

She tackled the pile of washing up in the scullery with vigour, only breaking off when the bell went for her to clear the pudding plates and add to the pile. Mr Kirby was pouring port and talking heatedly to Blake about the price of things. Miss Kirby had left for the drawing room, where Lissie had left a small pot of coffee and the best tiny china cups.

Lissie could go to bed when she had finished all the pots and pans, and put everything safely away. She took her biscuits out of the bottom oven and left them to cool on the freshly scrubbed kitchen table. It was a hot sticky evening and the airless scullery was stifling. The attic would be even hotter and stickier, so she wandered down to the orchard to cool off before going to her bed.

The orchard was her own private place after dark. No one else went there and she sat under the trees to enjoy the silence. She leaned against the fissured trunk of an old, gnarled pear tree and took off her boots and stockings to enjoy the cool fresh grass between her toes. It was a clear night, with bright stars and a half moon.

She thought that Blake would probably not mention to the Kirbys that he knew her or Miriam. His appearance was that of a young gentleman now, so, Lissie reckoned, he would not want the Kirbys to know that he had been working on the canals until recently.

The back of the house was now in darkness, except for a tiny yellow glow of a candle stub through the attic skylight. It was late. She would have to go inside soon.

Another yellow glow appeared in one of the back bedrooms, then it disappeared and reappeared a few minutes later in the kitchen. The door opened quietly and she glimpsed a white shirt in the darkness. It must be Blake. Mr Kirby did not come into the garden except to talk to George. And George had gone to his bed.

He strolled down the path to the horse trough and scooped up a handful of water that he threw over his face, spreading it through his hair and round the back of his neck with his fingers.

Lissie held her breath in case he heard her. Though why she was worried about that she did not know. She had as much reason to be out here as he had. He meandered along the rows of vegetables and fruit bushes and eventually sat down on a stone garden bench at the edge of the orchard. Lissie would have to walk by him to go back into the house.

Well, she couldn't stay here all night. As she scrambled to her feet her starched cotton petticoats and full skirts rustled in the quiet of the night. He turned his head to listen.

'Who's there?' he called.

She stayed silent, not sure what to do.

'Is that you, Lissie?'

Still she did not reply.

'Are you going to hide in the orchard all night? Why don't you come and sit by me? The honeysuckle smells particularly sweet in this corner of the garden.'

She walked slowly towards the stone bench, carrying her boots and stockings in her hand.

'Good evening,' he said politely. 'How are you?'

'I'm well, thank you. Are you?'

He murmured something in response and she stopped walking, keeping what she considered to be a safe distance from him. 'What are you doing here?' she asked.

'I'm trying to cool off. The house is very warm tonight.'

'I mean what are you doing staying here? What do you want?' she asked bluntly.

'I want you to come and sit by me. And to talk to me.'

'What about?'

'About you. Tell me, is Lissie your proper name?'

'Yes.'

'Lissie, short for . . . ?'

'Short for nothing. Just Lissie.'

He stood up and she took a step back.

He said, 'Look, I'll move to one end of the seat and you can have the other.' He sat down again. 'There. Is that far enough away for you?'

She sat on the bench and pushed her feet into her stockings.

'Mr Svenson—' she began.

'My name is Blake. You know that.'

'Miss Kirby would never allow me to call you that here.'

'Miss Kirby is probably fast asleep in bed by now.'

They sat in silence for a while, then Lissie asked, 'Have you given up the fly boats?'

'I have. I have been going to classes at the Institute in town. That is where I met Mr Kirby.'

'He often talks of the Institute. What is it, exactly?'

'A school. Like this one. Well, not quite like this one. It's for men to learn how to be engineers and manu-facturers.'

'How do you learn about that?'

'By reading books.'

'Oh, I love reading books. Miss Kirby lets me read all her books.'

'Do you like your position here?'

She thought for a few seconds and then replied frankly. 'Yes. But I wouldn't like it half so much without Miss Kirby's books to read.'

'What kind of books do you like?'

'Oh, all of them.' Her stockings were around her ankles and she wondered if, in the darkness, it would be all right to lift her skirt hem so that she could secure her garters. She decided not and folded her stockings over instead. Then she pushed her feet into her boots and stood up.

He got up quickly and caught her hand. 'Don't go yet.'

She should have shaken off his hand and gone into the house that minute. But she didn't. She allowed him to pull her closer and bend his head to hers. She allowed him to kiss her and it was the most wonderful feeling in the whole wide world. He held her tightly against him as his lips searched hers for a response. A response that came from her slowly at first, and then more passionately as her heart began to thump uncontrollably.

She put her arms around his neck, feeling the cool dampness of his skin and hair, grasping his head with her hands so as not to let him go. Her body moulded into his and his hands roamed her back and waist and hips, searching through the folds of her skirt. A strange uneasy flutter spread through her legs and stomach and she wanted him to go on like this, to go on for ever and ever. But suddenly he stopped. He took her hands from around his neck and placed them by her sides.

'Lissie, Lissie,' he groaned.

'What is it? What's wrong?' *He does not like me after all,* she thought.

'I did not wish for this to happen.'

'Oh.'

He was shaking his head. 'You don't understand, I should not have done that.'

Lissie's heart plummeted. 'But you did.'

'I know. I am sorry. I—'

'I see.' She was right. He did not like her. She turned to walk away.

'No you don't see!' He caught hold of her hand again, but this time she shook it off. She remembered what Eliza had said to her. *You want to watch them bargeboys. They don't call 'em fly-by-nights for nothing.*

'Good night, Mr Svenson,' she said. She gathered up her skirts so that she could escape from him as quickly as possible. How could he? How could he take her in his arms like that and then reject her? The man was a fraud. A foreigner masquerading as a gentleman! She hoped he would not be staying long at the Kirbys.

A lamp was on the kitchen table, turned down low. Her little almond biscuits were now quite cold on their baking tray. There were two tiny gaps where someone – Blake, it must have been Blake – had sampled them. She could not understand why this made her so angry, so – so beside herself with vexation. She tipped the remaining biscuits on to a tin plate and carried them upstairs.

The dormitories were quiet, although Lissie knew the older pupils were still awake. She put her finger to her lips and went round with the biscuits, leaving one by the pillow for those who were asleep. Finally, she shushed the whispering and flopped on to her own bed, trying to understand why her body felt so shaky.

Hurt and confused, she fretted about the kiss. She hadn't asked him to do it. Welcomed it, yes, but he had stolen it from her. And then pushed her away. He was cruel and she did not like him for that.

Tired, upset and increasingly perplexed, she eventually fell into a restless sleep. She heard the early morning rooster crow, and an ox-cart rumbling along the road, then realisation dawned. Of course. It was Miriam he wanted. He had come here to court Miriam.

Chapter 18

'Have you heard the latest? Miss Kirby is taking a lodger.' Miriam came into the kitchen as soon as she arrived for school the following morning. She was wearing one of her best dresses. A pretty blue cotton one, too new for the schoolroom.

'Who told you that?' Lissie asked. She was sitting at the table writing her list for Miss Kirby.

'I heard it at my lodgings. Mr Kirby brought a gentleman from town home in the trap yesterday.'

'Yes, he did.'

Miriam's eyes widened. 'Did you see him? Who is he? What's he like?'

'Oh, I don't think he'll be staying. Not when Miss Kirby finds out who he really is.'

Intrigued, Miriam sat down at the table. 'What d' you mean, Lissie? Do you know him?'

Lissie kept her eyes on her list as she replied. 'He's that horseman from the flyer. The one whose horse lost a shoe. I bet he hasn't told Mr Kirby he used to work on the barges.'

'Oh, I remember him,' Miriam breathed, excited by this news. 'He was real handsome, he was.'

'He still is, if you like that sort,' Lissie replied shortly.

'You wouldn't tell on him, would you, Lissie?'

'No I wouldn't. Would you?' She stopped writing and put down her pencil, then finished cutting slices of bread and spreading it with dripping for Miriam's pupils. 'There, you can take that lot in for their breakfast.'

Miriam picked up a piece of bread and dripping for herself. 'Bring me a mug of tea in the schoolroom? Please, Lissie. You know I'm stuck in there all morning.'

Lissie sighed and shook her head. Miss Kirby did not allow tea in the schoolroom, but if Lissie didn't take her some, Miriam would land her with pupils who were hopeless in the kitchen and then Miss Kirby would blame Lissie for getting behind with her work.

When she took in the tea the schoolroom was a mess as Miriam had not tidied away last night's sewing before she had left the previous day.

'Miriam, get a move on! Miss Kirby will be in here soon and she'll be furious if she sees it like this.'

'You do it for me, Lissie. Go on, you're much quicker at these things.'

Lissie sighed. 'Are you sure you really want to be a teacher, Miriam?'

'Oh yes. It's better than working for me mam at the Navvy.'

'But you're no good at it!'

'I know,' her friend wailed. 'That's why I want you to 'elp me.'

Reluctantly, Lissie lined up all the pupils on one side of the room and gave the bigger girls brooms to sweep the floor then asked the smaller ones to pick up cutting-out debris from the worktable. Lissie was on her knees behind the tall teacher's desk when the door to the schoolroom opened. Oh no! Not Miss Kirby already! She held her breath and waited for Miriam to get rid of her, desperately thinking about what she would say if Miss Kirby found her there.

'Oh! G-Good morning.' Even in those short words Lissie could hear Miriam's demeanour change. It was as though someone had turned a key in her back. There was no whining, no pleading, as she went on, 'Can I help you, er – sir?'

Slowly, Lissie sat back on her heels and watched as Miriam got down from the high teacher's chair and sauntered towards Blake at the door.

He was dressed for town in his high boots and long black coat and was carrying a tall black hat and gloves. 'I heard voices,' he said. 'This must be the schoolroom.' He looked around with interest.

'They can be untidy little b-blighters sometimes,' Miriam explained. 'Lissie was just giving me a hand.'

'Lissie? Is Lissie in here?' Blake stepped forward into the room and let the door close behind him.

'She was just leaving. Weren't you, Lissie?' Miriam directed.

'Yes. Gladly.' Lissie got up off her knees and dusted down her calico apron with her hands. 'Good morning,

Mr Svenson,' she said and bustled past him with her head
held high.

He didn't answer but stepped aside and let her pass.

Lissie fumed silently in the kitchen and kicked the
big iron fender in frustration. Infuriating man! Miriam
had looked really pretty this morning in her blue cotton
dress with lace at the cuffs and throat, and with her
honey-blonde curls escaping and mingling with her cap
strings.

She fingered the plain brown twill of her morning
work dress and wondered if she should curl her hair.
One thing was certain, if she did, Miss Kirby would not
like to see tendrils of black hair showing beneath her
cap when she was in the kitchen. She went to clear the
dining room and saw Mr Kirby in his pony and trap
outside the front of the house. Blake dashed out of the
front door, climbed up beside him and they left for town.

Miss Kirby did not allow pupils in the front rooms
of her house, so Lissie set them to work in her kitchen
and started on the cleaning herself. She left Blake's
bedchamber until last. He was tidy, she noticed. He had
made the bed and left his nightshirt neatly folded on
the pillow. She picked it up and hugged it to her breast,
burying her face deep in the folds of cotton. She wished
it was him. She wished he was here, in the room with
her, alone with her, kissing her again.

He had books in his room. They were stacked on the
mantelshelf and she lingered, looking at the titles. There
was a horsehair armchair by the fireplace and she sat
down for a moment to flick through one of his books.
It was all about how to make things from iron and other

metals and it had drawings in it with numbers and letters on them. Still nursing his nightshirt, she stroked the pages, imagining him reading the book and writing a note on the small table by his right arm.

She felt rather than heard Miss Kirby enter the room, and when she looked up, Miss Kirby's fury was obvious.

'What do you think you are doing?'

'I . . . I was just looking, ma'am.'

'How . . . how dare you? Give me that nightshirt this instant! Mr Svenson is a guest in this house and a gentleman. You are here to look after him, not pry into his private papers.'

'No . . . I . . . er . . . I wasn't, I mean, I was only—'

'Prying. You were prying. I should dismiss you this minute.'

'No, no please, ma'am, please don't send me back home.'

'I shall not discuss it now. Finish here immediately and go down to the schoolroom. One of the children is ill.'

Miriam was in a panic because one of the new boarding pupils had been sick on the schoolroom floor. Lissie cleaned up the mess and took the little girl outside. She sat her in the shade and pumped some fresh water for her to drink. Miss Kirby came out and decided that the pupil could lie down for the rest of the day and the crisis was over.

'I shall see you in the morning room now,' she said to Lissie.

Lissie stood in the middle of the small room and waited for her employer to speak.

'You have disappointed me, Lissie. Going through a gentleman's possessions indeed! What have you got to say for yourself?' Miss Kirby was very angry.

'I . . . I was only reading one of his books, ma'am.'

Miss Kirby had learned how to glare like her brother did. She had the same beady brown eyes and they stared unblinkingly at her.

'I . . . I'm sorry, ma'am. It won't happen again.'

There was another silence.

'Very well. You will forfeit your next half day and will clean every knife in the house before you go to bed tonight. That is all, you may go.'

Dejected, Lissie went back to her work, wondering how she would tell her dad that she could not come home this month. By good fortune, Miss Kirby did not want a cooked tea that evening. Her brother and his guest were staying in town for an evening lecture at the Institute and she had asked for a light supper on a tray in her morning room. Lissie spent the afternoon cleaning kitchen knives with an old cork and some sand. She hated knife cleaning as it made her finger ends so sore.

By evening she was tired and missing the sleep she did not get the night before. Her last duty was to leave out the gentlemen's late supper in the dining room. She arranged cold cuts of pickled tongue, Yorkshire cured ham, plum relish and fresh-pulled lettuce hearts under muslin cages on the table. She had made a cherry pie especially and left it with a bowl of fresh clotted cream from Eliza's dairy. Miriam came into the kitchen for some bread and cheese before she went back to her lodgings.

'Are they all in bed?' Lissie asked.

'They should be. I sent 'em up there half an hour ago.'

'Haven't you been up to check?'

'No point. You'll be going up soon. I've not seen George with the trap yet. Where's Mr Kirby tonight?'

'You mean where is Blake. They are at a lecture in town until late.'

'Oh. I'll get off then.' Miriam cut another piece of bread and cheese, wrapped them in her handkerchief and left.

In the attic most of the little ones were asleep with their day clothes heaped on their boxes. It was a long day for them and they were always tired out by nightfall. A few older girls were whispering and giggling and one was systematically folding all the discarded pinafores and dresses. Lissie broke up two who were squabbling about where the candle should be.

Luckily, the sick child had improved, but she complained of being thirsty so Lissie poured her some water from the washstand ewer. She closed the dormitory doors thankfully, put on her own nightgown and brushed out her long black hair. A light breeze came in through the attic window that she propped open permanently in summer, and she heard the pony and trap coming down the drive.

Tired as she was, Lissie lay on her back with her eyes wide open, imagining Blake and Mr Kirby in the dining room enjoying their supper. She hoped they – he – would like her cherry pie and then chided herself for being foolish. The house went quiet. She got out of bed to check that the candles in the dormitories had been blown out.

The sick girl, like her, was wide-eyed and restless. 'I'm not sleepy now, miss,' she said.

'Hush. You'll wake the others. Would you like some more water?'

'I'm hungry, miss.'

'Did you eat some tea?' Lissie whispered.

'No, miss. Miss Jackson didn't bring me any.'

'Do you mean you haven't eaten since dinner?'

'I didn't have any dinner neither. I didn't feel like any then. I'm hungry, miss.'

Lissie put her fingers to her lips. 'You must be very quiet. Go and climb into my bed on the landing and I'll fetch you something from the kitchen.'

'Some bread and dripping, please, miss,' the girl said immediately.

'Not dripping, not after you've been sick. How about some bread and honey?'

'Yes, please, miss.'

'As long as you are very quiet.'

Lissie pulled on felt slippers that she had made herself, took her lamp and crept down the back stairs to the kitchen. Some of the empty dishes from the dining room had been placed on the kitchen table. She could smell cigar smoke and realised that one of the gentlemen had carried them through. Mr Kirby had not done anything like that in the past. She jumped, startled, as the door to the garden opened.

'I saw the lamp.' Blake stood in the open doorway. He was not wearing a jacket and his shirt was open at the neck. 'I've been down to the orchard. You were not there tonight.'

She went into the scullery immediately to fetch her shawl from the nail behind the door and wrapped it around her thin cotton nightgown. 'One of the pupils has been poorly,' she muttered as she sat down to prepare the food.

'May I talk to you while you work?' he asked.

'What about?'

'You. Why are you being like this with me?'

'Like what?'

'Ignoring me.'

'I'm not ignoring you. I'm busy.'

'Lissie, you are not busy now!' he exclaimed. 'For heaven's sake! It's the middle of the night!'

'So go to bed then.'

He walked across the room, took the bread knife from her hand and placed it carefully on the table. 'Stop and listen to me for a minute. Please?'

She pulled her shawl tighter around her nightgown. 'What do you want?'

'You, Lissie. I want you. I wasn't going to tell you. I was going to wait until you were older and I had proper work in the Riding. But I can't. I can't wait for you.'

She forgot the bread and honey, and the poor child waiting hungrily in the attic. 'B–but you pushed me away.'

'I told you. I planned to wait.' He took both her hands and pulled her gently to her feet. Her shawl fell away. He pushed his fingers through the long silky curtain of her hair and let it fall gracefully on to her thinly clad shoulders.

She was shaking. She could not believe this. He was saying he wanted her. *Her.* Not Miriam after all.

He held her chin lightly and traced the contours of her eyes, nose and mouth with his fingers. His thumb lingered on her lips and she parted them and nibbled at it, ever so slowly, with her teeth. In the glow of the lamp his face looked dark and stormy – no, not stormy, hungry – his face looked hungry.

She twined her hands around his neck and stretched up to kiss him. Her lips parted and his mouth and tongue searched hers with a passion that she returned. His arms snaked around her. His hands were all over her body and her blood was pounding in her head. She tottered backwards and he clasped her tighter, closer. She was acutely aware of his hard body against hers, of his muscled thighs, his rising manhood and his firm chest against her softness. Together, they pushed against the table, rattling crockery and dislodging a dish that fell to the stone flags and shattered.

He stopped kissing her for a moment and simply held her close, her head pressed against his chest, whispering breathlessly, 'I want you, Lissie. I need you. Tell me you feel the same.'

Every inch of her skin was alive with a passion that left her speechless. She was in a turmoil, drawn into a vortex of desire that she could not understand, let alone control. She had no resistance when his hands searched under the thin cotton of her nightgown for her soft, yielding flesh. Or when his lips lowered to her throat, and then to her breasts . . .

'*Stop this at once!*'

They froze. Slowly, Blake disentangled himself from Lissie's nightgown, picked up her shawl and wrapped it around her.

Mr Kirby, clothed in his dressing robe, stepped into the kitchen. His sister hovered behind him in the passage. The ensuing silence lengthened.

Finally, Blake swallowed and said, 'I am the cause of this, sir. This is my doing.'

'Be quiet, Mr Svenson. Lissie, I am ashamed to have you in my house. My sister has told me of your behaviour in Mr Svenson's bedchamber today. You are dismissed. You will pay for the broken china out of your wages. Pack your box in the morning and leave.'

Blake took a step forward. 'No, Mr Kirby, do not do this. Sir, this is all my fault. You cannot blame Lissie. She is innocent here.'

'I asked you to be quiet, Mr Svenson!'

'No, sir. I shall not stand by and let this blameless young woman suffer for my weakness.' Blake hesitated for a moment before going on, 'You are a man yourself, sir, and you know of men's urges . . .'

'How – how *dare* you speak of such things before my sister!' His face was so flushed that Lissie thought Mr Kirby was going to explode.

'But, sir, I know you understand these things, you—'

Mr Kirby raised his arm to strike Blake, but Miss Kirby stilled it from behind with her hand and said, 'No, brother, dear. That is not so wise.'

Lissie saw that Blake's fists were clenching and unclenching by his side.

Mr Kirby dropped his arm and said, 'I am shocked,

deeply shocked, by your behaviour, Mr Svenson. I invited you into my home as a guest and this is how I am repaid!'

'It's . . . it's not his fault, sir,' Lissie stammered. 'I came down for—'

Mr Kirby's fury was rekindled. 'I think I know very well what you came down for! I warned my dear sister not to employ you . . . you . . . you . . . it is very clear to me what kind of woman you are!'

'No, sir. You are wrong!' Blake protested. But he knew that Kirby was not a man that he could reason with, especially after wine and port.

'And you, Mr Svenson, should know better than to give in to the temptation of . . . of *harlots*. I will not have you under my roof. Leave this house immediately!'

'Now, sir? In the middle of the night?'

Mr Kirby waved his arms around and shouted, 'Get out of my house! Get out, I say!'

Blake glanced at Lissie with naked despair in his eyes then left. Lissie moved to follow him into the garden.

'Stay where you are, you little trollop! Sister, fetch my cane.'

Luckily for Lissie, Miss Kirby came forward and calmed her brother with entreaties not to wake her pupils and to save any punishment until morning. However, she was just as angry as he was and said, 'Lissie, go back upstairs this minute.'

Lissie, her head now as cold and clear as day, obeyed instantly. She picked up the bread and honey and folded the pieces together.

'Leave that where it is!' Miss Kirby snapped.

'It's . . . it's for the sick pupil, she—'

Miss Kirby glared at her. 'Very well, take it. Go now.'

As she hurried into the passage and up the back stairs, Miss Kirby added, 'You will have your box ready to leave before breakfast.'

'I am sorry, Lissie, love,' Eliza said. 'It was that lad off the flyer, wasn't it? I saw him leave with Mr Kirby in the trap yesterday morning. I was just taking milk to the doctor's house when they went off. I tell you, he was a bit of a surprise to me, he was, because he looked quite the gentleman, all dressed up for town.'

Lissie sat in silence on the stone steps of the dairy. She was thinking of those stolen moments in Blake's arms last night and how much she wanted to repeat them, and how she did not regret her actions for one minute. She hoped, desperately, that she would see him before she left Fordham for good.

She had sent a message to her dad and he might be back on a barge this afternoon, someone had said. She had not seen anything of Blake this morning. Unable to sleep, she had carried her box down from the attic herself and left it outside the kitchen door before daybreak.

Eliza was sympathetic and went on, 'You can stay with us at the farm. For as long as you like. You know that, don't you?'

'Thanks, Eliza. But I'll have to go home with my dad when he gets here. I expect I'll find work at the Navigator.'

'Look, why don't you leave your things in the dairy and come back to the farmhouse with me? I'll leave word at the alehouse where you are. If your dad – er – or that lad – comes looking for you, they'll know where to find you.'

'What will your husband say?'

'You leave him to me. He'll not cause any bother.'

'Thanks, Eliza.'

Chapter 19

Luther Dearne's first stop when he climbed off the barge at Fordham was the alehouse, where he heard all about the to-do at the school the night before. He hurried up to the school hoping to talk Miss Kirby round with a few yards of Nottingham lace. He was not even allowed in the kitchen door. Old George came outside and told him firmly to take Lissie's box and leave or Mr Kirby would send for the constable.

Luther retreated to the alehouse.

Blake slept in the trap at the coach house. George went in the house to pack his belongings and agreed to keep them until he found somewhere to stay nearby. Finding lodgings was not easy for Blake as word had spread quickly and no one wanted to upset Mr Kirby by taking him in. All he thought of was Lissie and what he would say to her when he found her. Where was she?

His mind was distracted when he saw Luther Dearne

going into the alehouse. He recognised him straight away. He had seen him from a distance at the wharf in town, and a local bargeman that Blake knew had confirmed his identity. His blood began to pound in his head. All the frustration and anger that he had for Mr Kirby and his imperious manner was suddenly refocused on this ghost from his past.

His deep-rooted grief bubbled to the surface. Everything was Dearne's fault! It all went back to his crooked dealings that had led, ultimately, to his father's death. His rage focused on this man who had murdered his father and got away with it. Well, not for much longer, he resolved. He was never more ready than now to confront him. Blake wanted his revenge more than ever as he followed Luther Dearne to the alehouse.

Luther was thinking about where he would get the rent at quarter day, now that Lissie had lost her position. He was already up to his eyeballs in debt and Lissie would not be able to earn the same skivvying for Annie Jackson at the Navigator.

It sounded to him as if his little girl had grown up faster than he had realised. He didn't think she was interested in lads. And she was a bonny lass. All the fellas at the Navvy said so. But she was a good girl and did as she was told when it came to staying away from the bargeboys and such. She never encouraged them like that Miriam did. And they knew better than to mess with the Jackson lass, or her little friend. Mickey saw to that.

Well, at least his little Lissie wasn't turning out to be a dried-up old prune like Edie! Still, the tincture was doing the trick for Edie. It quietened her and it was cheaper than gin. But she was no use to man or beast these days. If his Lissie came back home he could kick out Edie and she could go and live with that Rosa woman.

Thick as thieves those two were. If you asked him, Luther thought that Rosa was a witch, and she was only tolerated at Mexton Lock because she was good with the sick. Like Edie, in a way. Folk only put up with her loony ways because she was Luther's wife. Well, he didn't care about her any more, but he reckoned his Lissie wouldn't let him kick her out.

Where the hell was he going to get the rent? A bolt of cloth might pay Mickey his dues for drink and food, but it was not enough for rent. Perhaps he could find a husband for Lissie? He had been prepared to pay a good price for her as a babby. There must be some barge owner around looking for a woman. A widower would do. With a few shillings to spare to keep his pretty young wife's parents off the streets.

Luther thought this was one of his better ideas and he slapped a coin on the alehouse counter. 'A pint of your best, landlord,' he said.

He was staring at his half-empty tankard when Blake walked in. Blake bought himself a pint and retired to an opposite corner where he could watch Luther's drinking and movements. A group of farm labourers came in from the fields to slake their thirsts and blocked his line of vision.

Blake decided it would be best to tackle Luther outside. He finished his ale, slipped out through the back door and surveyed the cobbled yard at the back. It was almost totally enclosed by stone walls and outhouses on each side. But, like the much bigger Navigator Inn at Mexton, it had a privy opposite, across the cobbles. He stepped into the shade, leaned against the wall, and waited.

After the evening milking, one of the milkmaids came to tell Lissie that her dad was in the alehouse and she hurried to find him. The day was overcast and dark grey rain clouds were blowing up from the west. Luther was on his third pint when she sat down beside him.

'Dad, Dad! Have they told you what happened? Oh Dad, I'm ever so sorry!'

'Nay, lass. It can't be 'elped. Did he do owt to you though? Tell me if he did and I'll kill him, I will.'

'No, Dad, he didn't. He didn't do anything wrong, honest.'

'Mr Kirby thinks 'e did, or 'e wouldn't have kicked the both of you out like that!'

'We had a kiss, that's all. You know what Mr Kirby's like! He's a chapel-goer and he doesn't hold with that sort of thing.'

'It were just a kiss, then?'

'Honest it was. We were in the kitchen.'

'Well, whoever 'e was, 'e seems to 'ave scarpered now.'

Lissie sighed, feeling dejected. Where had Blake gone? She didn't want to go off home with her dad without talking to Blake first.

'You'll 'ave to get work somewhere, lass,' her dad said. 'Trade's real bad fer me nowadays.'

'I could go into town and find something. You must know people there, Dad.'

'Aye, I do that. But I'll not have yer working in town. It's too far away from me and yer mam. She's allus said 'ow much she wants yer back home.'

'But I won't be earning if I'm at home with Mam.'

'There's work at the Navigator for now. Summat else'll come along. Your old dad'll see to that.'

Just as she thought. Lissie sighed again. 'How is me mam?'

'Same as always. No use to anybody. You'll have to cook t' dinner for us when we get back. I've time for another pint afore we go though.'

After his fourth pint, Luther pushed his way through the throng of thirsty farm workers to find the privy across the yard. He stumbled about in the gloom until he had relieved himself, then made his way outside to go back to his ale.

He came face to face with a young, well-built fellow whose piercing stare left him feeling cold. His heart seemed to flutter in his chest, then it missed a beat and he panicked silently. Luther had done enough dodgy dealing in his life to be very wary of strangers who took an interest in him. There was another man in the privy, but only the two of them in the yard.

He glanced around. Behind him was the stinking privy and a stone wall. On either side of the yard the stone-built stores were locked and barred. His only way out was across the yard down a narrow alley and he'd have to get past this young tyke to get there.

Luther became anxious. This man was tall, with broad shoulders and big fists already tightly clenched by his sides. He looked as though he meant business, business that Luther didn't want to get involved in. He noticed he was dressed smart, for town. He wouldn't want a fight, would he? He wouldn't want to muck up those nice clothes, would he?

Luther stepped briskly to one side with a casual remark, 'It's the door behind me, squire, but you'll need to hold your nose as well as your cock.'

Blake covered his escape route with one easy stride.

'Look here,' spluttered Luther, 'I don't know who you are, but—'

'Svenson. My name is Svenson.'

Luther felt his heart turn over again and he began to sweat. Svenson! Bugger! It must be nearly six years since he'd seen off old Svenson, but it still worried him from time to time. Who was *this* Svenson then? Surely not that skinny kid? Nay, it couldn't be!

'Never 'eard of yer, mate,' Luther grunted as he tried, again, to push by. Bloody hell, the fellow was rock solid! He thought he saw a movement at the back door of the alehouse and swivelled his glance. But if anyone was there they had melted back into the shadows. Luther raised his voice, just in case. 'Out of my way, man. I have no business with you.'

A strong arm barred his escape route. 'I have business with you, Dearne. You murdered my father. You shot him in cold blood to cover your thieving ways and now you are going to pay for it.'

'Not me, mate. I don't know what you're talking about.'

One of those large fists gripped his shoulder and pushed him backwards, throwing him against the rough stone wall. Luther's hands were clammy and he could feel the sweat trickle down the sides of his face. Yet he felt strangely cold, as cold as ice, and reality seemed to be slipping away from him.

A voice, strangely disembodied to his ears, sent the chill deeper into his head. 'I have searched and watched and waited for you. You're a murderer, Dearne, and if the magistrates won't make you admit it, then I shall.'

Luther was winded. His arm was hurting where he had banged it against the wall. What was happening to him? He felt pain grip him like a tight belt around his chest. The fellow must have struck him right in his guts. He hadn't felt it in the guts, it was his arm, his arm . . . His knees buckled beneath him and he choked for air. The belt around his chest became tighter, as if he was being throttled, he couldn't breathe, he couldn't see, he couldn't hear . . .

It all happened much more quickly than Blake had planned. His words were strong, but when he saw the older man close up, Blake could see that there would be no contest in a fight. The man was heavy with belly, not muscle, and his face was jowly and florid. Blake had pushed him against the wall and threatened him, raising his fist. When he saw the fear in Dearne's eyes, he pulled his punch and was sure that he had not struck him. But Luther Dearne went down before him, clutching his arm, spluttering and choking.

This was not how Blake had planned it at all. He had planned to overpower him, yes, then march him down to the canal, to a more isolated spot where he would extricate the truth about his father's murder. Maybe he would have to rough him up a bit, but not enough to floor the man.

Blake stood over Luther with his shoulders hunched and fists clenched. Luther, helpless on his back, gurgled like a baby. One of the farm labourers came out of the privy door, with his eyes wary and wide, and edged cautiously around Luther's motionless bulk.

Lissie had pushed through the men in the alehouse, ignoring their coarse remarks about her sullied reputation. If she waylaid her dad in the yard, she might persuade him not to go back into the alehouse and they could set off for home. She heard raised voices from the direction of the privy and slowed her pace. If drunken men were arguing, she had best stay out of it.

But from the shadow of the open doorway she was shocked to recognise the voices and figures of Blake and her dad across the yard. Blake had his back towards her. Dad had his back to the stone wall. She thought she saw another figure in the gloom at the entrance to the privy.

She inhaled sharply. Dad had found out it was Blake at the Kirbys last night and was going to thump him! She must stop him! Her dad was no match for Blake – Blake would kill him! She was too late. She saw Blake's clenched fist raised in anger. She heard her dad's strangled cry and saw him sink to the ground.

'Stop! Stop it! Get away from him!' she cried. She picked up a piece of wood and ran across the cobbles. 'Get away from him! What have you done to him?' She hit Blake across his body again and again with the wood.

'Lissie!' His surprise to see her there was mingled with

confusion as he tried to dodge the blows. 'What are you doing?'

'Leave him alone, you brute!'

He caught hold of the end of the wood and wrenched it from her grasp, protesting, 'Stop this, Lissie. It's nothing to do with you!'

'You hit him! You knocked him down!' she accused shrilly.

'No! I didn't touch him!'

'Liar! You're a liar! I saw you!' She fell to her knees on the cobbles. Her dad lay motionless on his back. His eyes were closed and a choking, gurgling sound came from his throat. She took hold of his shoulders and shook them vigorously, crying, 'Wake up, Dad! It's me, it's Lissie! Wake up! Wake up!' But the gurgling was fading and his corpulent body lay still. His right arm fell from across his chest to the ground. Lissie's heart missed a beat and her throat closed as she realised what had happened.

Blake's face was stony and his eyes wide. He stared at the scene before him, unable to believe this was happening. Lissie had called this man 'Dad'.

'No, no, don't die, please don't die,' she whimpered to the twisted purple face of her darling dad. What had Blake done to him? Kneeling beside his still form, she continued to shake his shoulders. 'Open your eyes, Dad. Open your eyes for me. It's Lissie, your Lissie. Don't leave me. Not now. I couldn't bear to lose you now!'

But she knew that it was too late. Her anguish and grief spilled over and she turned her head to look up at Blake and screamed, 'Murderer! Murderer! You've killed him!' She began to sob, cradling her dad's lifeless head in her arms, rocking backwards and forwards as she knelt beside him. 'You killed him, you killed him,' she choked. 'You've killed my dad.'

Blake continued to stare uncomprehendingly at the scene. He was frowning and shaking his head. This couldn't be true. How could this be? When he found his voice again it was a hoarse whisper in his throat. 'I don't understand, Lissie. Is this man your father? But he can't be. He can't be! He murd . . .' He stopped talking, horrified by this realisation. No, he did not believe it. This man was his father's murderer. He was nothing to do with his beloved Lissie. He couldn't be!

'Of course he's my dad,' she sobbed. 'My darling, darling dad. And you've killed him! You've killed my dad.' She was weeping now, her shoulders sagged and shook as she whispered, 'How could you do this? I loved you. I would have done anything for you.' She inhaled raggedly, her grief and anger mingling uncontrollably. 'You'll pay for this. I'll make you pay for this. I'll see you hang for what you've done.'

Blake's anguish mixed with an increasing bewilderment. 'Lissie — no. Listen to me,' he begged, 'I didn't touch him. I swear I didn't. He can't be dead, he can't be!'

Two men from the alehouse had come out to investigate the commotion and as they drew near, Lissie replied angrily, 'I saw you. I saw you hit him with your fist, and then . . . and then he went down, he fell down at your feet. I saw it all. I did.' She turned her head to the two men. 'Did you hear me? I saw him murder my dad. Fetch the constable.'

Blake protested, 'No, Lissie, no, you've got this wrong.'

One of the men came forward and took Blake's arm. 'Best come with us, lad, until the constable gets here.'

'Let go of me!' Blake stepped back and out of his grasp, but the other one barred his way. 'It's young Svenson, isn't it? The one who's come to lodge at the schoolhouse?'

The other man added, 'Oh yes, I 'eard about him. The young gentleman who's bin taking liberties with the girls there.'

'Yes, that's him,' Lissie interrupted shrilly. 'But he's not a gentleman. He's a bargeman off the flyers!' She turned her grief on Blake and cried, 'You're a liar and a fraud! You come here, all dressed up in your fancy gentleman's clothes, with your fancy way of talking and you're nothing but a common bargeman. A common *murdering* bargeman!' She choked and spluttered on her words but she meant every one of them. 'I hope they hang you for this.'

The two men closed in on him, one for each arm. Blake was too quick for them. He elbowed one in the stomach and winded the other with his fist, then turned smartly and disappeared down the narrow alley at the side of the alehouse. He sprinted along the street, over a low stone wall and into the woodland beyond. He moved so quickly that neither Lissie nor the two men realised what was happening until it was too late and he had gone.

'Don't worry m'dear,' one said to Lissie. 'The constable's men'll catch up with him tomorrow. He won't get far once word gets round.'

Lissie didn't care any more. Her whole world had fallen apart. Nothing would bring back her dad. And Blake? She had thought she'd found a friend in Blake, and a man that she could love. She had thought he cared for her. He said he did. But it was all a pretence.

Why had he done this to her beloved dad? Her dad was an old man and Blake was young and strong. He was no gentleman. He was just a thug like Mickey Jackson and his lads at the Navigator. How could she have thought she loved him? Blake Svenson was nothing more than a cold-blooded killer and she hoped he'd rot in hell.

Chapter 20

Blake moved quietly, hacking his way through the scrubby undergrowth that grew thickly in the woods surrounding Fordham. His lack of confidence in the local constable and magistrate ran deep, and had done so since the injustice of his papa's death. If the constable caught up with him he would be doomed. He was known as a bargeman. Even worse, he was a foreigner.

Had Lissie known all along who he was, who his father was? Had her father put her up to this charade? Had she deliberately led him into a trap that would end with him in the hands of the constable? No, she would not have wanted her father to die. That part, he was sure, was not planned.

But if he were in jail, Luther Dearne would be free for ever! Had Lissie been deceiving him all this time? Oh God, he thought. She was Dearne's daughter. His flesh and blood. His beautiful Lissie was the daughter of a murderer. His father's murderer.

He was breathing heavily and his heart was thumping when he reached the waterway. It was a dark, dank night and he was frightened. If the constable's men caught up with him he would be locked up, with no chance to prove his innocence, to find out what had really happened.

A ghostly silence blanketed the canal. Tethered horses stood quietly on the towpath and a string of sleeping barges lined the bank. He stared at the still, black water and wondered, fleetingly, how cold it was and how long it would take him to die. Dying was better than rotting in an English jail until he was hanged for a murder he did not commit!

But giving up was not his way. He was Blake Svenson and proud to be him. He was a fighter and a survivor, and he was innocent. He had not killed Luther Dearne. He was certain of that. However Dearne had died, it had not been his doing. Even so, the man was dead and his darling Lissie hated him with a vengeance for it.

Blake anguished, wrestling with his conscience. He had wanted Dearne dead. He had lain in wait for him. He had prepared to fight him and then drag a confession out of him, so that the magistrates would hang him for his papa's murder.

What should he do now? Flee downstream to the coast? He could be on a ship to Sweden within the week. He could start a new life. His mother had cousins there, he would not be alone. But he would have to leave England for good. Leave the South Riding and above all, leave Lissie for ever.

His head was in turmoil. The shock of realising his

lovely Lissie was the daughter of Luther Dearne was too much for him to bear. How could such a dear, sweet creature be the offspring of that vicious manipulative crook? It didn't make sense. A growling groan escaped from his throat as he sank to his knees beside the inky water.

How could she continue to want him, thinking that he had killed her father? Lissie hated and despised him. She wanted him dead. She wanted him incarcerated and hanged. He had to get away from here, but where could he go?

Blake staggered to his feet and set off. He walked through the night, following the waterways upstream towards town and then he waited under a bridge for the flyer to come by. The horseman knew him and Thomas was resting in the cockpit, so they welcomed him as a passenger without question. His physical exhaustion ensured that sleep quickly overtook him.

But not for long. His mind continued to churn with bad dreams of Lissie tempting him into her bedchamber and then transforming herself into a hooded hangman. He even felt the rope around his neck when he woke from his nightmares, anxious and sweating, and grateful to continue his journey.

He left the fly boat before it reached Tinsley and walked cross-country, skirting the ironworks and terraces of labourers' houses in the town. He knew the landscape and travelled with a purpose, avoiding known roadways and farms. He knew where he was going. He was going to a place of refuge away from prying eyes, where everyone was always discreet. Always.

He reached Grace's late, as nightfall approached, after walking since dawn. His shirt was grubby and his coat and boots scuffed and dusty. He was exhausted, hungry and, most of all, thirsty.

'Let me in.' He rapped on the scullery door of Grace's and whispered as loudly as he dared, 'It's Blake. Open the door, quickly.'

A young female voice whispered back, 'Go away. It's all locked up back here. You can't come in.'

'Who are you?'

'Why do you want to know?'

'I won't harm you, I promise. But please, please let me in. I must see Clara tonight.'

There was a short silence, then the young voice replied more loudly, 'Gentlemen callers round the front, if you please, or I'll have to get madam.'

'Do that then! Call her, you silly girl!' Blake stopped and took a deep breath. 'I'm sorry,' he went on. 'It's just that I am so very tired. Madam Grace knows me and I don't want any of Clara's services. I just need to . . . to talk to her.' He slumped against the door, almost fainting with thirst and fatigue. 'Please . . .' he begged.

He must have closed his eyes or fainted, or he simply fell asleep on the back step. The next thing he knew he was falling over on to the quarry-tiled floor as the scullery door swung back.

He heard a distant voice say, 'It's him all right. Looks as if he's walked across the Pennines. Mary, pull the day bed out in the kitchen and fetch some coals for the range. Then get yourself off upstairs till morning. Go on, girl, you can sleep in my bed. Get on with it!'

Blake prised open his eyes. 'Clara? Is that you, Clara?'

'It is that, my lad. And what have you been up to since I last set eyes on you?'

'It's a long story . . .' His voice faded. 'Can I have some water?'

Clara went to the scullery sink and started pumping. When he had drunk a tankardful she said, 'I think you had best get some sleep first. Can you stand? There's a bed in the kitchen and a drop o' brandy in the cupboard if you need it. Come on, lad, on your feet now.'

The water and brandy revived him. 'Thanks,' he murmured. 'Stay with me, Clara. Please. I need to talk – I'm in a bit of trouble.'

'I guessed as much. Why would you be here looking like this if you weren't? You're not going anywhere else tonight, that's for sure, so we'll talk when you are properly rested.'

The welcoming warmth of the kitchen range soon took over and he collapsed gratefully on to his makeshift bed. It was pitch dark when he woke. For a second he wondered where he was, and then the memories rushed into his mind and he knew why he was here. A fire glowed across the room and there was an oil lamp on the dresser behind him. The bed was little more than a pallet pulled out from the bottom of a cupboard. But there was plenty of padding underneath him, even if his feet did hang over the end. He pushed away a rough woollen blanket that was keeping him warm.

Someone was moving around, over by the range, and he heard the heavy clunk of a drinking mug. He craned his neck to see around the table legs. 'Clara. Is that you?'

'Blake! You're awake. Well, this is a fine carry on, isn't it? I expect you'd like something hot to drink. It's just mashed.'

Her level, matter-of-fact tone reassured him. He would be safe here.

'What time is it?'

'Four o'clock. The last client has just left. We have had some good spenders in tonight. Grace is really happy, which is just as well for you. Are you getting up for this tea? There's bread and cheese as well.'

Blake realised how starving hungry he was. When the bread and cheese was gone Clara fetched the remains of a plum pie from the pantry and he demolished that with some thick cream.

'Another brew?' Clara asked as he finished.

Blake nodded. 'Thanks.'

Clara set the refilled mug in front of him and asked, 'What happened?'

He shook his head slowly. 'I don't know. I don't know how everything went so wrong.'

'Surely things can't be that bad,' Clara smiled optimistically.

Yes they can, he thought miserably.

Clara waited a few minutes then prompted him. 'I heard you were doing all right for yourself on the fly boats. What went wrong?'

'Nothing really. I came off them and went to the Institute and . . . and . . .' Oh God, his life was such a mess! He changed the subject. 'How is Grace keeping?'

Clara went along with him, thinking that things were probably worse than she realised. She replied, 'Grace is in fine fettle. She had a nasty fever last winter, but pulled through all right and she'll be with us for a good few years yet. Tough as old boots is our Grace.'

Blake raised a smile at last. 'I'm pleased to hear that. And you, Clara, how have you been?'

'Oh, you know, surviving.'

'Are you happy?'

'Sometimes.'

'Aren't you ready to do something different? You must have a bit put by.'

'It's a good living,' she replied sharply. 'Besides, I do what Grace wants to do. I wouldn't go off and leave her now. I'd be dead if it wasn't for her. I'd have starved to death on the streets. And . . . and . . . well, she is getting on in years a bit and she kind of thinks of me as a daughter, you know.'

'Does she have no family of her own?'

'I don't think so. She was brought up in the work-house and married a sailor who was lost at Trafalgar. Mind, she may have had a baby once, one that died, I think. She says she's never had any, but sometimes she talks about how she got out of service and she talks about a baby. And then she shuts up and asks for some brandy.' Clara paused and sipped her tea. 'Have you been to see your own mother lately?'

'She went back to Sweden to see her cousins. I had a letter from her. She had it delivered to our warehouse on the Humber and Ephraim, who runs the business for us, sent it to the flyer office for me.'

'Is she well?'

'The crossing was rough, but she says she has recovered.

Lucy, her maid, is with her. She writes cheerfully, considering . . .'

'I am sure that she misses you very much. I would if you were mine. Have you written to her?'

'Twice. The last time just recently when I came off the flyers and enrolled at the Mechanics Institute. I know that will please her. But now . . . this . . . she cannot know about this.'

'I don't see what can be so wrong that you cannot tell your own mother!'

Blake, revived by the hot drink and food, took a deep breath and began, 'I'm in a bit of trouble, Clara. I just need to disappear for a while.'

'I guessed as much. Sweden seems as good a place as any.'

'No. I've got to stay and clear my name somehow. I didn't do it, I swear. And there's this girl I told you about. Oh, Clara, you should meet her. Her name is Lissie and she is such a darling. She sparkles like the stars in the night sky and . . . and . . . now she thinks I killed her father. I . . . I . . .' He gave an exhausted sigh.

Clara got up to put more coal on the fire. 'You'd better tell me all about it.'

Blake floundered, his emotions churning again. 'I . . . I don't know where to start.'

'Try the beginning.'

The beginning – where was that? All those years ago when Dearne shot his father? Or, more recently, when he had searched out Kirby at the Institute to effect an introduction to his home?

'I . . . she . . .' he began. 'Do you remember when I

told you about my father's death? Her father was his murderer. He was a liar and a cheat and a thief. And he shot my father.' Blake ran his fingers through his hair and his shoulders sagged. 'How could that ruffian produce such a bright, beautiful girl like Lissie? How, Clara? How?'

Clara stretched her arm across the table to hold his hand and listened to his tale. It was breaking dawn when he finished talking. Luckily the household did not stir until later when Mary got up to see to the range and get the hot water going. Grace stayed in bed until noon and Clara dealt with the household's affairs until teatime, when Grace would be dressed and ready to receive her visitors.

Clara was a good woman, Blake reflected. She deserved better than this for her life. But it was what she wanted. If he had loved her he would have taken her away from here and not worried about the difference in their years. But he did not love her, not in that man and woman way. Clara was a friend. And Blake desperately needed a friend.

'But you can't stay here, Blake!' Clara protested. 'Some of our clients are well-known townsmen. They guard their reputations and Grace guarantees them absolute discretion. If you were seen and – God help us – recognised as a wanted fugitive, there would be hell to pay. Are you sure that Sweden is not the best place for you until it all blows over?'

'That was my first instinct. But they will be looking for me on the waterways down to the coast. And . . . and I really do not want anyone over there to know.' He ran his fingers agitatedly through his thick hair. 'If my mother finds out, it will break her heart.'

'But you didn't kill that man! You told me you didn't do it!'

'I was there though. And everybody thinks I did! Clara, you have to help me, I don't know what to do. I didn't kill him, I swear I didn't. But he did die. He died before my eyes — he just crumpled up and fell to the ground. I don't understand it, I pushed him back against the wall. That's all I did. I didn't punch him, I didn't!'

'Well, you are a strong man, Blake. And you're a good fighter, I'm told. How well known was Dearne anyway?'

'He had friends up and down the canals. Been around for years, but was known to be crooked and untrust-worthy.'

'There you are then. The magistrate will understand.'

'Understand what? That I killed him?'

'No. They'll see that he had it coming to him.'

'So you *do* think I killed him.'

'No, Blake. You're twisting my words. You know what I mean.'

'Well the magistrate doesn't know what happened either. He only knows what others tell them. I'm worried, Clara. Luther Dearne had a lot of local friends.'

'Where is he from then?'

'Mexton Lock. He is as thick as thieves with the land-lord of the inn there.'

Clara stared at him in horror. 'Not the Jacksons from the Navigator? You don't want to make enemies of them.'

'Too late. I already have. They are not all bad though,' he added, thinking of Pete, the horse marine.

'If you say so.'

There was something in Clara's tone that made him pause and he glanced at her face. 'They don't come here, do they?'

'Of course not! Grace wouldn't allow that sort over the threshold. No, it's not that, though they do come into town fairly regularly – especially the father and his eldest son.'

'And?'

Clara faltered, as if she regretted opening this line of conversation. 'He's . . . he's well known for being brutal with his women.'

Blake's eyes rounded. 'With you? Mickey Jackson has attacked you?'

'No, I've never met him, but I know his reputation. He . . . he, well, my stepfather was like him. The local street girls all stay well clear of him.' Clara choked slightly on her words. 'But I expect he finds his pleasure some-where else now, with some poor unfortunate . . .'

Blake came over to comfort her. 'I'm sorry. Don't upset yourself. I've heard tales of the two older boys being like their father, but the youngest works with horses and he is kindness itself. And his girl, Miriam, well she is wayward but she is settled as a pupil teacher now. She's a cocky wench to be sure, who'll get herself into trouble before long, but I don't think she has suffered like you did. Her mother got her away from the inn.'

Clara recovered. 'You know quite a lot about them.'

'I've been asking around.' Blake thought for a second. 'I can't do that any more. That's why I need you.'

Clara heaved a sigh. 'It's no good. Grace will not let

you stay here. What if someone like Sir William found out?' There was another short silence, then Clara went on, 'Of course, Sir William might help.'

'I haven't had contact with him since – since that first night I came here.'

'But he has news of you! He knew you were on the flyers and that you had been at the Institute. He took a liking to you that night.'

'How do you know that?'

Clara gave him a long, steady gaze. Finally she rose to her feet and picked up the tray before her. 'I'll just take this tea upstairs for Grace. She'll be awake now. Why don't you have a wash in the scullery and then we'll toast some bread by the fire?'

Refreshed by cold water, Blake's head cleared and he was sitting by the glowing coals when Clara came back. The morning was dark and damp with a cold rain lashing at the windows. Blake handed the toasted bread to Clara who spread it with butter and honey. She brought more cushions to sit by him in front of the range.

'Grace agrees with me. I'll ask Sir William's advice.'

'I shouldn't think he would want to get involved.'

'Oh, he doesn't like crooks any more than you or I. But I won't say why you want to go to ground. He's a man of the world and he'll accept that you have a good reason.'

'But I have only met him the once—'

'He remembers you and . . . and . . . well, he knows that you have called here.'

'How is that, Clara?'

'I tell him everything.'

'Everything? You mean about your clients?'

'Oh, Blake, for a man of your education you can be very slow about some things.'

'What on earth do you mean?'

'Sir William *is* my only client. He pays well to keep it that way.'

'Then, I – er – we . . .'

She nodded. 'You did not realise how privileged you were that night. You . . . I . . . we needed his permission.'

'Yes, I remember.'

'He once said that he wished he had a son like you, a son with your spirit and courage.'

'Well, well. But he is married, is he not? Does he not have any sons?'

'He has no children at all – it is his greatest sadness.'

'Yes, I can understand that.'

'There is a persistent rumour about a bastard that he fathered when he was a young man. It caused quite a scandal at the time. He has always been a man full of life and ideas. Grace's provides a discreet outlet for his energy.'

'But his wife, Lady Swinborough – does she know about you?'

'I believe so, and by all accounts she turns a blind eye to his visits. She is an invalid, you see, worn out by too many miscarriages and stillborn births. They were slowly killing her and the doctor advised no more. People have to deal with their lives as best they can. It is no good being too idealistic, is it, Blake?' Clara gave a wry grimace. 'Don't judge him too harshly. His wife has the best doctor he could find. He always hoped for an answer but she is too old now. Sir William still loves her. Maybe you'll understand when you're older.'

He was beginning to understand something. To understand what it was like to want someone so much that it hurt. And then to have your belief in them, and theirs in you, shattered. Was this the answer? To seek solace elsewhere as Sir William had?

Not for Blake it wasn't. He still held a memory of Lissie. A painful memory. A memory of her body close to his, and his desire to possess her made him ache with longing. How could this have happened to him? He had had everything to live for, and it had all been snatched from his grasp. Now, all he could hope for was jail at best and the gallows at worst.

In despair, he covered his face with his hands and wept silently. Clara held him close until his grief eased for the present. When he was more composed he continued, 'You must believe me, Clara. I didn't want Luther Dearne to die by my hand. I only wanted him to admit what he had done to my father. I only wanted the truth!'

'I do believe you, Blake. Now calm yourself. What is done is done and we have to make the best of it.'

But he wasn't listening. Consumed by despair, he was reliving all the grief of his childhood. It was tearing his heart out and he couldn't stop himself. He began to talk again, to ramble. 'I tried to get a doctor for my father. Peter Jackson was just a boy like me, but he helped. He lent me a horse and I rode over to Fordham. But the doctor was not there. His housekeeper said he was at Swinborough Hall and wouldn't leave. I might have saved him if only I could have brought the doctor!'

'You did your best.'

'My father died, Clara! My father died because I failed!'

'It wasn't your fault. You must stop blaming yourself! It is eating away at you and that is why you wanted this revenge. Well, you have what you wanted. Luther Dearne is dead. You can move on now.'

'To where? What can I do?'

'I don't know and neither do you. But we have to get you away from here, so that you can lie low until they stop looking for you.'

'Why would they stop?'

'We'll put out word that you have gone back to Sweden. That will satisfy the constable. Now, have you ever worked down the pit?'

'Down the pit?'

'Yes. Down a coal mine. Or any sort of mine?'

'No, but I'm willing to try it.'

'Sir William's estate is vast and he has some drift mines in the hills. There are no deep shafts. They are safe and the teams are reliable. The coal keeps the furnaces going in Sir William's ironworks.'

'Where are these pits?'

'They are well away from town, and from the canal. All the coal is brought down in narrow boats on a private cut that links to the canal. So you'll be able to lie low until the panic dies down.'

'Where would I live?'

'Sir William is a good landlord. He has built rows of cottages near the pits for the colliers and their families and you'll easily find lodging with one of them.'

'Sounds perfect for me.'

'Well, we'll have to get Sir William to take you on, but I'm sure he will when I ask him.'

'Thanks, Clara. You're a true friend.' He reached out for her hand. 'I have to prove that I didn't kill him and I don't know how. Help me, Clara. Please. Help me to prove my innocence.'

Chapter 21

'Dad, oh Dad,' Lissie sobbed. 'What'll I do now? What'll I do without you?'

It was a week after he'd been killed and, still numb with shock, Lissie stood outside the stables at the Navigator and listened to the hammering as the lid on her dad's coffin was secured in place.

Somebody came and helped her into the back of the cart where the coffin rested. She rode with it over the stone bridge and along the woodland track to home. The day went by in a blur, just as all the other days had since her journey from Fordham with her dad's body.

They had left him in the stables until the coffin was ready. Miriam's dad from the Navigator took charge of everything. Lissie had never been very much aware of him as he was usually in the saloon of his inn. But now he was organising things and he kept asking her if she was all right.

Lissie did not answer. She had no words to say. She

had lost her bonnet and her hair was tumbled. Her dress needed mending, but she no longer cared. All she wanted was her dad back. They placed the coffin in their front room, resting it across their two best chairs with one end on the horsehair sofa. He was a big man, her dad, and it took three of them to carry him.

Someone shoved a little glass of spirits into her hand. She didn't see who. She didn't see anything. The next thing she knew Miriam's dad was stroking her hair and saying to her, 'You tell your mam not to worry. Mickey will take care of everything.'

Lissie wondered why he couldn't tell her mam himself as he was there, in the house. Then she realised that her mam was already dead drunk and fast asleep by the cold ashes in the grate. Lissie stood there, lost, in the untidy kitchen and wondered how she would cope with her mam now her dad was gone.

Mickey lingered a moment, looking at her. 'You've grown up proper while you've been working at that school. Your ma'll be pleased to 'ave you 'ome again. Tell 'er I'll call back tomorrer.'

He seemed not to want to leave. He stared at her and Lissie just stared back at him blankly, unaware of time or feeling. Then Mickey said more briskly, 'Yes, tomorrer. I'll drop by tomorrer.'

Lissie climbed the stairs, took off her boots and crawled fully clothed under the bedcovers. She sobbed herself into an eventual sleep.

Mickey Jackson continued his unusual half-friendly behaviour after the funeral. Edie always made him welcome because he brought her bottles of gin from the

Navigator. Edie liked the tincture from the apothecary as well though, and she told Lissie to go and ask Rosa to get some.

'I'll have to pay for it, Mam,' Lissie said, holding out her palm.

'Tek 'er yer dad's timepiece chain from the cupboard. It's gold so she'll get a good bit for that in town.'

'But it was me dad's! You can't sell it!'

'I've no use fer it and he sold his timepiece months ago.'

Lissie did not know that things had got so bad at home. She did as her mam asked and Rosa was very kind about it all. She gave her two bottles of Mam's tincture saying, 'It's laudanum, lass. It's like medicine for 'er now. Gi' her a few drops in a glass of wine, if yer 'ave it. I'll get as much as I can fer the chain. 'Ow is she?'

'Same as always. Mickey Jackson seems to be taking care of most things. Why don't you come and see her, Rosa? Mam would like that.'

Rosa shook her head. 'Better not. Not while Mickey's around. Treating you all right, is he?'

'Oh yes,' Lissie replied, thinking of the gin.

'You tell yer ma from me that she can allus come here if things get bad.'

'Thanks, Rosa. We'll be all right though, as soon as I get some work.'

But Rosa did go to see Edie. On the day that Mickey went off with his eldest lad to see Peter and go to the races at Doncaster. They set off early and were gone all day. Lissie took her chance and went over to the Navigator to ask Annie for a day's work in exchange for

some meat trimmings and drink for Edie. Rosa saw her
go by, reached for her shawl and went off to see her
friend.

'Edie, ducks, 'ow are yer doing?'

'Oh, Rosa, I'm right glad to see you. Come and sit
by the fire. Our Lissie made it up wi' a log from the
wood afore she went.'

'I've brought yer some o' yer medicine.' Rosa placed
the small brown bottle of laudanum by Edie's tin mug
on the hearth.

'Put some in there fer me, will yer?'

Rosa picked up the mug. 'It's empty. 'A'n't yer got
owt to drink?'

'Not till our Lissie gets back from the Navvy.'

'Not even any ale?'

Edie shook her head.

'I thought Mickey Jackson were looking after you?'

'Last time he called he said I had to pay 'im 'is dues
somehow.'

'Can't your Lissie earn it at the Navvy?'

'If their Annie'll 'ave her there. She says it'll encourage
me to go over and cause trouble.'

'Aye, well, me ducks, she might be right there. Is there
any hot water in this?' Rosa lifted the blackened kettle
off the swing hob, poured some water into Edie's mug
and added a few drops of her laudanum. She looked
around her as Edie drank and said, 'Nice little house this,
it'd be a pity to lose it. You'll 'ave to give Mickey what
'e wants.'

'Oh aye? How?'

'Oh, Edie, you know 'ow 'e likes women. Save 'im

going inter town if 'e can come 'ere fer it. Do you want some o' my henna fer yer 'air?'

'Oh not that, Rosa. I couldn't stand that wi' Luther, let alone Mickey.'

'Yer just shut yer eyes and do it. Wi' men like 'im, yer don't even 'ave to tek off yer drawers.'

'Eh?'

'Yer do it wi' yer 'ands. Or yer gob.'

'Me gob?'

'Well, not yer gob wi' 'im. I heard tell that he 'as a right big 'un and nearly choked one of the lasses in town.'

Edie's voice rose to a squeak. ''Ow d'yer know that?'

'Edie, ducks, 'ow d'yer think I get me rent on quarter day?'

'Yer go to t' market and sells yer salve, don't you?'

'That on'y buys me flour and lard. I 'ave to do a bit of whoring fer the rent.'

'But yer told me yer di'n't like doin' it wi' men!'

'I don't. That makes it easier fer me to charge 'em. Anyroad, like I said, I do it wi' me hands or me gob. You could give it a try.'

'Oh I don't know. Perhaps I could ask the parish to pay me rent.'

'Yer don't want them poking their noses inter everything!' Rosa protested. Edie had been a good friend to her over the years, sharing any coppers Luther left behind when he went on the canals. She liked Edie and Edie liked her. Rosa continued, 'They'll find out what we get up to together and they won't like it.'

'Oh, Rosa, they wouldn't stop us, would they?'

'Oh aye. I'd rather pay me own rent and do what I want.'

Edie didn't reply. She swallowed the rest of her warm water and laudanum and fell silent.

Lissie found her dozing by the fire, tucked up in Lissie's old school cloak. She saw the laudanum bottle and guessed Rosa had called. It was a relief to her that Mam was asleep because Annie had not given her any work. Instead she had told her to stay away, on their own side of the canal, and not to talk to their Miriam again.

But she had calmed down a bit when her lad, who was minding the inn for Mickey, went to check on his beer in the outhouse, and added, 'I'm sorry about yer dad, lass. Tek this bacon knuckle fer yer mam. There's a bit o' meat left on it.'

Lissie had hurried home. She cut off the meat and boiled up the bone with some barley and vegetables from the garden. They had a feast for dinner that day and her mam was quite placid now she had her medicine.

'I'll try further afield for work, Mam,' she said after they had eaten.

'No,' her mam replied. 'Get this place clean an' tidy fer when Mickey calls. I wants ter keep 'im sweet.'

'How long has Mickey Jackson been coming over here?' she asked.

'It were when yer dad couldn't get work and had nowt to spend at the Navvy. He took to coming over wi' a few bottles or a jug o' draught. And a drop o' gin fer me.'

Lissie realised that this was where all the money had gone, because Mickey would want paying one way or another. She wondered how Mam was going to afford her gin, now there was nothing coming in.

'Mam, why can't I go out to work somewhere?' she pleaded.

'I want you 'ere,' her mam whined. 'I needs looking after now.'

That was true. But she needed her laudanum now as well. As long as she had that, Lissie realised, her mam didn't complain. It could have been anybody banking up the fire and cooking the dinner for her. Lissie got the house and bit of garden organised, but they needed coal, and flour for bread.

'Haven't you got any coppers anywhere?' she asked.

'No. I told you we 'a'n't got no money,' her mam scowled. 'Yer dad left nowt except debts.'

'Then let me go and earn some money by working!'

'Nay, lass. Mickey says yer don't have ter. He says – he says yer can stay and look after yer old ma.'

'What on earth has it got to do with him?' Lissie demanded.

''E owns the 'ouse now.'

'What? This house? Dad left him our house?'

'Nayow! It were already 'is. He bought it off yer dad years ago, when the canal trade was bad and yer dad got into a bit o' bother. Kept him outta prison, Mickey did. We paid 'im rent, like. But we 'a'n't got no money now yer dad's gone.'

Lissie became even more anxious. 'But it's past quarter day and we haven't paid any rent! I'll have to go out and work for it!'

'Yer don't listen ter me, do yer?' Mam cried. 'Yer never

listen! That's what I'm saying. You don't 'ave to go out ter work. You can stay 'ere, Mickey says.'

'Mam! Mickey Jackson won't let us live here rent-free, believe me. He'll turn us out. We'll be in the work-house.'

'Mickey won't let that happen.'

'You seem very sure of him, Mam.'

'I've bin thinking.'

'About what?'

'Things. Just things.'

Lissie could get no more sense out of her. The house was growing cold and there was no more food apart from vegetables from the garden. To lose their house Dad must have borrowed heavily from Mickey during hard times and not paid it back when trade was good. Edie always had her gin and Lissie had never wanted for boots or a working dress. But now Mickey Jackson seemed to own everything about them.

'Mickey's been good to us,' Mam told her.

'Well he's not being very good now,' Lissie remarked pointedly. 'Is he going to turn us out or what? We'll end up on the streets!'

''E promised it wouldn't come to that. 'E promised me.'

Lissie shrugged. Mickey and her dad had been as thick as thieves for years. There would be things she didn't know, and most likely her mam wouldn't know either. Mam had never questioned Dad about where the money and the gin came from.

Lissie looked at her steadily. Her mam had aged in the few years she had been at the Kirbys. She looked old and worn out, and her skin was shrivelling on her bones. But she was her mam and Lissie knew what her duty was. She would have to look after her, whatever happened.

'I'll take the rugs out and beat them, Mam; I need something to keep me busy now the funeral and mourning is over and done with. But we can't live on fresh air.'

'We won't 'ave to.'

'Then where is the money coming from?' Lissie wailed.

'Mickey allus said ter me he'd help out, if I were nice to him. Rosa's told me what he means. He'll likely bring some meat wi' 'im next time he calls and he can 'ave 'is dinner wi' us. Can you cook a dinner fer us, love?'

'Doesn't he eat Annie's dinner at the Navigator?'

'He likes to get away from there sometimes. You know, into town and that.'

'Well, coming here isn't going into town! Still, if he brings us some meat, I'll cook it for us.'

'You're a good lass, love.'

As Lissie scrubbed and polished, she realised that was the first time her mam had ever called her 'love'. Maybe she was softening in her old age.

If she scrubbed by day, Lissie cried by night. She grieved for her dad, and anguished over Blake. She heard from the Navigator that he had disappeared. The constable's men did not catch him and they said he had left the country.

Well good riddance, she thought. But she grieved for him also. She *had* loved him. And now he was gone there was just an emptiness inside her, a void where her love for him should be.

Her mam was unreliable so it was up to Lissie to keep body and soul together. Mickey was probably only being nice to them because her dad had been a good friend of his. He had a reputation for being rough and tough though, so she did not expect his good nature to last. Even so, he sent round some flour and pig fat, and a couple of pheasants for dinner. Lissie found vegetables to go with them, and there was some fruit on the trees in the garden.

'What's he coming for, Mam?' she asked as she rolled out suet pastry for a pudding.

'To see 'ow we're getting on, o' course.'

'But why?'

'Well, he's our landlord now and 'e wants to see we keep the place nice an' that. So we 'as to be nice back to him.'

And he brings you gin, Lissie thought. Mickey must have taken a shine to her mam when he was visiting her dad. Mam seemed to be happy with the arrangement so who was Lissie to question it?

'He likes you then, Mam?' Lissie queried.

'Well, I wouldn't say that exactly.'

'What then?'

'Come on, Lissie. You know what I mean. You're a grown woman now. I 'eard the stories about you and that lodger at the Kirbys.'

'You mean the one that killed dad?'

'That's the one. Miriam told her ma that you'd been found in his bedchamber in on'y yer nightgown. Miriam said you knew, all right, what men wanted.'

'It's not true. Not like that, anyway.'

'But Mr Kirby did catch you in bed wi' the lodger, didn't he?'

'No, Mam. I wasn't in bed with him. I was kissing him, that's all.'

'Oh! That's not what I 'eard. Anyroad, you know what it's all about now, don't you?' Her mam sounded irritated by her denial.

'Yes, Mam,' Lissie sighed. 'I know what you mean.'

So that was how her mam paid for her gin. In that brief moment Lissie felt sorry for her. From things her dad had said, Mam didn't like the bedchamber side of being wed and never had. So providing those kind of favours for Mickey Jackson must be hard on her. But she needed her gin every day, she couldn't live without it, so perhaps Mam was grateful that Mickey had taken a shine to her.

Lissie wondered if Mickey's wife knew about this arrangement. Miriam's mum had been like Miriam when she was younger, but she had grown stout during her years working in the kitchen at the Navigator. Perhaps Mickey had tired of her and preferred his women skinny like her mam.

When Mickey came for his dinner it was just like the old days. Just like when Lissie lived at home and dad was alive. There were pot-roasted pheasants, done slowly with celery and herbs in the bake oven, and Mam's favourite apple pudding to follow, all served up in the kitchen at the scrubbed wooden table.

Mickey was a big man like her dad, but he hadn't run to fat. He was broad and muscular, from a family of strong, labouring men who had built the canals years ago. When he arrived he gave Mam her gin and had a present for Lissie, just like her dad used to. It was wrapped up in old calico and he said, 'It's not new, but it's made o' good stuff. Used to belong to the missus, on'y she's too big for it now. Go on, try it on.'

'It's a dress, Mam,' Lissie squealed in surprise as she opened the parcel. 'Oh, it's really pretty, and just look at this lace!'

Her mam came over to feel the material. 'Oh aye. That is a nice bit o' stuff. Go on then, lass. Put it on.'

'What? Now?'

'Aye,' her mam nodded. 'It's all right. I'll see to t' cooking.'

The dress material was a beautiful, soft, floral sprigged cotton, with lace trims at the neckline, sleeves and hem. It fitted her well at the waist and billowed out over her boots to skim the floor. The bodice was a bit tight, but the shoulders were fine. She pulled at the lace to cover where she was bulging out of the low neckline. She wondered if she dare go to the Navigator in it after tea. Mickey and her mam were sure to want her out of the house.

Mam shouted upstairs. 'Tea's on t' table. Let's be having you.'

Lissie felt like a real lady for the very first time in her life. If only her dad could see her, he'd be so proud. She clattered down the stairs and floated into the kitchen, holding her skirts off the floor as she came into the room.

Mam looked at her, nodded briefly, and said, 'Very nice. Sit down and eat up then.'

Mickey stared at her for a bit then poured her some ale from the bottles he'd brought with him without saying a word. He pushed a glass across to her.

'Drink up, lass.'

She took a sip and he repeated, 'I *said* drink up.'

'Do as he says, love,' her mam added, finishing off her own drink.

Lissie emptied her glass and he refilled it immediately.

When he'd finished his meal, he belched loudly and said, 'That were a tasty bit o' pheasant, Edie. I'll just have a pipe and another tankard.'

Lissie picked up the hint and volunteered, 'Shall I go out? I could go to the Navigator if you like.'

'Nay, lass,' her mam said quickly. 'Go and sit in t' front room. I'll clear the table. You wouldn't want to dirty that dress, would you?'

'No, Mam. If you're sure . . .' It wasn't like her mam to be so nice. Must be because Mickey was here.

It was chilly in the front room and Lissie sat on the old horsehair sofa and pretended she had rung for a maid to bring her some tea. She thought that this was a nice way to carry on and maybe things might get better with Mickey around. She was just beginning to wonder if her mam and Mickey would be going upstairs when Mickey came into the room.

'Well, Lissie, my lass. You look a pretty picture sitting there in that fine dress.'

Lissie smiled and said, 'Thank you ever so much, Mr Jackson. It's lovely.'

He lumbered over, took hold of her hand and pulled her to her feet. She slammed into his chest, which smelled of stale ale and kitchen grease. Then, as his other arm held her jaw, he pressed his foul, slobbering mouth over hers.

She squealed and struggled to get away but he held on to her firmly.

'Stop wriggling, lass. It's time for a proper thank you now. Come on.' Mickey dragged her across the room and into the tiny hall. 'Get up those stairs and look sharp about it.'

Shocked and frightened, Lissie yelled, 'No, I won't! What are you doing?'

He gave her a painful shove from behind. 'Don't start playing about now.'

'No, no, not me! It's my mam you want! Mam! Mam! Where are you, Mam?'

Edie's flushed face appeared at the kitchen door. Mickey turned his head and said, 'You told her, Edie, didn't you?'

''Course I did. She knows what to do.'

'Mam, what? What did you tell me?'

'Y'know. About what men want.'

'B–but I thought that was you. I thought it was you he wanted!'

'Don't be daft.' Mickey pushed her again and she fell up the first few stairs. 'What would a red-blooded man like me want with a wizen old crow like Edie? Gerrup there and tek that dress off.'

'Mam! No! No, Mam, I can't. I won't. You can't make me.'

'Can't I?' Mickey growled.

Edie frowned. 'I don't know, Mickey. If she don't want to . . .'

'Oh she does, all right. You can see just by looking at this one that she does. Besides, I like 'em spirited. You leave her to me, Edie. She'll come round.'

'She's on'y a young 'un, Mickey . . .'

'I like 'em young. You should know that by now.' Mickey gave Lissie another hard push up the stairs. 'Come on, lass, let's try out the goods.'

One of his arms circled her waist easily and he lifted her bodily off the stairs to drag her the rest of the way. Ignoring her kicking and protesting, he threw her into the front bedchamber where her mam and dad had slept and slammed the door shut behind him. There was no key in the lock so he dragged their heavy oak chest across the door.

'Now then, lass, let's you and me have a bit o' fun.'

Horrified, Lissie scrambled to the window, but she knew before trying that it would not open. The wood had swollen and warped over the years and it did not budge.

Mickey laughed and made an animal-like growling noise in his throat. 'Go on then, lass, gi' us a bit of a fight. I like a bit of a fight. It makes it all the sweeter in the end.'

She shook her head, so frightened that she was unable to speak and cowered against the wall until he said, 'What are you waiting for? Get that dress off.'

When she did not move he took off his leather belt and flicked the end at her, whipping her arm. She flinched at the stinging pain and rubbed the spot with her other hand. He flicked the belt again, catching the back of her hand and she let out a cry.

'All right!'

Her fingers fumbled with the tiny buttons at the front of her bodice. Whenever she stopped undressing he flicked her again with the belt until the dress and her petticoats had dropped to the floor.

Then he threw down the belt and tore away the rest of her flimsy undergarments until she stood completely naked by the bed.

'Please don't do this,' she whimpered, but he seemed not to hear her.

He pushed her roughly on to the bed. When she tried to cover herself with the blanket, he took both her hands in one fist and lifted them above her head so that every inch of her unclothed body was exposed to him. He stared at her for a long time.

And then he smiled, showing his broken, stained teeth. He let her go and she thought he had changed his mind. Weak with relief, she tried to roll from the bed, away from him. But he clawed her back and hit her hard across the face.

'Stay where you are,' he growled.

He had stopped only so that he could take off his own clothes and as he pressed his coarse swarthy body on hers he snarled like a starved, caged animal.

He terrified her. 'Please don't,' she begged. 'I . . . I haven't done this before.'

'That's not what I 'eard. I 'eard you've bin goin' wi' one o' the bargemen.'

'It's not true,' she croaked.

She pushed at his body and tried to wriggle out from under him. This only served to inflame him further and he slapped her hard with the flat of his hand, knocking her almost senseless. Her defeated, flaccid body flopped back on to the ticking mattress.

Then his coarse hands and foul mouth were all over her, pinching, prodding and poking, and then he drove into her again and again, forcing her flesh apart and covering her mouth with his to stifle her screams.

She must have fainted at that point because the next thing she knew he was holding her head and telling her to take a drink. The brandy trickled into her mouth and revived her. She wished it had not, for that was only the first of several attacks on her that night.

When she struggled against him he became on fire. His eyes burned and his nostrils flared as his brutal assault overcame her weakening resistance. If she tried to escape in the quiet interludes when he was recovering his strength, he hit her.

Eventually, he became exhausted by his efforts and fell into a noisy slumber. Lissie thought that he had had enough of her and would let her leave. Cautiously, she slid away from him in the tumbled bed. But the pain and stiffness, and exhaustion of her bruised, aching body, made her groan involuntarily as she moved, and he woke up.

He revived quickly and began the kissing and stroking again. Except that it wasn't stroking, it was grasping and kneading, then nipping with his teeth at her most sensitive parts. She yelped instinctively, tried to push him off her and then cringed, waiting for the blows.

He grunted. 'You're a strong young wench, I'll gi' yer

that. Don't fight me so much, then I'll not 'ave to hurt
yer.'

Already she could feel his arousal pushing at her side
and managed to croak, 'Please, no more. It hurts so much
and I am so sore . . .'

He growled into her breasts. 'Aye well, if as you say
it's t' first time, it will 'urt. It allus 'urts t' first time. You'll
start to enjoy it now . . . I told yer not to fight too much,
di'n't I?'

His swarthy heavy body was over her again, stabbing
at her, tearing her flesh, again and again. This time it
seemed to go on for ever, until the sweat ran off him
on to her face, filling her nostrils with the stale stench
of his body and the ale on his breath.

After that, he became too exhausted to throw his hairy
body across hers, so he took her hands and guided them
to his private parts.

'Come on, lass. Play wi' 'im. He needs a bit o' coaxing
now. Put a bit o' life back inter 'im.'

She recoiled in disgust as her fingers tangled with his
sticky, matted body hair and warm quivering flesh. She
felt sick at the thought. Then he put a large calloused
hand around the back of her head and pushed it down
towards his feeble arousal.

Oh God, she thought, did he expect her to kiss it?

'Open your gob, love,' he ordered. 'Put him in yer
gob and gi' 'im a good suck.'

Not in her mouth, surely? She gagged at the thought
and when he shoved her face over it she felt the bile
rise in her throat and she retched. She would have
vomited over him if he had not yanked back her head.

'Not ready for that yet, lass? Ee lass, tha's got t' learn a bit more if yer wants to keep yer ma's rent paid. I 'ope yer not goin' to be like yer ma in the bedroom. Like a dead crow she was, just a bag o' bones and no idea at all. A man likes a bit o' playing around in the bedchamber. Aye, a bit o' playing around. I reckon thee an' me can have a good bit o' fun together, once yer know what to do, like.'

She lay there, the taste of vomit in her throat and thought, So this is what hell is like.

It was still dark when she woke again. Every muscle and bone in her body ached and screeched at her as she moved. The sheets were damp and smelly where they had lain. She tasted blood on her lips and hoped some of it was Mickey's, from where she had bitten him. But she guessed that it was hers, and that the dragging pain deep within her stomach had been caused by Mickey's relentless assault.

She felt dirty, soiled and ashamed. Ashamed that she had let this happen, that she did not fight harder. She remembered how Blake had held her in his arms, how his hands had been so gentle, and how he had controlled his urges during that first kiss in the orchard. She thought of what might have been with Blake and she wept.

Dawn was breaking and a candle flickered on the oak chest that was still in place across the door. A bottle of brandy and a glass stood on the mantelshelf and beside it a phial of her mam's laudanum. Mickey snored loudly as she crept out of bed as quickly as she dared.

He stirred and snorted. 'Get back in 'ere, now,' he yawned.

'Just getting a drop of brandy,' she replied. 'I thought it might revive me.'

She picked up the bottle. 'Why don't you have a drop? To get your strength up, eh?' She tried to sound coquettish and persuasive and it worked.

He leered at her. 'Don't mind if I do.'

Her hands shook as she poured out the brandy and then added what was left of her mam's laudanum, stirring it round with her finger before she turned towards him. She kept a fixed smile on her face until he had drained the glass and fallen back on to the pillow. It was easy for her to sit quite still on the bed while the laudanum took effect and his snoring returned.

Ignoring her aches and pains, she heaved back the oak chest inch by inch. It scraped along the floorboards but Mickey did not wake up. Downstairs was quiet too. She gathered up what was left of her clothes and crept across the landing to dress.

Mam had raked out the ashes and left them on the hearth plate for Lissie to take outside. She must have been downstairs all night for the fire was going and there was a full kettle on the hob. Now Mam was nodding off in her chair with a tin mug by her side. And another bottle of laudanum, Lissie noticed. No wonder they had no money for food! Lissie stole quietly across the kitchen.

'Is that you, Lissie?'

'Yes, Mam.'

'You're up early. Mek us a brew, will yer?'

Mam did not even ask how she was or if she wanted

hot water for a wash. Lissie waited until she saw her
eyelids droop again, then dropped some of her laudanum
into her tin mug and topped it up with gin.

'You have another drink, Mam,' she said. 'And a nice
rest. I'm just having a wash in the scullery.' She handed
the mug to her mam and hovered behind her chair as
she drank.

Then she took the kettle, poured some hot water into
a tin bowl, stripped off her clothes and washed herself
all over, standing on an old sack at the stone sink. Every
part of her felt bruised and tender and there was blood
coming out of her as if her bleeding had started early
that month. Her insides hurt and she felt as if she was
being torn in two. From the kitchen cupboard she fetched
the strips of linen that she used to line her under-drawers
and pulled on her brown work dress and shawl.

Then she took her dad's old leather hunting bag from
the front room and began systematically to pack a few
clothes and some bread and cheese. As she moved around
she felt the bleeding again. With some satisfaction, she
tore up the pretty dress that Mickey had brought for
her. The plain underskirts would do for more padding
to stem the blood. The soft cotton felt comforting in
her under-drawers but the aching and tearing still
dragged at her insides. She wondered, briefly, how long
the pain would take to go away and, on impulse, took
the laudanum bottle as well.

Feeling exhausted and weak, she took a draught of
water and chewed on a heel of bread. Hopefully that
would revive her enough to put a safe distance between
her and Mickey Jackson before he came round. The

laudanum was safely tucked away in her bag, along with a few coins that Mickey had left to buy more flour and lard. She put on her old comfy boots that were kept for the garden and tied her new ones by the laces to the broad leather shoulder strap of the hunting bag. The bag felt heavy and it hurt her shoulder as she slung it across her bruised and battered body.

When she was ready she filled her pockets with good apples from the outhouse and left. This had been her home but she felt no remorse. She did not belong here. Miriam had been right all along. Her mam wasn't really her mam and even if her dad was her own dad he was gone now. Gone for ever.

And Blake? She tried to push all thoughts of him from her mind. He had had no right to kill her dad in cold blood like that. She had hoped the constable's men would catch up with him and that he would hang for his evil deed. But he had been too wily for them and had escaped to his native Sweden where he belonged.

When Lissie thought of him a void opened in her body, a cold emptiness that ached with yearning for him. It reinforced her pain and made her despise him more for doing this to her. She took one last look at the little house and the untidy garden that had been her home. It held nothing for her now. Nothing. Whatever unknown lay in store for her, it had to be better than a life as Mickey Jackson's whore.

The tears streamed down her face as she resolutely put one foot in front of the other, forcing herself to move on. She would survive this, she would! There had to be something better for her somewhere. She could live with hardship and was not afraid of work. There had to be a way for her.

Her instinct was to take the track down to the canal and reach the towns from the towpath. But Mickey or one of his boys might see her and bring her back. So instead, Lissie disappeared into the woods at the end of the garden, putting as much distance as she could between her, the canal and the Navigator Inn.

She knew the woods well and soon found a pathway through the undergrowth to where the turnpike skirted the trees. The turnpike was the safest route; most of the people who knew her used the cheaper canals and cuts for getting about. Travellers on the turnpike were noisier too. She was bound to hear horse riders approaching, and carriages if anyone came after her. Traps and hand-carts were quieter, but they were slower and she'd be able to see them coming in time to leave the road and hide in the trees or fields that lay on either side.

But as she trudged through the trees, hardly recognising the path as tears blurred her eyes, her aching became a nagging pain again and the increasing stickiness between her legs warned her that the bleeding had not stopped.

She must reach the turnpike! If she could get to the turnpike before she rested she might take a sip of the laudanum to ease the pain. Perhaps not though, for she had to push on and get further away from Mexton Lock before nightfall. Her dad had often said a man could lose himself in the towns, and that nobody would find him if he didn't want them to. Well, perhaps a woman could lose herself as well.

No, she would not rest, she would stand the pain and save the laudanum for night when it would deaden the cold as well as the pain and let her sleep. She only had to reach the turnpike . . .

As her bruised and torn body protested, her mind became numb and her thoughts were frozen. She had no idea of where she would go or what she would do, only that she had to get away from Mickey Jackson. She knew that she had to survive.

She had bread, cheese and apples for two days and could get fresh water from springs and horse troughs by the road. An isolated barn or cowshed would give her shelter for the night, hopefully with some straw to warm her.

Also, she had a little money now. She felt sick to her stomach as she reasoned that she had earned it. But she would need it when she reached the towns. The knowledge of it there, secreted away in a small drawstring pouch, gave her a feeling of security and determination that urged her battered body forwards.

She had nothing else in this world, save the things she carried with her. She was alone and frightened, frightened of what might happen to her, of who would come after her to drag her back to a life of violation and servitude. She had no notion of what might happen to her in the future but she knew she had had to make a choice, to stay for Mickey Jackson's pleasure or leave the woman who called herself her mam. A woman who had sold her to their landlord for the price of the rent and a bottle of gin.

Lissie knew that whether she lived or died now was

down to her and her alone. What happened to her in the future would be because of what she had chosen to do. This was not her mam's choice, or Miss Kirby's, or Mickey Jackson's. It was hers. Her choice.

But could she survive? She knew she was injured and realised, too late, that she should have gone to Rosa's first, for help. But there had not been enough time. The bleeding was getting worse and she was beginning to feel faint. The pain in the pit of her stomach was increasing and walking seemed to be pulling her apart.

What should she do now? Lie down in a ditch, give up and die? Or stay alive? Stay alive by moving on? Keep going, keep putting one foot in front of the other as each step would put a greater distance between her and a life she had to escape.

She had to block it out of her mind. It never happened. It had been a bad dream and she would wake up soon to hear her dad whistling his way up from the canal carrying a sack over his shoulder and calling for her to come and see what he'd brought her . . .

Chapter 22

Lissie thought she must have fallen as she could not remember leaving the woods. The trees had thinned and now only thick hedges and drystone walls edged the turn-pike. She was in the ditch beside the road, her back against the loose stones of the wall. Through a gap she could see that the fields behind had been harvested and the rooks were down, feeding on the gleanings. Nearby, at the edge of the road, a lone carrion crow tore at a dead rabbit knocked senseless by the hooves of carriage horses.

Perhaps she had thrown herself into this ditch to avoid an express stage coach? She was so thirsty. And so cold. Thankfully, the sun had not yet set and there was still warmth in its rays. The bottom of the ditch was damp and chilly, but she didn't want to move. It hurt so much to move. But she knew that if she stayed and let herself slip into a faint again she would die. She clawed at the grass, hauled herself out of the ditch and forced herself onward.

The turnpike was nearing the track that led down to Fordham, and Miss Kirby's school. Lissie had been at her happiest there, helping to look after the pupils, going to chapel and, most of all, meeting Eliza. She choked back a sob as she realised that she would never see Eliza and Job again.

Nervously, she drank from the stone trough at the top of the rise and moved on. The clear cold water revived her and she was able to push herself more, biting on the leather strap of her bag when the pain became too much to bear. She stumbled along the turnpike ruts until her hunger and weakness melded with pain and exhaustion. A break in the endless drystone walls let her into a field of springy turf that smelled clean and fresh. She ate some bread and cheese, then pushed her best boots beneath her head and allowed herself to sleep.

Her slumbers were short-lived as she was aroused by raucous laughter and the creaking and clattering of a cart on the flinty surface of the turnpike. She heard two men shouting, worse for drink she guessed, as they stopped to feed their horse. Lissie froze and shrank back against the stone wall, listening to their coarse language.

Eventually they quietened and when she heard a snore she stretched her neck to see over the wall. The heavy draught horse was chomping from a nosebag and the men – no, not men, for they were just boys really – were out cold, sprawled on the road beside a brownstone ale flagon, on its side and empty. The cart was loaded with straw, warm dry straw, destined for winter bedding at some farm along the way.

Lissie saw her chance and took it. Ignoring the pain and bleeding, she clambered on to the back of the cart and buried herself in the straw. It warmed her stiffening joints and the cart would take her further from Mexton Lock than her weary legs ever could . . .

Later she was vaguely aware of the cart moving. She heard the boys urgently gee-up the horse. But they were quieter now, having slept off their youthful inebriation. If they found her, she would explain to them how . . . why she was here . . . Warmed by the straw and exhausted by her fight to keep going, she gave in to sleep.

It was dark when she woke up. The cart was turning and it jolted dangerously as it hit a rock in the road. Lissie pushed the straw aside and saw the turnpike receding into the distance as the cart bumped its way down a narrow farm track. She would be discovered! The straw would be forked out into stables or the like and those two coarse and vulgar youths would find her! Terrified of what they might do to her she gathered together her meagre possessions and slid silently off the straw, a bent, shadowy figure clutching the ache in her stomach. Slowly and painfully she retraced the track back to the highway.

She had no idea where she was, only that she was off the turnpike. This highway was smaller and without deep ruts from coaches. Tracks and byways criss-crossed the South Riding as far as Sheffield and beyond. The dark eerie silence was broken by a night rider and the thumping of horse's hooves as he galloped by. She was damp all over from the dank night air and chilled to the bone. Frightened, she tried to quicken her pace so that she would warm up a little, but within yards had keeled over, groaning with weakness and pain. Her toes would not move inside her boots and her fingers did not have the strength to grip the buckle of her bag and open it. She rubbed them frantically and blew on them to get them moving. She must keep going otherwise she might fall into a faint and freeze to death!

As she began her weary trudge onward, Lissie realised it was not the night air that was icy, it was only her own body that was getting colder and colder as it slowed down in its fight to keep going. She must find shelter and warmth where she could rest safely for the remainder of the night. There was no moon or stars that night to light her way and the countryside was not familiar. She must find water to drink. She was so thirsty . . . all the time, so thirsty . . .

There was a fork in the road. The highway stretched in front of her, but to one side lay a track through sparsely wooded land that sloped down from the road, and, hopefully, hopefully, a sleeping farm with barns for shelter. She sat on a tree stump for a long time to gather her strength. In the darkness, she made out a cottage, a large one, built of stone with a slate roof. It had a well-kept garden and cinder paths. The track continued past the cottage and disappeared into more woodland beyond. A vixen screeched and an owl hooted but no sounds came from the cottage, no light burned in its windows.

At one side, there was a long, low building of the sort that houses animals. It was also stone built and in good repair, but firmly shut, its stout wooden doors padlocked against intruders. But, Lissie knew, animals needed water and she crept around until she found a water butt at the back.

Water gave her a second wind and she thought she might climb in through one of the high windows and bed down with the animals. But as she clambered on to a grassy stone and then the damp wooden lid of the butt she felt her flesh tearing again and the familiar warm stickiness of fresh blood between her legs.

Her head felt light and dizzy and she stumbled, falling from the water butt and crying out in pain. Her shawl snagged and tore and her bag fell open, spilling out its meagre contents. From inside the barn she heard a horse whinny and fret at the commotion. She leaned motionless against the rough stone wall and sank slowly to the cold wet ground. The laudanum bottle rolled at her feet. Laudanum! The laudanum would help. It would take the pain away, take the cold away, take the world away.

Just one small sip, that's all, to help her through the night. She winced at the bitterness from the one sip, but gradually her damp and chilly corner seemed a better place. Her aches and pains drifted away and her bleeding seemed to ease. A warm feeling seeped through her veins and her eyelids drooped. She sank further into the ground and drifted into her own oblivion.

She was aroused at dawn by the sound of a horse and cart on the cinder path. She caught a glimpse of it disappearing towards the highway, laden with baskets of livestock and sacks. A man and woman sat upfront, hunched against a chilly wind.

There was a strange tinny taste in her mouth and she

was thirsty again. She was stiff with cold and unable to move her limbs until an early morning sun shed its warmth. Her legs felt like lead weights and her head was feverish and befuddled as she staggered towards the cottage. It had a long covered porch, standing proud of the front door. The porch was well built of old oak posts, with a roof to keep off the winter hail and snow. The door itself looked heavy and was patterned with iron-work studs.

She had to get inside, to warmth, shelter and food, or she would die. She did not want to die. The cottage was quiet and the dawn sun was now hidden by dark clouds that were banking up from the west. She fell with both hands against the stout wooden door and tried to raise a cry or two. No one was home. No one heard her beat the wood with her hands and plead for some help. She trudged silently back to the water butt to drink. The effort made her almost faint and her legs buckled under her. There was no help for her here. She had to move on.

Desperately she tried to focus her eyes on the track. Why did her head feel so light and her legs so heavy? A steady drizzle wet her through and made her already damaged body chilled and even weaker. She couldn't go on, she knew she couldn't. But if she lay down here she might die from the cold and wet. Yet she must rest, other-wise she would bleed to death.

Her head was spinning, the trees were swimming around and the ground kept coming up to meet her and then receding. She felt dizzy. Sick and dizzy. She clung on to an oak post for support. She was back at the cottage, under the porch. Her feet had carried her down the track instead of up towards the highway. It was meant to be, to rest here. Just a short while until her strength returned again . . . The cottage would have a fire . . . a warm fire . . . and perhaps some bread and milk . . . She had money . . . she could pay . . . if only they would let her stay by their fire . . . until the rain eased . . . then she would be on her way . . .

The post was slipping away from her, she couldn't hold on any more. She was mumbling to herself, garbled words that tumbled out. Yes, I have a long way to go . . . right on into town to find work . . . Yes, I am a good worker . . . I have worked in a school . . . I can read and write . . . Please let me in . . . just for a few minutes to warm myself by the fire . . . please . . .

But nobody came as she muttered her pleas through the thick wooden door and beat her hands helplessly against the studded oak. Her back was racked with pain and her life blood was ebbing away into the makeshift bandages between her legs. She began to shiver uncontrollably and her eyes blurred, making her unable to see properly.

She fumbled in her bag for the laudanum and took a sip, then another and another slipped easily down the back of her throat before the small brown bottle slid from her fingers. Her legs buckled beneath her and a cloud of oblivion enveloped her bruised and battered body and soul.

She remembered the pain easing. And then the rain, the ceaseless, soaking rain, and the wind blowing puddles on to the draughty porch, making the fired clay tiles so muddy and slippery that she could not get back on her feet. She remembered the reddish-brown hue of the tiles, and, as the rain seeped through her clothes, the same reddish-brown of her blood as it smeared its way down her legs and spread through her skirts. And then she remembered nothing, only a welcoming blackness releasing her from her suffering.

After the blackness came the horror. Her dad was here, her beloved dad was holding her and kissing her cheeks and hair. But when she looked at his face it wasn't her dad, it was Mickey Jackson and he was laughing at her. Her mam was here too, laughing with Mickey and drinking his gin. Then someone knocked the bottle out of her hand and started beating Mickey with his fists until Mickey fell in a senseless heap on the floor, and when Lissie ran over to look, it was Blake standing there and the man on the floor was her dad and he was dead. Dead. And then she was screaming and yelling at Blake, 'Murderer! Murderer!' over and over again until she floated away.

She felt hot. She was burning alive. Water. She needed water from the pump. Fetch water from the pump. More water. More water. And then there was water all over her and she was icy, icy cold. She must be in her grave, in the cold, cold earth. She was dead. This is what it was like to be dead. Cold and more cold all around her.

Her hands and feet were pinched and nithered and there was no fire because she hadn't cleaned the grate and Miss Kirby was shouting at her to get the fire going. But it wouldn't light and her fingers were too numb to strike the flint. There was a heavy weight on her chest that felt so tight she couldn't breathe. She was suffocating. She was in her coffin, suffocating.

She beat her fists against the sides and they yielded, strangely soft, letting in more cold wet air. She was fighting, fighting for air. She wanted to breathe. She didn't want to die. She wouldn't die. She wouldn't. Somebody help me. Take my hand. Somebody, take my hand, don't let me die.

And in her fever someone did take her hand and held on to it, dragging her back from the brink of death, holding on to her, keeping her safe. The heavy weight bearing down upon her chest eased and she could breathe again. Roused from her delirium, she felt the softness of a feather bed and pillows beneath her.

This must be Heaven, she thought, as someone raised her head and gently offered a cup of water to her parched lips. She drank, then sank back into the gentle haze of garden lavender beneath her head. And in her new found comfort, at last, she slumbered peacefully.

She woke up facing a small window that looked out on to a grey sky. It had proper curtains made of some heavy, green material. They were pulled back now to let in daylight. The room was small but it had a chair and a washstand holding folded linen and torn strips next to a row of small pots and bottles. She could smell the salve, the strong odour of wintergreen overpowered her lavender pillow.

There was a fireplace with cupboards fitted into alcoves on either side. A fire burned in the grate and an earthenware pitcher stood on the hearth. The bed was wide and very soft. Lissie fingered the sheets. They were old, but made of linen, like Miss Kirby's sheets, and the bedcover was made up of the same stuff as the curtains. The wooden bedstead creaked as Lissie tried to sit up. Shortly afterwards she heard footsteps on the stairs and the bedroom door opened.

'Well, well, you pulled through after all. You've had me fair worried these past few days.'

A large-boned woman with greying brown hair under a lace cap and wearing a coarse-textured grey work dress stood in the doorway. She had striking features and held herself well, giving an overall effect of being handsome rather than beautiful. Her expression was a mixture of curiosity and anxiety as she looked critically at Lissie.

Lissie tried again to lever herself up into a sitting position. 'Who . . . who are you? Where am I?' she croaked. Her throat was parched.

'Don't try and get up, you're too weak still. You've been very ill and you must rest.'

'How did I get here? I can't remember . . .'

'You will in time. Don't fret yourself, you're safe here.'

Safe? Suddenly, Lissie was stricken by panic and her eyes widened in alarm. 'Has he found me? Where is he? Has he been here? Don't let him in! Please don't let him . . .' She tried to turn back the covers. 'I should go, move away from here . . .' But her arms weren't strong enough to shift the heavy blankets and her legs would not move.

The woman came forward quickly and placed her hand over Lissie's as it clutched the bedcovers. 'Stay calm. You have to stay calm to get better.'

Her quiet insistence was reassuring and Lissie fell back against the pillows.

'You'll be in bed a while yet, my girl. It was touch and go for some time.'

'How long? How long have I been here?'

'There'll be plenty of time for questions when you're better. You have to concentrate on getting your strength back for now.'

'But what happened to me?'

The older woman grimaced sympathetically. 'You'll remember when you're ready to. And I'll be here for you.' She hesitated, before adding, 'You lost a lot of blood and then you caught a raging fever. But you're over it now and you'll get well again.' The grimace turned into a smile. 'You will get well, I promise you, if you try. But only if you try. You will try, won't you?'

Lissie nodded. Snatches of her nightmares pushed themselves forward in her head. 'It was raining, I remember it was raining . . . and . . .' As the memories flooded back, tears welled up in her eyes.

Again the woman held her hand. 'Don't dwell on it now. It's over and you're on the mend. Your body will heal and you must be strong in yourself to help it along.' After a minute or two she added briskly, 'Now, I'll bring you some beef tea and bread to begin with – er – what do I call you, what's your name?'

'Lissie. Lissie D— Er – just Lissie.'

'Well, I suppose that "just Lissie" will have to do for now. I'm Martha. Martha Thorogood.'

'Thank you, Mrs Thorogood.' Her voice croaked again and she coughed.

'Call me Martha. Please. We don't stand on ceremony at this farm.' She frowned slightly. The girl was still very weak. 'You rest now. I'll fetch your soup.'

'I can come downstairs,' Lissie volunteered. 'I don't want to trouble you.' She made a supreme effort to sit up and realised that every part of her body hurt and her insides felt as though they were being mangled. She fell back. Martha was right, she had no strength.

'It's no trouble. And if you move around you'll start the bleeding again so it's best for you to stay put.' Martha gave her another reassuring smile. 'You've a long way to go yet, lass, before you can get up.'

Lissie again allowed herself to sink back into the feather pillows and mattress. She remained there, motionless, until Martha returned. Looking around the room at the linen and salves, she realised that Martha had taken very good care of her. Her nightgown was beautifully soft and white, with lots of smocking, drawn-thread work on the sleeves and ribbon ties at the neck.

She pushed back the gathered cuffs to expose her wrists and forearms and noticed with a shock how thin and bony they had become. And pale. Her skin was so white it looked like marble.

Martha came back with her beef tea and some toasted bread on a wooden tray that had large handles at either side. She put the tray on a wooden chest at the foot of the bed while she helped Lissie sit up, stuffing more soft pillows behind her so that she felt comfortable. Then she placed the tray across her knees and said, 'If you can take some of the toast, soaked in beef tea, it will help you get stronger. And there's warm milk and honey in the tankard.'

Lissie realised she had little appetite for any food. However, she knew that she must try otherwise she'd just waste away. She picked up the spoon. The beef tea was surprisingly good and the delicate savoury taste perked up her palate. She took another spoonful and a little of the soaked toast. 'Thank you, Martha. You have been so kind to me. Why would you be so good to a total stranger?'

Martha moved a pile of clean linen to the wooden box and drew up the only chair nearer to the bed. 'Ee, lass! I couldn't let you die on my doorstep. When I got back from market that day I thought you were already gone. You were just a soggy wet heap on my front porch. And there was blood all over, where the rain had spread it through your clothes and over my tiles.'

'I'm sorry . . . I . . . I . . . don't know what happened to me. I think I fainted.'

'Fainted? You were in a stupor for days. No blood left in your veins at all to be sure. I think it was all soaked into your clothes instead. It took a while to get out, but it's not too bad now, just a dark patch here and there. Doesn't show too much on that brown dress of yours.' Martha tossed her head, indicating the alcoves behind her. 'All your things are safe and sound in the cupboard there. I cleaned up what I could.'

Lissie felt Martha's keen brown eyes watching her as she spoke. She remembered it all now. Mickey Jackson, the attack and feeling so soiled, so dirty and ashamed, and walking out on her mam. She prayed that she would never have to see Mickey Jackson again. Ever.

'I . . . I can't go back. I can't,' she stammered.

'No, I expect not. But you didn't do yourself any good being on the road, walking and out in all that rain. And I didn't know how much of that laudanum stuff you'd taken – I found an empty bottle on the porch. You were very weak from the bleeding – and then you caught a fever, a nasty one, which had me very worried. I didn't know whether you'd have enough strength left to fight it.'

'I was in a lot of pain. The laudanum helped. It just took it away so I felt I could go on.'

'Oh aye, it does that all right. But it cannot stop you catching the fever. You had to ride out the fever yourself. And being in a weakened state, taking no nourishment, it was touch and go for a while.' Martha watched quietly for a few moments as Lissie took her beef tea and toast and then added, 'You must be a strong young woman underneath to come through this like you have. I've seen women die of much less.'

Lissie laid down her spoon. 'I am so grateful to you, Martha. I had nowhere to go. But, believe me, nowhere was better than staying where I was. I can't thank you enough for taking me in.'

The older woman smiled. 'I don't know what you're running from, but I've been looking after you for two weeks now and I've seen the bruising and the tearing so I know more or less what's happened to you. How old are you?'

'Nearly sixteen.'

'And you've no wedding ring, so the man that did this to you was not your husband. Well, I'll not ask you to relive it, but if you want to tell me, I'll listen.'

Lissie felt mortified with shame at the memory. 'I can't . . . I can't talk about it. It's too painful, too awful . . .'

'Aye well, then it's best forgot if you can. I'll leave you to finish your beef tea and get some more rest. That's the best medicine for you now.'

Alone with her thoughts Lissie ate as much as she could manage and took a little of the milk and honey. Within minutes she felt exhausted again and her eyelids drooped. Half-asleep, she thought she heard doors opening and closing downstairs and the clatter of crockery. An aroma of meat stew drifted up the stairs and under her bedroom door.

The house was unusually quiet. No voices, no family – just Martha perhaps? But she had seen a man, hadn't she? A big man, driving the farm cart off to market that day. He was a fair bit younger than Martha. Maybe her son? Or just a farm hand? She couldn't tell. Nervously, she wondered where he was now and what would happen if he came upstairs when she was alone.

Martha tended to her needs well and Lissie grew stronger by the day. She worried for the older woman constantly climbing up and down the stairs for her and begged to come downstairs. But Martha would hear none of it.

'You can get down all right but you would do yourself some damage climbing back up the stairs to be sure. You don't want to set off the bleeding all over again.'

'How bad am I, Martha? You know, inside me?'

'Hard to tell, really. It looked worse than anything I've seen before. But you are young and young bodies mend better than old ones.' She hesitated before continuing, 'Your flesh was badly torn and I don't know how much you were damaged right inside. I'll be right in thinking you've not had any babies yet?'

Lissie shook her head. 'I'd never been with a man before. Not like that – and he was so . . . so brutal . . .' She choked on the memory.

'Aye well, it was painful for you because you were still a maid. You are a pretty one though. And men do like to bed pretty maids.'

'I tried to fight him off.'

'That would've made it worse for you, but you weren't to know. Your flesh will heal with time, and we shall have to wait and see about a baby.'

Lissie's mouth dropped open. 'A baby?'

'Aye, lass. It does happen when you lie with a man. You could be with child. His child.'

'No! No, I can't be! I didn't want to do it! He made me do it! He forced me!'

'Makes no difference to God's will. If God wants you to have a baby then you'll have one. But you need not fret so. In my experience it's unlikely you'll have kept it, what with all that bleeding going on and you being so ill with the fever. You never can tell though. You've got a strong heart underneath that pallid skin, and you're healing well.'

Martha thought for a moment, then went on. 'I suppose you could try coming downstairs awhile. If you did, John could carry you back upstairs.'

Lissie clutched the bedding and drew it up to her throat.

'Who is John? Is he your husband?'

'Nay, lass,' Martha laughed. 'My husband is long gone to his grave. John is my son and he works the farm for me. He lives with me here but spends most of his time outdoors. He loves the outdoors does my John, like his father before him I suppose.'

Her face softened and she smiled. 'John won't do you any harm, my dear, though he does sometimes lose his rag when things go wrong. He's a gentle giant. But he can't speak like you or me. He was born like it. I had a putrid fever when he were in the womb and they say that caused it. He's stone deaf, you see. So he never learned to talk right.

'He has good eyes though,' Martha continued, 'and he's quick on the uptake. You only have to show him something once and away he goes. And strong. Like his father. His father was a big strong man. But he was old when John was born so he never really saw him grow up. Gone to his grave now, God rest his soul.'

She gently unclasped Lissie's hands from the bunched up bedding. 'John won't hurt you, love. He wouldn't hurt a fly.'

Lissie smoothed down the sheets and Martha asked, 'This man, the one that did this to you, who was he?'

Lissie considered lying. It would be so much easier to say he was a stranger who had attacked her on the road. But Martha deserved the truth, Lissie decided and so she said, 'He was someone my mam and dad knew. Mam said – I thought she said – she said he was going to look after us.'

Martha gazed at Lissie steadily for a long time before

she went on. 'When you had the fever, you were delirious and you talked. You said things.'

'What things?'

'Most of the time it made no sense, but, well,' Martha heaved a sigh, 'you talked about a killing, a murder. Did you kill him, Lissie? I have to know. Did you kill the man who did this to you?'

'No.' Her answer came out with a long sigh. 'I wish I had. Him and my mam together. The pair of them are evil and I hate them both.'

'Your mam? You wished you'd killed your mam? Did your dad kill him, then?'

Lissie shook her head and the tears welled in her large green eyes. 'No, nothing like that. No. It's my dad who is dead. All this would not have happened if my dad had still been alive. He was murdered, you see. It was my dad who was murdered.'

'Your dad. I see. By this man? Did this man kill your dad?'

Lissie's heart turned over as she thought: No, my dad was murdered by someone else. By a man I thought I loved. But he was a fraud and a liar and just using me to get at my dad. How could I have been taken in by Blake? she thought. He seemed so genuine. Best forget I ever met him. If I can.

She stared at the lime-washed plaster walls and said, 'No, it's just that when my dad was killed we had no money and my mam said I had to . . .' she choked on the words '. . . to go with him to pay the rent.'

'Your own mam. Oh, I'm so sorry, Lissie.'

She began to cry. 'She was at her wits' end and she

needed her gin and she said I wasn't to work at the inn.' It was the first time she had cried about the attack and her tears began to flow freely down her face. 'He bought me a dress and I thought he was being nice to me because he wanted my mam. But all the time it was me he wanted. And Mam said she'd explained it to me but she hadn't really. And he dragged me up the stairs and pulled the chest across the door so I couldn't get out.'

The sobs were rattling from her throat in shudders as she relived the horror. Martha held her until she calmed and Lissie carried on, her voice wavering with hiccups. 'She – she's not my real mam. She never wanted me, I can see that now. I . . . I don't know who my real mam is. Nobody does, but my dad has always looked after me and he was nice to me. He let me go to school when he had the money, but it ran out and then I worked there in the kitchen and seeing to the house for the schoolmistress and her brother.' She heaved in a noisy breath. 'They were strict about everything but it was a nice house. Like this one.'

'Hush, now. Talk about it if you must, but you don't have to tell me if you don't want to.'

Lissie's grief spilled out. 'Bl . . . Bla . . . this friend of Mr Kirby's came to stay and I had met him before and I liked him a lot. I thought he liked me as well but it turned out that he was putting on an act. He was after my dad and he killed him in a fight.' She wiped her eyes with the back of her hand and inhaled shakily. 'After that, Mam had no money for the rent. The man that – that did this to me had bought our house off Dad years ago when the canal trade was bad. So it was him, you see, and we had to pay him his dues . . .' The memories were too vivid. Her words stuck in her throat and she gave herself up to her tears.

Martha's soothing voice interrupted her, 'And that's enough for the moment. You're too upset and I see why now. It's too much for a body to deal with. You have to take your mind off what's happened, otherwise you'll not get better. You can come down for your dinner today and John will bring you back up afterwards. Wrap yourself in my big shawl and put these goatskin slippers on your feet.'

Chapter 23

Lissie's recovery was slow and steady, and soon she was pulling a skirt on over her nightgown and tying a shawl round her shoulders so that she could stay downstairs for dinner and tea.

'You must remember that John can't hear you,' Martha explained. 'And try not to rile him because he can go off in a tantrum sometimes. He sees really well, so if you want his attention, wave one of these calico cloths outside. He can catch sight of it from as far away as the top pasture.'

She looked at the young woman sitting in her rocking chair by the kitchen range and was pleased with the improvement in her colour. 'Well, now you are feeling stronger, we'll kill a fowl for dinner. I've got two of them not laying and I reckon one of them can go in the pot.'

Lissie thought that Martha's husband must have been fairly well off for a tenant farmer. Farmers in the South Riding were usually tenants if they were not gentry. It was good land by all accounts, just at the edge of a big estate and only a few miles from the ironworks towns in the valley.

As Lissie's strength returned, she was able to help Martha run the farmhouse. There was always a good fire and Martha was a capable housekeeper. Her high tea of home-cured ham and new-laid eggs marked the end of the working day for John and he came in, ruddy from the fresh air, and, as always, hungry and thirsty. Martha made real tea to go with the meal every day and they drank it with fresh-baked bread or scones, and jam made from the orchard fruit.

The autumn evening closed in chilly as Martha mulled a tankard of ale for John and put out cold pie for his supper. Although he could not speak, Lissie could tell from his face how he was feeling. He was cheerful tonight, but yesterday he had been frustrated about something out on the farm and had made angry noises in his throat to try and tell them about it. He had thumped the table making the knives jump and rattle. Martha became cross with him in turn and shouted at him to stop. Even though he could not hear her, he knew from her countenance that she was angry.

Lissie realised then that his frustration was not about the farm. He had been angry with himself for not being able to speak.

'Martha?' Lissie asked.

'What now, lass? I'm a bit tired tonight.'

'Have you got a slate and some soft chalkstone?'

'Yes, I have. I use them for the prices when we go to market. They're in the cart in the barn.'

'I think I'll just go out and fetch them.'

'Not in this cold wind, you're not. You'll catch your death,' Martha protested.

'I was fine tying up raspberry canes in the garden this morning.'

'You're always the same when you get a bee in your bonnet! Well, take my big shawl. And John, to hold the lamp.'

They were soon back in the kitchen, at the scrubbed wooden table with slates and chalk. Lissie drew a picture of a pig and showed it to John. Then she chalked the word 'pig' underneath and got him to copy the letters on his slate. She did the same for a cow. He laughed about her drawing but knew what it was.

'What are you two doing over there?' Martha asked.

'I'm teaching him to read,' Lissie replied. 'If he can read and write he can as good as talk to us, and then he won't lose his temper. He only loses it when he gets frustrated.'

'Do you think he will be able to learn though?'

'Oh yes, Martha. I am sure he will. I know he can't speak, but he can think all right.'

'Well, would you believe it! After all these years!'

'Martha, he will be able to do his numbers as well,' Lissie added excitedly. 'I know he will!'

'Well, this is the best news I have ever heard!' Martha exclaimed. 'If he can do all that I shall be able to make over the farm to him properly. My husband only left it to me because of John's affliction.'

Martha watched Lissie teaching her adult son to read. She was so much better now. This was just what she wanted to take her mind off her ordeal. But the girl also needed something to take her outside of the farm and meet up with other folk.

Lissie looked up and saw Martha staring. They exchanged easy, comforting smiles and Martha thought that she would not want Lissie to leave them.

John learned quickly during the dark evenings of that winter, and soon moved on from slate and chalk. However, when spring arrived, his work on the farm soon took him away from his lessons. One evening the following autumn, he was writing something on paper that Martha had brought in from her bureau in the front parlour. Sitting at the kitchen table he bent over his task, concentrating hard, dipping his quill frequently in the inkpot and scratching away at the paper.

'Don't you be spilling any ink on that fresh-scrubbed table, my lad,' Martha warned. 'I have to knead the bread on there.'

'I'll get him to fashion a board to write on,' Lissie suggested. 'He needs a writing slope anyway because he is too big to sit hunched up here. Miss Kirby had one at the school. If I draw what I mean on a slate, he'll make it in no time.'

Lissie and Martha were sitting by the fire at the end of their working day. It had been a particularly busy day for all of them as tomorrow was market day and they had been loading the farm cart to take into town at first light. As usual there was plenty of produce to sell, vegetables that they could spare from the garden and some apples off the trees. Martha's chickens had bred well that year and she had surplus hens and cocks, which always fetched a good price.

But this time they had something different to offer. It had been Lissie's idea. As she regained her strength she wanted to help out Martha and John in any way she could. Martha had said it was enough teaching John to read and write, but Lissie could only do this at the end of the day when he came in from the fields. Even then, he was sometimes too tired to do much.

So she needed something to occupy her during the day. There was planting and hoeing to be done in the vegetable patch when John was busy on the farm. She had also helped Martha with preserving and storing her fruit and vegetables to see them through the winter months. And there was always bread to bake, meals to prepare and rooms to clean, an aspect of life at which both Lissie and Martha excelled.

But it was not enough for Lissie just to earn her keep. She wanted to give more to the woman who had saved her life. Martha needed a new woollen dress before the winter set in and Lissie planned to earn enough to buy some good cloth for both of them.

'What is John doing at the table? I thought he'd be too tired for any book work tonight,' Martha commented as she threw another log on to the range.

'I don't know, but he'll show us when he's done.'

It didn't take long before he brought the single sheet of paper over to Martha. On it he had written, in beautiful copperplate script, the word 'Mother' and underneath 'I love you'. Tears came into her eyes as she nodded her appreciation to him and he went back to the table.

A few minutes later he returned to the fireside, this time to show Lissie his work. Again a sheet of paper, this time with her name and underneath 'I love you'.

Lissie was slightly taken aback, but John was grinning and holding up his left hand to signal her to wait. He went back to the table and wrote some more before showing her the paper again. Now it read 'Lissie. I love your pies.' Lissie giggled and passed the paper across to Martha.

'Yes well,' Martha smiled, 'you do make a tasty pie, I'll give you that. And my John knows a good pie when it's about.'

'Let's hope the townsfolk think the same.'

'Oh, I think they will,' Martha responded. 'They work hard in the furnaces and forges in town and they do like to fill their bellies. The womenfolk are always looking for something tasty for tea.'

Lissie's expression was a cross between pleasure and pensiveness. She'd loved making her pies but couldn't believe anyone would be paying good money for them when they could just as easily bake them themselves.

Martha, with her wisdom gained from years of selling produce in the town market, knew different. She was convinced Lissie's pies would sell. She had already cleared the front parlour table to make up the wool into new dresses.

That night Lissie slept well, having had a hard day baking. She dreamed of making raised pie crust and boiling pigs' trotters for jelly. It was a relief to wake up and know that her pies were cooked and cold now, and wrapped in calico cloths in baskets already on the cart in the barn.

Today, for the first time, Lissie would go with Martha and John to town for the market. Town! She had heard so much about life in town, but Fordham had been the nearest she had ventured and that had only been one street of big houses with side roads of cottages. Town! And with her own pork pies to sell in the market square!

They left at dawn and the early-morning mist had cleared by the time their farm cart reached the top of the final hill before town. Already the factory chimneys were smoking and plumes were swirling about the rooftops. Town had its own smell too, that was different from the farm; a stench of decaying animal and vegetable waste mixed with chimney smoke from coal fires was overlaid by a thicker acrid atmosphere belched out by the works. It rose up the hill to meet them, making Lissie catch her breath and cough.

'It's a clear day,' Martha commented as they rode side by side next to John urging on their horse, 'and once we're down in town we'll be out of this smoke. It's bad when it rains though. The clouds bring the smoke down on you and you can't breathe then.'

Lissie had never in her life seen so many houses all at once. Rows and rows of them, mostly brick and slate and not like the warm stone of the villages that she knew. And so many people too, out early, going to labour in the ironworks, pits and forges, or going to market as they were.

They approached the centre of town and the noise became louder for the road was cobbled. Horses and carts rattled along and the boots of so many people clacked and clattered after them. The market square was already busy when they arrived, with fretting livestock unsettled by their journey and penned in by unfamiliar hurdles.

John drew up on the edge of the town square, where another road came in from the other side of town, and set up their pitch. He gave their horse a nosebag and let down the back of the cart, taking out two empty barrels across which he stretched planks of wood. On top of this he heaved down the baskets filled with Lissie's pies and she began to unpack them.

She had little ones for selling whole, and bigger round ones for cutting into wedges with Martha's sharpened kitchen knife. Martha stacked her apples and garden vegetables next to them. Her chickens were kept in wickerwork baskets on the cart. John went off to look at the stock pens, his familiar face soon recognised by old friends who slapped him on the back and muttered things he couldn't hear.

There were people all over, more than Lissie had ever seen in her life before. And they kept coming; talking, laughing, shouting, arguing and sometimes fighting, especially around the two alehouses that fronted the square. Someone started playing a flute and a few men, influenced by drink, began dancing, their boots ringing on the cobbles. Lissie chalked on a slate that she propped up by her basket, *Pork Pies. Best in the South Riding.*

She had sold out before midday. Most of the garden produce had gone as well, and all of Martha's chickens. Lissie was amazed. She could have sold her pies all over again. Easily! There were so many people with money to spend!

'They've got families to feed and no farm like we have,' Martha explained. 'And there are inns and boarding houses in town. Innkeepers like a decent chicken for the pot when they can get one. There's an even bigger town past Tinsley, right at the end of the canal. They make knives and tools and stuff that goes all the way to London to be sold. But this place is big enough for us.'

'I'll say,' Lissie enthused. 'Look how much we've got to buy our cloth.'

'Aye, you've done well. At this rate we'll be buying silk next time instead of wool. The draper will stay open late today, so why don't you have a stroll round the market and town for an hour or so. Then we'll have our bread and cheese afore we do our own marketing.'

Lissie wandered about looking at other wares and listening to the auctioneer shouting the bids as the stock pens emptied and new owners led their animals away. She ventured down a side street or two but found them unsavoury places, especially around the inns and going down to the canal.

There was a big dirty ironworks on an island there, where the river went one side and a canal had been cut the other side for the barges. The barges brought the iron ore in and took bar iron out to forges where it was worked into axles for railway engines and the like. There were some forges nearby, and the slamming of drop hammers made her head rattle when she got too close!

There were women too. She had seen the women in the square early on and knew what they were about. They pulled down the necks of their bodices and took out any lace or muslin to expose their throats and swelling breasts. One had hitched up one side of her long skirts to show off a shapely ankle and slender leg as she waited.

They loitered for men to come out of the alehouses, flushed with drink and, hopefully, with money still in their pockets. Then the two of them would disappear down an alley for their own special bit of marketing.

Lissie recognised one of them with a start as she realised how far from home the woman was. She had put some stuff on her hair to make sure that she was noticed. It was gaudy, Lissie thought, more like the colour of Martha's copper kitchen pans, than hair. She watched her for a while, fascinated by her appearance, then approached her.

'Rosa? It is Rosa, isn't it?' she asked tentatively.

The older woman turned slowly to face her, her eyes unusually bright and her lips red with French rouge. 'What?' she said abruptly. 'What do you want? This is my patch. Clear off.'

'It's Lissie. You must remember me. Edie's girl.'

Rosa blinked and looked her up and down. 'What? Lissie Dearne? Little Lissie Dearne? So it is. Not so little now, are yo'? You come to work 'ere an' all?'

'No ... I ... er ... I wondered how ... how Mam was getting on?'

'As if you care! She could be dead and gone for all you know. Some lass you turned out to be, deserting your dear old mam in her hour of need, wi' your poor ol' dad hardly cold in the ground. It's lucky she had me to look out for her, else she'd 'a' bin in the workhouse long ago.'

'How is she, Rosa?'

'She i'n't that well. What do you think I'm here fo'? She needs her medicine and it costs money. Now, if you're here to work an' all, I'll thank you to clear off to your own patch.'

A brawny man in dirty breeches and a greasy coat came out of the inn and saw the two women together. He obviously knew Rosa and came right up to them both.

'Well, well. You got an apprentice now, Rosie? How much for the young 'un?'

Quick as a flash Rosa replied, 'A guinea.'

'Don't be daft!'

'You can afford it, Jethro Baines, and you can have her for the night for that.'

His eyes lit up. 'What? Tek her home wi' me?' Then his face fell. 'What'd the missus say?'

'Lucky bugger, probably,' Rosa sneered. 'Are you buying or not?'

'Only the young 'un.'

'I'm not for sale,' Lissie broke in firmly.

'Oooh! Hoity-toity an' all! I'll gi' thee a shilling. Tek it or leave it.'

'I *said* I'm not for sale.' Lissie turned to walk away but Rosa gripped her arm with a surprising strength and stopped her.

'You 'eard the lass,' Rosa added. 'Clear off, Jethro.'

'Huh. Some company you keep these days, Rosie me girl. I'll find missenn a decent tart down by the cut.' He went off with a jaunty stride, whistling to himself.

Rosa was still holding on to Lissie's arm. 'We thought you were dead,' she said. 'Going off like that and never coming back. Why did y' do that to yer old mam?'

'She didn't tell you then?'

'Tell me what? That you didn't want to work for your keep? We all 'as to work for our keep and if you 'a'n't got no man to fend fo' you, you 'as to find summat.'

Lissie realised that without money for rent, Mickey Jackson would have turned her mam out. 'I . . . I didn't know what else to do. I couldn't . . .' She choked on the words, unable, even after all this time, to talk about that dreadful night. 'Where is she now?'

'She's wi' me o' course. Where else would she be? We allus looked after each other an' I i'n't gi'ing up on 'er now.'

'How bad is she, Rosa?'

'She's got no strength, but I reckon there's a year or two left in her yet. She talks about yer sometimes. She says your name. Why don't you come and see her for yerssenn? You'd better make it soon though, if you wants 'er to talk any sense.'

The parish clock struck the hour and Lissie realised Martha and John would be waiting for her. 'I've got to go now, Rosa. Will you tell Mam I'll come and see her? Before Christmastide, if the snows keep away.'

Rosa looked doubtful and said, 'I'm not saying owt to 'er if yer don't mean it.'

'I do mean it. I promise.'

'All right then. Clear off now and let me get on wi' me business.'

Lissie retraced her steps back to the market square. She wondered how far it was from Martha's farm to Mexton Lock. Maybe a day's journey if she took a carrier along the turnpike and walked down through the wood.

But her inner journey, she thought, would be the longest one of her life.

She discussed it with Martha a few days later. 'I want to see her, Martha. For all her faults she was the mam that brought me up. And I did walk out and leave her.'

'Well, if you have the strength to go, you must do it,' Martha advised, keeping her eyes on the sewing in her hands.

'I am frightened though,' Lissie admitted.

'What of? Your mam?'

'No. Him. You know, the one that . . .'

'Do you think he'll try it again?'

'Well no. Mam's living with her friend Rosa now, so she's not beholden to him any more. He generally picks his women from the ones that hang around the Navigator.'

'Best stay away from there, then. Will Rosa be able to put you up?'

Lissie thought she would. 'I'll stay on the woodland side of Mexton Lock while I'm there.'

'Maybe John should go with you and take the cart?'

'Oh no, I couldn't ask him to do that,' Lissie replied. 'He's needed for the ploughing before the winter frosts set in. Mind, he could take me as far as the turnpike where I can get the morning carrier.'

Martha sighed. 'Well, if you are set on it you'd better not delay. T' weather can easily turn nasty at this time of year.' She gave a small smile at last. 'I'll make up your new winter dress while you're gone. It'll be something to bring you back to me.'

Lissie detected a wistful tone in Martha's voice and

looked at her sharply. 'But of course I'll come back to you, Martha,' she said. 'Do you think I won't? There is nothing for me now at Mexton Lock. The house is gone and Mam has never wanted me. My true family, the one that I love, is here.'

Martha's eyes glistened with tears. 'Just make sure you do, lass.'

Lissie walked over to her chair and put her arm around Martha's shoulders. 'I wouldn't leave you and John. You're all I have.'

Martha put down her sewing and took a deep breath. 'Well, as long as that's settled, I'll get on and make some beef tea for you to take to your mam. And fetch in some new laid eggs and butter for her. And how about one of your pies for Rosa?'

'Oh, Martha, you are so good to me. I do love you.'

Then Martha did something she had never done before. She took Lissie in her arms and gave her a long lingering hug. Her voice was squeaky and hoarse as she whispered, 'Just make sure you come back to us safe and sound. All right?'

'I'll be back, I promise you, Martha. And don't you go fretting about me, I'll be all right. I will.'

Chapter 24

Retracing that journey, now a lifetime away for Lissie, affected her more than she had thought it would. It started as soon as she reached the turnpike and waved goodbye to John. The jolting carrier cart brought back memories of the straw wagon, the cold, the pain and the bleeding. The memories worsened as she passed the wall where she had hidden and waited for the two lads to fall asleep after their flagon of ale. They became even worse when she approached the familiar woods, pulled her box down from the carrier, and searched for the track down to the canal.

The track was wider now, and the trees thinner as more lumber had been cut in her absence. The walk seemed shorter and the woods smaller than she remembered. Her world had grown in the time she had been away. She realised that she had grown in her worldliness as well. She had had a woman's body then, but without a woman's wisdom. Now she had the benefit of Martha's wise counsel. She hoped that it would help her to survive this visit.

As the track passed her former home she shivered at the memory of her last night under that roof. She had pushed áll those dark thoughts to the back of her mind. She had locked them away in a box in her head for good. But her body shuddered as she hurried by.

The house was occupied. There was clean washing on a line strung out between two of the apple trees in the back garden. Small clothes and bedsheets blew about in the breeze. She recognised a pretty woman with frizzy carroty hair tending the vegetable patch. As she straightened, rubbing her back, Lissie saw she was with child. She had been walking out with Mickey's eldest two years ago. They must be married now and living in the house. She hoped the woman had not seen her and scuttled on, the dragging weight of her box pulling her down.

The lock looked exactly the same. Why should it look any different, Lissie thought? Still the piles of coals and heaps of logs. Still the Navigator Inn and its surrounding buildings over on the other side. Still the slow steady progress of the barges through the lock, filling and emptying, filling and emptying, as it had always done. Over the sound of water rushing through the sluices she could hear the ringing of the blacksmith's hammer on his anvil as he worked. Nothing had changed. Why should it? Why should it have changed just because she had gone away?

Rosa was surprised to see her, but welcomed her, and seemed genuinely pleased with the beef tea and food from the dairy. There was broth on the hob and Lissie

sat down gratefully to a steaming bowlful of it with a
heel from a stale loaf. She broke up the bread and dropped
a piece in the broth to soak.

'How is my mam?' Lissie asked.

'Fair. She talks about yer sometimes. Well, mostly
rambles on these days, but she keeps saying yer name.
And she goes on about Luther.' Rosa paused. 'She says
you were his and not really hers.'

'Well, I sort of knew that anyway. She always told me
when I was naughty that she'd sell me back to the gypsies.'

'Aye well, y' 'ave that look about yer. She knows more
than that though. After Luther died and . . . and then yer
cleared off, she 'ad to sell his things to try and pay t'
rent – most of t' furniture, his garden spade an' fork. An'
his gun.'

Lissie looked down. If only her mam had talked to
her earlier about paying the rent, she might have thought
of that herself. The gun alone would have fetched enough
to keep them going for quite a while.

'It weren't enough for Mickey Jackson,' Rosa
continued. 'He wanted that house for his eldest lad
and . . . and, well, your mam spent all her money on gin
anyroad. She moved in 'ere wi' me and my earnings from
t' herbals kept us going for a bit. But even that's not
enough for yer ma's laudanum. She gets through quite
a bit o' that nowadays. Still, I goes to market day in town
every now and then,' she shot a sideways glance at Lissie,
'as yer know. Usually at quarter day when t' rent's due,
and we manage.'

'You do that for my mam?'

'We go back a long way, me and yer mam. She were

allus a good friend to me and I'd do owt for her. It's no skin off my nose. Men are all the same anyroad, an' I can tek 'em or leave 'em. Me and yer mam get along fine. Leastways we did till she took poorly this summer. She's lost a lot o' her strength now, but she rallies every now and then and comes downstairs.'

'She should have told me about Mickey.'

'She said she did.'

'I didn't realise what she meant. I could have found another way.'

'Oh aye? 'Ow? 'E allus gets what he wants. 'E wanted you, not 'er.'

Lissie accepted that this was true and tried to calm down. 'Well, I was mad with her.'

'She were mad wi' you an' all.'

'Will she want to see me after all this time?'

'Oh aye, she'll see yer. She been asking for yer since she cleared out o' t' house. She found some bits and pieces o' Luther's, along wi' 'is gun in the old clock. From yer real ma, she says.'

Lissie felt suddenly weak and shaky. She had not expected this. Maybe her dad had been married before and he'd held on to a few keepsakes. Dad had been soft like that, she recalled, more so than her mam.

The beef tea was sizzling in a small copper pan on the hob. Rosa stirred it and said, 'I'll tek this upstairs and tell 'er yer 'ere. Come upstairs in a bit and she'll be all right to talk. Five minutes only. She 'a'n't got much attention now.'

Lissie was shocked by Edie's appearance. Her tiny, bird-like frame was now just a bag of bones held together by her sagging, yellowing skin. Her eyes were sunk deep into their sockets and circled by dark brown shadows. The bedding was old and the sheets grey, and the room was filled with an unsavoury smell of sickness and the chamber pot.

Lissie gagged as she entered. It brought back stark memories of her own near demise at Martha's, except that her mam's room did not have that underlying salty smell of blood-soaked rags.

There was a table near the bed, covered in tiny bottles and pots of potions and salves that were Rosa's stock-in-trade. Lissie noticed that the empty ones were mostly brown laudanum containers from the apothecary, and not gin. Rosa was sitting on a rickety wooden chair, coaxing the beef tea down her mam's throat.

'Come on, Edie, ducks, try this for me. Just a few spoonfuls for yer old Rosie. Yer got a visitor today. Your Lissie's 'ere. 'Ow 'bout that then? She 'eard y' were poorly, like, an' 'as come to see yer.'

A spoonful of the beef tea gurgled in Edie's throat and eventually slid down.

'Lissie? Our Lissie's 'ere?' Edie wheezed.

'Aye. D'yer want to see 'er?'

'Must tell 'er. Luther. Luther said . . .'

'Take yer time, Edie, love. Here, sit up a bit now. I've got this cushion fo' yer back.'

Rosa made Edie as comfy as she could and then nodded to Lissie to move closer to the bed.

'Lissie? It is you, i'n't it?'

'Yes, Mam. I'm sorry you're poorly.'

'Left me all on me own, you did. Wi' that mate o'

yer dad's. He were a wrong 'un, he were. Still is. I 'ad nowt left, y'know. Nowt.' Her eyes had an artificial brightness as they darted about, taking in Lissie's appearance. 'Still an 'andsome lass, I see,' she went on. 'Always were an 'andsome lass. 'Ave yer brought some more o' me medicine?'

Lissie glanced at Rosa who nodded towards the table. 'Put a few drops o' that laudanum in that glass o' water. She'll drink it down herssenn.'

After a few minutes, Edie continued. 'Luther said 'e'd tell you when you were grown up, but 'e never did. 'E were drunk when he told me. 'E said your real mam were a proper lady.' Edie made a grunting noise from the back of her throat. 'One o' the gentry, he said.'

'Mam? Are you sure about this?'

'I never believed him, o' course. Allus coming home telling tales, were yer dad. But after he were gone an' we 'ad to sell 'is stuff I found yer bits and pieces in t' old clock. And she said we 'ad to keep 'em for you.'

Lissie flashed a grateful smile at Rosa. Edie, calmed by her medicine, took another sip and lay back on the pillows. 'Fancy that. Fancy yer real mam being a lady. Fancy that, eh?'

'Mam? Did Dad say who she was?'

Edie sighed, her eyes were glazed and she was smiling a secretive little smile to herself.

Lissie persisted. 'Did he say, Mam? Did Dad say who my real mam was?'

Rosa came forward. 'Edie, love, tell 'er what Luther told yer about where he got 'er from.' Rosa turned to Lissie. 'She's often said it.'

Edie wheezed again. 'Bought you from some woman, 'e said—'

'*Bought me, did you say*?' Lissie's voice came out as a hoarse whisper. Her dad had bought her? Paid somebody money for her? Someone – her mother – oh God, please no, not her real mother – had *sold* her? Please God, don't let her say my real mother did not want me either. She coughed a little and asked, 'Rosa, could I sit in that chair awhile, please?'

Rosa shifted the tin soup bowl and old tray, saying, 'Bit of a shock is it, lass? Yer could 'a' done a lot worse, yer know.'

Edie muttered on. 'Bought you,' 'e said. When 'e were down t' canals on t' coast. Good days they were. Plenty o' money. Plenty o' coal fer t' fire. He came back wi' you one day. Pleased as punch he were. Pleased as punch. Some right pretty things you 'ad wi' yer an' all. Bonnet and shawl like a proper gentry babby. I suppose if yer mam were a lady, then—'

Rosa broke into Edie's ramblings. 'She said Luther told 'er 'e'd bought yer from a woman staying at an inn over on the Humber. An' when we found yer things, it seemed he'd been telling t' truth all along. I'll show you.'

It was a pouch made of oiled cloth and inside was a wooden cigar box, old and with the label worn away. The box contained an empty silver locket on a delicate neck chain and a silver picture case with a likeness inside. There was also some fine lacework and a piece of paper, a billhead for the North Star, in Hull. And a date. Several months after her birthday. A date on a bill for staying and eating at the inn and written in Luther's hand was a sum of money and *For Lissie*. On the back was scrawled *Mrs Beighton* and *Saltby*.

Lissie stared at the contents. 'Do you think Mrs Beighton was my real mam?'

Rosa placed a comforting hand on her shoulder. 'If she were a lady then it's more than likely Mrs Beighton were 'er nursemaid who looked after you.'

Lissie opened the picture case again. 'Is this my real mam, then?'

'She looks like a lady ter me,' Rosa speculated. 'Young though. T' likeness is yer mam, all right. You got her black hair and big eyes an' all.'

Lissie let out an exhausted sigh. This was too much to take in. Her real mam was a lady. A lady who was not able to keep her. Lissie guessed the reason. Not wed and probably disowned by her family, Lissie was lucky that she hadn't ended up in the workhouse! What would she have done if Mickey Jackson had left her with child?

As Lissie examined the likeness, Edie rallied and wheezed, 'She died. Luther said she died, yer mam, when she 'ad you.'

Lissie suddenly felt very sad, for a lost life, for her mother and – and – for herself. A realisation dawned on her that, if her dad had bought her, he wasn't her real father either.

'Mam?' she asked quietly. 'Did Dad say who my proper father was?'

'It wa'n't him. I were wrong there,' Edie replied.

'Who then?'

Rosa answered. 'Luther di'n't know.'

'Maybe this Mrs Beighton did?' Lissie suggested.

'Where's Saltby?' Her mother's family may not have wanted her but her father might! Did she have a proper father somewhere? Maybe uncles and aunts too? Where are they? she wondered. In Saltby?

Rosa put a hand on hers and answered, 'Lissie, ducks. Like as not 'e never knew nowt about yer. Them secrets are best kept quiet. You wer all right wi' Luther, weren't yer?'

'Yes. He was a good dad to me,' Lissie conceded.

Rosa was right. No one had wanted her when she was born. But to be sold as an infant, like a hireling on market day! She could never have done that to a tiny baby, whatever the circumstances. She would have found a way! She would!

Her head drooped. Not wanted by her real family, or even by her mam here. The only dad she had ever known was dead, murdered by a man she thought she loved. Lissie had never felt so alone.

She fingered the few trinkets feeling her sadness wash over her. 'Can I keep these, Mam?'

Her mam nodded and Rosa spoke for her. 'Oh aye. That's why yer ma wanted to see yer. They're yorn anyroad.'

'Thank you. Both of you. I know how difficult things have been, and – and – well, you could have sold them.'

'Ee lass, even if yer'd come 'ere dripping gold you couldn't do much to help yer mam now. It's just t' laudanum that keeps 'er going and I can earn enough for that.'

'You're a true friend to her, Rosa.'

'She were allus good to me when Luther were flushed wi' money.'

'Yes. It was like that with Dad. Either plenty or a famine. But he was generous when he had it. And he did his best for me, with sending me to Miss Kirby's and getting the position there. I'll always be grateful for that.'

'Aye, well, 'e's gone now, God rest his soul.'

Lissie swallowed hard before her next question. 'Do you know — I mean, did they ever find him — his murderer, that is?'

'Didn't you 'ear, lass?' Rosa exclaimed. 'That foreign lad never touched 'im. A bloke coming out o' t' privy saw it all. They di'n't find no bruises or nowt on Luther. He just died. T'old doctor said it were a seizure, like. Nay, they stopped looking for that foreigner ages ago, but I 'eard 'e'd gone back to 'is home country anyroad.'

Lissie covered her eyes with her hand. *Blake. Blake. He didn't do it. Blake didn't kill my father. And now he's gone. Gone away. Across the seas. I've lost him. Lost him for ever. Help! Oh help me, someone! This is too much to take in. Too much.*

Rosa continued, 'If you'd 'a' stayed around a bit longer, you'd 'a' known that.'

Lissie nodded silently and sagged weakly against the bed.

'You all right, ducks?' Rosa asked.

'Yes, thanks. Well no, not really. All this about my mother . . . and Luther buying me, it's . . . it's unsettling. And now this about the way Dad died . . . I . . . I hadn't heard anything where I was.'

'You found somewhere ter live, then?' Rosa asked.

'On a farm over Swinborough way. I help keep the place going and make pies to sell on market day.'

'Oh. Is that what yer were doin' there that day in town?'

Lissie nodded. 'I'm happy there, Rosa. I promised I'd go back. But if you need help with Mam, I can stay for a bit.'

'Nay, lass. Yer ma's no trouble ter me. Stay on fer a bit if yer want. But I can allus send for yer if she teks a turn for the worse. Look, she's dropped off ter sleep now. Shall we go down and have ussenns a drink?'

Rosa brewed up one of her garden-herb mixtures that tasted slightly bitter. She sweetened it with honey and they drank it out of bowls in Rosa's cluttered kitchen. Lissie found it reviving and calming at the same time.

'Will you be staying 'ere, or a' yer goin' t' tek a room at t' Navvy?' Rosa asked.

'No! Not the Navigator! I can't stay there!' Lissie exclaimed. 'I . . . I mean . . . I . . . I don't want to stay there. Can I stay here, Rosa? I'll sleep in the chair by the fire if you've got a spare blanket.'

Rosa raised her eyebrows. 'Still worried about Mickey, are yer? 'E'll 'ave moved on from you by now. 'E's got brass in 'is pocket, so there's plenty willin' ter go wi' 'im fer that. Mind, they're not as young and 'andsome as you, me duck.'

Lissie preferred not to risk it. 'I'd much rather stay this side of the canal if I can. It was always nicer on this side.'

'You're right there, lass. You're right there.'

'Who's the horse marine these days?'

'T' old fella's back. Young Peter Jackson went off ter some fancy racing stables near Donnie. An' Mickey's eldest lives in Edie's old house now, wi' his missus and babby.'

'Yes, I saw her on my way down. Another one on the way.'

'Middle lad is still working for his dad. Good brewer, 'e is. Folk wh' 'as got t' money comes from all ovver fer a keg or two fer their own cellars. Brews a good tankard o' ale, 'e does.'

The evening closed in and they sat by the light of the kitchen fire. A copper kettle rumbled on the swing hob and a blackened pot hung from a hook over the coals.

'That broth I had earlier was tasty, Edie,' Lissie commented.

'Aye. I boiled up a bacon hock and some barley.'

'Shall I make a bacon pudding with the meat?'

'Go on, then. Put some cabbage in wi' it.'

Lissie cleared a space on Rosa's rickety table and set to work. When the pudding wrapped in greased calico, and the cabbage stuffed into a net were simmering in the pot, Lissie asked, 'Is Miriam still at the school?'

'Miriam? Oh 'er! Right little madam she turned out t' be! She left soon after you went. She go' a position as a nursemaid at a big 'ouse in Derbyshire. Never comes 'ome ter see her mam at all now. Just writes letters saying 'ow grand everything is.'

'But I thought her dad had a bond for her at the Kirbys?'

'There were a bit of a to-do wi' followers,' Rosa explained. 'An' after all that wi' you and that lad off the barges, ol' man Kirby got rid.'

Lissie sighed. 'Poor Miriam. The Kirbys were very strict though.'

'*He* were!' Rosa scoffed. 'Two-faced bugger, if yer ask me!'

'What do you mean?'

'We-e-e-ll,' Rosa scorned, 'he reckoned he were a chapel man an' all that, but I know different. Allus in the Lion drinking, and gamblin' at t' races wi' all the gentry. And women!'

'Women?' Lissie queried.

'Oh aye, 'e likes 'is women does ol' man Kirby.'

Lissie remembered that night at the school, when Mr Kirby had had a builder doing out the new schoolroom, and she had bathed in the scullery. She remembered the way he'd looked at her, all over, as she stood dripping wet and naked on the stone scullery floor. He had called her a harlot, and pawed at her breasts, and she remembered being frightened of what he might do next. But, fortunately for her, he went off into town, presumably to one of his women.

'He never brought any lady friends to meet his sister,' Lissie said.

'Like I say,' Rosa sneered, 'two-faced.'

Lissie made herself as comfortable as she was able for the night by the fire in Rosa's small kitchen. Her limbs and body ached from the journey and from the tension that was gradually spreading through her veins. She must have dozed from time to time but her mind was too full to sleep.

She had more or less known that Edie wasn't her real mother, but had never dreamed she had been a lady. She wondered again who her real father was and whether he had been told about her. It would be nice to know. But not if he had been the one to sell her! Rosa was right. She had been lucky. She had been sold to Luther. He had been a good dad to her and she wouldn't have changed that.

The loneliness and emptiness crept over her as Rosa's kitchen fire died down and the air became chilled. She missed Martha's wise counsel and John's good humour. They would have helped her cope with all this. Martha had warned she might find it difficult to return here, and Lissie had ignored her. She thought she was strong enough to deal with it. But she had reckoned without all this about her birth. She wished Luther was still alive so she could ask him all the questions buzzing about in her head.

The hardest part to take in was finding out that her dad had not been murdered after all. Not murdered! Blake was innocent. She had accused him of murder and he was innocent. No wonder he had taken off like that! She had called for the constable's men to take him away. It was her fault. Her fault that he had left.

She rocked backwards and forwards in Rosa's kitchen chair, aching with misery. She had shut him from her mind, told herself she could not love a liar and a murderer. And since then she had been trying to close the void it left inside her. She had not been successful. She knew that now. It was as though all her efforts had been in vain and this awful, awful emptiness was consuming her. She folded her arms across her body as she rocked but the void remained. A void, she knew, that only Blake could fill.

If only she had known before that he was innocent! Now it was too late. He had gone from her life. He was the only thing, *the only thing*, she wanted from her past. Even worse, she had been the cause of his disappearance. What had she done? Her life was in pieces and it was her own doing.

'Blake. Blake.' She whispered his name over and over again. 'Where have you gone? I need you so much. Where are you?'

As she tormented herself with these feelings of remorse, she wondered if he ever thought of her.

Chapter 25

Blake racked his brain to work out a way of proving his innocence. Who would believe him? His fists had been ready to fight. Witnesses had heard him and Luther Dearne shouting at each other in the alehouse yard. And they had seen Dearne fall senseless to the ground! On top of all that, Lissie was Dearne's daughter! How come? he asked himself. How come that lovely girl is the daughter of a murderer?

'Get a move on, Blake!'

'Just waiting for young Eddie to catch up!' Blake called in return.

The two latecomers hurried forward to join big Eddie and his mates for their day at the coalface. Their metal-tipped clogs crunched and rang on the rocky surface as they made their way down the slope of Kimberhill drift, steadily descending into blackness.

'I didn't know the Swinborough estates stretched this far out,' Blake commented to Eddie as they walked.

'Swinboroughs have owned all this part o' t' South Riding for generations. Used to be iron an' all but most o' the best ore is worked out now,' Eddie replied.

'Good coal round 'ere though, an' it's everywhere. Coal seams like Kimberhill's fair jump outta t' ground. Old Swinborough only had to dig down into the hill-sides and carry it away!'

'He owns ironworks in town as well, doesn't he?'

Eddie clicked his teeth and jerked his head to one side. 'Shrewd man is Sir William. All t' coal we mine goes down t' cut to t' furnaces. His grandfather dug t' cut when t' main canal were built.'

'I met Sir William once,' Blake said. 'At a prize fight.'

'You a fist-fighter?'

'Not really. I did some sparring once.'

'Hear that, lads?' Eddie shouted. 'This 'un 's done some bare-knuckle scrapping. We'd better watch out then, 'a'n't we?'

A ripple of laughter ran through the men as they followed wagon rail tracks down the long black slope to their labour. Blake laughed with them as they trudged.

After a year or more with this gang, he was pleased that he fitted in now. They were suspicious of him at first, wary of the way he spoke, and they kept their distance from him. But he lodged with Eddie, his wife and young Eddie, just fourteen, and the men respected Eddie, so Blake was accepted.

'Your cottage looks fairly new to me,' Blake continued.

'Aye. Sir William built 'em so we w'u'n't have to walk as far to t' pit. Now t' word's got around, everybody wants to work at Kimberhill so they can 'ave one o' t' cottages. Womenfolk like 'em, y' see. They got indoor pumps fo' t' watter and new ranges in t' kitchen. And cellars fo' t' coal.'

'That steam engine back there must have cost him.'

Eddie nodded. 'We 'ad pit ponies pulling t' wagons afore that. But t' coalface is a long way down now, so 'e 'ad t' engine put in. Goes for owt new, does Sir William. You bin on one o' them railways yet?'

'No, not yet.'

'Well, they'll be ovver this way soon, they say.'

The gang reached the bottom of the slope and set up their lamps. A train of wagons stood empty, waiting to be filled with coal dug out by pick and shovel and the sweat of a man's back.

'Get stuck in, lads! It's already raining outside!'

Blake welcomed the labour. It took his mind off the outside world and the fact that he was a wanted man. He was eternally grateful to Clara for using her influence with Sir William and locating this place for him. It was a good choice, well out of the way of town folk. She had promised to find out what she could about the search for him, and to get word to him somehow. The only person he could trust was Clara. She would never betray him.

He thought a great deal about Lissie and Luther Dearne, his own actions on that day and how he had messed up his life for good. He was well rid of them both! A cold-blooded killer whose blood ran in the veins of his lovely daughter! She was a siren, a temptress, and he was glad that he had found out sooner rather than later. Even so, at times he wished he could go and find

Lissie and explain that he wasn't a murderer like her
father. Foolish thoughts! He was a wanted fugitive and
the constable's men would be waiting on every corner
for him!

Blake considered himself to be a strong man. Working
on the fly boats had given him stamina. But, he swiftly
realised at Kimberhill drift, he was nothing compared to
the strength and stamina of his fellow colliers.

The top ones were stocky men, short and thickset,
with huge, muscled arms and even brawnier legs. They
kept going in the worst of conditions for long, long
hours. They toiled on when they were worn out, in the
heat or in the cold, in the dark and in the wet.

The older ones were best, they had courage, and a
determination that kept them strong, with some to spare
for the younger, inexperienced men who became angry
with their tools when they were exhausted at the end
of their day. They looked out for each other at all times,
as Eddie did for Blake.

Blake was taller than the others, and agile with a good
reach. His suppleness in cramped conditions made up
for his inconvenient height, and his quick thinking and
speedy reactions made up for his inexperience.

Coal mining was dangerous work. The men at
Kimberhill drift knew the main risk was flood; when
the rain seeped in all over, an icy enemy, making your
clothes wet and your tools rusty. The soil above their
heads became clogged and the wooden pit props creaked.
The coal became heavier to haul and the air dank and
suffocating. Experienced colliers were seasoned weather-
watchers and knew before they went down when the

day would be short and the steam whistle would call them out early.

They had to be quick to hitch the wagons before they were hauled away, screeching and rumbling up the metal tracks, drowning out any conversation between the men. With their heads well down and their bodies bowed in the small space, the gang followed their wagons, planning what they could do with the rest of the day as they toiled back to the surface.

On that day a coupling pin was loose. In their haste the last wagon had not been properly hitched and, as the steam-driven pulleys dragged the train to the surface, it suddenly broke free, fully loaded, and rumbled back down the slope to the men trudging wearily in its wake. There was not much room in the tunnel. As soon as Blake realised what was happening, he yelled a warning, pushing his mates out of the way with his elbows and his legs. But young Eddie was in front of him and he froze as the wagon gathered speed.

He didn't move a muscle. Perhaps he couldn't.

Blake yelled again. 'Jump, Eddie, for God's sake, jump!'

Blake darted forward, grabbed the lad by the waist, twisting his body to protect him, and leaped sideways with all the strength his legs could muster. The loaded wagon rumbled past them, gathering speed, crumpling and crushing hastily discarded tools until a mesh of picks and shovels locked the wheels on one side and with a screech and a thunder, it toppled, spilling its load and raising a choking, blinding fog of coal dust.

Then everything was quiet except for the distant chugging of the steam engine winding the remaining wagons to the surface. One by one the men called each other's names and, between the coughing and the groaning, one by one, they answered.

'Harry?'

''Ere.'

'Ezra?'

'Right.'

'George?'

'Aye.'

'Eddie?'

'That's me.'

'Young Eddie?'

Silence.

'Young Eddie?' The second time his father called him there was fear in his voice.

Then Eddie heard his son cough and reply, 'I'm over here, Dad. I'm all right. I hurt a bit where I fell but I'm all right. It's Blake though. He's sort of laid on top o' me and he i'n't moving.'

'You stay where you are, lad, till I get to you. D' yo' 'ear me? You keep still now.'

'Yes, Dad.'

Slowly, gradually, the dust settled and the air cleared. A single lamp, miraculously, still glowed. The men moved cautiously, shaken, bruised and cut, but alive and able to walk. All except Blake, who lay motionless where the wagon had clipped his outstretched foot, throwing him off-balance and head-first against the solid, rocky wall.

Blood trickled from his temple and his left foot lay at an awkward angle. Rain was already seeping through the seam and it ran in rivulets down the walls of the mine and coursed away to the coalface. Soon the icy water would be ankle-deep and rising.

'Where's Joe?'

''E's gone for the medicine box. No need to panic, lads. They'll 'ave 'eard what's 'appened on t' surface.'

It was a half-hour trek to the surface, but on the way out there was an alcove carved out for housing tools and drinking water to supplement their cans of cold tea. They also kept poles and canvas for splinting limbs and carrying back injured men. Mining, as they knew, was a dangerous calling.

Joe was a bone-setter and he came back with the tools of his trade. He'd learned about bones from his dad who'd learned it from his dad.

'Let the dog see the rabbit,' he ordered gruffly as he set about his task of feeling and prodding and straightening, and then splinting Blake's foot and strapping him to the canvas stretched between two poles.

'He's a long 'un, to be sure,' Joe said, rolling him over on to his makeshift stretcher.

Blake groaned and his eyelids flickered in the dim glow of the mining lamp. 'Good sign,' muttered Joe, 'but keep 'im as still as you can, lads. Best get moving. Water's rising fast.'

They carried him out through the pouring rain to Eddie's small terraced cottage, and, somehow, got him up the narrow stairs to his bed. Eddie cleaned him up while his wife saw to the cuts and bruises on their son. Young Eddie would be all right after a drink of negus and a long sleep.

His mother made the negus with port wine, honey

and hot water and it always worked for her children. She was used to tending cuts and bruises and knew her menfolk were tough. This young lodger was a different breed though. Strong enough and a good worker by all accounts, but not from real mining stock, she thought. You 'ad to 'ave it in your blood to survive working in the pits.

Eddie sighed wearily and watched his wife clear up the bowl of water and bloody rags. 'Joe says he'll be up there a while, lass. Broke his ankle and taken a knock to the 'ead. Can you manage all right?'

'Oh aye. Joe's wife 'll come round to lend a hand if needs be. I've seen a lot worse.'

'Aye, me too.'

He listened to the ceaseless rain coming down in torrents. 'Reckon we'll be rained off for a week at this rate. We got plenty o' coal in?'

'Cellar's full. Bank up the fire and get them wet clothes off. You'll catch your death.'

The heavy rain continued and Kimberhill mine was flooded for more than a month. The men walked five miles morning and night to another pit for work while they waited for the water to go down. Blake drifted in and out of consciousness for several days until one morning, when he opened his eyes and saw young Eddie staring at him from the bedroom doorway.

'Dad! Dad! He's woke up! Blake's woke up, Dad!'

Blake frowned as he collected his thoughts. He had been vaguely aware of pain and of people fussing round him and, as he lay there feeling too exhausted to move, he remembered the accident. His head was thumping and his ankle hurt. He tried to move it and it hurt even more. He fingered his head where it was sore and tender. He'd taken a fair crack and there was a swelling to show for it and, he guessed, a deep cut and some colourful bruising.

His ankle was bound, done up with plastered bandages from calf to toes, and propped up on a bolster at the bottom of the bed. His toes felt cold but he could wiggle them all right. Damn! He was going to be like this for a long time while it mended. Well, at least young Eddie was all right. He hoped the others were too.

Young Eddie came back with his dad. Eddie's hands were dirty with soil from his garden at the back. It must be a Sunday. Young Eddie put some coal on the fire from a bucket on the hearth. His dad splayed his hands to show the soil still on them.

'Just digging a few parsnips to go round t' meat. By gum, I'm right pleased you've come round. 'Ow you feeling now?'

'My leg hurts a bit and my head's thumping like mad.'

Eddie poured some water into a tin mug from a can on the mantelpiece. 'Drink some water. Your leg's not too bad. It's t' ankle, Joe said. It'll be as good as new once it's mended, if you can keep off it, like. Heads are funny though. Can you see all right?'

'If that's young Eddie by the fire there, then yes, I can.'

'That's good. Thanks for what you did for our Eddie.'

Young Eddie jumped forward. 'Yes. Thanks, Blake. You saved my life.'

'Off you go now, lad. Fetch those parsnips in for your

mam.' Eddie sat on the only chair in the room. A heavy, wide, wooden thing that had seen better days. 'We're missing you in our gang but it can't be helped. You have to stay off that ankle if it's to mend proper, like. You'll be laid off a good few weeks and then we'll be into winter.'

'What does that mean?'

'Kimberhill drift floods a lot more in winter. Most of us goes off to other pits. Pit manager's dropping by to say hello after chapel today. Then we'll 'ave us dinner. You hungry?'

'I could eat a horse.'

Eddie grinned. 'That's a good sign. I reckon you'll do. You'll 'ave to stay up here a while, but you'll do all right. Joe'll bring round a crutch for you to get about and you'll be able to shuffle down the stairs on yer backside soon.'

He stood up and turned round, lifting the wooden seat of his chair to reveal a chipped chamber pot. 'Talking o' backsides, Joe's missus sent this round for you to use, and she says if you 'as trouble going she's got something in her cupboard for you.'

'I'll bet she has,' Blake replied ruefully. 'When's Joe coming round with the crutch? I'll go mad cooped up here all the time.'

The rains continued for several weeks, causing major problems at Kimberhill drift. Blake followed Joe's advice and his injuries healed well. He helped out around the house and Eddie's garden where he could, and spent much of his time reading. Eventually, he was able to get out using the crutch and made his way to the offices at the mine.

'Come in and sit down, lad. How's the ankle now?'

Blake hobbled into the pit manager's small office, grimy with ingrained coal dust. He carried a well-thumbed book in his free hand, which he placed on the manager's worn and grubby desk.

'It's coming on nicely, sir. Joe says I'll be putting my full weight on it soon.'

Blake had met this man only once before. He was one of the gaffers who travelled around on horseback, checking up on Sir William's various works, sorting out problems and feeding through information. He'd been to the pit to see about the accident and had already had a chat with Blake. That was how he knew about Blake's interest in steel and how he had come to lend him the book.

The manager was a brisk, no nonsense man, a bit like Sir William, Blake thought. He nodded briefly, seemingly satisfied with Blake's response.

'Thanks for the loan of the book,' Blake went on. 'We do need to keep producing iron to forge, but I've always thought there was a future for steel as well.'

'So I believe. You've spoken of it to others. How did you learn about it?'

'From the Institute. When I came off the flyers I did some classes there and went to some lectures.'

'Why the interest in iron and steel?'

'I reckon it's in my blood. My great-grandfather dug iron ore out of the mountainside in Sweden. My grandfather smelted it and hauled it. My father shipped pig iron over here. I want to be part of its future.'

'I would have thought that shipping iron, like your father, would be a better line of work for an educated man like you. It's clean and it's profitable.'

'It's not for me. I'm no clerk.'

'You're no collier either, lad!' The manager got to his feet to emphasise his point.

Blake put his hands on the chair arms to lever himself up and then thought better of it. 'You're not laying me off because of one lousy accident, surely?' he protested. 'I'm a good worker, ask any of my mates.'

'Oh aye, I have already. And they all speak very highly of you. But you can do better than this.'

'What do you mean? Mining coal is good work and it pays well. Besides, I like hard graft. Always have. I want to stay down the mine.'

'Yes, that's what your mates say too.' The manager came round his desk to face him and leaned back against it. 'Come on, lad. You're educated! You've been to school and you can read. Not just the news-sheets, but proper books about new processes and materials. You're wasted down the pit!'

'I want to stay. I have my reasons.'

'Well I have my reasons for shifting you,' the manager snapped. 'We mine this coal here to keep the furnaces going in the valley. And we can't keep 'em going wi'out getting the coals down there. I can use a decent man like you, one who knows what he's doing.'

'I thought production at Kimberhill had stopped.'

'D' yo' think I don't know that! Since the big flood at Kimberhill I've been bringing coals over from Mexton. I can't get Kimberhill back to full production until Sir

William has installed a bigger steam engine to pump out the water. I've got empty barges standing idle, and furnaces cooling off for lack o' coals!'

Blake grimaced and sighed.

The manager continued, 'As soon as you're walking proper again I'm putting you on the narrow boats bringing the coals from Mexton down to the works.'

Blake scowled as he realised there was no choice for him. The irony was, he thought bitterly, he *wanted* to be out of the pits, back on the canals or working on a furnace in the ironworks. But he dare not risk it. Not yet. There could be a drawing of him as a wanted man on every street corner in town. He'd be better off staying here, well out of the town.

The manager was staring hard at him, expecting an answer. 'Look, lad, you came here with a nod from Sir William and I never asked no questions. So why don't you tell me the real reason you came to Kimberhill drift. I may be able to help. You can't spend the rest of your life holed up here. Besides, I want men like you in the ironworks. You'll have to live in town then.'

When Blake did not respond he tried again. 'I heard you had a sweetheart down Fordham way. Still waiting for you, is she? You could wed her and be living in a manager's house before long, if you'd only listen to what I'm saying.'

Blake covered his face with his hands and heaved a sigh. If only, he thought, if only. He looked up and said frankly, 'I killed a man.'

Visibly shocked, the manager went back to his chair behind the desk. 'God no. Nob'dy said it were that serious. You'd better tell me about it.'

Blake did. All of it. The truth about his own father, the Kirbys and Lissie, and how Lissie's father had died. The manager listened to him in silence, pursing his lips as the story unfolded. Finally, Blake shrugged, saying, 'A friend of Sir William's told me about Kimberhill drift and I wanted to keep away from town and lie low.'

'For how long though?'

'I don't know,' Blake groaned. 'Oh God, I don't know.' He watched as the manager gave a weary sigh and chewed at his lip, pulling his mouth sideways.

'I'll do anything to stay—' Blake continued.

'Shut up, I'm thinking!'

Blake looked down at his hands, worker's hands with scars and calluses. They were not a clerk's hands. They were hands that he was proud of.

The silence lengthened until the manager broke it by saying briskly, 'Right. Two things. I've not heard about this murder of Luther Dearne and, believe me, I know most that goes on in these parts. We've had no constable's men around the works or the pits asking questions. I would know if they were looking for you, lad. And they're not. Still, I'll find out what I can for you.'

Surprised at this response, Blake muttered, 'Th-thanks – er – thank you, sir. And the other thing? You said there were two things.'

'The other? Oh yes. I already said it. I need a capable man like you on the Mexton run. The sooner, the better. So when do yo' think you'll be fit enough to handle a narrow boat?'

Chapter 26

At Mexton Lock, Lissie was staring at her mam's tray on Rosa's rickety kitchen table. A glass of port wine with a few drops of laudanum helped her mam sleep. She gazed at the small brown bottle and wondered how many more sleepless nights she could take.

Rosa's horsehair chair was comfy enough, and she had a stool for her feet. But the memories kept coming back – painful recollections that pushed at the lid of the sealed black box in her mind.

Rosa had not asked Lissie to go over to the Navigator for anything, not even when their ale ran low. The older woman carried the cans over the bridge and back by herself. Lissie was grateful for that. Instead, she borrowed a sacking apron and with Rosa's approval, set about cleaning her small cottage.

This morning she had pumped water at the trough behind the row of woodmen's cottages and filled the boiler at the side of Rosa's kitchen fire. When the water was hot she carried it in a bucket through to a tub in the scullery and washed all the linen she could find in hot water and real soap. Then she took Rosa's rag rugs outside, draped them over tree branches and bushes and beat them clean for all she was worth.

It was while she was doing this that she saw Mickey Jackson go by. He was carrying a jute tool bag. She guessed he was going to see his daughter-in-law and grandchild. She held her breath and her heart stopped as she watched him and prayed that he would not turn and see her. He didn't and she breathed out raggedly as he disappeared up the track through the woods.

But her stomach churned. Fear and loathing rose in her gullet and she gagged at the bitter gall in her throat as she remembered the smell of him and the feel of his gross swarthy body invading hers.

As she retched she realised how much she still hated him, how much she had pushed the bad memories to the back of her mind and imagined him dead and gone from this world. But he wasn't. He was carrying on as if nothing had happened, visiting his family, probably mending the window in the very same room he had degraded and defiled her.

She retched again and hated herself for the continuing effect he had on her. She leaned over and pumped cold fresh water over her face to wash away the bile. Her dress became wet and she went inside to dry out, sitting very still, alone by the fire, saying nothing, watching the daylight fade through Rosa's small kitchen window.

Why hadn't she thought before of how much

returning here would bring back that dreadful, dreadful time? What could she do to take away the memory, to forget how loathsome he had been and what he had done to her?

The battered wooden tray was on the table, ready for Rosa to take up to her mam. Lissie stared at the small brown bottle on the tray. She had taken laudanum when she fled from here. Martha had also given her a little to help the pain of her injuries after the attack. She remembered the blissful floating euphoria that helped her survive the hurt and humiliation. Just a few drops in a glass of wine, she thought, would be enough to dull her mind, enough to blot out this resurrected hell that threatened to blight her life for ever.

She stood up and moved towards the table. The evening was drawing in. Another long, dark and sleepless night lay ahead of her, reliving the torment. How long would the memory take to fade again? Maybe she would be all right tomorrow? Perhaps she just needed to get through this night? Just a few drops would help, she was sure. She picked up the small brown bottle and took out the cork.

'Nay, lass, it's too early for that! Yer mam won't be awake for her supper if yer gi'es it 'er now.' Rosa burst in the door with a can of ale and two bottles of porter. 'By gum, them cans get heavier.' She flopped down on to her fireside chair, rubbing her shoulder.

Lissie's hand shook as she pushed back the cork and replaced the bottle on the tray. 'I – er, I haven't started to cook anything yet.'

'Aye, well, yer don't have ter tonight. Annie Jackson

wants some o' me green salve for her hands and she were roasting mutton for t' inn so I did a deal wi' 'er.'

Lissie pushed her shaking hands behind her back and asked sharply, 'What sort of deal?'

'Two pots o' salve fo' three roast dinners! What do yer think o' that then?'

Lissie moved away from the table, trying to sound normal. 'That sounds like a good deal, Rosa.'

'Aye. She wants to send some to their Miriam.' Rosa smiled and added, 'Yer mam likes a slice o' roast mutton wi' a 'tater.'

'You are good with her, Rosa.'

'I do me best. Mind you, I'm tired out tonight. Been up and down them stairs all day. And this shoulder's playing up again. Can you tek the salve over to the Navvy for us? And tek a tin fo' t' dinners?'

Lissie closed her eyes and swallowed. *No! Please no, not tonight. Just not tonight.*

'Yer'll be all right,' Rosa prompted. 'Mickey'll be serving ale in the saloon. Yer on'y 'as ter nip in and outta t' kitchen. Won't tek yer a minute.'

Lissie inhaled deeply. She had to go over there sometime. Just as long as she could keep away from Mickey Jackson! She said, 'Of course. I'll get my shawl.'

It was twilight, early evening, with only half a moon and no one had lit any flares. A couple of working men were busy marshalling a train of narrow boats slowly through the lock. They were loaded with coal and pulled by a brace of heavy horses. As she crossed the bridge and looked upstream her eyes grew accustomed to the gloom.

She frowned. It was the way he moved. There was a man, a tall man, commanding another of the narrow boats and organising the horses beyond the lock gates. She watched him cross the far set of lock gates and talk to the lock keeper. A flare was lit. There was a train of three barges to get through the lock that evening.

At first she was sure it was him, the man she once thought that she loved, the man she believed had killed her dad. Then she shook her head and moved on. Her mind was playing tricks on her. He had gone away she had heard, out of the country. Since seeing Mickey Jackson all her thoughts were befuddled by bad memories. This man too was a bad memory now.

She went round the back of the inn to avoid going through the saloon where Mickey would be. The meat and potatoes were not quite ready. Annie was busy and said, 'Why don't you go into the saloon for a tankard while you wait?'

'No thank you, Mrs Jackson. I'll stay in the kitchen.'

'Well, I can't be doing with you! I've a group of travellers in tonight, all baying for their food. Go and stand out there.'

Lissie hovered outside the kitchen, on the cobbled yard that led to the brew house. A light glowed through the half-open door. After a few minutes two men came out, one carrying a lamp, and walked across the yard to the kitchen. Lissie recognised them and shrank back into the shadows.

'Well, well, well. Look 'ere, lad. Look who we' got 'ere.' Mickey Jackson held up the lamp to see her face.

'It's Edie Dearne's lass. Come back to say sorry to me and yer old ma, 'ave yer?'

Lissie pressed her back against the rough stone wall. 'Keep away from me,' she said.

'Or what?' Mickey moved closer, slowly lowering and raising the lamp. 'Still a fine-looking lass, I see. Always was a fine-looking lass, was our Lissie.'

'I'm not your Lissie.'

'No? Your ma said you were, and you owe me summat from then, lass.' He pushed his grimy fingers through the folds of her skirt to between her thighs. 'Some more o' that,' he sneered.

He stood so close to her that she could smell the ale and tobacco on his breath and feel the heat of the lantern against her cheeks. His bloodshot eyes and flushed unshaven face leered at her in the yellow glow. Coils of lank greying hair hung greasily from under his grubby cap. The stench of stale sweat in her nostrils overtook the yeasty fumes from the brew house.

Suddenly he swung the lantern to one side and barked, 'Here, tek this inside, son, and see to t' men in t' saloon. I've got some unfinished business 'ere.'

Mickey's son disappeared fast, leaving Mickey standing in front of her. He was breathing deeply, and he placed a hand on the stone wall each side of her head. 'Still got that fight in yer, 'ave yer? Or 'as some young stallion knocked it out o' yer yet?'

Lissie's throat closed with fear. Her stomach knotted and, again, she felt the bile rise in her gullet. 'Keep your filthy hands away from me, you evil man!' she hissed.

He smiled. It was a crooked, lopsided grin that showed

his stained and broken teeth. 'That's my girl,' he whispered, as his foul breath closed in on her mouth.

She lifted her knee as hard as she could into his groin and pushed him away with her hands. Her effect on him was minimal but she realised that she had startled him, and quickly she ducked under his arms to escape. As she struggled to break free he caught hold of the fabric of her gown and she heard it tear as she pulled away from him. She gathered up her skirts and ran as fast as she could around the corner of the inn towards the canal and the bridge.

But the back of her skirt, torn away from the waist as it was, trailed on the ground behind her. In the darkness she missed her footing, caught the heel of her boot in the fabric and fell, winded, on the bank side.

Mickey Jackson was right behind her, grabbing the back of her skirt, ripping it away and pinning her down on the ground with his body. He pushed her face into the soggy soil, tainted with coal dust and machine oil, and she felt his hand fumbling with the buttoning of his breeches.

She twisted her neck, scratching her face in the gritty sludge and yelled as loud as she could, 'Help me! Somebody, please help me!' Through the darkness she made out the top of a laden narrow barge in the lock, the last one waiting for the sluices to be opened and empty the lock. Someone must be around! The lock keeper might hear her. 'Help!' she cried. 'Please help!'

But her words were lost as Mickey shoved her head further into the mud. His body was a dead weight on top of her. He had torn away the back of her drawers and she felt his hardened arousal press into the soft flesh of her rump. He pushed one of his hands under her stomach to lift her rear away from the ground. Desperately, *desperately*, she clenched her muscles and tried to squirm away from him.

The scream in her throat spluttered out through coal grit and soil, but she kept trying. She struggled with all her ebbing strength to heave him off her back, twisting her body this way and that, but he was too heavy, too strong and too inflamed with his greedy needs to stop now.

Then suddenly, quite suddenly, she was free.

'Get away from her, you animal, or so help me, I'll kill you!'

His heavy weight was lifted from her back. Cold air breezed across the naked flesh of her bottom and legs. She heard the thud of fists on flesh and the cries and groans of fighting men. She rolled over in the sludge to see who it was.

It *was* Blake! No, it couldn't be! Not him. Here? At Mexton Lock? She must have knocked her head when she fell. She must be hallucinating.

But no, she wasn't, her head was clear and it *was* him! He had freed her from this vile beast and was making a good job of knocking Mickey senseless.

She sat up and pulled the fabric of her torn skirt around her. Blake was dusting himself down with his hands and walking over to where Mickey was flat on his back and groaning.

But as she sat up two figures loomed out of the darkness and punched Blake low in the back. His knees buckled

and he staggered but did not fall. Mickey's sons set about
Blake with a vengeance, throwing punches and kicks indis-
criminately. Lissie watched in horror as he cowered against
the blows with his arms encircling his head.

Then Blake retaliated. He had the advantage of height
and reach. He placed his punches accurately and knocked
down first one brother and then the other. But they
were also young, strong men and they each recovered in
turn to fight back. The blacksmith landed a heavy blow
to the side of Blake's head that sent him reeling. The
younger son grabbed his arm and quickly the other arm
was seized in a vice-like grip by the blacksmith. Blake
struggled at first but they held on to his arms tightly
and eventually he stopped.

Mickey clambered slowly to his feet and Lissie, behind
him by the edge of the canal, saw him approach Blake
with his raised clenched fists. Mickey would kill him! Blake
had no chance against him with his arms pinioned by the
Jackson brothers! She stood up and cast about looking for
a weapon. Her boot struck a discarded winding handle
used for raising and lowering the sluices in the lock gates.

She bent to pick it up. It was an old one, made of
rusting iron and heavy in her hand. No one was looking
at her. She took it in both her hands, not caring that
her skirt fell away and her drawers were torn, and using
all her might, swung it round to strike Mickey's head.

He let out an animal howl and turned, startled, but
did not fall. She had missed and struck his shoulder rather
than his head or neck. He swayed, recovered, and then
began to approach her again. She had not even winded
him.

Blake yelled, 'No, leave her alone.' He was struggling again to free himself and crying, 'Run! Run for it!'

She could not. Her legs wouldn't move. Fear froze her to the spot.

Mickey was just a few yards away and she heard a growl in his throat as he lumbered towards her. His breeches were still undone and his hands were already pulling the buttons aside to expose his renewed arousal. She took a step backwards, glancing nervously over her shoulder at the nearness of the oily dark water. At that split second, the cold deep water was preferable to whatever Mickey Jackson had in mind for her.

Blake yelled again, 'Keep away from her, you animal! Leave her . . .' His words were lost in a strangled groan as he was punched into silence.

Lissie's instinct for survival took over. She had nearly died because of what this man had done to her in the past. She remembered the belt. And the tearing injuries to her insides. Injuries that were worse because she had tried to fight him. She still had the winding handle in her hands, but it had been no good to her and Mickey could easily wrench it off her and use it on her in his anger.

Her head cleared and she knew what she had to do. She looked at him and she smiled. She held the iron handle at arm's length and dropped it into the lock, listening for a thud as it landed on a loaded coal barge or a splash if it hit the water. She heard a splash. The narrow barge had drifted to the far side of the lock.

She was ready for him. She smiled again. She tore away the remainder of her skirt to expose the front of her drawers and placed both her hands in the waistband to push them down and offer him what he wanted.

He growled again and lurched forward. He would have fallen against her if she had not stepped smartly to one side. Mickey realised his mistake and arched his back, flinging his arms over his head. But he was too late. He carried too much weight, too much momentum, and could not stop himself from moving forward that extra step, the step that took him over the edge.

Lissie watched him as he tottered, desperately trying to fling himself backwards. It seemed a long time to her as he wavered like a tree in the wind, until, eventually, he toppled forward into the lock and, after a second, hit the black water beneath.

It all happened very slowly and she watched every second of it. A muscled, heavy man, he made a big splash in the lock, causing waves that hit the stone-built sides. The stern of the coal-laden narrow barge hit the wall and bounced very slowly away from the far side.

Mickey coughed and spluttered and yelped as the water soaked into his clothes and dragged him down. There was an iron ladder cut into the lock wall and he struck out for it as best he could. The second he disappeared over the side, his sons dropped their grip on Blake's arms and rushed to the lock side.

'Fetch a rope,' one yelled. 'I'll go down the ladder.'

Mickey thrashed and splashed in desperation to reach the ladder. The stern of the heavy boat, glistening blackly in the moonlight, bounced gracefully away from the far side of the lock and swung slowly towards Mickey. Nothing and no one could deter its gentle drift until it connected with Mickey's screaming, heaving bulk and crushed him against the wall. Mickey's son stopped his descent as he realised that he too might be crushed.

Mickey's agonised screams echoed through the night. Lissie choked with horror. Tons of floating coal were grinding against the stone wall of the lock and squeezing the life out of Mickey Jackson, leaving his anguished haunting cries a mere gurgle in the water.

Lissie stared as the wayward barge slowly recoiled and released Mickey's crushed and lifeless body, a body that sank silently beneath the water's undulating surface.

It was over. Finished. She had wanted to kill him and she had.

She began to cry. Tears of relief ran down her cheeks. He was dead. Mickey Jackson was dead. Someone had retrieved the torn skirt of her dress and was wrapping it around her. He turned her round to face him, gathering up the fabric and knotting it firmly in place.

'Lissie?' he said. 'It *is* you!'

'Blake?' she said vacantly, her senses dulled by shock. 'You're in Sweden, aren't you?'

He shook his head silently.

'M-Mickey J-Jackson, he fell. He just fell,' she muttered. What was Blake doing here?

'I know. I saw him.' Blake took off his corduroy working jacket and placed it around her shoulders.

'I didn't kill your father,' he said. Even though he shot mine, he thought. How could he look at her and not remember that?

She pulled the coat around her trembling shoulders. 'I know. Rosa told me. She told me lots of things.' Lissie let out a long shuddering sigh. 'He wasn't my real father anyway. I didn't know that until yesterday. He bought me. When I was a baby. Who would want to sell their own baby? Any baby?'

'I'm sorry your father died.' Blake realised that he meant it. And, though he still grieved for his own father, revenge no longer simmered in his breast. He had worked out his vengeance with the coal he had mined at Kimberhill. Did it matter any more, he thought? Did anything matter except that he had found his Lissie again, and she was safe. She was the same Lissie to him, whoever her father was and whatever he had done.

After a second she added, 'He was the only father I ever knew and I loved him. I didn't want him to die.'

But I did at the time, thought Blake. And Lissie knows that. Will she ever forgive me?

Someone lit flares. Rosa came over the bridge to find her, saw the commotion and retreated to her cottage. Drinkers came out of the Navigator to find out what was going on. Lissie recognised Eliza from the dairy farm at Fordham. She was arm in arm with her husband Job.

'Lissie? Is it you, Lissie?' Eliza came forward, concerned. 'Oh, what has happened to you, you poor love?' She looked up at Blake's bruised, bleeding face and torn clothing. 'This isn't your doing, is it?'

'N–No, Eliza,' Lissie said. She was feeling strange, chilled and shivery and numb. It took a huge effort for her to add, 'The Jacksons beat him up. He was – he was trying to protect me.'

Eliza put her arms around both of them. 'Come home with us,' she said.

Job added, 'I've got our farm cart round the back of the Navigator — if you don't mind sharing it with a keg of ale and some straw?'

Lissie nodded, too exhausted to speak. Her face was scratched and sore. She was feeling very cold and starting to shiver.

Blake lifted her on to the straw bedding in the cart and climbed in beside her.

'It's not far,' Eliza called over her shoulder as the horse pulled them forwards.

The farm cart rumbled through the night air, following rutted tracks to the dairy at Fordham. Lissie, wrapped in Blake's heavy jacket, curled up and shivered in spite of the warmth of the soft barley straw around her.

Blake stretched out beside her, and placed an arm above her head. 'Let me hold you. The heat from my body will warm you.'

'No!' It was the first syllable she had uttered since the shivering started. It came out as a strangled whisper, forced through her closed throat. She turned away from him, curled her body tighter and pulled the jacket closer in a vain attempt to shield herself.

Blake lifted his arm away and covered his eyes with his hand. Rejection. Was that all he could hope for? He could not blame her. She had come through a dreadful ordeal. But he did want to hold her, to warm her, to make her well again. Her shivering was becoming worse. He could hear her teeth chattering. He took off his flannel work shirt and draped it over her.

He wondered how he looked. His jaw felt swollen and he had a cut over one eye. There were livid patches and grazes on his arms. No doubt there would be more hidden beneath his undershirt. The bruises from his beating were already stiffening up into nagging aches. He was tough though, he would recover. But Lissie, she was not so strong. She had been running away from Mickey Jackson and he had no idea what Mickey had done to her before he heard her cries.

'Is it much further, Mr Dacre?' Blake twisted his neck to speak to Job.

'No, lad. Just down by the big field and over t' canal bridge an' we'll be 'ome. You two all right back there?'

'Lissie's very cold. She can't stop shivering.'

Eliza pressed her husband's arm gently. 'Can you go a bit faster, Job? Lissie's had a really bad time.'

'Hold on tight then. Not far now.' He flicked the reins and his dappled grey mare broke into a trot.

Lissie clenched her jaw in a vain attempt to stop her teeth chattering. She was unable to think straight, unable to talk and hardly able to breathe. Her breath came in short rasps and she felt that she could not fill her lungs with air no matter how hard she tried. She curled up tighter and felt another covering drop over her. The extra warmth was no help. She could not stop the shivering.

It was Blake who had rescued her. She had not been imagining it when she had seen his silhouette in the light of the flare by the lock gates. He had been there all the time during her ordeal, marshalling coal barges through the lock. Her spirits had lifted when he loomed out of the darkness to tackle her attacker.

Now, in the aftermath, her fighting spirit had deserted her. A numbness of body crept over her and she struggled to arrange her thoughts in her mind. She felt detached from the world, closed off from reality. It's easier to let go, she thought. If she let go, the shivering would stop and the pain would go away. Yes . . . the . . . pain . . . will . . . go . . . away . . . Lissie thought idly as she slipped silently into a faint.

Blake carried her from the cart into Job and Eliza's low, stone-built farmhouse and gently lowered her on to the parlour couch. He winced as he straightened. Those Jackson thugs had cracked a rib or two, no doubt. He was bruised and cut but he'd suffered worse in the past and right now he was more worried about Lissie. Her beautiful black hair was tumbled and knotted, and the delicate skin of her face had been bruised and cut during her attack. Now Blake was alarmed by her pallor under the streaks of dried sludge and coal dust.

'Have you got another blanket for her, Eliza?' he asked. 'Her skin is icy cold.'

Eliza took charge of the situation and despatched her husband to open the damper and draw the kitchen fire, light oil lamps and fill a warming pan with coals for the spare bed upstairs.

'Here, put this over her,' Eliza suggested, handing Blake a thick woollen rug. 'A drop of brandy might help. You look as if you could do with one yourself.'

'Yes, I could.'

'In the dresser cupboard.' Eliza nodded in the direction of a large oak sideboard displaying a variety of plates and pots. 'Me and Job'll have one an' all.'

Blake sat beside Lissie and supported her head while he coaxed brandy through her pallid lips. She coughed

and spluttered but revived and managed to swallow some
of it. Warmth began to course through her veins and her
shivering eased.

'Th-thank you,' she muttered. 'I . . . I don't know what
came over me.'

'It's only to be expected after what you've been
through,' Eliza replied in her usual common sense way.
'You'll stay with us tonight. Blake, you can have the
couch if you like.'

Blake ran his fingers through his coal-streaked fair
hair. 'I wish I could stay. I was taking a train of coal
barges through the lock when I heard Lissie's cries for
help. I've left them with a young lad. He's only a nipper.
He won't be able to manage them on his own, not with
two Cleveland Bays hauling.'

'You'd best get off, then. I'll look after Lissie,' Eliza
responded.

Lissie made a huge effort to speak. 'Will you . . . will
you come back?' she croaked.

He hated leaving her like this. His heart ached to hold
her close and make her well again. His throat closed and
he simply nodded, whispering, 'If you want me to.' He
bent over to kiss the top of her head, blocking the light
from the lamp.

The shadow of his broad shoulders covered her face
and Lissie smelled the coal grit on his clothes. She tasted
again the wet gritty dust in her mouth and she relived
the horror of her attack, her face being pushed into the
black sludge and the weight of Mickey Jackson squeezing
the breath out of her body.

'No!' She recoiled from Blake's lips, pressing her back

in to the couch and, helpless with distress, saw the
surprise, the anguish and then the naked hurt in his eyes.

Job came forward with another lamp, illuminating the
panic in Lissie's frightened eyes. He placed a gentle hand
on Blake's shoulder. 'Leave her be, for now. Give her
some time. The lass was all but raped and . . . and . . . well,
she saw the man perish. Nasty way to go, being slowly
crushed by a coal barge. That sort o' thing is hard for a
young 'un to deal with.'

Eliza echoed her husband's wisdom. 'We'll look after
her well, Blake. You can rely on us. Come and see how
she is on Sunday, if you can.'

Blake straightened up. The pain from his bruised ribs
was nothing compared to the pain in his heart. Lissie
could not bear him even to touch her. His blue eyes
were bright with tears as he stepped out into the cold
night air.

When he left the mine at Kimberhill he had harboured
hopes of finding Lissie at Mexton Lock. The lock keeper
had told him that she had gone away after her father
died and the house had changed hands. No one knew
where she was, but her mother was still around, living
with Rosa in Woodmill Row.

He remembered Rosa. She had helped him when his
father was shot. Maybe Lissie had found a position in
service somewhere and come back to Mexton to see
her mother?

Blake hoped, desperately, that Lissie was going to be
all right. She had been cruelly attacked by that rogue.
Men like that deserved everything they got! But Mickey
Jackson's death had been particularly nasty. It was one

of Blake's barges that had crushed him to death. He shivered at the memory of the man's screams. He was glad that young Eddie had been up stream from the lock with the horses and not seen what had happened.

Young Eddie would be wondering where he was. It was late. Painfully, he broke into a run on the towpath until he had sight of his horses tethered and waiting, munching slowly from their nose cans.

'Am I glad to see you,' Eddie exclaimed. 'The lock keeper gave me a hand with this last barge. He said you were in a fight. And t' inn keeper drowned in t' lock! Flipping 'eck! Did you knock 'im down, Blake?'

'No I did not. He fell. It was an accident.'

'Oh.' Young Eddie sounded disappointed.

'Have they taken his body out yet?'

'Aye. We had to wait till he were out afore we could shift t' last barge. I watched 'em fish 'im out. The lock keeper had to fetch a winch from t' mill and they hooked him up just like a big fat pike. Wait till I tell me dad about this!'

'That's enough, Eddie,' Blake snapped. 'Get the harnesses on the horses while I check the tow ropes. We've lost too much time already!'

'All right! Keep your 'air on!'

Normally sure-footed, Blake winced in pain as he clambered from one barge to another on the string of three, and misjudged his footing twice. After hearing a second curse from Blake, Eddie called, 'I can do that fo' you, if you like.'

'I told you to look to the horses, Eddie. Make sure the harness is secure.'

'Yeh, yeh. Did yo' know that girl then, Blake? The one he were after?'

'I said drop it, Eddie! We have no time for gossip. This coal has to be in the works by morning.'

The heavy horses moved on and their floating cargo edged forwards into the night. As they glided past the dairy at Fordham, Blake hoped and prayed that Lissie would be all right.

The farmhouse was quiet when Lissie woke the next morning after her brandy-induced slumber. Job and Eliza were long gone to milk their cows. She felt as though she would break in two if someone pushed her, and climbed out of her big feather bed carefully.

Eliza had draped clean clothes over the wooden bedstead for her to dress. The sun was already high in the sky as she pulled back the shutters. Her bedchamber overlooked a backyard, where chickens scratched and a few geese cropped the grass. She sat on the edge of the bed with sagging shoulders and a drooping head.

Mickey Jackson was dead. She was rid of him at last. Or would this image of his evil crooked face be for ever etched in her mind? It had seemed a lifetime since he had raped her, until last night. Now she felt as if it had happened all over again. Last night's attack had resurrected the memories, just as vivid and just as horrific. But she had come through it, and now she was over the shock she felt stronger.

Blake only knew of last night's attack. He did not know about her earlier ordeal. Would he still be interested in her as a woman if he did? She remembered that look in his eyes last night when he had turned away from her, confused, unsure about her, and who would not be? In despair, she poured water from the ewer into a bowl on the washstand. She did not allow her mind to dwell on the past or what the future might hold for her. It would take all her courage to face the day.

Eliza came back to their farmhouse for breakfast. Lissie cut bread and butter and mashed tea and found more strength in the daily routine.

Eliza fried eggs on an iron griddle over the fire and commented, 'Job's brought one of the cows in for the night. He's out there with her now.'

'Shall I call him in for you? You look exhausted.'

'I'm used to it, dairy folk always have early starts. I often go to bed soon after tea.'

'Let me help you with the chores. Tell me what you want doing for dinner.'

'No, you rest up for a few days and get yourself back to normal.'

'Thanks, Eliza, but I need to be up and doing. Otherwise I shall dwell too much on last night.'

'Oh! All right, if you say so,' Eliza replied. 'As long as you don't go wearing yourself out.'

'It will help me to sleep,' Lissie said simply.

'Well, if you're sure. The brewer at the alehouse in Fordham killed a pig t' other day and a quarter of it is ours. Tastes good an' all, because he feeds it on the butter-milk left over from my churning. There's a nice piece of the belly in the larder. It's my Job's favourite, he says it's the sweetest o' the lot. We can have it for dinner if

you set it to roast in the slow oven. Job likes his crack-
ling really crisp.'

'You've got some apples ready on your tree out there,
I'll make some sauce to go with it,' suggested Lissie. 'You
have a sit down. The dairy is a lot of work for just the
two of you.'

Eliza agreed. 'I had an old woman from the village to
help me in the farmhouse until she died, bless 'er. I think
I can manage through this winter on my own, but after
calving next spring Job is giving me a proper dairymaid.
Mind you, she'll take some getting used to, I've been
working the dairy on my own since I were knee-high.'

'Well, you can show her what to do. I was showing
young 'uns what to do all the time when I worked at
the school. Were you born on this farm, Eliza?'

'No. My mam came here as dairymaid after my father
was killed in the pit. I was a babe in arms then, but she
was a good dairymaid, my mam. She married the farmer,
old Mr Dacre, when I was about eight. Then one winter
him and my mam caught a fever that took them both
so I was left on my own. I was twelve by then, but I'd
been working in the dairy with my mam since I could
walk, so I knew what to do.'

'Everybody says you're the best dairymaid around
here.'

Eliza smiled, proud of her achievement. 'I try to keep
it as my mam did.'

'But you wouldn't have been able to look after the
cows as well, not on your own,' Lissie commented.

'No, well, what happened was that old Mr Dacre had
wanted to leave the farm to my mam and my mam had

wanted me to have it, and everybody thought that would happen when they died.'

'Do you mean the farm is yours, not Job's?' Lissie exclaimed.

'No, there was some family will that entailed the land. My Job is a cousin to old Mr Dacre, and it came to him. He was a tenant farmer before and very pleased to have his own land. But when he found out about me he said he couldn't let me stay.'

'He turned you out? Job turned you out?'

'Heavens no! I had nowhere to go. What he was saying was that I could only stay if we got wed. We could not live on the farm together unless we were wed. So I became Mrs Dacre. I've been Mrs Dacre for eight years now.'

'Do you like being Mrs Dacre?' Lissie asked.

'I do. My Job is the kindest, gentlest man I know and I love him dearly. He was insistent that he would not take me into his bed until I was older. And even then he said I had to want to, like, y' know, want him as my husband.' Eliza blushed and glanced at her friend. 'I am sorry, I should not be talking of such things.'

Lissie stopped cutting bread and gazed vacantly at the slices in front of her. Her heart cried for what she had lost. She had not experienced such compassion at her own introduction to the desires of men. Her initiation had been brutal and painful, wrenched from her unprepared body as she was beaten into submission.

The fear that Mickey Jackson would repeat his attack last night had terrified her so much that she was not sorry he was dead! But his death could not take away the wretched memory. Or give her back what she had lost.

She remembered when Blake had first held her in his arms, in the orchard at Miss Kirby's house. He had said he wanted her when Mr Kirby had caught them kissing in the kitchen.

But there were things that Blake did not know about her, things that had happened to her in the time between. Would he still want her if he knew? And what of her? Could she ever let a man near her after her experiences at the hands of Mickey Jackson? Any man? Even Blake?

Chapter 27

The following Sunday dawned bright and sunny. A day to lift the heart, Eliza thought as they walked back for breakfast after morning milking. 'Are you coming to chapel with us?' she asked her husband.

'You know what I think about chapel.'

'But you enjoy the hymns. And you've got a good voice on you.'

'Aye, I like the singing all right.'

'Well then?'

'It's that preacher. He goes on and on about the alehouse. I don't like it. Farming is thirsty work and a man likes a drink after a hard day's labouring.'

'I know. But he'll be going on about something different this week I expect,' Eliza replied. 'I think it might do Lissie some good if she went.'

'Raise her spirits a bit, you mean?'

'Yes. Give her an appetite for her dinner.'

'Go on then. I'll wash off the cow muck and put on my Sunday suit for the pair of you.'

Lissie wasn't keen on the idea. But she managed a smile and hadn't the heart to refuse Eliza. Her friend had done so much for her and, yes, they both liked going to chapel. It cheered them up.

They set off in a buoyant mood to walk the short distance along Fordham's main thoroughfare to chapel. Lissie looked well in Eliza's second-best dress. It was a sage green colour that matched her eyes and she wore a pretty bonnet trimmed to go with it. Lissie noticed a few dark glances cast in her direction and the small congregation were whispering between hymns more than usual. They all fell silent for the sermon as the preacher climbed up the steps of his plain wooden pulpit.

He started quietly as he always did. Job looked down at his hymn book for most of the sermon. Eliza and Lissie liked to watch his performance. He was a man of middle years with a round florid face and unruly coppery hair that flopped about as he became more animated.

It was when the preacher made a reference to the *carnal* attractions of alehouses that Job raised his head. This was a new slant on an old argument, he thought. Lissie stared straight ahead. She recognised the backs of two people in the front pew. Miss Kirby and her brother, sitting side by side in their Sunday finery.

The preacher was raising his voice . . . *the harlots who frequent these places and bring down decent hardworking men* . . .

Job stole a glance at his wife who raised her eyebrows.

. . . the sins that belong to Jezebel who flaunts her temptation . . .

Eliza, sitting between her husband and her friend, turned her head towards Lissie, whose expression had frozen on her face. She reached across to hold her friend's hand.

. . . that a man should die while this temptress moves among us . . .

Job leaned over to whisper in his wife's ear. 'I've heard enough of this. We're going.' He put his hand under her elbow.

'We can't walk out in the middle,' Eliza replied quietly.

'Yes we can.'

'What about Lissie? It'll make it worse for her. Everybody will look at her.'

'No they won't. They're all watching the preacher.'

'They'll hear us.' One or two of the congregation had already turned round, scowling, to see who was whispering. 'Sshh, Job. He's nearly finished.'

Lissie was mortified. Frozen to the hard wooden pew, she continued to stare blankly ahead. The preacher blamed her. They all blamed her for what had happened. Men were men, and decent women should not put temptation in their way. It was her fault that Mickey Jackson had died.

Eliza held both their hands tightly and whispered, 'Sit still and don't say anything. We won't move until everyone else has gone.'

The small congregation filed out. A few ignored them, but most looked pointedly in their direction, shook their heads and tutted at each other.

The Kirbys were the last to leave. They stood up slowly and paced down the stone flagged aisle. Miss Kirby was dressed in a plain gown made of delicately printed challis that looked new. She wore a small bonnet tied with silk ribbons and walked deferentially behind her brother. She hovered by his shoulder, with a cross expression on her face, when Mr Kirby stopped to address Job.

Mr Kirby's coat looked new as well, and he had a fine tweed waistcoat underneath with a heavy gold watch chain across it. He was carrying a tall hat and some kidskin gloves. The pair of them certainly looked better off than when Lissie had worked at their school.

'I expected better of you, Job Dacre,' Mr Kirby began. 'When you took over the Dacre farm you did right by your young wife, and our small community has held you in good esteem. But her youthful ways have turned your head and it is a man's duty to see that his wife keeps good company.'

Lissie knew that Mr Kirby would brook no argument about her. As a child in school he had identified her to be in danger of moral decay. And her behaviour with Blake had served to reinforce this opinion.

All three kept their eyes firmly fixed on the pulpit at the front. Eliza held on to her husband's and her friend's hands and squeezed them again.

Mr Kirby continued, 'This village does not want,' he sneered with distaste, 'does not want . . . that sort of woman in its midst, the kind that lusts after men and leads them into temptation without restraint or shame. These are evil, wicked women, who bring down the good name of decent men. You were a respected man

in this village until you offered shelter to . . . to . . . that
Jezebel.' His face was going red and he fingered his tight
Sunday collar. 'I am sure your good wife, young as she
is, does not wish for such a temptress under her roof.
Perhaps she, too, has been bewitched by the harlot's ways.'

He stopped, expecting a grovelling assurance that Lissie
would be cast out from his home. When Job remained
silent, Mr Kirby went on, 'Yes, I see she has already
worked her evil spell on you. Well, if that is the case, we
shall not be needing any of your supplies from your dairy
to the schoolhouse while that . . . that woman . . . is
lodging beneath your roof. You will find that others in
this village will follow my example. Do I make myself
clear?'

He marched off, not waiting for a reply. Miss Kirby,
unable to add to her brother's tirade, uttered just one
word as she passed their pew. 'Harlot!' she breathed, then
hurried after her brother.

Only Eliza saw Job's eyes narrow with anger. She
squeezed his hand hard and he remained silent.

Lissie stared straight ahead, her eyes glassy with unshed
tears. It was her fault that Mickey Jackson had died. She
had tempted him and as a result he was dead. She was
a killer as well as a harlot. And now her friends would
lose their livelihood. Everyone had to suffer because of
her. They would all be better off if she just went away.

The thunder of hooves outside her front-room window
made Eliza look up from her sewing. She got up and
crossed to the window. It was nightfall and Job was out
in the cowshed with his sick cow.

Blake had come to see Lissie as he'd promised. He
was riding a glossy chestnut hunter and dismounted
quickly. He held on to the reins and met Eliza at her
front door.

'She isn't here, Blake. We tried to stop her leaving,
but she would have none of it. It was Mr Kirby, you see.
He has set everybody against her.'

'That damned hypocrite!' Blake exploded. 'No wonder
he lost his ironworks!' He took a deep breath. 'Sorry,
Eliza. I didn't mean to curse. I got here as soon as I
could. When did she leave?'

'After we got back from chapel this morning. She
wouldn't even stay for her dinner.'

'Do you know where she went?'

'Back to Rosa's, she said.'

'Thanks, Eliza.'

He re-mounted and galloped off over the small stone
bridge and down the towpath to Mexton Lock. He was
not going to let her get away from him this time! Since
moving down from Kimberhill, Blake's life had taken a
turn for the better. He lodged with Sir William's works'
manager in their neat house, a little way out of town on
the valley road. It was brick built with a single attic room
for servants, a young couple who looked after the
manager, his wife, three children, a horse, and now Blake.

Blake had written immediately to his mama and to
Ephraim. He had taken both letters down to the flyer
office and found a small dusty packet waiting for him.
It contained a letter from his mama and two from
Ephraim, the last one pleading for a reply with his where-
abouts. Ingrid Svenson and her maid Lucy were coming

home the following summer, and bringing two of his cousins to visit.

To have found Lissie again had made his life perfect. He could not wait to see her and he spurred on the hunter. The horse was sweating when he arrived at Rosa's cottage and rapped at the door.

Rosa glanced through the window, straightened her apron and patted her hair. Thoroughbred horses were rare on this side of the canal. She answered the door and put on her best voice. 'Can I help you, sir?'

'Is Lissie Dearne here? I need to talk to her.'

'Lissie Dearne? Well, who shall I say is asking for her?'

'Tell her it's Blake. Blake Svenson.'

Rosa stared at him. She had a good memory for names, especially unusual ones. It was a Svenson that Luther Dearne had shot all those years ago. What did he want with Lissie? She had enough on her plate already!

Blake noticed the stare. He cocked his head to one side. 'You have met me before, when I was a boy. You took in and cared for my father when he had been shot.'

Rosa frowned. She did not want any trouble. 'I remember. What would you be wanting with Luther Dearne's daughter?'

'I mean her no harm!' Blake's patience was running out. 'Just let me see her. Please.'

Rosa was thinking, My God is this that little boy? He has grown into a fine handsome fellow. He had been here the other night, at the fight, when Mickey Jackson drowned in the lock. Lissie seemed to know him, all right, and they had gone off together with Job and Eliza Dacre. Good people, were the Dacres.

'Rosa! Please?' Blake repeated impatiently.

'Are you a friend of Lissie's, then?' she asked.

'*For God's sake, woman, I love her!*'

'Oh!' Rosa's mouth dropped open and her eyes widened. Well, what a turn of events! This prosperous-looking gentleman in love with little Lissie!

She said, 'Oh, you've missed her. She collected her things and left. In a hurry she was, to catch the evening carrier on the turnpike.'

'Dammit, no! Which way was she heading?' The horse was spooked by Blake's raised voice and he whinnied and pulled at the reins.

'Search me! She never said. But she's been living on a farm somewhere since . . . since her father died.'

'How many farms are there in the South Riding?' he groaned.

'Look here, sir,' Rosa suggested. 'There's no point in chasing after her now. That horse needs a rub down and you need to calm down a bit too. All I can tell you is that she sometimes goes to market in town. She told me she makes pies and has a stall there.'

Town? In town? He lived near the town now! The market square was just up the hill from Sir William's ironworks. He could find her. He *would* find her.

Martha saw Lissie struggling down the track with her travelling box. It was early morning and she had just unbolted the front door and stepped out on to the porch.

'Lissie! Oh, Lissie, what happened? You look tired out!'

'I came on the night carrier. And walked from the turnpike.'

'You walked? All that way on your own! Come inside, there's porridge on the hob. Here, let me take your cloak.'

After porridge with milk and honey in their warm farmhouse kitchen, Lissie felt better and was able to tell Martha everything that had happened to her.

'I should have been with you,' Martha commented.

'At least I know a little about my birth now. That was quite a shock and then the attack . . .' She shuddered. 'It was horrible and I did have a feverish reaction. It brought back all the memories of that first attack. But Mickey Jackson's dead now and he can't hurt me any more. What's done is done. I have had time to think on the long walk from the turnpike.'

'And?'

Lissie paused and took a deep breath. 'I have to move on. I shall go and see Edie as often as I can, and Eliza will always be my friend, but I have to look forward now and make something of my life.'

Martha's heart turned over. She did not want Lissie to leave. She nodded silently and waited for her to go on.

'The man who I believed had killed my dad was there and it was him, Martha, who rescued me and stayed with me until I was safe at Eliza's.' Lissie covered her face with her hands. 'I pushed him away, Martha. He only wanted to care for me, to be kind to me, and I pushed him away. He went off then. Said he had to get back to work. I didn't want him to leave me. I didn't.'

'You'd had a rough time of it. He'll understand, I am sure.'

'But I love him! I love him and I could not stand for

him to touch me. Twice, Martha, I turned away from him twice. He'll not come looking for me again.' Lissie gazed into the red glow of the fire and let out a long sigh. 'I don't know if I'll ever be able to let . . . let him touch me.'

Martha reached across the table to hold her hand. 'There are good, kind men in this world, Lissie, love. He sounds like one of them. You have to give yourself time. He will too.'

'But what if . . . what if . . . I mean, would I have to tell him about . . . about the rape?'

'Yes, my dear. You have to be honest with each other.'

'But he won't want me then, will he? What will he do when I tell him?'

'It will be hard for both of you. But if you are right for each other, you'll come through it together.'

'He is right for me, Martha. But I'm frightened that he has left me for good now.'

'He doesn't sound to me like a man who gives up easily. Are you sure you really love him?'

Lissie nodded silently.

'Then we shall have to see what we can do. Where is he now?'

She shrugged. 'In town, I suppose, or hauling coals on the canal. I was so . . . so numbed by events that I could barely speak to him.'

Martha tried to cheer her. 'Why don't you show me your mother's things?'

Lissie took the pouch out of her box.

'There's nothing about your real father?'

Lissie shook her head. 'These are all the things I have.

I expect Rosa was right and he didn't know — or didn't want to know about me.'

Martha examined the trinkets. 'You look a lot like your mother. Pity there's nothing about your father.'

'I don't think I shall ever know now, Martha. But Luther Dearne was a good dad to me and I loved him. He did his best for me and Edie, even though Edie was like she was. I know my real mother was a lady. But she's been dead and gone since I was born and her family hasn't come looking for me.' She looked directly into Martha's brown eyes. 'My real family is here, Martha.'

'Welcome home, Lissie,' the older woman replied tearfully.

They celebrated that evening when John came in from the fields. Martha killed a fowl which Lissie plucked and drew and stuffed with sage and onions to roast in the bake oven. John tapped a new barrel of ale in the cellar and they both complimented him on his brew.

'The sow has farrowed,' Martha commented as they finished up stewed pears and clotted cream. 'I thought we might keep more of the piglets this time, to fatten for your pie meat.'

'What a clever idea! I'll look after them. Can we give them more buttermilk and whey in their feed? It makes for very tasty pork.' Lissie sat back in her chair at the kitchen table. 'Oh, it is good to be home again.'

'I'll be taking the rest of the litter to market as soon as they're weaned. You know, now you're here to stay, we could go to market more often.' Martha cast her a knowing glance. 'You need to get to know the folk in town better now. Find a friend or two of your own age. When you're ready.'

'Oh, I am ready, Martha. Quite ready. When is the next market day? I should make a start on my pies.'

Market day was breezy and sunny. The smoke and grime had been blown over to the east and the air was clear. Gusts of wind ruffled Lissie's skirts about and she had to tie her bonnet on with an extra-broad ribbon. She looked for Rosa to give her some of the pie money for Edie, but there was no sign of her that day. Next time, Lissie resolved, for already she was planning a weekly stall for her pork pies.

The cobbled market square was thriving with pens of cattle, sheep and pigs. Live poultry squawked in baskets and farmers' wives displayed their garden produce for sale. Trade was good and there was talk of Sir William starting up new furnaces and more work for the towns-folk. John went off to watch the livestock auction while Martha and Lissie looked after the stall.

'This breeze is a bit parky today,' Lissie commented as it swirled round her head.

'Why don't you go into the Lion for some soup?' Martha suggested. 'It'll warm you up a bit. Don't go in the tap room though, it's rough there. The saloon will have ladies in today, it being market day.'

'Thanks, I shall.'

The Lion was busy and noisy. She took her bowl of soup and found a chair at a table in the window, oppo-site two women who were warming themselves with brandy.

'Good morning,' she said breathlessly. 'Can I sit with you?'

The women were squashed together in the window seat, their full skirts taking up all the space. They nodded and smiled at her. The older one had grey hair under her bonnet and a plain, lined face. But her dark dress was made of good woollen cloth and she had a matching small cape with a grey silk lining. Her companion was younger, her daughter maybe, Lissie thought. She had a lovely face and wore fashionable ribbons on her bonnet that were echoed by the trimmings on her maroon dress.

She returned their smile tentatively and drank her soup. After a few minutes she was aware that the older woman was staring at her intently. Eventually, the woman said, 'I hope you don't mind me asking, but do you come from round here?'

'Swinborough way,' Lissie answered politely. 'Just past Sir William's estates. On the way to Mexton.' After a pause, she added, 'I'm Lissie,' and offered her hand.

'Lissie, did you say?' the younger woman enquired slowly. 'Are you fr—'

'Grace,' the older woman interrupted quickly, taking Lissie's hand. 'And this is Clara, my niece.'

Sitting opposite her, Grace thought that Lissie was the image of her mother. Same glossy black hair, coiled and tamed under her bonnet. Same green eyes and delicate white skin. Thank goodness she didn't have her father's jaw to spoil it! She had inherited the beauty of her mother and the upright bearing of her grand-father. She looked reasonably well turned out too.

Grace recognised that the stuff of her gown was one of this year's woollens from the draper's shop on the high street.

'Have you come for the market?'

'I've brought my pork pies in to sell.'

'Clara,' Grace added briskly, 'why don't you get me another brandy? Would you like one, dear?'

'Oh, no thank you,' Lissie replied. 'This soup is enough for me.'

As Clara left, Lissie was jostled from behind and a male voice said, 'Excuse me.'

She turned to face Mr Kirby, well dressed in a tweed suit, fancy silk waistcoat and polished boots. He held a glass of whisky in his hand and it was clear to Lissie that he had already drunk several before that one.

'Well, well,' he sneered. 'The Lion is indeed honoured today. The ladies of the town, all gathered together to ply their trade.'

Grace leaned forward. 'Don't take any notice, dear. This man is drunk.' She turned to Mr Kirby and added, 'If you carry on like this, you'll get through your new money like you got through your father's.'

'Mind your own business,' he slurred.

'I'll do that all right,' Grace replied smartly.

'I heard you were selling up, anyway.'

'Now where did you hear that, Mr Kirby?'

'And it's not before time! We don't need your sort here,' he replied belligerently.

'No, well *you* don't. Not now you're a respected alderman. But I remember when you were very happy to visit . . .' She stopped, glanced across at Lissie, then finished lightly, 'You wouldn't like me to talk to your sister, would you, or that preacher friend of yours?'

He had been a regular afternoon visitor to Grace's, when he told his sister he was at the Institute. Grace wondered how he would continue to satisfy his appetites now that he no longer called.

He spluttered into his whisky. 'I'll have you run out of town, you—'

'No need, Mr Kirby. You will be pleased to hear that you are right and I am leaving.' Grace patted her throat. 'The smoke from the furnaces is not good for me. Clara and I are moving to Harrogate for my health. They have healing waters there.'

Mr Kirby made an impatient, grunting response and moved on.

'So sorry, my dear,' Grace apologised.

'Oh him! Don't be sorry about him. He's always laying down the law for other folk!'

'Do you know him?' asked Grace, surprised.

'I was a pupil at his sister's school and when their housekeeper died I was given her position.'

'Oh?' Luther had looked after her little Lissie well, she thought. 'What did you think of Mr Kirby?'

'I didn't like him. He was strict with everyone except himself.' Lissie shook her head. 'Strange fellow, if you ask me! I couldn't fathom him at all. Where has he got all his new money from anyway? Not the school, surely?'

Grace laughed. She knew that he had been responsible for the furnaces closing down and the buildings being rented out. Sir William had bought them up and taken on young Blake Svenson, who would run the new ironworks one day.

Grace also knew that, for all his self-righteous preaching, any money Mr Kirby had gained from the sale of his father's ironworks would soon be spent on drink and gambling and women.

She answered, 'No, not the school. He sold his father's bankrupt ironworks to Sir William. It's about time those furnaces got going again.'

Lissie finished her soup and got up to leave. Martha needed a break, also. She gave Grace a brief nod and said, 'I have to get back to my stall. Thank you for your company. I wish you well in Harrogate. Good day.'

Out in the square, with its animal smells and noise, Lissie thought how much she wanted to stay here. She liked it here. It had a future and so did she. What had happened to her in the past had been harrowing and, yes, it had wounded her. But wounds can heal and although the scars, whether they were visible or hidden, would always be there, they gave her protection from further damage and reminded her that she had healed. She could go on, she would go on and be part of this town, with its ironworks and forges, its people and its future. She had an extra strength now because she knew she could survive. No matter what happened in the future, she would be able to endure it.

Blake reined in his horse just before he reached the market square. He winced a little as he dismounted. But the aches in his muscles were nothing compared to the ache in his heart as he had searched for Lissie. The works' manager had lost patience with him and told him to take a day off to sort himself out.

He had asked around the town. A newcomer, he was looking for. A young woman, a beautiful young woman, you would remember her if you saw her, black hair and green eyes. The draper's assistant remembered because she had been there a while back, with widow Thorogood, for woollen cloth to make winter gowns. Yes, Mrs Thorogood lived on a farm on the edge of the Swinborough land. She was often here on a market day, had a stall with her son, big man he was, impossible to miss him . . .

Thorogood farm. It had to be where Lissie lived now! If she doesn't come to market today, I'll ride over there tonight.

The market crowds were thinning as Lissie threaded her way from the Lion through the pens and stalls. Farmers and butchers were herding off their newly purchased beasts. Martha and John were selling the last of their vegetables and preparing to pack the cart for their journey home. There was a man with them, holding a horse, a fine chestnut, and talking to Martha. Lissie recognised him at once and her heart rose in her breast.

She quickened her pace. Blake was here. In town. At the beast market. As she approached she heard Martha explaining about John and telling Blake how Lissie had taught him to read. Blake had his back towards her, bowing his head to John.

'Oh look,' Martha said. 'Here she is.'

Blake turned his head. He was smiling. How striking he looked when he smiled! She wanted to reach out

and touch his face, trace her fingers around his eyes and
nose and lips and kiss him, right there, in the market
square.

'Lissie!' He had found her at last. He dropped the
reins. His arms came forward to hold her and she did
not flinch from him. Gently, he rested his hands lightly
on her upper arms and gazed at her. She had a radiance
about her that made his heart turn over. She was smiling!
She was pleased to see him! It took all his will-power
to stop himself scooping her up and carrying her away
that minute.

'Blake! Oh Blake! You're here, you're here.' Her face
was beaming. She could barely get the words out. She
loved him so much that her heart was swelling in her
breast and her throat was closing with emotion. How
could she have ever rejected him? 'You have recovered
from the beating?' she asked.

'Oh yes. Eliza told me what happened in the chapel
last Sunday. How could the preacher be so cruel? It's
that Kirby fellow! I could tell you a thing or two about
him!'

John took the reins of Blake's horse, smoothing his
hands over its nose and neck and flanks in a close exam-
ination of its form. Martha busied herself tidying the
cart. Lissie sat on their makeshift stall as they talked. The
noise and bustle of the beast market faded into oblivion.
She loved listening to Blake. She loved everything about
him. 'Have you settled in the Riding for good, now?'
she asked.

'Sir William has taken me on in his new ironworks,'
he said. 'I'll be manager one day and live in my own

house.' How could he wait until then? He desperately wanted to have her to himself *now*, to hoist her up on his horse and ride away with her to the hills. But he knew she needed time, healing time, and he could wait. It would be hard for him but he had time. *They* had time. Time to be together, and to grow together.

He went on, 'Will you go back to Mexton?'

'Only to see Mam and Rosa. I live with Martha and John now.'

Martha glanced up at them and smiled.

'Mrs Thorogood,' Blake asked, 'may I come and visit you — all of you — out on the farm?'

'Of course you may,' Martha replied. 'It's no distance at all on horseback if you cut through Sir William's estate. I'm sure he'll not object.'

'Thanks.' He turned to Lissie. 'Promise me that you will never run off from Martha's like you did from Eliza's.'

'I promise,' Lissie agreed solemnly.

He put his arm round Lissie's shoulders and gently kissed her cheek. She did not recoil. She did not reject him and his heart soared.

Lissie leaned against him, soaking in the warmth of his body. This is where I belong, she thought. With him. With Blake.

Grace stumbled on the cobbles as she left the Lion.

'Here. Take my arm,' Clara said.

'It's this stiff hip of mine,' Grace complained.

'You'll be better when we get to Harrogate. Does wonders, apparently.'

'We'll see,' Grace responded sceptically.

Across the market square they saw Blake and Lissie talking together, his arm resting comfortably around her.

Clara said, 'Look, Grace, there's Blake. He's with that young woman we met in the Lion. Lissie, wasn't it? He talked of a girl he had met when he was working on the flyers. Do you think it is her?'

'Fine-looking woman,' Grace added. 'They make a handsome couple, don't they?'

'Mmmm, yes,' Clara responded. 'He is a gentleman, is Blake. I hope she is worthy of him.'

'Oh yes. She is,' Grace answered. 'She has good blood in her veins. And he will look after her all right. He'll go far, he will. He's already secured Sir William's patronage.'

They walked on to their waiting carriage.

'How do you know about her blood?' Clara ventured.

'It's a long story, Clara. I'll tell you when we get to Harrogate.'

But Clara was not put off. 'Is it her?' she pressed.

'Who?'

'That baby you talk of sometimes. Is Lissie that baby?'

'Might be.'

Clara was aghast. 'She isn't yours, is she?'

'No, my dear. Not mine.'

'Then whose? Come on, Grace! You can tell me.'

Grace gave a rare smile. 'Yes, you're right and I shall. One day. Her mother was a real lady, you know.'

'What about her father?' Clara urged.

'I've never told a soul about him and I don't think I should start now. She doesn't need him. She's in good hands with Blake.'

'She would want to know who her father was, surely?'

'Perhaps. But he would never own her. He did not know about her and he married and had other children. He is a gentleman though,' Grace replied.

'*Is* a gentleman?' Clara pursued. 'He is still alive, then?'

Very much so, Grace thought. Lissie's grandfather had been a successful iron master in the South Riding and his only son, Lissie's father, had gone on to build all kinds of new things with it. He was famous now, for his railways and his bridges. News-sheets reported his progress. He lived in London with his family and had travelled to the Americas twice.

But she would not risk his rejection of Lissie, as reject her he surely would if ever the truth came out. He had been a highly charged and active young man when he had been a visitor to the Admiral's home in London, a trait he had carried on into adulthood with his ideas and his work. Now, no doubt, he valued his exalted position in society too much to lose it.

Lissie's future was secure with Blake. She hoped fervently that they would have a long and happy life together, with children and grandchildren. They were young, strong and had each other. If any couple could survive in this danger-strewn world of the nineteenth century, they could.

Grace said, 'Did I say her father *is* a gentleman, Clara? Slip of the tongue. He *was* a gentleman. He's dead now.'